THE MOON AND MORE
& JUST LISTEN

SARAH DESSEN

THE MOON AND MORE & JUST LISTEN

PENGUIN BOOKS

PENGUIN BOOKS
An imprint of Penguin Random House LLC, New York

Just Listen first published in the United States of America by Viking,
an imprint of Penguin Random House LLC, 2006
Published by Speak, an imprint of Penguin Group (USA) LLC, 2008, 2012
The Moon and More first published in the United States of America by Viking,
an imprint of Penguin Random House LLC, 2013
Published by Speak, an imprint of Penguin Group (USA) LLC, 2015
This omnibus edition published by Penguin Books, an imprint of Penguin Random House LLC, 2020

Just Listen copyright © 2006 by Sarah Dessen
The Moon and More copyright © 2013 by Sarah Dessen

Visit us online at penguinrandomhouse.com

THE LIBRARY OF CONGRESS HAS CATALOGED THE VIKING EDITIONS AS FOLLOWS:
Dessen, Sarah.
The moon and more / by Sarah Dessen.
p. cm.
Summary: "During her last summer at home before leaving for college, Emaline begins a whirlwind
romance with Theo, an assistant documentary filmmaker who is in town to make a movie"
—Provided by publisher.
ISBN: 978-0-670-78560-5 (hardcover)
[1. Coming of age—Fiction. 2. Resorts—Fiction. 3. Beaches—Fiction.
4. Family-owned business enterprises—Fiction. 5. Dating (Social customs)—Fiction.
6. Fathers and daughters—Fiction. 7. Documentary films—Production and direction—Fiction.]
I. Title. PZ7.D455Moo 2013 [Fic]—dc23 2012035720

Dessen, Sarah.
Just listen : a novel / by Sarah Dessen.
p. cm.
Summary: Isolated from friends who believe the worst because she has not been truthful with them,
sixteen-year-old Annabel finds an ally in classmate Owen, whose honesty and passion for music help
her to face and share what really happened at the end-of-the-year party that changed her life.
ISBN: 978-0-670-06105-1 (hardcover)
[1. Self-actualization—Fiction. 2. Interpersonal relations—Fiction.
3. Models (Persons)—Fiction. 4. Family problems—Fiction.
5. High schools—Fiction. 6. Schools—Fiction.] I. Title.
PZ7.D455Jus 2006 [Fic]—dc22 2006000472

Omnibus edition ISBN 9780593203064

Printed in the United States of America

1 3 5 7 9 10 8 6 4 2

THE MOON AND MORE
& JUST LISTEN

THE MOON AND MORE

For Jay and Sasha,
my world

1

HERE THEY COME.

"—or I promise you, we'll turn right around and go back to Paterson!" the woman behind the wheel of the burgundy minivan was shouting as it pulled up beside me. She had her head turned towards the backseat, where I could see three kids, two boys and a girl, staring back at her. A vein in her neck was bulging, looking not unlike the interstate, thick and unmissable, on the map held by the man in the passenger seat beside her. "I am serious. I have *had it*."

The kids didn't say anything. After a moment of glaring at them, she turned to look at me. She had on big sunglasses with bedazzled frames. A large fountain drink, the straw tinged with lipstick, was parked between her legs.

"Welcome to the beach," I said to her, in my best Colby Realty employee voice. "May I—"

"The directions on your Web site are garbage," she informed me. Behind her, I saw one of the kids frog-punch another, who emitted a stifled shriek. "We've gotten lost three times since getting off the interstate."

"I'm so sorry to hear that," I replied. "If you'd like to give me your name, I'll grab you your keys and get you on the way to your rental."

"Webster," she told me.

I turned, reaching into the small rattan bin that held all the envelopes for that day's check-ins. Miller, Tubman, Simone, Wallace . . . Webster.

"Heron's Call," I read off the envelope, before opening it to make sure the keys were both in it. "That's a great property."

In reply, she stuck out her hand. I gave the envelope to her, along with her complimentary beach bag full of all the free stuff—Colby Realty pen, giveaway postcard, area guide, and cheap drink cooler—that I knew the cleaning crew would most likely find untouched when they checked out. "Have a great week," I told her. "Enjoy the beach!"

Now she gave me a wry smile, although it was hard to tell if she was truly thankful or just felt sorry for me. After all, I was standing in a glorified sandbox in the middle of a parking lot, with three cars lined up behind her, most likely full of people in the exact same kind of mood. When the final stop on a trip is paradise, being the second to last is no picnic.

Not that I had time to really think about this as they pulled away, signal already blinking for their turn onto the main road. It was three ten, and the next car, a blue sedan with one of those carriers on top, was waiting. I kicked what sand I could out of my shoes and took a deep breath.

"Welcome to the beach," I said, as they pulled up beside me. "Name, please?"

* * *

"Well," my sister Margo said when I came into the office, sweat-soaked and depleted, two hours later. "How did it go?"

"I have sand in my shoes," I told her, going straight to the water cooler, where I filled up a cup, downed it, and then did the same with two more.

"You're at the beach, Emaline," she pointed out.

"No, I'm at the *office*," I replied, wiping my mouth with the back of my hand. "The beach is two miles away. People will get to the sand soon enough. I don't see why we have to have it here, too."

"Because," she replied, in the cool voice of someone who had spent the day in air-conditioning, "we are one of the first impressions our visitors get of Colby. We want them to feel that the moment they turn into our parking lot, they are officially on vacation."

"What does that have to do with me standing in a sandbox?"

"It's not a sandbox," she said, and I rolled my eyes, because that's exactly what it was, and we both knew it. "It's a sandbar, and it's meant to evoke the majesty of the coast."

I didn't even know what to say to this. Ever since Margo had graduated from East U the year before with a double degree in hospitality and business, she'd been insufferable. Or more insufferable, actually. My family had owned Colby Realty for over fifty years; our grandparents started it right after they got married. We'd been doing just fine, thank you, before Margo and her sandbox or sandbar, or whatever. But she was the first one in our family so far to get a college degree, so she got to do whatever she wanted.

Which was why, a few weeks earlier, she had this sandbox/
Tiki Hut/whatever it was made and put it in our office parking
lot. About four feet by four feet, with waist-high walls, it was
like a wooden tollbooth, with a truckload of playground sand
dumped in and around it for good measure. Nobody ques-
tioned the need for this except me. Then again, no one else
had to work in it.

I heard a snicker, muffled, and looked over. Sure enough,
it was my grandmother, behind her own desk, making a phone
call. She winked at me and I couldn't help but smile.

"Don't forget about the VIP rounds," Margo called out, as I
headed in that direction, chucking my cup in the trash on the
way. "You need to start promptly at five thirty. And double-
check the fruit and cheese platters before you deliver them.
Amber did them and you know how she is."

Amber was my other sister. She was in hair school, worked
for the realty company only under duress, and expressed her
annoyance by doing everything in as slipshod a way as possible.

"Ten-four," I replied, and Margo exhaled, annoyed. She'd
told me ten times that it sounded so unprofessional, like
trucker talk. Which was exactly why I kept saying it.

My grandmother's office was right at the front of the
building, with a big window looking out onto the main road,
now packed with beach traffic. She was still on the phone but
waved me in when she saw me in her doorway.

"Well, yes, Roger, I sympathize, believe me," she was saying as I pushed some brochures aside to sit down in the chair
opposite her desk. It was messy as always, piled with papers,

file folders, and several open packs of Rolos. She always misplaced one after opening it, only to do the same with the next, and the one after that. "But the bottom line is, in rental houses, door handles get a lot of use. Especially back door handles that lead to the beach. We can fix them as much as possible, but sometimes you just have to replace the hardware."

Roger said something, his voice booming from the receiver. My grandmother helped herself to a Rolo, then extended the pack to me. I shook my head.

"The report I received was that the handle fell off, inside, after the door was locked. The guests couldn't get back in. That's when they called us." A pause. Then she said, "Well, I'm sure they could have climbed in through a window. But when you're paying five grand for a week, you can claim certain privileges."

As Roger responded, she chewed her Rolo. The candy wasn't the best habit, but it was better than cigarettes, which she had smoked up until about six years earlier. My mother claimed that when she was a kid, a constant cloud had hung in this office, like its own personal weather system. Weirdly enough, even after multiple cleanings, new curtains and carpet, you could still smell the smoke. It's faint, but it was there.

"Of course. It's always something when you're a landlord," she said now, leaning back in her chair and rubbing her neck. "We'll take care of it and send the bill. All right?" Roger started to say something else. "Great! Thanks for the call."

She hung up, shaking her head. Behind her, another minivan was pulling into our parking lot. "Some people," she said, popping out another Rolo, "should just not own beach houses."

This is one of her favorite mantras, running a close second to "Some people should just not rent beach houses." I've often told her we should have it needlepointed and framed, not that we could hang it up anywhere in this office.

"Another busted handle?" I asked.

"Third one this week. You know how it goes. It's the beginning of the season. That means wear and tear." She started digging around on her desk, knocking papers to the floor. "How did check-in go?"

"Fine," I said. "Only two early birds, and both their places were already cleaned."

"And you're doing the vips today?"

I smiled. The VIP package was another one of Margo's recent brainstorms. For an added charge, people who were renting what we called our Beach Palaces—the fanciest properties, with elevators and pools and all the amenities—got a welcome spread of cheese and fruit, along with a bottle of wine. Margo first pitched the idea at the Friday Morning Meeting, another thing she'd instituted, which basically forced us all to sit around the conference table once a week to say everything we'd normally discuss while actually working. That day, she'd handed out a printed agenda, with bullet points, one of which said "VIP Treatment." My grandmother, squinting at it without her glasses, said, "What's a vip?" To Margo's annoyance, it stuck, and now the rest of us refused to call it anything else.

"Just leaving now," I told her. "Any special instructions?"

She finally found the sheet she'd been looking for and scanned it quickly. "Dune's Dream is a good regular client," she said. "Bon Voyage is new, as is Casa Blu. And whoever's in Sand Dollars is there for two months."

"*Months?*" I said. "Seriously?"

Sand Dollars was one of our priciest properties, a big house way out on the Tip, the very edge of town. Just a week would break most budgets. "Yep. So make sure they get a good platter. All right?"

I nodded, then got to my feet. I was just about to the door when she said, "And Emaline?"

"Yes?"

"You looked pretty cute in that sandbox this afternoon. Brought back memories."

I smiled, just as Margo yelled from outside, "It's a *sandbar*, Grandmother!"

Down the hallway in the back storage room, I collected the four platters Amber had assembled earlier. Sure enough, the cheese and fruit were all jumbled up, as if thrown from a distance. After spending a good fifteen minutes making them presentable, I took them out to my car, which was about a million degrees even though I parked in the shade. All I could do was pile them on the passenger seat, point every A/C vent in their direction, and hope for the best.

At the first house, Dune's Dream, no one answered even after I rang the bell and paged them from the outside intercom. I walked around the extensive deck, peering down. There was a group of people around the pool below, as well as a couple walking down the long boardwalk to the beach. I tried the door—unlocked—and stepped inside.

"Hello?" I called out in a friendly voice. "Colby Realty,

VIP delivery?" When you had to come into people's houses—even if they'd only just moved in, and then just for the week—you learned not only to announce yourself but to do so loudly and repeatedly. All it took was catching one person unaware and partially clothed to bang this lesson home. Yes, people were supposed to let it all hang out on vacation. But that didn't mean I wanted to see it. "Colby Realty? VIP delivery?"

Silence. Quickly, I moved up to the third-floor kitchen, where the views were spectacular. On the speckled granite island, I arranged the platter, chilled bottle of wine, and a handwritten card welcoming them to Colby and reminding them to contact us if they needed anything at all. Then it was on to the next house.

At Bon Voyage, the door was locked, the guests most likely out for an early dinner. I set up the platter and wine in the kitchen, where the blender was still plugged in, the carafe in the sink smelling of something sweet and tropical. It was always so weird to come into these houses once people were actually staying there, especially if I'd just been in the same morning to check after the cleaners. The entire energy was different, like the difference between something being off and on.

At Casa Blu, the door was answered by a short woman with a deep tan, wearing a bikini that was, honestly, not really age appropriate. This was not to say I *knew* how old she was as much as that, even at eighteen, I wouldn't have attempted the same skimpy pink number. There was a white sheen of sunscreen on her face, a beer in a bright yellow cozy in her free hand.

"Colby Realty, VIP delivery," I said. "I have a welcome gift for you?"

She took a sip of her beer. "Great," she said, in a flat, nasal tone. "Come on in."

I followed her up to the next level, trying not to look at her bikini bottom, which was riding up, up, up as we climbed the stairs. "Is it the stripper?" someone called out as I stepped onto the landing. It was another woman around the same age, midforties, maybe, wearing a bikini top, a flowy skirt, and a thick, gold braided necklace. When she saw me, she laughed. "Guess not!"

"It's something from the rental place," Pink Bikini explained to her and a third woman in a shorty bathrobe holding a wine glass, her hair in a messy topknot, who were looking down from the deck at something below. "A welcome gift."

"Oh," the bathrobe woman said. "I thought *this* was our present."

There was a burst of laughter as the woman who let me in walked over to join them, looking as well. I arranged my platter and bottle, put up the card, and was about to leave discreetly when I heard one of them say, "Wouldn't you just love to take a big bite of that, Elinor?"

"Mmmm," she replied. "I say we dump dirt in the pool, so he has to come back tomorrow."

"And the next day!" Flowy Skirt said. Then they all laughed again, clinking their glasses.

"Enjoy your stay," I called out as I left, but of course they didn't hear me. Halfway down the stairs to the front door, I glanced out one of the big windows, spotting the object of their ogling: a tall, very tan guy with curly blond hair, shirt-less, wielding a long, awfully phallic looking pool brush. I could hear them still whooping as I went out the door, easing it shut behind me.

Back in the car, I pulled my hair up in a ponytail, secured it with one of the elastics hanging around my gearshift, and sat for a moment in the driveway, watching the waves. I had one more stop and plenty of time, so I was still there when the pool guy let himself out of the fence and headed back to his truck, parked beside me.

"Hey," I called out, as he climbed up into the open bed, coiling a couple of hoses. "You could make some big money this week, if your morals are loose enough and you like older women."

He grinned, flashing white teeth. "Think so?"

"They'd devour you, given the chance."

Another smile as he hopped down, shutting the tailgate, and came over to my open window. He leaned down on it, so his head was level with mine. "Not my type," he told me. "Plus, I'm already taken."

"Lucky girl," I said.

"You should tell her that. I think she takes me for granted."

I made a face. "I think it's mutual."

He leaned in and kissed me. I could taste the tiny bit of sweat above his lip. As he pulled back, I said, "You're not kid-ding anyone, you know. You are fully capable of wearing a shirt when you work."

"It's hot out here!" he told me, but I just rolled my eyes,

cranking my engine. Ever since he'd taken up running and got all cut, you couldn't keep a top on the boy. This was not the first house that had noticed. "So we still on for tonight?"

"What's tonight?"

"Emaline." He shook his head. "Don't even try to act like you've forgotten."

I thought hard. Nothing. Then he hummed the first few bars of "Here Comes the Bride," and I groaned. "Oh, right. The cookout thing."

"The shower-slash-barbecue," he corrected me. "Otherwise known as my mother's full-time obsession for the last two months?"

Oops. In my defense, however, this was the *third* of four showers that were being held in preparation for the wedding of Luke's sister Brooke. Ever since she'd gotten engaged the previous fall, it had been all wedding all the time at his house. Since I spent much of my time there, it was like being forced into an immersion program for a language I had no interest in learning. Plus, since Luke and I had been together since ninth grade, there was also the issue of everyone making jokes about how we'd be next, and his parents should go ahead and get a two-for-one deal. Ha, ha.

"Seven o'clock," Luke said now, kissing my forehead. "See you then. I'll be the one with the shirt on."

I smiled, shifting into reverse. Then it was back down the long driveway, onto the main road, and up to the end of the Tip, to Sand Dollars.

This was one of the newer houses we managed, and

probably the nicest. Eight bedrooms, ten and a half baths, pool and hot tub, private boardwalk to the beach, screening room downstairs with real theater seats and surround sound. It was so new, in fact, that only a couple of weeks ago there had still been a Porta-John outside, the contractor rushing to finish the last inspections before the season began. While they did punch-list and turnkey stuff, Margo and I had been putting away all the utensils and dishes the decorator had bought at Park Mart, bags and bags of which had been left in the garage. It was the oddest thing, furnishing a whole house all at once. There was no history to anything. All rental houses feel anonymous, but this one was where I'd felt it the most. So much so that even with the pretty view, it always kind of gave me the creeps. I liked a little past to things.

As I came up the drive, there was a lot of activity. A white van with tinted windows and an SUV were parked out front, the van's back doors open. Inside, I could see stacks of Rubbermaid bins and cardboard boxes, clearly in the process of being unloaded.

I got out of my car, collecting the VIP stuff. As I started up the stairs to the front door, it opened, and two guys about my age came out. Within seconds, we recognized each other.

"Emaline," Rick Mason, our former class president, called out to me. Behind him was Trent Dobash, who played football. The three of us were not friends, but our school was so small you knew everyone, whether you liked it or not. "Fancy meeting you here."

"You're renting this place?" I was shocked.

"I wish," he scoffed. "We were just down surfing and got offered a hundred each to unload this stuff."

"Oh," I said, as they passed me, moving down to the open van. "Right. What's in the boxes?"

"No idea," he replied, lifting one of the bins out and handing it to Trent. "Could be drugs or firearms. I don't care as long as I get my money."

This was exactly the kind of sentiment that had made Rick such a lousy class president. Then again, his only competition had been a girl who recently moved from California whom everyone hated, so it wasn't like we had a lot of options.

Inside the open front door, another guy was moving around in the huge living room, organizing the stuff that had already been brought in. He, however, was not from here, something I discerned with one glance. First, he had on Oyster jeans—dark wash, with the signature O on the back pockets—which I hadn't even known they made for guys. Second, he had a knit cap pulled down over his ears, even though it was early June. It was like pulling teeth to get Luke or any of his friends to wear anything but shorts, regardless of the temperature: beach guys don't do winter wear, even in winter.

I knocked, but he didn't hear me, too busy opening up one of the bins. I tried again, this time adding, "Colby Realty? VIP delivery?"

He turned, taking in the wine and the cheese. "Great," he replied, all business. "Just put it anywhere."

I walked over to the kitchen, where a couple of weeks ago I had been pulling price tags off spatulas and colanders, and arranged the tray, wine, and my card. I was just turning to leave when I caught a flutter of movement out of the corner of my eye. Then the yelling began.

"I don't *care* what time it is, I needed that delivery today! It's what I arranged and therefore what I expected and I won't accept anything else!" At first, the source of this was just a blur. A beat later, though, it slowed enough for me to make out a woman wearing black jeans, a short-sleeved black sweater, and ballet flats. She had hair so blonde it was almost white, and a cell phone was clamped to her ear. "I ordered four tables, I want four tables. They should be here in the next hour and my account is to be adjusted accordingly for their lateness. I am spending too much money to put up with this bullshit!"

I looked at the guy in the Oyster jeans, still busy with the bins across the room, who appeared to not even be fazed by this. I, however, was transfixed, the way you are whenever you see crazy people up close. You just can't look away, even when you know you should.

"No, that's not going to work for me. No. No. Today, or forget the entire thing." Now that she was standing still, I noted the set of her jaw, as well as the angular way her cheek and collar bones protruded. She was downright prickly, like one of those predator plants you see in deserts. "Fine. I'll expect my deposit to be refunded on my card by tomorrow morning or you'll be hearing from my attorney. Goodbye."

She jabbed at the phone, turning it off. Then, as I watched, she threw it across the room, where it crashed against the wall that just had just been painted on Memorial Day weekend, leaving a black mark. Holy shit.

"Idiots," she announced, her voice loud even in this big room. "Prestige Party Rental my *ass*. I *knew* the minute we crossed the Mason-Dixon Line it would be like working in the third world."

Now, the guy looked at her, then at me, which of course made her finally notice me as well. "Who is this?" she snapped.

"From the realty place," he told her. "VIP something or other."

She looked mystified, so I pointed at the wine and cheese. "A welcome gift," I said. "From Colby Realty."

"It would have been better if you'd brought tables," she grumbled, walking over to the platter and lifting the wrap. After peering down at it, she ate a grape, then shook her head. "Honestly, Theo, I'm already wondering if this was a mistake. What was I thinking?"

"We'll find another place to rent tables," he told her, in a voice that made it clear he was used to these kinds of tirades. He'd already picked up her phone, which he was now checking for damage. The wall, like me, was ignored.

"Where? This place is backwoods. There's probably not another one for a hundred miles. God, I need a drink." She picked up the wine I had brought, squinting at the bottle. "Cheap and Australian. Of course."

I watched her as she started pulling open drawers, obviously looking for a corkscrew. I let her look in all the wrong places, just out of spite, before I finally moved over to the wet bar by the pantry to get it.

"Here." I handed it to her, then grabbed the pen and paper we always left with the housekeeping card. "Prestige has a habit of screwing up orders. You should call Everything Island. They're open until eight."

I wrote down the number, then pushed it towards her. She just looked at it, then at me. She didn't pick it up.

As I started towards the stairs, where Rick and Trent were banging up with another load, neither of the renters said anything. I was used to that. As far as they were concerned, this was their place now, with me as much scenery as the water. But when I spotted a price tag still on a little wicker basket by the door, I stopped and pulled it off anyway.

2

MY BEDROOM DOOR was open. Again.

"So I'm like," I heard my sister Amber saying as I got closer, already feeling my blood pressure rising, "'I understand you want to look like a model. I want to win the lottery so I don't have to do this job. Let's just both lower our expectations, okay?'"

"I hope you didn't really say that," my mother murmured. I swore I heard pages turning. If she was reading that issue of *Hollyworld* I hadn't even cracked yet, my head was going to explode.

"I wanted to. But instead I gave her the bangs she insisted on, even though they made her look about thirty-five years old."

"Watch it."

"You know what I mean."

"Do I?"

I slapped my hand on the half-open door, pushing it wide into the room. Sure enough, they were on my bed. My mom was, in fact, reading my *Hollyworld*, while Amber—sporting yet another new hair color, this time a carrot orange—was in the process of taking a sip off a huge fountain Diet Coke from the Gas/Gro. Between them was an open can of cocktail nuts. "Get out," I said, my voice low. "Now."

"Oh, Emaline," Amber began.

My mom, knowing better, had already put the magazine back in my drawer, and was digging around in my duvet—*which I had just washed*—for the top to the nuts. When she couldn't find it, she gave up, getting to her feet with a guilty look on her face.

"You know what it's like upstairs right now."

"That has nothing to do with me," I replied, walking over to my TV, which was showing some rerun of a modeling reality show, and turning it off. "This is my room. *My room*. You are not allowed to just come down here and trash it."

"We weren't trashing it," my mom said, as she stepped behind me on her way to the door. "Just sitting here having a conversation."

I ignored this, instead going over to my bed, where my sister was for some reason still sitting. I dug under my pillow until I found the top to the nuts. I held it up, evidence.

My mom sighed. "I was hungry."

"Then eat in the kitchen."

"We have no kitchen!" Amber protested. Now she was finally moving, although, as usual, she took her sweet time. "Have you been up there lately, Miss Private Entrance? It's like a war zone."

"It's not a private entrance," I replied. "It's the garage."

"Whatever! Daddy's torn out everything. There's no place to sit, no place for the TV . . ."

As if in support of her point, I heard the pop of a compressor from upstairs, making us all jump. My dad had been doing carpentry for so long big noises no longer affected him. The rest of us, though, were still nervous as cats once he started up with the nail gun.

"What about *your* room?" I asked Amber, as my mom passed behind me, stopping briefly to tuck in the tag of my shirt, which apparently had been sticking out all afternoon. Great.

"It's too messy," she replied as she slowly made her way to the door, knocking a pile of folded laundry off the bureau on the way.

"Wonder why," I said, but she ignored me. Sighing, I bent down to pick it up. A beat later my mom, still silent, joined me. Amber and her traffic-cone hair had left the building, sighing melodramatically as she went. Though older than me, she'd once been the youngest. Now, all these years later, she still acted like a baby, although we now all blamed it on her being the middle child.

"You're in a mood," my mom finally said. It was typical of her manner, as well as her approach. Where my sisters and I tended towards loud and bombastic, she was always understated and quiet. It was like raising us just sucked all the fight right out of her.

"I've been yelled at too much today," I told her, getting to my feet. "And you know I hate when you guys come in here."

"I'm sorry." She held out the nuts to me, a peace offering. I shook my head, but still couldn't help but pick an almond out of the mix.

"No strip-mining," she said, helping herself to a handful. Selecting just the good stuff was one of her biggest pet peeves. "So isn't that engagement thing tonight?"

The nail gun popped again upstairs, once, twice. "Brooke and Andy's. Yeah."

"Maureen must be beside herself."

"She is. It's like wedding planning is a drug and she's always jonesing for a fix."

"Emaline," she said, but she was smiling. She and Luke's mom had both grown up in Colby, although my mom was seven years younger. Still, everyone knew that Mrs. Templeton had been on the pep squad and dated the captain of the football team, while my mom got pregnant the summer after junior year by a tourist boy. People didn't forget anything in a small town.

"I'm serious," I told her. "You should hear the stuff they are all saying about me and Luke. It's like they expect us to announce our engagement at the wedding, or something."

Her eyes got wide, the nuts in her hand frozen in midair. "*Don't*," she said, in a rare stern tone, "even *joke* about that."

"Don't hang out in my room," I replied.

"It's hardly the same offense." She was still giving me the evil eye. "Take it back."

"Mom, honestly. Take-backs at your age? Really?"

"Do it."

She wasn't kidding. That's the thing about someone who rarely gets upset: when they do, you notice. I cleared my throat. "I'm sorry. I was just making a stupid joke. Of course Luke and I aren't getting engaged this summer."

"Thank you." She ate a nut.

"We'll definitely wait until after freshman year," I continued. "I think I'll need to be adjusted to college before I start all the planning."

She just looked at me, chewing. All right, not funny.

"Mom, come on," I said, but she ignored me, going out into the hallway as there was another pop from upstairs. "I'm sorry. I'm just . . ."

She was still walking, towards the sound of the nail gun.

". . . being stupid. Okay?"

After a beat, she turned around. From this distance, you never would have guessed she was thirty-six. With the same long, brown hair that I had, her body toned from regular workouts, she looked closer to late twenties, if that. It was the reason she was more often taken for Amber and Margo's sister rather than their stepmother, why when we were kids she always got That Look at supermarkets and bank lines as people tried to do the math. They could never figure it out.

"You know," she said finally, "I only get upset because I want you to have everything I didn't."

"The moon and more," I said, and she nodded.

This was our thing, from the days before my dad, Amber, and Margo came into the picture, the days I didn't even really remember. But she'd told me often of a book she read aloud every night when I was a baby, about a mother bear and her little cub who won't go to sleep.

What if I get hungry? he asks.

I'll bring you a snack, she tells him.

What if I'm thirsty?

I'll fetch you water.

What if I get scared?

I'll order all the monsters away.

Finally he asks, *What if that's not enough? What if I need something else?*

And she replies, *Whatever you need, I will find a way to get it to you. I will give you the moon, and more.*

This, she always said, was how she felt as a teenage single mother, raising me alone. She had nothing, but wanted everything for me. Still did.

Now, she pointed at me with her free hand. "You behave yourself at that party. This is about Brooke and Andy, not you and your opinions."

"You know," I said, as she turned around again, "contrary to what you believe, I don't actually think everything's about me."

Her only response was a snort, and then she was gone. The gun continued to pop as she climbed the stairs, but a moment later, it stopped. In the quiet following, I heard her say something, and my dad laughed. Typical. We might make fun of her, but when they were together, the joke was always on us.

"I heard that," I yelled, even though I didn't. More laughter.

Back in my room, I surveyed the damage, which was easy because that morning, like always, I'd left the place spotless: bed made, drawers shut, nothing on the floor or bureau tops. Now, I spotted Amber's keys and sunglasses on my desk, my mom's flip-flops parked under my bedside table. There was also a crumpled piece of paper on the floor beside my trash can. I sighed, then walked over and picked it up. I was just about to toss it in when I saw my mom's handwriting and smoothed it out instead.

It was from one of the Colby Realty giveaway notepads, which were all over our house; you'd be hard-pressed to find anything else to write on. In her neat script it said simply, *Your father called. 4:15 p.m.*

I looked at my watch. It was 6:30, which meant I had less than a half hour before I needed to leave for Luke's and the party. But this was more important. I took the note and went upstairs.

The first thing I saw when I stepped into the war zone that was currently our kitchen was my dad, shooting a nail into a piece of shoe molding by the pantry door. The kitchen itself was empty, as it had been since he'd been refinishing the floors. My mom was watching him from atop our new dishwasher, which was functioning as furniture, island, and catchall area until it got installed.

Bam! went the nail gun, and I jumped. My mom looked over at me, clearly thinking I'd come up to continue our conversation from earlier. When I held up the note, though, her expression changed.

"I was going to"—*Bam!*—"tell you," she replied.

"But you didn't."

Bam! "I know. It was a mistake. I just got distracted when you came in all upset about—"

Bam! Bam!

I held up my hand, stopping her. "Dad!" I yelled. Another pop. "*Dad!*"

Finally, he stopped, then turned around, seeing me. "Well,

hey there, Emaline," he said, smiling. "How was your day?"

"Can you stop that for just one second?"

"Stop working?" he asked.

"Would you mind?"

He glanced at my mom, who stress-ate another handful of nuts. "All right," he said, as easygoing as always, and put the nail gun down, trading it for a Mountain Dew sitting on the dishwasher. My mom and I were both quiet as he twisted off the top, taking a big sip. He looked at me, at her, then back at me. "Whoa. What'd I miss?"

"Nothing," my mom replied.

"She didn't tell me my father called," I said at the same time.

My dad looked at her, a weary expression on his face. "This again?" he said. "Really?"

"I forgot," she told us both. "It was a mistake."

I looked at him, making my doubt about this clear. He put down the bottle. "But you *did* get the message. Right?"

"Only because she threw it all crumpled up on my floor."

He shrugged, as if this actually was the same thing. "What matters is that now you know."

I exhaled, shaking my head. Thick as thieves, these two were. I had never been right enough for him to take my side on *anything*. "I just don't understand why you're so weird about this," I said to my mom.

"Yeah, you do," my dad said.

We were all quiet for a moment. All I could hear was the TV in Amber's room, which worked just fine, in case you were wondering. "I took the message," my mom said finally, "then brought it down there to leave it for you. But when I heard you coming, I trashed it, figuring I'd tell you myself. But I . . . didn't. I'm sorry."

The thing is, I knew this was true. She was sorry. In her real life, she was a capable and responsible mom, wife, and daughter. But when it came to my father, it was like she was eighteen all over again, and she always acted like it.

I looked down at the note. "Did he say what he wanted?"

She shook her head. "Just to call him when you get a chance."

"Okay." I checked my watch: 6:40. Crap. "I have to go. I'm already late."

"Have fun," she called after me as I headed back to my room. It was a peace offering, and a little bit too late, but I nodded and waved anyway, so she knew we were okay. They were quiet as I went down the stairs and started down the hallway to my room. Once there, though, I could hear their voices, muffled overhead, as she gave him the explanation she just couldn't ever seem to relay to me. Whatever it was, it was short. By the time I was in the shower, the nail gun was popping again.

* * *

There's a difference between the words *father* and *dad*. And it's more than three letters.

Up until the age of ten, I didn't know this. I also didn't know much about where I'd come from, other than my mom had me when she was a senior in high school, which was why she was so much younger than the mothers of all my friends.

Then, one day in fifth grade, my teacher Mr. Champion got up in front of the whiteboard and wrote, *My Family Tree*. And just like that, things got complicated.

I'd always loved everything about school, from checking out the maximum number of books allowed from the library to organizing my notebooks into neat, labeled sections. Even at ten, I took my assignments very seriously, which was why I was not content to put my stepdad down next to my mom on the top of my tree, even though he'd adopted me when I was three.

"It's supposed to reflect my accurate, genetic family," I told my mom when she suggested this. "I need details."

I could tell she wasn't happy about it. But to her credit, she gave them to me. Some I had heard before, others were new. The bottom line was that she didn't get too far into the story before I realized my tree wasn't going to look like everyone else's.

My mom met my father when she was seventeen, just after her junior year of high school. She was working at the realty office; he, a year older and heading off to college in the fall, had come down from Connecticut to spend the summer with an aunt who lived in nearby North Reddemane. In any other world, they never would have met. But this was the summer at the beach, and the standard rules, then as now, didn't always apply.

They couldn't have been more different. His parents were wealthy—his father a doctor and his mother a realtor—and he attended private school, where he'd studied Latin and played lacrosse. She was the second of three daughters of a working-class family with a business that was mostly seasonal and always struggling to stay afloat. My mom was pretty, a known beauty; she'd dated only jocks and heartthrobs. He was a brain bordering on a smart aleck. They had nothing in common, but one night, she was heading to a party with her best friend, whose boyfriend brought along the mouthy Northerner he washed dishes alongside at Shrimpboats, a local fried seafood joint: my father. My mom was not looking for a boyfriend. What she got in the end was, well, me.

It wasn't just a hookup: I've seen the pictures. They were In Love, inseparable the entire summer. He left in mid-August to go home and get ready for college, but not before they made firm travel plans to see each other again as soon as possible. The goodbye was tearful, followed by a couple of weeks of serious long-distance bills—all your typical summer romance stuff. Then my mom missed a period.

Suddenly it was no longer a romance, or even a relationship, but a crisis. Her parents were devastated, his were horrified, and what had been a singular relationship between two people became much more complicated. Calls were made, arrangements discussed. My mom had never gone into much detail, but I did know there were people on both sides who did not want her to keep me. In the end, though, she did.

For the first part of the pregnancy, she and my father remained in regular contact. But as the months passed and her belly grew, they started to drift apart. Maybe it would have happened anyway, even without a baby in the picture; maybe that baby should have prevented it. My mom, to her credit, never assigned full blame for this to my father. He was so young, she told me again and again, away at college with parents who so disapproved of the situation. They had all those miles between them and only a summer in common. It would have been hard enough for him to relate to her world—one now focused on buying onesies and reading books on labor and delivery—even without his friends in his other ear, nagging him to go to keg parties.

By the time of my birth their contact had gone from rare to nonexistent. He was listed on the birth certificate, but didn't meet me until I was six weeks old, when he came down with his parents for what was by all accounts a massively awkward visit.

My mom said my father's dad couldn't even make eye contact as she held me, instead just always looking off to her left, as if trying to see around us. To him, more than anything, we represented a wrong turn, one that if acknowledged would make their entire family that much more lost. As for my father, he was nervous and distant, so different from the boy she'd met the year before. Funny how it was only when he was finally right there in front of her, she said, that she knew for sure he was already gone. After that visit, she wouldn't see him again for ten years.

The only good thing that came out of the whole thing, my mom always said, was a discussion about child support. She, like her parents, hated the thought of any kind of handout, but she was in high school, and diapers and childcare weren't cheap, so an amount was set, a schedule made. My father might not have been reliable, but the money—in the form of a check, signed by my father's father's secretary—

always was. After graduating, my mother went to work full-time at Colby Realty, dropping me every morning with my great-aunt Sylvie, who rocked and fed me while she watched her soaps. Later, she would say these were the hardest years of her life.

So that was my father. As for my dad, *he* came into the picture when I was two years old. A widower with two small girls of his own, he was set up with my mom by mutual friends for a blind date. Both were young and single with small children: it seemed the perfect match. Instead, she hated his humor and the way he ate, while he thought she was stuck-up and didn't smile enough. Six months later, though, my mom's car broke down on the single two-lane road that ran through Colby. My dad was the first one who stopped.

They'd been together ever since. He always said she just needed to see him with tools to fall hard. She maintained he was not all wrong.

And so, just like that, we were a family. I was two years old, Amber four, Margo six. I had no real memory of a life without them as my sisters, just as they didn't recall much that happened before my mom became theirs as well. After the wedding, we'd moved into the same house our dad had been adding onto and tearing apart ever since. Even without the constant construction, it was chaotic and loud, not peaceful by a long shot. But it was what I knew.

So while my dad was present for most of my childhood, my father was more like Bigfoot or the Loch Ness Monster. There had been sightings, other people claimed he was real, but the proof was all secondhand: old pictures, ancient conversations, the checks that my mom had put a stop to when my dad adopted me. Then, though, Mr. Champion wrote those three words on the board, and I was determined to fill in my own blanks.

"I want to write to him," I told her, that first day I came home with the assignment. "Ask some questions."

"Oh, honey," my mom had said, getting that heavy, tired look that always came over her face on the rare times this subject came up. "I don't think that's a good idea."

"He's my father," I said. "It's my story. I need to know it."

I remember she glanced at my dad for support. He was quiet for a moment—he never spoke without thinking first—then said, "Emaline, he might not write you back. You need to be ready for that."

"I will be," I said. My mom gave me a doubtful look. "I *will*. You have to let me at least try."

In the end, she did, sitting silently across from me as I wrote first a draft—always the perfectionist when it came to school—then a final copy of the letter. I slid it into an envelope, then watched as she flipped through her address book until she found the one that had been on the top right corner of all those checks. She read it aloud, I wrote it down, and we took it to the mailbox together.

It could have ended like that. Nobody, including me, would have been that surprised. But two weeks later, an envelope arrived with my name on it. Inside was a typed letter on thick paper. JOEL PENDLETON, it said at the top. No more Loch Ness. He was real.

Dear Emaline,

*Thank you so much for writing me. I have
thought of you so often, wondering how you were
doing and what you were like, but never thought
it was my right or place to try to find out. I would
love to answer the questions for your project and,
if you were so inclined, tell you a bit about myself
as well. I know I can never expect to be your father.
But it is my hope that maybe, someday, we might
be friends.*

The letter went on. He gave me everything I needed of
his family history—answering each of my questions in order
and detail—before moving onto his own. He was working as a
freelance journalist and married, he said, five years now, to a
wonderful woman named Leah. They had a two-year-old boy:
Benji. Maybe, someday, I could meet him. On the last page,
just before his scribbled signature, was an e-mail address. He
didn't say to write him, or that he was waiting to hear from
me. It was just there, like an offering.

That was the first time I saw my mom get that particular
mix of worry and sadness on her face. Now, I could spot it
from across a room. He'd hurt her so much all those years ago.
Her greatest fear was that she'd let him get in a place where
he'd be able to do the same to me.

I finished my project and handed it in, receiving an A.
Then I filed it away. (I was a kid with files, even back then;
once a school-supply nerd, always a school-supply nerd.) The

letter I kept in the drawer of my bedside table, where I'd take it out and look at it every once in a while. The stationery was so thick, his monogram raised. Like even paper was different, somehow, in his world. Finally, a few weeks later, I opened up my e-mail, typed in the address he'd provided, and wrote to him, thanking him for his help and telling him I'd gotten a good grade. Within a few hours, there was a response.

That is great news, he wrote. *What else are you studying in school?*

Really, it was in those last seven words that our relationship, whatever it was or would be, began. School was a common ground, something he knew so much about, more than my mom and dad, more than even some of my teachers. Math, history, literature, science—he had experience with them all, and was always ready and eager to provide me with his opinions, links to articles, books I should think about reading. Learning became our common language, and suddenly we were writing regularly.

A few months and many e-mails later, he wrote saying he and his wife and son would be coming down to North Reddemane. They hoped to meet me, if my parents agreed. When I told my mom, she bit her lip, and I saw that look again.

Nobody thought she should do it. Her family said he had done nothing for us and deserved the same in return, that it would just confuse and upset me. But my mom had read all the e-mails. Despite her misgivings, she understood that he was somehow filling a void we might have not even known was there. So a couple of months after the letter arrived, a visit was arranged. My father, his wife, and Benji came down to stay with his now-elderly aunt, and we made plans to all meet for dinner at Shrimpboats. In the days preceding this, my mother was so nervous she threw up repeatedly, which I'd never seen her do before—or since, actually. Your past holds on to everything, apparently, even your gut.

When the day arrived, we showed up at the restaurant and were led to a table by the window, where a tall man in glasses and a woman, a chubby toddler on her lap, were waiting for us. Personally, all I remember from the visit was how different my father was than in his e-mails. He seemed uncomfortable and awkward, and would not stop looking at me. He openly stared pretty much from when we said our hellos (stiff handshakes, awkward mumblings) until the merciful moment about an hour and a half later when we finally parted. It was like he was trying to make up for his own father, all those years ago, in seeing me.

His wife Leah, a toothy, friendly brunette, engineered the entire conversation, talking constantly to fill in any and all awkward silences. The boy, Benji, my half brother, was cute and thought everything I did was hilarious. I had popcorn shrimp. My dad talked entirely too much about the building business. My mom drank ginger ale and eyed the restroom. And then it was over. When we said goodbye, my father gave me a wrapped package, which I opened up, somewhat self-consciously, as everyone else watched. It was a copy of *Adventures of Huckleberry Finn*, his favorite book when he was my age.

"You may not like it," he said, by way of explanation. "Which is fine. Just try it and see."

On the way home, I sat with it in my lap, watching from the backseat as my mom exhaled, resting her head against the closed window. My dad reached over from behind the wheel, and squeezed her shoulder. "So that's that," he said, and she nodded.

Well, not exactly. It took me a week to read *Huckleberry Finn*, another to figure out what to say to him about it. In the end, I decided just to be honest, telling him that it was kind of boring, had weird language, too much river. I wondered if I'd offend him, or if how strange he'd been at our meeting meant I wouldn't get any reply at all. The next day, though, just like clockwork, there was this:

What else did you think?

As it turned out, that lunch wasn't the end for us. But it wasn't the beginning of some beautiful relationship, either. More like a door being opened a tiny crack to let a sliver of light in. It wasn't enough to see clearly by, but from then on, we would never be fully in the dark again.

We e-mailed regularly, talking about what I was studying and reading. Once a summer, they'd come down to North Reddemane and a meeting would be arranged. There was mini golf, more popcorn shrimp, the aquarium and Maritime Museum with Benji as he grew. Cards came for my birthday, gifts neatly wrapped (I knew by Leah) for Christmas. All the while I continued battling with my sisters, being with my friends, and doing all the other things that constituted my Real Life, the one I had, very happily, without them. Then, during a visit the summer I was sixteen, something changed.

It began with a simple comment, lobbed across the table

as we sat at Igor's, the lone Italian place in town. (My dad swore their slogan was "For when you can't eat seafood one more time!" although this was not actually the case.) My father took a sip of his wine, then looked at me. "So," he said. "Have you thought at all about college?"

I blinked at him. "Um," I replied. "Not yet. They don't start doing stuff at school for it until next year."

"But you do plan to go," he continued. "Right?"

He was a stranger in so many ways, but one thing I knew was that where he came from, higher learning was expected. This was unlike in my own family, where at that time college graduates numbered exactly zero. This difference was clear just by looking at Benji, who wanted the crayons the waitress offered when we sat down, but was told to do a word puzzle—Leah carried a book with her everywhere—instead. "Challenge yourself," she'd told him, opening it up and pushing it across the table.

I glanced over at my half brother, watching his face as he studied the little squares. When I looked back at my father, he was still staring at me, just like the first time we'd met, but it felt different now. This was our thing, our shared interest. Maybe it was weird there was only one. But I'd take it.

"Yeah," I told him. "Absolutely. I mean, that's the plan."

"Good." He nodded, pleased. "Glad to hear it."

A week later, the first book arrived. *Test Best: Preparing for the S.A.T.*, I think it was called, although in the months following he sent so many more it was hard to keep them all straight. Books about taking tests, writing powerful essays, making your application stand out. About picking a college, calculating your chances, making sure you had the right backup and safety school. One by one, they crowded out my novels and magazines, taking over the entire shelf to the point where it sagged in the middle. I wasn't stupid. I knew that with all these words, bound between covers, he was building me a way out of Colby, one book at a time.

The thing was, even though I was a good student, the schools where he wanted me to apply—Dartmouth, Cornell, Columbia—were ones my guidance counselor hadn't even suggested. Plus there was the question of money, always tight. "Don't worry," he assured me, whenever I got up the nerve to broach this subject. "Leave the finances to me. You just concentrate on getting in."

It was a big promise, though, coming from someone who did not exactly have the best track record. This was something my mom, in particular, could not ignore. Our e-mail relationship was one thing; at least there, he was still at a distance, existing to me only, really, in cyberspace. But money and promises were real. As was the disappointment I'd feel if he wasn't able to deliver.

"I just don't want you to get your hopes up," she told me. "When I knew Joel he was a big talker, but not so big on delivering."

"Mom, he was *my* age then," I pointed out. "Would you want to be judged based on how you were at eighteen?"

"I didn't really have a choice," she said. "I had a child."

Point taken. And I got where she was coming from. She'd done everything she could to make sure I didn't have the same experience, on any level, that she did. Luckily, I had some people on my side.

"Stop worrying," my grandmother said to her more than once, when I overheard them discussing this behind a door that was supposed to muffle their words. "He wants to get her there and pay for it, let him. You've done everything else."

"I don't want her to get let down," my mom replied. "The whole idea of being a parent is your kid *not* repeating your mistakes."

"People do change, Emily. He's a grown man now," my grandmother told her. "And anyway, no matter what happens, she has you and Rob. She'll be fine."

The books, essay prep, and hard work all paid off: I got into three of my top five schools, and my safety, East U, offered me a full ride. It wasn't until the e-mail came from our first choice, Columbia, however, that I finally let myself exhale. The first thing I did was hit Compose and type in my father's address.

Columbia, I wrote in the subject line. Then, below, without a greeting or closing, only, *I got in*. Then I hit Send.

I expected a quick response, as, like me, he checked his messages almost constantly. Instead, it was about five hours later that he wrote back. *Great news*, the e-mail said. *Congratulations*.

It wasn't like he'd ever been that effusive in our exchanges. But I had expected a bit more excitement—or something—at this particular news. He'd written me pages about *Huckleberry Finn*. This was only three words.

I tried not to think about this, though, as I hit Reply and

thanked him, saying I'd be sending along some links to financial and admissions stuff we needed to work out. No response.
In fact, the next time I heard from him was three weeks later.

Emaline,
    I am so sorry to have to tell you this, but due to
unforseen circumstances, I will not be able to supplement your tuition to Columbia. It was always my hope
and intention to help you, but some things have occurred that make it impossible. I hope you understand.

Supplement? I thought. Not only was the deal off, it had
never been what I thought in the first place. Also, I couldn't
help but notice that the tone—distant, almost automated—
sounded not unlike messages I'd received from the schools
that had rejected me. All that was missing was a *We regret to
inform you.*

So that was that. Columbia had been a long shot. I'd gotten there, and now it was being pulled away again. Sucker. To
make matters worse, it was too late to apply for financial aid,
which I'd assumed I wouldn't need. And while we theoreti-
cally could have taken out a loan, all I could think of was my
dad, who never bought anything on credit, paid his bills in
full each month, and expected all of us to avoid debt with the
same vigilance we did pedophiles and rabid animals. I could
only imagine his face when I told him we'd need to borrow
about as much as he'd make in a full year. Luckily, I didn't
have to. When he and my mom sat me down after dinner the
next night and told me there was no way we could afford Co-

lumbia, I wasn't surprised. After all, it had never been their promise.

So East U it was. I had a full ride, it was a good school: you didn't have to have a degree to see it was a no-brainer. That night, I sat at my desk, looking at that full shelf of college prep books, all lined up in a row. Thanks to ongoing budget cuts, they numbered more than the entire collection on the subject in my school's media center. Just as I thought this, I had a flash of my mom graduating eighteen years earlier, while I watched from my grandmother's arms. How different our lives were, then and now. She'd wanted so much for me: the moon and more. But maybe, right now, the moon was enough.

So it seemed fitting, really, that the moon was out and shining through the corner of my window as I pulled up the Columbia Web site and notified them I wouldn't be attending in the fall. After all that hard work, it was so easy. Just a couple of clicks, some keystrokes, and done.

As for my father, there were no more e-mails, no explanations: he was just gone, Bigfoot all over again. At times, I found myself questioning his very existence, even though I knew I had, in fact, spotted him, with my own eyes.

And while I kept my initial acceptance message from Columbia in my inbox for a while, looking at it didn't really make me sad. Instead, it was the lack of e-mails. How pathetic I felt logging in to my account, hoping to see my father's address atop the new messages. The weirdness of donating all those books to the media center, now that I didn't need them anymore.

Mostly, I felt stupid for falling for his big talk, the very thing my mother had warned me about. Even from a distance he'd taken me in, and I'd gone, gullibly and willingly. In my less masochistic moments, I reminded myself that I, a girl from Colby High, had gotten into an Ivy League school. That had to count for something. I just wasn't sure what it was.

But life went on. And the one person who knew that best of all, always, hadn't gone anywhere. She was always bragging, telling anyone who would listen about my full scholarship to a great school. Squeezing my shoulder as she passed by me as I sat on the couch watching TV. Smiling from across the dinner table when Amber said something typically ridiculous. Stopping outside my closed bedroom door for only a moment, yet always just long enough so I knew for sure she was there.

3

"I'D JUST LIKE to say again how thrilled we are that Andy will be joining our family in August. Here's to the bride and groom!"

There was a burst of applause as Mr. Templeton held up his glass, followed by a collective "*Awwww*" as the happy couple leaned in for a kiss. Off to the right, Luke's mom stood watching, face flushed, tears visible in her eyes. A beautiful moment.

I looked over at Luke, who was standing beside me in a collared shirt I was sure he had put on only under serious duress. "I am so glad we are going to college," he said. "Because this next year, at this house, when all this is over and my mom has nothing to do? It's going to be *scary*."

"That," I said, as his parents hugged Andy, then Brooke, "is a really poor attitude."

"My mother," he said in response, "has already told me that I have to wear tails to this wedding. *Tails*. In Colby. We'll be like all those people we mock."

He meant the ones who came here for destination weddings, most often in spring and summer. They set up chairs and little arches decorated with flowers on the beach, then were surprised when it was windy and the bride's veil took flight and everyone looked ruffled in the pictures. After complaining endlessly about all our caterers and vendors—hopelessly backwards compared to wherever they came from—they more often than not left wedding cake smeared into the furniture and a trail of broken dishes behind in their rentals. There was no denying people like this were part of an industry many in Colby depended on for their living. Which did not mean we couldn't make fun of them, at least a little bit.

"Maybe," I said, as there was another round of applause, "she'll ditch that idea and let you all wear Hawaiian shirts and white pants instead."

"Only if the bridesmaids wear flip-flops and carry single sunflowers," he replied. These were things we had witnessed so far this summer alone.

"I would be happy," I offered, "to decorate a bunch of shells with their initials and wedding date to scatter across the beach. Oh, and fill a bunch of little bags with sand for favors."

He held up his hand, stopping me. "You joke, but they're talking about releasing butterflies."

I raised my eyebrows. "You're kidding, right?"

"Told you," he said, shuddering. "Scary stuff."

Really, it was kind of fun to see Luke bent out of shape. Spend enough time—like three years of your life—with Mr. Easygoing, it was hard not to feel superneurotic in comparison. His attitude, though, was one of my favorite things about him, even if did make me examine my own psyche more than I preferred to. He was not bad to look at, either.

I stepped closer to him, kissing his cheek, and got a familiar whiff of chlorine and sunshine. I loved that smell. "You poor baby. I hope you survive this."

"I think I'll need extra emotional support," he said, then gave me a real kiss, right in view of some elderly relatives passing by on the way to the appetizers. I could see their startled faces from the corner of my eye as he was pulling me in, but once his lips hit mine, relatives and everything else fell away. All this time and he could still make my heart jump, just like that first kiss in the fall of freshman year. Best-looking guy in school—no, just best *guy* in school—and he wanted me. Sometimes I still couldn't believe it.

"I think I know who's next," someone trilled from behind us, breaking this thought even as I was having it.

Luke pulled back, grinning at me. "Look at that. Engagements are contagious."

"So is the plague," I said, and he laughed out loud.

"Luke? Honey?" A beat later, his mom was beside us, one hand on his arm. "We're running low on ice. Can you run down to the Gas/Gro and get some?"

"Sure thing," he said. Mr. Accommodating. To me he said, "Want to ride along?"

"Not so fast," Mrs. Templeton said, switching her grip to *my* arm. She was a grabber, always had been. "I think you two can stand to be apart for ten minutes. I need Emaline's help in the kitchen if we ever want to serve this dinner. Some of these workers the caterers brought are *worthless*."

Uh-oh, I thought. Luke gave me a look, which I ignored, focusing instead on his mom's perfect updo, which was bouncing slightly in front of me as she led me up to the house. As we climbed the side steps to the kitchen, I saw it was crowded with people: Luke's dad was arranging steak and salmon on a platter, his younger sister Stacey was taking pans from the oven, and a woman in black and white, clearly hired, was busy piling rolls in a big basket. Only one person was standing still, doing nothing, and of course it was Morris.

"We've got to get this food out," Luke's mom said to me over her shoulder. "Can you find the salads and bring them to the table? Oh, and there are a couple more bottles of wine in the pantry, I think the bartender might need them by now."

"Right," I said, negotiating around Luke's dad, who gave me a wink, hoisting his tray of meat and fish. I spotted the salads on the counter by the fridge and made a beeline over to them, grabbing one before walking up to my best friend, who was busy holding up the fridge and examining his fingernails. "Morris," I hissed. "What are you doing?"

He looked up at me. "What do you mean?"

I shoved the salad into his hands, hard, making him jump. "Do you realize you are the only one in this entire room not working right now?"

"I'm working," he said. This I ignored, grabbing the other salad bowl and sticking it under my arm before ducking into the pantry to grab the wine.

"Come on," I said. He just looked at me. "*Now.*"

We went out onto the deck and down the stairs, heading to the rows of tables that were set up in the backyard, tiki torches lined up between them. All the way, just behind me, I could hear Morris's signature shuffle-lope. It was a sound I knew well, mostly because despite the fact that we'd known each other since grade school, he had not once *ever* been in front of me. He was that freaking slow.

"What's your problem?" he asked as I plunked the salad bowl onto a table by a stack of plates. He was still holding his, would not put it down unless directly instructed to do so. "You and Luke in a fight or something?"

"Do you even know how much I had to stick my neck out for you to get this gig?" I demanded. "Robin did *not* want to hire you. I basically begged her."

"Why'd you do that?"

I couldn't take it anymore: I grabbed his salad, putting it on the table. "Because," I said, "Daisy told me you were desperate for work."

"I wouldn't say *desperate*," he replied.

"Clearly not. Because if you were, you'd actually be, you know, *working*."

Most people, having been spoken to this way, would be chastened. Or at least react. But this was Morris, so he just looked at me. "She told me to bring in the salads and bread. I did. I was awaiting further instruction."

I rolled my eyes. "Do you really always have to be specifically told everything? You can't see a need and jump in to meet it?"

"Do what?"

"Morris?" I turned. It was Robin, the owner of Roberts

Family Catering, who had owed me a favor. Now I was pretty sure I was in *her* debt. "Did you unload those napkins and plates from the van?"

"Uh-huh," he told her.

"*Yes*," I corrected him, not that he heard me.

"Are they"—she glanced at the serving station, now lined with platters of food—"here?"

"You didn't tell me where to put them."

Dear God, I thought, as Robin—and I—looked over at the driveway where, sure enough, the plates and napkins were stacked on the pavement, right next to the van. "Go," I said to him. "Go *get* them and *bring* them *to* her."

"You *are* in a bad mood," he observed, but now, finally, he was moving. Shuffle-lope, shuffle-lope. I shook my head, then headed over to Robin, who was busy pulling foil and cling wrap off her various dishes.

"Don't say it," she said, before I could even begin to apologize. "I'm too busy right now."

"Let me help, at least," I told her, coming around the table. I found some tongs, stuck them in the dishes, then lined up the dressing cruets someone else had just dropped off.

"You just did more than he has in two hours," she said in a tired voice.

"I'm sorry."

"He's worthless."

"I know."

Now she stopped, giving me an incredulous look. "Then why in the world did you ask me to hire him for a big job like this?"

"I was trying to help . . ." I trailed off as Morris approached, the napkins and plates in hand, "a friend."

"Must be a good one," she said.

I nodded as she gestured to Morris to put the stuff he was carrying at the end of the table. Then I went over to stand beside him and began opening up the plates. After a beat—or three—he joined me.

I wished this was the first time I'd taken heat for Morris, but our entire relationship—forged in third grade, when he and his mom briefly lived next door—had pretty much revolved around him screwing up and me making excuses for him. The best I could figure is that I never got to have a puppy, and being friends with Morris was kind of like the same thing. He could be cute, and fun, but also at any moment ruin your favorite shoes and pee all over your floor. So to speak.

Still, I should have known better, especially after last summer. That was when I'd had the bright idea of convincing my dad to hire Morris to tote boards and supplies and be a general gofer on his job sites. He'd had back surgery in the spring—twenty years of driving nails takes its toll—and the doctor told him he needed to take it easy, or at least easier. Morris had just been let go from his job at Jumbo Smoothie for eating too many toppings, among other things, so I went to bat with my dad, convincing him to give him a shot. The first day, Morris backed the company truck into a gas pump, left half the crew's lunch order on the counter at Sliders & Subs, and took, by my dad's count, approximately fourteen water breaks. I wanted to die.

"He moves *so slowly*," my dad said that evening, popping his ritual first beer. He still seemed incredulous, even hours later. "It's like he's got a disease or something."

"I'm sorry," I said.

"And you have to tell him everything," he continued, not hearing me. "Not just, say, 'go fill the gas tank.' More like: 'Park the truck. Remove gas cap. Fill tank with gas. Remove pump. Replace gas cap. And don't hit anything on your way out.'"

"I'm sorry," I said again.

He shook his head, downing another sip. "I was going to let him go, but I told him he needed to work off the cost of getting that dent fixed. So I guess I'm stuck with him."

"I'm—" He gave me a look, and I stopped myself from apologizing again. "I'll pay the dent cost. It's my fault he was there in the first place."

"No, no," he said, waving me off. "You've done enough for him. I'll deal with it."

I expected Morris to be fired by the next week. But he wasn't. Instead, my dad kept him on, which was worse, because I had to hear him complain about Morris every single night. How slow he was. How he couldn't bang a nail without hitting his own hand or someone else's. He couldn't dig a decent hole, remember a simple order, drive a stick shift. The list went on and on, and every item on it made me cringe.

"So fire him," I said finally, over dinner in mid-June. "Please. I'm begging you. I can't take this anymore."

Across the table, Amber snorted. If Margo was the goody-goody and I was the perfectionist brain, she was the wild child. Prone to tattooed older boyfriends, never making it home by curfew, and blowing all her money on beer or clothes, she was usually the one getting it from one or both parents, and loved it on the rare occasions when someone else was.

"Oh, I will," my dad said. "I'm just waiting until I find someone else to replace him. He's better than nothing." A pause. "I think."

The weird thing was, he never did let him go. The excuses evolved: it was too much trouble to train someone new, another guy quit, and then the summer was practically over. But even after all the complaining, Morris was still doing odd jobs around the house after school and on weekends. Maybe my dad kept him around because he knew his backstory— no father in the picture, Mom less than invested, to say the least. Or perhaps he just had the same helping gene I did, even though we weren't blood related. Whatever the reason, I didn't question his tolerance of Morris, if only because of how much I hated it when anyone did the same to me.

Now, I glanced over at him. He was putting forks in a basket, one at a time. "Morris. Please. Just dump the box in, okay?

"Huh?"

"Forget it."

I could see Luke now, pulling up with the ice. He parked, then got out of the car and went around to the trunk, laughing as someone called out to him. It's funny how two people can grow up in the same town, go to the same school, have the same friends, and end up so totally different. Family, or lack of it, counts for more than you'd think.

"You sure you're okay?" Morris said, opening another box of forks. "You seem . . . weird."

I swallowed, glancing over at Robin, who was barking orders. "My father called today."

"Really." I nodded. "What'd he want?"

"Don't know. Haven't called him back."

He considered this, then said, "Maybe he has a graduation present for you."

I made a face. "Kind of late, don't you think?"

He shrugged. "Better late than never."

This, ladies and gentlemen, was basically Morris's mantra. But that was the weird thing: I could handle *him* being slack because, well, it was just how he was. I expected more from everyone else. Especially my father.

With the college issue finally settled, life had slowly gotten back to normal, as much as it could with the final days of high school winding down. Even though we'd left things awkwardly weeks earlier—to say the least—my father had been instrumental in my college process, and I'd always intended to invite him, Leah, and Benji to graduation. So in late May, I wrote their address on one of the thick, creamy envelopes and popped it with the others into the mailbox. He never responded. Whatever it was we'd shared all those months, clearly, it was over.

Or so I'd thought. *Call when you get a chance*, the message had said. I could understand my mother's first instinct, to toss it away. Fool me once, shame on you. Fool me twice, I was just a fool. This was the girl I was, this was where I was from, and East U was where I was going. What could he possibly say that would change any of that now? Nothing.

And yet, I hated to leave anything open and unfinished,

so I wondered. All through dinner, as I sat with Luke's arm loosely around my shoulders, trying not to track Morris's work—or lack of it—from a distance. As it grew dark, and the tiki torches took on a mild, warm glow, bugs circling them. For the entire drive home that I knew by heart, four turns, two stop signs, one flashing yellow light. It was like a voice barely in earshot, whispering just loud enough to make you want to lean closer so you could make it out. When I finally got to my house, I cut the engine, then slid my feet out of my shoes. We were blocks from the beach, just like the office was, but no matter. The first thing I felt on my bare feet, like always, was sand.

* * *

The next day was Sunday, which meant another round of checkouts and arrivals. So much for a day of rest. For me, the last day of the week always meant follow-up duty.

Colby Realty didn't employ their own housekeeping staff. Instead, we subcontracted out to several cleaning companies, each of which handled certain houses each week. It was hard work, and you had to do it quickly: checkout was at ten, check-in at four. Which left six hours to make houses fully used by folks on vacation appear pristine and untouched. Not everyone could pull it off, which was why Grandmother insisted that we check behind every crew for quality control before the keys went back out. The Sunday shift of this was the least desirable job at the agency. Which was why it was usually part of mine.

The first place on my list that day was Summer Daydream, a peach-colored house on the second row back from the oceanfront. I parked, then climbed the stairs to the front door and followed the sound of a vacuum through the entryway and into the TV room. There I saw one of our longtime cleaners, Lolly, chasing dust bunnies with her canister and hose.

"Emaline," Lolly called out to me as I passed by the living room. When I doubled back, she cut off the vaccuum, picking up a Windex bottle.

"Hey," I said. "How's it going?"

She sighed, spritzing a big glass coffee table covered in smudges and cup rings. Here we go. "Well, you know how I put out my back last month. Went to the doctor finally and they sent me for an MRI. You ever have one of those?"

I shook my head. Lolly was a talker, and I'd learned that the less I responded, the better chance I had of actually extracting myself at some point.

"Awful," she said, spritzing the table again. "You have to lay in this metal tube and be totally still. I thought I was going to have a panic attack. And then they tell me that my L4 and L5 are totally shot. Gonna need surgery. Like I have time for that."

"Wow," I said. "I'm sorry."

She waved her paper towel at me, shrugging. "First Ron's prostate thing, now this. And you know our insurance won't cover it all. Plus Tracy's moved back in with the kids since her divorce, so we don't get a moment's peace."

I nodded, then shot a look at my car, wondering how I could get out there.

Lolly sighed again, then started back on the table. "Tell your mom the towel rack in the master bathroom finally fell off. It won't take another bolt, they're going to have to replace the whole thing."

"Okay."

"And there's a big scratch on the game room wall, a black one. Magic Eraser won't take it out."

"Got it."

She started dragging the vacuum and canister towards me. Behind her, the room now looked perfect: couch cushions fluffed, table with not a streak or mark, clean lines on the carpet. Ready for vacation. Again.

"Janice," she hollered into the kitchen. "I'm packing up. You about done?"

"Yep," another voice replied. "Meet you outside in ten."

I did my quick pass through the house, checking that all beds were made, bathrooms were clean, and towels had been distributed, as well as everything else on the checklist I knew by heart. By the time I was done, Lolly and her friend were wrapping up as well, their stuff piled up on the front steps.

"Catch you later at Tidal Wave?" she called out.

I nodded, then went to get into my car. I was just pulling the door open when I heard footsteps on the road behind me. I turned. It was a tall guy with glasses, jogging, wearing an iPod. He looked familiar, somehow, but no name came to mind, so I went back to what I was doing.

"Hey," he called out. I turned again to see he was slowing to a walk, taking out his headphones. "You're from the realty place. Right?"

I squinted at his face, trying to remember him. Before I could, though, he said, "You told us about the table place. When you brought the wine and cheese."

The vips, I thought. Of course. He was the one with the obnoxious woman at Sand Dollars. "Oh, yeah. Right. That was me."

"Theo," he said, pointing to himself. Then he stuck out his hand. "I forgot your name."

I was pretty sure we hadn't gotten to this level of familiarity during our previous meeting, but I shook anyway. "Emaline."

He nodded, then looked behind me. "So this is where you live?"

I glanced at Summer Daydream, which was an eight-bedroom, ten-bath, four-story monstrosity sporting a pool and triple garage. "Uh, no," I said. "Just working."

"On Sunday morning?"

"The rental industry never sleeps." I wasn't even sure why he was talking to me, especially since it meant cutting his run short. Who does that? "Half our houses turn over on Sunday."

"Oh, right," he said. "So, look. About yesterday. My boss . . . she's kind of intense. She doesn't mean to be rude."

"No?"

He smiled, barely. "Okay, maybe she does. But it's kind of a New York reflex. Not entirely her fault."

"It's fine," I told him. "I'm used to it."

"She's just really stressed about the time crunch we're under with this thing, doing the editing and filming . . ." He trailed off, as if suddenly realizing that I was just standing there, waiting to leave. "She's really talented."

"She makes movies?"

"Documentaries." He ran a hand through his hair. He was a bit on the skinny side, not really my type, but I could see that for some girls he'd be cute. "We're finishing up this project about a local artist that she's been working on for three years now."

"Artist?" I said. "Who's that?"

"Clyde Conaway."

"The guy that owns the bike shop?"

"Among other things," he said. "You know him?"

"As much as anybody here does," I replied. "Since when is he an artist?"

"You don't know his story?"

I shook my head.

"Oh, man, it's extraordinary. Colby kid becomes hot modern artist, then abandons all to move back to small coastal town and become local eccentric, even as his work is still in serious demand? There's a real mystery there. Everyone wants to know why."

"Because he's Clyde," I told him. "Nothing he does makes any sense."

He pointed at me. "We should interview you. I'm going to talk to Ivy about it."

I smiled, shaking my head as I slid into my seat. "Believe me, I'd be no help. I don't know anything about him. Thanks anyway, though."

When I cranked the engine, though, he didn't move. He just stood there, so I had to go right past him. When I did he smiled, putting his earbuds back in. "Nice talking to you, Emaline."

"You too. Enjoy your stay."

He nodded, and I headed down the street. At the next stop sign, though, I looked back. He was still standing there in front of Summer Daydream, looking up at it. What kind of person would think a girl like me would live in a house like that? The same kind who thought there'd be interest in a movie about Clyde Conaway. In other words: Not From Around Here.

4

"HOLD ON. DID you hear that?"

Luke groaned right into my ear, then rolled off me. "Emaline."

"I'm serious. Listen."

We lay there, side by side, completely quiet. In the distance, like always, there was the ocean. Nothing else.

"You know," he said after a moment, "it's getting hard not to take this personally."

"Do you want a repeat of what happened in April?"

"No," he replied. "But I also don't want to waste the only time alone we've had in months being paranoid."

"It has *not* been months," I pointed out, but he wasn't listening, already too busy migrating back to my pillow, one hand smoothing over my stomach, then hip bone.

"Feels like it," he mumbled into my neck.

I rolled my eyes. Luke and I didn't differ on much, but when it came to this one issue, we were often at odds. If you asked him, I was a dull prude. As far as I was concerned, he was a sex addict who could never get enough. Somewhere in the middle was the truth, not that we'd ever gotten close enough to see it.

"It was last week," I pointed out, as he unbuttoned my jeans, picking up where he'd left off. "Wednesday or Thursday."

"It was the week before," he said, shifting his weight so I could slide them down over my legs.

"Do you realize you are picking the wrong moment to split hairs?"

"Do you realize we can't have a moment at all as long as you're talking?"

I loved my boyfriend. I really, really did. But ever since my mom had come home unexpectedly this spring while we were spending our lunch hour doing pretty much this same thing, I'd been skittish. One minute we were happily occupied, secure in the knowledge that we had the whole house to ourselves, and the next she was pushing open my bedroom door to get a full-on view of something none of us ever wanted her to see. I still got red-faced thinking about it, while my mom was so traumatized she couldn't look at me in the eye for over a week. I would have pointed out that this was yet another reason she should stay out of my room, if either of us could talk about it without the risk of exploding from shared embarrassment. In fact, we'd never discussed it at all beyond a curt conversation (lacking eye contact) during which she confirmed that 1) I was on birth control and 2) I knew I was never, ever to do it under this roof again.

And we didn't. At least for a while. But when you're in a committed relationship with someone you love, fooling around in a parked car or in the dunes at the beach just feels . . . dirty. Not to mention uncomfortable. Add in the fact that Luke's mom was *always* home—this was not an exaggeration, she worked from home and had no hobbies other than her family—and it wasn't too long before we ended up playing with this particular fire again. Now, though, even when we were alone, something was different.

If I was honest, though, there was probably more to this than just what happened in April. Like the fact that while, for the first year or so we were together, Luke and I were all about falling in love—the stuff that happens pre-walking into the sunset—we'd now crossed over, right to the little irritations that crop up in relationships after that. Like the other person drives too fast (or slow), watches too much football (or not enough), or wants to fool around all the time (or never). He was such a great guy, I knew that any other girl would be able to overlook any of his not-so-great aspects. But I was me. Unfortunately.

Plus there were the various stresses of the last year, with both of us applying for school. We hadn't ever talked about it, but I could tell all the college stuff I'd done with my father—applying to Ivy League schools far away from Colby and, by extension, Luke himself—he'd taken a little personally. I mean, why wouldn't I go to East U, where I'd get a free ride *and* we'd be together? For him, that was perfect. And even though he never said as much, I knew he wondered, more than once, why it wasn't for me.

"Wait." I pushed myself up on my elbows. "I swear, I think I just heard a car door."

"There is nobody here."

"Just listen for a second."

This time, he didn't move, just stopped. As he humored

me, I looked up at his face, familiar and gorgeous. I could not imagine my life without him, and I thought I'd kill any girl who tried to come between us. And yet, I knew he was right: it was the week before last.

He looked at me. "I don't hear anything."

"Okay. Sorry."

For a moment, we stayed right where we were, him above, me below, our eyes locked. *I love you,* I thought, but instead of saying this, I slid my arms around his neck, pulling him closer. He whispered my name and then his lips were on mine, erasing the space between us and everything it encompasses and doesn't. At least for now.

* * *

"You just take a shower?"

I blinked, startled. I didn't know what it was about Mrs. Ye, my best girlfriend Daisy's mom, but she had this way of totally disarming me. Even about something so simple as having damp hair at twelve thirty on a weekday.

"Um, yeah," I said, as she went back to applying hot pink polish to a woman wearing a terry cloth beach cover-up. "I got hot cleaning up the storeroom at work. Plus it's filthy in there."

"Hmmh," she replied, the meaning of which even without the language barrier—which was sizeable—was impossible to decipher. Then she said something to Daisy in their native Vietnamese, the undecipherable words flowing off her tongue as quickly as the polish off the brush.

"Okay," Daisy replied. "Do you want mayonnaise?"

Her mom added something else, again so quickly I couldn't have caught it even if it was in a language I spoke. This time, Daisy said nothing, only giving a quick nod of her head. I followed her out into the parking lot of Coastal Plaza, where her parents' salon, Wave Nails, was located right between a liquor store and AZ Grocery. Booze, food, and pampering. What else did you need on vacation?

"Hot," Daisy said, putting on her huge sunglasses as we started down to the other end of the mall to Da Vinci's Pizza and Subs. "Too hot."

"Well," I pointed out, "you're not exactly dressed for summer."

She turned, leveling her eyes at me. Daisy had been my closest girlfriend since her family had moved here in seventh grade, but her beauty could still totally disarm me at random moments. My style was slapdash at best, but she was always photo ready, cribbing styles from the fashion magazines she read nonstop. She was small, with delicate features she made even more stunning with the makeup she got up early to apply carefully every morning. Nobody dressed like her, mostly because she produced most of her looks at her mom's sewing machine, which she'd taught herself how to use when she was twelve. Colby was not exactly New York or Paris when it came to fashion, but you wouldn't know this by looking at Daisy. She was dressing for the life she wanted, not the one she had.

Which was why, while I was sporting my basic summer uniform of cutoff shorts, tank top, and flip-flops, she had on a black sleeveless dress and platform wedges, her hair pulled back in a neat chignon. Like Audrey Hepburn, if she passed Tiffany's and headed south. Very south.

"What you don't understand," she said now, smoothing her small hands over her dress, "is that this is the perfect dress."

"It's black and long and it's ninety degrees out."

She sighed. After Daisy spent much of the first year we knew each other trying to get me to be even *slightly* fashionable, we decided for the sake of our friendship to agree to disagree. Which we did pretty much constantly.

"Black and long," she repeated, her voice flat. "That's really how you describe this?"

"Am I wrong?"

"It's a vintage A-line, Emaline. It's classic. Knows no season."

"It's a dress," I replied. "It doesn't know anything."

This she didn't even dignify with a response. Despite our sartorial differences, the reason we'd bonded, at least initially, was our shared perfectionism when it came to school. Before she arrived, I'd regularly been near the top or the best student in just about every class I took. Then, suddenly, there was this new girl, whip smart, better read, *and* bilingual. If we hadn't hit it off I was pretty sure we would have hated each other.

Now she adjusted her sunglasses as a guy on a moped passed us, engine whining like a gnat. I hated mopeds, but for whatever reason they were ubiquitous here, like saltwater taffy and hermit crabs being sold as pets.

Daisy wrinkled her nose. "God, I *hate* mopeds."

I smiled. "You better talk to Morris, then. He's still making noises about getting one."

"That boy needs a car, not a toy," she said, sighing. "But

first he needs a job. Did you hear he got let go from that catering gig?"

"No," I said, not that I was surprised. Since Daisy and Morris started dating—around the same time hell froze over, pigs flew, and bears began relieving themselves in other places than wooded areas—I'd learned that I couldn't talk about him the way I once had. Used to be, he was My Friend Morris and I was free to complain about his slackness as much as I wanted. Now he was Her Boyfriend and different rules applied. We were still working out what they were, however.

The truth is, anyone would be lucky to date Daisy. First, she was gorgeous and smart, clearly headed for what she and I referred to as GTBC: Great Things Beyond Colby. This was in comparison to the other category we created, AGN: Ain't Going Nowhere. Which, if we're honest, is where Morris would fall instantly if he wasn't someone we cared about. This shorthand began as a kind of game, a way of passing the time while pouring over our slim yearbook. But in the last year, as college loomed and then overtook us, it got real, and now two categories weren't even really enough. A lot of people were going Beyond Colby, but not necessarily headed for Great Things. Like myself, actually. Columbia would have gotten me to Great Things, for sure, just like the Savannah College of Art and Design, where Daisy would enroll at the end of the summer, earned her a spot. East U, however, was a more lateral move. But at least I was moving.

Morris, like about thirty percent of our class, would be going to Coastal Tech, the community college twenty minutes past the bridge over to the mainland. There was a good four-year school just past North Reddemane, Weymar College, but locals rarely went there: it was pricey and private, not to mention geared towards the arts, which our high school didn't have the funds or faculty to provide beyond the basics. Coastal Tech, however, was affordable and offered both day and night classes in subjects like office administration and dental assisting, things that could get you employed right out of the box. Unlike my slate of fall classes, which would likely include Spanish-American history, a required overview of English literature, and an introduction to psychology. I could only imagine what would have been at Columbia.

Morris wanted to get a degree in automotive systems technology, with an eye towards getting a job at one of the local dealerships or repair shops. Which was very ambitious. It was also not as much his idea as that of our lone guidance counselor, Mr. Markham, who was young and energetic, and took Morris on as a personal project senior year. "Transport is a human need. People always have to get from here to there," he said over and over again, pushing the Coastal Tech brochure across his desk. So Morris planned to enroll. Then again, he had also planned to work for Robin at Roberts Family Catering. Not that I could really say this to Daisy.

"He says," she continued now, as the Da Vinci's Pizza and Subs sign—featuring the Mona Lisa chowing down on a slice—came into view up ahead, "that they let him go because the owner wanted to hire her nephew."

I had a flash of Morris, leaning up against the fridge in Luke's kitchen as everyone moved around him. "Her nephew already works for her."

"He does?"

She was looking at me, but I kept my gaze on the Mona Lisa. "Yeah."

Daisy exhaled, a low, whistle-like sound. It was the same noise I'd heard her mom make often in response to a chattering customer. Some things were the same in every language. "He's still working with your dad, though, right?"

"I think so," I replied, although in truth I couldn't remember the last time I'd seen Morris show up at 6:30 a.m. for a ride to the job site. Just because I hadn't witnessed it, though, did not mean it wasn't happening. Technically.

We came up to the door of Da Vinci's, which was steamed over slightly, and I pulled it open, instantly smelling dough and pepperoni. It was just before twelve, so the place was packed with a mix of tourists in beachwear and locals on lunch break. We got in line, right behind three girls in bikini tops and shorts looking up at the wall menu and talking loudly.

"I can't believe I still have a headache," one of them was saying.

"I can't believe you hooked up with that guy last night," one of the others replied. "Since when are you into chest hair?"

"He did not have chest hair."

Her friends burst out laughing, clearly disputing this. "Deidre," one finally said, "it was like *fur*."

They started giggling again, while the girl with the headache sighed. "I think you guys are forgetting the vacation code we decided on during the trip down here."

"Code?" the girl on her right asked.

"We said," her friend continued, "that what happened here, this week, would not be part of our permanent record. Pizza at last call, chest hair, belly shots—they all apply. They're to be filed away and forgotten."

"Belly shots?" the girl on the left said.

The other two looked at her. "You don't remember the belly shots?"

"Who, me? No *way*. I would never do that." They kept staring. "Would I?"

"Next in line!" the guy behind the counter called out, and they moved up. I smiled at Daisy, who was shaking her head disapprovingly.

"Oh, come on," I said. "You have to admit, it would probably be fun."

"What?" she replied. "Belly shots?"

"No, that whole down-for-a-week, anything-goes, summer-fling thing."

"Please don't start up about how the tourists have more fun than us again," she warned me. "I can't take it today."

"I'm not saying they have more fun," I replied. She gave me a doubtful look. "I'm saying that, you know, we never get to go to the beach and just, you know, let loose. Fall in love and be different, with no permanent record. We *live* in our permanent record."

"There are other beaches besides here," she said.

"I know. But we've never gone to any of them, have we?"

"Emaline, I look at the ocean all year long," she told me. "If I travel, I want to do something different."

"Which is exactly what I'm saying. You go on vacation, you

can be different. We see people do it all the time. But we're always just supporting players in someone else's summer, so we stay the same."

"I like my same, though," she said. "And don't forget, things are about to change, in just a month or two, with college. Right?"

I nodded, but really, that was different. College was for four years, not one week. It was permanent, whereas a vacation—like the ones I saw beginning, in progress, and ending all around me, every day—had a set duration, only a finite amount of time before it was gone for good. Just once, I would have liked to find out how it felt to come to a place like Colby, have the time of my life, and then leave, taking nothing but memories with me. Maybe someday.

"Next!" the heavyset guy behind the counter called out. We stepped forward. "Crazy Daisy, my favorite customer."

"Eddie Spaghetti," she replied. "How's it going?"

"Wednesday," he said with a shrug, like this was an answer.

She put down a twenty-dollar bill. "She wants her usual. No mayo."

"You got it," he said, scribbling something on his order pad. "You guys eating?"

"Slice of cheese," I told him, and Daisy held up two fingers. I reached for my money, but she shook her head, sliding the bill towards him. "Hey. I can pay."

"I know."

Eddie comped us two fountain drinks, which we got before claiming a booth to wait for our food. "So," Daisy said, unwrapping her straw, "why'd you really just take a shower?"

I raised my eyebrows. "Does there have to be a reason?"

"For you, yes." She flicked her eyes to the TV over my head, then back at me. "I know for a fact you've been up since six thirty, at work at eight sharp. Last I checked you didn't take bathing breaks."

I poked at my ice. "Luke and I, um, met up for lunch at my house."

She exhaled, shaking her head. "I thought you said never again."

"I did. Apparently this is never."

"Apparently you *want* to get caught."

"I really don't," I told her. She made a face, clearly doubting this. "But it's not like we have a lot of options."

"Other people manage."

I held up my hand. "Stop right there. Remember what I told you. I don't want to hear about you and Morris."

"I'm not talking about *me*," she replied, offended. "I don't sneak around like that."

"You do it in the car or dunes instead?"

"I don't do *it*, period. You know that." This was true. Daisy was a virgin, and planned to remain one until marriage. While the reasons for this tended to vary from person to person, among the people we know it was usually religion based. Daisy, however, was not a churchgoer. But her family was her faith. Mr. and Mrs. Ye, first-generation immigrants, were upstanding, hardworking, morally centered people who expected their children, especially their oldest daughter, to follow suit. In their family, there was no rebellion, no back talk, no sneaking a boy home at lunch. These things just Did

Not Exist. My mom, battling with my sisters and me through-
out middle and high school, once asked Mrs. Ye how she managed to keep her kids so in line. She just looked at her. "They
are children," she said. "You are adult." It was just that simple.
At least at their house.

"Order up!" Eddie yelled, hitting the little bell by the register. Daisy started to move but I shook my head, going over to
pick up our slices and her mom's sandwich. I was just sliding
into my seat when the front door beeped again. Looking over,
I saw my dad, Morris, and a couple of other guys from Dad's
crew coming in. Morris headed right over, but my dad just
waved en route to the counter. I waved back, wondering if my
hair looked damp from a distance.

"Hey, girl," Morris said as he plopped down beside Daisy,
sliding an arm around her waist. She presented her cheek for
a kiss. Two months together and they were like an old married couple.

"Morris!" my dad called out. He and the other guys were
up at the counter ordering. "You eating or what?"

"Yeah," Morris replied. "Get me—"

I kicked him squarely in the shin, as hard as I could. He
squeaked, then looked at me. "What?"

"Are you seriously asking him to order for you?"

He glanced at my dad, who I could tell, even from this
distance, was annoyed bordering on irritated. Next step was
pissed, and nobody wanted that.

"*Go over there*," I said, my eyes level on him. "*Now*."

Morris slid away from Daisy, shooting me a look, then
loped back to the rest of the crew. My dad watched him ap-

proach and order, his expression flat. When Eddie was done ringing everyone up, my dad slid some bills across the counter. He'd told me a million times there was no such thing as a free lunch, but somehow Morris managed to get one. If it wasn't too much trouble to order it himself.

I looked at Daisy, who was chewing a bite of pizza, her eyes on the parking lot. "Don't say I'm too hard on him," I told her. "He needs to learn this stuff."

"I'm not saying anything," she said. I was never that fond of any of Daisy's other boyfriends—a volleyball player, a guy who may or may not have been gay, a creative writing student at Weymar who wrote about nothing but aliens—mostly because I never thought any of them were good enough for her. Times like this, though, I would gladly have welcomed any or all back.

"Emaline."

I turned to see my dad a few tables away, standing while the rest of his crew, Morris included, got settled with their slices and drinks. "Yes?"

"Got a minute?"

I nodded. "Sure."

As I got up to follow him outside, I was braced for any number of conversational possibilities. There was my damp hair, and the fact that I might be busted, again. Also, there was Morris, who had provided yet another reason he should never have been hired. Both were uncomfortable topics, but at least Morris was secondary shame, so I knew which one I had my money on. Once we were face to face by the newspaper boxes, though, he broached neither, instead handing me a slip of paper with a phone number scrawled on it.

"What's this?" I asked him, as that same moped whined past, going the other way.

"Your father's number. He called again when I was just at the house."

There was always a weird moment when he referred to anyone else as my father. Like we'd entered an alternate universe, or something. "I have his number."

"That's his cell. I was going to drop it by the office with your mom to give you on my way back to the job." When I just looked at him, confused, he added, "He said it was important."

Important. I had a flash of my graduation invitation, never responded to. It was like I hadn't even sent it.

"Just call him, get it over with," my dad said. "Okay?"

"Sure," I said, as he pulled the door open. "I'll do it right now."

"Good girl. See you tonight." I watched him go back inside and cross the restaurant, his walk slow, but not for the same reasons as Morris. Twenty-plus years of carpentry and roofing had taken a toll, although his body wasn't as broken as some. At my age, he'd worked days framing, then played guitar in a bar band at night, one good enough to get close to a record deal. But close is just close, especially in Colby.

Inside, Daisy was looking at me, so I pulled out my phone and held it up so she'd know what I was doing. She pointed at my mostly empty plate. When I shook my head, she gathered it up, along with her own, and tossed both in the trash. I was just starting to dial the number when she came outside.

"Everything okay?" she asked, putting on her sunglasses.

"I'll let you know in a minute."

She nodded, then started walking back up to the salon, the bag with her mom's lunch hanging from her hand. In my ear, the phone was now ringing. Once. Twice. Three times. I was expecting a voice-mail greeting, but then, suddenly, he was on the line.

"Hello?"

"Hi," I said. "Um, it's Emaline. My dad said you called?"

"Yes," he replied. A pause. "You're a hard girl to catch up with."

"Sorry," I said, then immediately regretted this easy, knee-jerk apology. "Is everything . . . okay?"

"Benji and I are headed your way," he told me. "We just crossed into Virginia, should be there in . . . four hours? Five?"

"You're coming here?"

"My aunt passed away a couple of months back. We're cleaning out her place to get it ready to go on the market."

"I'm sorry." This time I meant it. I'd met her a few times. She was always nice to me.

"She'd been sick awhile. It was for the best." He cleared his throat. "Anyway, I figured it would be a great opportunity for a road trip. A pilgrimage of sorts, just us guys."

"Leah isn't with you?"

A beat. Then, "I figure we'll be crossing over the bridge right around dinnertime, give or take whatever traffic holds us up. I know it's short notice, but I was hoping you could meet us for a quick bite."

I wanted to tell him no, make an excuse, then get off the phone. But it was one thing to be cold over distance, another entirely when they were in your same zip code. "Um . . . sure. Just call me when you get close."

"Will do. See you soon, Emaline."

And with that, he was gone, again. The great disappearing act, that was my father. No mention of school, plus he didn't answer any of the questions I asked him. It made me think of Mrs. Ye and all the things she said that I couldn't figure out. She and I at least spoke different languages, though. With my father, the words themselves were clear. I got every one. But somehow, I still didn't understand.

* * *

News travels fast in a small town like Colby. Between my parents, though, it was more like warp speed.

"You need me to do a towel delivery?"

My mom glanced at me, then put down the pencil she was holding. "Oh, right . . . yes. Towels. I do."

I just looked at her. It was not exactly a bad trait, but my mother was the worst liar ever. "Where?"

She swallowed, then pushed a few papers around on her desk, searching for a Post-it or piece of paper I was almost positive did not exist. "Let me see . . . I think it was over in Sandbar Cove. . . ."

Behind me, I heard Margo, who was in the next office, snort. One look at her face—biting back a smile as she studied her computer screen—and I knew my hunch was correct. I turned back to my mom. "He told you about the phone message, didn't he?"

"What?"

"Mom. Come on."

Finally, she stopped pretending to look, instead sitting back in her chair. By now Margo had moved to the doorway as well, all the better to hear every word. "He *might* have mentioned that your father had something important to tell you."

If hearing this made me nervous, I can only imagine what it did to my mom. In fact, if I'd opened up her top desk drawer right then, I knew I'd find all the saltier, crunchier offerings of the office vending machine, partially consumed. She was a stress eater from way back. Lucky for her, worry also boosted her metabolism, so it usually balanced out.

"He's on his way here," I told her. "With Benji."

She just looked at me. Margo said, "That's the kid, right?"

"What about Leah?" my mom asked.

I shook my head. "Didn't mention her. All he said was that his aunt died and they're putting her house on the market."

"Miss Ruth passed away?" my mom said, looking genuinely sad.

"Do they have a realtor?" That was Margo. Because of course this was the most pressing question.

"She'd been sick awhile," I told my mom. "Apparently."

"Who's Miss Ruth?"

I turned, and there was Amber, holding a paper sack from Amigos, the Mexican place up the road. "What are you doing here?"

"I got an SOS call," she replied, pushing past me to walk over to my mom's desk, where she deposited the bag, which already had grease staining the bottom. "Someone needed a taco, stat."

"You deliver now?" I asked.

"If someone else is paying. I'm broke and hungry," she replied, plopping down in the chair opposite my mom. "Who's Miss Ruth?"

"Emaline's father's aunt," Margo informed her.

You could literally see Amber figuring out this relationship, her brain wheels spinning. Then she said, "The one he used to stay with, in North Reddemane?"

My mom, unwrapping a taco, nodded. "Such a nice lady. She made the best chicken salad. It was to die for."

"How long's he staying?" Margo asked me.

"He didn't say."

Silence. Which was rare when we were all together, if not unheard of. "Maybe," Amber said, "he's planning to apologize for being such a jerk about the college thing, win you over, and be your favorite parent again."

My sister did not have that many talents. One she *had* cultivated, however, was the ability to zero in on the single thing someone absolutely does not want to hear and then say it aloud. I looked at my mom, who, sure enough, was already stuffing the back end of her taco into her mouth.

"Not happening," I said. "And besides, this isn't about me. His aunt died and he's taking his kid on a road trip."

"Do they need a place to rent?" Margo again. Who else?

"I'm sure they're staying at Miss Ruth's," my mom told her, chewing.

"She's dead," Amber pointed out.

"But her house isn't," Margo replied.

"Maybe," Amber said, "we should offer them *our* guest room."

"Stop it," I told her, and she snorted. To my mom I said, "Do you have a delivery for me to do or not?"

A pause. Then she shook her head, slowly, still chewing. I sighed, turned on my heel, and headed for the door. "I'm sorry," she called after me, once she'd swallowed. "I just really wondered what he wanted."

"If he needs a good realtor," Margo said to me as I passed her, holding out a business card, "put him in touch with me, okay?"

"You people are ridiculous," I said, but I took the card, stuffing it into my pocket.

"Don't be mad!" my mom yelled, halfheartedly, as I walked across the office. I didn't answer her.

As I headed out the door, I saw an older guy in cargo shorts and a COLBY BEACH T-shirt opening the complimentary ice cream cooler in our lobby. He reached in, helping himself to a Popsicle and a Nutty Buddy cone, then held them both out to a little girl in a pink bathing suit and princess cover-up.

"Which one?" he asked. She pointed at the cone. After he unwrapped it, handed it to her, and opened the Popsicle for himself, they both wandered over to the big map on the wall, staring up at it as they ate.

WHERE'S HOME FOR YOU? said the letters over the map, this year in bright yellow. The previous year it had been red.

You could still see tiny traces of the color, like faint shadows, especially around the curvier letters. Scrape down to the wall itself, through the fifty years of layers, and you'd surely find every other color of the rainbow as well. Not too much changed in Colby or even our office itself, but the map was new and the letters freshly painted, every single season.

It was my grandfather, way back in the day, who had first put them there. Then he added a YOU ARE HERE over Colby's spot, put a cupful of pushpins nearby, and let people leave their mark. Pretty soon, for many families, it was part of the vacation tradition, just like getting ice cream when they got their keys, and coffee when they dropped them off. You just had to put in a pin, marking the place you would return to when your time with us, in this place, was over.

As the man and his daughter headed into the office—her ice cream dripping, also per tradition, across our floor—I stopped by the map, checking its progress so far this season. Like normal around this time of the summer, there were a lot of pins within our own state, several in the ones above and below, and a scattering of others beyond. Someone had been here from Los Angeles; another, from Austin, Texas. There were several, all crammed together, in western Illinois—a wedding, most likely—and two placed neatly, meeting at the tip, over Toronto, Canada. So many different places, different routes to and back from this same place.

As for Colby itself, though it was my home and everyone else's that worked here, there was no pin. Just a circle, a star, and the YOU ARE HERE I'd written myself when I repainted the sign back in May. I *was* here, always, and in many ways loved it. But every time I passed the map and this reminder, it kind of made me sad.

Why, though, was hard to say. Just as it was difficult, back when all the college stuff started, to explain to my parents, Luke, and just about everyone else why I'd want to go to anywhere other than East U. It was barely a millimeter away on this map, so close, and yet it still felt like enough distance to them. In Colby I'd found that people either wanted to stay forever (and usually did) or couldn't wait to get gone and never look back (ditto). For me, however, it was a mix of the two, this constant push and pull. I loved it here. But I'd been in that circle and star for my entire life, and I so wanted to know what it would feel like to claim another distant spot as my own, if only for a little while. Someday.

Outside, Daisy was sitting on the hood of my car, waiting for me. "I thought you were getting towels," she said, as I pulled open my door.

"So did I. Turns out my mom just wanted to know what was going on." She laughed. "It's not funny. They are all such psychos. They can't stay out of my life. Or my room."

"Because your life and your room are much more interesting than theirs."

I rolled my eyes. "If that's what you really think," I said as I cranked the engine, "why don't *you* tag along for dinner tonight?"

"I totally would, as my life is not interesting either," she replied. "But I'm on gyno from four to close."

Gyno was Daisy's shorthand for bikini wax, her specialty

at Wave Nails. There were other girls there who did it, but because she brought to this task the same dedication and meticulousness with which she did everything else, she had a rabid local following. Her clients were so numerous (and hairy, I guess) that she had to keep special post-workday hours to accommodate them all. Personally, I couldn't understand how she stomached the, um, awkwardness of the situation, but Daisy was nothing if not professional. Seen one, she said, seen them all. All right, then.

"Want to trade?" I asked her now.

"Depends. Where's he taking you for dinner?"

"No idea. They're just calling when they get closer."

"Tell him to meet you at Melisma."

That was the nicest restaurant in Colby. I'd been there only once, for prom, when I could barely afford to order more than a salad. It was a really good salad, though. "I don't think that's what he has in mind."

"Too bad. It's the least he can do for blowing off your graduation."

"Yeah, well, we didn't talk about that."

"Think you will?"

I sighed, then tipped my head back and looked up at the ceiling. The car was hot and I needed to take Daisy to her other job, at a local boutique, so I could do a round of midweek drive-bys of our properties. We did this to make sure nobody was up to anything crazy, like moving a couch onto the balcony, neglecting to report a small fire, or packing forty people into a house that sleeps twelve. Truthfully, I would have rather dealt with all of these problems at once than have to broach the subject of my graduation with my father.

"If he doesn't mention it, neither will I," I told her. "It's over. There's no point."

Daisy was quiet for a moment, long enough that I turned to look at her. Once I did, she said, "He really hurt you, though, Emaline. You should tell him so."

"It won't change anything," I replied. "And if I was any other girl, I would have gotten over it by now anyway."

Now, her eyes narrowed. "You know I hate when you say that."

"What?"

"That any-other-girl thing." She flipped her hand, as if literally swatting the words away. "People are not uniform, Emaline. There is no such thing as any other girl. So stop holding yourself to some ridiculous high standard, would you please? It's okay if you're still upset. I would be."

My phone beeped suddenly, announcing an incoming text. I flipped it over and looked at the screen. I'm sorry, it said. My mom. Forgive me?

I looked up at the rental office, where I could just see her window. I didn't know if she realized I hadn't left, or was watching me as I typed back three letters: Yes.

The irony of this was not lost on me as I cranked the engine, then backed out of the lot and turned towards the boardwalk. But making up with my mom was easy: It wasn't the first time one of us had screwed up and had to apologize. Not even the first time this week, probably. Behavior and apologies could be taught, learned over time. Eventually, it became habit, second nature. But my father and I didn't have that. It would take more than three letters to fix this. Which brought me to the real truth, the one that had sat on my chest since I heard him pick up the phone an hour earlier: I was thinking that maybe, by this point, I liked it better broken.

* * *

I planned just to drop Daisy at the entrance to the boardwalk and start my drive-bys, but once I pulled in, I changed my mind, parking instead. If a couch was on the roof already, another half an hour wouldn't make much of a difference. I needed to clear my head.

The boardwalk was crowded, the beach below it even more so. In the winter, we often had this entire stretch to ourselves, save for some circling birds, but the difference between then and now was as vast as the ocean alongside. A band was playing at the grandstand, the outdoor tables filled with people eating and drinking. The boardwalk itself was a solid mass of strollers, folks in bathing suits and cover-ups, and more beach-related stuff for sale—shot glasses, picture frames dotted with shells, and COLBY BEACH T-shirts in every possible design and color—than anyone would ever want to buy.

I'd barely taken two steps when a guy wearing sunglasses and a baseball hat suddenly appeared square in my path. "Ladies' night tonight!" he barked, thrusting a piece of paper at me. "Free entrance and two-dollar cocktails! All at Tallyho, hottest club in Colby!"

I shook my head, dodging him, but Daisy wasn't so quick and ended up with one. She flipped it over as we picked our way through the crowd. "Tallyho is the hottest club in Colby? Since when?"

"It probably just means the air conditioner's busted," I told her. Clearly we were not the only ones lacking interest, as discarded fliers littered the boardwalk ahead of us. A step later, I got a strong, sudden whiff of cotton candy, sugar incarnate filling my lungs. If I had to bottle the boardwalk, it would be a mix of this and sunscreen, with a tinge of sweat mixed in. Lovely.

"On your right!" I heard a voice say, and a second later a bike was moving past me, ridden by a shirtless guy in swim trunks. Behind him was a girl in a bikini, a woven bag over one shoulder with a rolled up towel sticking out of it. They went a little farther before stopping in front of Abe's Bikes, where a girl with curly brown hair in a bright pink T-shirt was standing with a clipboard. Behind her a sign said QUICK, EASY BIKE RENTALS! PAY AND RIDE AWAY! She waved at us, and as we passed, Daisy tried to hand off the flier to her. She shook her head.

"Come on, Maggie," Daisy said. "It's the hottest club in Colby."

"Since when?" Maggie replied. "No, no, no to Tallyho. Nice try, though."

"I hate that somehow I'm responsible for killing this tree." Daisy sighed, crumpling up the paper and tossing it into a nearby trash can.

"You going to do the window?" Maggie asked her.

"Yep," Daisy said. "Florals are *so* last month."

"You would know," Maggie said, taking the bikes as the

riders dismounted. She was just asking them if they were *sure* they didn't want another hour—at half price!—as we came up on Clementine's. Sure enough, the mannequins in the window were all in flowered dresses, with petals scattered around their feet.

"Looks pretty cute for something already passé," I said to Daisy as I pulled the door open.

"It is," she agreed. "But it's time for a change. I'm thinking robots."

"What?" I said, but she was already walking past me inside, the chime sounding over our heads announcing our arrival.

"There she is," I heard a voice call out from behind the register. I looked over to see Heidi, the owner, sorting bills into the drawer, while her stepdaughter Auden pegged stretchy bead bracelets with a pricing gun. "Our fashionista has arrived."

"You know I hate that word," Daisy replied. "It makes me sound like I'm starting a revolution."

"Aren't you?" Auden asked. The gun stuck suddenly. She banged it on the counter, once, twice.

"One robot at a time," I said.

"Robots?" Heidi raised her eyebrows. "Really?"

Daisy nodded. "Silver, futuristic. Metallics. Contrasted with deep skin tones, plus maybe some bead or sequin trim for texture."

Heidi nodded. "I like it."

"I," Auden said, picking a stray sticker off her shirt, "have no idea what you guys are talking about."

"Which is why you're not doing the window," Heidi told her. To me she said, "You here to help? You know I'm hiring, if your mom would ever let you jump ship on the family business."

"Unlikely," I told her. My mom and Heidi knew each other from the chamber of commerce, where they always seemed to end up on one committee or another together. They were the younger members, often joining forces against long-timers like my grandmother and her friends. Everything was small in Colby except the personalities. "I'm just procrastinating."

"Doesn't sound like you," Heidi observed.

"I'm starting a revolution," I told her, and she smiled.

Just then, the door chimed from behind us, announcing the arrival of two girls in bikini tops and sarongs. As Auden put down the gun to go greet them, I followed Daisy as she made her way back to the storeroom, stopping along the way to pluck pieces that caught her eye.

Before she'd taken the job, Clementine's window, like that of any other beach clothing store, featured a few mannequins and lots of bathing suits. Now, it was a local institution. She did zombies (in bikinis) for Halloween, a tableau based entirely on coal for Christmas, a slasher theme in deep reds for Valentine's Day. It had been pointed out to Heidi more than once that Daisy's windows might be a bit too "visionary" for the Colby boardwalk, but she maintained that whatever else, they made people stop in front of the store. And once they stopped, they were that much more likely to come in.

Now, Daisy assembled an armful of shiny bathing suits, then fetched the oversize tackle box where she kept all her pins and props. As she got to work, I sat in the doorway that led into the window, alternately watching her and the crowds passing by. En masse like this, the tourists all blended together into types: younger folks moving in packs; parents with strollers, toting huge beach bags full of gear; older couples, walking slowly. The only constants were sunglasses and the feel of spare time. Again, it occurred to me how weird it was to be permanent in a place that to everyone else was only temporary. Like I could never be sure if they were the ones who weren't real, or if I was.

"I think I'm going to need a few metal rulers," Daisy said, holding up a gold bikini top and squinting at it. "And maybe some saw blades."

"Sounds dangerous," I told her, as a group of girls walked by, outright gawking in at us. It was like they didn't realize we could see them as well. "I thought this was about robots."

"Dangerous robots," she murmured. She was getting into the zone, that quiet place where her ideas came together. No need for me to stick around. Pretty soon she'd forget I was there anyway.

"I gotta go," I told her, getting to my feet. "I'll call you later?"

She nodded, and I slipped out of the store, waving at Auden and Heidi. As I headed back to the parking lot, it was nearing two p.m., which gave me about two hours before my father and Benji crossed the bridge over here to my side.

I got in the car, rolled down all the windows, then turned around to the backseat floor to dig for my drive-by list. Just beneath it, I saw a piece of card stock poking out and grabbed it as well. It was one of my graduation announcements, left over and forgotten. I ran a finger over it, reading the letters of my name and my high school. It had been such a big deal at the time, like the finish line of a race I'd been running for as long as I could remember. My mom and dad were there, my sisters, my grandmother, all of my friends. But as was so often the case, it was the one person missing who you thought about more than the ones who were right in front of you.

Stupid, I thought now, tossing it back behind me and turning my attention to the drive-by list again. House after house, their names like fairy tales: Gull's Cry, Carolina Dream, Driftwood Escape, Tide Traveler. I'd hit them all, slowing down to peer again from the outside at someone else's vacation, looking for anything amiss or suspect. But if they happened to glance out, they wouldn't even realize this. To them, I was just another girl passing by.

5

I ONLY CHEWED gum when I was nervous, and could always gauge the stress level of anything by how many sticks it took to calm me down. Sitting outside the Reef Room that evening waiting for my father and Benji, I was up to four and counting.

This was not where I wanted to be. It had been a long day, and Morris and I had planned to go to the movies, then meet Daisy when her shift ended to hit whatever parties were going on down at the Tip. Instead, I was in my car with a sore jaw, wondering how dirty a person could actually get from cleaning pools all day.

I hadn't planned to bring reinforcements, figuring this would be weird enough without throwing anyone else into the mix. But then, as I was leaving my house, I panicked.

"Are you chewing gum?" was the first thing Luke said to me when I finally got hold of him. I'd already left two what I'd hoped were casual-sounding voice mails, but clearly he could hear the Big Red in my voice.

"What's weird about that?" I shot back, entirely defensive. "You chew gum sometimes, you know."

He was quiet for a moment, so I could fully absorb how crazy I sounded. Then he said, "What's going on?"

I told him. And opened another piece. By the time I'd stuffed it into my mouth, he'd assured me he would get back to his house, take the fastest shower possible, and meet me as soon as he could. Now, though, as a Subaru wagon with Connecticut plates pulled into the lot, I knew it wasn't soon enough.

I hadn't seen my father since the previous September, when he, Benji, and Leah were down over Labor Day weekend. They'd stayed at Miss Ruth's, although she'd already moved to an assisted living facility by then, and we'd had dinner together at this same restaurant. I was in the thick of my pre-application madness then, so my father and I spent much of the meal strategizing. So much so that I'd actually felt kind of bad for Leah and Benji, who, clearly not as enthused about the subject of power essays and early admissions as we were, left to take a walk on the pier when they'd had enough. I had to admit, though, I'd liked having his full attention, as well as this project in common. I was happy to share anything, actually, other than our weird, somewhat shameful origin story.

Fast-forward to April, and that last e-mail, followed by the long stretch of silence, and the memory took on a different tinge. As he parked a few rows over, I opened another stick of gum. But with my jaw already aching, one cheek protruding, for once I knew better than to make a bad situation worse. So I put the stick on the dash instead, then spit my wad of gum into a tissue. Without it, my mouth suddenly felt light and huge, like I could say anything.

I'd just gotten out of my car when I saw Theo, the guy from Sand Dollars. Just my luck. He was climbing out of a white van a few spaces over, a cell phone pressed to his ear.

"Right," I heard him say as I shut my door. "Two orders of the chicken satay, the big Caesar with no olives, one Margherita pizza. Got it. Anything else?"

If I started towards the restaurant now, he'd see me, and I had enough on my mind. So I stalled as he passed, checking my reflection in my fingerprint-smudged back window. Who had been touching the outside of my car like this? It was tempting to blame Morris, but I knew that was just reflex.

"Emaline?"

Crap, I thought, even as I arranged a surprised look on my face and turned to face him. "Oh, hi," I said. "Theo. Right?"

He nodded. "We have to stop meeting like this."

It was a weird line, which—judging by the slight flush over his face—I was pretty sure he realized about the same time I did. It made him look kind of cute, though: like embarrassment worked for him. "So," I said, "how's the Clyde project going?"

"Good, really good," he replied, stepping aside so a BMW searching for a space could pass on his right. "We've gotten some great interviews with locals this week. Up until now there'd been a lot of resistance, for whatever reason."

"Really."

He nodded. "Ivy says it's often like that in rural areas

when you come in asking questions. There's a sense of protectiveness of the subject, a need to keep away outsiders."

"Or maybe," I said, "it's just that nobody has anything to say."

"Oh, I doubt that." He brushed a hand through his hair. "Clyde Conaway has a real story. Even if part of it is that no one wants to tell it. Actually, I was thinking that I needed to get in touch—"

"Emaline!"

I turned, and there was Benji, about a foot taller than the last time I saw him, running in that sloppy, ten-year-old way right towards me. He was grinning and his hair was too long, hanging in his face. When he was about an arm's length away, he launched himself right at me, throwing his arms around my waist.

"Hey," I said, surprised by this sudden show of affection. Benji had always been sweet, but we'd seen each other only a handful of times, each separated by multiple months. "How are you?"

"Good," he said, still hugging me tight. I looked over his head, to the Subaru, where my father was standing watching us, his keys in one hand. As soon as our eyes met, he started walking, as if he had to be sure it was me first. "We've been in the car *forever*."

"I bet." I ruffled his hair, because that's what you do with kids this age (I thought). Must be, because he loosened his grip, stepped back, then looked squarely at Theo. I had not been planning any introductions, but now they seemed unavoidable.

"Um," I said, very much aware of my father coming ever closer, "this is my brother, Benji. Benji, this is Theo."

They exchanged hellos, and then my father was joining us. Unlike Benji, he didn't look all that different from the last time we were here. Same black-framed glasses, same kind of clothes: a white button-down shirt, jeans and loafers, no socks. "Hello," he said to me, and then somehow we were hugging, quickly and awkwardly. "How are you?"

"Good," I said, already stepping back. "How was the trip?"

"Great. The hardest part was getting out of the city. The GW was backed up for miles."

Theo smiled. "It always is."

My father looked at him for a moment, then extended his hand. "Luke, right?"

"Actually, no," I said quickly. "This is Theo. He's down for the summer."

"From the city," my father said, clarifying.

"I'm in school at NYU," Theo told him.

"Studying what?"

"Filmmaking. I'm down here doing an internship with a documentary filmmaker."

"Really." My father looked surprised. And oddly, pleased. "I know a few of those. Who is it?"

"Ivy Mendelson."

"*Cooper's Way,*" my father said. Theo smiled, nodding. "I saw that a couple of years back at the Tribeca Film Festival. What brings her to Colby?"

"This artist, Clyde Conaway?" Theo replied. "He's from here. So we're doing background, interviews, getting footage."

"Right, right." My father looked at me and smiled. I was not sure what was going on here. Then he said, "So . . . are you joining us?"

Just then, I heard a beep, followed by an engine approaching. I didn't even have to turn around to know it was Luke: his truck had had a loose tailpipe for months now, and I could hear it loud and clear as he pulled into a space somewhere behind me. There was a bang, and the sound of rattling keys. He was a jingler, too.

"I'm just picking up some food, actually," Theo finished. "For the third night in a row. Ivy thinks this is the only place on the island where she can get anything other than a shrimp burger."

"She's right," my father—who had not lived here since before my birth—told him.

"Did somebody say shrimp burger?"

Of course that was Luke, ambling up behind me. His hair was damp, his skin pink from a day in the sun. I couldn't help but notice that he and I were the only adults not wearing designer eyewear. "Hey," I said, as he wrapped one hand around mine.

For a beat we all just stood there, staring at each other. Then Luke, who was capable of being social in any situation, stuck out his free hand to Theo. "Luke," he said.

"Theo."

"You must be Emaline's father," Luke said next. They shook, formally, and then he pointed at Benji. "Little man. Benji, right?"

"Yup," Benji said, already grinning. Dogs and children loved my boyfriend. It was a simple fact.

"How was the drive?" Luke asked my father.

"Too much traffic on the bridge," Theo said.

"Oh, that always happens around quitting time," Luke replied. "Everyone trying to get back home on the island at once."

I bit my lip, not wanting to correct him. A bridge was a bridge. Right? "We should go in," I said instead. "They fill up fast here."

"They do," Theo agreed.

"It's the snobbier tourists," Luke said. "They think this is the only place that makes anything for their refined palates."

I didn't look, but I was pretty sure my father and Theo exchanged a glance, hearing this. I said, "Well, my palate isn't refined, but I love the olive bread."

No reply from anyone. We all started walking to the restaurant, Benji falling in beside me and taking my other hand. I was not sure what this sudden burst of sibling affection was all about, but it was kind of sweet. Plus, there was safety in numbers.

The hostess, a high school girl with visible tan lines, smiled at us as we came in. "Welcome to the Reef Room! Five for dinner?"

"I'm not eating, just getting takeout," Theo told her, then turned to my father and Luke. "Nice meeting you both."

"And you as well," my father said. "I'll keep an eye out for the finished doc."

"Do that."

Then Theo waved and was gone, going into the half-filled bar. As the hostess gathered menus, then led us to a large booth by the window, Luke leaned down to my ear. "What's the story with Girl Jeans?"

Of course this was the first thing he noticed. "I met him doing vips the other day. He's down working for some film-maker."

"Ivy Mendelson," my father said from behind us. "She's a very talented director."

"Who likes the chicken satay here," I added. The hostess smiled widely at me. Not for the first time since we got here, I wished I had more gum. "Let's sit down."

I slid in by the window, and before I knew it, Benji was beside me. Which left Luke to join my father on the other side. It was like the oddest of double dates.

"I want a shrimp burger," Benji announced, without even opening his menu.

"That's my boy," Luke said, holding up his hand for a high five. They slapped. "They have good ones here. Not too bready, light on the cocktail sauce. Skip the onion rings, though. Too thin."

Now my father looked at him, as if not sure exactly what kind of species he was. "Luke's kind of an expert when it comes to shrimp burgers," I explained.

"The key is the size of the shrimp, the amount of bread-ing, and how much mayo is in the slaw," Luke added. "You have to get all three right, and then . . . *perfection*."

Benji laughed. "I like anything fried."

"Agreed," Luke said. "I had fried Oreos at the fair last year. They were great."

My father looked over at the bar, apparently missing Theo already. "You had a burger at lunch," he said to Benji. "I think you'd better go with salad and a lean protein now."

"But I want a shrimp burger."

"Benji." There's was the slightest edge to his voice. "Salad and protein. Get fish or chicken. *Not* fried."

I felt a nudge in the middle of my shin, but didn't look up to meet Luke's eyes. I could imagine his expression without the visual. Between this and Girl Jeans, we were not off to a good start. Benji, for his part, looked on the verge of tears.

"The chicken satay *is* good," I told him. "That's what I always get."

Luke was looking at me, I knew, as this was an outright lie. Thankfully, a beat later, he said, "She's right. It's pretty awesome."

"So, Luke," my father said suddenly, folding up his own menu. "Are you off to college this fall as well?"

"Yes, sir. To East U. Just like Emaline."

Luke was the most-good natured person I knew, but even without that, it was clear from his tone and expression this was just an honest, polite answer to the question. From my father's face, however, you would have thought he'd reached across the table and punched him. His face reddened, he coughed, then quickly looked down at his menu. *You brought it up,* I thought. *Don't ask if you can't handle being told.*

For a minute we just sat there, in a silence that felt heavy like a blanket. On the one hand, I got some satisfaction that the subject at least made him uncomfortable. But then the awkwardness became excruciating. *Please, God,* I thought, *let us talk about something else. Anything.*

Apparently, God was listening, as right then I heard a cell phone trill, the melody oddly (and irritatingly) familiar. It was "The Mexican Hat Dance."

I looked at Luke—who was known for terrible ringtone choices—but he shook his head. It couldn't be my father's. Could it? Then Benji pulled something from his pocket.

"Not at the table," my father said automatically.

"It's Mom, though." For a moment they just looked at each other, Luke and I in the periphery. Then Benji answered. "Hello? Yeah, hi. No, we just sat down to dinner . . ."

My father turned around in his seat, scanning the room. "Do we have a waitress here?"

"I'll find someone," Luke said. "I need to hit the restroom anyway."

With that, he was up and gone, and I wished more than anything I could go with him. Benji was still talking.

"—a shrimp burger, but Dad said I had to get chicken satay." My father looked at him, now clearly annoyed. "What? Oh, Emaline and her boyfriend. Luke."

"Benji."

"He's really cool. He—"

"Benji."

This time, Benji stopped talking. "What?"

"We don't use the phone in the restaurant. Take it outside. Or at least up front."

Benji looked at me, as if needing confirmation of this. When I didn't give it, though—not my place, not even really my family—he got up anyway.

My father watched him, his mouth a thin line, as he wove through the tables towards the hostess stand. "That phone. It drives me crazy."

"I didn't realize kids his age even had them these days."

"It's relatively recent. Since we decided to separate. We figured it would make it easier for Leah and me to stay close to him."

Separate?

"Can I get you something to drink?" the waitress, finally appearing, asked from the end of the table.

"Water for me," I blurted out, too quickly. My father, after consulting the beer list, asked for some microbrew I'd never heard of. As she went to the bar, we were both quiet for a moment. Then I swallowed and said, "I didn't realize you and Leah had . . ."

He looked up from the beer menu, meeting my eyes. Suddenly the more tired expression, how he seemed older somehow, made sense. "We only decided a few months ago. Benji doesn't know yet."

I nodded, all the while doing the math in my head. A few months ago had been just after my acceptance to Columbia. This, then, was the Unforeseen Circumstance that had forced his own *We regret to inform you.*

"I'm sorry."

"Well." He cleared his throat. "Yes. Thanks."

Our waitress, now working at warp speed, came back with our drinks. Once they were distributed, she said, "Are we waiting for two more?"

"They're here," I told her. "Just—"

"Give us five more minutes," my father said. She nodded, retreating again, and I watched him glance at Benji, who was now sitting on a bench by the front entrance, picking at his shoe as he talked to Leah.

"How's Benji doing?" I asked, nodding in his direction.

"He's been aware of the tension, for sure." He took a sip of his beer, which had a label like an abstract painting, all swirly reds and blues. "We'll see how he does on this trip, though. With the distance, and the time away from his mom, as well."

I wasn't clear what he meant, and even less sure I wanted to ask. But I did. "So . . . you're here for more than a visit?"

He took another sip. "For the summer, probably. In the fall, I'll be finding an apartment and moving to the city, and just have him weekends. He doesn't know that yet, though."

I looked at Benji again, thinking of his face when he couldn't order what he wanted. And that was just a shrimp burger.

"What'd I miss?" Luke asked, sliding back into his seat. He spotted the drinks. "Other than the waitress."

Instead of answering right away, I turned my head and looked out at the parking lot. In the distance, you could just make out the bridge to the mainland, arcing across the blue of the sky. Cars were coming, cars were going. A bridge was just a bridge, indeed. All that mattered was that somehow, it carries precious cargo from one piece of solid ground to another, safely over everything and anything that might lay below.

* * *

"Man," Morris said. "That is just crackers."

We were sitting at the Tip, a strip of beach on the west end of Colby that was slowly being eaten away by the ocean. There wasn't much there except the end of an access road, bonfire remnants, and, on weekend and summer nights, just about everyone from my high school.

This evening was no exception. A pile of driftwood was just catching about a hundred feet from us, a keg sitting lopsided on the sand adjacent. People were milling around, but Morris and I had a small stretch of sand all to ourselves.

"Crackers?" I repeated. "What the hell does that mean?"

He tipped up his red plastic cup, finishing it off. "Crackers. You know, like, crazy. Bizarre. Weird."

"You just made that up."

"Nope."

I just looked at him, not fully convinced. Morris was always coming up with his own expressions, then swearing they were part of the general lexicon, as if just by appearing in his own head they indeed existed for the rest of us. Crackers, indeed.

I didn't want to be thinking about the contents of Morris's head, though. I didn't want to think at all, which was why I was here in the first place, a heavy cup of cheap draft beer parked between my feet. It was my second one, but I still couldn't get the bad taste of my dinner at the Reef Room out of my mouth. And it wasn't just the chicken satay.

It was just so weird, from the very start. Seeing Theo in the parking lot, Benji's sudden attachment to me, and then, the capper: my father dropping the bomb that his marriage was over. Suddenly, it all made sense: his weird response to my acceptance, the sudden rescinding of all he'd promised. But why hadn't he just told me? Plus there was the fact that when he left my half-brother to move to New York, Benji would be not that much older than I was when my father first decided to come back into my life. There was a symbolism in that, but I was trying not to think about it. I picked up my beer and took another big gulp instead.

Earlier, after the bombshell, my father had moved on to inquiring politely about how my family was doing. I, in turn, asked him about his plans for the summer. Safe and easy topics for all of us as we ate our food, with the booths, bar, and tables filling up all around us. When we got the check, the restaurant was packed and noisy, with a crowd of people waiting to be seated.

"Wow," my father said as we wound through the mob to the front door. "This is a popular place."

"High season," I replied. "Everything's crowded."

I was right behind him, with Benji holding my hand, Luke bringing up the rear. I'd been so worried about how dinner would go and whether it would be awkward, but once my father told me about the separation I couldn't think about anything else. Why did I have to know something about Benji's life that he didn't? Not the position I wanted to be in, even before he'd attached himself to my side. Maybe it was my father's way of apologizing to me about everything that had happened, without actually doing it: he could dodge that obligation, as well. I wished, yet again, that things with him could just be clear cut. But none of this was my choice anyway.

Once in the parking lot, he pulled out his keys. "Well, I suppose we should be on our way to North Reddemane. We've paid to have the house cleaned since the renters left, but there's no telling what kind of state we'll actually find it in."

"Renters are hell on houses," Luke said, as Benji skipped beside me in that awkward, bouncy, little-kid way.

"Is that so," my father said.

"According to Emaline's grandmother, anyway." Luke pulled out his keys and started jingling them as his truck came into sight. Seriously, it was like a reflex with him. "Most likely it's nothing you can't fix up yourself, though."

"I don't know about that," my father said. "I'm not exactly handy."

I saw Luke give him a look, slightly pitying. It's one I never would have expected a couple of hours earlier, when this evening began. Then, he and Theo were the experts, and Luke stuck out. But here, now, it was reversed, and I suddenly saw my father the way I realized my boyfriend had from the beginning, like he was the one who should be embarrassed. Which, in turn, embarrassed me. Apparently, I was responsible for everyone now.

"Nice to meet you," Luke told him, extending a hand. My father shook it. "And thanks for dinner."

"Of course."

"Are you coming back to the house with us?" Benji asked me.

"Um," I said, glancing at Luke, "I don't think so. Not tonight, anyway."

"Emaline's got her own life," my father said. "She was very kind to meet us on such short notice."

Benji looked at me, his eyes squinty in the setting sun. He was more my sibling than Amber or Margo, at least if you went by genetics. But I didn't know him at all.

"I'll see you soon," I told him. "We'll go play minigolf, or something."

"Yeah?" he said, excited. "That would be so cool!"

"Watch this one with a golf club," Luke told him, cocking a finger at me. "She's lethal."

"That was just one time," I said.

Benji's eyes widened. "What happened?"

I looked at Luke. "I kind of nailed him on the forehead on the windmill hole."

"Hit one of the spokes and shot right back at me," he added, ever cheerfully. He stuck a finger in the center of his tanned forehead. "Had a circle mark here for *weeks*."

Benji laughed, because of course this was just the kind of thing ten-year-olds loved to hear about. My father forced a smile. "All right, buddy," he said. "Let's get going."

"Okay." Benji crossed over to where my father was standing, leaving us in two separate camps. The natural order, resumed. "See you guys later."

"Count on it," Luke said.

"Drive safe," I added. And then, finally, it was over. It had only been an hour and a half, but I was exhausted. I could feel it in my bones.

Even so, after a few steps, I turned back and looked at them again. Benji had run out ahead to the Subaru, my father walking behind him slowly, almost heavily. As I watched, he reached up and rubbed the back of his neck.

"Check the doorknobs," I called out.

He turned around. "What?"

I cleared my throat. "The doorknobs. They get the most wear and tear in a rental. Especially any onto the beach side. You don't want them falling off and locking you out."

He just looked at me for a moment, and I wondered why I was even telling him this. In the distance, Benji was lifting his arms to the breeze coming off the causeway, his hair blowing back from his face.

"Okay," my father said. "Thanks."

I nodded, then started back towards my car, where Luke was waiting for me. *Doorknobs?* I was thinking. *Really?* And yet it wasn't like I was proficient in his language, had any idea how to speak to him. You stick with what you know.

Now, back at the Tip, Morris picked up his beer again. "It's not your problem," he told me.

I looked at him. "What isn't?"

"His marriage. Or his relationship with his kid." He took a sip, then swallowed. "Any of it."

Morris might have been dense. Okay, Morris *was* dense, most of the time. But just about when I was totally ready to give up on him, he'd say something out of nowhere that surprised me. And, even more surprisingly, helped.

"So why do I feel like it is?" I asked.

"Because he dumped all that shit on you. Totally uncool." Another gulp. God only knew how many he'd had. Morris never seemed to get drunk, just talked even more slowly. When he was really wasted, he was flat out silent. That's how you knew. "He wasn't around for you when you needed him, you don't have to be there for him. Bottom line."

I was quiet, aware as I always was when we crept close to the issue of his own father. All I knew of him was the lowered Monte Carlo he'd always driven to see Morris back when we were neighbors, years ago. It was red, supershiny, with a stereo that had bass rumbling loud enough to set your teeth chattering. You could tell the car was its owner's baby, absolutely loved and cared for. This was in stark contrast to how he treated his actual child, who, more often than not, sat waiting on the front steps for weekend visits for hours before finally disappearing back inside, dragging his overnight bag behind him. After Morris and his mom moved, his dad relocated somewhere up north and hadn't been in touch since. It was not something we talked about much. What I did know was that in the weeks leading up to graduation, when I found myself haunting my mailbox for responses to my invites, it was Morris who said to cut it out, that it wasn't worth the time. He might have been ignorant on some fronts, but the boy knew about the futility of waiting around.

Unlike Luke, who was now suddenly behind me, his hands sliding down over my shoulders. "What are you guys doing over here, looking so serious?" he asked. "Contemplating the universe?"

I glanced at Morris, who was downing the last of his beer. "Sort of."

"Screw the universe," he said. "I'm just checking out the ocean."

Luke guffawed, then plopped down next to me and pulled me into his arms. I knew he was buzzed and just being sweet, but like too often lately, it grated; he'd come at the wrong moment. I tried to shake this off as Morris got to his feet.

"Getting a refill," he announced. He looked at me. "You need one?"

I shook my head. "Talk later?"

"Talk later," he repeated.

It was what we had always said, our version of goodbye, going all the way back to the days when he lived next door. Back then, when we were kids and time was long, we spent just about every day together— riding the bus to school, coming home, then playing by the causeway behind our houses. More often than not, he'd then end up at our house for dinner and TV afterwards, leaving only when it was time for me to go to bed. But as he finally went out the door, walking the short distance across the grass to his rental house, it was never a full stop. More like a pause, until we started up the next day. Talk later. We always did.

Now he nodded, then was gone, loping across the sand. As I watched him go, Luke pulled me in even closer and kissed the back of my head. "You did look pretty serious over here. Everything okay?"

"I guess." I picked at a piece of driftwood by my foot. "Just kind of freaked about my dad and everything, still."

"Right." He was quiet for a moment. Then he said, "I know it's weird. But the fact that he did tell you . . . it's kind of cool. Like he's, you know, letting you in."

I felt myself blink, processing this. "Into what?"

He shrugged. "I don't know. His life, his marriage. I mean, that's progress in some way, don't you think? That after pulling away like he did, he wants to include you now?"

No, I thought. Out loud I said, "Maybe."

It was so different from what Morris had said, the complete opposite in fact, that I wanted him to explain himself. But then he was sliding his hands around my waist, over the small of my back, kissing my neck again. "My parents are out tonight," he said into my collarbone. "Want to see if we can get busted at my place this time?"

It was a fair offer, one I most likely would have jumped at any other day. But now, it just felt off. Sometimes I thought Luke knew me better than anyone. This wasn't one of them.

"Maybe," I said again, leaving all of my doubt to hover in this one word between us. I didn't know if he heard me or not, as the wind was picking up, carrying voices from behind us with it. There were so many sounds near the ocean. Water, air, even sand blowing. As you got farther inland, nature subsided, muted by concrete and the landscape. Here on the Tip, though, you could always count on it to drown just about anything out.

*　*　*

Of course, Luke's parents didn't catch us. He had always been the lucky one.

I was heading home just after midnight when my gas light came on. Now I'd be late for curfew for sure, I thought, as I turned into the Gas/Gro. I'd just started filling up when a dusty, dented pickup pulled up to the other side of the pump. The door creaked open and an older guy with graying hair, wearing a worn baseball cap that simply said FISH, climbed out.

It was one of those hot summer nights, with a breeze that didn't even come close to cooling you off, even when it hit you right in the face. Inside the Gas/Gro, the attendant had his cell phone tucked between his ear and shoulder as he stocked cigarettes, sliding in one box at a time.

When my pump read twenty bucks, I slowed it down, watching the numbers carefully so I wouldn't go over what I had in my pocket. In my peripheral vision, I saw the guy slide his credit card, then twist off his gas cap. He started filling up as well, and for a moment we just stood there, the only sound the ticking of gallons and dollars going in.

"Hey, Clyde," I finally said.

He glanced up. "Emaline. How's it going?"

I nodded for my answer and we were silent for another minute or so. Then I said, "You know there's some people down here shooting a documentary about you, right?"

He didn't take his eyes off the pump. "I believe I have ignored some phone messages to that effect."

"They seem pretty persistent."

He shrugged. "We'll see."

When I hit twenty-five bucks, I stopped pumping and re-placed my gas cap. As I did so, I looked at Clyde, who was as much an institution in Colby as the pier and the bacon at the Last Chance Café. He'd grown up in Colby, worked do-ing maintenance for my grandmother in the summers, ran a framing crew my dad was on in high school. I'd met him hang-ing around the bike shop by Clementine's, which he owned and had run until a couple of years earlier. He was recognized and referred to by all of us, and yet nobody really knew him that well, which was just the way he'd liked it since he moved back from New York about ten years ago.

On my way in to pay, he nodded at me, and I waved. From inside, I watched him climb into his truck, crank it up, and pull onto the main road. Maybe he was going back to the sound-side house where he lived, or to check on the Wash-room, the all-night Laundromat/café he owned. Whatever it was, though, it was his business.

That's what Theo didn't understand, what I couldn't tell him when he first starting asking me questions. It was one thing for all of us here to wonder about Clyde, speculate what his story might be. This was a small town, and that's what people did. When someone from outside started prodding around, though, it was different. This was the coast. We un-derstood about secrets. And Clyde's, whatever they might be, would always be safe with us.

6

"OH MY GOD. Look at *that*."

There was an appreciative murmur. "Oooh, the scenery here just keeps getting better and better!"

"Melissa, the beach is in the other direction!"

With that, the four girls gathered at the check-in desk burst into loud, squealing giggles. I was pretty sure I knew what they were gawking at, but just to be sure, I glanced out the window. Sure enough, there was Luke, moving some stuff around in his truck bed in the parking lot, shirtless.

"Honestly," Margo said out loud, adding a couple of cluck-cluck noises as she tapped away at her computer. "Can't you keep him dressed in public, at least?"

"It's not up to me," I said, glancing at the girls again. They were here for a wedding, or so they announced when they'd come in a few minutes earlier. We were used to the kind of pre-vacation exuberance that people let loose after being cooped up in a car for a few hours: voices raised, footsteps hard, the lid to the ice cream cooler being banged, not eased, shut. Everything took a beating in high season.

"Have you stayed with us at Fancy Free before?" Rebecca, one of our reservation specialists, was saying to them now.

"Never," the tall brunette who first noticed Luke replied. She had that deep brown tan that you just knew was cultivated in a bed all winter. "We usually go to Hilton Head. We could barely find this place! Leave it to Tara to decide to get hitched in the middle of nowhere."

Margo tsked again, shaking her head. I agreed with her, sort of—not only did these girls show up demanding early check-in, now they were insulting our beach—but she still sounded like an old woman. Then again, as long as she was distracted by them she wasn't noticing that I was here and not out in the sandbox, where I was technically supposed to be.

The front door banged and Luke came in, pulling a shirt over his head as he walked. He had a sheaf of papers in one hand.

"Oh, no," too-tan Melissa said to him as he passed her. "Don't do that!"

Luke yanked it the rest of the way down, then smiled at her. "Sorry?"

"Your shirt," she replied, nodding at it. "You don't really *need* it, do you?"

"Afraid so," Luke told her. "No shirt, no shoes, no service. You know the drill."

"I hate rules," she said, smiling at him. Her friends, behind her, exchanged looks as he kept walking, over to my grandmother's open office door. She was on the phone, so he stopped just outside, smoothing his hair down with one hand.

"Hey," I called out, my voice low. He looked over, surprised; he hadn't seen me. "What do you need?"

He glanced at the girls, his face flushing slightly, then held up the papers. "Invoices from my jobs this week. Carl said I needed to come by and get a check."

"She might be on forever," I said, nodded at my grand-mother, who was talking shop with one of our more chatty owners. "Come on over to my mom's. Are they readable, at least?"

"Yes," he said, sounding annoyed. I doubted it, though. We both knew his handwriting was the absolute worst.

As he followed me across the office, I was distinctly aware of the girls watching not only him but me as well. I was not the jealous type, but that didn't mean I didn't notice. I said, "Your fan club just keeps growing."

"Hardly," he replied. "They're on vacation, would look at anybody."

"Not everybody's putting on a show, though."

I felt him slow his steps, and instantly hated how petty I sounded. More and more lately, we kept hitting each other with these little jabs. Like we were siblings or bickering friends, not a couple supposedly in love. "It's hot and I work outside, Emaline."

"I know."

My mom was behind her desk, bent over some papers, a pen in one hand. A fountain drink cup from the Gas/Gro was sweating through a napkin beside her. "Hey," I said, and she looked up. "Luke needs a check."

"Doesn't everyone." She sighed, waved him in, then looked at her watch. "Aren't you due to do check-ins?"

"Just about." Luke handed her the invoices and, as I ex-pected, she squinted at them like they were written in

Sanskrit. "But Grandmother said she had an errand for me to run first, so I was waiting around."

"Remind her of the time. You need to get out there," she said, reaching for the checkbook she kept in her bottom drawer. To Luke she said, "Dear God, this is practically illegible. Is that a six or a b?"

I shot Luke a look—he ignored me—as I went back to my grandmother, through the office, which was now quiet. It was three, though, which meant people would start showing up in rapid-fire style soon. Luckily, she was off the phone now, busy opening a Rolo.

"I have to start handing out keys," I told her. "Did you need me?"

"Yes," she replied, reaching down for a Park Mart bag beside her. "The owners of Foam Free apparently didn't trust us to purchase a new doorknob for the property, so they dropped off their own. Maintenance is already there. Can you run it over?"

"Sure," I said, taking it from her. "Anything else?"

She shook her head, and I headed out to my car and Foam Free, an older property a few blocks down from the office. It should have been a short, easy trip, but I got bogged down en route and coming back by a fender bender on the main road. By the time I pulled back into the office lot, there was a line of cars backed up from the sandbox.

I groaned out loud, already picturing how pissed Margo must be, having to fill in for me. When I got out of my car and sprinted over, though, I found Morris instead, squinting at the box of welcome packets like they were written in code.

"Baker," a man in a Mercedes, clearly annoyed, was saying to him. "Bay-kurr. B-A-K-E-R."

"Right," Morris repeated, still looking. S-L-O-W-L-Y. "Ummm . . ."

I reached around him, finding the envelope, then grabbed it and the complimentary Colby Realty bag and handed them over. "Here you go, sir. Have you stayed with us at the Jolly Pirate before?"

"No," he said, taking the bag and envelope from me.

"It's a fantastic property. Our number is on there if you have any questions or problems. Have a great week!"

He grumbled a goodbye, then pulled away, making room for a Cadillac packed with people.

"What are *you* doing here?" I asked Morris.

"Margo was freaking," he replied, helping himself to a water bottle from the cooler.

I didn't doubt this, but it still didn't answer my question. "Yeah, but why were you here in the first place? Looking for me?"

He shook his head as the Cadillac rattled to a stop beside us. "I came for my other job."

"McAdams," a red-haired older woman with a deep tan announced from the passenger seat of the Caddy, skipping a greeting entirely. "We're renting Sea Door."

"Right." I found the envelope, got them a bag, and handed both over. "Have you stayed with us before?"

"Yep," she replied. "Just hope the air conditioner works this year."

"Call us with any problems. Have a great week!" They

drove off. I looked at Morris, saying, "You have another job? Since when? And doing what?"

He nodded towards the front of the office. "Working for them."

A minivan, radio blaring, was pulling up right as he said this. So it was with the number one song of the summer so far—a bouncy dance track called "Mr. Right Now"—playing in my ear that I looked over to see Theo and his boss, Ivy, standing by their white van. They were talking to Margo, and all of them were looking right at me.

* * *

"I told you," I said again. "I don't even know Clyde."

We were inside now, in the conference room. Normally I would have been thrilled to be relieved of sandbox duty—Rebecca was suffering temporarily instead—but this kind of third degree was not really an improvement.

"Theo was under the impression that you did," Ivy said. She wore jeans and a black tank top, her arms pale and sinewy, and she folded and unfolded her sunglasses. "And we could really use some help reaching out to him.

"Why don't *you* get in touch with him?" I asked Margo.

"I've been away at school for four years," she replied, glancing at Ivy. She was so clearly starstruck, or New York–struck, or just struck, it was embarrassing. All it took was the word *movie* or something similar and she threw Clyde, and me, right under the bus. "I don't know anybody here anymore."

I would have liked to point out, for the record, that she'd

only been a couple of hours away, not overseas. "I don't know Clyde either," I said again.

Ivy looked at Theo, her expression displeased.

"So you've never had contact with him?" he asked me. For the first time, I realized he looked kind of nervous. There was that flush again. "Because I thought—"

"I mean, I've met him a few times," I said. Which was a huge mistake, because they both literally leaned forward, hearing this. "But he's a pretty private person."

"This is a ridiculously small town, though," Ivy pointed out. "Can't be too private."

I glanced at Margo, to see if she was equally offended by the use of the word *ridiculously*, but she was too busy checking out Ivy's bag, a big leather number with a bunch of buckles. "He does a pretty good job flying under the radar."

"Which is why," she replied, leaning forward again, "we need *you*, Emaline. We're not from here, don't know the back roads and locals. If we want that part of Clyde's life accurately represented, we need someone to help us get to them."

I could practically feel Margo breathing, she was so excited by this prospect. Bet she was sorry now she claimed to be all worldly and distanced from Colby. I couldn't savor this, though, because I was looking at Theo, whose expression could only be described as pleading. Crap.

"I can't bring you to Clyde," I told them both. Theo's shoulders slumped, just slightly, and Ivy shot him a look. I swallowed. "But I can . . . I mean, I guess I could show you around Colby."

The minute I said this, I knew it was a mistake. I didn't know Ivy well, but I had a hunch that once you gave her something approximating what she wanted, she wouldn't let up until she got it all.

"Wonderful," she said now, smiling at me. "We'll start this afternoon. Yes?"

"I have to work here," I say.

"Only until six," Margo piped up, clearly having now moved on to directing the bus in what was, exactly, the best way to run me over.

"Then why don't you come over to the house around seven." Ivy pushed out her chair, getting to her feet. "We'll talk, figure out a game plan. Yes?"

I didn't answer, not that she was waiting for me to do so. As Theo moved to follow her, I started to glare at Margo, only to realize he was trying to catch my eye. Ivy was already halfway down the hallway as he mouthed the words *thank you*. I nodded, despite myself, and then he was jogging after her, towards the exit.

"Well, isn't that something," Margo said, watching them go. "Someone's shooting a movie right here in Colby."

"It's not a movie, it's a documentary," I told her.

"Either way, it's interesting." She craned her neck, keeping them in sight as they got in the van.

I saw Morris was with them as well, sliding open the back door. Earlier, he'd explained to me that he was in the Wave Nails parking lot, having just visited Daisy, when Theo approached and asked if he wanted to make some quick money toting boxes. Fifteen minutes later, he was at the Shipping

Depot, unloading cartons. When Theo asked him if he knew anyone who was really familiar with either Clyde or Colby in general, Morris immediately thought of me. What a coincidence.

"I didn't know you were already friends," he'd said, as I handed over another envelope to a family in a car with Delaware plates.

"We're not," I'd told him. "We just met when I did a vip drop-off over there."

He looked at Theo again, then back at me. "Huh."

Morris was not one for innuendo. It was pretty much beyond him. What you saw was what you got, which was alternately refreshing or frustrating, depending on the situation. "What?"

"I dunno," he said, as the next car pulled up. "He just acted like he knew you well, or something."

"Really."

"Yeah." He shrugged. "But maybe he's just like that with everyone."

Saying this, he had been assuming a lot himself, but I figured it wasn't worth pointing it out. Still, now, as I watched them leave, I wondered how, exactly, I'd come to feel like I owed Theo anything, especially something I couldn't even promise to deliver. It couldn't just be that he was cute when he blushed. And what a weird coincidence that Morris now, too, had been sucked into his orbit, making our paths cross once more. On the flip side, it wasn't like it was so difficult to find connections. This was, after all, a ridiculously small town.

* * *

At six thirty, I finally left the sandbox to go home, exhausted. I was so worn out, in fact, that when I started down the hallway towards my room and saw the door ajar, the sound of a TV drifting out, all I could muster was a loud sigh.

"Look!" Amber said, as I stepped into the doorway. She was on my bed, the orange hair now gone, replaced with a jet-black dye job. Not for the first time, I wondered if she ever did anything at cosmetology school besides adjust her own look. My mom, sipping a light beer, was beside her. "It's the movie star!"

I just looked at them. "I can't believe you guys."

"Fumes," my mother explained.

"Excuse me?"

"Your dad is doing something upstairs with the floors and epoxy. We can't breathe it, it's dangerous."

"Dangerous," Amber echoed, flipping a page of one of my magazines.

I walked over to my (crowded) bed, kicked off my shoes, and flopped facedown across the only space remaining. After a moment, a foot nudged my shoulder blade. "You okay?" my mom asked.

"Margo totally sold me out," I replied, my voice muffled by the pillow.

"She'll do that," Amber said. "Especially if there's money involved."

"But I thought that boy was your friend," my mom said. "That's what he said, anyway."

I lifted my head. "Said?"

"When he came in. I was there. He said he was a friend of yours, wanted to talk to you about Clyde and Colby."

"I've met him twice." I put my head back down. "Three times, max."

"Around here, that's practically dating," Amber said.

"He's not from here, though."

"Then maybe you *should* date him." A pause. "Is he cute?"

"Emaline has Luke," my mom reminded her.

"Yeah, but high school romances never last." The bed wiggled as, I assumed, my mom gave her a shove. "What? Did yours?"

We were all quiet for a moment, the only sound some mobile phone commercial on the TV. Then my mom said, "Oh, before I forget. Benji called."

I was so tired, my brain cluttered with Theo and Clyde, that it took a second for my half brother's face to pop up and pair itself with this name. "Really." I sat up. "What did he say?"

My mom, clearly proud of herself, picked up a pad of paper. "He wanted to know when you could play minigolf. Left a number and everything. He was very sweet. How old is he now, eight?"

"Ten," I said, as she handed over the pad.

"Is Leah with them?"

"Not this trip."

My mom nodded, taking another sip of her beer. Watching her, I felt a weird twinge, aware that I hadn't yet told her about my father being separated. It wasn't a trust thing, or that he swore me to silence: I just hadn't mentioned it. The more time that passed, though, the bigger a deal it seemed.

My phone buzzed in my pocket and I slid it out. It was a number I didn't recognize. "Hello?"

"Emaline, hey. It's Theo."

"Oh," I said, turning myself slightly towards the door. "Hey."

Despite this attempt at subterfuge, I now had Amber's full attention. She made this clear as she asked, loudly, "Is that him? He *sounds* cute."

I slid off the bed, going out into and down the hallway. "Sorry to bug you," Theo was saying, "but I just wanted to confirm our meeting tonight, here at the house, at seven? Ivy's got a conference call with some backers, so it'll just be us at first."

"Seven," I said, sitting down on the bottom step of the stairs leading to the second floor. "Right. I'll be there."

"Great." He sounded relieved, making me wonder if he'd thought I'd change my mind. I wished I'd known it was an option, but oh well. Too late now. "I really appreciate it. I've been trying to get her to give me some more, you know, hands-on responsibility, and this is . . . a good first step. So thanks. I, um, owe you one."

"Sure," I said. "It's no—"

And that was as far as I got before the smell of whatever my dad was using on the floors upstairs suddenly hit me. It was harsh, stank of chemicals, and filled my throat immediately, spurring a hacking cough. One minute I was having a conversation, the next I was about to puke my guts out. Whoa.

"Emaline?" Theo sounded worried. "Are you . . . is everything all right?"

I heard footsteps, then looked up to see my mom in the hallway in front of me. "Fumes," she said, gesturing for me to get up and come towards her. I did, still hacking away, and she grabbed my elbow, leading me outside to the fresh air. Theo was still talking as I gave my mom the phone, bending over to put my hands on my knees.

"Hello?" she said into it, watching me with a worried look. "No, this is her mom. She's fine, just . . . hold on a second."

I could only imagine what Theo was thinking in the moments that passed before I felt relatively sure I wasn't going to pass out. Finally, though, I motioned for my mom to return the phone to me. "I'll be there at seven," I croaked into it. "Okay?"

"Sure, great," he replied, hurriedly. "See you then."

I hung up, then bent over again, taking in few more deep breaths. My pulse, which had been beating wildly at my temple, was finally slowing down. "You weren't kidding," I said to my mom. "That stuff is lethal."

"Yep," she replied, rubbing a hand over my back. It was nice and familiar, the same way freshly cut grass and chicken soup were, and I wished I could just stay there, deep in it, forever. But it was creeping close to seven, and I'd made promises. So when I could breathe on my own again, I stood up straight and we walked back inside, together.

7

WHEN I PULLED up to Sand Dollars a couple of minutes past seven, the first thing I saw was Ivy. She was on the side deck of one of the master suites, dressed in jeans and a tank top, phone clamped to her ear. Not shockingly, whatever conversation she was having appeared to be heated, involving hand flipping, facial contortions, and constant pacing. I sat and watched her go back and forth—ocean to sound view and repeat—until I started to feel hypnotized. Then I shook my head, hard, and got out of the car.

Theo was waiting for me at the door. I knew this because he opened it as soon as I knocked, instead of me having to cool my heels for however long it would have taken to get there from either upstairs or downstairs. This struck me as cute, for some reason, and made him, again, seem sort of cute as well.

"Hey," he said. "I was watching for you."

Like I said: cute.

"Yeah?"

Now, he flushed, as if only just realizing how eager he seemed. "The doorbell doesn't work. Between the ocean and the size of this place people can knock forever before we hear them."

"The doorbell's busted?" He nodded as I leaned in, inspecting it.

"That's not good. Did you call the office to let them know?"

He shrugged. "It's not a big deal. Ivy's a light sleeper. If it did work she'd probably be even crankier."

"Yeah, but this place is brand-new. Nothing should be broken. Yet, anyway." I pushed the Call button. Nothing: no buzz, no click, no annoying blast of mariachi-like music that came as the default chime.

"This house is new?" Theo asked.

"Yeah. Just built this year."

He looked around the foyer as I came inside. "Wow. I didn't even realize."

"You'd notice the difference if you went into one that had been around awhile. Wear and tear and all that." I checked out the inside console, hitting buttons. Still nothing. "I'll let maintenance know about this tomorrow. It's probably just a fuse or something."

"Do you ever stop thinking about work?" he said, shutting the door and motioning for me to follow him upstairs.

"Doesn't feel like it, no." I wanted to add that this visit *also* felt like being on the clock, but I held my tongue. Hopefully they'd realize soon enough I was of no use to them and go bother someone else.

The third and main floor, which housed the kitchen and living room, had been transformed since my last visit. Gone were the couches and coffee table—making me wonder (1) where they had put them and (2) if the floors/walls were scratched during the process—replaced by a row of foldout tables lined with computers, video equipment, and several half-full bottles of Diet Coke. The kitchen was equally cluttered, with to-go containers and newspapers piled on the counters. By the dishwasher, three different cell phones were plugged in and charging, a row of tiny lights.

"Sorry about the mess," Theo said, pushing aside a plastic crate of cords with one foot so we could pass. "We've been working nonstop the last couple of days. Have a seat."

The only chairs were also folding ones, lined up along the tables. I pulled one out, only to see a stack of thick books piled on the seat. *Urban/Rural: A Retrospective* was the title of one, with a shot of a brick wall on the cover. Another, *Modern Coast*, featured a close-up of a painting of what looked like sand magnified into tiny grains.

"Cool, huh?" he said when he saw me checking it out. "You've seen that before, right?"

"What?"

"Clyde's painting."

I shook my head. "This is his?"

"Yeah." He reached across me, flipping the book open and turning to a page marked with a sticky note, which featured the same sand image. Here, though, it was just a small center square, surrounded by a cityscape: slabs of concrete, brick wall, and storefronts. The street view was dark and grimy, and in contrast the tiny piece of beach almost glowed. "His early stuff was more collage, standard cutouts. But after a couple of years, he started this contrast series. It's what he's best known for."

"Really," I repeated, turning to the next page and another painting, this one featuring alternating squares of dune grass and barbed wire. "I didn't even know about this stuff."

"That's not really an accident. Just going by our New York interviews and the personal history we've been able to gather, it's pretty clear he'd prefer to keep this part of his life to himself."

"If that's true," I said, "why are you guys chasing him down?"

"We're not," he replied, sounding somewhat defensive. Upstairs, a door banged. "We want to tell his story, give his work the attention it deserves. That's what's so maddening about his resistance. I mean, he put this out there. Why not own it?"

I flipped back to the sand painting, looking at it again. "Maybe because it's part of his life he'd rather forget?"

"Most painters *spend* their lives looking for this kind of attention for their work."

"But he's not a painter anymore. Right?"

Theo drew in a breath, ready to reply to this. Before he got the chance, though, Ivy's voice came booming down the stairs at full volume. "*Theo!*"

I jumped, startled both by the volume and her impatient tone. It sounded like a third or fourth attempt at contact, not an initial one. But he hardly seemed ruffled as he said, "Yes?"

"Didn't I ask you to contact that guy from here who was at Parsons? The one cited in that article?"

"You did."

"And?"

"I've called and e-mailed. No response yet."

There was a bang, followed by a thud. What was she doing up there? "God!" she shouted. "What the hell is *wrong* with the people down here? Are they so backward they can't even tell when someone's trying to do something *good* for them?"

I raised my eyebrows, looking at Theo. He bit his lip, then walked over to the stairs, taking them two at a time to disappear upstairs.

"What?" I heard Ivy say a moment later. He said something to her. "Oh, for God's sake. Fine. I'll be right down."

That's it, I thought. I grabbed my bag from the table and started for the door. I was almost there when he came back down, spotting me in mid-escape. "Hey, hold on," he said. "Don't—"

"Find someone else to 'help' you, okay? I'm not your girl." Upstairs, there was another loud thud. I pointed at the ceiling, adding, "And while you're at it, you might want to tell your boss to reread the rental contract she signed. If this house is damaged in any way, she *will* pay for it."

"Hey, hey," he said.

I shook my head, pulling the door open.

"I'm sorry, okay? She's just really stressed right now."

"No, she's rude. And I have better things to do than stand here and be insulted."

"I know." He reached out, putting a hand on my arm. "Look, just . . . give me five seconds, okay? Please?"

I didn't say anything. But I didn't leave either.

"Five seconds," he repeated, pointing at me. Then he went inside, shutting the door behind him.

Stupid, I thought, as I stood there, watching a family cross the street and start up the public access path to the beach. The kids, two of them, ran ahead, while the parents hung back, holding hands. The sun was just beginning to go down.

My phone beeped. I pulled it out of my purse and glanced at the screen. One missed call, one text, both from Luke. The latter said simply, Eat?

I looked inside at Sand Dollars, all lit up. I still wasn't exactly sure what I was doing here, and even less certain I could explain it to Luke. Instead I wrote, Still working. Will call soon.

I'd just hit Send when Theo stepped out, now wearing a jacket, a handheld video camera in one hand. He smiled at me. "Ready?"

"That depends. Where are we going?" I asked him, as he went down the stairs ahead of me.

"You're the local," he said over his shoulder. "You tell me."

"I don't know what you want to see."

"Colby. And not the tourist spots. The real stuff."

He was at my passenger door now, waiting to get in. "This isn't New York," I warned him. "The grand tour is not exactly . . . grand. We could cover it all in about fifteen minutes."

"Which is fifteen more than we have so far." He popped the cap of the camera lens, pointing it at me. A little red light came on, and I felt a bolt of nervousness, unexpected. Then he smiled at me. "Let's go."

* * *

I had standard answers when clients or tourists asked me for suggestions for things to do in Colby besides hitting the beach. Walk up the boardwalk. Visit the aquarium and Maritime Museum. Eat the famous onion rings at the Last Chance Café. Rent bikes from Abe's and follow the sound-side paths that wound past the marshes and tidal pools. As Theo and I waited to turn onto the main road, though, none of my go-to choices felt right.

Real, I repeated to myself, as my turn signal ticked. He was still holding the camera, pointing it out at the traffic passing. When the light changed, I went left, driving a couple of miles, then took a right. Two blocks down a gravel road, the fish house came into view. Just like most nights around this time, the lot was crowded with trucks backed up to the ramp and slips, people moving between them. I pulled into a spot and cut the engine.

"What's this?" Theo asked.

"You want local. This is about as local as it gets." I opened my door and got out. He followed, the camera still in his hand. "You might want to put that away, for now. These folks don't really crave publicity."

He nodded, slipping it into his jacket pocket, then fell into step behind me as we crossed the lot, the gravel crunching under our feet. We were still about a hundred feet from the first row of trucks when the smell hit.

"Whoa," I heard him say, right on schedule. "That's pungent."

"Fish. You'll get used to it in a minute." I cut between

two pickups, then down the walkway to the main door. Inside, the smell was even stronger, filling the one small, open room, mostly bare except for a few tables and several garbage cans. A counter along the far wall was lined with coolers, guys moving around them packing that day's haul and dumping ice from plastic bags. Through the back doors, which opened out into the boatyard, I could see more people at cleaning stations, cutting and scaling.

"That's red drum," I said to Theo, pointing at a pile of fish on newspaper on one of the tables. "There's also usually shrimp this time of year. Sometimes cobia. And . . . that looks like bluefish."

"Striper," a tall guy wearing rubber boots, who was loading a cooler, corrected me. He was wearing a Finz Bar and Grill baseball hat, the closest thing to labeling yourself a local. Tourists never went there.

"Striper," I repeated. To Theo I added, "This is the stuff you'll be eating at the Reef Room this weekend. And just about everywhere else you order fish."

"You better hope so, anyway," a guy on my other side said, shaking some ice into a cooler. "Better than last week's."

Theo stuck his hand into his jacket pocket, raising his eyebrows at me. I cleared my throat, then said to the guy in the Finz cap, "Okay if my friend shoots some video? He's trying to get footage of the 'real' Colby."

As I expected, the guy—and those hearing this around him—immediately looked wary. "Real," he repeated, narrowing his eyes at Theo. "For what?"

"It's a documentary," Theo told them. "By Ivy Mendelson? She did *Cooper's Way*?"

They all just looked at him.

"It's about some New York artist who claims Colby inspires him," I explained.

This, of course, brought a round of guffaws. "Inspired, huh?" our friend in the Finz hat said. "Hey, I'm inspired, too. Every day, by my mortgage statement."

"And my power bill," someone else chimed in.

"And my wife's credit card!" another voice added, as a blast of fish smell wafted across us.

I smiled. "It's okay, then? We'll stay out of your way."

"Yeah, why not," the guy said, shaking more ice out of a bag. "Just be sure to get my good side, okay?"

I nodded at Theo, who slipped out the camera and turned it on. Then I moved back, giving him room, as he carefully panned the counter, taking in each of the piles as the fisherman worked over them. Around him, the conversation, razzing, and jokes continued as he slowly documented the entire scene, moving easily around his subjects. I had to give him credit. He might have stood out like a sore thumb in this crowd initially, but in work mode, he managed to almost disappear, separating himself cleanly and easily from what he was taking in. After about fifteen minutes, he walked back over to me.

"This was great," he said, putting the camera back into his pocket. "Ivy keeps saying that we need more local b-roll. But whenever we try to film, people get skittish."

"Maybe it's your approach," I said, as we started towards the door.

"Meaning what?"

I looked over my shoulder at him. "Just from what I've seen, Ivy doesn't exactly have the best people skills."

He immediately got that sort of flustered look I'd already come to recognize when he was feeling defensive. "I'll admit she comes on strong. But she's actually really good at what she does."

"As good as she is at condescending to just about everyone she interacts with?"

"She's not like that with everyone. It's just that that the people here . . ." He trailed off suddenly. I took another couple of steps, waiting for him to continue. He didn't. I turned back.

"The people here what?"

He swallowed. "They're not what she's used to."

We were at my car now, facing each other over the roof. "Meaning, they're ignorant and stupid?"

"No. They just take her demeanor personally. And it's not personal."

I raised my eyebrows.

"No offense, Emaline, but you haven't exactly put out the welcome mat for her either."

"I don't even know her," I said.

"Exactly. Which has not stopped you from assuming a lot, and none of it good. She's not the only one who's stereotyping here."

Hearing this, I felt that strange mix of annoyance and

shame. Like when you hear something you don't want to be true, but have a feeling probably is. I kind of had to give Theo credit for pointing it out. He wasn't so easy to read, after all.

"This is my home," I told him now. "I'm protective of it."

"And Ivy's my boss and my mentor," he said. "Even if she could use some etiquette lessons. Okay?"

"Yeah." I nodded. "Okay."

"Thanks."

I opened up my door and got in, and he did the same on his side. As I started the engine and pulled out of the fish house lot, neither of us spoke. I was wondering if it was going to be weird from then on, when Theo said, "Can I ask you what I hope is a not-insulting, not-personal question?"

"When you preface it like that," I replied, "I don't know how I could say no."

He smiled, then pointed at my right hand, which was resting on the gearshift. "I've seen those bracelets a lot lately. On you, your sister the other day, the guys who helped us move in. Are they a local thing?"

I looked down at the thin braided piece I was wearing. It was studded with red beads and a single scallop shell, and was frayed so badly in places it would take hardly a tug to break it free. The other one I'd been wearing since about Valentine's Day had just broken off the week before.

"Yeah," I said. "You could say that."

"Local as in private," he replied, confirming. "Off limits?"

"No." I put on my blinker. "Just sad."

* * *

It was just about fully dark when we pulled into Gert's Surf Shop, a small combination tackle/convenience/gift shop that was one of the last surviving businesses in North Reddemane. Open twenty-four hours, it was a landmark I always looked for on my way back from Cape Frost. That was the biggest town on the island, where we traveled to go to the (admittedly still small) mall and a wider variety of restaurants, among other things. It was thirty miles from Colby, and the only way to get there was to take a two-lane highway with nothing much to look at but beach on one side and sound on the other. North Reddemane, and the always-on light at Gert's, broke up the monotony of the ride back, always letting me know I was that much closer to home.

"Gert's," Theo said, as we got out of the car. "Short for Gertrude?"

"Nope."

I walked over to the door and pulled it open. Bells over-head jangled. Inside, it smelled of burnt coffee, as always. Be-hind the counter, a heavyset man sat watching a portable TV, drumming his fingers on the counter.

"Hi, Mr. Gertmann," I said as we walked past him, and he nodded at me, then turned his attention back to the small screen. Unlike the Gas/Gro and just about every other convenience store I knew, the lighting was dim, the aisles narrow. Gert's sold a little bit of everything: tackle supplies, groceries (mostly canned, many expired), beer (stocked regularly, unlike the groceries), and touristy crap like visors, beach chairs, and sunscreen. As we walked past an old Coca-Cola cooler stocked with glass bottles, I heard Theo let out a low whistle.

"Wow, check it out," he said. He reached out, touching the pocked metal of the machine. "This is seriously vintage. I know a place in Brooklyn that would pay a fortune for it."

"I doubt it's for sale," I said. "If it's like everything else, it's been here for generations."

"Family business, huh?"

"Since the turn of the last century." I nodded towards a back door. "It's only about ten steps to their house from here. See?"

Sure enough, visible through the screen was the white clapboard of the Gertmanns' place. Just like most every night, a light was on in the living room. In one window, a girl sat, head bent, working on something at a table.

I went over to a nearby cooler, taking out a water. The floor creaked beneath my feet as I moved, making a sound like a moan. "You want anything?"

Theo shook his head and I let the door drop shut and started up to the counter. Mr. Gertmann looked up at me as I put the water down. "How's your mom, Emaline?"

"She's good. How's Rachel doing?"

He punched a couple of buttons on the register. Behind him, on the TV, a row of army tanks was rolling down a road. "About the same."

I nodded, quiet, as I slid two bills across to him. While he made change, I said, "My friend here is filming a documentary about Colby. You know, the history and all of the area. We were wondering if maybe he could shoot a little bit of footage of the store?"

I felt Theo's surprise as I said this, since I'd not mentioned anything about it to him. "Don't see why not," Mr. Gertmann said, handing me my change. "We're not exactly busy right now."

I looked at Theo, who was already taking out his camera. "Thanks so much," he said, turning it on. "This will really provide some great local color, a sense of the staying power of local businesses, and . . ."

He trailed off as Mr. Gertmann turned back to the TV screen, clearly more interested in whatever he was watching than the living history around him. I gave Theo an encouraging look, and he set off towards the Coke cooler. As he began to film it, I pulled over the small ceramic dish that sat right by the register, a sign taped to it. HANDMADE BRACELETS, it read. $7. TWO FOR $12. Inside the dish were about six bracelets similar to mine, woven from thin rope and dotted with beads and shells. As I picked through them, I could hear Theo walking around, the floor making its wheezings beneath him.

"Wow," he said after a few minutes. I looked up to see him peering closely at a stack of plastic milk crates, piled up just by the front door. "Do these . . . does this really say Craint Farms?"

I pushed the bowl back where it had been and walked over to see. "Looks like it. Why?"

"Because . . ." He shook his head for a second. "They're prominently featured in one of Clyde's contrast pieces. One of the early ones. But most critics have assumed the name was intended to be meaningful. Like a metaphor."

"Craint?" I said.

"*Cray*," he corrected me. "It's French. Means 'feared.'"

"You think he was afraid of milk crates?"

"No," Theo said, shooting me a look. I smiled as he squatted down to look closer at the stack, which, judging by the cobwebs around it, had been there for a while. "The most accepted criticism is that it represents how the agricultural world feared the encroachment of urban industry. But because the piece had both worlds overlapping and, therefore, interdependent, the fear was necessary, and, actually, shared."

Whoa, I thought. Before I could reply—or even begin to think of something to say—Mr. Gertmann said, "The Craints farmed out off of William Crossroads for years. Sold to a developer about five years ago. Condos going in there now."

"So the Craints were a real family?" Theo asked him, shooting footage of the crates from one side, then leaning in closer from another. "With a real farm?"

Mr. Gertmann looked at me. I shrugged, making it clear Theo was on his own, wherever he was going with this. "Doubt it's a farm anymore. Think they at least got it perked before the bubble burst."

Now it was Theo who glanced my way, wanting a translation. "They started building," I explained. "Then ran out of money. Pretty common around here in the last few years."

"It has been written that Clyde might have worked on a dairy farm when he was in high school. But if this is a connection that clear, it's pretty amazing. Ivy's going to freak." He looked back over at Mr. Gertmann. "Any chance these might be for sale?"

"You want to buy my milk crates?"

"He's from New York," I told him, like this explained everything.

"Maybe just one of them?" Theo said, ignoring me. "I'll give you fifty bucks for it."

Mr. Gertmann looked at the stack, taking his time. Finally, he shrugged. "Why not. Doubt the supplier will miss it."

"Great," Theo said, a big smile breaking across his face. He walked over to the counter, pulling out a wad of bills from his pocket. Mr. Gertmann and I both watched as he peeled off a few twenties. He was just about to hand them over when he saw the bowl of bracelets. "Oh, and, um . . . one of these. Actually, I'll take two."

"Milk crate and two bracelets," Mr. Gertmann said, punching buttons. "Sixty-two even."

Theo pulled out a couple more bills, then slid the pile across. Mr. Gertmann turned his attention back to the TV, now showing a car dealership commercial, as Theo picked through the bowl to make his selections.

"Have a good night, Mr. Gertmann," I called out, as we started for the door. After a quick survey of the crates, Theo selected one from the middle of the stack, then arranged the remaining ones neatly, how they'd been, the cobwebs barely disturbed. He might have been long-winded, but the boy did have an eye for detail.

"Thank you!" Theo added. Neither of us got a response.

Back in the car, I realized he was beaming. Like, literally grinning ear to ear as he turned the crate in his hands. "This is *amazing*," he said. "I mean, seriously. I never would have even hoped to find anything like this."

I laughed. "It's a milk crate, Theo."

"It's a huge find in terms of Clyde's backstory!" He shook his head, still smiling, then turned to me. "Thank you, Emaline. Seriously. You just helped me impress Ivy, which is *not* easy to do. I could kiss you right now."

I blinked. "Don't do that," I said. "It's really not necessary."

"I just meant . . . I'm just . . ." He stopped talking, thankfully, as his face flushed pink, then a deeper red. "Sorry. It was just an expression."

"I know," I said. He was still pink. "I'm just joking around."

"Oh." He cleared his throat, then gave me a smile. "Anyway, it's just been sort of a hard trip so far. This will help. Thank you."

"You're welcome."

I started the engine and we pulled away from Gert's, back onto the highway towards Colby. I'd driven a couple of blocks before I said, "So which bracelets did you pick?"

"Bracelets?" A beat. "Oh, right! Yeah, the bracelets. These two." He held up one with green beads, another with white. "I wasn't going to buy any. But they looked sort of sad, set up like they were there."

I kept my eyes on the road ahead, which was dark, no coming traffic. "His daughter makes them. Rachel. She went to school with my sister Amber until she had this accident the summer before eleventh grade."

"Accident," he repeated.

I nodded.

"What happened?"

I tucked a piece of hair behind my ear. "She was riding her bike home from her boyfriend's one night and got hit by a drunk driver."

Theo looked back down at his bracelets. "God. That's awful."

"It was. The guy that hit her just left her in the road, like an animal." I cleared my throat. "Went back to his hotel, parked his bashed-up car, then passed out in his room. Didn't even remember getting behind the wheel when the cops finally tracked him down."

"He was a tourist?"

I nodded. "She recovered in some ways, but her head injury was pretty severe. She started making the bracelets when she was in rehab. There's something in the patterns, the braiding, the colors . . . it helps her. Or so her mom says."

We were coming up to the outer edge of Colby now, where neighborhoods began and lights gradually became more and more visible. I tried to think of all the times I'd driven down this road, coming back home from one place or another. It seemed it was always this time of night, the air sweet and warm whistling through my half-open window, but I knew that wasn't true. There were winters and falls and springs, too. I just never remembered them.

I was so lost, thinking this, that when I heard a horn give out a long *beeeeeep* as it passed us, I jumped. Glancing in my rearview, I saw Luke's truck. I slowed down.

"Everything okay?" Theo asked me.

"Yeah, it's fine," I said, glancing back again. Luke had turned around, was behind now, catching up fast. He flicked his headlights, brights on and off, and I put on my signal, turning into the empty lot of Coastal Federal Bank. A beat after I parked, he pulled up beside us.

"What's with the beeping?" I said to him, rolling down my window.

"What's with not answering my text?" he replied, equally annoyed. He leaned forward, looking at Theo and his milk crate. "I thought we were doing dinner."

"I told you I had to work late."

"When?"

"When I texted you back?" He shook his head. I sighed, then pulled out my phone to show him proof. There, on the screen, was my response to his message. Unsent.

"Whoops," I said, holding it up. "It didn't go through."

"You don't say," he replied. I made a face, which he gave right back to me. "So you were working. Doing what? Delivering milk?"

I just looked at him. "Luke."

"Actually," Theo said—as I watched a wave of irritation move across Luke's face at the sound of his voice—"Emaline was showing me some local places. For our documentary? She took me to this store, where I found this, which references directly some of Clyde's work. It's pretty amazing, actually."

Luke just stared at him for a second, then turned his attention back to me. "I'm going home. Call me later?"

I nodded. "Yeah."

With that, he shifted into reverse and backed away from us. I watched him pull back out onto the road, tires squealing slightly. Then he punched it and was gone.

Theo and I sat there, right beneath the Coastal Federal sign, as it informed us that it was 9:07 and 81 degrees. Then twice. Three times. Finally he said, "Well, that was a bit awkward."

"It's nothing," I said, although in truth, it was unlike Luke to be visibly annoyed, ever, about anything.

"I'm sorry if hanging out tonight caused a problem for you," Theo said.

"It didn't," I said.

"He didn't seem very happy."

"He'll be fine."

I backed up, then turned onto the main road. Now that we were close to town, there were more cars, there was more life, people coming home from dinner or going out to the clubs. As we pulled up to a stoplight, Theo said, "You guys been together a long time."

It wasn't a question. But I answered it like it was, saying, "Since ninth grade."

"Wow." He sat back, exhaling. "I can't even imagine still being with any of the girls I liked back in ninth grade."

"No?"

He winced. "Ugh. No. But then again, I was into the skinny, mean types. Who've probably just gotten skinnier and meaner."

"Or fatter and nicer."

"Maybe." He looked down at the bracelets resting over the edge of the milk crate. "Don't have an interest in finding out, though. I'd be happy if I never had to see anyone from high school again."

"Really," I said. "Aren't you only, like, a couple of years out, though?"

"Doesn't matter. Even in ten years, I still won't want to see any of those people."

The light changed and we moved forward.

"Sounds like it was pretty bad."

"There just wasn't much for me there," he said. "It was jock-centric, seriously elitist. As a computer geek into the history of cinema and my trombone, I functioned mostly as a school-wide joke or a punching bag. Usually both."

I glanced over at him. "Trombone? Really?"

"It's an incredibly underappreciated member of the brass family."

I didn't even know what to say to that.

"I know." He sighed. "I had no idea how to be cool. It was like I wanted to be beat up."

"I wouldn't say that."

"You don't have to. I heard it plenty, usually just before someone slammed my face into a locker." His phone buzzed and he pulled it out, glancing at the screen. "College, though, is awesome. Plenty of geeks. No lockers. Much better."

"Good to hear," I replied. "I leave at the end of August."

"You'll love it," he told me. "A whole new world. I promise."

I nodded, slowing for a light as he typed a response to whatever text he'd gotten. I knew I should have told him that, really, the next four years wouldn't exactly be that kind of sea change for me. Not at East U, anyway. But it was one thing for me to share my past in Colby with Theo; the future, as always, was different. I thought of the guys at the fish house, Rachel Gertmann at her table. It seemed like things either stayed just the same or changed irrevocably. And like most times I found myself with hard choices, I just wished there was something clear and easy, right in between.

8

"WHERE'S LUKE?"

This, apparently, was the million-dollar question, although I hadn't expected Benji to ask it. At least, not the very first second he saw me. I hadn't even gotten all the way up Miss Ruth's walk yet.

"He got called into work," I said. "Pool cleaning emergency."

Benji gave me a doubtful look. I knew this was a bad lie, but I didn't know where Luke was, as he was not returning my phone calls or texts. Mr. Easygoing apparently was not so much right now, at least when it came to bumping into me and Theo.

"If you ask me, he's just being a big baby," Morris had said earlier, when I'd told him and Daisy about what happened. We were on a bench outside Wave Nails, where Daisy was about to start her gyno shift.

"I didn't ask you," I told him.

"I think," Daisy said, speaking around the bobby pin in her mouth as she twisted her hair up in a knot, "that Luke did overreact, a bit. But look at it from his side. You ignored his text to go out with another guy. He was upset."

"Like a big ol' baby," Morris added.

I ignored this, turning back to Daisy. "I told him it was a mistake, that I thought the text went through. I didn't even want to take Theo out in the first place. I got totally pushed into it."

"I know that." She removed the bobby pin, reaching up to slide it into the knot. "But Luke didn't until *after* he saw you. So he'd already had a chance to take things his way."

I rolled my eyes. Behind us, a moped whined past. Morris watched it, then said, "You know, they're really not that annoying."

"Yes, they are," Daisy and I said in unison.

"If he insists on ignoring me, though," I went on, "I can't apologize. So what *do* I do?"

"Just give him some space and time to cool off," Daisy told me. "You know he will. It's Luke."

She was right, of course. It was just a misunderstanding, exacerbated by both of us being tired at the end of a long workday. No big deal. And yet, I still felt uneasy as I walked up the steps to Miss Ruth's wide front porch, where Benji was waiting for me in the porch swing. He, too, looked down in the dumps. Apparently, all the men in my life had PMS.

"Where's your dad?" I asked him.

Benji tilted his head towards the front door, which was slightly ajar, the screen closed over it. "On the phone with Mom."

"How's she doing?"

He shrugged, kicking at the floor with his sneakers. The swing creaked as he pushed himself back a bit. "They always end up on the phone *forever*."

"Oh." I looked at the door again. "Maybe I'll just stick my head in, tell him we're going out for a bit?"

This got his attention. "Really? We can go ahead and go?"

"Can't hurt to ask. Wait here." I went over to the door, eased the screen open, and stepped inside. The house was dimly lit, but looked pretty much the same as I remembered it: dark hardwood floors, gauzy window treatments, furniture that looked heavy. Remembering my previous conversation with my father, I checked the doorknob. It was fine.

"—just don't see the point, is what I'm saying," I heard him say suddenly, from the other end of the hallway. I stopped, not wanting to eavesdrop even as I realized I already was. "It's a long trip to make for just a couple of days, and I thought we agreed . . . well, that was my understanding. It's not working. You coming down here, no matter the pretense, won't change that."

Yikes, I thought, looking back out at Benji. My father was quiet for a moment, but I could hear him in the kitchen, pacing as he talked.

"Yes, I know. I don't want to do that either. But do you really think we can be here, together, and have him not be aware of what's happening? That was the whole idea behind this trip, to work out the details while . . ." He paused. "Well, I did. I assumed we were on the same page."

I knew I should just turn around and go back outside, wait until he was done. But I couldn't stand knowing Benji might be able to hear any of this. "Hello?" I called out, louder than necessary. A beat later, he appeared in the open kitchen doorway, the phone to his ear. "Oh, sorry," I whispered, like I hadn't realized. "I was just . . ."

"Hold on, Leah." He covered the phone with his hand. "Emaline. I didn't know you were here."

"I'm just going to take Benji to minigolf, if that's okay," I said, still keeping my voice low. "I'll bring him back in an hour or two?"

He looked at me for a moment, then at the slightly open door behind me. "Yes, of course," he said. And then, "Thanks."

I slipped back outside, then smiled at Benji. "We're in business. Let's go."

"Awesome!" he said, hopping off the swing. He darted ahead of me, down the stairs and onto the walk. Watching him, I felt a pang of sadness, thinking of everything he didn't know yet. The least I could do was spring for eighteen holes.

At SafariLand, he picked out a blue putter, while I, out of habit, grabbed a yellow one. As a kid, I was always yellow, Amber red, Margo blue. It's funny the things you remember. We headed out to the first hole, the easiest, a straight shot right into the cup.

"All right," I said, waving my club. "You're up."

Benji put down his ball, then readied his stance, wiggling his hips a little bit. I tried not to smile. Which quickly morphed into trying not to gasp as he swung the putter backwards, up, up, up over his head, before hitting the ball with full force. *Crack!* It went flying, soaring through the air to land in the bushes by the eighth hole.

"Whoa," I managed, as the people currently *on* that hole

looked at us, alarmed. I smiled, waving to acknowledge that, yes, we were responsible for the projectile. "Easy now."

"Sorry," he said.

I jogged over to retrieve the ball, jumping a small river on the way. I felt around in the bushes for a minute, trying not to think about all the other trash that was probably down there, before finding it. SafariLand was older than I was, and not exactly known for its cleanliness standards.

Benji looked cowed as I returned. "I didn't mean to . . ." he began, then stopped, kicking at the grass. "That's just how they do it on TV."

"I know. But a hit like that is more for long drives at the Masters," I told him, putting the ball back down on black starting mat. "Putt-putt requires a more gentle touch. Right?"

"I don't know. I've never done it before."

I tried not to look surprised. "No?"

He shook his head. "It's not something we . . ." He paused, then set up again, giving the ball a cautious tap. It rolled forward, perfectly centered, right into the cup. "No."

I had a flash of him at the table with Leah a couple of years earlier, wanting crayons but being told to do word puzzles instead. "Right. Well, there's a first time for everything. And there will be some holes later when you need to give it a good whack."

"Yeah?" he said.

I nodded, then put down my ball to take my shot. I couldn't even begin to imagine how many times I'd played this very same course: as a kid, then a middle schooler, all the way up to when I, too, had gotten overenthusiastic and hit Luke in the forehead. My dad had always been all about family activities and certain nights at SafariLand kids golfed free. It didn't matter (to him, anyway) that my sisters and I were quickly bored with the course and bickering, dragging our clubs along behind us or swinging them at each other. If it was a collective outing, you went, like it or not. Yet now, as Benji and I moved to the next hole, I realized the memories I had weren't bad. Not at all.

At the windmill, for sentimentality's sake, I called Luke. No answer. So I shot a picture of Benji putting towards it. Wish you were here, I typed beneath it. This time, I made sure the text went through.

Because Benji was a novice, I stopped keeping score about hole seven and just let him go at it, rules forgotten. By the time he knocked his ball into the clown's nose on the eighteenth hole (after ten or so tries, from multiple angles) he was miles away from the surly kid in the porch swing earlier.

"Wanna play again?" he asked me, once the siren and circus music of the game finale died down.

"Nah," I said. "Let's go to the arcade or something."

"Arcade?" His face lit up. "Awesome!"

I opened up my wallet, digging around to see if I had any SafariLand cards. When I was a kid, they'd issued the old-fashioned paper tickets when you scored points, which you could then exchange for your pick among the toys and prizes kept in a dusty case by the snack bar. Sometime during the last few years, though, they'd switched over to a debit card system for both playing the games and keeping track of credits. I always had at least one floating around the bottom of my purse, usually coated in lint and half-melted sticks of gum.

"Aha!" I said, extracting a card featuring a smiling lion. I unwrapped a hair elastic that was tangled around it, wiped it on my shorts, then slid it through the slot of the skee-ball machine beside me to check the balance. "Seven seventy-nine," I told Benji, as the number popped up on the display. I handed it to him. "Should keep you busy for a while."

"I can spend all of it?"

"Sure," I said. "Word of advice, though: Don't bother with the toy grabber thing. It's totally rigged. I've never seen anyone win anything there. Not even Luke, and he aced all these games, like, years ago."

Benji looked at the machine, which was full of stuffed animals that looked deceptively easy to snag with the metal pinchers that hung above them. "Right. I like the video ones better anyway."

"Perfect. I'm just going to grab a drink, okay? I'll come find you."

He nodded, then was off, moving down the rows of loud, blinking machines, the card in his hand. I walked over to the snack bar, checking my phone on the way. No reply from Luke, at least not yet.

I went to the snack bar and got a drink, then tried Luke once more, hanging up when it again went to voice mail. What was it about suspecting someone was deliberately not answering that made you that much more desperate to reach them? I told myself to calm down and put my phone away.

After a brief search, I spotted Benji at one of the driving games, wrenching the wheel back and forth as the screen flickered in front of him. I was almost to him when my phone buzzed in my pocket. Finally, I thought, grabbing it and hitting the Talk button.

"Hey," I said, cupping my hand over my other ear to drown out the array of noises around me. "You missed it. Benji's got a lethal swing. Must run in the family."

There was a pause. Then, "Emaline?"

It was Theo. Whoops. "Oh, hey. Sorry. I—"

"What?"

"Hang on a sec." I walked over to the do-it-yourself photo booth and slipped inside. It wasn't silent, but still an improvement. "Okay. Can you hear me?"

"Yeah. Much better," he replied. "Where are you?"

I looked at the display of pictures on the wall opposite where I was sitting, all staged snapshots meant to look casual and spontaneous. A girl holding two fingers behind another girl's head; a family crammed in together, all of them making faces. Meanwhile, in the reflective lens, I just saw myself, looking tired. "I'm hanging out with my . . . with Benji."

He was my half brother. I knew that. But calling him that, or anything really, felt more than half-weird.

"Oh, right," Theo said. "So . . . I was just calling to tell you Ivy went crazy over that milk crate. She couldn't believe it."

"Really."

"Oh, yeah. I got some major brownie points. I owe you big."

I looked at the pictures again, each in strips of four. At the top of one, a boy closed his eyes as a girl kissed his cheek. Next shot, she kissed his lips. Then they both faced the camera for the last two, one smiling, one laughing. "No problem."

We were both quiet for a moment. Outside I could hear Benji's computerized car squealing its tires, then crashing into something. Theo said, "So I wondered if you might be up for playing tour guide again sometime. I mean, at your convenience."

I eased the curtain aside, looking over at Benji. GAME OVER, said his screen. He kept turning the wheel anyway. I sat back again.

"I don't know," I said, thinking of the look on Luke's face the night before when he'd pulled up beside us. "I'm really busy with work right now, and . . ."

Theo waited a second, as if I might finish this thought. When I didn't, he said, "Oh, right, sure. I understand. I figured you had a lot going on."

I nodded at my own reflection. "Yeah. I do."

"Emaline?"

I glanced over to see two skinny ankles clad in socks and Nikes at the bottom of the curtain. I opened it and looked up at Benji. "Hey. I'll be off in a sec."

"Cool," he said. "Can I come in?"

Before I could answer, he was sliding in beside me onto the short bench, leaning forward to look at the camera lens. His arm was warm next to mine, one foot already tapping the floor. "I better go," I told Theo, as Benji pulled out the Safari-Land card I'd given him and swiped it through the slot. A row of lights appeared on the screen behind the camera, blinking.

"Oh, right," he replied hurriedly. "I'm sure I'll see you around, or something."

"Small town," I agreed.

"Yeah." A pause. Everything seemed awkward, for some reason. "Bye, Emaline."

"Bye." I hung up, then put my phone in my lap. Over the camera, the screen now directed us to SMILE! and began to count down from five with a series of beeps. Benji stuck his tongue out as the first flash went off. *Pop.*

"Do something silly," he told me, demonstrating by pushing his nose up to make it into a pig snout. But even as I watched him, I couldn't think of anything in time. *Pop.* Two more to go.

"One serious," I said, sliding my arm over his skinny shoulder. "For me." He crossed his eyes anyway. *Pop.* I poked him with my free hand.

"Okay, okay," he said, giggling. The machine was counting down again. As it did, I looked up at all those other pictures, happy and laughing, loving and sweet, all tiny manufactured moments in imagined lives. I felt suddenly, and inexplicably, sad. But then I looked at Benji, who was smiling, just as I'd told him to. So I fixed my own face, just in time. *Pop.*

* * *

An hour or so later, I dropped Benji off in front of Miss Ruth's. Then I sat in the car, watching him as he walked up to the house, the paddle ball game he'd cashed in points for in one hand, three of our four pictures in the other. Once he was safe inside, I tucked the final one, which I'd kept, over my gas gauge before pulling away from the curb.

It was a warm night, steamy almost, but I kept my windows down, needing fresh air after breathing in arcade smells for so long. I'd still not heard from Luke, which was now not just annoying but unsettling, so I went to look for him.

My first stop was the parking lot at the end of the boardwalk, in case he was at Abe's Bikes or Last Chance. When I had no luck there, I headed out to the Tip, which was pretty dead save for a group of freshman girls hanging out in the back of an SUV. Doubling back, I cut through his neighborhood, on the off chance he was home. He wasn't. I was driving towards my own house, trying to figure out where to look next, when I saw his truck parked outside of Finz, right next to his buddy Will's Land Cruiser.

I pulled in on the other side, then cut my engine and sat there to think. I knew I needed to just go in and work this out. But Will was one of those gossipy types (a trait I disliked even more in guys than girls), which meant any visible tension between me and Luke would go public almost immediately. So instead, I got out and walked over to the truck and tested the driver's-side door. When I found it unlocked, I got in, found a pencil in the console, and started looking for something to write on.

There was a Double Burger wrapper on the floor, but it was greasy, so I opened the glove box and dug around. After a moment, I unearthed a slip of white paper with something scribbled on one side. The other was blank, so I smoothed it out on the dash. I was sitting there, trying to figure out exactly what I wanted to say, when it occurred to me to double-check that whatever was on the reverse wasn't important. I turned it back over.

Really. You look better without it (your shirt).
Melissa 919-555-2323

I had a flash of the dark-haired girl from the office, sliding this under the wiper. He hadn't discarded it, but folded
it neatly and tucked it away, like something precious. Then
I noticed the bit of faint scribbling in pencil below her message. It was hard to read, as always, total chicken scratch.
But, unlike most people, I had experience deciphering Luke's
penmanship. So it only took a moment for the message, and
the situation, to become clear.

Fancy Free, he'd written. *Till Sunday*

Probably, he'd used the same pencil I was now holding to
jot down this information after he called her. But when had he
done that? That day? Or since he'd seen me and Theo?

I put the pencil back in the console, then folded the paper
up again. It was like I was watching someone else as I got back
out of the truck. I had left the paper on the seat, where he'd
see it first thing. Another message from me he could ignore, if
he chose. But I had a feeling he wouldn't.

When I got home and pulled into my driveway, I could
see lights on upstairs in the house. As I came in and walked
down the hallway to my room, though, there was for once no
sound or signs of occupation. Just my bed as I'd left it, made,
the towel I'd used for my shower that morning hanging from
the hook on the bathroom door. I should have been happy that

my mother and sister had finally given me the solitude and re-spect for my space that I'd been demanding for ages. Instead, I found myself listening for any sound of life from upstairs. A footstep, a voice, a door being shut. Just something to let me know I wasn't really as alone as I suspected.

* * *

"Coffee?"

I nodded, then flipped my mug over and moved it closer to the edge of the table. The waitress—a girl with a lip ring and a tattoo of what looked like a circle of protractors on her bicep—filled it up. "Thanks."

"Sure. Still waiting for one more?"

"Yeah."

Still waiting, I thought, as she moved on to the next table. I glanced at my watch. It was just before eight a.m., almost twelve hours since this whole nightmare had started. Although calling it that made it sound like sleeping had been involved at some point, which was not the case. Even after Luke and I had arranged to meet for breakfast, I'd tossed and turned until daybreak, tracking the hours one by one in the red numbers of the clock beside my bed.

"Hey," he'd said when he finally called the night before, around eleven. "It's me."

"Hi."

The awkwardness was like thin air, making it hard to breathe or think.

"I guess," he said after a long pause, "that we need to talk."

"Yeah. I guess so." I swallowed, wondering if he could tell

I'd been crying. I honestly, still, could not believe that any of this was happening. A lot of people lied and cheated, I knew that. But Luke was one of the good ones. Then again, I'd also been sure he was mine. "Did you . . . you called her?"

"Emaline," he said, sounding sad.

"Just tell me."

Another pause. Too long, I knew, to be followed by anything I wanted to hear. "Yes. I called her."

"Why?" I asked.

In the quiet that followed I thought, for some reason, of the first days we'd been dating, way back in ninth grade. How just seeing him coming towards me in the crowded hallway before first period made me nervous and insanely happy all at once. My throat got tight, and I cleared it. I was all too aware that he still hadn't answered me.

"I think we need to talk face to face," he said. "Not like this."

I bit my lip. "All right. When?"

"Before work tomorrow? Last Chance? Like, at eight?"

"Okay."

Too much silence, I thought, as we endured another pause. Luke and I were a lot of things, but quiet had never been one of them. Now, I'd had nothing *but* quiet in the hours since, most of which I spent shuffling the events of the last two days as I knew them, trying to make them add up to something else. But all I could see, again and again, was that girl—dropping his wiper back down over her note. *Thwack.*

Now, I pulled my coffee towards me and took a sip. I was just putting it back on the table when the bells over the front door jangled and Luke came in.

He glanced around, his expression businesslike. Then he saw me, and something softened in his features, triggering the same reaction in my own. *Oh my God*, I thought. *Please, no. No.* But then he was sliding in across from me, and it was already happening.

"I'm sorry," he said, immediately. The words came out rushed, like he'd been holding them in with his breath. "I'm so sorry, Emaline."

I swallowed, hard, as the waitress returned with the coffeepot. Luke turned over his cup, she filled it, and then, thankfully, moved on. "I don't even know what you're apologizing for yet."

He ran a hand over his hair, then looked outside at the boardwalk, the ocean beyond it. It was a cloudy day, the sky gray and flat bordering the horizon. I waited for him to speak again. He didn't.

"Okay," I said finally. "You were pissed about me not returning your text because I was with Theo. So you called her. I get it. I'm not happy, and clearly it's a sign of a bigger issue. But—"

"It was before that."

I took me a minute to actually hear this. Like the letters or sounds were scrambled and had to rearrange themselves. "What?"

He shifted his gaze slowly away from the window, then found my face. "I called her before I saw you with him."

"You—" I stopped, realizing I was sputtering. "Why?"

"I don't know," he replied.

"That's not an acceptable answer," I told him, like this was a game show and he'd phrased it incorrectly. "Try again."

I watched him exhale, his chest falling. "You know we haven't been hanging out so much lately. Things have been . . . weird. Kind of off, you know. And then she left that note . . ."

"And you decided to cheat on me," I finished for him.

"It wasn't like that." He reached up, pinching at the skin between his closed eyes. "Look, I'm not sure why I called. I just did. And she said she was going out that night with her friends, and I should meet them. I wasn't going to do it. At least, I don't think I was."

I held my breath, scared that even the smallest sound might cause him to say what I so did not want to hear.

"But then," he went on, dropping his hand, "I *did* see you, after you'd blown off my text. I was pissed off. So I went."

"You met her," I said, clarifying. He nodded, not looking at me. "Did you sleep with her?"

"No!" he said, sounding surprised. "God, Emaline. Do you really think I'd do that?"

"I don't know what to think about you anymore!" A woman at another booth turned, slightly, to glance at us. I lowered my voice. "Seriously. How could you *do* this?"

"I'm not the only one who's been acting questionably here. You were hanging out with another guy, remember?"

"That was work related."

"Oh, right," he said, rolling his eyes. "Because you're always driving around after dark with some dude on official company business."

"I didn't do anything with Theo *but* drive him around," I shot back. "We weren't at some club together. Where did you go, anyway? Tallyho?"

I'd been joking, not that any of this was funny. When he stared back at me, though, flushing slightly, all I wanted to do was cry.

"Oh my God," I said. "Luke. Really?"

And it was then, of course, that the waitress appeared at the end of the table, her pad in hand. "Okay. Ready to order?"

Food was the last thing I wanted. But somehow, I asked for my usual scrambled eggs, bacon, and toast. Luke got a bacon and egg biscuit, like always. Even when nothing was normal, breakfast apparently did not change.

Once the waitress was gone, neither of us said anything for a while, instead just sitting there as the sounds of the restaurant—forks clinking against plates, other conversations from the tables and counter customers, the door chime sounding again—filled the air around us. Finally, I said, "So what now? We break up?"

"I don't know." He picked at his napkin, fraying the edge. "Maybe we just spend a little time apart, to think."

"God, that is such a cliché." I shook my head, looking out at the water again. "Next you'll be saying that it's not me, it's you."

He sighed, letting this pass without comment. "Look. We've been together since ninth grade, Emaline. We go to college in a few weeks. I just wonder if, you know, this is happening for a reason. Like maybe we both were missing out on something."

"Like a date with some tourist at Tallyho?" I asked. "Oh, no, wait. You did that already."

He shot me a look. "Fine. You don't have to agree with me. But I bet, if you think about it, you might actually get what I'm talking about."

"Don't hold your breath." I tucked a piece of hair behind my ear, glancing outside again. Just another Friday, or so it would seem from the outside. But down deeper, something I'd seen as solid—not perfect, but solid—was suddenly crumbling. I felt like I was falling to pieces right along with it. "I don't need to get anything, Luke. *You* did this."

He didn't say anything. But I could feel him watching me, that heaviness of someone's scrutiny, as I focused solely on a sea tern outside, floating above the boardwalk. Its wings were outstretched as it rode the breeze, up and down, up and down.

"I'm sorry," I heard him say again. Then, out of the corner of my eye, I saw a sudden blur of movement as he slid out of his seat, left some bills for the breakfast he wouldn't eat, and walked away. And as he did, I thought again of those mornings in the hallway at school, way back in ninth grade. Everything had started in such sharp detail, each aspect pronounced and clear. Obviously, endings were different. Harder to see, full of shapes that could be one thing or another, with all the things that you were once so sure of suddenly not familiar, if they were even recognizable at all.

9

I SHOWED UP at work a half hour later with a small plastic take-out box, Luke's uneaten biscuit wrapped up inside. I'd tried to just leave it, but the waitress, for whatever reason, was determined that I bring it with me.

"They actually keep pretty well, if you stick them in the fridge," she explained as she folded a piece of wax paper carefully around it. "When you're ready to eat it, microwave it on low for, like, thirty seconds only."

I nodded. This must be what shock feels like, I thought, as I paid, tipped her, then carried the box to my car. I passed three garbage cans on the way, and told myself at each one I should toss it in. But I didn't. Like that box held the last little piece of what was normal, and I wasn't ready to give it up just yet.

Once at the office, I put on my busy face and headed inside, intending to go straight to the back storage room to get the towels and whatever else needed delivering to clients who had requested them. Then I saw everyone gathered in the conference room. It was Friday at nine a.m., which meant another one of Margo's mandatory meetings. Crap.

"So nice of you to join us, Emaline," she said as I came in. "Did you bring food for everyone, or just you?"

I ignored this, taking a seat next to my mom, who was busy typing something on her phone, her morning Mountain Dew from the Gas/Gro on the table beside her.

"Well, I guess we can start now," Margo said, shuffling some papers in front of her.

"What about Mrs. Merritt?" Rebecca asked. Despite having been with us only six months, even she knew any meeting was useless without my grandmother, who, despite Margo's posturing, was the real boss here.

"I have a printed agenda that will catch her up," Margo replied, passing the stack of papers over to my mom, who was still busy with her phone. They sat there on the table, untouched, until my sister finally picked them up again, handing them out to us one by one with a bit too much gusto. "All right. Let's start with item one. Staff food storage and rules."

My mom finally put down her phone, then nodded hello to me. I nodded back, very aware of her looking at the take-out box, my face, then the box again. I concentrated on the stupid agenda, not wanting to risk full eye contact.

Margo cleared her throat. "It has come to my attention that certain employees are not showing the proper respect for other people's foodstuffs."

"Foodwhat?" Rebecca asked.

"All drinks, snacks, and lunches in the office kitchen area brought from home," Margo replied. "As I've reminded everyone here multiple times, they should be labeled with the owner's name, to be removed and/or consumed by that person *only*."

My mom sighed. "Is this about your coconut juice?"

"It's coconut *water*, Mother, and no, it isn't," my sister snapped. "It's about the simple concept of respect for other people's property."

"What happened?" I asked.

"Her drink vanished," my mom said. "She thinks it was you."

Of course she did. "I don't even know what coconut juice is."

"It's *coconut water*," Margo said. "And it was clearly labeled with my name when someone took it from the fridge. It's not the first time, either. Clearly, the issue needs to be addressed."

"And it has been. So move on," my mom said, waving her hand. Then, to me, she added, "What's in that box, anyway? It smells fantastic."

Rebecca nodded. "It really does."

"It's a biscuit from Last Chance," I told them.

"Bacon and egg?" my mom asked. I told her yes, and she sighed. "I knew it. I could just *tell*."

"Item number two," Margo continued, loudly. "New staff uniform guidelines."

"Oh, God," I said. "Not this again."

"I thought we tabled this?" Rebecca said.

"We did. Until now." Margo cleared her throat. "Now, I'm aware that this is not a popular issue. But the core of uniformity is *uniform*. It's important that we as a staff are always easily identified by our clients."

"If you start talking about khaki pants and denim shirts," I warned her, "I am walking right out of here."

"Emaline," she shot back, "I am sick of you always trying to bully me out of making needed changes. As my employee—"

"I don't work for *you*," I said. "I work for the office."

"I am the office!"

"Girls," my mom said, in a tired voice. I couldn't really blame her; Margo and I butting heads was a part of just about every meeting, if not every day. Despite the fact that I was the youngest, we'd always argued with each other more than either of us did with Amber, mostly because she was too lazy to get that riled up. We'd both gotten a work ethic; the stubborn gene was just a lucky bonus.

"Khaki and denim is the perfect combination for a beach rental office!" she said now, pulling a glossy catalog from her stack of papers and waving it at us. A picture of a woman in black pants and a white shirt balancing wine glasses on a tray was on the cover. "And there are options here that are practical for every department, from us all the way down to the service contractors."

"The service contractors?" I said. "What, you're going to make the cleaners and maintenance people wear them as well?"

"Anyone who interacts with our clients on our behalf is representing Colby Realty. If they are in uniform, there's no question who the person is who suddenly appears at your rental house to clean your pool. He's easily identifiable, not some shirtless, barefoot stranger."

"Shirtless?" my mom asked. "Who's shirtless?"

I was pretty sure I knew. I looked again at the to-go container, feeling sick.

"Here in the office," Margo was saying now, "we'll be in khaki pants or skirts, with denim shirts in long or short sleeves, embroidered with our logo. Contractors will wear shorts and polo shirts or, in certain cases, T-shirts." She folded back a page of the catalog, then pushed it towards Rebecca. "Everyone will know all the options available to them before they're asked to purchase them."

"What?" I said. "We have to pay for these out of our own pockets?"

"Emaline," she said, looking tired, "I think you and your boyfriend can afford a couple of polo shirts."

"He's not my boyfriend anymore," I muttered. "And anyway—"

And that was when I realized two things: what I'd said, and that it was too late to take it back. Hearing this, my mother literally jerked in her seat, as if this news was an electric charge, straight from me to her.

"What did you just say?" she asked.

I closed my eyes, silently cursing myself. There were probably worse places for me to announce this than right in front of my mom, my nosiest sister, and Rebecca, who spent most of her time at work gossiping with her friends. But right then, I was hard-pressed to think of any of them.

"Nothing," I said, reaching over to grab the catalog from Margo, as if looking at the available options of button-down shirts was the most crucial thing at that second. "I didn't say anything."

"Wow," Margo said, her eyes wide. "I figured you'd probably break up in the fall, at school, but—"

"Hush," my mom told her, then turned to me. "When did this happen?"

I shook my head, knowing I couldn't even begin to talk about it. Just saying this out loud had made it more real than I was ready to acknowledge.

"Oh, my goodness. Is it Friday already?"

I looked up to see my grandmother in the conference room doorway, car keys in one hand, her purse in the other. Once again, she was saving me.

"It is," Margo replied. "We've only just started, though."

"What a relief," my grandmother said, in her classic way that made it impossible to tell if she was being gracious or sarcastic. "I'll be right back, just let me put this stuff away."

She disappeared down the hallway, where we could hear her turning on lights in her office and pushing her creaking chair back from the desk before going into the kitchen for something. Meanwhile, we all just sat there, with everyone looking at me while I pretended they weren't. Finally, my grandmother bustled back in.

"Okay, I'm here." She sat down at the other end of the table, her regular spot, then plunked a bottled water in front of her and twisted off the cap. "What did I miss?"

"The short version?" I said. "People are stealing food and we have to buy our own uniforms."

"The talking points are in detail here," Margo added, shooting me a look as she pushed an agenda to Rebecca to pass down to her. My grandmother squinted at it over her reading glasses.

"Uniforms," she said, taking a sip of her water. "Didn't we already decide against this?"

"We tabled it for further discussion," Margo said slowly. "Is that . . . are you drinking a coconut water?"

My grandmother glanced down at the bottle's label. "I don't know, it was in the fridge. They're pretty good. Would you like a taste?"

Rebecca bit her lip, then looked down at the table. My mother said, "Margo is of the mind that the subcontractors should also be in company-chosen attire."

"You want the pool guys in uniform?" my grandmother said. "We're lucky to get them to wear shirts."

"They wear shirts," I said, a bit too defensively.

"Not usually," she replied. "And who's paying for all this?"

"Employees will be asked to purchase their own work ensembles," Margo told her. She sounded uncommonly flustered, although whether by the water issue or this one was hard to say. "It's standard business practice."

"Maybe so, but it's a bad one," my grandmother told her. "We'll be breeding resentment among the people who have the closest contact with the clients during their vacations."

"Those same clients need to know who they are dealing with when someone shows up at their rental house," Margo said, rallying a bit.

"Then we order T-shirts with our company logo and make them the uniform. Cheaper and easier."

"This is a professional environment," Margo argued. "We can't be wearing T-shirts."

"But maybe we wouldn't have to," my mom pointed out. "I mean, we're here at the office. There's no question who we work for. Margo's right, there should be no confusion who is at the properties. So we do T-shirts for everyone who is making house calls, and we just continue as we are."

This, in a nutshell, was how every Friday meeting went. Margo came in swinging with some Big Idea and she and I got into it. Then my grandmother shot her down, and my mom worked out a compromise. You'd think we would have figured out a shortcut, but for whatever reason, we still had to do it like this, every single time.

"So it's decided," my grandmother said, downing a bit more of Margo's water. "Let's get a quote from that T-shirt place we like. You know the one that we used for those give-aways last year."

"Threadbare," my mother said. "Over on Plexton."

"Right. Margo, you'll get some logos together for them?"

Margo nodded, but she didn't look happy, the expression on her face the same one as when we were kids and me and Amber picked on her. Which was pretty often, if I was totally honest. Then, like now, she just made it too easy.

My mom and grandmother had already moved on, discussing some plumbing issue with one of the properties. I leaned over to Margo. "You know," I said, as she sulkily crossed something off her agenda, "personally, I'd like having a required T-shirt. Then in the morning I wouldn't even have to think about what to wear."

She eyed my tank top. "Are you saying you do that now?"

And there you had it. No good deed—or kind word—goes unpunished. "Forget it," I said, moving back again.

"Hey, I'm kidding." She smiled at me, barely, then added, "I'm sorry about you and Luke."

I nodded. "Me, too."

"You think it's really over, or just a fight?"

"I don't know," I told her. "It's just really weird."

She gave me a sympathetic look, then reached over and squeezed my hand. Say what you would about Margo—and I said more than anyone—she was still my sister.

"Margo," my grandmother said now, "can we go ahead and move through the rest of these items? I've got to be at the building department at nine thirty to make nice with that inspector about walkway setbacks."

"Right." Margo shuffled her papers, back in charge. "Next item: the new additional linen inventory system. If you'll flip over your agenda, you'll see that I've incorporated a new process for managing and documenting client towel requests. If we can all look at diagram A, I'll . . ."

She kept talking, going on about towels and allotments and overhead. I tried to listen, but my mind kept drifting, back to the events of the night I'd gone out with Theo. What if that text had gone through? Maybe he would have called that girl, but it wouldn't have gone any further. And what was one stupid phone call, really, in the grand scheme of things?

Well—a lot. I knew that. And trying to break it down this way, to minor and major offenses, maybes and what-ifs, was like arguing over the origin of cracks in a broken egg. It was done. How it happened didn't matter anymore.

When the meeting was finally over, my grandmother left for the building department, Rebecca returned to reception, and my mom and sister started talking about some homeowner who was unhappy with a bill he'd been sent. Well aware that at any moment they'd be descending on me for more details about Luke, I took advantage of this diversion and left for the storeroom, biscuit box in hand.

My first job of the day was to run items to whatever properties had requested them since end of business the day before. I grabbed the list from where we kept it, on a clipboard on the door, and got busy getting what I needed.

As always, lots of people wanted more towels. Someone needed a bathmat. A smoke detector was beeping for new batteries at one house, multiple light bulbs had blown out apparently simultaneously at another. In other words, nothing very surprising until I got to the end of the list, where I saw this:

> *Functioning, high-end brand-name toaster oven with temperature-adjust feature and varied toast doneness options. Only new from box acceptable. ASAP!*

Even before I ran my finger across the page to the column listing what houses requested what, I knew what I would find opposite this item. Sure enough: Sand Dollars.

Sighing, I propped open the back door, stuck my bag and biscuit in my car, then doubled back for the towels and everything else. Then I went to my mom's office for further instructions. I found her on the phone, sipping at her fountain drink.

"No, she wouldn't tell me," she was saying. She listened for a moment. "Of course I did. But—"

"Mom."

She clapped a hand over the receiver, a guilty look on her face. "Oh, Emaline, hi. Yes?"

"That's Amber," I said, nodding at the phone. "Right?"

"You know what, it *is*," she said, like this was such a crazy coincidence. "We were just touching base about, um . . ."

I held up the list, mostly to spare us both whatever excuse she was scrambling to come up with. "What's the story with the toaster oven on here?"

"Sand Dollars?" she asked. I nodded. "I have a call in to the owner. If it needs to be replaced—"

"It's brand-new," I said. "I unpacked it myself."

She shrugged. "Could be a lemon. It happens. On vacation, people need their toast."

"I've dealt with this client plenty," I told her. "I'd bet you big money it's just not up to her standards."

"Well, she is paying ten grand a month," she pointed out.

"Then she can afford her own high-end, temperature-adjusted, varied-doneness toaster oven. We shouldn't have to cater to her every freaking whim."

Through the speaker of the phone, I heard Amber say, "*Someone's* in a bad mood."

"I'll send maintenance over to check the current machine,"

my mom said, sliding her hand to cover the receiver. "Okay? And then we'll go from there."

"I'll do it," I said, turning on my heel. "It's just stupid, is all I'm saying."

"You know," my mom called out, as I walked away, "maybe you'd be happier doing reception today? I can send Rebecca to—"

I waved her off, shaking my head. Dealing with Ivy and her appliance standards was in no way ideal. But being stuck at a desk, a sitting target for everyone's curiosity, would be much worse.

I got into my car and cranked the engine, then pulled out onto the main road, headed towards the Tip. I'd gone about a block when I saw a familiar figure loping in a very familiar way down the shoulder ahead. I pulled up slowly, waiting until I was right behind Morris before leaning on my horn, hard. Anyone else would have leapt right from their skin, but true to form, he didn't even jump.

"Hey," he said when he turned and saw me, all casual, like it was common for people to try to scare him to death during rush hour on a weekday. "What's up?"

"You want a ride?"

He considered this, like he actually preferred walking, before saying, "Sure."

I unlocked the passenger-side door, he slid in, and I eased back into traffic, neither of us saying anything for a moment. Finally, as we came up to a stoplight, he noticed the take-out box, sitting in the center of the dash. "That yours?"

"Luke's," I told him. "A biscuit from Last Chance."

"Huh."

Another silence. Traffic was really moving slowly. I said, "We broke up this morning."

I felt him look at me. This seemed to warrant actual surprise. "For real?"

"Think so. There's some other girl, apparently."

He directed his gaze forward again. "From here?"

I shook my head, then swallowed. "Nope."

We drove on a little farther, then had to merge left around some construction cones. As we did, the biscuit box slid a bit down the dash, the Styrofoam making a squeaking sound. Morris and I both watched it until it hit a vent, which stopped it.

"I'm so stupid," I said, embarrassed suddenly by the catch I heard in my throat. "I don't know why I'm still carrying that around. He didn't even want it. I need to just throw it away."

Morris considered this as we pulled up to a yellow light that was turning red. Then he reached forward and grabbed the box, unwrapped the biscuit, and stuffed the entire thing in his mouth, dispatching it with about three chomps. After swallowing, he crumpled the paper back into the box, threw it onto the floor at his feet, and said, "Asshole."

For some crazy reason, it was this—not the breakup itself, not the shock afterwards, not even Margo's kind words—that finally made me cry. The tears just came, blurring all the brake lights ahead. "Morris," I said.

"Cheating, no-shirt-wearing loser," he added, looking out the window. "He's a punk."

"He went out and met her at Tallyho," I managed, my voice breaking.

He made a disgusted noise. "Punk," he said again.

Now I was really crying, which would have been embarrassing had it been just about anyone else. But this was Morris, who had seen me bawl plenty, the first time being when we were eight and I fell out of the tree that bridged our two yards, breaking my wrist. He was the one who had sat with me in the back of my mom's car as she sped to the hospital in Cape Frost, his face stoic as I sobbed from the pain. Morris was not the type to offer a hug or even hold your hand. But there was something in his quiet indignation at the universe then—and Luke, now—that was just the kind of comfort I needed.

I was still blubbering, but trying to stop, as I saw the bridge up ahead. "I'm such a mess," I said. "We're almost off the island and I didn't even ask you where you were going."

He shrugged. "No place. Wherever you are."

I felt that lump in my throat again, swelling, and turned back to traffic to try to regain my composure. Meanwhile, Morris settled into his seat with his signature slouch, neither knowing nor caring where I was taking him. Like destinations, in general, were vastly overrated. And maybe they were. As long as you were moving, you were always going somewhere.

＊　＊　＊

"Well," Theo said, "I suppose that would depend on your specific definition of 'not working.'"

I looked at him, then back at the toaster oven sitting on the kitchen island between us. "You're saying there's more than one?"

"Definition?" he said, clarifying. I nodded. "Well, sure. On the one hand, it could mean, you know, that it's broken."

"Right," I said.

"But taken in a wider sense," he continued, "it could translate to the lack of a specific skill, i.e., an inability or outright refusal to perform required tasks."

"It's a toaster oven," I said. "Not the proletariat."

He laughed. "Wow. Impressive vocab you have there."

"What, just because I'm from here I can't use big words?"

He raised his eyebrows. "Um, no. That's just kind of an SAT word choice, not one you throw around in breakfast conversation."

Okay, so maybe I was a little bit on edge. "Sorry," I said. "Rough morning."

"It's okay." He rubbed a hand over his face, glancing at the stairs that led to the upper floors where, I assumed, Ivy was still sleeping. On his wrist was one of the bracelets he'd bought from Gert's, the slim, green one with the scallop shell. "Look, I know you think this whole toaster thing is ridiculous—"

"Because it is."

"But the bottom line is that Ivy likes things done in a certain way. If her breakfast, or anything else, isn't right, then it's my job to correct the problem."

"How can toast not be right?"

"As I've explained," he said, giving me a tired look, "there is no specific control for doneness on this thing. Your only choices are light, medium, and dark."

"You want more variation," I said. Then, before he could reply, I added, "I think that's the word that got me into college."

He smiled. "What I want is an adjustable dial. Light is too light, medium is too medium, and dark is too dark. Right now, we have black and white only, and we need gray."

"Gray toast?"

"Fine," he said, shaking his head. "Go ahead, mock. But I think you actually *do* know what I mean."

Hearing this, I had a flash of Luke earlier, saying the same thing, but about what our relationship was lacking. Apparently, it was obvious to everyone else what I did or did not know. Too bad I still felt so clueless.

"So what I'm hearing," I said, pushing this out of my head, "is that this machine is not broken, but still needs to be replaced."

"Pretty much." He sighed. Then, more confidently: "Yes."

As I looked back at the toaster oven, I could feel him studying me, the same way he'd been doing since I'd first turned up at his door fifteen minutes earlier. After I dropped Morris off at a nearby gas station—"Talk later," he'd told me, as always—I'd done my best to regain my composure, putting on lipstick and taking deep breaths. Unfortunately, I was cursed with the blotch-prone kind of skin that always made it obvious if I'd been crying. Theo hadn't asked me anything about this directly, though. Never had I been so happy to talk about breakfast foods.

"Look," I said, "normally, our policy is this: if an appliance is in working order but not up to the standards of the client, it's up to them to provide their own alternative."

Theo bit his lip, looking stressed. "Okay."

"However," I continued, slightly distracted by how this single word spread a sudden hopefulness over his features, "the owners of this particular property have been apprised of the situation and are willing to remedy it."

"So we get a new toaster oven? With an adjustable doneness setting?"

I glanced down at my phone, re-reading the text my mother had sent me only moments earlier. Since VIP, owners OK'd. Get what they want. Since I'd last checked it, another one had appeared beneath it. You need me, call. Love you.

I felt tears prick my eyes again—God, what was *wrong* with me?—and shoved my phone back into my pocket. "Looks like it," I said to Theo.

"Oh, man. That is *great*." He was actually beaming. At least for a second. Then he said, "When, do you think?"

"When . . ."

". . . can we get the replacement?"

I opened my mouth to answer, but before I could, he went on. "Today? This morning?"

"Um," I said slowly, "I guess it's really just a matter of going out and finding one that meets her specifications."

"But we could do that now, right?"

I just looked at him. "You are pushy, you know that?"

"Well, that depends on your definition of pushy," he replied, smiling. "Personally, I like to call myself driven. It's different."

I made a face, showing I wasn't so sure about this. "Well, Mr. Driven. Big Club opened at nine."

"Perfect. Just give me five seconds."

And with that, he was gone, jogging across the room and disappearing up the stairs. I wondered what time Ivy roused herself, if it was even possible to have the perfect toaster oven waiting for her when she did. Apparently, I was going to find out.

A few minutes later, Theo was easing the front door of Sand Dollars shut so slowly and gently, you would have thought there was a bomb attached to the knob. "Really?" I said. "She's that light a sleeper?"

"Apparently, I slam doors," he explained.

I watched him as he turned the lock, also with the utmost care and concentration. "Do you *like* your job, Theo?"

"Yeah," he replied. "Why?"

I shrugged, starting down the front steps. "I don't know. It just seems . . . really demeaning."

"Yes, but," he said, "all work has demeaning moments. Otherwise it would be called play."

"That sounds like a quote."

"I may have complained about certain tasks at various times." He cleared his throat. "There was a time when both her cats had simultaneous diarrhea. Not exactly what I had in mind when I applied."

"What was that, though?"

"Diarrhea?"

I made a face, pulling open my driver's side door. "Why did you want this job in the first place?"

"The experience," he replied. Not a moment of hesitation, not even a breath. "I want to be a filmmaker, and I get to spend all day with an award-winning one."

"Cleaning up her cat shit," I added.

"One very bad week, yes," he said. "But I've also watched her shoot, and edit raw footage. I've been there when she's taken meetings, begged for funding, somehow drawn out reluctant subjects to reveal things they never planned to. And now she's even letting me shoot b-roll, which is awesome."

"If you say so," I said, cranking the engine.

"Do I plan to include litter box fumigator and purveyor of toaster ovens on my résumé?" he said. "No. But you take the bad to get to the great. That's just how it works. Right?"

"Well," I said, "if that's true, I guess I'm going to have a freaking awesome day tomorrow."

This was out before I even realized it, and I instantly wondered what on earth compelled me to share it. Too late now, as Theo was looking over at me. "Not that it's any of my business, but you did seem kind of upset, earlier. You okay?"

"Fine," I said. "Nothing a trip to Big Club can't fix."

I'd meant this as a joke, but as we headed over the bridge in the tail-end of morning traffic, I actually did feel a sense of relief. Like I was leaving the morning, Luke, and everything else behind. In Colby, the roads were narrow, everything small and close together. But where the Big Club was, in Mc-Corkle, things were more spread out, and it felt nice to just get lost a little within them.

"Wow," Theo said, as I pulled into a space. "Look at the *size* of that shopping cart. It's epic!"

"Everything is huge here," I told him. "It's a bulk store."

"Still, that's insane," he said, still gawking at the cart, parked sideways in the return next to us. "It's bigger than my apartment."

I got out, then went to retrieve it, easing it out backwards. It had a loose wheel, of course. I'd yet to ever have one that didn't. That, too, was part of the Big Club experience. "Isn't everything in New York huge, though? Buildings, attitudes, shopping carts . . ."

"Common misconception," he replied, falling in beside me as I rattled towards the entrance. "The truth is, with so many people packed into such a small island, things have to be compact. It's, like, the ultimate dichotomy. Such largesse and tininess, all at once."

"Largesse? Who's studying for their SATs now?"

He made a face at me, and I laughed.

"Anyway, here everything's small. Except Big Club."

"Apparently," he replied, as we passed a woman pushing a cart piled with large boxes of laundry detergent. "Wow, did you see the sizes of those Tides? Who does that much laundry?"

"Everyone, eventually." The doors slid open, revealing a guy in a Big Club blue vest. He glanced at my membership card, then waved us through. "That's the whole idea. You buy big, but it costs less in the long run. It helps to have storage space, though."

"So we're buying multiple toaster ovens?"

I shook my head, pushing us past the candy section towards appliances. "They sell better names here than at Park

Mart. More chance we'll find one her highness approves of."

"Adjustable dial," he said, in a flat voice. "All I am asking for is an adjustable dial."

We found one on the third model we saw, a shiny chrome number that also sported slick black trim, an expanded-size broiler pan, and, inexplicably, a digital clock. "So you can time your toast, I guess?" I said.

"You can never have enough clocks in the kitchen," Theo told me, twisting the dial back and forth to test it. "It's where the entire day begins."

"Wow," I said. "You are, like, a motto machine. You should write bumper stickers or something."

"It's because of my parents," he explained. "They were old."

"What?"

"Older," he corrected himself, "than, you know, just about everyone else's mom and dad. My father was forty-eight when I was born. He wasn't the best on the basketball court, but he had a saying for everything."

"I don't think my father would have been much for basketball either," I said. "Even if he had been around."

"You didn't grow up with him?"

I shook my head. "Didn't even meet him until I was ten. My stepdad adopted me at three, did all the heavy lifting."

"Wow," he said. "I never would have guessed, just from meeting him in the parking lot that night. You two seemed close."

"Looks can be deceiving."

"That," he said, pointing at me, "is one of my father's fa-vorites."

I smiled, then nodded at the oven. "So, you think this will work? She'll approve?"

"Yep. We're good." He picked it up and slid it into the cart. Problem solved. If only they were all so easy. "You need a vat of Tide before we go?"

"Just stocked up last week," I said, as a guy in a baseball hat rounded the corner beside us, pushing a cart packed with paper towels and various cleaning supplies. He had his head ducked down, studying a list he was holding, but I still recognized Clyde instantly. "Yeah, so," I said, starting towards the register, "let's just get this back, and we'll see what—"

"Emaline?"

To say I was surprised that Clyde had spoken to me was an understatement: he wasn't exactly known for his outgoing nature. I glanced at Theo, who was reading the fine print on the oven's box, with no clue whatsoever to who was standing right in front of him. "Hi," I said, as casually as I could, "how are you?"

"I'd be better if that storm the other night hadn't busted a hole in the ceiling of the Washroom," he said. "Place is soaked. Your dad still doing some contracting?"

"Um, yeah," I replied, as Theo slid his hands in his pockets and stepped back to stand by politely. "He's framing a job over on Summerhill right now, I think."

"Sound or ocean end?"

"Sound."

"Maybe I can convince him to stop by, take a look. Can I get his number?"

"Sure," I said. He flipped his list over to the blank other side, grabbing a pen from behind his ear, then held both out to me. I wrote the number quickly, wondering if it was actually possible that we'd be able to part ways with no one the wiser. Then, though, just as I handed it back, Clyde gave Theo a polite nod. Next thing I knew, Theo was sticking out his hand.

"Theo Burns," he said.

"Clyde Conaway."

The shock that went through Theo as he heard this was like a gunshot: I literally *felt* it hit him, then reverberate all around us. "You're . . . " he said, then stopped. I could suddenly hear him breathing. "You're Clyde Conaway?"

"Well, we better go," I said quickly. "It was good to—"

"We're doing a film about you," Theo blurted out, a bit of spit flying along with it. Oh, dear. "A documentary. Ivy Mendelson is the director, she did *Cooper's Way*? We've been trying to reach you for months." He started digging in his pockets, for God knows what, still talking. "You have no idea how hard it's been to track you down. And now, here you are, with the toaster ovens. I mean, it's unbelievable, I can't even . . ."

He was still talking, still breathing, still searching for something on his person. Just a hot, sputtering mess, and I wanted to die, right there in Big Club. I looked at Clyde, trying to convey my deepest apology, but he was just studying Theo, his face impassive. Then, in a voice as casual as Theo's was on the verge of hysteria, he said, "Oh, right. The documentary. How's that going?"

"Oh, it's amazing! Just fantastic. I mean, we've hit some local opposition in terms of willingness for interviews and providing information. But apparently that's typical when a subject is, um, as private as, well . . . you are. Really, though, that's exactly why we came down here, to get a sense of the community, you know, immerse ourselves in your world, your people, and—"

I was beginning to think he was never going to stop talking, even though—judging by the raspiness of his voice and dropping volume—he desperately needed to take a breath. "Theo's very, um, passionate about the project," I said, hoping to give him a chance to do just that. "He's working really hard."

"And Emaline's been amazing!" Theo added, once bolstered by a quick shot of oxygen. "She took me some places I never would have found otherwise."

Clyde glanced at me, and I tried not to cringe. "Really."

"Oh, yeah," Theo went on. "The fish house, for starters, and also this local market, where we found this milk crate that was, like, *huge* in terms of your history."

"A milk crate," Clyde repeated. I kept waiting for him to get visibly annoyed, but instead he seemed almost amused. "Huh. How so?"

"Well, it was from Craint Farms," Theo explained. "And, of course, it's well known the word *craint* was prevalent in some of the collages in the Metal/Paper series of 1997. All the writing on the subject has assumed this was a reference to the French word for *fear*, denoting your feelings about how agriculture felt in the face of industry."

Clyde was just looking at him. It occurred to me that this had to be beyond bizarre, having your own work interpreted and analyzed by a total stranger. In Big Club.

"But then when I bought the crate," Theo was saying now, "the owner of the store said the Craints used to farm around here. So it's possible it was based on a real name, not a translation. Which is just—"

"Wait," Clyde said, holding a hand to stop him. "You actually bought a Craint Farms milk crate?"

"From Gert's," I explained.

"It's a huge find for the film," Theo added, "not to mention to the collection of your papers and interviews. Ivy said it really singularly confirms everything that brought us here. The sense that this town did shape you and your work, more than anyone realized."

Clyde looked at me again. "Old Gert must have thought you guys were nuts."

"Yeah," I said. "But he got fifty bucks out of it, so he wasn't exactly complaining."

"He does love a dollar," he agreed.

"You *have* to let us interview you," Theo told him, his voice suddenly grave, serious.

"Theo," I said, "I don't think—"

"What you could add to this film, with your input and cooperation," he continued, "would take it to a whole other level. I know you haven't exactly had good experiences with journalists in the past. I mean, we all remember that piece in the magazine of the *Times* in 1999."

"We do?" I said.

"But if you would just give us a chance," he went on, ignoring me, "we could in turn give you, and your legacy of work, the respect it deserves. Just meet with Ivy, give her a chance to explain her vision for the film. Please. I am *begging* you."

I could literally see him sweating now, he was so excited. Good Lord, I thought. No wonder he got beat up in high school. If a locker had been around right then, I would have pushed him into it, if only for his own good.

For a moment, we all just stood there, no one saying anything. In the silence, I found myself thinking of the other toaster oven, back at Sand Dollars. Perfectly fine, in good working order. If only it had that adjustable dial. It takes so little to change everything. If you really thought about it, it would scare you to death.

"All right," Clyde said finally, so casually you would have thought he was agreeing to a cup of coffee. "Set it up with your boss, name your place and time."

"Oh my God!" Theo said. Now he was damp, breathless, and shrieking. I put my hand over my face. "Thank you! You won't regret this, I promise. Just give me your number, and—"

"No." Clyde nodded at me. "Set it up with Emaline, have her contact me."

Me? I thought. But then Clyde was waving and walking away, just as easily as he'd turned up, down the wide aisle towards the paper plates.

At first, Theo and I just stood there, watching him go. Then he said, very quietly, "Please, for the love of God, tell me that did actually just happen."

"Think so," I said, readying to push the cart towards the

registers. "Can we go now? I have other clients waiting for towels."

He turned to face me, a smile slowly spreading across his face. Behind him, toaster ovens and microwaves were stacked up high over us, facing mini fridges on the other side. And it was there, surrounded by low-priced appliances, that Theo suddenly stepped forward and kissed me. In a bulk store, with high ceilings and vast quantities, more of anything than you could ever really need. And the weirdest part was that in that moment—after feeling so small all morning—the tug I felt in my heart as I kissed him back was suddenly, inexplicably, very big as well.

10

"PICK A CARD. Any card."

This was how Benji greeted me at the door. No hello; just a command. I looked down at the playing cards, spread in a fan between his fingers, and reached for one in the middle. His brow furrowed.

"Not that one," he said. I drew back. "Pick another."

I did as I was told. This time, he just shook his head, looking frustrated.

"How about this," I said. "Let's just say that, in the interest of time, you give me some direction."

"More to the left," he told me. "Far left."

I picked the last card, a queen of hearts. Happy, he folded up the rest. "Okay," he said, then cleared his throat, closing his eyes. A beat. Then, "Your card is . . . the queen of hearts."

I flipped it over. "You're right! Wow. That's impressive."

"I'm just learning right now," he explained, unnecessarily, turning to go into the house. "I only got the kit yesterday."

"Kit?" I said, but once I was in the foyer, I understood. There, scattered across the huge, antique dining room table, was everything you'd require for putting on a magic show: top hat, stuffed rabbit, bag of balloons, interlocking rings, as well as several packs of cards. "Wow. Where'd you find this?"

"Park Mart," he told me, as he climbed up on one of the chairs, picking up the rings. "We've been going there, like, every day."

"Really," I said, picking up the rabbit and studying its small, whiskered face. "Why's that?"

He shrugged, letting the rings fall back to the table with a clank. "I'm really hard to keep entertained."

Hearing this, I thought of Theo, earlier in the day, relaying how he'd been told he slammed doors. His and Benji's expressions, sharing these things, were altogether similar: small and sort of rueful. Clearly truths they'd heard more than once.

Then, however, my brain shifted to another image of Theo, this time after I'd received the call from my dad asking if I could drop by when I had a chance. At that moment, he had still been apologizing for kissing me at Big Club.

"I can't believe I did that," he'd said, again, as we walked to the car. His entire face was pink, having faded from the bright red it had turned earlier when he first pulled away from me, when he suddenly realized what was happening. "Especially after last time, when you specifically told me *not* to kiss you. I swear, I'm not that guy."

"Theo—"

"You know, That Guy Everyone Hates. I don't make a habit of kissing girls with boyfriends. I'm not even a big PDA person! Or, I mean, I wouldn't be, if I'd ever had much of a relationship. Which I haven't. Maybe because I'm That Guy Everyone Hates?"

"Theo."

"Emaline, you have a *boyfriend*. Whom I *met*. Who *already* doesn't like me. It's like I want him to kick my ass. And I swear to you, I don't. I've never been in a fight. Like, not even once."

"*Theo.*"

This time, thankfully, he shut up. Which left me with the floor before I was ready to know what to do with it. So, equally ungracefully, I said, "Luke's not my boyfriend anymore. We broke up this morning."

He stopped dead in his tracks, the cart he was pushing rattling to a sudden stop. Then he looked at me. "You split up today?"

"Yep."

"That's why you were upset, when you came over!" he said, pointing at me. I nodded. A big grin spread across his face. "Oh, man. That is *great*!"

"Well," I said diplomatically, "I wouldn't say—"

"I mean, it's not, of course not," he added quickly, fixing his expression. "It's terrible. For Luke. And your, you know, long relationship, which was clearly very important and meaningful."

"True," I told him.

"But for me," he said, smiling again, "it's good news. Because, number one, I am not That Guy Everyone Hates. Or totally him."

"Always a good thing," I agreed.

"And two," he said, grinning wider, "I can do it again. I mean, we can. And it'll be okay."

I smiled at him. He was such a dork, one thing I could safely say Luke, for all his charms, had always been too confident to be considered. "It wasn't so bad the first time, actually."

Another grin. And then, he leaned over the cart—awkwardly, sweetly—and kissed me once more. Clearly, despite the jumbled way it had all happened, that first time was no fluke. It was more than okay.

By the time I pulled into the driveway at Sand Dollars, though, the guilt was starting to set in. I mean, this had to be the quickest rebound on record. Actually, it was more of a crazy, errant hard bounce, right back into the basket. So when he leaned down into my open driver's-side window, toaster oven box in his arms, to make it a three before walking up the steps of Sand Dollars, I pulled back.

"Uh-oh," he said, looking worried as I put my hand over my mouth. "That's never good."

"No, I'm fine," I said. "I—"

"Usually I get at *least* twenty-four hours before people regret kissing me," he said, shifting the box in his arms. "Just so, you know, you're aware of the averages."

I shook my head. "It's not you. It's—"

He winced, already bracing himself for what came next.

"Luke and I were together for a long time," I continued. "I like you. But I have to be careful not to go too—"

"Fast," he finished for me. I nodded. "Of course. I understand. You need a demarcation."

"Demarcation?" I asked.

"It means a clear separation between two things," he told

me. "A solid end before a clean beginning. No murky borders. Clarity."

I knew what it meant, but figured this was not the time to again flaunt my SAT verbal score. So I just said, "Exactly. The problem, I guess, is figuring out how to do that."

He considered this, shifting the toaster oven again. "It seems to me the only way is a do-over."

"Of . . ."

"This," he said, waving his free hand between us. "You and me. Start over, back at the beginning, with you as a happily single girl and me not That Guy Everyone Hates."

"And we do that by . . . what? Going back to Big Club?"

He considered this. "No. We just wait a little bit, then start over fresh. No looming boyfriends. No toasters. Just us."

"Okay," I said.

A car drove past and someone hollered in our direction, distracting us both momentarily. Another beat, and Theo said, "About how long?"

"Should we wait?" He nodded. "I don't know. A day or two?" His face fell. "You think?"

"You," I said, pointing at him, "are the expert on this demarcation thing. You tell me."

I watched as he thought for a minute, really considering it. Then he said, "Tomorrow. New day, new start."

"Okay," I repeated. "It's a date."

He smiled, just as the front door of Sand Dollars opened to reveal Ivy, in pajama bottoms and a tank top, her hair matted on one side. "Theo!" she barked. "Did I not ask for fresh-squeezed orange juice?"

"Fridge door, blue pitcher," he replied, ever cheerful. She huffed, then shut the door again. I raised my eyebrows and he said, "Vitamin C. She's a bear until she has it."

"Clearly." I reached down, cranking my engine, and he stepped back. "So I'll see you . . . tomorrow?"

"Count on it."

I'd smiled, and he went up the drive and into the house. I'd looked at the clock on my console. It was not even noon. Suddenly, I wasn't sure I'd ever have enough demarcation to figure out how all this had happened. What had I *done*?

Now, shaking this off—or trying to—I turned my attention back to Benji. "It's summer and you're at the beach, though. There's a million things to do here."

"Yeah?" he said. "Like what?"

I'd forgotten who I was dealing with: of course I'd be expected to expand on this. "Well," I said slowly, "there's, um, swimming."

"I'm only allowed to be in the sun two hours a day," he informed me, voice flat. "And I have to be accompanied by a responsible adult."

"Oh." I glanced back at the kitchen, wondering where said adult actually was at that moment. "Well, what about riding a bike around or something? I bet we could—"

"Because of my inner-ear problems, I have balance issues." He picked up the cards again and shuffled them. "I have to stay away from self-propelled wheeled activities."

Zero for two. "Well, you could read."

"That's all I've *been* doing. That and practicing my balloon twisting."

"Balloon twisting?" I asked.

He plucked a slim booklet from between a ring and the rabbit and held it out to me. "Making animals. It's part of the kit."

Twist Art: Easy Balloon Sculpting for All Ages! proclaimed the cover, which featured a bald guy with a handlebar moustache, a bright yellow balloon giraffe in one hand and an air pump in the other. I flipped through the pages, which provided step-by-step instructions for everything from beginner-level wiener dogs to incredibly elaborate rose bouquets, complete with stems and thorns. "Wow," I said. "This is really cool."

"It's noisy, though."

I raised my eyebrows. "Noisy?"

"When they pop. It could give a person a nervous breakdown." Again, this sounded like a direct quote. "So I had to stop and just do the card tricks for a while."

"Where *is* your dad, anyway?" I asked him.

"Upstairs," he replied, cutting the deck once, twice. Then he drew out a few cards, fanning them between his fingers. "He's on deadline."

"Deadline?" I repeated.

"It means he's grumpy. And stressed." He nodded at the cards. "Pick another one."

I reached for one on the far right. This time, he didn't stop me. Seven of spades.

"Okay." He folded the cards back into a stack, then closed his eyes, concentrating. "Your card is . . . the ten of diamonds."

I glanced at it. "You're right!"

"I am?"

I had no idea why I was lying to him, especially since the deception would be more than clear as soon as he looked at what was left in his hand. But there was something so sad about a little kid at this huge table, bored and alone. The least I could do was let him think he could do magic, if only for a little while.

"I'm going upstairs for a minute," I said, sliding the card in my pocket. "Keep practicing, okay?"

He nodded, shuffling the cards again, and I started up the stairs. It had been years since I'd been in this house, and I wasn't sure I'd ever made it to the second floor. Still, something about the climb felt familiar, as did turning to the left, not right, to reach the master bedroom.

Inside, I found my father sitting at a wooden desk by an open window. He had his back to me, but even without my seeing his face, the stress of being on deadline—whatever that really meant—was apparent. One hand was at his left temple, rubbing hard as if trying to polish it to gold, while the other tapped a pencil against the desk staccato-style, *rat-a-tat-tat*. Additionally, there were papers spread out all around him: on the desk, the floor, the bed. So much paper, so little order. It made me want to clean up, quick. I was almost to the door when he said, "Is it twelve fifteen? Because it *better* be."

I stopped where I was, glancing at my watch. "Um . . . no?"

He turned, his face irritated. Then he saw it was me and just looked tired. "Oh, sorry. I thought you were Benji."

What was the proper response to this? I didn't say anything.

"He's been up here constantly," he explained, rubbing a

hand over his face, "bugging me about one thing or another, even though he knows how I get when I'm working. It's driving me nuts. I told him I didn't want to see him until lunchtime, or else."

"I think he's just bored."

"Which is a first world problem," he replied. "This piece I'm working on? It's about the African famine. Suffice to say, I have very little sympathy."

Right, I thought. But this was not my business, so I said, "You said you wanted to talk to me about something?"

"What? Oh, yes." He gathered up one stack of papers, arranging them in a lopsided stack, and put them on the desk. "I'm totally swamped right now, trying to work out these estate issues and putting the house on the market, not to mention trying to work."

Downstairs, distantly, I was pretty sure I heard a balloon pop.

"I'm aware," he continued, "that you're very busy, working and getting ready for, um, school . . ."

With this, he started rubbing his temple again, rapidly. Like at the Reef Room, it was like this last word, and the subject it pertained to, spiked his blood pressure from flat to borderline widowmaker status. Even his face was flushed. It was beginning to make sense why I'd never heard more from him after that weird, formal e-mail. If just the thought of my college did this, a real, honest conversation might outright kill him.

"But I was hoping," he continued, rushing through the words as if they actually did put space between us and this issue, "that you might know someone who could help me out with Benji. Take him places, keep an eye on him, get him involved in some activities."

"You need a babysitter?"

"I need a lot of things," he said, picking up another stack of papers, glancing at it, and setting it aside. "But child care is the first thing I'm feeling up to tackling. I'm sure admitting this isn't going to win me any parenting awards, but I can't take this."

I just stood there, wondering if he expected me to reassure him about, of all things, his fatherhood skills. This day was just getting weirder and weirder.

"The thing is, I had an idea," he said, sighing, "that this trip would be the perfect bonding experience. Quality time for Benji and me, right before I had to move out. I had visions of him entertaining himself during the day, then us cooking gourmet meals together before reading our respective books by the fireplace in the evening."

"He's ten," I pointed out.

"Yes, I know," he replied, irritated. I felt a smile trying to creep onto my face and fought it back as best I could. But really, I couldn't help myself. At that moment, he looked more like Benji than I ever could have imagined: foolish, hopeful, and disappointed all at once. "I guess it's been a while since I've spent an extended amount of time with him without Leah. She does—did—a lot."

I didn't say anything. Another pop came from downstairs.

"Anyway," he said abruptly, shaking his head and looking

at me. "Child care. A few hours a day, just so I can get some work done. Do you know anyone?"

"Not off the top of my head," I said. His shoulders sank a bit. It reminded me of Theo, so quick to react, easy to read. Weird. "But I can think on it."

"That would be great," he said, so emphatically that you would have thought I'd given him ten names and numbers. "Thank you."

I nodded. "Well, I need to get back to work. I've got a ton of stops to make, and—"

"Of course. You're working." He grabbed a large envelope off the bed and slid some papers into it. "Which is what I should be doing. Instead, I'm making calls to realtors, trying to find someone to list this place. It never ends."

At least you're not suffering from the African famine, I thought, but resisted saying this aloud. "We actually have a really good realtor on staff at the office," I told him instead. "My sister Margo. She can handle a lot of the details for you."

"Really?"

I nodded, then fished around for the extra Colby Realty cards I kept stuffed in the outside pocket of my wallet. I found one, then handed it to him. "Just ask for her when you call."

He looked down at the card, then back at me. "I'll do that. Thanks."

"Sure. And I'll think about the babysitter thing."

I turned, then started down the hallway. On the stairs, with every step I took, it sank in a bit more that somehow, despite owing him exactly zero, I'd now not only committed to helping him out, but dragged my extended family in as well. How did *that* happen?

Downstairs, I found Benji at the table, gently forming a ball at one end of a black balloon. Watching him, I felt even more on edge, although it's not like you can ready yourself for a balloon popping. It's a spontaneous, sudden act, meant to startle, and all the preparation in the world won't change—

Pop! Despite my efforts, I jumped. From upstairs, there came a single word, bellowed: *"Benji!"*

He jumped up, quickly gathering the broken pieces of the balloon from where they'd scattered across the floor, then skulked back to the table.

"Well, I better go," I said, as he picked up his cards again. "I'll see you later, okay?"

He nodded. "Okay."

I walked to the door, pulling out my phone and making a note on the memo app to ask around about sitters. As I did so, I realized that ever since the Last Chance, I'd been burdening myself with more than was necessary. A breakfast sandwich, agreeing to being the bridge between Clyde and Theo, a kiss without demarcation, my father's child-care crisis. No wonder I felt so weighted down. On the flip side, it wasn't like one additional thing was going to make much of a difference.

"Hey," I called out to Benji. "Want to ride along?"

He looked up at me, his face hopeful. "Really?"

"If your dad says it's okay."

"He won't care," he said, abandoning the cards and literally running over to me, as if at any moment I might rescind the offer. "He probably won't even notice."

"Go ask him anyway."

I stood there, watching, as he ran up the stairs, taking them two at a time. On the landing, he cupped a hand to his mouth and yelled towards the bedroom, "I'm leaving! With Emaline!"

"What?" came my father's voice, muffled by the door.

"I'm leaving!" Benji repeated.

"What?"

"I'm leaving! Back later!"

The response to this—if there even was one—was lost in the din of him bounding back down the steps towards me. I figured if it wasn't okay, my father would emerge, but after a beat, it was still just us.

"All right," I said. "Guess it's a go."

"Awesome!" Benji hollered, pushing past me out the door and running down the front walk. He was so excited, even though he, like Morris, had no idea where we were going. I shut the door behind me, then followed him at a more subdued pace, wondering if my father was watching us from his window upstairs. All the way to the car I thought about turning back to look, but in the end, I decided against it.

* * *

"Wait a second." Daisy turned around, the wax applicator in one hand. "You did *what*?"

I glanced at the older woman on the table in front of her, who was lying flat on her back, purse in her lap, her hands folded over it. I'd only come back to the waxing room to let Daisy know I was outside waiting. Sharing my personal life in earshot of a stranger with a hair management problem was another thing entirely. "I'll just be outside, okay?"

"Why?"

I nodded towards the woman on the table. "You're kind of, um, busy?"

"Oh, Jean? Don't worry, she's really hard of hearing." She blew on the wax for a second, then leaned close to the woman's ear. *"I'm going to start now, okay? Are you ready?"*

The woman opened her eyes, blinked, then cupped her hand behind one ear, looking confused. Daisy held up the applicator. She nodded, smiled, then closed her eyes again.

"Okay." She bent down, carefully smoothing wax under the woman's already thin brow. "Now go back to the beginning. Because either I'm going deaf, too, or you just said something totally crackers."

Crackers, I thought. That was one word for it. "Well," I said, as she picked up a piece of muslin from the shelf beside her and carefully pressed it down on the wax, "Luke and I broke up this morning. And then I kissed someone else at Big Club."

She ripped off the paper, one quick stroke. On the table, Jean winced, but kept her eyes closed. "And this kiss, was it with someone you know, or just a random person?"

"It was Theo," I said.

I watched her dip into the wax again. "You kissed a guy you just met in Big Club?"

"We were buying a toaster oven," I said, like this explained everything.

She turned to look at me, blowing on the wax, her expression incredulous. "Are you *serious*?"

"It just kind of happened."

"Which part? Breaking up with your boyfriend of three years, or making out with someone else you barely know moments later?"

"It was not moments," I pointed out as she started on the other eyebrow. "There was at least a couple of hours in between."

"Oh, well, in that case," she said sarcastically.

There was a knock at the door of the waxing room. Before we could even ask who was there, Mrs. Ye was sticking her head in, looking at me. "You bring boy here?"

"What?"

"Little boy outside. He with you?"

"Oh," I said, suddenly remembering I'd left Benji up front, examining the array of polishes. "Yes. He's my brother."

Mrs. Ye nodded, then shut the door again without further comment. To Daisy, who was looking at me with a quizzical expression, I explained, "I'm sort of helping my father out. He's swamped with stuff right now."

She leaned over Jean's face, and started plucking, a series of quick little stabs. "Helping how?"

"Just entertaining Benji until we can find someone else to do it."

"Okay, wait a second," she said, holding up her free hand. The plucking continued with the other, at a quick speed. "So what you're saying is that since I saw you yesterday, you broke up with Luke, kissed Theo, *and* offered to help out your dead-beat, undeserving father."

I thought for a moment. "Yes. Oh, and I also introduced Theo to Clyde and agreed to help them get together for an interview."

Now, she stopped what she was doing and looked at me. "Do you understand how insane you sound right now? How could your whole life be so different in less than twenty-four hours?"

"Because that's the way it is around here," I told her. "Nothing happens for ages, and then all the changes come at once."

"Not *that* fast," she grumbled.

"Well, then, maybe I'm just actually having a summer," I offered. "You know, a big one where Things Actually Happen. Hey, it's like I'm a tourist or something!"

"Emaline, stop. Seriously." She shook her head, then switched to the other brow. Outside, I could hear Mrs. Ye barking at someone in Vietnamese. "Although I will admit you are acting like one. I can't believe you're already in a relationship. What's next, chest hair and Jell-O shots?"

I made a face. "It's not a relationship. Or Jell-O shots. It's one kiss."

"You were with Luke for more than three years."

"He cheated on me, Daisy. Went to meet some girl at Tallyho."

She looked at me again, this time with pity. "Oh, Emaline. Really?"

I nodded. You'd think each time I said this, it would hurt less. Nope. I felt tears gathering in my throat again. "Look, I should go. Benji's here, I have stuff to do. Can we talk later?"

"Wait, I'll walk out with you." She picked up a hand mirror, then leaned down to Jean again. *"I'm finished,"* she yelled, loudly and close enough to her ear to cause deafness, had it not already been accomplished. *"Would you like to take a look?"*

Jean opened her eyes. When she saw the mirror, she sat up, then took it, surveying her reflection. "You do such a lovely job," she told Daisy, in a normal tone. "Thank you."

"You're welcome," Daisy hollered back at her. *"Have a good day."*

Jean nodded, then slid off the table, still clutching her purse, and I stepped back to let her pass. Then I watched as Daisy ripped off and replaced the paper cover on the table, put the top back on the wax, then dropped the tweezers with a plunk into a container of cleaning solution. Just like that, everything was clean and reset. Unlike so much else in the world.

Outside in the salon, we found Benji examining the display of gel fill-ins. "Hey Emaline," he called out when he saw me. "Did you know they use wood sanders to file these things?"

"I did not," I replied.

"It's so cool! They have to wear masks and everything."

I smiled, then turned to Daisy, who was behind me. "Benji, this is my friend Daisy. Daisy, Benji."

He stuck out his hand. "Pleased to meet you."

Daisy, impressed, took it. "And you as well. I've heard a lot about you."

"I'm just along for the ride right now," he explained, all casual. "I'm hard to entertain."

She looked at me, raising her eyebrows. I shrugged, then said, "We're on our way to the office. There's some kind of towel crisis."

"Sounds serious," she said, as we started outside.

"Margo's got some new system, all computerized," I told her. "It's working as well as you'd expect."

"Well, maybe you can totally shake it up for her," she suggested. "Change everything, really quickly. Since you're on a roll with that today, and all."

I just looked at her. "I'm really not doing it on purpose."

"I know. It's just . . ." She glanced at Benji, choosing her words carefully. "A lot to take in."

"Tell me about it."

"Oh!" She snapped her fingers. "Before I forget. *This* will cheer you up. Wait right here." I watched her as she went back inside, over to the coat rack by the door, and removed a hanging bag. She unzipped it as she walked back. "Check these out. I found them last time I was at Dolly's, that vintage store in Durham I told you about? They're for the Beach Bash."

I looked at the contents, which appeared to be two very fluffy and ruffled dresses, one pink, one blue. They looked like something Little Bo Peep would wear. In Candy Land. "The thought of wearing this is supposed to cheer me up?"

"They won't look like *this*," she said, sounding offended. "Once I'm done, you won't even recognize them. But the colors are perfect, since I'm thinking of going with a candy theme."

"We're wearing candy?"

"The *theme*, the *vision*, is candy." She sighed, looking at Benji. "Do you know your sister has no sense of fashion-forwardness whatsoever?"

"What's fashion-forwardness?" he asked.

"Must be genetic," I said. She zipped the bag back up, turning her back to me. "Hey, hey, I'm just joking. I know they'll be great. They always are. You're a genius, Daze."

This made her smile. "We do have a reputation to uphold."

"*You* do," I said. "All I have to do is wear what I'm told and show up."

The truth was, I would have liked to be able to take some credit for the fact that Daisy and I had won the Best-Dressed Couple award at the annual Colby Beach Bash for two years running. But it was *all* Daisy, ever since we'd started attending together in middle school. She was the one who spent the year searching out fabrics, patterns, and inspiration in order to come up with the perfect vision, which she then executed, single-handedly, to her typical high standards. I just got fitted a few times and poked with the occasional straight pin, a small price to pay for half the bragging rights.

"I can't believe the Beach Bash is happening so soon," I said to Daisy now, as she hung the garment bag over one arm. "I feel like we just graduated."

"Thirty-six days to go," she told me. There was that exactness again; the girl lived by her calendar, with several back-ups. She was like NASA she was so organized. "Not that I'm keeping track."

"Can I do anything to help?"

She gave me a sympathetic look. "Maybe explain to your brother what fashion-forward means."

"I will," I told her. "As soon as I figure it out myself."

She smiled, then stepped forward and wrapped her arms around me. "Call me as soon as you get off work. You hear me?"

I hugged her back. "I hear you."

"Nice to meet you, Benji," she said, turning to go back inside.

"You, too!" he replied. And then, again, he was running out ahead of me to the car, like a dog on one of those retractable leashes, grabbing all the distance possible before he got pulled back.

In the car, I checked my messages. Besides the text earlier from Margo in response to my inquiry about more towels—No towels. Come back for further instruction—I had two new voice mails.

"Emaline, hello, it's me." Pause. "Um, Theo." Another pause, during which I could think of nothing but that kiss among the toasters. "I just spoke to Ivy and she'd really like us to go ahead and nail Clyde down for an interview as soon as possible. I mean, you know, at his convenience, of course. But today. Preferably soon? So if you could"—here, someone in the background was saying something—"call him and set that up, we'd really appreciate it." More direction from Ivy. Then, "Just call me back as soon as you can. Thanks!"

I hit Delete, looking at Benji, who was fidgeting in his seat, tapping one foot while drumming two fingers on the open window. The next message began.

"Emaline, it's me again. Theo." I sighed, then cranked the engine. "So Ivy thinks it would be best if we could just get Clyde's direct number? So that we don't have to bother you with these requests? I explained to her that he preferred to go through you, but"—muffled noises, voices, static—"anyway, if that's possible, you can just text his info to me and I'll take it from there. But if not, you know, just call me back"—more muffling—"as soon as you can. Thanks!"

"Oh for God's sake," I said out loud. Pushy, driven, whatever they chose to call it: it was still annoying.

Instantly, Benji froze, dropping his drumming fingers, silencing the bouncing leg. "Sorry," he said quietly.

"No, no." I waved my phone at him. "Them, not you."

"Oh." He brightened visibly. "Okay."

We pulled out into the traffic, and I looked over at him again. He was such a kid, all impulse and emotion, but he was young; it made sense he was so easy to read. I could only imagine how he'd take the news that his parents were divorcing, whenever they did finally tell him. It broke my heart just thinking about it.

When we got to the office, we found Margo in the conference room, sitting at her laptop. All around her, on the table, chairs, and every other flat surface, were towels. All white, all sizes: bath, washcloth, hand, mats. It was like the linen closet had exploded, albeit very neatly.

"I thought we were out of towels?" I said.

She looked up at me, her expression irritated. "I didn't say that. I said there were no towels for *you*."

"Okay," I said. "But I don't actually *need* any. The clients do."

"This morning, at the meeting," she said, in a way that made it clear a scolding was to follow, "I carefully detailed the new, computerized system I have implemented for inventory of the towels. Ten minutes later, you went back to the storeroom and took a bunch, ignoring everything I said. "

Beside me, Benji was watching this exchange, looking at Margo, then me, then back at her again. I nodded in his direction, saying, "You remember Benji, right?"

She gave him a glance. "Oh, yes. Hello."

"Hi," he said. "That's a lot of towels."

"Yes, Benji," she replied, in the same know-it-all tone, "yes, it is. It is, in fact, all the towels we have here at Colby Realty for midweek replenishment for renters. I'm sure you'll agree that it's necessary to have this many so we can always be sure we can meet the needs of our guests."

"Margo," I said, "he's a kid. He doesn't care about this."

"The point is," she continued, ignoring me, "I developed a system to ensure we always know how many of each kind of towels we have at our disposal. All that is required to *make* the system work is that each employee who checks a towel out logs it in the database. Is that so complicated?"

"Yes," I said.

"No," Benji replied obediently, at the same time.

"We don't need an exact count, just a general idea," I said. "It's towels, not radioactive material."

"And you are not in charge here," she shot back. "I say we are using this system, so we are. End of conversation. Now come in here and get a refresher course so I can get back to work."

For a moment, I just stared at her, and she held my gaze, just as fiercely. Under other circumstances, I would have held my ground like I usually did. But beside me, Benji was fidgeting again.

"Fine." I stepped into the conference room. "Refresh me."

"Gladly." She pushed out the chair beside her, and I slid in, gesturing for Benji to sit as well. "Now, we've put a computer in the storage room for inventory use. What you'll do, when you need towels, is open up this Excel file labeled 'Linens,' and then . . ."

Fifteen minutes later—which was about fourteen more than was necessary—she was done. I stifled one last yawn. "Got it. Anything else I need to know right now?"

Margo glanced around her. "No, I don't think so. Just put all these towels back in the storage room, sep᾿rated by type, and we should be good to go."

"Me?" I said. "Why do I have to put them back?"

"Because it's your fault I had to do this exercise in the first place. If you'd been paying attention this morning, none of this would have been necessary."

Not for the first time that day, I was sorely tempted to pull her hair or frog-punch her, like when we were kids. Instead, I just reminded myself that, soon enough, I'd be gone from here, with towels—and Margo—no longer my daily cross to bear. Then I picked up a stack of washcloths.

"I can help," Benji said, grabbing another pile from the table. "Where do they go?"

"Thanks," I said. "Follow me."

I was on my second trip to the storeroom when my phone rang. I shifted the tall stack of mats I was carrying to the other hand, then fished it out of my back pocket. "Hello?"

"Hey, Emaline, it's me." A pause. "Theo."

"Hi," I said, navigating the hallway. "Sorry I haven't been able to get back to you. Things are sort of—"

"So look, Ivy really feels," he broke in over me, "that it would be best if you just gave us Clyde's contact information. She's concerned that having you as a go-between will, um, complicate things."

Of course she was. "No," I said, "what will complicate things is if he won't talk to you because you've deliberately chosen to ignore the parameters he set up."

I waited for a crack about this word being an SAT basic. Instead, there was just silence. Then, "True. But as a film-maker and documentarian, her relationship with her subject is crucial. Anything that diffuses or distorts it can endanger the project."

"Say whatever you want, but I'm not going against his wishes," I said. "And neither should you."

There was that muffled noise again, and then suddenly his voice was lower, closer to the receiver. "Look, I'm not try-ing to hassle you, okay? She's just angling, it's what she does. I'm sorry. I'm so grateful to you for everything this morning."

"Theo."

"Not the kiss," he said quickly. "I mean, that was great, too, don't get me wrong. I haven't been able to stop thinking about it. Even though I know we're, um, not talking about it. Until tomorrow." Now I was blushing, right there in the hallway. "But introducing me to Clyde, finessing that connection . . . that was amazing. I can't thank you enough."

"You don't have to," I replied. "Just don't let her ruin it. Okay?"

"Okay." He cleared his throat. "So, um . . . I am still going to see you, though, tomorrow, right? In a non-work-related way?"

I looked at Benji, scooting past me in the narrow hallway, toting a bunch of washcloths. He'd already cleared half the table, making twice as many trips as I had. Clearly, all that preteen energy, properly channeled, could be a serious resource.

"Yeah," I said to Theo. "I'll be in touch, on both counts, soon. All right?"

"Sounds good," he replied. "Bye, Emaline."

I smiled, then hung up, pushing my phone back into my pocket. Then I turned around, to the storeroom, only to find Luke standing there, his eyes level with mine over the towering pile in my arms. I jumped, startled, and the towels collapsed between us in a blur of white.

"Oh my God," I said, putting a hand to my chest as one last washcloth fluttered past in my side vision. "You scared the crap out of me."

"Sorry."

I dropped down to collect the towels and he joined me on the floor, grabbing a few that were closer to him.

"What's going on here? Some kind of spa day or something?"

"Margo's got a new system," I told him. "What are you doing here?"

He ran a hand through his hair. "Well, actually, I was hoping to—"

"Luke!" I heard Benji yelp, and then he was running towards us, footsteps thumping across the carpet. "I didn't know you were here!"

"Just walked in, bud." Luke held up his hand for a high five, which Benji delivered with a loud slap. "She's got you working, huh?"

"Inventory," Benji explained. "It's a lot of towels."

"I can see that." Luke looked at me, grinning. I almost smiled back at him out of habit, until I remembered what had happened only a matter of hours ago. "Hey, give me a quick sec to talk to Emaline, okay?"

"Sure," Benji said. "I still have a lot of stuff to move. See ya!"

And with that, he was gone, back into the conference room. Luke looked at me. "Can we—"

"I'm actually really busy," I told him.

"Ten minutes." He lowered his voice. "It's important."

I glanced across the office where, sure enough, both Margo and my mother were watching us. "Five. And not here."

He nodded, then followed me as I dropped my pile back in the conference room and walked out to the front porch of the office. Once the door swung shut behind us, I hopped up on a newspaper box. "All right," I said, crossing my arms. "Talk."

Luke glanced away, at the traffic passing, then back at me.

"Look, so, this morning . . . it didn't go they way I planned. None of this has. I made a mistake."

"When?" I said. "Meeting that girl at Tallyho? Or dumping me this morning?"

Instead of answering, he ran a hand over his face again, something he always did when he was stressed out. I knew this, like so many of his tells, as well as I did my own. "I didn't dump you," he said. "I said we might need a break."

"So why are you here?" I asked.

"Because," he replied, "because ever since I walked out of the diner away from you, I've felt sick. Like something's really wrong and I need to fix it."

I bit my lip, not saying anything.

"I'm not saying things have been perfect between us for the last few months," he continued. "But I want to be with you."

"You didn't feel that way when you decided to go to Tallyho."

"Are you ever going to stop with the Tallyho thing? I was trying to be honest with you!" he replied, his voice rising. "I told you the truth. That I was tempted, and acted on it, but not in a way you thought. Now I'm telling you I regret every-thing. You've got to give me something for that."

"Like what?"

Instead of answering, he stepped forward to stand be-tween my open knees, sliding his hands up my neck in that way that was familiar and thrilling, all at once. As he put his lips on mine, I turned my face up and just a bit to the right, so we fit perfectly, a skill honed from a million kisses over the years. When he finally drew back, he moved his mouth to my ear. "I love you, Emaline."

My head was swimming. All I wanted, all I ever wanted in moments like this, was to keep kissing him. But somehow, I managed to put my hands on his chest and pushed him back. "I . . . I can't."

"Why not?" he asked.

"Things have changed," I said.

"I told you I was sorry, I made a mistake." He moved in closer, again. "I'll fix it. And the other problems we've had, we'll work on them, too."

I shook my head, looking down at my hands. "It's not just about all that."

"Then what?"

I didn't say anything. All I could think about was toasters.

"Something you did?" he asked. Long, awkward pause. Where was that waitress to interrupt when I really needed her? "Emaline, I just saw you, like, four hours ago. What could possibly have happened since then?"

It's always very pure, that last moment before an ugly, unsettling truth hits someone. The most stark of before-and-afters. I sat there and watched Luke's face change, right before me. "Oh my God," he said, stepping back. "It's that guy, isn't it? Theo. Did you—"

"Luke," I said quietly.

"What the hell? You went running to him the minute you left the diner?"

"Hey." I pointed a finger at him. "You walked out on *me*, remember? As far as I knew, you were gone for good."

"Which must have been so convenient," he shot back. "You could finally jump into bed with Girl Jeans without even having to feel bad about it."

"I didn't jump into bed with anyone," I replied. "God. What are you even saying?"

"What are *you* saying?" he replied. "The minute our three-year relationship hit a rough patch, you hooked up with someone else?"

"At least I waited until it was over."

The look on his face as he heard this—hurt, surprised, vulnerable—made *me* feel sick. I tried to reach out for him, to blunt it somehow, but he stepped farther away, leaving me flailing.

For a moment, we just stood there, this huge space between us. "You said it yourself," I said finally. "Things haven't been great in a while. If they had been, neither one of us would have done anything. It means something was wrong."

Judging by the pained look on his face, though, it was easier to say this than to hear it. "I just can't . . ." He trailed off. "I can't believe this."

"I know," I said. "Me neither."

We were both silent for a minute, the only sound cars passing on the road. I thought again of what I'd said to Daisy: nothing changes for three years, and then suddenly everything does, all at once. Maybe those other people's summers I'd envied weren't all fun either. You never really know anything until it's happening to you.

"Well," he said finally. "I guess . . . that's that."

Breaking up earlier had been hard enough. Doing it again,

and this time because of me, was like torture. "I didn't plan any of this," I said softly. "It just happened."

"Yeah. Well." He couldn't even look at me. "I should . . . I'm leaving."

And then, for the second time since sunrise, I sat and watched the only love of my life walk away from me. As he did, oddly enough, I kept thinking of Benji, running up the stairs to the outskirts of my father's earshot earlier, these same words repeated like a spell.

I'm leaving.

I'm leaving.

I'm leaving.

It wasn't really necessary to say, especially if you were already walking away. Almost redundant. And yet, there was a comfort in there being no question, no room for doubt. I'd assumed I had that earlier from Luke. But I was sure of it now.

11

"OKAY, SO, UM . . . I guess first, maybe just say and spell your name?"

Clyde looked at me, then back at the camera. "You don't know who I am?"

"No, no," Theo said quickly, "I do, of course. This is just a device to mark frame, have identification. It's—"

"Completely unnecessary right now," Ivy finished for him. "My apologies, Clyde. He's an intern and a novice. Let's just get started."

Glancing at Theo, who was squinting through the camera lens, I saw the tips of his ears and much of his face were now red. Maybe you didn't need to know someone forever to be able to read them from a distance after all. Nervous myself, I stuck another piece of gum in my mouth.

Meanwhile, Clyde was still studying Ivy with the same flat, unreadable expression he'd had since meeting her about a half hour earlier. Finally, he looked back at Theo. "My name is Clyde Conaway. C-L-Y-D-E C-O-N-A-W-A-Y."

I smiled, then glanced across the Washroom, the Laundromat/café Clyde owned, to check on Benji, who was eating a piece of pie. Theo and Ivy had been so gung ho to get going on the interview that we'd come straight from the office, so I'd arranged for my father to pick him up from here. Until then, I was plying him with Clyde's homemade sweets and hoping for the best.

In the end, I had not had to hunt Clyde down; he called me. Or the office, actually, where he was at first just a single line blinking on the phone that Rebecca pushed across the desk. I'd just come back with Benji from a late lunch at Casa Sandbar on the boardwalk and was still chewing my complimentary mint.

"For me?" I said, and she nodded. "Who is it?"

"Didn't say," she replied. "Just that it was important."

I was expecting Theo, since I knew he and Ivy were going nuts over at Sand Castles, wishing I'd go ahead and jump now that they'd told me how high. So it was with some trepidation, to say the least, that I pushed the button and said hello.

"Emaline," a voice said in response. "It's Clyde. Got a minute?"

I did. And it took not much longer than that to set up this very interview. Quick and dirty, as my dad would say. He named the time and place, I assured him they'd find it, now here we were. What happened from this point on, however, was anybody's guess. Which was why I was glad I'd found a fresh pack of Big Red in my purse.

"I'd like to begin," Ivy was saying now, "with summarizing your personal details. Where were you born?"

"North Reddemane. November twenty-first, nineteen sixty-eight."

"And your parents were farmers, yes?"

"My father kept dairy cows," Clyde replied. "Holsteins. My mother taught third grade at Sacred Heart Catholic School in Cape Frost."

"Which is where?"

Again, Clyde looked at me. It had been clear since I arrived that, as far as he was concerned, there was a clear division here between Us and Them. It made me wonder, yet again, why he'd agreed to do this. Then again, it had been me who told Theo that nothing Clyde did made any sense. At least he was consistent.

"Cape Frost is about twenty-five miles east of here," he was saying now. "Closest thing to a city we had then. And now, really."

"And Sacred Heart, was that the school you attended?" Ivy asked.

Clyde snorted. "Nobody from North Reddemane went there. Except the Guadaleris. Right, Emaline?"

"The who?" Ivy asked.

I smiled. "The Guadaleris. Rich and super-Catholic. They could afford the tuition and gas."

Ivy turned, looking at me. "It would be best if we kept this conversation between ourselves. We're fine with you observing, but—"

"Hey," Clyde said, cutting her off. "I asked her something. She was answering."

She blinked at him. "I understand that. But in a documentary setup, we need the subject to have a relationship only with the camera, not people off screen."

"Well, maybe she should be on screen," Clyde said.

Ivy's expression darkened. Ever since she'd arrived to find Clyde and the situation not exactly to her specifications, she'd been simmering, close to a boil. I would have enjoyed it more had I not been so worried about all of this collapsing for Theo.

"Actually," I said, holding up my phone. "I need to step out anyway."

I got up and slid behind the camera setup and out the back door. I could hear Ivy as she took a deep breath, then said, "All right. So you attended school here in town. Was that for all twelve grades?"

Outside, where it was considerably less tense, I returned a text from Daisy (You OK? Call me!), then looked around to see if my father had shown up yet. There was no sign of the Subaru, though, just Clyde's beat-up truck, my car, and Ivy and Theo's van, from which they'd earlier unloaded what seemed like an awful lot of equipment for just a single interview.

"Looks like they're moving in for the duration," Clyde had said to me then, as we stood in the café watching them run cords around the dryers in the next room. He'd just given Benji the pie menu, which he was studying with such focus it was like he expected to be quizzed on it later.

"They didn't say how long it would take," I'd told him. "I think, though, they'll talk to you as long as you're willing."

"Huh," he said in response, cryptic as always.

"Seriously, though," I said. "Thanks for doing this. You pretty much made Theo's life when you agreed to it."

"Theo?"

I leaned my head towards the dryers. "My friend, from the Big Club this morning. Ivy's not, um, the easiest boss to impress."

"Oh." He nodded. "Right."

"Razzleberry," Benji had said, putting down the menu. "Although it was *not* an easy choice."

"Good pick," Clyde told him. "Made it fresh last night."

As Clyde reached into the glass case behind him, I looked back at Theo, who was now adjusting a large light he'd set up behind a folding station. After a second, he glanced up and, seeing me, smiled. Behind him, Ivy, clad in black jeans and a black fitted T-shirt, was flipping through some notes on a clipboard. She looked at him, then at me, her eyes narrowing. I turned back around.

Now, I heard gravel crunching and looked up, expecting to see my father pulling into the lot. Instead, it was my dad. He parked beside my car, then opened the truck door and eased himself out with a familiar end-of-a-long-workday groan.

"Hey," I said. "What are you doing here?"

"I was about to ask you the same thing," he replied. "Aren't you supposed to be at the office?"

"Got an early reprieve."

"Really." I nodded. "From what I heard, sounds like you might have earned it, though."

"Mom told you about Margo being on the warpath about the towel thing?" I shook my head. "I swear, you have no idea how hard she is to work for. Or even *with*. It's craziness."

"Margo?" he repeated.

"Yeah. Isn't that what you meant?"

Before he could answer, Clyde stuck his head out the door of the Laundromat. "Rob," he called out squinting at us. "Give me a sec and I'll show you that ceiling."

My dad nodded, waving at him, and Clyde disappeared back inside. Just beyond him, I could see Ivy and Theo huddled together. She was talking quickly, gesturing with one hand, while he just nodded. I saw my dad take them in, too, as well as the cords, lights, and equipment.

"They're shooting a documentary," I explained.

"Who is?"

I nodded at them. "My friend Theo and his boss, Ivy. It's about Clyde. They just started interviewing him today."

"They're making a movie about Clyde?"

"And his art career. Did you know he was a big deal in New York at one time?"

He looked back inside. "I vaguely remember hearing something about it. Long time ago, though."

"Yeah," I said. "I guess it was."

A car was pulling in behind us now, slowly navigating the small and somewhat crowded lot. Sure enough, it was the Subaru. When my father saw me, he lifted a hand in greeting.

"Is that Joel?" my dad asked.

"Yeah. I've been hanging out with Benji. He's here to pick him up."

There was a definite awkwardness, standing there with him as my father got out of the car and approached us. It was the same feeling I remembered from those childhood lunches at Shrimpboats, years ago, with me and my mom and dad on one side of a booth and my father, Leah, and Benji on the other. Us and Them, again.

"Robert," my father said as he walked up. He stuck out his hand. "Good to see you."

"You too," my dad said, shaking it. "How's Leah?"

"Good," my father replied, then glanced at me. "What'd you do with your brother?"

"He's eating pie inside."

"Pie?" He glanced at his watch. "For dinner?"

Whoops. "It's berry pie," I said, like that made a difference.

"Sorry about that." Clyde came walking up, joining the confab. "Your daughter got me into this documentary thing. Did she tell you?"

They both looked at him, then back at me. And here I thought this couldn't get *more* awkward. "She did not," my father said finally. "Is this the Ivy Mendelson project?"

Clyde, clearly confused, looked at my dad, who explained, "This is Joel. Emaline's father. Joel, Clyde Conaway."

"Oh," Clyde said. "Sorry. I didn't—"

"It's fine," I said quickly. "It's kind of confusing, all of us together."

"Clyde?" Ivy stuck her head out the door, squinting in the sunlight. "Can I get an idea of when you'll be able to start up again? We've got quite a bit we'd like to cover."

"Not too long. Gotta talk to a man about some drywall." She looked confused, as if not sure if this was a euphemism for something. "Fifteen minutes."

She nodded, not exactly looking pleased, and went back inside. Clyde said to me, "She's really something, huh?"

"*Exceptionally* talented," my father agreed, as if this was what he'd meant. "I saw *Cooper's Way* at the Tribeca festival. Just riveting."

My dad and Clyde just looked at him. The silence was so excruciating I finally broke it myself. "So Benji's inside, and . . ."

"The spot's in the café," Clyde finished, turning back to the door. "No crack yet, but it's sagging. Hate to think what's weighing it down."

"Either loose pipe or a leaking one," my dad replied. "We'll have to cut in to know for sure."

We went in single file, Clyde and my dad first, my father and I bringing up the rear. Ivy and Theo, who were watching something on the monitor, barely glanced up. I, however, was more than aware of the oddness of this little parade.

"Watch your step through here," Clyde said over his shoulder as we wound through the maze of cords. "Emaline's boyfriend and his boss have the place wired up like you wouldn't believe."

"Boyfriend?" my father said from behind me at the exact same moment my dad, up ahead, glanced back.

"There's Benji," I said, loudly, like increased volume might change the subject even faster. "He's been a big help to me today."

Benji, who'd just stuffed a heaping forkful of pie into his mouth, chewed for a moment, then explained, "There was a towel situation. The new system involves spreadsheets and everything."

"Really," my father said.

"Yeah, but Emaline didn't use it? So her sister got really mad and had to give us a refresher course."

My father looked at me. "Sounds exciting."

"Oh, you know the realty business," I told him. "Never a dull moment."

He smiled, and I felt myself relax, relieved he'd apparently let the whole boyfriend comment slide without further comment. Then I glanced at my dad. He was still looking right at me.

With a lot of loud rattling noises, Clyde dragged a ladder out from a storeroom and set it up at the end of the counter. We all watched as my dad climbed up, pulling a flashlight from his pocket once he reached the top. As he tipped his head back, examining the spot, Clyde observed from below with more attention than I'd seen from him since we'd started this whole thing.

I looked over at Theo and Ivy, wondering if they'd noticed this as well. He was crouched down, adjusting some plugs on a power strip while she sat on a dryer, studying her phone. I walked over, leaving Benji regaling my father with more towel details.

"So," I said to Theo. "How's it going, you think?"

"Good," he replied. "I mean, he's not the most cooperative subject. We knew not to expect that, though."

"At least he's answering the questions," I pointed out.

"Oh, yeah. I think Ivy just needs to get some momentum with him. All these interruptions . . ." He looked over at my dad, on the ladder, then back at the plugs. "It just makes it hard to get a good rhythm."

"This shouldn't take long," I told him. "And we'll all be out of your hair pretty soon."

"All of you?" He got to his feet and came closer. "Because I was thinking, you know, that maybe we could . . ."

"What happened to tomorrow?" I said.

He ran a hand through his hair, looking over at the counter. "Well, really, tomorrow actually *starts* tonight. If you actually think about it."

"You're messing with my demarcation," I pointed out.

"You're right, you're right." He stepped back, holding up his hands. "Sorry."

Neither of us spoke for a second, the only sound my dad moving the ladder, triggering another round of clattering and scraping. When it was finally quiet, Theo said, "All I'm saying is that, you know, we could hang out tonight. Just as friends, at least until—"

"Midnight," I finished for him. "And then we turn into something else, like Cinderella after the ball? Pumpkins, maybe?"

"Fine," he said, shaking his head. "Forget it. Demarcate away. I'll see you tomorrow, in daylight. Not a moment before."

I smiled, stepping a little closer to him. "I didn't say no. I just made a princess reference."

"I have no sisters and sparse girlfriend experience," he said. "I don't know what that *means*."

"It means," I said, as Ivy slid off the dryer and started coming towards us, "that I might see you later."

He smiled, surprised and pleased, at least until Ivy said, "Are we ready to shoot when he is? Because if you're gabbing over here, we ought to be."

"All set on this end," Theo told her cheerfully.

"Well, that's half the battle," she replied, sliding her phone back into her pocket. She looked over at Clyde, standing at the base of the ladder, then at me. "How long does this sort of thing take, again?"

"Not really sure," I told her.

She sighed loudly, then said to Theo, "Just double-check we're set up and ready to go. We need to establish something here, and soon."

He nodded, turning his attention back to the camera. A beat later, I heard my father say my name. He and Benji were now walking towards me. "We should be getting back the house. Thanks again for the help today."

"No problem." To Benji I said, "It was fun, right?"

"Totally," he agreed. "Much better than practicing card tricks."

My father nodded at the camera. "Impressive setup you guys have here."

"Yep," Ivy said, not looking up, from her perch on the dryer. "All we need is the subject."

My father raised his eyebrows. I said, "Clyde's not exactly running on a schedule."

"The roof takes precedence," Ivy added, with a loud sigh.

"It's actually a ceiling," I said. I couldn't help myself.

"—send a crew by early next week to cut in, and then go from there," I heard my dad saying, flashlight still in hand, as he and Clyde came towards us now as well. "I'd plan on redoing that entire part of the ceiling, though. And that would be the best-case scenario. Get into more structural issues and—"

"A burst pipe would be the least of my problems," Clyde finished for him.

My dad nodded, then started out the door, but not before shooting me a look making it clear I should follow. Outside, after my father and Benji said their good-byes, he walked over to his truck and tossed the flashlight onto the passenger seat. "Did I hear you right?" he asked me. "That kid's your boyfriend now?"

"I didn't say that," I pointed out. "Clyde did."

He just looked at me. This was not his department, and we both knew it. In our house the divisions were clear: my mother handled all things relationship, menstruation, and fashion related, while his arena was oil changes, finances, and plumbing problems. But this was too big to ignore.

"He's not my boyfriend," I said. "It's just been a really weird day."

"Tell me about it." He ran a hand over his face—up, down, then up again—another one of his end-of-workday moves. "You headed home soon? Your mom's worried about you."

"It's my next stop."

"Good." He climbed in the truck and pulled the door shut with a bang. "I'll see you there."

I really had planned to go right home. But once I was in the car, I realized how badly I needed some perspective. When

I saw the boardwalk in the distance, I knew exactly where to find it.

Five minutes later, I was walking up to the ticket booth at Surfside, the rundown little amusement park that had been right on Colby's beach since my mom was a kid. It had none of the high-tech attractions of SafariLand: no dancing or driving games, no laser tag, not even go-karts. Instead, there was just a rickety building that housed a decrepit snack bar and skeeball, duckpin bowling, and basketball tosses. Outside was a merry-go-round, a roller coaster that had been Closed for Repairs since I was in middle school, and the Ferris wheel.

When I walked up to get tickets, pulling a couple of bills from my pocket, Josh Elliott, who worked there most days, waved me off. "You know your money's no good here, Emaline."

"You never let me pay," I said to him, as he grabbed a ring of keys on his way outside.

"High School Special," he replied. Which was what he always said, even though he'd been on his second senior year when I was a freshman, and even then never graduated. "Hop on."

I walked over to the wheel, climbed onto the bucket nearest the ground, then pulled the door shut behind me. Josh disappeared into the booth, and a moment later the engine started up and I began to rise.

There might have been more beautiful places than the top of the Surfside Ferris wheel, but I didn't know of any. I'd always felt something magical as I got higher and higher above the boardwalk, beach, and ocean. It was like resetting myself, and I'd come here often during the last year when the stuff with my father and college was weighing heavily. It calmed me, a reminder there was something else to this world than just Colby. I always knew, logically, this was true. But some days, I needed to see it to be sure.

When I reached the highest point, Josh stopped the wheel so I could sit there for a while. At first, I traced my day from a distance, finding the Washroom, the office, Wave Nails, Big Club, Sand Dollars, Last Chance. Then I turned and looked at the ocean, amazed, as always, by this greatest of contrasts. One side was populated, housing everything, and the other, nothing but blue. In between and high above, I did all I could to soak up the stillness while it lasted.

✳ ✳ ✳

When I knocked on the door of Sand Dollars later that night, at first there was no answer. Then, finally, the intercom—fixed, thanks to my call to maintenance—buzzed.

"Yes? Who is it?" I heard Theo say.

"Cinderella," I answered. I heard him laugh. Then there was a buzz, and the door clicked open.

Inside, I found the entire place dark, the only light coming from the pool sconces outside. I came up the stairs, then stood for just a minute on the landing, letting my eyes adjust. Finally, I made him out, over at one of the tables, a pair of headphones around his neck.

"Hey," I said. "You're in the dark."

"It's part of the job." There was a click and a monitor came on; now I could see him. He waved me over to where he was sitting. "Come check this out."

I went, relieved to see no sign of Ivy. Over at the table, he moved some books off the chair beside his, then gestured for me to take a seat.

"He was a little stiff, but it was the first interview," he said, reaching forward to the keyboard in front of him. The screen came to life before me, showing Clyde in a freeze-frame. A couple of keystrokes, and he was talking.

"—never planned on it for a living," he said. "People didn't do that around here."

Then came Ivy's voice, off camera. "But you did."

"Well, someone's got to be first to buck the trend," Clyde said with a shrug. "Might as well be me."

"And Henrikson? He was part of that as well?"

I felt Theo lean closer to my ear, his voice low. "That's Dale Henrikson. Abstract painter, worked mostly in the late nineteen fifties. Very well esteemed, until he lost his tenured position at Cal Arts after a scandal involving a student who was a minor at the time. He ended up teaching Clyde here at Weymar."

I nodded. "Right."

"Not that he," Clyde was saying on the screen now, "was exactly at the height of his own career. I didn't know that, though. Had no idea who he was. Only ended up in that class because welding was full."

"You wanted to be a welder?"

"I wanted to be anything but a farmer. And I liked fire."

I felt Theo shift. When I turned to look at him, he was grinning. "See that?" he said, nodding at the screen. "You can just see him warming up. It's *golden*."

He rewound the clip again, and we both watched Clyde move in reverse, taking back these words. "So it went well," I said.

"Oh, yeah. Ivy was really happy. And she's never happy." He paused the tape again, then pushed back from the table. "And you know what? I'm happy, too."

"Yeah?"

He nodded. "Sure. You're here."

I felt myself blush, then redden even more as I realized it. Theo might have been dorky in some ways, but he'd already emoted more than Luke had in our first three months of dating. Maybe it was true: outside of Colby, everything and everyone moved faster.

As if to emphasize this, Theo leaned in and brushed my hair back. He was just leaning in closer when I said, "What time is it, exactly?"

He sighed, then looked at the computer screen. "I had a feeling you might point that out. Eleven forty-six. And thirty seconds."

"So," I said, "it's not tomorrow."

"Not technically, no." He sat back in his chair. "Although if we were in Australia, I could make a compelling argument for us to have been together long enough to be engaged."

I raised my eyebrows, startled at this. Clearly I wasn't the only one. Even in the dark, I could see him redden. "Well," I said, swallowing. "I guess it's a good thing we're here, then. Because that would be crackers."

"Be what?"

I cleared my throat. "Crackers. You know, crazy. Insane."

"I've never heard that term before," he commented.

"I'm pretty sure it's a Morris original."

"A what?'

"Never mind." I looked at the clock again. "Anyway, you do make a good point. Time is relative, right? At least in physics. What's fourteen minutes, really, in the great scheme of things?"

"Thirteen," he corrected me, nodding at the clock.

I snapped my fingers. "Exactly."

At this, he grinned, and I found myself smiling back. He had one of those faces, so wide and open that whatever expression he made, you couldn't help but mirror it. "No, no," he said, shaking his head. "You're right. Demarcation is important. We'll just keep busy until midnight."

I looked around the dark room. "Doing . . . ?"

"Whatever it is platonic friends who have no romantic involvement yet do together," he said.

"Like watch the clock and discuss physics?"

"It's worked so far."

We sat there for a moment, in silence. Finally he said, "Well, that was a short run."

"Totally," I agreed. "We make awful platonic friends."

"It's a good thing we only have to do it for another eleven minutes." He leaned forward, resting his elbows on his knees, and studied me. "Maybe it's just that we don't know each other all that well yet. Tell me something about yourself."

"What?" I replied.

"Anything."

I just looked at him.

"What's your favorite condiment?"

"*Condiment?*" I asked. "You have everything in the world to choose from and you ask me that?"

"Look, all I really want to do is kiss you. And I can't for another—" He glanced at the clock. "Ten minutes. I'm doing my best."

"Fine. It's mustard."

He cocked his head to the side. "Mustard? Really."

"What's so surprising about mustard?"

"I don't know," he said, with a shrug. "I kind of figured you for a ketchup girl."

"Why?"

"Not sure. Just a hunch."

I rolled my eyes. "What's yours?"

"Soy sauce," he said, without missing a beat. "I can eat it on anything. Even ice cream."

"That," I said, "is disgusting."

"I disagree, but we'll move on," he replied. "Favorite room in the house?"

"Bedroom," I replied. "I like to sleep. You?"

"I'm into cooking. Kitchen."

"You can never have enough clocks there," I said.

There was that grin again. "Novels or poetry?"

"Novels," I said. "Most poems are too short and cryptic for my taste."

He pointed at himself. "Totally opposite. Love haikus and free verse, low tolerance for long-winded prose. Salt or pepper?"

"Can't I like both?"

He made a face.

"Fine. Salt."

"I'm all about pepper. See, opposites *do* attract!"

We both looked at the computer clock again. Seven minutes.

"I feel like I'm in school, time is passing so slowly," I said, leaning my head back and looking at the ceiling. That made me think of something. "Favorite subject."

"Computer programming, closely followed by commercial design," he answered easily. "What's yours?"

"History," I told him. "And geometry and trig. Love angles and protractors."

"That," he said, pointing at me, "is *so* mustard of you."

"Favorite SAT word?" I asked him.

He thought for a second. "Pernicious. Because it looks like it would mean something pretty, but instead is all malicious and dangerous. You?"

"Omphaloskepsis," I said. "The art of studying your belly button. Because that was totally what I would have preferred to do instead of learning to spell that word."

He laughed, then snorted, which made me laugh.

"You're a *snorter*?"

"Hey, you picked mustard," he reminded me. "Okay, let's get topical: favorite tomorrow-related quote."

This I had to think about for a moment. Finally I said, "'Everything will look better in the morning.'"

"Who said that?"

"My mom. Usually when I was in tears over something school related right before I went to bed. What about you?"

He didn't have to think. "It's John Wayne. 'Tomorrow is

the most important thing in life. Comes into us at midnight very clean. It's perfect when it arrives and puts itself in our hands. It hopes we've learned something from yesterday.'"

"Wow," I said. "That's great."

"I know." He smiled. "I like yours, too."

We sat there a second, looking at each other. *I don't know you,* I thought. *And yet I do.* It was the weirdest feeling.

"Next question," he said, and I sat up, ready. "Do you know what time it is?"

I looked at the clock: 12:02. "It's morning."

"Tomorrow," he agreed. "How about that."

And then he leaned forward, carefully, slowly, pulled me onto his lap, and kissed me. No toasters this time, just this dark room, the pool glowing blue in the distance, and Clyde, frozen in front of us. It was really nice, and worth the wait. Until the lights suddenly came on.

"Theo! Hello?" An annoyed sigh. "I need some help here."

We broke apart, sloppily. I put my hand over my mouth, then turned to see Ivy on the landing, a large box in her arms. She gestured at Theo impatiently, and he eased me off his lap, getting to his feet.

"I thought you were just wrapping things up," he said, crossing the room. "What's this?"

She handed him the box without comment, then walked into the kitchen, tossing down her purse and keys with a clank. Despite myself, I thought of the (at least previously) nick-free countertop. Once a realty employee, always a realty employee, even after hours.

"Mr. Conaway suggested," she was saying now, as she pulled open the fridge and took out an opened bottle of white wine, "that I do some 'reading up' before we meet again."

"Reading up?" Theo repeated, carrying the box over to the table. "On his work? But you've already—"

"Not his work," she cut him off, getting herself a glass. She poured it more than half full, then took a large gulp. "This place."

Theo opened the lid and took out a few books. I saw what looked like an atlas and some other volume with a visible layer of dust, spotted with fingerprints. "The town?"

"Yes, Theo. The town," she said, her voice flat. "Apparently, my questions today did not convey an understanding of that particular part of his personal history. I suppose he'd be more comfortable with someone who can name-check the Gualalupes."

"The who?" Theo asked, confused.

"That Catholic family." Ivy waved a hand in my direction. "She knows."

Now they were both looking at me. I said, "The Guadaleris."

"Exactly." She took another gulp of her wine, then walked over and picked up the dusty book. "He was kind enough to provide me with some items from his personal library for my perusal."

"Those are Clyde's books?" I asked.

"Oh, yes. He has *volumes*." To Theo she said, "Anyway, if you need me for the next twelve hours, I'll be studying."

"I can help," Theo offered.

"I know. The rest are for you. We'll regroup tomorrow and compare notes." She glanced at me again, then added, "You probably should get started."

"Oh." Theo swallowed. "Sure. Right. I'll get on it."

"Good boy."

And then, with a dramatic sigh, she stuck the book under her arm, grabbed the wine bottle, and shuffled off down the hallway. I watched her go, yet again shocked by the way she talked to Theo. But when I turned to say as much to him, he'd already emptied the rest of the box and found a legal pad and a pen.

"You're serious?" I looked at my watch. "After all that work we did to get to midnight? Don't you ever clock out?"

He shrugged. "I told you, it's not that kind of a job."

"So you have to pull an all-nighter because she didn't do her homework?"

"I have to pull an all-nighter," he corrected me, "because we weren't fully prepared for the interview."

I walked over to him and picked up another one of the books, a blue one with a warped cover. The title, once embossed but now worn and faded, read *Our Fair Town: A Local's Remembrance.* It had been penned by someone named Irma Jean Rankles. I said, "Either way, I have to say right now working at Colby Realty feels like hitting the jackpot."

"You really think delivering towels is better than this?"

"I think," I replied, "that I spent half of fourth grade studying the history of Colby. It's not exactly compelling stuff."

He cleared a space for himself at the table, sliding a monitor aside. "Well, obviously Clyde feels differently."

Instead of responding, I flipped through the first few pages of *Our Fair Town*, something that—judging by their smell and yellow pallor—no one had done since Irma Jean's days. "So you're . . . I should go. Right?"

He looked up at me. "You don't have to. We could read together. This stuff might be fascinating, now that you're not, you know, nine."

"Doubt it." I put the book on the top of the stack. "It's late. I need to get home anyway."

"Oh. Right." He tucked the pen he was holding behind his ear, then reached forward, looped his arms around my waist, and pulled me closer. "Look, I promise. Tomorrow night, we'll get together. No town history, no work stuff. No demarcation. Deal?"

It was hard to say no when he said it like that. "Deal."

He smiled, then cracked the atlas and flipped the legal pad to a clean sheet. The good student, personified. I hung around as he turned through the early pages of town maps, his brow furrowed with concentration. Pretty quickly, though, I felt a yawn coming on and slipped away to the door.

Outside, there was a warm breeze blowing, and I had that stiff spot in my neck I knew would only be cured by sleep, and lots of it. I opened my car door and was about to slide in when I heard Ivy say from somewhere above me, "You're leaving."

I looked up to see her up on the deck off the master bedroom, the glowing tip of a cigarette visible in her hand. Unnecessarily, I told her, "Theo's got a lot of work to do."

She exhaled, not saying anything for a minute. "So you're . . . together now. Yes?"

It was hard to gauge her tone, saying this. Maybe it was the wind, or the angle, but I couldn't tell if she was being condescending, annoyed, or a mix of both. "We're just hanging out," I told her.

"Ah." Another drag. "Not sure that's the best idea."

No mistake this time: I felt myself bristle, hackles rising. "Meaning what? You're the boss of his personal life now, too?"

"Just making an observation," she said mildly, shrugging.

"Well, I'm not on your clock. So you can save your breath."

I slid into my car and pulled the door shut with a bang. I made a point not to look up at the house at all as I cranked the engine and backed out, glancing back only once I was pulling away. By then, though, she was gone, the only thing visible on the deck the half-filled wine glass, a cigarette butt bobbing within it. Which pissed me off more, if that was even possible.

I rolled down my windows as I drove into town, trying to cool off. When I passed the Washroom and spotted the back door open, light spilling through, I doubled back.

Anywhere else in town on a summer Friday night at this hour would have been crowded, if not outright packed. But the Washroom wasn't exactly Tallyho. In the Laundromat, a girl tapped away on a laptop, waiting for her clothes, while a guy across the room thumbed through a paperback. Over on the café side, Clyde was behind the counter, talking to a guy who was reading the newspaper and eating a piece of pie. When he saw me, he smiled.

"Emaline," he said. "What'd you do with those New York friends of yours?"

"The better question," I replied, walking over, "is what did *you* do?"

"Me?" he said, all innocent.

I just looked at him. "*Our Fair Town: A Local's Remembrance*? Really?"

"What? It's a very informative volume."

"So you've read it," I said, clarifying.

"It's part of my own personal collection."

"Since when? Lunchtime?" I asked. He blinked at me. "I saw the stamp, Clyde. You got it today, along with the rest of them."

There was nothing he could say; we both knew he was busted. He'd been safe assuming Ivy and Theo wouldn't know about the Colby library's budget crisis, and how they were selling older books to try to generate revenue to buy newer ones. But as an avid reader who regularly haunted both the library's stacks and their clearance room, I knew well the red circle with a date inside that meant final sale.

"Okay, fine," he said now. "It is sort of mean. But she had so little respect for this place and everyone in it. I had to do something."

"So you attacked with Irma Jean Rankles."

"Or," he countered, "I encouraged her to educate herself and provided the means for doing so."

The guy eating the pie snorted.

"Good night, Clyde," I said, shaking my head.

"Oh, don't leave angry," he called out as I started back towards the door. "It wasn't targeted at your boyfriend. He seems like a good kid."

"He's not my boyfriend."

"No? Well, can't say I'm not relieved."

I turned around, looking at him. First Ivy, then Clyde, not to mention every other volley from the peanut gallery all day. What was it about me that made people think my love life was up for their debate? "You just said he seems decent."

"He does," he said, shrugging. "But still, you know the drill. Those things never end well."

"What things?" I said. "Relationships? That's a pretty sweeping generalization, don't you think?"

"You're right," he agreed. "Can't speak for all. And I'm not. But when it comes to folks like that and people like us? Not a lot of happy endings."

I had a flash of Amber saying the same thing about Luke and my long-term chances. So the odds weren't good for me and a boy I knew or one not from here. Which meant what: I'd never be happy with anyone?

"Well," I said, with a shrug, "someone's gotta be first to buck the trend, right? Might as well be me."

Clyde just looked at me for a long moment. Then he smiled. "Good point."

"Good night," I replied. And this time, I walked out the door.

12

"DON'T LOOK YET. Are you looking?"

I blinked again against Theo's hand, which was pressed over my eyes. "I'm not looking."

"Good. Just a little bit farther. We're almost there."

Even though I was basically blindfolded, I knew we were outside and walking in sand. Which narrowed the location of Theo's Super Secret Surprise Best First True Date Ever to, well, just about anywhere in Colby. I was also pretty sure I'd just gotten a whiff of popcorn, which meant we were somewhere near the boardwalk, but the wind was blowing too hard for me to be any more specific.

"Okay, now, step up one step." I did, feeling his hand support my elbow. "And one more. Perfect. Now take two steps back, keep your eyes closed, and count to ten."

"Theo," I protested, as he dropped his hand. "Do we really—"

"To ten!" he repeated, his voice now farther away.

"One, two, three," I began. Some sand blew in my face. "Four, five, six . . ."

"Go more slowly!"

"Se-ven. Eight. Ni-ine . . ."

Suddenly he was back beside me, sliding his hand over mine. When I got to ten, I opened my eyes.

The first thing I saw, no surprise, was the ocean. Then I realized we were on a wooden platform, dusted with sand, that held a small wooden table and chairs. The table was set with a bottle of wine, two glasses, and a white paper bag. I looked behind me, expecting to see a house, but there was only a rise of dune, dotted with driftwood.

"Wow," I said. "Is this—"

"Isn't it *great?* I found it while I was running the other morning. It's like this perfect spot in the middle of nowhere. The table and chairs were just tossed to the side, so I pulled them over."

"It's beautiful," I told him.

He squeezed my hand, clearly pleased with himself. "Well, there's much more to come. This is only the beginning of the Best First True Date Ever. Here, let me get us some wine."

He walked over to the table, pulling the cork from the bottle there. As he busied himself pouring, I turned slightly, hoping so much that the walkway he'd led me down from the car was *not* lined with a white fence. It was. Worse, there were still scraps of yellow ribbon tied to it.

In the two weeks or so since Theo and I started hanging out regularly, I'd learned a few things about him. First, he liked pomp. Everything was an Event, with a Specific and Special Moniker. Hence, our first kiss was referred to as the Big Club Big Moment, our developing relationship part of his Best Summer Ever. Likewise, this evening, which he'd planned to compensate for the rushed and somewhat chaotic state of our getting together, was our First True Date. After being with Luke, who had to be reminded of any and all occasions and still forgot my birthday regularly, I found this kind of adorable.

At the same time, for all his incredibly sweet intentions, Theo's surprises and Big Moments were often, for me at least, tinged with a sense of awkwardness. Everything he found novel, charming, and amazing here, I'd known my whole life. Which meant knowing the backstory of them all as well.

Like, for instance, this spot. It was not a table in the middle of nowhere; in fact, a year earlier, there had been a set of stairs attached to this platform, which was in turn attached to a house. Both had been swept away by a freak storm that had hit us fast and hard in September—between ostensibly "more serious" hurricanes—that also claimed a life of a neighbor, who was hit by a flying deck board while trying to save the family's loose dog. Bad enough to lose your house to something big and scary enough to have its own name. But this was nothing anyone really saw coming. Of course, Theo had no way of knowing this. To him, it was just a pretty place, not sacred ground.

This same thing had happened, albeit on lesser levels, the other times he'd tried to put together Big Impressive Moments. There was his discovery of the "great hole-in-the-wall restaurant" where I'd actually eaten with Luke on one of our first dates, not to mention many after. His excitement about the dusty Island Drive-In Movie Theatre—complete with old-timey speakers!—which I associated only with peach brandy and my first hangover. Also the lagoon behind the mall, where for a quarter you could buy some dog kibble to throw to the voracious snapping turtles. They rose up from below the water, looking positively primordial, and had been a favorite of mine for as long as I could remember. Which made it considerably harder to feign the level of excitement he clearly felt showing them to me, although I did my best.

That was the thing about Theo, though. His enthusiasm *was* contagious. There was something so genuine and honest about how pumped up he got over the smallest things. I'd seen glimpses of it with the milk crate at Gert's, as well as him meeting Clyde the day of the Big Club Big Moment. Now that we were together regularly, however, I understood it to be a core part of his personality. He didn't play it cool. He didn't play at anything. He just *was*, and it made me want to be, too. Even if I sometimes felt a bit guilty doing so.

"Okay," he said now, holding out a plastic cup of wine to me. I walked over to him, taking it, and sat down at the table. He cleared his throat. "A toast. To the Best Summer Ever. And to you."

"To you," I repeated. We clinked glasses and drank, with me wincing a bit at the taste. I was used to watered-down keg beer, and Theo's love of wine, red in particular, was something I was still adjusting to.

"Oh! Almost forgot." He put down his glass and reached forward for the folded paper bag. "I brought snacks and apps, as well."

"Snacks and apps?"

"Cocktail food," he explained, opening the bag. "That's what my parents called it. Every night between five and six, they had drinks, snacks, and apps. Usually martinis, olives, and either herring or salmon dip with rice crackers."

I had not eaten one of these things, ever. Instead of sharing this, though, I said, "Really."

He nodded, taking a carryout box from the bag. "But don't worry. That's not what I brought. I know it's not exactly for everyone."

I smiled, watching as he removed two other small boxes from the bag. While he opened and arranged them neatly in a row on the table, I tried not to think of my dad and the two cold beers he drank most evenings. But it wasn't like I'd envisioned our families being similar. Nothing else was.

Theo had grown up in both New York and Connecticut, attending private schools. His father was a psychiatrist, his mother an editor at a publishing house that specialized in travel and art books. They'd had him late—he claimed "our pleasant surprise" was his family nickname—and he'd been raised making the rounds of art openings, symphony performances, and operas. They did not have a television when he was a kid, and never kept junk food in the house. He'd actually had his first Cheez Doodle a few days earlier, with me.

It wasn't like I'd planned on indoctrinating him in the orange delights that were my favorite snack food. I'd just picked up a bag from the Gas/Gro after a hard day at work and brought them with me when I went to pick him up. That was the other thing: Theo didn't drive, at least not confidently. He had a license, but because he spent most of his time in the city, he didn't use it much, and was much more comfortable riding shotgun than behind the wheel. Which didn't bother me, since I was the exact opposite. Riding made me nervous. It had been a running joke between Luke and me how uncomfortable I was in the passenger seat, always looking both ways in tandem with him and eyeing the speedometer when it crept higher than I thought it should be going.

That day, when I pulled up to Sand Dollars, Theo came out and got in the car, then leaned over to kiss me. When we finally broke apart, he eyed the Doodles in my lap. "Is that your dinner?"

"Nope. Just a snack," I said, popping one into my mouth. "You want one?"

"Okay."

I held out the bag, then watched as he carefully extracted one. After examining as if it was an artifact from another civilization, he finally popped it into his mouth. Then he chewed, a pensive look on his face, before swallowing and saying, "Huh. Interesting."

"What is?" I asked, putting the car in reverse.

"That . . . whatever it is," he said, gesturing to the bag. "Cheese Bomb?"

"Cheez Doodle." I glanced over at him. "What, does it taste weird or something?"

"I don't know. It's the first one I've ever eaten."

This statement warranted a full stop of the car. I turned to face him. "You've never had a Cheez Doodle before?"

"Well, I have *now*," he said.

"You're twenty-one years old," I said slowly. "And that was your first?"

"Yeah." He smiled. "What? Is that weird?"

Yes, I thought. Out loud I said, "Not weird. Just uncommon. These things were, like, part of our regular diet in our house when we were kids."

"Really." He glanced at the bag again. "Wow. They're, um, awfully orange."

I looked at the bag. "That's the cheese."

"Oh, right. Of course."

We backed down the rest of the driveway, and I ate another Doodle, surprised at how self-conscious I suddenly felt. Now, though, with this mention of the herring dip and olives, it made more sense. His life was a long way from mine. But we *were* getting closer. One piece of junk food and glass of wine at a time.

"Okay," he said now, with the voice I'd come to recognize as his ceremonious one. "Snacks and apps. These are all from the Reef Room. We have their homemade wasabi peas and peanuts mix, shrimp puffs, and, your favorite, the chicken satay."

"Wow," I said, looking across the spread. Actually, I was more a shrimp burger girl and hated horseradish in any form. Still, as he fixed a little plate for me on the top of one of the containers, I didn't say any of this. "This looks great."

"Is that your phone?"

"What?"

He nodded at my pocket, adding another shrimp puff. "Your phone. I think it's ringing."

"Oh. Sorry." I slid it out and glanced at the screen, then hit the mute button. "It's just my father. He'll leave a message."

"You don't want talk to him?"

I tried a wasabi pea. Ugh. I took a sip of wine, which didn't help matters. "I rarely do, actually."

"I'm surprised," he observed, now making his own plate. "You seemed pretty close the other night at the Laundromat, when he came to help Clyde with that hole in the ceiling."

I picked up a piece of chicken. "That was my dad."

"Your . . . ?" He looked confused. Then, "Oh, right. I keep forgetting you have two."

"Only one dad. And one father."

"Similar words," he pointed out.

"But not similar things. At least not in my life." I was feeling myself getting less and less hungry by the second, discussing this. "It's a long story."

"We've got time." He took a sip of his wine, savoring it. "I mean, if you feel like talking about it."

I didn't, actually. But since I was also now keenly aware of a woman in a Finz shirt power walking down the beach past our little date, eyeing us disapprovingly, I needed a distraction. "My father got my mom pregnant the summer before her senior year of high school. He disappeared from our lives pretty soon after. She married my *dad* when I was three. My father and I haven't ever been close, really. The only stuff we've ever had in common has been school related."

"School," he repeated, pouring some more wine.

I nodded. "First just what I was learning, reading, that kind of thing. But when I was sixteen and started looking into colleges, he was suddenly very invested. Said he would handle tuition, bought me books, coached me about applications and essays. He really wanted me to go to an Ivy, or someplace of equal stature."

"And that's a bad thing?"

I glanced up at him. He was listening while swishing around the wine in his glass, something I'd noticed was a habit of his. It was like it tasted better if he kept it moving, or something. "No. But then, when I did get into Columbia, he told me he actually couldn't pay after all. And then instead of explaining why, or really saying anything, he just disappeared. Again."

Now, he looked up at me. "You got into Columbia?"

I wasn't sure if I should be flattered or insulted by how surprised he sounded. "Yeah."

"Wow. You weren't kidding about the SAT thing," he said. "You must have seriously aced that verbal."

I had. Not that I needed to tell him that, so instead, I shrugged. "I did okay."

"Why aren't you going there?"

"I couldn't afford it."

"That's what student loans are for, though," he said. "Debt is part of education."

"Well," I said. "Not in my family, I guess."

"Your parents didn't want you to go to Columbia?" he asked. "That's crazy. Do they even know how hard it is to get into?"

"My dad's a contractor," I pointed out. "And East U gave me a full scholarship. It made no sense to go into some huge debt."

"Yes, but they're not the same caliber of school. I mean, no offense, but really . . ." He shook his head. "Not even close."

"Yeah." I bit my lip. "I guess not."

He looked at me, but I just turned my head to the ocean, forcing myself to take a deep breath. Here I was, sitting on the remains of someone's house, drinking wine I didn't like, with food I could barely tolerate, while rehashing the worst part of the past year. There are just moments when you look up from any one place and realize, suddenly, you have no idea how you got there.

"Wow," Theo said after a moment. I was still studying the waves, crashing in front of us. A few tern circling overhead, taking occasional dives. "Our First Fight. And it only took ten days."

Even after such a short time, I could say that this sentence was pretty much Theo encapsulated. Not only did he know the exact duration of Our Time Together, but our first fractious moment already had a moniker. "Are we fighting?"

"I offended you." It was a statement, not a question. I turned to look at him. "I'm sorry, Emaline. I just . . . education is a big deal in my family. It arouses passions."

I nodded. "We feel that way about college football."

I was kidding, although I realized, a beat later, he might not have realized it. We sat there another moment in silence while I tried another wasabi peanut. Still kind of gross. But the wine, surprisingly, was kind of growing on me.

"And," he added, "I didn't get into Columbia."

I raised my eyebrows. "No?"

"My verbal was nothing to sneeze at, either." He sighed. "It was my first choice."

"No way."

"Yep." Another wrist flick, sending the wine swishing. "Don't get me wrong, I love NYU. But it still nags at me sometimes."

I didn't say anything. Instead I just looked down at the table and the faint layer of sand covering it. I drew a circle in it with my finger, slowly. "I know a lot of people would have found a way to make Columbia work. But it just wasn't going to happen for me. But the fact that he never explained what happened and disappeared . . . it just made it worse."

"It's a big promise to break," Theo agreed.

"He blew off my graduation, too. Never responded to the invite. I didn't hear from him until that day you saw us at the Reef Room."

"What, a couple of weeks ago?" I nodded. "Ouch."

"I know."

He was quiet for a minute. "Did he ever tell you what happened? Like, why he suddenly couldn't pay?"

I shook my head. "Now I know his marriage was falling apart. But he never gave that as a reason. He can't even talk about it, period. The couple of times the subject of college has come up, even fleetingly, he looks like he might implode or something."

A pause. Then he said, "Man. He's probably embarrassed."

I raised my eyebrows. "How do you figure?"

"It makes sense," he said. "This is a guy who had never

lived up to his obligation as a parent, right? Finally here's his chance. He's going to help you get into college and pay for it. Does it make up for everything? No. But it *is* Columbia. A dream come true, right?"

It wasn't my dream, though, I thought. But I didn't say this.

"But then," he continued, "he screws *that* up, too. Talk about humiliating. Man."

It was taking me a minute to catch up with this reasoning; there was a delay, like on live broadcasts. Finally I said, "But I was fine with going to East U, even after all we'd done. I didn't care about Columbia. I would have told him that, if he'd just stuck around and been honest with me."

"Maybe. But I bet for him, it wasn't just about getting you into any old school," Theo told me. "This was a chance he could give you that no one else in your life could. Something that could change *everything*. He was so close to redeeming himself. Which made it even worse when he didn't."

"It wasn't about him, though."

"True. But the bottom line is that, as humans, we are by nature selfish creatures. The only way we care about anything, really, is by making it about us." He leaned forward a bit, looking more closely at me. "Look, I'm not saying he handled the whole thing well. I'm just saying . . . maybe there was more to it than you think."

By this point, I felt unsettled, like my view of something I'd taken as fact was suddenly being shifted, and in doing so was skewing everything else I believed as well. Beneath all that, barely but still there, something else. This tiny feeling that maybe, just maybe, he might be right.

"If that's what he was feeling, he should have said as much," I managed finally. "He's a grown-up. He can use his words."

"Absolutely," he agreed. "Again: not handled well. But he's here now, right? Maybe he wants to make amends somehow."

"Maybe. But I'm not holding my breath."

He ate a shrimp puff. "Sorry. My optimism can be very annoying."

Hearing this, I again had a flash of Benji, telling me he was hard to entertain. Now that I thought about it, they were pretty similar, at least by the numbers: parent professions, where they were raised. There was probably something meaningful to them both converging on me simultaneously. Not that I was in the mood, right then, to figure out what it was.

"It's not annoying," I told him. "Just different. Like the Cheez Doodle thing."

He smiled at me, then got up, coming over to where I was sitting, his glass in hand. He held it out, and I did the same. "To optimism. And junk food."

We clinked glasses and drank. Then he leaned down, cupping my chin in his hand, and kissed me. I closed my eyes, letting myself forget where I was and what I was doing, temporarily, to just sink into it. It was almost easy to do, except for the fine grains of sand I felt blow up and over us every now and again. Light and drifting, tiny granules you couldn't even see. But as always, they were there.

*   *   *

The next morning, when I woke up, someone was moving the furniture.

I could hear it immediately, the sound of large objects being pushed and pulled. I pressed my pillow over my ears, trying to dip back into dreaming, but no luck. Saturday morning, seven thirty. I was up.

More scraping, more dragging, followed by a large thud as something hit the floor. I threw off the covers, got out of bed, and went to investigate. When I pushed open my door, however, it moved only about an inch before meeting something solid and refusing to go farther.

I tried again. No luck. Finally, by using my entire body weight, I managed to get it open enough to see out, only to find myself facing the glass doors of the breakfront from our dining room.

"What the hell?" I said, to my own face, dimly reflected back at me. It wasn't just the china cabinet that had relocated; there was also the coffee table, the dining room table, several chairs, and my dad's beloved recliner—all packed into the narrow hall outside my bedroom, as if, en masse, they were making a run for it.

"Hello?" I called down the hallway towards the stairs. With all the noise, though, nobody heard me. I considered just staying put until whatever project was going on was finished, but then my tendency towards claustrophobia hit. I tried the door again. It moved another millimeter. The window it was.

There is probably something more humiliating than climbing out of your own bedroom window in full view of the neighbors early on a weekend morning. But really, I was hard-pressed to think of what it might be as I wriggled through, landed on my behind in the damp grass in my pajamas, and turned to see that Mr. Varance, the elderly widower to our right, had caught the whole show. He raised up his rose clippers in greeting; I waved back. Then I got to my feet and went around the house to the back door.

My mother was at the sink, already dressed, rinsing out a coffee cup. She didn't see me until she was turning off the water, at which point she shrieked, jumping backwards and disappearing, momentarily, from my view. When she popped up again, she was pissed.

"What are you doing?" she huffed at me, through the glass. "You scared me to death!"

"I was barricaded in my room," I replied. "The window was the only way out."

In response, she turned, looking behind her at my dad, who was at that very moment carrying the couch onto the side deck. Morris, at the opposite end, was already outside. "Oh," she said. "Sorry. I think he thought—"

"Can you let me in, please?" I interrupted her, aware of my damp backside and the fact that Mr. Varance could probably still see it.

She scurried over to the door and unlocked it, then held it open as I came in. "I think he thought," she said again, "that you were already gone."

"My car is here," I pointed out. "And it's not even eight on a Saturday."

"I'm not driving this train," she said, holding up one hand. "Take it up with him."

When I turned to my dad to do just that, I instead found myself facing Morris, who was grinning. "Nice jammies," he said. "You always sleep in the grass?"

I looked down. There were green clippings all across my tank top and midsection. Of course the lawn had been mowed yesterday. "What are you even doing here?" I asked him.

"Working," he replied, as if this was something he actually did, ever.

"All right, let's get that love seat out and that should do it," my dad said, walking back into the room. When he saw me, he said, "Whoa. What happened to you?"

"I had to climb out the window," I replied.

"Why's that?" I just looked at him. "Oh, right. The hallway. Well, you knew the floors were getting started today. Can't do them with the furniture here."

"How was I supposed to know that, again?"

He bent over one end of the love seat, gesturing for Morris to get the other one. "About the floors?"

"Yes."

"Because," he said, squaring his shoulders and lifting, "we did the trim, then painted. Floors are next."

As if I had some kind of flow chart in my mind, keeping up with every step of this never-ending remodel. "I'm not a contractor, Dad."

"No," he said, holding up his end of the couch, "but you are in our way. Scoot, now, we've got work to do."

I moved aside as they passed by, taking the love seat out the door I'd come in. My mom, standing across the empty room, held up two coffee mugs, a questioning look of her face. When I nodded, she gestured for me to follow her down the hall to Amber's room.

"You'd think," I said as we walked, "he could leave me a note or something."

"I think the plan was to let you know when you got home last night," she replied. "But you were . . . late."

Whoops. I bit my lip, remembering how far past curfew I'd actually walked in from the First True Date the evening before. Late enough that my dad had gone to bed, something he rarely did before everyone was in and accounted for.

"I lost track of the time," I said. "Sorry."

She said nothing to this as she pushed the door open, revealing Amber, her now-blonde head buried under the covers. We walked over to the bed, where my mom nudged her aside, making a narrow space for us to share. She pulled up the comforter over our legs, handed me my coffee, and we settled in.

"I don't understand," I said, after a couple of sips, "why he can't just let it be."

"Who?"

"Dad. And the house. Why is this"—I swirled my hand in the general direction of the door—"always going on?"

She shrugged. "Don Quixote had windmills. The Wright

brothers had the sky. Your dad has home improvement."

"But it was fine like it was before the *last* project. And the one before that, actually."

"Well, fine is a relative term. And your dad has always wanted better than that for us." She twisted her cup in her hands. "You see a perfectly good dining room and kitchen. He sees the potential for a great one."

"Right now I just see furniture in the hallway and us in Amber's bed."

"Which," my sister's voice came, muffled by the pillow, "I bet is looking pretty good to you right now, huh, Miss Get-Out-of-My-Room-or-Else?"

I kicked her, albeit gently, with my foot. "You owe me."

"Says you." She grunted, turning over. "And for the record, I was actually sleeping before you two decided to pig-pile in here. Some of us have to work today, you know."

Amber, as part of her cosmetology school training, spent one morning a week shampooing and sweeping up hair at a local salon. From the way she talked about it, you would have thought it was the chain gang. I kicked her again. This time, she kicked me back.

"Girls," my mom said, in the same tired voice I'd heard her utter this word at least a million times before.

For a moment, we just sat there not talking, the only sound the sputtering of some kind of machine starting up down in the living room. Finally my mom said, "The floor issue aside, Emaline, you really haven't been around here much lately. I miss you."

"You see me at work every day."

"True," she agreed. "But it's not the same. And with you leaving at the end of the summer . . ."

"It's still June," I pointed out now. "I leave in August. We've got weeks."

"And you have a new boyfriend," she replied, taking a sip of her coffee.

I looked at her. "This isn't about Theo."

"No, it's about Mom being codependent," Amber said from underneath the comforter, her voice muffled. "God, you'd think she was going to be left on a desert island alone or something. Hello, the rest of us will still be here. Only Emaline is going anyplace."

My mom sniffed. "But she is going."

"You did fine when Margo left," I told her.

"I gained fifteen pounds!"

Whoops. I'd forgotten about the onset of her sudden, and serious, Twix bar habit. "It's not fair to make me feel bad for going to school. You would have killed me if I hadn't gone."

"Says the Smart One and the Favorite," Amber added.

"I have no favorites," my mom said, another of her mantras. To me she added, "I just thought you'd be home more this summer. And then you and Luke broke up, and . . ."

"So this *is* about Theo," I said.

"Yep," Amber replied.

"Not exactly," my mom protested. "He seems perfectly nice. And I do want you to be happy. But it's just . . . different. And so suddenly so."

I felt tired just hearing this. Mostly because, even though

I was perfectly happy with my life and love life as it was, I seemed to be the only one. Luke had his faults, too, but at least he'd been familiar. Theo was Not From Here, didn't drive, wore girl jeans, and was monopolizing my time, all of which were apparently punishable offenses. The thing was, he wasn't getting penalized. Just me.

"Luke cheated on me," I reminded my mother, again. "With a girl he met at Tallyho."

"Plus," Amber added, "he's already got a new girlfriend anyway."

I turned, looking down at her. "What?"

"You didn't know?" she asked. I shook my head. "Oh. Sorry."

"Who is she?"

"This friend of Brooke's, Jacqueline Best. She was my year. You know her, red hair, really pretty. Drives that black convertible."

None of these were ringing bells, for which I was actually kind of grateful. In some cases, and especially small towns, it's better when it's the devil—or girl—you don't know.

"My yearbook's over on that shelf," Amber offered. "If you want, you can look her up, critique her outfit, black out her eyes."

Which is just what she would have done—half the girls' pictures in her class had already been defaced in this way. Amber was known for having a long, ever-changing list of enemies. "No, thanks," I said. "I've moved on, too, remember?"

She shrugged. "Up to you."

I pushed myself off the bed, taking my mug with me. Immediately, Amber took up the space I'd vacated, burying her head again. I said to my mom, "You know, I thought you'd be glad I'm not dragging around all summer, crying about my broken heart."

"Of course I am," she replied. "It's just . . ." She trailed off, shaking her head. The half-finished sentences were the worst, as if she expected me to somehow fill in the blanks for her.

I forced myself to take a breath before saying, "Just what?"

I was standing in the half-open door now, with her still on the bed, her legs pulled up to her chest. I watched as she closed her eyes, then looked up at the ceiling for a long moment. Finally, she said, "You're my baby. And I'm just really going to miss you, honey. That's all."

I bit my lip. "I'm going to miss you, too. But I'm not gone yet. Okay?"

She nodded, her eyes filling with tears. Oh, for God's sake, I thought, but just like that, I was gone, too, my vision blurring. I could handle just about anything but seeing my mother cry. It struck at something deep and primal in me, flipping a switch I couldn't reach no matter how I contorted myself. I put my mug down, then walked over to the bed and slid in beside her, looping my arms around her waist.

"I love you," she whispered into my hair. "To the moon and more."

This time, it was easy to know what to say. "The moon and more."

We stayed like that for a minute, the sounds from the living room muffled in the distance. Finally, Amber broke the silence. "Whenever you all are done, I could *really* use some coffee. I think it's the least you can do for co-opting my bed."

My mom elbowed her—more gently than I would have—then laughed. "Fine. But only because I need to get going anyway."

We started down the hallway, where the sputtering was still going. The living room, kitchen, and dining room were all empty now, sunlight slanting in on the bare floors. Morris and my dad were bent over some kind of compressor, a big floor sander now between them. From what I could see, the hardwood was just fine. Then again, I'd just see a windmill and an open sky, too, never feeling the need to conquer either. You think it's all obvious and straightforward, this world. But really, it's all in who is doing the looking.

13

"OKAY, SO WHAT I was thinking was that we'd take out these prints, and you could . . ."

"Holy crap. Is that *marble* over there on those counter-tops?"

Ivy pressed her lips together, which meant she was doing her best not to scream, berate, or otherwise verbally abuse someone. This was an effort that, in my experience at least, she made only when it came to Clyde.

"I have no idea," she told him, her voice flat. "But as I was saying, about the prints . . ."

"It can't be marble," Clyde said, craning his neck to look at the kitchen again. "Nobody would be stupid enough to spend money on that for a rental, would they, Emaline?"

I glanced at Ivy again, having learned my lesson about commentary from the peanut gallery while she was filming. She sighed, giving me a nod. I said, "It's granite."

"You sure?"

"Yep. It's on the Web site write-up."

"Man." Clyde whistled between his teeth. "Granite. Add that up with just the fridge over there and you've got more money than the value of my entire house."

"I'm sure that's not true," Ivy said.

"Pretty close."

"Would you like to prove it? I'll grab a camera and we can go there right now."

Now I bit *my* lip, ducking over the payroll sheet I was filling out at the kitchen island. It was odd to admit, but at times like this, I actually felt kind of bad for Ivy. She was so desperate to get into Clyde's head, to win his trust and open access to his world, and yet she kept doing things that did the exact opposite. Like when he balked at her suggestion that they do interviews at his home, she told him to come here. Bad, bad idea.

"Why?" Theo had asked me earlier, when I'd come with the sandwiches from Da Vinci's I'd picked up for our lunch, only to find him busy getting the main room set up for filming. "This is a great space."

"This is a mansion."

He put down the light he was carrying, then glanced around, as if seeing it all for the first time. "You think?"

"You don't?"

"It's a rental house," he replied, shrugging. "I mean, it's nice. But it's not a Central Park penthouse."

"Clyde grew up on a dairy farm, Theo."

"And went on to be a successful artist in New York. He's no stranger to money, if the names of the collections that have bought his work are any indication." He nodded at *Modern Coast*, the large, glossy book with pictures of many of Clyde's paintings that I was flipping through. "He's seen fancier than this, I promise you."

"Maybe in New York," I said. "But this is Colby. It's going to be a distraction."

"I don't think you give him enough credit," he replied. "It'll be fine."

Now, I glanced over at Theo, who had studiously avoided eye contact with me since Clyde's arrival. Which, sure enough, had been followed by him insisting on the full house tour, during which he expressed awe, shock, and amazement over everything from the crown molding to the large soaking tubs in every bathroom. I kept quiet. Nobody likes to hear "I told you so."

"Emaline," Clyde called out now, gesturing at the long, double-story-height windows beside him, "you have any idea what the window budget was for this place?"

"No, can't say I do."

"Had to be at *least* one hundred and fifty, I'm guessing," he mused. "I mean, you look at how much glass and it's already gonna be a lot. But the sizes of these big ones? And the shapes of some had to be custom—"

"We get it," Ivy said loudly, cutting him off. "The house is grand and opulent, entirely excessive, and therefore we are offensive for living in it. Can we talk about your work now?"

He looked at her, surprised. I think we all were. So far, Ivy had played all of Clyde's games, from reading Irma Jean Rankles to, most recently, enduring a hands-on fish-cleaning tutorial he insisted was crucial for understanding of his collage technique. Now, suddenly and finally, she'd had enough.

I expected Clyde to get up and leave, or at least fire back.

Instead, for the first time I could remember on camera, he smiled. "You think I'm saying you're offensive?"

"I think," Ivy replied, "that considering how much you talk about wasting money, you have absolutely no problem with wasting time. Especially mine."

Yikes, I thought. Now Theo did look at me, both of us totally on edge. I was beginning to wish I'd eaten lunch at the office.

"I'm wasting your time," Clyde repeated. He was still smiling. In fact, he looked more comfortable than I'd seen him so far in this entire process.

"From day one," Ivy replied, clearly emboldened now. "It's one thing if you have no respect for your own work. But by diminishing the value of both our passion for it and the project we are making *out* of that passion, you insult us both. And frankly, I'm tired of pretending otherwise. So if you want to talk about windows, or countertops—"

"Tell me what you want to know," Clyde said. "Right now. Tell me."

Ivy leaned forward, over the clipboard in her lap. "Why did you leave New York and stop making art?"

A beat. Then another, before Clyde replied, "I sold a painting for a half a million dollars. It made me sick to my stomach. I was twenty-seven years old and I didn't know who I was anymore."

Silence. All I could hear was the ocean outside. When I swallowed, it sounded deafening. Ivy said, "This was *Terns*?"

"Yeah." Clyde picked up the book I'd been looking at earlier and flipped through the pages. It was weird for this to be the only noise in this huge house. He found the page, then looked at it for a long moment. "It's canvas, ground shells, plaster, some tubes of paint. You think that's worth a half a million bucks?"

"I think it was the centerpiece of your first solo show. I think it put you, officially, on the map as one of the rising stars of the art world at the time."

"You're not answering my question."

"I'm not sure I understand it."

Clyde looked back down at the photo, and I realized I was holding my breath. "The last year before he sold the farm, my father made thirty thousand dollars. And that was a *good* year. Farming is back-breaking, soul-killing work. His body was ravaged by the time he was sixty."

Nobody said anything. Outside, some kids were running along the water, a kite bobbing over them. Clyde lifted up the book, turning it so Ivy could see the picture. "Canvas. Ground shells. Plaster. Paint. It was like an insult to him. *I* felt like an insult to him."

From where I was sitting, the photo was just a blur of grays and blacks. Ivy studied it for a moment. "But you were his son, and that was your work. You were getting paid for it. He could have taken it as partially his accomplishment as well, no?"

No, I thought, at the same moment that Clyde shook his head. It would have been the same with my own parents. No matter how proud they were, that much money would change the balance, not only affecting how they viewed me but also making them assume I viewed them differently as well. Even if I didn't.

"If I stayed in New York and lived that life, making that

kind of money from then on, I knew I'd become an asshole," Clyde said now. "But turning away and coming back here . . . that made me one, too. I couldn't win."

Ivy said, "But you did come back."

"Yeah." He looked out the window, at the kite bobbing, barely visible above the deck rail. "And I'm such an asshole."

No one contested this. Not then, and not in the next half hour that I remained there, watching silently as they continued to talk. Clyde said a lot more about his work, his choices, his regrets. Glimpses here and there of things he might have done differently, or not, like a collage of words instead of materials. He didn't speak to anyone but Ivy. He didn't take breaks or ask questions about the house. And at one o'clock, when I slipped out the door to go back to work, I was pretty sure he didn't even notice.

* * *

When I pulled up at the office, my father's Subaru—recognizable by both color and its Connecticut plates—was parked right outside. I passed the open space beside it, which I would have taken otherwise, and parked around back instead. Then I came in through the supply room, as quietly as possible, so I could see what was going on.

As it was early afternoon on a Monday, things were pretty slow. My grandmother was on the phone, Rebecca sat picking at a salad at the front desk, and my mom was nowhere to be seen. I could hear my father in Margo's office, so I dodged it, ducking into my grandmother's instead, where I slid into a chair that gave me a clear view while still being hidden myself.

"Rolo?" she asked me, nodding at a half-open pack on the corner of the desk. I took one, sneaking a quick look at Margo, who was now getting to her feet as my father did the same. As they left her office and headed for the door, she suddenly glanced over, spotting me, and I ducked back out of sight. But not quickly enough.

The front door of the office swung shut. A moment later, though, I could just *feel* her in my grandmother's doorway, even with the file cabinet solidly between us. "What *is* it with you two? He's not a monster, you know."

My grandmother grabbed another Rolo. "He's not Santa, either."

"Who else is hiding from him?" I asked.

"Your mother," they said in unison. My grandmother pointed at me. "She was in that same spot until he turned his back long enough for her to escape."

"Personally, I'm thrilled he's here," Margo said, adjusting her purse. "We're going to North Reddemane to look at that house. If it's half as nice as he thinks, I'm looking at a good chance for a decent commission."

"It is," I told her. "I was just there last week, when I was hanging out with Benji."

"Is that the little boy that was here?" my grandmother asked.

"My half brother. He's ten." I looked at Margo. "Where is he now?"

"I sent him out with Morris," Margo said.

"With who?"

"Morris," she said, as if this was just the most normal

thing you could do with a child. "What? He stopped by looking for you, the kid was bored, and we needed to talk business. I gave him ten bucks, told him to go get ice cream or something."

Ice cream. She would not have had to tell him twice. Morris would do about anything for a fudge ripple from the Squeeze Serve.

"What I need from you," Margo continued, "is to keep an eye on him while we do this house thing, then bring him back to North Reddemane. Say, in an hour or so."

"What?" I said. "I have a job to do also, you know."

"Babysitting for a client who might make the agency money *is* your job," she replied. "Besides, he's your brother, Emaline. Honestly."

She turned, heading out of the office, and my grandmother watched her go, an amused look on her face. I pulled aside the nearby blind, looking out at my father, who was standing by his car, squinting in the sun. I knew it probably did look weird I'd gone to such lengths to avoid him. But ever since I'd discussed everything that had happened between us with Theo, the thought of seeing him made me more nervous than usual. It was one thing to be angry with him; that, I could handle. Pitying him, however, was an entirely new ball game, one I was not up for playing. At least not yet.

Once the coast was clear, I went outside just in time to catch Benji and Morris darting across the main road, ice cream in hand. "Squeeze Serve, huh?" I called out. "That's a serious Colby delicacy."

"Morris said fudge ripple is obligatory," Benji informed me.

"He used the word 'obligatory'?"

"Any other flavor's for punks," Morris told me, pretty much confirming my suspicions. "Is Margo still inside? I have her change. But it's not much. Squeeze Serve ain't cheap."

"She went to North Reddemane, to see the house," I told him. "I'm supposed to bring Benji back up there in a bit."

"I can take him, if you want," Morris offered. "I need to go to Gert's anyway."

"Yeah!" Benji said. "I can show you my magic set, like I told you about."

I looked at Morris. "You have a car? Since when?"

"Ivy said I could take the van. She wants me to go buy up all their milk crates, or something."

"Ivy?"

He turned, glancing at me. "Theo's boss. Remember her?"

"Yes, of course." I hated when anyone made me feel stupid, but when it was Morris it burned especially. "I just didn't realize you were still doing work for her."

"When she needs it. Which seems to be a lot lately. Seems your boyfriend's not much for heavy lifting."

"He's not my boyfriend," I muttered.

Just as I said this, the top of Benji's cone rolled off and down the front of his shirt, leaving a smear of chocolate sauce behind it. "Whoops," he said, and Morris snorted. Boys.

"Bathroom's inside, just down the hall and to the right," I told him.

"Right," he said, handing off the cone to me. I held it at arm's length, not wanting to risk my own shirt, as Morris and I sat down on the steps to wait for him.

"Thanks for taking him," I said. "I'm sure he loved it."

"He'd never been before," he replied. "Every kid needs a Squeeze Serve."

I thought of Theo, with his Cheez Doodle. It was a summer of firsts, apparently. "He's a good kid."

Morris nodded, not replying. We sat there a moment, just watching the traffic, before he said, "He knows about the divorce, you know."

It took me a minute to understand. "What? When did they tell him?"

"They didn't." He leaned back, resting one knobby elbow on the next step and folding the other behind his head. "But he's not stupid. He can tell what's going on."

"He told you that?"

"He told me his parents are splitting, that his dad is moving out when they get back."

I thought of Benji, feeling a pang in my stomach. "God. That sucks."

Morris shrugged. "He doesn't seem too broken up about it."

"I doubt he'd tell you if he was. He just met you."

"Yeah," he agreed, "but when you go for Squeeze Serve with someone, it's a safe zone. What's said there, stays there."

I looked at him. "I think that's Las Vegas."

"That, too."

I rolled my eyes, leaning back beside him. I had no memory of my father with my mother, and therefore no feelings when it came to thinking of them apart. But my mom with my dad—that was different. Even when I was ten, and they'd been married only a few years, to lose my sense of my immediate family would have been devastating. If I was honest, actually, it wouldn't be much easier now. Then I thought of something.

"You were around that age, right?" I asked him. "When your parents split?"

"Nine," he replied.

"I think it's going to be hard for him," I said now, keeping my eyes on the sky overhead. "You know?"

"Maybe," he said. "Or maybe not. Staying together isn't always better."

He didn't elaborate. Morris wasn't much on talking about his past—or anything, really—but from what I'd been able to cobble together, his life had been a lot different before the divorce. His parents owned their house and he spent a lot of time with his dad's extended family, most of whom lived in Cape Frost. I'd even seen a few pictures of him with a black cat, obviously a beloved pet, in the one box of photographs they kept on their coffee table. He'd never mentioned any of these things, though. Like when the marriage ended, they did as well.

I nudged his foot with mine. "You know, I'm going to miss you."

"I'm just going to Gert's," he said.

I sighed. "I meant in the fall, moron."

I heard the office door chime sound, then footsteps. A beat later, Benji appeared, looking up at us. "You guys sunbathing?"

"Something like that," I said, getting up and handing him his now-melty cone. "You ready to go?"

"Yep. I got some Rolos for the ride." He held out his hand, showing me. "Want one?"

"Nah," I said, ruffling his hair. Like always, he leaned into me slightly, like a dog. "Thanks, though."

"Morris?" Benji asked.

"Heck yeah. Toss me one." A Rolo went flying over my head and Morris grabbed it. "Thanks."

The candy tossing, and other stupid behavior, went on pretty much all the way to Sand Castles. Having two sisters, I wasn't used to so much boy around me all the time. By the time we pulled into the driveway, I was more than ready to be rid of them.

"I'll see you soon, okay?" I said to Benji, as we all got out. "We'll go golfing again, or something."

"Yeah? Awesome!"

I waved, then started up towards the house to say hello to Theo. I was almost to the steps when Morris called out, "Hey. Emaline."

"Yeah?"

"You know I'll miss you, too."

"Yeah, I know." I smiled. "Talk later."

"Talk later."

So ridiculous, I thought, swallowing over the lump that was suddenly in the back of my throat as he backed down the driveway. I climbed up the stairs and knocked on the door, taking a few deep breaths. But even with my best efforts, and knowing how silly the reason, when Theo opened the door he still had to ask me why I was crying.

14

MOST PLACES IN town were not open at eight thirty a.m. on a Saturday. But the Colby Fitplex was not like most places.

It was a gym, although in my experience, there was never that much actual working out going on. This morning, for instance, as I got on the treadmill, the group I'd dubbed the Coffee Klatch was already at the tables by the front door. Senior citizens who gathered bright and early every day at the Fitplex, ostensibly to exercise, but mostly to shoot the breeze, their routine never varied. It went like this: fill coffee cup, drink slowly while seated and discussing town gossip and news, drag yourself over to ride the bike for five minutes or do one set on a machine on the lowest-weight setting; repeat.

There were some people exercising. Like the diminutive woman in her early sixties who always showed up clad in a leotard, tights, and a headband of varying neon colors. She'd stretch extensively, then do a routine with five-pound dumbbells, facing the mirror, with the seriousness and exertion level of an Olympic power lifter. There were grunts, gasps, and dramatic drops at the end of the set that sent the dumbbells bouncing across the floor to bump anyone who happened to be standing nearby. Which, more often than not, was an older fishing boat captain who showed up with his mat every morning, spreading it out to do the downward dogs and sun salutations he'd tell anyone who would listen had saved his bum knee from needing surgery.

Really, that was the true workout, avoiding the Klatch and the talkers so you could actually break a sweat.

I'd started coming to the Fitplex the previous fall, just as all my college stuff was really heating up. I kept waking up in the middle of the night, heart racing, panicking about essays and applications, unable to get back to sleep. I tried not eating before bed, giving up coffee, and making other major sacrifices, but nothing worked. Finally, my mom convinced me to go to the doctor, who diagnosed "situational anxiety" and told me to get some exercise. From then on, when I woke up super-early and couldn't calm down, I came here.

There was something oddly soothing about working out while the rest of the world was asleep. I drove down empty streets, past dark houses, the only stoplights blinking yellow. The Fitplex opened at six sharp, and invariably some of the Klatch was already there, getting the coffeemaker going, as I slipped in, scanned my membership card, and untangled my headphones from around my iPod. On the most stressful days, I hit the treadmill and ran for three or four miles. Other days, I did the elliptical or the bike. As long as I was moving, my heart pumping for reasons I could understand, I felt better. So much so that, once all the applications were in and I started sleeping through the night more regularly, I still dragged myself out of bed to work out a couple of mornings a week.

Now, as the older woman flexed her wiry, bird-like biceps at her reflection, I got on one of the open treadmills and cranked up the speed, starting with an easy jog. Because it was Saturday, and later than I normally showed up, the place was a bit more crowded, with people dotting the rows of machines here and there. The line of TVs were all on, some turned to morning news, one to a foodie show (which always seemed counterintuitive to me, watching people cook while running), another to a rerun of the same modeling reality show Amber always watched. With my music filling my ears, I alternated among them, which resulted in one crazy quilt of a show: headlines, celebrities, photo shoots, and corn bread preparation. When it got to be too much, I upped my speed and stared straight ahead at nothing. That's when I saw Luke's mom.

She was on one of the leg machines, doing a Klatch-like light and short set. As always, she looked totally put together: stretchy black pants, an East U T-shirt, and bright white running shoes, her hair pulled back in a pert ponytail. I suspected it was one of her first times at the Fitplex, both because I'd never seen her there before and by the workout she was doing, the same one they set up everyone with on the welcome tour. After a minute, I stopped watching her and put my head down, hoping that somehow this would also make me invisible to her.

No luck. Around mile two and a half, I happened to glance up at the clock on the opposite wall just as she was passing in front of it. Our eyes met, and I instantly felt my face flush even more. Before I could look away again, she was headed over.

This didn't surprise me. If Mrs. Templeton was anything, it was polite; she wasn't the type to dodge anyone due to awkwardness, or any other reason for that matter. I did my best to channel the same as she got closer, making myself smile as I slid off my headphones. Still, I didn't break stride.

"Emaline," she said warmly, smiling at me. "I didn't know you were a member here."

"I come for the treadmills," I replied. "Also, there aren't a lot of other gym options."

"So I discovered when I decided to get in shape for the wedding." She looked around the room, over at the Klatch, then back at me. "I'm determined to wear a sleeveless dress and *not* have my arms all jiggly. Although it may be a losing fight."

"No way," I told her. "You can build arms quickly. At least, that's what the magazines say."

She smiled at me, and I could just feel the Talking About Anything but Luke part of the conversation coming to an end. Sure enough, the next thing she said was, "We sure do miss you around the house lately."

I actually felt myself start running faster in reaction to this, and had to force a slowdown. "I miss you all, too."

It was true. I'd spent much of the last three years of my life over at the Templetons', sharing dinners, weekend barbecues, and holidays. I'd even been the one who named their dachshund: she was Grace, which was my grandmother's name. I *loved* that dog. It was such a weird thing how a breakup stretched much wider than you expected. You didn't just lose a person, but their entire world as well.

"Brooke is really hoping you'll still make the wedding," she continued, as I worried fleetingly if I was splattering sweat on her. She was the kind of person who prompted this sort of concern. I slowed down. "I hope you know we want you to be there. Regardless of what is going on with—"

"Of course," I said quickly, cutting her off. I felt so light-headed, suddenly. I wasn't even sure I could bear to hear her say his name, much less finish this sentence. "I wouldn't miss it."

She smiled at me, just as the woman in the leotard again dropped her weights with a clank, distracting both of us. When we regrouped, I nodded at the treadmill console and said, "Well, I should probably . . ."

"Oh, of course!" She laughed. "Forgive me. I couldn't even say one word while running at that speed, much less carry on a conversation."

I smiled, slipping my headphones back into my ears. "It's good to see you. Good luck with the workouts."

"I think I'll need it." And then, before I could react, she reached out to my sweaty right hand and patted it gently with her own. "You take care, honey."

I nodded, and then, thankfully, she was walking away, over towards the triceps machines. I found my spot on the wall again, cranked the speed up another two notches, and ran the last mile hard, almost wishing, at times like this, that I still had my applications to distract me. By the time I was done, she was gone.

* * *

"Okay. Keep your eyes closed."

Another date with Theo, another Big Surprise. It was embarrassing enough be sitting there, blind, in a public place. This time, though, I had an audience.

"Are you looking? Don't look."

"I'm not looking," I murmured, although I was sure everyone else was.

"Okay, one more second." I felt Theo back moving beside me; something bumped my elbow. "And . . . now. Open your eyes!"

I did. The first thing I saw was Morris, across from me, a bored, slightly annoyed look on his face. Beside him, Daisy appeared slightly alarmed. And then there was the sparkler.

It wasn't like I could miss it. It was one of those big ones, lit and spitting in all directions. At its base was a small, heart-shaped chocolate cake that had something written on it in pink icing, not that I could make it out through the pyrotechnics. I wasn't sure if I was supposed to blow this thing out or just let it run its course, so I just sat there watching it burn down, down, down until it ended with a fizzle, leaving a cloud of smoke behind.

"Wow," I said, as Daisy coughed, politely covering her mouth with her hand. "What's the occasion?"

"You don't know?" Theo asked me. A large group of tourists, sporting sunburns and fresh bathing-suit strap marks, were all watching us from the next table over. "It's our two week anniversary today."

"Oh, right," I said quickly, looking at him and smiling. "I just . . . the sparkler distracted me. Happy, um, anniversary."

"Happy anniversary," he repeated, then he leaned forward and kissed me. A real kiss, not the kind you normally engage in on a date with another couple when half the restaurant is watching. I felt so bad about forgetting the date, however, that I felt like I couldn't pull away as quickly as I would have liked. When we did finally break, I did everything to avoid seeing Daisy's face. She hated public displays of affection even more than mopeds and mom jeans.

Instead, I focused on removing the sparkler and setting it aside so I could read the message on the cake. WILL YOU . . . ? it said, the question mark ending in a fancy curlicue.

"Will I . . ." I repeated, glancing at Theo, "what?"

"That's the second part of the surprise," he replied, reaching inside his sport jacket and pulling out a pink piece of paper with a bow on it. "Here."

"Theo," I said. "This is too much."

"What? It's our anniversary. Open it."

Now I did risk a look at Daisy, only to see on her face something worse than offense or annoyance: pity. Oh, God, I thought. All I'd wanted, with this double date, was to show her and Morris why they were wrong about Theo. If I could just get us all together for one meal, I'd reasoned, they would quickly see he was not, as they thought, an obnoxious summer person, know-it-all, or big-city snob. Despite my best effort, though, so far I'd proven just the opposite.

It had started with the sport coat. Actually, scratch that. It had started with the restaurant. My idea was to go to the Inlet Drive-In, which had some of the best shrimp burgers in town, and just eat at the picnic tables there. We'd get some of our favorite food, and Theo would get to experience a bit of the real Colby, done our way. Win-win. But he had other ideas.

"A double date! Sounds great," he'd replied. "I just read about this new pan-Asian place in the paper. I'll make us a reservation."

"Pan-Asian?" I'd repeated. "In Colby?"

"No, it's somewhere else." He turned around from the kitchen sink, where he was busy washing some huge grapes Ivy apparently required to have on hand at all times, picking up his phone. After pushing a few buttons, he said, "Cape Frost. That's not far, right?"

"It's not close, exactly."

He squinted at the screen, reading off of it. "'Offering a range of both traditional and modern Asian fare, Haiku boasts an extensive sushi bar, a wide array of sake choices, and one of the best vegetarian menus in the area.' Great, right?"

"I guess," I said, sounding uncertain even to myself. "But it might be easier if we just, you know, stay closer to home and keep it simple."

"It doesn't get much simpler than sushi," he pointed out, going back to his grapes. "Fish. Rice. Seaweed."

"I don't think Morris is much of a fan of that."

"What about Daisy? I'm sure she has a more adventurous palate, right?"

"Why? Because she's Asian?"

He gave me a look. "Emaline. I don't stereotype."

"I'm just saying—"

"What I meant," he continued, over me, "is that Daisy, from what you've said, has a very urban sensibility when it comes to fashion. I figured that might apply to cuisine as well."

Now I felt like the one stereotyping, which was why I didn't tell him Daisy, for all her reading of *Vogue* and *Harper's Bazaar*, preferred pizza above just about all other food. "Sorry."

"It's okay." He was drying the grapes now, carefully, with a paper towel. "Look, just let me make a reservation. I promise, they'll like it."

So earlier that evening, I'd put on jeans and one of my nicer tops, pulled back my hair, and worn some eyeliner—all things I never would even think of doing for a shrimp burger at the Inlet. Because I was dressed differently, I probably shouldn't have been surprised to see Theo do the same. But the sport jacket still felt like a bit much.

He *was* wearing it casually, with jeans and a button-down white oxford shirt, expensive sneakers on his feet. Personally, though—and I knew this said more about me than him—I associated any kind of dress jacket with formals and funerals, not dinner. I could only hope Morris wasn't in shorts.

He was. And a T-shirt, albeit what looked like either a new or newly laundered one. Daisy, true to form, looked gorgeous in a floral dress and sandals, a simple white eyelet cardigan over her shoulders. When they walked out of the house, Theo jumped from his seat, opening the back door for her. Morris, not noticing, got in first.

Oh, dear, I thought. Out loud I said, "Everybody ready for a road trip?"

"Let's go to the Inlet," Morris asked. "I could *dominate* on a shrimp burger right now."

"We're going for sushi, remember?" Daisy said to him.

"I don't eat raw fish," he grumbled.

"You'll like this," Theo assured him. "They have a mix of modern and traditional fare."

Like this would be a selling point to Morris, who subsisted mainly on Nabs crackers, Mountain Dew, and sausage biscuits. Instead of thinking about this, I concentrated on the road. The next sign we passed said CAPE FROST: 32 MILES. Even though I risked a certain ticket going above the speed limit, I still felt every one of them.

Once at Haiku, I hoped for a reset, a chance to start things fresh. But as soon as we were seated, Morris looked at the menu and announced there was nothing on it he liked.

"It's, like, ten pages long," I pointed out to him.

"I don't eat raw food," he said again.

"It's not all raw."

"Look," Daisy said, turning to one of the last pages. "They have a basic burger, it's just got Asian slaw."

"Oh, no ordering off the For the Americanos section!" Theo said. "That's against table rules!"

We all just looked at him. I said, "The what section?"

He took a sip of his water. "For the Americanos. That's what my dad called the section on a menu that's specifically for people who won't try anything out of their comfort zone. In our family, you weren't allowed to get anything like that. You had to go native, or go home."

"I'd love to go home," Morris muttered, but I was pretty sure Theo didn't hear him.

"I'm not the most adventurous eater either," Daisy, always the peacemaker, said more audibly. "Maybe we can both pick something a bit different but not *too* radical?"

"Just let me order some appetizers for the table," Theo said, opening his own menu. "I promise, you'll like them."

He wasn't all wrong. The edamame was great (although Morris, who was not a believer in vegetables other than pickles, avoided it on principle), the tempura shrimp a hit all around. The cabbage dumplings were tolerable, once dunked in soy sauce. Not so much the seaweed salad, which, despite Theo's insistence that we all try a bite of everything, remained on three out of four plates as they were cleared. One course down, I thought. It had only been thirty minutes.

For dinner, only I'd agreed to sushi. Daisy had gone with a dish that looked not unlike standard chicken and broccoli, which I knew because I was looking at it longingly while forcing down my hurricane and spider rolls. Morris, out of spite if nothing else, had gone all-out Americanos with a burger and fries. Worse, when Theo gave us a detailed tutorial on how use our chopsticks, he'd made a big show of using his to dip his fries in a pond of ketchup. I'd been so ready for dessert, if only because I figured by then we'd be past the worst of it.

Now, I looked down at the folded piece of paper with the bow on it, then back at Theo. "Open it," he said, nudging me with his shoulder. "It's not a bomb."

I glanced at Daisy—who, by her expression, was not convinced of this—then slid my finger under the single piece of tape, letting the paper fall open.

DANCING! MOONLIGHT! PRIZES! GET FORMAL FOR A GOOD CAUSE! it said in big block letters over a background of a picture of a retro-style couple waltzing. I couldn't even read the rest of it, as I was too busy anticipating the oncoming explosion. Ka-boom.

"It's this dinner and dancing thing," Theo was saying excitedly from beside me. "I kept seeing flyers all over the place, so I went into this clothing shop and asked about it."

"The Beach Bash," I said.

"From what the girl there said, it's pretty awesome," he went on, clearly unaware of the silence from the rest of us. "So I bought us VIP tickets. We get a sit-down dinner before. Just like the prom! I'll have to rustle up a tux somewhere."

I had a flash of those poufy, ruffled dresses Daisy had shown me a few weeks earlier. I hadn't had a fitting yet, but I knew by now one had to be on the dressmaker form in her bedroom, covered in pins and chalk marks, at least halfway to something fabulous.

"Wow," Daisy said quietly. "I didn't even know they had a VIP option."

"Because you'd never do it," Morris told her.

"You guys have been to this before?" Theo asked.

"They go every year," Morris told him, gesturing to me and Daisy. "Together. It's a tradition."

"Oh." Theo looked at Daisy, then at me. "Wow, sorry. I didn't mean to step on any—"

"It's fine," she said quickly, forcing a smile. "I normally make our dresses and I've been so busy getting ready for school I've totally dropped the ball this year."

I looked at her, surprised. "Really?"

She nodded. "I just didn't want to tell you, because I feel

so slack. I was kind of hoping, you know, we could let the whole going-for-the-win thing slide this year."

I so, so wanted to believe this. But I knew Daisy. First of all, when it came to dresses and vision, she was never slack. Secondly, and more tellingly, she was always unerringly, over-whelmingly polite. Even if it meant lying about something important to her.

"Why don't we buy another pair of tickets?" Theo said to her. "We can double-date!"

"She already bought tickets," Morris said. Clearly, Theo feeling bad was not his concern. "Weeks ago."

I swallowed, looking back down at the cake. After everything I'd forced myself to try, I couldn't deny the truth: it looked delicious.

"Hey, I'm sorry," Theo said to Daisy, clearly meaning it. "I had no idea. The last thing I want to do is, you know, get in the way of something that's important to you guys."

"It's really fine," Daisy assured him again.

We all just sat there for a second, the awkwardness like another person at the table. What a disaster, I thought. Beside us, the tourists were laughing, having a blast. Of course.

"It's just," Theo said, finally, "the thing is, I, um, didn't really get to do the dinner-dance, prom thing in high school. Like, at all. I know all this fanfare was kind of stupid, with the cake and sparklers, the big reveal . . ."

"Yep," Morris said. I kicked him, hard.

"But," Theo continued, reddening slightly, "when I saw this flyer, I thought it was my chance for a do-over. To have that memory, that kind of touchstone moment. The one I didn't have because I was at home, dateless, watching French films with my parents."

I saw Daisy's face soften at this. There, I thought. *This* is the boy I wanted you to meet.

"I mean, seriously," Theo was saying now, "back then someone like Emaline wouldn't even have looked at me, much less agreed to going to something like this."

"Theo," I said quietly.

"What?" he replied. "You're special, Emaline. You're not just any other girl."

He had no way of knowing, I was sure, what I felt hearing these last three words. Like it was a code or password, unlocking a secret, distant part of my heart. All this time, I'd seen it from the other side, as a way of focusing on all the things I wasn't. But to him, to be different was the better choice, even ideal. Yet again, he was giving me another view, and I liked how I looked from here. A summer of firsts, indeed.

"I think it's really sweet," Daisy said to Theo now. "It'll be great, really fun."

I looked at her, trying to catch her eye so I could let her know how much I appreciated this. Okay, it had been kind of an awful night. But it wasn't like when I was with Luke we were all one big happy group either. And I *was* happy now.

"Here," I said to him, cutting a large piece of the cake. "This is for you."

He smiled, pleased. "Yeah? Thanks."

"Thank you." And despite Morris and Daisy watching right across the table, despite everything, I kissed his lips.

And then, I slid that piece of my heart on the plate with a flourish, making it an event, and gave it to him.

* * *

The ride back home was considerably better. Maybe it was what Theo had said, or the cake, or the fact that Morris dozed off shortly after we left Cape Frost. Whatever the reason, we rode in amiable silence, with just the radio on. Every once in a while, I'd look over at Theo, who was sitting beside me, one hand resting on my knee, and smile.

The trip from Cape Frost to Colby was all one two-lane road, with a few stretches where there was nothing but scrub brush and mile markers. It was along one of these that we came upon a stopped blue truck with its hazards on and a U-Haul trailer attached. One of the trailer's tires was flat. The driver, in a beat-up baseball hat and a flannel shirt, was pulling out a jack from the truck box to change it. I slowed down.

"What are you doing?" Theo asked.

"I'm going to see if he needs any help," I replied.

"Emaline, I don't know . . ." He paused. "It's kind of late, don't you think? And there's not much around here."

"Exactly," I said. "If he doesn't have a phone he's screwed."

"Everyone has a phone these days."

"Not in Colby. Roll down your window."

He hesitated, his hand on the button. The guy still hadn't seen us. "I'm serious. I don't think it's a good idea."

"Theo. The guy's stranded out here in the middle of nowhere and there are four of us."

"He's got a weapon, though."

"That's a *jack*," I told him. "And there's a Finz sticker on that truck bumper, as well as a Colby beach permit. He's a local."

"But you don't recognize him."

"I'm sure it's fine."

"I don't know," he said again.

Now we were coming right up next to the guy, and Theo still hadn't even cracked the window. I turned to look at Morris, who was in the backseat, asleep, his mouth hanging open. To Daisy I said, "Wake him up, will you?"

She shook his shoulder. He came to quickly, the way I knew he would: Morris could sleep anywhere, deeply, and upon waking go right back to whatever he'd been doing without missing a beat, a skill he'd perfected in high school. "What's going on?"

"This guy's broken down," I said.

Immediately, Morris lowered his window. "Hey, man. You need some help?"

The guy turned, the jack in his hand, and squinted at us. "Yeah, that'd be great. I know there's a spare for this thing but I'm not sure where it is."

I reversed, then pulled behind the truck, and Morris hopped out. We sat there in silence, watching as the driver opened the back of the trailer to check on whatever he was hauling. It was crammed full of what appeared to be canvases or . . . paintings. Lots of paintings. I looked at his face again, more closely this time.

"Holy crap," I said. I got out of the car.

"Hey!" Theo called out, worried. "I don't think you should—"

I walked over to the trailer, and the driver looked at me. "Emaline! What are you doing here?"

"I'm with him," I said, gesturing at Morris. "You know Clyde, Morris?"

Morris glanced at him. "Oh, yeah. Right. Hey."

"Hey," Clyde said. He looked back at my car. "You guys out tonight, huh?"

"We went to Haiku for contemporary Asian fare," Morris told him.

"What the hell is that?" Clyde asked.

"Exactly," Morris replied. "Emaline, you got a flashlight? I think the spare's actually up front."

"In the car," I said. "Hang on."

I walked back over to my door, then got in, reaching across Theo to the glove compartment. "I know you think you know everyone here," he said. "But that guy could be a serial killer."

"Or one of the most noted collage artists of the nineteen nineties."

It took him a minute. Then he looked back at the truck. "That's Clyde?"

"Yep." I shut the glove box. "Be right back."

This time, he didn't hesitate. He was out of the car in a flash, falling in step behind me as I walked back over to the trailer. "Clyde," he called out. "What's the problem?"

"Who's that?" Clyde asked Morris, squinting into the dark.

"Mr. Sushi."

I handed Morris the flashlight, and he went around the front of the trailer, picking up the toolbox on his way.

Theo was just looking at the paintings, his eyes wide. "These are yours?"

"Yeah," Clyde replied, his attention on Morris. "Just emptying out an old storage unit over in the Cape. Hey, you need any help up there?"

There was a clank. "Nah, I'm good. I found it."

"These are . . ." Theo said, approaching the trailer and running his finger along the edges of the canvases. "There are so many of them. I can't really make out the details, but I don't think I've ever seen—"

"Got it," Morris called out, reappearing. Clyde stepped in front of Theo, cutting him off both in view and midsentence, then reached out for the spare as Morris handed it out. "It's not in great shape. The ones on rentals never are. But it should get you there."

"Great," Clyde said. "Thanks."

"You need help putting it on?" I asked. It was one of my dad's rules that all of us girls had to be able to aptly change a tire before he'd hand over the keys to any of his cars.

"Nah, I'll be fine."

Morris and I looked at each other. "It'll go faster with two pairs of hands," Morris said, picking up the jack.

"Oh, and I can help, too," Theo offered. However, as Morris squatted down by the flat tire, Clyde beside him, Theo didn't move. He was still looking at the paintings.

"This is," he whispered to me as they got the jack into place, "seriously amazing. Seriously. I don't think Ivy, or anyone else for that matter, had any idea he had work that hadn't been seen and cataloged. The possibilities for this are mind-boggling."

"Or," I said, "they could all be nothing, which is why he never showed them to anyone."

"This is Clyde Conaway. As far as anyone knows, he has a very limited oeuvre."

"Which means . . . ?"

"Even if they're nothing," he replied, "they're something."

There was a clank. "Shit," I heard Morris mutter.

Clyde adjusted the flashlight. "Better?"

"Yeah. Thanks. This lug nut's just being a bitch."

Of course it was a female. I sighed.

Theo said, "Ivy's going to *freak*. Especially if this means he might be considering the idea of a tour."

"A tour? Of what?"

He took a quick glance at Clyde, who had his back to us, before moving closer and inching aside the drop cloth over the side of one painting so he could study it. "We figured it was the longest of long shots. But she's been pressing him to consider participating in some kind of exhibition to be timed with the release of the film."

"Really," I said.

"It would, of course, be very limited. Exclusive. A handful of dates in major cities. The interest is there. It's just been a matter of persuading him. Which it looks like maybe we did." He pulled out his phone. "I've got to call Ivy."

I looked back at Clyde, who was helping Morris slide the spare onto the wheel base. "Theo . . . I don't think you should do that until you—"

"Hey, Ivy," he said, either not hearing or just choosing not to, that drive or pushiness again drowning everything else out. "It's me. Listen, you're not going to believe this . . ."

He walked away, still talking, into the darkness. I glanced back at Clyde and Morris, then at the paintings, lined up lengthwise in front of me. Who even knew what was on those canvases, or if any of us were supposed to see them at all. There was a reason people did things alone, under the cover of darkness. I shut the trailer doors.

"That should do it," I heard Morris say a moment later. He was getting to his feet, wiping his hands on a rag. "Just don't ride it too hard."

"Will do," Clyde told him. "Not going much farther anyway. Can I give you some cash or something, for your trouble?"

"Nah, I'm good," Morris said, heading back over to me. "Where's Sushi?"

"On the phone," I said.

He grunted, as if this just figured, then walked back to the car. As I watched him go, Clyde joined me, locking the trailer doors.

"He's a good kid," he observed.

"He has his moments."

I could see Theo now, walking back up into the light. He was still on his phone, his face animated. I thought of that night back at Gert's with the milk crate, when I didn't yet understand any of this. I wasn't sure I did now, actually. But I knew enough to say, "You should know . . . he's talking to Ivy. About the paintings. I tried to stop him."

"It's all right," he said. "I figured as much as soon as I saw him get out of the car."

"He thinks you might go on tour."

I expected him to laugh, or dispute this. Instead, he just said, "Does he, now."

"That's crazy, right? I mean, you wouldn't . . ." I studied his face, trying to read his expression. "You couldn't really do something like that. Would you?"

He didn't answer, and then Theo was right up on us, sliding his phone into his pocket. He seemed übercheerful as he said, "How we doing? Need any more help?"

"All fixed," Clyde told him. "Thanks, though."

"Sure. You want us to follow you back, help you unload?"

Clyde looked at me for a moment, then shook his head. "Nah. I'm good. I'll just see you guys tomorrow."

"Washroom, nine a.m.," Theo said, pointing at him. "See you then!"

And then, Clyde was walking away, to his truck. Theo, still clearly on a high, basically bounced, Benji-like, back to my car. I was following him when I heard Clyde say, "Emaline."

I turned around. "Yes?"

"You be careful out here, okay?" he said. "It's late."

I nodded. Even though it was only just after ten, I was pretty sure I knew what he meant. It was not all that different from Theo's concern when we'd seen him. And yet totally not the same thing.

I started back to my car, where, at this distance, Theo, Daisy, and Morris were just outlines, not distinguishable from one another. You can never be sure of anyone until you're close enough to see them clearly. Now I did the best I could, squinting into the oncoming headlights of someone else as they, too, made their way down this long, dark road.

15

JUST ANOTHER DAY in the sandbox. But at least this time I had company.

"Name, please?" I asked the woman driving the long car beside me. She was in a bathing suit and cover up, her shoulders that first-day-of-vacation pink, indicating they'd arrived early to hit the beach before check-in.

"Hopper," she replied. Her husband, beside her, was chomping on an unlit cigar.

"Hopper," I repeated, then reached behind me. A beat later, the envelope and welcome packet were in my hand. "Here you go. Can I offer you a cold drink for the ride?"

"Got a beer in there?" the husband asked, around his cigar.

"No, sorry," I said cheerfully. "Just water, cola, or juice."

"I'll take a water," the woman said.

One appeared by my elbow, and I gave it to her. "And you, sir?"

"Cola sounds good."

Boom, and the bottle was in my hands. I delivered it, then smiled. "Any questions or concerns, our number is in bold on the front of the envelope. Enjoy your vacation!"

"Thank you," the woman said, rolling up her window, and then they pulled away. Another happy customer.

I looked down at Benji, sitting on the stool behind me. "I think you're improving on your time with every car."

He smiled, pleased, then gestured to the cooler and milk crate full of envelopes in front of him, both within easy and quick reach. "It was just a matter of creating a more efficient system."

"Or any system," I pointed out. "I didn't exactly have one."

"We're a good team," he said.

"That we are," I agreed, as the next car, a black Cadillac SUV, pulled up.

In the end, it had taken me only a couple of days to find my father a sitter for Benji. One of Rebecca's friends, busy studying for the LSAT, was looking for something flexible. In truth, though, I kind of liked having him around, so I'd taken to picking him up myself a couple of days a week and giving him odd jobs around the office. Sure, he was ten, and couldn't be trusted with any of the heavy lifting, figuratively or literally. But when it came to an extra set of hands and a fast response time, there was no one better.

"Name?" I asked the man in the SUV now.

"Perkins. Is it always this hot here?"

"Not always," I replied, as Benji handed me the envelope and the bag. "But July can be pretty toasty. Can I offer you a cold drink for the ride to your property?"

The man, who was heavyset and had the A/C blasting hard enough that I could feel it from where I was standing, wiped a hand across his face. "Water," he said, like someone who had just crawled across the desert. Benji handed me one, which I delivered, and the guy cracked it and took a big gulp. "Man! That's *cold*. Really hits the spot. Thanks."

I nodded, then looked down at Benji, who gave me a thumbs-up. It had been his idea to partially freeze the waters on these superhot days before we came out. "Enjoy your vacation."

The SUV pulled away, and I wiped a hand across my own forehead. It *was* hot, even for mid-July. Which I honestly couldn't believe was already here. The summer was always too short, but this year it felt especially fast. Especially if I did it by the numbers.

Days since Luke and I had broken up: twenty-nine. Days Theo and I had been together: Also twenty-nine. (I wasn't proud of this, but the numbers didn't lie. I couldn't really count the demarcation, as nice as it was.) Days until the Beach Bash: twenty-eight. Days until I left for school: well, that one I wasn't exactly counting. Even though I probably should have been.

When I *did* make myself think about it, my heart raced in that familiar way I remembered from the height of my application stress. But this wasn't about what my future might be, like back then; it was about what it actually *was*. On some day in mid-August (I really needed to write it down) I'd be packing up my car with all my stuff and heading to East U, with this summer, like all the others of my life, behind me. I couldn't even begin to picture that. So I wasn't. Obviously.

I was not totally kidding myself, though. Despite the fact that I'd never before had a summer romance, I knew how the majority of them ended. Most of the girls I knew, other than Daisy, had fallen for a tourist boy at least once, with a few believing it was actually forever. Quickly—usually by October at the latest—they learned otherwise. Then, all they could do was hang out at Jump Java on the boardwalk, where everyone who'd been dumped long-distance convened in the fall, like some big, tremulous support group. Even if I had been planning to be in Colby, I did not intend to count myself among them.

Theo was going back to New York. I was leaving for East U. Done and done. If I wanted—and I didn't—I could chart exactly how it would go if we tried to stay together. Lots of phone calls/Hi There! chats at first. Plans made for trips to visit each other, one of which *might* actually occur, although probably right before the Very End. Which would come after a marked trailing off of communication by one person—usually the tourist, although not always—followed by an awkward confrontation you could only *hope* would not be on video chat. Nobody looks good sobbing in screen resolution size. Just ask the girls at the table with the tissue box at Jump Java.

I was not up for this. Which was why the way things were with Theo and me now was just perfect for me. The summer would end, we'd go our separate ways, and that was that. If I was sad, I'd have all of our Best Memories Ever, painstakingly created, to flip through whenever I wanted. Until then, though, I chose to think about it as little as possible.

Still, I couldn't ignore the fact that it was only a matter of time before our events went from the Best Fill-in-the-Blank Ever to the Last One. Which made me even more conscious of the *other* things I needed to be doing, like spending enough time with my mom so she didn't sigh as dramatically or loudly whenever I left the house, seeing Daisy and Morris both together and separately, working extra hours at the office to make money for school, and hanging out with Benji. At least now, I could do these last two at once.

"Emaline," I heard him say now. I looked down, and he nodded behind me. "Car."

"Right." I shook my head, getting back on track as a black convertible pulled up beside us. "Name, please?"

"You already forgot? Man. That's *harsh*, Emaline."

It was Luke. That he was even in the check-in line, in a car I didn't recognize, was only one of the things that immediately threw me off. Add in the fact that he was dressed in a shirt and tie and the girl driving was a very pretty redhead, and I was unsettled.

"Sorry," I said. "I just didn't expect—"

"Luke!" Benji hollered, popping up beside me.

Luke jumped, surprised, and despite myself, I laughed. The fact that he was easily scared was legendary. Leaping out at him from behind things just to hear him shriek like a little girl—we called it Gotcha!, a game he'd learned from his cousins Wes and Bert—had been one of my favorite pastimes. "Whoa," he said, flushing, then laughed as well. "You scared me, dude!"

"Sorry," Benji told him. He was literally jumping up and down, like a dog, to get a glimpse of him. "Guess what? I'm working with Emaline now!"

"Really?" Luke said. Beside him, the girl—who was wearing a short flowered dress and cowboy boots and did, actually, look sort of familiar—smiled. "Hope she's paying you the big bucks."

"Kinda." Benji looked at me. "Did you ask their name yet?"

"Um . . ." I said.

"Best," the girl said. "I think the property's called Emerald Belle or something?"

Quick as a flash, Benji handed her the envelope. "Do you want a cold drink, too? We have water, juice, and soda. But no beer."

Luke looked at me, raising his eyebrows. I said, "I know. He's good. With him here, they won't even notice when I leave next month."

"Oh, I doubt that," he replied. Which was nice enough to distract me from wondering how serious this relationship had gotten, considering he was actually wearing a tie for her. For about two seconds. "So. How you doing, Emaline?"

"I'm good," I said. "You?"

"Can't complain," he said with a shrug. "Actually, I can. I'm in a tie here."

"I noticed," I said, raising my eyebrows. "What's the occasion?"

I was not being nosy, just making conversation. Okay, maybe being a little nosy. But he'd brought it up first. God, this was weird. He said, "Brooke's bachelorette weekend. We're heading up the transportation team, getting the rental settled, and doing airport runs."

"In a tie," I said.

"My mother's idea."

"I'm so surprised."

"Aren't you, though?"

I laughed again. It was so odd that after a month apart— and an awkward split, to boot—Luke and I could be right back like this within moments. Maybe it was just part of growing up with someone. Once you have a rhythm and stay with it long enough, it's not hard to find again.

I gestured for Benji to hand me a water, then handed it to the girl. "You should have a great week. Although kind of a hot one."

"Emaline, this is Jacqueline," Luke said. "Jacqueline, Emaline."

We smiled and nodded at each other. I said to Benji, "You have a Mountain Dew in there?"

"Yup!"

He handed me one, and I passed it across to Luke. "Your favorite breakfast."

"And lunch and dinner," he agreed, setting it in the holder. "We better head on. If I don't get out of this tie soon I'm going to choke."

"Just keep your shirt on," I told him. He made a face, Jacqueline waved, and then they were pulling away, ending our first true run-in since the breakup. He seemed to be doing just fine. Which was what I wanted. Because I was fine, too. Right?

We had two cars in a row behind them, one with a million questions about vegetarian options on the island, the other a minivan that cleared out our remaining drink supply. Forget wiping my forehead; by the time we had another break, I was outright sweating.

"This is brutal," I said to Benji. "I feel like we're being punished or something."

"Cold towel?" he asked me.

"What?"

He opened up the cooler and rummaged around before pulling a rolled-up washcloth from the ice. "Try this."

I did, putting it to my face, and almost moaned it felt so good. "Wow. That's *amazing*. Thank you."

"You're welcome." He shut the cooler, then sat down on it, propping his head in his hands. "Do you miss Luke?"

I always forgot, when I was with Benji, that at ten he had not quite mastered the art of the smooth conversational segue. I took the towel off my face. "Yeah. I do. Not as much as I did when we first broke up, but . . . we were together a long time."

"He kissed another girl," he told me.

I looked at him. "Who told you that?"

"Morris." Also, apparently, not a whole lot of vagueness or dodging. If you knew it, you said it. "Were you mad?"

This one was easy to answer. "Yes. Very. And sad, too."

Benji looked in the direction where the car had gone. "But you're happy now, with Theo. Right?"

"Yep."

All these answers, I realized, made the whole thing seem very cut-and-dry, when really it was anything but. Yes, I had kissed Theo the same day Luke and I split, and yes, I was happy with him. But even with that in play, I still had moments and even days when I was really sad about Luke. Who would have thought that grieving an old relationship and enjoying a new one could happen simultaneously, in parallel? Yet another thing you only find out once it's happening to you.

We sat there for another moment, both of us silent. It was so steamy that across the parking lot, the cars looked wavery, the heat changing the very air.

"Emaline?"

"Yeah?" I said, wiping my face again.

"I don't want go home."

I glanced at my watch, then the road in front of the office. "Well, that's good, because we have at least another hour out here. If we don't die of heatstroke first."

"No, I mean *home*. Connecticut," he said, studying his hands. "I don't want to go back."

I looked at him, feeling a pang in my chest. "Now, I bet that's not totally true."

"It is," he said glumly.

"You must miss your mom. And your friends. Right?"

He shrugged. "I don't have a lot of friends. And my mom's really sad right now, which makes me sad. So no."

I hesitated, not sure what to say to this. Despite what Morris had told me about Benji knowing about it, I didn't want to bring up the separation. I took a breath, then said, "I know how you feel. I don't really want the summer to end, either."

He looked up. "You don't?"

I shook my head. "Because when it does, I have to go off to college, which is kind of scary. And I won't get to see Theo anymore. At least not for a while."

"He's in New York."

"Yup." I pulled out the water I'd claimed earlier and took a sip. It was lukewarm by now. "That he is."

"You could come visit him," he said. He thought for a second. "Hey, you could stay with me! It's a really short train ride to the city. We do it all the time."

"Yeah?"

He nodded.

"That would be great. I'd love that."

This seemed to cheer him up, at least temporarily. For a moment, we didn't talk, and I just watched him pick at the chipping paint on the cooler, sending tiny flakes flying.

"My parents are getting a divorce," he said finally, as matter-of-factly as he'd reported Luke's indiscretion.

I blinked, then took another sip of my water. "Are they?"

He glanced up at me. "You didn't know?"

"I knew that, um . . ." I looked over at the office, wondering when, exactly, my father and Margo would be returning from their latest trip to North Reddemane, this time to meet with painters before the house was listed. "I knew they were having problems."

He nodded. "They fight a lot. And yell."

"Really?"

"Yeah. She says his expectations are unrealistic. He says she nitpicks instead of focusing on the big picture."

No question: these were direct quotes. "That's no fun."

"Do your mom and dad fight, too?"

I thought of my parents, their easy compatibility. Arguing was not something that happened much, if ever. My mom was so stubborn, my dad had learned to choose his battles, which were few and far between. "Sometimes. Not too much, though."

"You're lucky," he said, picking again. "With mine, it was all the time. At least until we came here. Now they just do it on the phone, when they think I'm asleep."

"Is that better?" I asked him.

"It's still yelling," he replied. "Just one voice, not two."

I nodded, fighting the urge to reach out and brush back the hair that had fallen into his face, just to be able to do *something* in that moment. Instead, I said, "You know what? I think you and I need to make a pact."

This got his attention, and interest, immediately. "A pact?"

I thought for a second. "Yeah. Let's agree, that as of right now"—I looked at my watch—"July fourteenth at four-oh-five p.m., we won't talk about the summer ending, at least with each other, for a full month. Unless we absolutely *have* to before then."

"And if we do?" he asked.

"Then we have to pay a dollar into . . ." I glanced around, spotting my almost-empty water bottle. I took off the top, dumped it, then wiped the mouth on my shorts. "This bottle. Then, on August fourteenth, we'll take all the money we've collected and put it towards something awesome."

"Like shrimp burgers?"

I wagged a finger at him. "Can't tell you for a month. My secret. Do we have a deal?"

"Deal."

He stuck out his hand, I stuck out mine, and we shook. Then, to seal it, I pulled a wrinkled bill from my pocket and stuffed it in the bottle. "Hopefully, that will be the only dollar in there. Right? Because we are not talking about that thing that we aren't talking about."

"Nope," he said. "We are not."

Another car was pulling up now, the radio blasting. I pushed my hair back from my face and turned towards them as Benji took his position by the cooler. This would be good, I told myself. There was plenty of time still left for both of us.

"Hello," I said, as the window rolled down in front of me. "Welcome to Colby. Name, please?"

* * *

"I *knew* it."

Daisy turned, startled at the sound of my voice. When she saw it was me in her bedroom doorway, her shoulders sank. "Okay, fine," she said, waving a hand at the dressmaker dummy in front of her. "I lied. But I did it for a good reason."

Of course the dress was beautiful. Gone were the ruffles and cascading layers. All that remained of the original was the powder blue color. It had been reshaped into cocktail length with a slightly flared skirt. The neckline was trimmed with beads the color and shape of peppermint candies. The pink version, cut but not yet sewn, was spread out on the bed.

"Daze," I said quietly, walking over to it. "This is beautiful."

"It's nice, right?" She reached out to the bottom hem, adjusting it, then stepped back, narrowing her eyes. "I'm still working out how far to take the candy theme. I don't want it to be totally crazy, but I think I need something sort of fun for the trim. Maybe some silver, to look like Kisses or something."

"You're making two," I observed, as she removed a pin, then replaced it. "Does this mean I still get to wear one?"

She looked at me. "Emaline. You're entitled to have your own plans and your own dress. I swear, it's not a big deal."

"Big enough for you to tell a lie," I pointed out. "And you *never* lie."

It was true. Daisy was unfailingly honest, which could be both wonderful and awful. On the one hand, she would always tell you when an outfit didn't look good or you were making a bad choice. On the other, she would always tell you when an outfit didn't look good . . . or you were making a bad choice. How you felt about it might vary. But she never did.

"You were so happy that night when Theo asked you to the Beach Bash," she said now. "And it's just a dress."

"A gorgeous dress," I added. She smiled, pleased. "I'd love to have the chance to wear it. *If* you'll allow me to."

"Of course!" she said. "Who else is going to wear it? Morris?"

I looked at the dress again. "Blue's not his color. Also, the sleeves would look bad with hairy arms."

"Agreed. But I am getting him to wear long pants this year, if it kills me."

She bent down over her sewing box, taking out something, and I took my normal place in the chair by the window, out of her creative space but still close enough to talk. I'd seen her through a lot of projects: we had our rituals.

"You want Morris to wear long pants," I said, "and I'm just hoping I can convince Theo not to get a tux. Want to trade?"

"Nope," she said. Immediately, she looked at me, worried. "I didn't mean how that sounded. I just—"

"I understand," I said, nodding. "Theo's . . . well, he's not for everyone."

Wisely, she didn't comment on this, instead bending down to pin something on the hem. From where I was sitting, all I could see was that it was sparkly, catching the bit of light slanting through her window. Finally she said, "He's really nice. Just . . ."

I waited, but she didn't continue. "Not from here," I finished for her.

She looked over her shoulder at me. "It's just a big switch from Luke, is all. I think I need a little bit longer to get used to it."

"Don't take too long," I told her. "We're only going to be together for another few weeks, at most."

"Emaline!" She looked dismayed. "Don't say that."

"Why not? It's true."

"You don't know that." She turned back to the dress, sliding a pin into the hem.

"I think I do," I said. "I don't really see us in a long-distance relationship."

"Why not?"

"Because they never work?" I asked.

"Some do."

"Who? My mom and father? Or just about anyone else we know who's had one?"

"Still, they don't all fail," she said, her back still to me.

"The odds aren't good."

To this, she said nothing. So it was in total, awkward silence that I finally became aware of how fully and completely I had just stuck my foot in my own big, stupid mouth. Whoops.

"Daisy," I said. "I was talking about me and Theo, not—"

"It's fine," she replied, but the stiffness in her voice erased any doubt I'd struck a nerve.

I got up and walked over to her to stand next to the *other* dummy. "It's not. I'm sorry. Look, Theo and I have been together, like, four weeks. You and Morris are long-term."

She bit her lip, focusing on folding back a piece of the neckline. "No, you're right. Nobody ever stays together long-distance. And having a boyfriend when you go off to school . . . it's a terrible idea."

"Everyone's different," I offered. Lamely.

"I'm going to school over seven hours away," she pointed out. "He's staying here and taking classes at Coastal Tech. And that's if he can get his act together. Which is a big if. I love

Morris, but I can't fix him. Especially from Georgia."

This was the first time, ever, I'd heard her use the L Word. I had a flash of Morris, walking down the side of the main road, lumbering along. Who was going to take care of him when we were both gone?

"Anyway, my point is that I need to take a lesson from you. Just enjoy things while they last, then be done with it."

"It's a bit easier to do when you've only been dating twenty-nine days," I said. "Also, I'm dealing with someone Not From Here. Who wants to wear a tuxedo to the Beach Bash."

This made her smile, thank God. "It is kind of ridiculous."

"I know."

She moved around to the other side of the dress and bent down to the hem again. I looked at the pink version, stretched out across the bed, then around the room itself. I had spent so many hours in this same place, watching her sew while the sound of the Weather Channel (always on, her mom and dad were obsessed with it) wafted in from the living room. It felt like I'd taken everything for granted up until just right now, when suddenly my entire world and all in it became precious and fleeting. I should have paid more attention, soaked it in more. Which you always realize once it's getting too late to do just that.

"So," she said, in the voice that made it clear she was ready to switch topics, "what are you doing here, anyway? Don't you have big plans tonight, or something?"

I did. As big a plan as I got these days, which was hanging out at the Washroom or one of Clyde's other haunts, waiting for Theo to be done with work. After Benji left the office with my dad, I'd been en route to do just that when I passed the entrance to Daisy's neighborhood and stopped in, on impulse. I was glad I had.

"Not really," I said, taking my seat by the window again. "You?"

"You're looking at it." She turned back to me. "Can you hand me those scissors? The small pair, not the big."

I bent over her sewing box, finding the ones she wanted, then handed them off to her. She thanked me, then went to her work. In no time, she'd get into that place where she'd forget I was there, but no matter. I knew we were together, at least for now. And right then, while I still could, it was exactly where I wanted to be.

16

"SO THE PLAN," my father said, gesturing to the living room, "is to keep only the basic furnishings here until mid-August, when we go back home. Of course, if we're very lucky, we might get an offer by—"

"Dollar!" Benji called out, interrupting him. "You owe me a dollar!"

My father looked at him. "Benji. I'm talking."

"You mentioned the end of the summer, so you have to pay the tax. It's the rule! Right, Emaline?"

Now, everyone looked at me. "Um, I think that just applies to us two only. Not everyone else."

Benji made a face. "Fine. But *I* don't want to hear about it. I'm going outside."

And with that, he left, letting the front screen door fall shut with a bang behind him. We all watched him stomp down the front walk, wildly swatting at the no-see-'ems that hung around the bushes out front as they descended upon him.

My father cleared his throat. "Obviously, he's not taking the separation well."

"It's hard on kids," Margo murmured, in her realtor voice.

"Anyway, as I was saying . . ." he continued, starting to walk again. She fell in behind him, scribbling on her ever-present notepad, but I hung back, looking out at Benji. He was now sitting on the steps by the mailbox, looking down the empty street as if waiting on something that should be show-ing up soon, any minute now. The no-see-'ems had returned to the bushes, swirling around each other in a big, buzzing cloud.

By the time I caught up with my father and Margo, they were in the kitchen, which was cluttered with boxes and pack-ing supplies. "I really need to get the bulk of this stuff boxed," he was saying. "But dealing with Benji and this deadline I'm on for my article, it's been impossible."

"We can look into prices for packers," Margo suggested.

"Paying movers is expensive enough."

My sister considered this. "Well, then Emaline could do it."

"Me?" I said. "I'm supposed to be at work *now*."

"This *is* your work," she said to me.

"Does that mean you're going to do the towel runs and organize the request checks when we get back? Because I'm leaving the office right at five today, whether they're done or not."

"Emaline," she said. She glanced at my father, who had picked up his phone from the counter and was now studying its screen, then lowered her voice. "What have I told you about discussing personnel issues in front of clients?"

"He's my father," I reminded her. "And you can't just dump everything on me."

"Fine. I'll ask Morris." She made a note on her pad, then

said, "Joel, I'm just going to make a few calls. The first movers should be here in a few minutes for that estimate."

"What?" My father looked up. "Oh, right. Thanks."

Margo smiled, then picked up her purse from the chair beside her and stepped out onto the screened side porch. Within moments, I could hear her on the phone, talking too loudly as always. I tipped my head back, looking up at the ceiling as if there might be strength there.

"He informed me this morning," my father said after a moment, "that when I take him back to Connecticut, it will in effect ruin his entire life as we know it."

I was startled, not least because I'd thought my father was absorbed in whatever text he was reading or sending. "Benji did?" I asked stupidly. Like it would be anyone else.

"To say he was disappointed when I said I'd be doing it regardless is a massive understatement." He sighed, pulling out a chair from the table and sitting down. I did the same. "He's become very fond of you. Obviously."

"Well, that's sweet," I said. "But I don't think it's only about me."

"I don't think you give yourself enough credit."

"Maybe not." I looked out at Margo, pacing around the porch, phone to her ear. "But really, I think it's Colby, the summer . . . the whole package. He just doesn't want to think about everything changing."

"Change is inevitable, though," he replied. "As is disappointment. Best to get used to it now."

"How can you get used to it?" I asked. "It's always changing."

At this, he smiled, and I realized how few times I'd actually seen him do so, especially on this trip. "You've always been a smart one, Emaline."

"I think I can just relate," I said. "With him and me, there's a lot of big stuff ahead. My whole life is changing at the end of summer, too, with school and all."

I really wasn't thinking as I said this; it just came naturally, as truths tend to do. It was only after the words left my mouth that I realized what I'd said, and to whom I'd said it. Sure enough, his face was already reddening, his discomfort obvious.

"Yes, well," he stammered, then coughed into his hand. "Again, it's part of life in general. One must learn to adapt, move on."

Move on. This, clearly, was when I was supposed to do just that. Back off again, sparing him all the discomfort he had easily caused me. But I'd already waded out this far. For once, I decided to dive in.

"The truth is," I began, then paused as he shifted, still noticeably uncomfortable, in his chair, "I've been wanting to talk to you about that. My going to school, and what happened between us, back in the spring."

And there it was. The elephant in our collective room, the shared albatross around our necks, recognized and out in the open. This was my moment to ask him all my questions, just like the ones I'd written out for Mr. Champion's class all those years ago. No time for drafts or polish, though. I just had to do it.

"Oh," he said quickly, shifting again. "Well, I'm not sure this is the right place or—"

"I just never really understood why you didn't answer my messages," I pressed on. "And then when you didn't respond to my graduation invitation, after all the work we'd done . . . I felt like I'd done something wrong."

"Emaline." He held up a hand, palm flat out to me. "Not now."

"But I just—"

"*No.*"

In that one word, two letters, I heard it: the sharp, final tone I associated with my actual parents, the one that let you know when something went from a *maybe* to *no chance* and keeping up pushing would most likely lead to a punishment. No talking. No explanation. Just: no.

"Think I just heard the movers pull up," Margo reported, coming in from the side porch. "And they're on time. Early, even! That's a good sign. I'll go let them in."

She started for the door, and I just looked at him, his red face, the way, without me even really noticing, he'd at some point pulled back from the table, putting that much more space between us. I just knew that if I said another word he'd be gone from the room; another sentence, from the house. This was the way it had to be, or so I was figuring out. When it came to the two of us, it didn't matter if it was the summer, this past year, or all our lives. The one constant, beside change, was that we played by his rules. Otherwise, the game was over.

* * *

Back at the office, I threw myself into work for a solid three hours, organizing towels, making deliveries, and doing check-ups. Then, at a minute to five, I clocked out and went home to change.

Theo was getting off work early, for once, and he'd made plans for us to have what he called the Best Outdoor Date Ever. All I knew was I'd been instructed to be at the Washroom at 6 p.m. sharp and wear flats. Which was in itself hilarious, as I never wore anything else. But Theo liked to cover all his bases when it came to his Best Evers. The least I could do was follow directions.

At my house, I let myself in and headed down the hallway to my room. The door was slightly ajar, and I could hear voices just beyond it. *Dammit*, I thought, feeling that familiar annoyance rise up in me. I pushed it open.

There, on the bed, were Morris and Amber. They were sharing a bowl of popcorn, watching my TV, and both of them had their shoes on. I did not even know where to start.

"Why are you in my room?" I demanded.

Morris swallowed the popcorn he'd been chewing. "You weren't home yet."

"Dad's painting the kitchen trim," Amber said. Today, suddenly, she was wearing hair extensions, rounding out a retro-feathered look. "It stinks up there."

"So you made popcorn and got into my bed with your dirty shoes on."

"My shoes aren't dirty," my sister, who knew better than to vouch for Morris, said. She held out the bowl to me. "Want some? It's still warm."

I glared at her. Then I remembered I'd skipped lunch because of Margo. Experience had taught me that I really only had the energy to be annoyed with one sister at a time, so I took a handful. "I'm still not happy about this."

"I know," she said, as if she'd had nothing to do with it. Morris, beside her, helped himself to some more as well. "Why are you home so early?"

"I told you," Morris said. "She's got a date."

"She always has a date these days," Amber told him, like I wasn't even there. Then she tossed her fake hair, a move she'd clearly been practicing. "She's seeing a dater."

"A dater?" I repeated, getting my towel and stepping into the bathroom. The door was superthin, so I could still hear every word.

"A guy who likes to date," she explained, chewing. "As opposed to one who just wants to hang out."

"What's the difference?" Morris asked.

"Do you plan extravagant events and outings that make for special moments?" she asked him.

"What do you think?" I called out, stripping off my shirt.

"Exactly," Amber said. "A dater likes dates. Theo's a dater. The guys I get involved with just like to hang out. Preferably with cheap beer or video games involved. Ideally, both."

"What's wrong with video games?" Morris said.

"They're passive. Dating is active. Which means you don't do it sitting on the couch." I heard her eat another handful of popcorn. "Which is why I, myself, am not a dater. I *like* the couch. And the beer and video games. And I *love* the boys who love them."

Usually, I found Amber's theories to be far-fetched, if not outright ludicrous. But this one, I realized as I started the water, was not so off. Theo was the planner, the cruise director of our relationship. He planned, he paid, he engineered the Best Memories Ever. And on days like this, especially, I was really fortunate to have him.

When I got out of the shower, my sister had vanished, leaving just Morris and the now-empty bowl of popcorn. "Where's the dating expert?"

"Went to get another Diet Coke," he replied, studiously avoiding looking at me, even though I was wearing a towel that covered everything. Having a guy for a best friend required certain modifications, especially when it came to undressing. But Morris and I had been best friends a long time. Like me and Daisy, we had our rituals.

I grabbed my clothes, then went back into the bathroom, leaving the door only a crack open. "What are you doing here, anyway?"

"Wanted to talk to you."

I raised my eyebrows at my own reflection. "About what?"

"Daisy."

"Oh." This sounded serious. "Okay. I'll just be a sec."

I got dressed, then combed my wet hair, put on some makeup, and dug my nicer sandals out from behind the hamper. When I returned, he was sitting on the edge of the bed, looking at his phone. I joined him, then waited. Morris talked, as he did everything, at his own pace and on his own schedule. Finally he said, "I have to break up with her."

"Excuse me?"

"Daisy. I have to break up with her."

"Why?" I turned to face him, narrowing my eyes. "I swear to God. If you fooled around with another girl—"

"Of course not." He sat back, leaning on his palms. "She's going to college in, like, four weeks. Once she gets there, she'll want nothing to do with her stupid loser high school boyfriend."

I felt a pang just hearing this. "Morris. Don't—"

"We both know it's the truth," he said, cutting me off. "And Daisy's so sweet, she'd feel like crap having to dump me, especially long-distance. She'd be miserable. Someone's gotta be the bad guy. I'm better at it."

I bit my lip, thinking of Daisy studying her dress dummy, acknowledging in her own way how far-fetched their chances of staying together were. Different languages, same message.

"She's not leaving yet," I told him quietly.

"But she will." He cleared his throat. "It's like Amber said. She needs a dater, and I'm a couch guy. That's never gonna change."

"You don't know that." He made a face, doubting this. "You don't. You have your whole life ahead of you."

"Maybe," he said. "But even that's not long enough to be the person she deserves. I just think it's probably time to let her get started finding whoever that is."

It was the most twisted, sad, Morris-esque logic. And yet I understood it completely. Some people—like myself and Theo, say—would let the flame burn as long as possible, squelching it only when it was just about going to go out anyway. But Morris, despite his lack of long-term goals, still had a way of seeing the bigger view.

I could hear Amber coming back down the stairs. Aware he probably didn't want this public conversation or knowledge, I said, "So when are you going to do it?"

"I don't know." He looked down at his hands. "All I'm sure of is that it's gonna *really* suck."

I reached over and squeezed his hand. "You're a good guy, Morris."

"Naw, I'm an asshole," he replied, pushing himself to his feet. "But at least this time I can say I have a good reason."

Again, this made me think of Daisy, and her white lie about the dresses. We were willing to do so much for the people we loved, even if it meant hurting ourselves. Maybe that, in the end, was what love—all kinds—was really all about.

Amber came back in, carrying a can of Diet Coke, which she popped as she crossed the threshold. When she saw Morris headed for the door, she said, "Don't leave on my account."

"This isn't your room," I pointed out.

"Gotta go," he told her. To me he said, "Talk later?"

"Talk later."

He left, and a moment later I heard the door fall shut behind him.

"I told him to take his shoes off," Amber informed me. "Just so you know."

"And yet, you kept yours on."

"Mine are clean."

I rolled my eyes, then picked up my brush and gave my hair a few good strokes. "He's such a good guy."

"I don't know about that," she replied, scraping the bottom

of the popcorn bowl for the last few kernels there. "But he's a *very* good Morris."

I smiled at this, bending down to grab my purse. "Don't leave that bowl in here."

"Do I ever?"

This I chose to ignore, instead just waving as I headed out myself.

"Have fun with the dater!"

"Thank you," I called over my shoulder. I figured I'd catch Morris walking down the driveway, give him a lift to wherever he was headed, or at least partway there. But when I got outside, he was nowhere in sight. I looked both ways, drove an extra loop around the neighborhood. No luck. Weird. Someone who normally moved so slowly, this time, for once, was long gone.

＊ ＊ ＊

When I walked into the Washroom at the appointed time, I was surprised to find that Theo wasn't there. Instead there was just Clyde, alone, perusing a cookbook in the small booth that doubled as his office.

"Where's Ivy and Theo?" I asked.

"No idea," he replied. "They left for lunch, never came back."

"Lunch?" I glanced at my watch. "When was that?"

He flipped a page. I caught a glimpse of a piecrust, the top woven lattice style. "Two thirty or so."

I sat down opposite him. "Doesn't sound like Ivy."

"Nope. Maybe I scared her off for good."

I watched him turn another page. The pictures of the pies looked amazing. I realized I was starving. "I'd heard just the opposite, actually."

Now, I had his attention. He shut the book. "Which means what?"

"Just that you're being really on board with the whole film thing these days," I said. "Cooperating more, and now there's talk about a tour . . ."

I let this last part trail off, thinking he'd dispute it. But, like the night we'd stopped to fix his tire, he didn't. Instead, he sat back. "Nothing's definite about a tour yet."

"Yet? So you are doing it?"

"You sound shocked at the very thought," he observed.

"Because I am," I said. He raised his eyebrows. "I mean, at the beginning of the summer, you wouldn't even *talk* to them. Now you're thinking of coming out of retirement and taking your show on the road?"

"I'm not a circus clown, Emaline."

"You're not an artist anymore, either," I said. "At least, I didn't think you were."

"This wouldn't be about new work," he pointed out. "Just a way of giving my older stuff another chance. I mean, an opportunity to do things differently, with the benefit of hindsight? That's a hard thing to turn down."

"A do-over," I said. He nodded. "I get that. In fact, I was kind of hoping for one of my own, earlier. Didn't happen, though."

"No?"

I shook my head. "I'm starting to think, though, that some things never get that. The replay, and all. So at some point you have to make peace with it as it is, not keep waiting for a chance to change it."

"I don't know about that." He looked down at the table, scraping at a spot there. "You're pretty young to be talking in nevers."

I thought of my father, back in his kitchen. "Some people would say disappointment is a good thing to learn young."

"True," he agreed. "But some people are assholes."

I smiled. "I seem to remember you calling yourself that, not too long ago."

"True. So you don't have to listen to anything I say, either," he said. "But for what it's worth, Emaline, I'll tell you this: Life is long. Just because you don't get your chance right when you want or expect it doesn't mean it won't come. Fate doesn't punch a time clock or consult a schedule. Look at me. Forty-two and talking about showing my art again. Didn't see *that* one coming."

"Which is probably just why it did," I said.

He pointed at me. "Smart girl."

So now it was a consensus. Too bad I still felt like a victim of my own dumb luck. Speaking of which, right then, Ivy walked through the door.

"Well, there's an entire working afternoon shot," she said, as if she'd been carrying on this conversation without us prior to her arrival. She walked over to the counter, peering across it at the cooler on the other side. "You'd think I would learn. This is what happens when you don't hire professionals. You sell beer here, right?"

"No," Clyde said.

"You're kidding." She exhaled dramatically. "That is so unfortunate. Because I *really* need a drink right now."

I glanced at the door she'd just come through. "Where's Theo?"

She held up her hand, palm facing me. "Don't say that name to me right now. Especially if there is truly no beer here."

"There's a bar across the street," Clyde told her. "The margaritas suck. But they are powerfully strong."

"You had me at margarita," she replied, turning on her heel. "Let's go."

Clyde and I looked at each other, and he got out of the booth. "The woman wants a drink," he said with a shrug. "As a Southern gentleman, I must oblige."

Ivy was already halfway out the door, the sun now slanting through into the dark room, making the dust in the air dance.

"Do you need me to lock up or something?" I called after Clyde.

"Nah. Just shut the door tight if you leave," he replied. Which, in downtown Colby at least, counted as a basic security measure. Add an actual lock or alarm system, and you were in full-on bunker mode, as far as anyone was concerned.

Now, alone, I looked at my watch: it was ten after six. Something was definitely up. I picked up my phone and texted Theo. A moment later, he replied.

Change of plans. Boardwalk and bikes in ten.

Bikes, I thought. Well, that explained the flat shoes. I told him I was on my way and left, giving the door a good yank behind me.

It was still early for the boardwalk, the crowds a mix of people wrapping up a day at the beach—toting bags, umbrellas, floats, and pink-cheeked children—and those out for an early dinner. I picked my way through the crowd, towards Abe's Bikes. About halfway there, a beefy guy in a tight black T-shirt thrust a piece of bright pink paper at me.

"Ladies' night at Tallyho!" he said. "Quarter shots! Bring a friend for the most fun on the beach!"

I shook my head—no, no—dodging around him. As I passed Clementine's, I looked in the open door to see Auden and Maggie folding jeans at a clearance table. They waved, gesturing for me to come in, but I motioned up ahead, mouthing I'd see them later. I had just caught sight of Theo.

He was in front of Abe's, wearing his sport coat and jeans, scanning the crowd. Awfully dressy for a bike date, I thought. I didn't see the bags at his feet until I was right in front of him.

"There she is!" he said, stepping forward and picking me up off the ground, one big swoop. Startled, I lost a shoe. I heard it hit the ground with a *thwack*. "Ready for our Best Outside Date Ever That Has Now Become Even More Epic?"

"Um, yeah," I said, trying to gracefully find my footing again. Behind him, Wallace, who worked at the shop, was standing next to a pair of bikes, watching us with a bemused expression. "Are you okay?" I asked Theo.

"Fantastic." He put me down, then smiled at me. His

cheeks were flushed, a faint sweat visible on his brow. "Just had the biggest blow-up with Ivy. Whew! You should have seen her. She was *livid*."

"Are those yours?" I asked, looking down at the large duffel and backpack on the ground between us.

"Yep. Got thrown out." He laughed. "That was part of the whole livid thing."

"She threw you out?" I asked.

"I'll explain everything. Let's just ride first, okay?" He turned to Wallace, reaching into his pocket for his wallet. "So that's . . . two-hour rental for the bikes, right? And I can leave this big bag behind the counter?"

"Sure," Wallace said. Theo handed him a few bills. "Let me get your change."

"Keep it," he told him. Then he took the smaller bike and wheeled it closer to me. "Your chariot awaits."

Wallace looked at me again. I was pretty sure I knew what he, all the guys at the shop, and everyone at Clementine's would be talking about after work that night. If not the second we were out of sight.

"Are you sure you're all right?" I asked Theo.

"I'm fine," he assured me. "Hop on."

I did, if only because I was eager to be rid of our audience. It had been a while since I'd been on a bike, and navigating the shifting crowd wasn't exactly easy, but after a moment I found a narrow, somewhat empty stretch. I looked behind me at Theo, who was now on his own bike. "Where are we going?"

"Follow me!" he said, and then he was zooming up beside and past me, backpack now on, his sport coat flapping out behind him. I tried my best to keep up as he zigzagged along, braking sharply whenever someone stepped in front of him. Finally, after a traffic jam at the Pavilion, where some terrible-sounding band was playing—SPINNERBAIT! according to the banner they had tacked up, crookedly, behind them—we emerged onto a more empty stretch. Theo picked up speed, glancing back at me.

"Not far now," he said. "You're going to *love* this."

We were getting closer to the pier now, with people dangling fishing poles dotting it all the way out over the water. Beyond that, there was nothing but sand, hardly conducive to riding. Just as I was about to point this out, Theo suddenly took a sharp right, onto the road that led to the unpaved campground area.

"Hey," I called out, my voice wobbling as we bumped over a large pothole, RVs and trailers on either side of us. "I think you went the wrong way?"

"Nope. This is right. We're almost there."

I was, in a word, hesitant. Colby was a pretty safe place, but the pier campground was notoriously sketchy. So much so it made the small, rundown motel adjacent—which, despite lacking one, was called the Sea View—look positively decadent in comparison. Home to mostly seasonal fishermen and a rougher set of tourists, it was a known mostly as an epicenter for drunk and disorderly conduct and fighting arrests. Not a place you went on the Best Outdoor Date Ever. Or ever, if you could help it.

The road was steadily getting worse, with more holes and now the occasional beer bottle to avoid. Every once in a while we'd pass someone, usually shirtless and/or smoking, who followed us, unsmiling, with narrowed eyes. If my dad knew I was anywhere near here, he'd kill me. If I wasn't murdered first.

"Um, Theo," I called out, cautiously. "I think—"

"Here we are!" He jerked his bike to a stop, kicking up a cloud of dust, then jumped off. I pulled up beside him, but stayed on mine, watching from there as he gestured grandly at the small, beat-up camper in front of us. "Home sweet home. Lucky number seven."

I looked at it, then at him. "Whose house is this?"

"Mine," he replied, as if it was the most natural thing in the world. "I mean, it's a rental, of course. Twenty-five bucks a night, first three nights free with a month commitment. What's not to love?"

I could think of a long list. Which would begin, most likely, with the trailer next door, which was listing noticeably to one side, had its door hanging open, and appeared to be pelted with bullet holes. Yikes. "You rented this for a month?"

"Yup." He wheeled his bike up to the door, parking it. "Which I figure is long enough to get myself where I need to be work-wise, hang with you, and hit the Beach Bash in great fashion. Preferably in that order. Come on, check out the inside."

He shrugged off his backpack and pulled out a keychain, from which he selected a tiny key. He fit it into the Master lock that hung from the camper's door. It stuck at first, but eventually he got it open, although it protested with a shriek-like sound. It was only because a car was approaching, the driver apparently not planning to slow down despite the fact that I was in his path, that I finally moved to join him.

"Watch your step," he said, extending a hand out to me as I got closer. I ducked into the narrow doorway, letting him pull me up to the camper proper. One of those kinds designed to be towed behind a truck, it was small, seemed ancient, and smelled strongly of bleach. Which had to be covering the scent of something else, although I didn't even want to think about what that might be. Theo, apparently not noticing this, had already begun the grand tour. "Now, this is the sleeping area, down here. Cool shelves, right? And then, behind you, there's the dining area, kitchenette, and social space."

I could barely turn around fully to see all this, it was so small. "I can't believe you're going from Sand Castles to this."

"Hey, I'm a New Yorker," he said, hardly bothered. "Small living space is what I'm accustomed to. And I'm already getting settled in. Have a seat!"

I looked where he was pointing. There, overturned, was one of the milk crates from Gert's. In typical Theo style, he'd draped a brightly colored cloth napkin over it. Even here, there would be pomp. I sat, simply for the head room.

"And now, we celebrate," he said, pulling over a beat-up wooden stool plastered with fishing reel stickers and settling in. He unzipped his backpack and took out a bottle of wine, already opened and corked, as well as two clear plastic cups, a jar of cocktail olives, and a small can of salted nuts. He poured a glass for me, then one for himself, arranging the food on the backpack's surface.

"What are we celebrating, exactly?" I asked.

He held up his cup, clearing his throat. "To freedom. And new beginnings."

I repeated this, and we tapped glasses. Despite my dislike for red wine, I took a big gulp, quickly followed by another one. "Are you going to tell me what happened now?"

He opened the olives. "You mean with Ivy?"

"I mean . . ." I looked around the camper again, then out the narrow door. The ocean was behind us, with many other vehicles in between. The only real view was the back of another RV, which had been in its spot long enough to have scrub and vines tangled around it. "There have clearly been some changes since I saw you last night."

"There have indeed." He grinned, then sat back, swishing his wine around his glass. "Okay. So the biggest news is that Clyde's going out on tour, in conjunction with the film's release early next year."

"I thought that wasn't definite."

"Oh, no. It's definite." He took a sip of his wine, closing his eyes. "What's not clear is what kind of support he'll need in terms of getting the work ready, dealing with the press, handling the publicity. Which is where I come in."

"You?" I said. "What about Ivy?"

"Well, there's the rub." He helped himself to a nut, then an olive. "My feeling was that, by the time this would all be happening, she'd be done with the film and have little need for me. But apparently, she felt differently."

I thought back to what she'd said when she arrived at the Washroom. "Feeling differently" was clearly an understatement. "So she threw you out?"

"Not initially," he replied. "When I first told her I wanted to go ahead and give my month's notice to pursue other opportunities, she was just really pissed. Said I was screwing her over, abandoning her. You know, her typical rant. But then when it came out those opportunities involved Clyde . . . that's when she went ballistic."

I watched him help himself to another olive. Drinks and snacks, so civilized, even in this most uncivilized of places. "Why, though?"

He shrugged. "Oh, she thinks I used her to get access to him. That I always intended the job with her to be a conduit to something bigger."

I couldn't help but notice how casual he was about all this. The one time I'd gotten fired—from a retail job at a dollar store in a now-defunct strip mall—I'd been totally freaked. "But that's not true. I mean, how could you have even have known Clyde would come around?"

He smiled. "I didn't. It was just a good hunch."

I looked at him, confused. "Wait. So you—you *did* sort of plan on this?"

"This?" He looked around the camper. "No. In my mind, it did not end like this. But I told you, Emaline: I'm driven. I don't settle. If I see something better within reach, I go for it."

"Even if it gets you fired?"

"Risk is part of ambition," he replied. "If living here is what I have to do, I'll take it, if the next step is my working for, and with, Clyde. I don't need a mansion, or Ivy for that matter, to make my play for the Best Job Ever. In fact, this might turn out to be the best thing that could have happened to me."

Now, I was really lost. "How do you figure?"

"You said it yourself," he replied. "He's Clyde Conaway. Which do you think he'd respect more: me living in that house, or this one?"

Something wasn't right here. It was like the smell of the bleach, obvious and nebulous at the same time, one thing covering another. "I think Clyde would see if you were trying to be something you're not."

"Maybe. Or maybe not." He smiled, then picked up the bottle, refilling both our glasses. "Regardless, the Best Summer Ever is about to become Better Than Ever. No more Ivy to deal with. We *have* to drink to that."

He held out his cup, and, slowly, I did the same. But as we pressed them together, I felt that same hesitancy, a bad feeling I could not name or shake. It stayed with me even after we left Lucky Number Seven (as I knew it would now forever be called) to return the bikes and get my car. Theo locked the camper, put his backpack on, then began pedaling back toward the pier, and I followed. Maybe it was the wine, or the freedom, but this time he was moving fast, as if lighter, and within very little time he'd sped out pretty far ahead of me. I waited for him to notice this and slow down, maybe even turn back. When it became clear he wasn't going to, I just pedaled faster, suddenly aware that the last thing I wanted was to be left behind.

17

IN THE DREAM, I was back in Theo's camper. Now, though, it was vast, huge, and I was looking for the door and unable to find it. As I searched, growing ever more frantic, the smell of bleach grew stronger and stronger, until I was coughing too hard to even see. When I woke up, I was gasping for air.

"Emaline?" Still fuzzy from sleep, I could barely make out my bedroom door opening in the morning light. Then my dad, a mask covering his own mouth, was beside my bed, pulling the covers back. "You're not supposed to be here."

"It's the middle of the night," I said, still coughing. "Where else would I be?"

"It's seven a.m." He eased me into a sitting position, then off the bed. "And when I checked around five thirty, you weren't here. Come on."

It was a good thing I was still half-asleep, not to mention coughing too hard to be expected to explain, because I was *busted*. I'd planned to make it home by curfew, only to fall asleep listening to music in the camper with Theo. Too much wine and olives, not enough of anything else. At any rate, when I'd finally woken up, I didn't want to leave the campground alone, waiting instead until it was light. Which had been, well, about an hour earlier. Whoops.

Luckily, my dad was too focused on getting me out of whatever toxic cloud he'd created to start in on me yet. Still, as he guided me over my threshold and down the hallway, I could hear him muttering.

"—specific point to make sure everyone was out of the house when the sealant was being applied," he was saying as I finally hit the fresh air and sucked in a deep breath. With the mask on, he looked like a surgeon delivering bad news. "Did you not get your mother's multiple messages?"

Now that I thought of it, I *had* seen a few texts on my phone. But then, the battery conked out. Theo's camper, among its many charms, had exactly one working—albeit ancient—outlet, which he needed for his computer, so I'd been out of luck. And incommunicado. "Sorry," I mumbled. "My battery died."

He sighed, annoyed with both me and this excuse: my phone was a common scapegoat. "You might have, too, if I hadn't heard you coughing."

"Is it seriously that dangerous?" I said. I mean, I got his whole renovation obsession thing, but there had to be limits.

"No," he grumbled. "But you don't want to be breathing it in for hours on end. Here, drink something."

He glanced around, then spotted a fountain drink, a straw sticking out, in my car console. As he opened the door to get it, it was like I could just *see* the next minute unfolding in front of me, and it was not going to be pretty. Quickly, I took it from him.

"Thanks," I said, sucking down a big, watery gulp of what had once been soda. "Whew. Much better."

And that was the exact moment that, despite my attempts to cover it with my hand, he saw the words on the side of the cup: CONROY PIER FISH/TACKLE. I'd told Theo this was not a safe place to go after dark—or really ever, as it was housed basically in a metal box beside the Sea View motel—but he'd insisted he was street smart and went for provisions anyway. "What could happen in Colby, really?" he'd asked, before disappearing into the dark. Now, I was pretty sure I was about to find out.

"Conroy," my dad said, looking at the cup, then at me. He still had on the mask, but now looked like an angry surgeon, one you definitely didn't want anywhere near you with a scalpel. "You were at the campground?"

I'd been hoping he'd ask if I'd been at the store itself. That way, I could answer honestly and say no. Just my luck. "Well," I said. "Sort of."

"Sort of," he repeated. I heard a car engine, and we both looked over to see my mom pulling into the driveway. She waved cheerfully. Neither of us waved back. "Which means yes."

"I was with Theo," I said, like this was going to win me any arguments.

"Why was *he* there? I thought he lived in a mansion out on the Tip."

"He did, with his boss. But his work and, um, living situation has changed." My mom was getting out of the car now, carrying bags from my dad's favorite breakfast place. Called

Roy's, it was known mostly for its sausage biscuit, which was so huge and greasy you needed a shower after eating one. "He's just renting a place for the rest of the summer."

"At the campground," he said, as my mom approached. "And you were there, all last night."

I nodded. He looked furious. On an unrelated note, now I could smell sausage.

"Good morning!" my mom said to me. "I didn't expect to see you here for breakfast. I figured you were still asleep at Daisy's."

"Nope," my dad said.

Just this single word, in this specific tone, clued her in that something was up. She looked at him, then at me. "What's going on?"

Neither of us replied. My dad was still glaring at me. Finally, he said, "Emaline spent the night at the campground. Apparently."

"What?" she demanded. My mom was a reactor: she could go from zero to seriously pissed in seconds. "Are you *crazy*?"

"Mom—"

"Do you even know what goes on there? It's basically lawless!" She thrust the bag at my dad, then focused again on me. "Now, I know you're about to leave for college and basically an adult. But I didn't raise you to be stupid, no matter how old you are."

Ouch. I knew better than to protest or defend myself, though. Like a storm, the best bet was to take whatever cover possible and wait for it to pass.

"She didn't get your messages," my dad added, taking out

a biscuit, the paper covering it wet with grease. "I just found her in her bed, breathing in fumes."

"I *was* coughing," I pointed out, as if this, again, was going to somehow win me points.

"You were in the house?" Then she turned to face Dad. "I thought you double-checked everyone was out before you started."

"I did. She came in after that."

I just looked at him. It wasn't like I'd expected him to break rank here—mostly because it had never happened that I could remember—but he was *really* not helping me. Unfazed, he pushed up his mask, meeting my gaze, then took a bite of his breakfast.

"Emaline," my mom was saying now, "I sent you several messages about the sealant. You *knew* not to be here this morning."

I waited for my dad to say I'd ignored her texts. Now, though, he was silent, leaving me to offer a lame, "My phone died."

"At the campground. In the middle of the night," my mom finished for me, not missing a beat. "What, do you have a death wish now, too?"

I was prepared to be berated about the phone and being out overnight. And if I'd been smart—or maybe just more awake—I would have just stood there and taken this with the rest of it. But stupidly, I said instead, "What's that supposed to mean?"

My mom took off her sunglasses, narrowing her eyes at me. "What did you just say?"

"You asked if I had a death wish now, *too*," I told her. "In addition to what else, exactly?"

My dad, having consumed an entire biscuit during this short exchange, crumpled up the paper in one hand and pulled the mask back down with the other. "I'm going in," he said to us. "Everyone else stays out here. Understood?"

"Yes," I told him. My mom said nothing. Then he walked away, leaving the Roy's bag on the hood of my car and us to it.

I knew she was waiting for me to speak first, backtrack somehow. Which was exactly why I didn't. Finally, she said, "God, Emaline. I just . . . I feel like I don't even know you anymore."

I had been expecting something harsh. But this went deeper than just anger or lashing out, and just like that, I felt small again.

"How can you say that?" I asked her. "Nothing's even changed yet."

"Are you kidding?" She held up a finger, counting off. "You broke up with Luke. You're out all hours. You don't return my calls or texts. You're going places you know *much* better than to be at any hour, much less late at night . . ."

"I'm eighteen," I said. "In a few weeks I'm leaving for college."

"But *not yet*," she shot back, now pointing the same finger at me. "And while you're here, you must follow our rules. I don't care if you have a new boyfriend, we're the same parents. And this is going to stop, right now."

"This isn't Theo's fault," I told her. "Just because you don't like him—"

"I don't know him!" she said. "You've never brought him home to meet us. We have no idea where he's from—"

"Unlike Luke, who you knew preconception," I finished for her.

"Stop it," she said, shaking her head.

"Seriously. If I'm only allowed to date people whose parents you went to high school with, I need to know that. It narrows the pool a bit."

"That is not what I'm saying."

"I hope not, because it was you, if I remember correctly, who was so adamant that I *not* end up tied down so young with someone from here. I mean, make up your mind. Do you *want* me to be like you, or not?"

I regretted these words the minute I said them. It was like I'd launched a missile, only to look down at the red button, scrambling for a way to unpress it. Her hurt expression, instant, was worse than anything she could have said. But she spoke anyway.

"What I did," she said, her voice strangely calm, even, "was give up everything for the wrong person. It was a mistake. I can't undo it. The closest I get, every day, is making sure you don't do the same thing."

"Mom," I said.

"But you're right. You're a big girl now. I can't protect you anymore from everything. Especially yourself." She looked away, then back at me, taking a step forward. "But know this, Emaline. The mistakes you make now count. Not for everything, and not forever. But they do matter, and they shape you. If you take nothing else from what I've been through, at least remember this: make your choices well. Because you'll always be accountable for them. That's what being an adult is all about."

And with that, she grabbed the bag off the car hood, turned, and walked away. I stood there, in my pajamas, watching her as she got in her car and drove off, not looking at me once. When she was gone, I glanced at my watch. Sure enough, now I was late for work. I went over to the front door, slightly ajar, and stuck my head in, looking for my dad.

"Hello?" I called out.

No answer.

"Is it safe for me to run in superfast and get dressed?"

Nothing.

"Dad?"

I stepped in, listening. I could hear him moving around upstairs and waited another beat for a response. When none came, I took a last deep breath of fresh air, then ventured in, hoping for the best. Clearly, now, I was on my own.

* * *

Fifteen minutes later, feeling light-headed but now appropriately attired, I headed to work. When I approached the lot, however, the first thing I saw was my mom's car, flanked by both Amber's and Margo's. Which meant they were already gathered at the conference table, eating biscuits and discussing me. No thanks. I kept driving.

And driving. Since it was early, the road to North Reddemane was clear, with most of the traffic going in the other direction. I wasn't even sure where I was going until I saw Gert's rising up in the distance. I put on my blinker and turned in.

Mr. Gertmann wasn't behind the counter, although he was clearly not far. The TV was on, a newspaper open by the register, one of those packaged sticky honey buns, half-eaten, beside it. I went to the cooler and got a soda, grabbed some crackers more from habit than anything else, then walked over to the back door and looked out at the house just behind the store. Like always, Rachel was at the table by the window, head bent, working on her bracelets. It was like she hadn't moved, or changed, since the night all those weeks ago I'd come here with Theo and found the milk crates. That made one of us.

I'd only been a kid when her accident had happened, but it was still an event that loomed large in my memory. I clearly recalled the bake sales and car washes that were held to raise money for her hospital expenses, as well as seeing her parents push her in a wheelchair into Da Vinci's for pizza. Even after the hospital and rehab, Rachel had looked the same, for the most part, a pretty, normal girl. At least on the outside. Within her mind, though, she'd remained sixteen, even as her body, friends, and family grew older. How weird that must be, to stay the same as everyone else changes. Even if you weren't able to understand, you had to notice.

For some reason, right then, I thought of my mom, seeing again her hurt face looking at me, once that missile was launched. She, too, had hit the pause button on her life, albeit in a different way, when she got pregnant with me. Left behind while everyone else grew up, moved away, moved on. Talk about accountability.

I sucked in a breath, putting my hand to my chest. I knew the sound could not have carried far, but across the backyard, Rachel suddenly looked up, seeing me. A half-finished Gert bracelet hung from one hand, a bead poised in the fingers of the other. After a moment, she looked away.

I turned, walking quickly to the front of the store. The TV was showing a clip of a guy holding up a huge marlin: RECORD BREAKER! the text below read. I pulled out a couple of bills, put them on the counter, and left.

Make your choices well, my mom had said. It was what she thought she hadn't done, what she hoped above everything I'd do differently. On the flip side, though, there was Clyde, telling me that there *were* second chances, even—and especially—when you've given up all hope of them. But maybe, when a life and summer was going so fast, you couldn't wait for fate to punch the time card. You had to do it yourself.

My father's house was only a few blocks from Gert's. When I turned in the driveway, the paper was still there, but the front door was open. Someone was already up.

Up on the porch, I peered through the screen, expecting to find Benji at the table with his laptop and other distractions. Instead, I saw only my father, a coffee mug in hand. He had his back to me and was sitting alone in the only chair remaining in the otherwise empty living room.

"Hello?" I called out.

He turned, squinting to make me out through the screen. "Who's there?"

"It's me," I replied. Then, to clarify: "Emaline."

"Oh." I saw him check his watch. "Come in."

I did, noting the loud creak of the screen door as I eased it open. I would have to tell Margo to grease that before she showed the house, although I was sure she'd already made a note of it, somewhere. "You're up early," I said.

"As are you," he replied, as I came into the living room. He glanced around. "I'd offer you a seat, but . . ."

"It's fine," I said, sitting down on the bare floor. "You weren't kidding when you said you were only keeping the minimum, were you?"

"I hadn't expected to go *quite* this sparse," he replied, looking around again. "Your sister, however, made a strong argument for having a 'blank slate' so possible buyers could 'create their own vision.'"

I smiled. "That sounds like Margo. Not only a realtor, but a force of nature."

"Not unlike another woman from the same family I know," he said, taking a sip from his mug.

"Mom can be hard to deal with," I agreed, pulling my legs up to my chest. "I can attest to that personally. Especially today."

"Mom?" He looked confused. "I was talking about you, actually."

"Me?" I said. He nodded. "Oh. Sorry. I—"

"Emily as a force of nature," he said slowly, as if trying out not only the words but the very concept. "Can't say that's the first thing that comes to mind when I think of her."

I had a feeling I knew what that first thing was. Sitting here in front of him, eighteen years later. I didn't say this, though. I'd start really talking when I was ready.

"Of course, she was young when I knew her. We both were. Just about your age, I guess. Wow." He sighed, was quiet for a moment. Then, suddenly, he smiled apologetically, as if just remembering I was there. "I'm sorry. You caught me in an entirely too introspective moment. All too common lately, I'm afraid."

"It's okay," I told him. "Seems to be going around."

He picked up his cup again. "Honestly, I thought I'd be thrilled to get an early offer on this place. But now that it might really happen, the thought of leaving it behind, for good . . . it's more bittersweet than I expected."

"You got an offer already?"

He looked at me, nodding. "Just yesterday. It's only been on the market three weeks. So much for the bust, huh?"

"Are you going to take it?"

"We very well might." He sat back, taking another sip. "It would really be ideal. We could get the paperwork going, then head back to the city. Benji would have time to get adjusted to me moving out before school starts . . ."

"He thinks he's here for a while longer, though," I said.

"I know. And he'll be disappointed. But we have to leave eventually. A few weeks one way or the other won't make that much of a difference."

I wasn't so sure about that. There may have only been a

certain number of days before I left myself for school—not that I had counted them out to the one—but if they were suddenly taken, I knew I'd feel cheated. And maybe a little scared. "I'm really . . ." I said. I swallowed. "I'll miss him."

He looked at me. "I know. And he'll miss you. You've been the one bright spot in what was otherwise a pretty hard summer for him. I appreciate all you've done."

"Of course," I said. "He's my brother."

At this, he smiled. Then, we just sat there for a moment, in silence. If they were really leaving, it was all the more reason to handle this one last piece of our unfinished business. Maybe this, right here, was fate giving me that in. Now I just had to be accountable for what I did with it.

"I'm really glad you guys came down here this summer," I began. "Even if the reason wasn't, you know, so ideal."

He smiled wryly, taking a sip of his coffee. "That's a kind understatement."

I took a deep breath. Here goes, I thought. "Truthfully, until that day you called, I was thinking I might never hear from you again."

Again, it was instant, how he reacted to this last sentence: his entire body tensed, from his face to his shoulders, directly into fight-or-flight mode. "I told you, we don't need to talk about all that," he said, his voice stiff. "It's in the past."

"Maybe," I replied. "But it was still really . . . hurtful to me. And confusing. I didn't understand why—"

"Because I was getting a divorce," he finished for me, his voice sharp. "Because I thought I would have the money, and then I didn't. That's why."

It took me a minute, but finally I spoke. "Money? You think that's what this is about?"

"I think," he said, "that it's bad enough that you're having to go to a state school after all the work we did to get you into Columbia. The only thing worse is that you continue to feel the need to berate me about it."

"Berate you?" I said. "You won't even *talk* about it."

He threw up his hands. "What are we doing right now, then?"

"This," I said, circling my own hands in the air between us, "is only because I came here and forced the conversation. If it was up to you, I'd just suck it up, all that hurt and confusion, all because you don't like feeling uncomfortable."

"What I don't like," he shot back, "is rehashing my failures. I tried to help you, I failed. There. Is that what you want? Happy now?"

For a moment, I was speechless. Finally I managed, "I got a full ride at a good school. That's not failing."

"It's not Columbia." He sighed, rubbing his face.

"Wait, so that's just it?" I asked. He looked at me, his expression weary. "Just because things aren't exactly what you wanted, they're nothing?"

"I was disappointed," he said.

"Disappointment," I reminded him, "is part of life. Just like change. You told me Benji should already understand that. Why can't you?"

"You don't understand!" he said, his voice rising. I'd never seen him upset, didn't know this side of him, and I felt my skin flush, my own fight or flight. But I stayed put. After all that silence, for so long, I was ready for some noise. "Columbia was my chance to fix everything for you. To get you out of here, give you a life not like your mother's, or grandmother's. And I *couldn't do it.*"

I swallowed, making myself take a breath. I felt eerily calm as I said, "I was never broken. I didn't need you to fix me."

He shook his head. "That's the whole point, Emaline. You don't *know* what you need."

"What I needed," I said, picking my words and tone carefully, "was for you to reply to my graduation invitation. To come watch me walk. To be proud of me no matter where I went to school."

"I wanted the best for you," he said, his voice clenched. "*Only* the best."

"Well, too bad," I said. "When you have a kid, you sign on for the whole package: good, bad, everything in between. You can't just dip in and out, picking and choosing the parts you want and quitting when it's not perfect."

"I was going to get you out of this place," he shot back.

"I'm still going!"

"Two hours away."

"Yes, at first," I said. "But from there, I can go anywhere. It's supposed to be a start, not a finish."

"You're so *young,*" he groaned, slapping a hand onto his forehead. "You have no idea how one bad choice, one stupid mistake, can change everything for you. And once it's done, believe me: it's *done.* But the sick part is, you'll *still* spend your whole life trying to fix it."

One bad choice. One big mistake. One summer. One girl. One Emaline.

"You say *it*," I said softly. "But you mean me. Right?"

He bit his lip, but didn't say anything. He didn't have to. Because right then, suddenly, irrevocably, I understood. All this time, from the day at Igor's when he'd first brought up the subject of college, I'd thought this was about what he wanted for my life, my future. But it was never about me.

My mom had taught me a lot of things. But one of the big ones was that if you made a mistake, you owned up to it, learned from it. My father, I saw now, wasn't able to do this; he couldn't even get past trying to fix it. That was his problem, though. No matter what he thought, I wasn't a problem or mistake. I was his daughter. And despite all of this, and him, I was going to be just fine.

For a moment, we just sat there, staring at each other. Like the next word would tip the balance, for good, forever. So it was a fortunate thing, maybe, that it was neither of us who said it.

"Hellooo!" A loud, cheerful voice came through the screen door. "Anybody home?"

It was Margo. My father held my gaze another moment, then turned. "We're in here. Come on in."

She did, the screen door squeaking loudly. "Have to get that greased before the next walk-through," I heard her say as she approached, heels clacking. "Among a thousand other things. But first, I have great news. The interested buyers want to—"

Whether she stopped talking and walking because she saw me or hit the wall of tension was hard to say. Either way, just like that, she, too, was silent. For about two seconds.

"Emaline," she said. "What are you doing here so early?"

I swallowed, trying to calm myself. "I was in the neighborhood."

"Oh." She looked more closely at my face, which I knew was flushed, then at my father. "Well, great. Then you'll hear it here first: the buyers are ready to sign a letter of intention!"

She was so excited and proud about this, she reminded me of Theo. Clearly, it was a moment for pomp and celebration. Which, unfortunately, was a bit harder to come by when you've just walked into a war zone. Still, I tried. "That's great, Margo."

"Isn't it?" She looked at my father. "At this rate, we can go ahead and get all the inspections started, then begin working up a contract and the other paperwork."

"Perfect," my father said, pushing himself to his feet. "Let's do it. It's time for us to get home."

"Oh, of course," Margo gushed, "and really, you won't want to be living here during all of this anyway, if you can help it. Now, I just realized I left my folder in the car—of course!—but let me just grab it, and we'll go over some preliminary details."

"Fine," he said, cutting her off. "I'll be in the kitchen."

And with that, he walked away. Down the hall, out of sight, gone once more. This time, though, unlike so many others, I didn't feel confused or wrong or angry. Just sad and disappointed. Like I was finally catching up to some Big Event of my own I'd been chasing, only to find it was over and done long ago.

I got to my feet and walked to the door. Margo followed me. "Are you okay? You seem—"

"I'm fine," I said, starting down the front walk.

"Were you arguing with him?"

"I have to go, Margo."

"Hey." She reached out and touched my shoulder. "Look at me."

I turned to face her. "Please. I'm really late for work, okay?"

"What happened, Emaline?"

"Nothing."

She cocked her head to the side, clearly doubting this, as I got into my car. But the thing was, it was the truth. *Nothing.* It had been what always happened when it came to my father, save for a few months where I mistook his ego for something else. That was the problem, though. When you've never gotten love from someone, you don't know what it might look like if it ever does appear. You look for it in everything: any bright light overhead could be a star.

All the way back to Colby, all I could think was that I'd lost something I never really had. And yet, the sadness in finally letting it go was as real as the tears filling and blurring my eyes. Worse, I had no idea where to go, or anyone who could understand. Not Theo, with whom this was already a loaded issue, or even Morris and Daisy, who had heard enough about my father to last us all the rest of our lifetimes.

If the light outside the realty office hadn't turned red, I was sure I would have driven right past and on, over the bridge, maybe even farther. But when it slipped to yellow, I eased on the brakes, wiping at my eyes. I'd only sat there a second when I looked over to the parking lot and saw my mother.

She was standing on the front porch of the office, scanning the approaching traffic. Clearly, Margo had called her. I waited; one beat, then another. Finally, she spotted my car. When our eyes met, she bit her lip, then came down the steps into the lot, crossing her arms over her chest. The light changed, and I put on my blinker and turned in, now sobbing. I'd disappointed her too that day, and an awful lot lately. But still, when I got out of the car, she was waiting for me.

18

IT WASN'T A cocktail maker. It was a monstrosity.

"You know," my mom said, from the open conference room door, "you don't have to do this today."

"It's been on the requested-items list for over a week now," I pointed out, climbing up on a chair with the box cutter and looking for a good angle to start in on the carton.

"Requested by the *owner,* not the tenant. They don't even know it's coming."

I looked at her. "Wouldn't *you* want this, if you knew it was available?"

She studied the picture on the front again, the sight of which, when UPS had dropped it off moments earlier, had left us all speechless. We'd seen it all. But never something like the Slusher Pro.

It was, at its basic core, a margarita machine. But this was like saying Mount Everest was a steep hill. It was *huge*, with one megablender, which, according to the box, held up to four gallons of mix, liquor, and ice. That alone was impressive. But it also had *five* different receptacles on its movable base so you could always have a fresh batch with the push of a button. No more constantly rinsing out the blender and refilling the alcohol to keep your guests adequately inebriated. Do it once, and the Slusher Pro did the rest.

"I still think," my mother said now, as I wrestled the box open, "that we need to have some kind of waiver involved with this. No good can come of that much tequila consumption."

"I don't know. Last time I saw Ivy, she sounded like she might need it."

It seemed both appropriate and ironic that it was the owners of Sand Dollars who had bought this mega-appliance, which had been on back order so long that both they and we had forgotten all about it. Once we looked at the paperwork, however, I remembered there being specific owner notes about leaving the space above the bar area open for "cocktail accessories." Which I'd assumed meant maybe a nice rack holding shakers and strainers. Silly me.

"Nobody needs this." She picked up a pack of shrink-wrapped papers. "Is this the manual? Good Lord, it's thicker than the one for the copy machine."

"You're not helping," I told her, freeing the huge engine-like base. "Can you make some room on the table there?'

She did, pushing aside the leftover biscuits and drinks from Roy's, which, as I expected, had been there when we came inside an hour earlier. Sausage had again been all I could smell as she'd led me to a chair, and made me sit, then fetching one of Benji's supercold Cokes and a box of tissues. I worked my way through both as I told her what had happened with my father, getting a headache from either a brain freeze or the copious amount of tears. Either way, by the time I finally stopped talking, I was a sniffling, caffeinated mess.

"That's it," she'd said, when I was done, reaching for her phone. "I'm calling him right now."

"*Don't*," I said. "This isn't your problem."

"How can you even *say* that?" She leaned forward, so we were knee to knee, her hands covering mine. "The one thing I've always prided myself on is that I always did my best to keep him from hurting you. And it keeps happening anyway."

"I'm a big girl," I told her. "I need to deal with him like one. Which means not having my mom fight my battles for me."

She'd done enough of that to last us both our lifetimes. And in truth, what she'd said in our fight earlier was still resonating with me, even if she'd forgotten. Eighteen years earlier, she'd given up her future for mine. That she'd ever think for a moment this might have been a mistake was enough to make me want to spend every day of it proving otherwise.

"He shouldn't be battling you, period," she said, clearly not convinced. "I can't *believe* he still acts like such a spoiled brat. I swear, it's like he never grew up at all."

"I'm okay, Mom," I told her.

"This is you okay?" she said, nodding at the pile of crumpled tissues on the table beside me.

"Yeah," I said. "It is."

I knew it sounded weird. But beneath the tears and the sobs, there'd been this sense of relief, a feeling that something long nagging at me was finally closed and finished. For months now I'd carried around all this hurt and confusion, not letting myself truly feel it. But in that drive from North Reddemane, I finally got it. We wouldn't have some big bonding moment, a sudden shift where he became everything I needed him to be. He wasn't a problem for me to fix, either. Instead, he was a truth to accept, just like the fact that he'd always be on that line of my family tree. There was a peace in that, just as there was in knowing that whether he became anything else would, in the end, be up to only me.

Now, as I pulled out the rest of the pieces of the Slusher Pro, I felt my phone buzz in my pocket. I pulled it out to find a message from Theo.

Phase one of Best Future Job Ever begins: now. Going to talk to Clyde.

Clearly, I was not the only one in a life-changing mode. I texted him back, wishing him luck, then climbed down from the chair. "Theo," I explained to my mom.

"Right," she said.

We were both quiet a minute as, channeling my dad—known at our house as the Great Assembler—I spread out all the parts neatly before opening the manual. Finally I said, "He's a really nice guy, you know."

"I'm sure he is," she replied. "But I still don't want you at the campground."

"How am I supposed to see him?"

"There's the entire rest of town," she said drily. "I'm sure you'll figure out something."

"So we can hang out in my room, then? I promise to lock the door."

She narrowed her eyes at me. "Not funny."

Still I laughed, and then she was leaving, sighing loudly as she went. I took a trip to the storeroom, where I dug around for the screwdrivers I needed, then got to work. Despite the

Slusher Pro's size and paperwork—half of which turned out to be drink recipes—it went quickly, and within about forty minutes it was done. Which brought me to my next problem.

"Oh, right," my mom said, after I called her back. "Moving it. Wait, will it fit through the door?"

"Don't even joke about that," I said. Of course I hadn't considered this. "It has to. My point is, I'm not going to be able to get it to Sand Dollars ' y myself."

"I'd help, but I have a ten o'clock," she said. She scanned the office through the conference room windows. "What about Rebecca?"

I gave her a doubtful look. "Have you ever seen her lift anything? Look at her biceps. They're spindly."

"True." She sighed. "Well, just leave it for now, I guess, and we'll—"

Just then, though, the cavalry arrived. Or, Morris and Benji did. Margo, who was also not known for her upper-body strength, was right behind them.

"Wow!" Benji said, as soon as he spotted the Slusher. "Is that a smoothie maker?"

"Sort of," I said.

"The Slusher Pro," Morris observed admiringly. "Cool."

"You know the Slusher Pro?"

"They have one at Tallyho," he told me. I just looked at him. "What? I've been picking up some shifts there."

"You have?"

"Don't sound so surprised," he said. "I do work, you know?"

"That does not sound like the Morris I know," I said, studying his face. "Who have you been talking to?"

"Nobody," he said.

I just looked at him.

"I bumped into Clyde at the Gas/Gro last night," he said with a shrug. "He said he had some odd jobs that needed doing. I figure between that, Tallyho, and Ivy, I'll be finally making some bank. Maybe enough for a trip to Savannah this fall."

"Savannah?" I raised my eyebrows. "So you're *not* doing that thing we talked about at my house the other day?"

"I don't know," he replied. "I just figured I'd try getting off the couch first, and go from there."

I smiled. "You just keep surprising me."

"Yeah, well." Morris was not one for mushy moments, especially in public or daylight. "Anyway, I'm headed over to the Washroom right now."

"Wow," I said, trying not to sound as shocked as I felt. "That's great. Although it leaves me out of luck. I was hoping you'd have time to help me take this to Ivy's."

"I can help!" Benji said, jumping up and down. "Can I help?"

"Absolutely," I told him. "But I think we *might* need more muscle than just us."

"Oh, right." He glanced at Rebecca, who looked back at us, surely wondering why we all kept looking at her, and her spindly arms, so disdainfully. "Hey, I know! We can ask Luke."

"Luke?" I said.

"Yeah. I just saw him outside. Hold on!"

And then, before I could stop him, he was running out the door, letting it slam behind him. A beat later, it opened again, revealing an attractive, dark-haired woman in black pants, a flowing shirt, and strappy sandals. When she saw me, she broke into a wide smile.

"Emaline! Hello!" As she came closer, I realized it was my stepmother. "Joel said you might be here. I'm so happy to see you!"

Over her shoulder I saw my mom trying to place her face. "Leah," I said, loud enough so she'd hear. "I didn't even know you were coming."

"No? Well, I suppose it was a bit last minute." She stepped back, holding me at arm's length. "Oh, you just look so grown up! I can't believe you're going to college in a few weeks. Are you excited? Nervous?'

"A bit of both, actually."

"I'm sure." As she squeezed my hands, still smiling warmly, I was reminded of how much I'd actually liked her, the few times we'd crossed paths. "But you'll do great. We're so proud of you."

Considering the events the morning, this was a bit hard to believe. Still, I appreciated her saying it. "Thanks."

"Of course. Oh! That reminds me. Before I forget . . ." She reached into her bag, digging around for a minute before finally pulling out a blue envelope. She held it to her chest, glancing at the door for a minute before saying, "First off, I have to say I know this is horrifically late. It's *so* embarrassing. But as I'm sure you've heard, we've been, um, dealing with a lot since the spring. And for what it's worth, I *have* had it since June. I just never quite got it in the mail."

She held out the envelope, and I took it, aware of the fact that both my mom and sister were now watching from their respective offices. I wanted to just thank her and open it later, in private, but she was looking at me so expectantly I knew she was waiting for the big reveal. I slid my finger under the flap and eased out a card.

ON YOUR GRADUATION, it said on the front, in raised, flowing script. Inside were a few equally overworded lines about "moving into the future with the greatest of hopes and dreams ahead," beneath which was a big *Congratulations! Love, Dad, Leah, and Benji.* A check, folded, was taped to the inside.

"You didn't have to do this," I said, suddenly embarrassed.

"Of course we did! It's a milestone." She pointed a finger at me. "Just promise me you'll spend it on something fun, okay? It doesn't have to be for books or school stuff. Unless, you know, you want it to be."

"Thank you," I said.

She smiled, nodding, and I was finally able to put the card in my pocket, just as Benji returned, this time with Luke in tow. Despite everything, I still got that same little jump in my gut at the sight of him. Like over all those years he'd worn a groove in my heart so deep it would always be there.

"Here he is!" Benji called out. "He was just about to leave but I stopped him."

"Too bad for you," I said to Luke.

"Hey, I was told margaritas were involved," he replied. "That's all I needed to hear."

"It's nine in the morning," I pointed out.

"Do you want my help or not?"

Leah reached out to Benji, pulling him into her hip. "What

do you say, bud? Ready to go get some breakfast?"

"But I'm helping Emaline and Luke," he protested.

"Oh, it's okay," I told him. "Breakfast sounds much better than dealing with this."

"But it's my job," Benji said, turning to me. "Right?"

Leah raised her eyebrows.

"He's been doing some stuff around here for me," I explained. "He's been a big help."

"I came up with a new drink and packet system," Benji chimed in. "I froze the waters!"

"That's great, honey," she said, glancing at me. "But I'm sure Emaline will understand if you want the day off to show me around Colby."

"Oh, sure," I said quickly. "Go have fun. Trust me, the work will still be here."

Benji did not look convinced or enthusiastic. But as his mom slid her arm over his shoulder, he allowed himself to be turned towards the door. Leah called out to Margo, "Did I sign everything you needed back at the house? Or is there more?"

"Nothing right now," my sister replied. "We'll get the rest of it when we meet this afternoon. In the meantime, I'll work on finding you all a place for the next few nights."

"Oh, that would be wonderful, thank you so much."

"My pleasure," Margo told her, and then they were leaving, Benji dragging his feet slightly as he went.

Once the door shut behind them, I asked Margo, "Did *you* know she was coming?"

"I knew it was planned for some point. But it was a surprise to see her today. It's good for getting the paperwork going though, so I'm glad." She lowered her voice. "Hey. Are you okay? That thing with your father seemed sort of intense earlier, back at the house."

"I'm fine," I told her. To Luke I said, "So you really think you're up for this?"

"Moving a margarita machine?" He snorted. "Please. How hard can it be?"

About twenty minutes later, outside of Sand Dollars, we were finding out. Not only was it heavy—blame that huge motor—but also of the most awkward size, really hard to get a good grip on, well, anywhere. At Colby Realty, we'd recruited a couple of maintenance guys and Rebecca and her spindly arms to help get it into the back of the truck. Here, though, we were on our own.

"If I get a hernia," Luke huffed from the step above me, trying to move backwards, "I am suing your entire family."

"Maybe it would help if you took your shirt off," I suggested. "It seems to work with the pool cleaning, yes?"

"Do you want me to drop this?" he asked, nodding at his end of the machine.

"Please, God, no," I said, laughing.

"I didn't think so." He grunted, going up another step. "So typical. We're together for a half hour and you're already trying to get me naked."

"Don't flatter yourself," I said. "Besides, don't you have a girlfriend?"

He glanced at me. "Where'd you hear that?"

"It's all the talk at Tallyho."

He rolled his eyes.

"I'm kidding. Amber told me. Plus, I did see you guys together, remember? You were in a tie for her."

"The tie was for my *mother*," he corrected me.

"Still," I said. There was a pause, which might have been awkward were we not already in duress. "I'm happy for you."

"Yeah, well," he said, clearly uncomfortable. He wasn't the only one. But it had to mean something that we'd gotten to this point. "Thanks."

By now, I was full-on sweating, both arms straining and burning, legs wobbly. I was pretty sure my lungs just popping like balloons was next. Just in time, we made it to the top of the steps. Hallelujah.

"Oh . . . my . . . God," Luke panted once we put the machine down. He bent over, hands on his knees. "And we're not even *done* yet."

"No more stairs," I told him. "Although we do have to deal with another difficulty."

"What's that?"

"Not what. Who."

I hit the doorbell. A moment later, the intercom crackled. "If you're selling something," a loud voice said, already annoyed, "I'm not interested. Actually, even if you're *not* selling anything. I'm not interested, period."

Luke raised his eyebrows.

"Hi, Ivy! It's me," I called out cheerfully. "Emaline."

Pause. Then, flatly, "Theo doesn't live here anymore."

"I'm here on official realty office business," I told her. "Can you buzz me in?"

A pause. Then, the lock clicked open. We were in.

Or the door was open. We still had to heave the machine over the threshold, then get it down the hallway to the wet-bar area in the living room. Compared to the stairs, it was much easier. Compared to just about anything else, though, it was not.

"How big *is* this room?" Luke, walking backwards, panted at me, as we passed one of the couches.

"Only a little farther," I told him. "You're going to need to turn right about . . . now."

He pivoted and I did the same, until we both were parallel with the countertop. "Hoisting and praying on three," he said. "One, two, three."

With all the strength I had left, which wasn't much, I pushed my end onto the counter. Finally. My arms were shaking again. Across from me, Luke's face was red, his shirt damp. We were both breathing hard, recovering, when I heard Ivy's voice.

"What the hell is *that*?" she demanded, from the hallway.

"Our cause of death," Luke told her. "Be sure to tell the coroner."

I laughed, still breathless, which made me start coughing. Pretty soon, it advanced to hacking. Luke glanced around, then grabbed a glass from the bar. He filled it and handed it to me. I sucked it down, then told Ivy, "It's a margarita machine."

"I don't need a margarita machine," she said.

"With something like this, is it really about *need*, though?" Luke asked her.

She just looked at him. "Let me rephrase. I don't want a margarita machine."

"Yes, but the owners of this house do. They ordered this way back in April." I turned, wiping a smudge from the main engine barrel. "You might use it."

"Unless it can shoot and edit footage and help run my production company, I doubt it," she grumbled. "Find me a machine that will do that, and I'll pay for it myself."

Luke looked at me. I said, "I think it just makes drinks, actually."

"Too bad." Ivy sighed as, from down the hallway, there was a loud bang, followed by another. She wiped at her face, seemingly not hearing it. One more bang. Finally, she saw we'd noticed and explained, "The screen door in my bedroom is busted. I get percussion when it's windy. Which is always."

"It's broken?" I asked. "Why didn't you call us to come fix it?"

"Oh, I don't know," she said, flipping her wrist. "Too busy dealing with arrogant artists and traitorous employees. A girl's only got so much time in the day."

"Wow," Luke said, under his breath.

Ivy looked at him. "Aren't you the pool guy?"

"Yep," he replied. "I wear many hats."

"That seems to be the norm around here," she observed, nodding at me. "This one has a habit of popping up everywhere I turn."

"She'll do that," he agreed. The door banged again, hard.

"Can I go take a look?" I asked her.

"Sure," she said, walking into the kitchen and pulling open the fridge. "Knock yourself out."

I started down the hallway, Luke following. When Ivy was out of earshot, I heard him say, "Man. She's a piece of work, huh?"

"You have *no* idea," I said. "She's—"

I had to stop there, as what I found myself facing struck me utterly, suddenly speechless. Oh my God.

The airy, expansive master bedroom I'd helped furnish back in May had been gorgeous, with creamy, white walls, a huge bed with a full ivory comforter and pillows, and matching dresser, chair, and bedside tables with pale wood accents. A framed, mirrored mosaic hung over the bed, with a flat-screen TV mounted on the wall opposite. The rest of the room was windows, huge, tall ones, showing the best view of the ocean. It was, seriously, one of the prettiest rooms I'd ever seen, like something from a magazine.

This room, however, was a pigsty: dim, cluttered, and smelling strongly of fried food. I couldn't even see the ocean, due to the black trash bags that had been put up—oh, God, please not with tape, I thought—to cover the windows entirely. The comforter lay in a heap on the floor, dotted with water and Diet Coke bottles, which also covered any other flat surface, often two or three deep. The floor was equally cluttered, with piles of papers, at least two different laptops, tangles of cords, and, inexplicably, many boxes of cereal, several of which were both open and spilling. And then, there was the banging.

The screen door, I saw as I peered into the dimness, was not just broken. It was hanging by only the top hinges, scraping the house's exterior each time a gust of wind blew up underneath it. Which, judging by the noise and the plentiful white paint chips piled up along the slim bit of view visible under the garbage bags—which were, in fact, attached with duct tape, oh dear Jesus—was pretty much constantly.

I couldn't even make a noise. Maybe I squeaked. It was Luke who said, "Oh, boy. Someone's not getting their deposit back."

"The windows . . ." I pointed, my finger shaking. "And . . . the carpet. Is that . . . is that *blood* over there?"

He stepped around me, gingerly, then navigated past a box of Froot Loops, two empty coffee mugs, and a huge pile of clothes to examine it. "Not blood. Cranberry juice, maybe?"

"I think I'm going to pass out," I said, reaching behind me for the wall. Instead, I hit a couple of plastic bottles, knocking them to the floor.

"Go ahead. I'm going to shut this door up before it makes me crazy." He picked his way across the floor, over the laptops and cords, and started feeling around under the garbage bags for the door handle. After searching a bit, he pulled the bag loose. And there was light.

I bent down, picking up the bottles I'd knocked over, an action not unlike removing a tablespoon of water from a tidal wave. "Who rents an ocean-view house . . . and then covers up the view?"

"The same person who lets a loose door scrape off half their siding, apparently," he reported, having finally gotten the sliding door open. Fresh air was coming in now, a stark contrast to the dankness. He stuck his head out, examining the damage. "Boy. Forget the deposit. She's in for more than that with this repair alone."

Now that I could see, I went over to the windows and carefully eased off a large piece of duct tape to take down another bag. It took up paint, leaving behind black, sticky residue. Still, the light made me feel better, so I started taking them all down. Luke pitched in, and soon the room was flooded with sunshine. Which, honestly, just made things look worse. The door was still banging.

"I'm going to get the toolbox from my truck," he said, as I surveyed the clutter and damage again. "I can at least take it off that hinge. Okay?"

I nodded, dumbly, and he headed to the door, clapping my shoulder on the way out. He knew better than to offer anything more positive.

I wasn't sure how long I stood there, just staring, before I heard Ivy behind me. She was just suddenly there. "What'd you do to the windows?"

I turned, slowly, to face her. "Me? What did *I* do to the windows?"

She pointed at them. "I had them covered for a reason."

"With garbage bags and duct tape?" I was pretty sure I was shrieking.

"I'm very light sensitive," she told me.

"Then sleep in a hole, not an oceanfront mansion!" Okay, I was shrieking. "I can't believe you did this to this room. It was perfect before you moved in. Pristine. And now—"

"Oh, it's not that bad," she said, looking around.

"Are you an *animal*?" I demanded. She looked at me, surprised. "Seriously. Because only animals live like this."

"It's just messy," she told me. "Calm down."

"Calm down?" I repeated. "The owners of this place are expecting to move in as soon as you leave. Which, by the looks of this, will probably be today."

"You can't kick me out," she said. "I have a contract."

"Read it," I said, gesturing around me. "You're in violation."

Now, she actually looked sort of worried. "I have to stay here until I finish this phase of the project. Especially since I'm working alone now."

"You should have thought about that before you trashed someone else's house."

In response, she picked up a Diet Coke bottle from the floor, then another one beside it, tucking them under her arm. "It's not trashed. It's just messy. Watch, I can fix it."

"The outside of the house is scraped clean of paint," I said, my voice flat. "Can you fix that?"

"Probably not," she admitted, still gathering up bottles, now at a faster clip. "But you can. Right?"

I just looked at her. "Why on earth would I help you?"

Her arms were full of bottles now. "You help everyone else."

"What?"

"You do!" she said, turning and dumping them out into the hallway. "You helped Theo, and Clyde . . ."

"That was different. They're my friends."

She looked up at me, one of the laptops now in her hands. "Oh, that's nice. Thank you so much."

"Ivy. We're not friends," I told her as she walked over to the bedside table, the laptop's cord dragging behind her, knocking bottles over as it went. Watching the plug approach an open box of Kix, I couldn't help myself. I went over and picked it up. "You don't even like me."

"That's not true," she said, dumping the laptop on the bed. I picked up another box of cereal, as well as a couple of more bottles. "I have no feelings about you whatsoever."

"The feeling's mutual." I picked up the two mugs. "Oh, for God's sake. I'm going to get a trash bag."

"Maybe bring the box," she called out, as I stomped down the hallway, passing Luke on his way back in with his toolbox.

"Are we leaving?" he asked.

"No. We're cleaning," I told him. Then I hit the laundry room closet, where just about everything I'd stocked at the beginning of the season—cleansers, wipes, mops, and sprays—remained basically untouched. Even the vacuum cleaner still had a plastic cover on the plug. Unbelievable.

Back in the bedroom, Ivy was still picking up things off the floor, while Luke was working on the hinge with a screwdriver. I walked over to the red stain with some carpet cleaner, taking out my aggression on the pump until it was totally saturated. "This better come up."

"It's just tomato juice," she told me.

"*Just?*" I said.

Outside the open door, Luke snickered. I looked at him,

and he reared back. "Sorry. No offense. But if you could see your face right now . . ." He trailed off, biting his lip.

"This is so not funny," I told him.

"You're exactly right," he replied, now straight-faced. "It's dire."

Now, Ivy laughed, and I glared at her. "Sorry. I laugh when I'm nervous. What? You are *really* kind of scary right now."

"If I were you, I'd stop talking," I told her. "Otherwise, I'm out of here and you can deal with this on your own."

For the next thirty minutes or so, we all worked quickly and silently. Luke got the door off, while Ivy and I filled trash bags, dealt with the carpet, and got everything off the floor. I plugged in the vacuum and pushed it at her, then made the bed with fresh sheets from the linen closet, which had also not been used yet. By the time we were all done, it slightly resembled the room I remembered. Which was honestly more than I expected.

"See?" she said, as we all stood by the door, surveying our work. "All better."

"Not all. And it's not like it could have gotten worse."

I heard a buzzing, and she pulled her phone from her pocket. "Hello? Oh, Clyde, hi. I'm on my way, just hit a little snag, so—What?" She glanced at her watch. "But we said ten thirty, so we could really get in some good time . . ."

Luke nudged me from behind. "You are a serious hard-ass, you know that?"

"What? She wrecked this entire place!"

Ivy shot me a look, then stepped out into the hallway. "All

right, then. Well, no, I wouldn't say I'm happy, but . . . let's just say three. But we'll start right then, yes?"

"It's just nice to know," he said, stepping around me to grab his toolbox, "that some things never change. Especially you, Emaline."

"That doesn't exactly sound like a compliment."

"It is," he replied, in that easy Luke way. The boy could flatter, I had to give him that. "I'll be outside."

Just then, as my own phone beeped. I slid it out and looked at the screen. Going to cape frost with Clyde, Theo had texted. Translation: so far so good.

"All right," Ivy said. I hurriedly slid the phone back into my pocket. "Let's just cut to the chase. Are you going to report me, or what?"

I looked at the room again. "That depends. Are you going to leave it like this *and* agree to pay for the damage to be repaired as soon as I can get someone here?"

"Yes," she said, without hesitating. She stuck out her hand.

"Not so fast. I reserve the right to check in on this room anytime I choose during the time you're still here. It creeps back anything close to what it was, and all bets are off."

"Fine." We shook, and then I turned and started down the hallway. I was going down the stairs when I heard her say, "You know, he's not wrong about you."

I looked up. She was on the landing above. "Who's that?"

"The pool guy," she said. "You *are* a hard-ass."

"But you don't mean that as a compliment, I'm sure."

"Actually, I do," she said. "It takes one to know one."

For a moment, we just looked at each other. It occurred to me that maybe under other, crazy circumstances, we might have become friends. But not these.

"Enjoy the view," I told her. I was pretty sure, however, that it was me she was still looking at as I pulled the door shut behind me.

* * *

"Just wait until you hear this," Theo said. "You'll totally understand why it called for the Best Al Fresco Celebration Ever."

Thirty minutes earlier, he'd sent me a text that said, simply, 5 p.m. You and me. The pavilion. Big news. I'd finished up the last few things I needed to do at the office, clocked out, and then headed over as instructed.

I was trying to move through the throng on the boardwalk when I spied a bouquet of multicolored balloons bobbing in the distance. As they grew closer, I saw that Theo, wearing his sport coat, was sitting right beneath them.

He'd spread a white cloth out on the bench beside him, upon which he'd arranged two champagne flutes and snacks: a tiny plate of crackers and cheeses, some mini-pickles, and a dish of olives. His backpack was at his feet, unzipped. When he saw me, he grinned.

"Surprise!" he said, attracting the attention of everyone else around me. I felt myself redden as I stepped away from the moving crowd, closer to him. "Have a seat."

I did, looking up at the balloons. "Where did you get those?"

"Helium Helpers, in Cape Frost," he replied, reaching into his bag and pulling out a bottle. He opened it—*pop!*—then began to pour. "Clyde told me about them. Nice, right?"

"We can't drink here," I said, looking around. Everyone passing was staring at us. "It's illegal."

"It's sparkling cider," he explained. "Which sounds *so* much better than fake champagne, don't you think? The snacks, however, are one hundred percent real. Olive?"

I took one, just because I knew he wanted me to. "So . . . what's all this about?"

"Ah!" He lifted his glass, then waited for me to do the same. Once I did, he cleared his throat. "To the Best Future Plan Ever."

"Which is what?"

"Drink first!" he said. "It's bad luck otherwise."

I drank, wincing at the sharp, fizzy taste. Theo put his glass down, then reached over and took my hands. "You," he said, "are looking at the new tour manager for world-renowned collagist and painter Clyde Conaway's long-anticipated upcoming museum shows."

This was a long title, not to mention quite a bit of information. "Clyde hired you?"

"Basically," he said, taking another sip of his cider. He picked up a piece of cheese and placed it on a cracker, then handed it to me before fixing one for himself. "Let's just say when you create the job description for a person who isn't even aware they need someone, you're already halfway hired."

"Halfway," I repeated. Above us, the balloons caught a gust, making squeaky, rubbing noises.

"The point is," he went on, "until today, Clyde had no idea all the help he was going to need for this tour. Now he does.

And he also already has, right in front of him, the perfect person for the job. It's just a matter of putting the two together."

"Which he did?" I asked, still confused.

"He *will*," he said. "We're having breakfast tomorrow, at which time I fully expect a job offer."

"Hold on," I said, putting my glass down. "But isn't this tour supposed to be happening sort of soon? What about school?"

"Emaline." He leaned closer to me, fixing me with a serious stare. "This will be Clyde's first display of work in over twenty years, in conjunction with the release of a documentary by an award-winning filmmaker. It's a once-in-a-lifetime chance. School will wait."

"That filmmaker's not too high on you right now," I pointed out.

"True," he replied, eating another olive. "But even if it *wasn't* in her best interest to support the tour, it and the film will be separate entities. But I know Ivy. She likes holding a grudge, but she *loves* publicity and media attention. Unless she works with me, not against me, she won't have the access to Clyde she wants."

"But . . ." I was trying to tread carefully here. "You don't even have the job yet."

"*Yet*," he repeated. "Today, I set the factors in motion. Now, all that's left is to wait for them to unfold. Hold on, that's my phone."

As he pulled it out and glanced at the screen, I downed another gulp of my cider, thinking that this all sounded awfully optimistic, if not a little bit arrogant. Then again, I kind

of had to admire his ability to go for what he wanted. I ago-
nized and worried before making the safest move; Theo saw
his opportunity and took it, risk be damned. No wonder he
couldn't believe I'd turned down Columbia. He would have
found a way to make it happen, money or no money.

"Sorry, this is Clyde," he said to me, typing something.

"Since when does he text?" I asked. "I didn't even think he
had a cell phone."

"He does. He just let the battery die and never recharged
it. It's been sitting in his truck until today, when I plugged it
in on the way to Cape Frost," he told me. "Then I explained
that texting means you don't have to talk to people, which
turned out to be a concept he could really get behind. Took
right to it."

"I don't know. It seems weird to me," I said, as his phone
beeped again. "Doesn't sound like something Clyde would
need."

"He doesn't know what he needs," he said. "That's what
I'm for."

That sounded a bit too familiar. Feeling unsettled, I looked
out at the water. The ocean had always been my constant and
usually all it took was finding it—on the horizon, over the
next hill, in the far corner of a window—to feel calmer and
know where I stood. Right then, though, with it front and center, even this oldest of tricks wasn't working. Something was
off. And I knew it even before Theo started talking again.

"Okay," he said, putting his phone down and turning back
to face me. "Here's the thing about the Best Future Plan Ever.
It's not just about the job."

That you don't have yet, I thought, but managed not to say this aloud. "It's not?"

He shook his head, smiling. "Since I'll be working closely with Clyde to get the exhibit together, I'll need to keep a base here, even as I'm going back and forth to the city to arrange dates and travel details."

"You're going to do this from the trailer?"

"No," he said, laughing. "I think with what Clyde will be paying me I'll be able to afford better than that. Nothing like Sand Dollars, of course. But since it'll be the off season, I'm sure we'll be able to find something nice and relatively inexpensive."

With all this big talk, it was ironic—or maybe not—that the one word that stuck out to me was a short one. "We?" I said. "But I'll be at school."

"Well, yeah, but only a couple of hours away." He picked up another olive, popping it in his mouth. "You'll be coming back weekends. Or I can get up there now and again, when Clyde doesn't need me here. Oh! That reminds me. I'm going to need to get a second-hand car. Hold on, that's probably him again."

He turned away, turning his attention back to his phone. I tried my ocean trick once more, even though I knew it wouldn't work. Between the *we* and the fact that apparently I was not moving to East U but basically commuting there, I'd need something bigger and more powerful than even the sea to quiet my now-racing heart.

Calm down, I told myself. He was just high on this whole job thing, not really thinking out what he was saying. Of course he didn't think I'd change my entire life trajectory based on one very nice, but very short, summer romance. Unless he did.

I turned my head. Sure enough, in the distance I could see the sign for Jump Java, the official gathering place of girls who also made assumptions, only to realize too late they were bad ones. I'd been so worried about being one of them, those left behind, that it hadn't occurred to me the flip side wouldn't be easy either. It doesn't matter whether you're the one having to douse a flame or helplessly watching it sputter. Either way, it goes out eventually.

I looked at Theo, who was typing something on his phone, a mild smile on his face. He was so happy, clearly, and even more so to share all of this news and future with me. I, however, felt anything but as, while he still texted, I pulled out my own phone and opened the calendar. I scrolled past the current month, into August, flipping past days until, on Saturday the eighteenth, I found what I was looking for. *Leave for school,* I'd entered way back when my first orientation materials had arrived. Before Luke and I'd split, before Theo, before my father had returned. It felt like an entire lifetime ago. But sitting there next to Theo, facing A Future I Hadn't Quite Expected, I knew that not only was it closer than ever, but I suddenly felt more ready than ever to meet it. It only took a moment to count the days: twenty-three. Now, I just had to figure out what to do with them.

19

THE NICE THING about a job like mine was that, because total chaos was never more than a phone call away, you could always be busy if you wanted to. I appreciated this especially as July folded into August. My own problems might have been too much to deal with, but I was more than happy to deal with someone else's.

"The whole thing started," the woman in the tennis skirt was saying as she led me downstairs, "because we love to grill out. When we're here at the beach, it's pretty much all we do for dinner."

"Right," I said, as we walked across the game room, past a dusty pool table and some beat-up leather chairs.

"So the first night," she continued, walking over to the back door and slowly easing the curtain aside, "we made this great grouper with a lime sauce. It was tangy, citrusy. Truly amazing."

I nodded, glancing down at my notes again. The request form, filled out by Rebecca, said only *Outdoor issue*. Which could have been anything. It was like choosing Manager's Special for your lunch: you really had no idea what you were going to get, only that, most likely, it would be good.

The woman was peering through the glass of the door now, looking first one way, then the other. "After dinner, we came out to clean up and noticed this sweet-looking kitten under the stairs, mewing at us."

Uh-oh, I thought.

"We're animal lovers," she explained, peering out again, "and the poor thing seemed so hungry. So we threw him a little bit of fish, then went inside and pretty much forgot about it."

"Until . . ." I said.

"Until the next time we tried to use this door, and this happened," she finished, flipping the lock and jiggling the handle. She kept the door closed. A moment later, she gestured for me to come take a look.

At first, there was just a gray cat, sitting at the base of the grill and staring at us. Then, another, tabby colored, crawled under the steps to join it. Followed by a fat brown one with a bum ear. When a fourth approached, mewing loudly, I dropped the curtain.

"First question: Has anyone been scratched or bitten?" I asked her.

She shook her head. "No. We haven't even opened the door. Where are they all *coming* from?"

"They're beach cats," I told her, writing this down next to *Outdoor issue*. "Feral and hungry. Like seagulls, but much worse. Give them food once and they never leave."

She lifted the curtain again. I didn't want to look, but couldn't help myself. At least ten cats were now milling around the patio, and when they saw motion, they all turned at once. I shuddered.

"What do we do?" she asked.

"All you have to worry about is not feeding them again. We'll handle the rest."

I started towards the door, already pulling out my phone to find the number for C.A.R.E.—Colby Animal Rescue and Education—the organization that did its best to trap, spay, and neuter the large population of feral cats in town. Run out of someone's garage, it operated on a shoestring budget, with just a few cages and two very brave women. I'd already had to call them twice this season, even though every packet I handed out at check-in had a page about not feeding the animals. Even the cute ones.

"I guess grilling is out of the question for the time being," the woman said, as we got back to the landing.

"I'll get someone here as soon as possible," I said. I reached into my folder, searching around until I found a voucher for a dinner for two at Finz. "But tonight, why don't you go out on us. Hopefully by tomorrow everything will be fine."

"Oh," she said. "That's so nice! Thank you."

"My pleasure," I told her.

Another satisfied customer, I thought, as I walked back to my car. This was why I'd been working pretty much whenever I could lately. I needed distractions, problems I could easily solve. Wild cats were never ideal, but now, I'd gladly take them.

It had been about a week since Theo's big news at the Pavilion, and things hadn't gone exactly as planned. At breakfast the following morning he was *not* offered the job, as he'd envisioned. Instead, Clyde asked for his help going through the work that had been in storage and piled up in a shed behind his house. In typical Theo style, he did not see this as a setback. Instead, he explained to me, it was Clyde's way of trying him out, testing his mettle, before handing over the real prize. *That* would happen a few days from now, at the press conference/cocktail party he and Ivy had planned before their split to celebrate the end of filming and the tour announcement. Between now and then, all he had to do was make himself indispensable, bond further with Clyde, and cement his standing as the most knowledgeable about the work, other than the artist himself.

"It's a win-win," he kept saying.

He wasn't the only one feeling confident. Not only had Margo listed my father's house in North Reddemane and gotten an offer in record time, but the negotiations and inspections had so far moved quickly, without a hitch. The furniture had all been packed up, the floors refinished, the septic and electrical checked out. My father and Benji had moved to a motel just down from Gert's, the Poseidon, with Leah in a room adjacent, to wait until the final repairs were done before heading home. While they both seemed eager to return to their lives, Benji, like me, was looking for distractions. Turned out he was pretty good at finding them.

It had started with some backtalk, not wanting to do the touristy things his mom had planned. He rolled his eyes at minigolf, claimed seasickness at ferry rides, and about the aquarium said only, "Fish are boring." This general bad attitude escalated once they moved to the Poseidon, manifesting itself in the slamming of doors, heavy, constant sighing, and complaints about the lack of decent channels on the TV. At first, Leah held her ground, dragging him on various expeditions even as he protested. After a couple of days, however, she caved to his near-constant requests and started dropping him off with me.

"I just don't get it," she'd said to me one day from her car, which he'd exited like a shot before it was even fully stopped. "I thought he'd just want to have fun the last few days here. What ten-year-old would rather work than go to the beach?"

"Got me," I said. "I'd love to be at the beach right now."

She sighed. "All I know is that I am *dreading* when we tell him we're leaving next week. He's been insufferable here. I can't imagine two days in the car."

"You haven't told him yet?"

She shook her head. "I mean, he knows it's coming, just not the exact day. Joel felt if we waited until the day before, it would be clear it was a fact, not something to be negotiated."

It was hard not to make a face, hearing this, but I did my best. I had not talked to my father since our argument, keeping my dealings to either Benji or Leah. He hadn't made any effort either. Now more than ever, it was no surprise to me that he'd preferred facts to negotiations whenever possible. Eliminate the opposing argument and you, too, always get to win.

With all this winning going on, someone had to lose. I'd really been hoping it wouldn't be me, but now I wasn't so sure about that either. If June was the beginning of a hopeful summer, and July the juicy middle, August was suddenly feeling like the bitter end. But it wasn't the end I'd expected, which had totally thrown me off.

What had I thought would happen in these three months? If I was honest, maybe a healing between my father and me, a beach backdrop as a bonus. Instead, we were back to where we'd been before his trip, if not further apart. I'd planned on a fun summer with a boy I'd long loved . . . who cheated on me. Adapting, I'd looked on the bright side, thinking a summer romance might be my fate. Now, though, even that was turning out to be more complicated than I ever imagined.

Theo and I had not talked again about plans for the fall, but only because he'd been so caught up making his come to fruition. Each day for the last week, he'd joined Clyde for his customary early bird breakfast at the Last Chance at six a.m. sharp, after which they set out in the truck together. After collecting collages and paintings from the various places Clyde had them squirreled away around town, they hauled them to the Pavilion, where the show and party was to be held. When Clyde was filming with Ivy, he left Theo there to catalog and organize, rejoining him when he was done. The upside of all this was that Theo was so busy that by the time we saw each other, he was too exhausted to discuss much of anything. The downside? Those twenty-three days I'd finally tallied were now seventeen and counting.

But the cats—the cats I had under control. After putting in a call to C.A.R.E., I headed back to the office, where I found

Rebecca on break, my mom and Margo gone, and Benji at my grandmother's computer, explaining the fine points of social networking on UMe.com.

"And, see, now that we've built the office's profile page," he was saying as I came into the doorway, "it's really easy to add various kinds of content."

"Content?" my grandmother repeated, peering over her reading glasses at the screen.

"Yeah. Like, say, pictures of some of the houses, in a kind of gallery? Or reviews from people who have rented from you. You can even set up a comment section, so people can ask questions in real time."

"Hmmm," my grandmother said. "Interesting."

"No fair," I called out, getting their attention. "I've been trying to get you to update the main Web site for two years, and now you're on UMe.com?"

"You haven't updated your Web site in two years?" Benji asked her.

"I told you, I'm a dinosaur." Grandmother helped herself to a Rolo, giving one to him as well, and they both turned back to the screen. "Okay, now tell me again what these pictures are of, on the side?"

"The people who have listed the page as a favorite," he explained. "Which means it's on *their* page for everyone to see as well. So far, since we just made it, it's me. But soon there will be others."

"Emaline," my grandmother called out, eating her Rolo. "Will you please make our page a favorite? Ask Rebecca, too. And everyone else you know."

"Done," I said, pulling out my phone and opening the UMe.com app. "Anything else?"

"No." She was still studying the screen, then suddenly she looked at me. "Oh, wait, yes. Someone's waiting to talk to you. In the conference room."

"The conference room?" I turned. The lights were on, the usual array of food and drinks cluttering the table's surface. At the very head, dressed in black with her head ducked over her own phone, was Ivy.

"What does she want?" I asked.

"She didn't say. But she's been waiting awhile." Grandmother narrowed her eyes at the screen. "Now, Benji, suppose we wanted to put up something about a rental special or promotion. Would we do it on this page, or another one?"

"Either," he replied, hitting a few keys. "But the best function would be this Newsflash button."

"Newsflash?"

"Yeah. See, how that works is . . ."

I walked over to the conference room door. I was wary of seeing Ivy under any circumstances, but glad for once to be in my own territory. "Can I help you?"

She looked up, her face grim. "I don't know. Can you finish the last of the filming for me, then wrap up everything here and coordinate the move of all of my equipment back to the city?"

"Nope," I said.

She looked back down at her phone, her shoulders sagging. "Yeah. I didn't think so."

Neither of us spoke for a moment. I came inside the

room and slid into a chair. "You need Theo," I said.

"I need a capable assistant with a working knowledge of filmmaking," she corrected me. "Which, in New York, are basically everywhere. Here, though . . ."

"Not so much," I finished for her.

"Nope."

Another silence. I wasn't sure what, exactly, I was supposed to be doing here, only that it felt odd enough to want to wrap it up, and quickly. "Well," I said, "I really should—"

"Look," she said, cutting me off. "I know you don't like me."

"Ivy."

"But right now, I need help. And I don't even know where to start finding it." She ran a hand through her hair, then looked at me. "The reason I'm here, humiliating as it is, is because I know you do."

"You want to hire me?" I asked, confused.

"I want to finish my film," she said. "I want *you* to find the people to do everything else that needs doing in the next week so I can do that."

"I have a job," I pointed out.

"I'll pay you well."

"There's only so much time in the day, though."

"True. But you're efficient." I must have looked particularly doubtful, because she quickly added, "Look, I know you're leaving for school soon, so you could use money. And if this is about Theo—"

"It's not," I told her. "I just . . . I'm kind of overwhelmed right now as it is."

She exhaled. "Emaline. Really. Do you *want* to see me beg?"

Truthfully, I kind of did. Not that I would have said so. So I was trying to figure out how to decline again, nicely, when I heard the front door open. A moment later, Margo came down the hall, my father behind her. He was carrying a folder, his face tense. When he saw me, it grew even more so.

"Just have a seat in my office," Margo said, turning on the lights and waving him in. "Leah should be here soon, and we'll get started."

He nodded, disappearing inside. I glanced over at my grandmother's office. She was on the phone, Benji still at the computer. He watched my father go inside, his own face darkening. *You owe me a dollar*, I thought. And then, I heard myself say something, this time aloud.

"Okay." I turned back to Ivy. "I'm in."

* * *

I clocked out at the office right at five. Ten minutes later, I was at the Pavilion, encountering the first of what I knew would be many awkward interactions.

"Hey," Theo called out when he saw me. "You're early."

I nodded, withholding further comment. I knew this room mostly from social functions like the Beach Bash, when it was decorated in one theme or another. Now, it was just big and empty, with paintings and collages leaning against the walls and stacked on folding tables. Theo was crouched next to a large painting, a close-up of four tall, vertical plants, done in exacting, perfect detail. His laptop was at his feet, some papers scattered around it.

"This is nice," I said, pointing at the canvas. "Very . . . earthy."

"Oh, it's amazing," he replied, turning to type something on the laptop. "When he first returned here, if my timeline is correct, Clyde really shifted his focus. He'd been doing so much with metals and scrap, but suddenly there's a lot of naturals, most in tight detail. I researched this one, and it's this obscure kind of wheat plant that grows only in certain kinds of Southern pastureland."

"Wow," I said.

"I know. I can't wait to see what people have to say about it. Hey, can you hand me that camera over there?"

I turned, seeing one with a zoom lens on the table behind me. I went over to retrieve it and brought it back. He took it, his eyes still on the screen, then said, "I thought we weren't meeting until later. I still have a lot of stuff to do here."

"Oh, I know," I said. "I, um, actually came to just check out the venue."

Now he glanced up, looking around. "Yeah. It's not much. But I think the sparcity will help to put the focus on the paintings. Honestly, though, I thought Ivy would have more stuff done here, with the opening so soon. She must be *freaking*."

And there's my opening, I thought. I cleared my throat. "Actually, I . . . sort of wanted to talk to you about that."

"Ivy? What about her?"

"Well," I said, "she came by the office today. Apparently, she really needs help with this event. And some other details."

"Ha! I bet she does." He grinned, bending back over the painting. "What, so she's looking for the rental agency to do that, now?"

"Not exactly."

Now I had his full attention. "Then what did she want?"

I swallowed. "She asked me to help her. Coordinate this event, hire people to do the other stuff she needs . . ."

"You?" He laughed. "Please. Like you'd ever help her after how she's treated you. And us."

I didn't say anything. In my pocket, my phone buzzed. I pulled it out, recognizing the number for Everything Island, the party supplier I'd told Ivy about all the way back on the first day I'd met her. "One sec," I told him. "I have to take this."

I put the phone to my ear, stepping a few feet away, his eyes still on me. There I had a clear view of his face, his expression increasingly incredulous, as I arranged for chairs and tables to be delivered to the Pavilion that coming Saturday morning. When I hung up, he shook his head.

"Oh my God," he said. "You took the job."

I sighed. "Theo. She's desperate."

"And she hates you! And you hate her!" He turned, shaking his head. "I can't believe this. I finally emancipate myself and you dive right into the shackles. And thwart everything I'm doing in the process."

"How can you say that?" I replied. "If this party's a bust, it hurts you and Clyde just as much as her."

"This party's in *Colby*," he said, waving his hand. "It doesn't count for anything, other than a chance for Ivy to get his new work on film while the locals gape. If this stuff ends up getting the attention I think it will, Clyde won't even need her little movie. In fact, we'll probably be better off without it."

Maybe it was the way he said the words *Colby* and *locals*, neither of them nicely. But I said, "We? I thought you didn't have the job yet."

"Why do you keep harping on that?"

"Because it's the truth?"

"Emaline," he said, sounding tired. "Jobs like this are earned, not given. It's not like bringing towels to people, okay?"

Ouch. "And you think that's all I do."

"I think," he said, picking up the camera again, "that you have no idea what it's like to live in the real world."

"Which is New York," I said, clarifying.

"Which is anywhere other than this small, coastal berg, where you know every single person by name and nothing ever changes."

"Berg?" I said.

He snapped a picture of the canvas. "It means small town."

"I know what it means. I did well on my verbal, remember?"

"Clearly. *You* got into Columbia."

"Who's harping now?" I asked. "And what does that have to do with this?"

"It has *everything* to do with this," he replied, turning to look at me. "Emaline, you're a really smart girl on paper. And it's not your fault you've done some not-so-smart things."

I was speechless. Literally: no words.

"But the truth is, you haven't had a lot of outside influences, people to show you there is another way," he continued.

"I'm here now. And I'm telling you, you do *not* want to take this job with Ivy. It will be a mistake."

"You think I made a mistake turning down Columbia." Now, apparently, I could talk. Barely.

He rolled his eyes. "You're a girl from Colby High School who got into the one of the best schools in the country. It was a dream come true."

"Not *my* dream, though."

Another eye roll. "This is exactly my point. You don't know what's out there, Emaline. If you even had the slightest idea, you'd understand what you're missing."

Instead of replying, I looked at him, closely, standing there before me. This boy, in his jeans and expensive fitted T-shirt, hipster sneakers, owner of sport coats. Someone to whom everything had to be Big and Special, or not worth his time.

But that is the hard thing about the grand gesture. Once you pull off one, what's left to do but start planning the next? Get used to pomp and anything less is just a disappointment. Why stop at the Best Summer Ever when you could try for the Best After Ever? The truth was, there was no way everything could be the Best. Sometimes, when it came to events and people, it had to be okay to just *be*. I'd already explained that to my father. I wasn't sure I had it in me to do it again.

And it was in that moment, a plain and simple one, that I knew what he'd said was right. I didn't know very many people like him. But I was beginning to think that was okay. One was probably enough.

"You know, I think I'm going to go now," I said. "I have a lot of work to do."

"So you're really going to do this to me," he called out, as I walked away. "You're taking the job."

"Yep," I said over my shoulder.

I heard him sigh. "You're not who I thought you were, Emaline."

Finally. Something we could agree on. "No," I told him. "I'm not."

And then I was walking, towards that open door that looked out on the boardwalk. It was late afternoon, still sunny, and I could see ocean. Funny how now that I knew I didn't have to make the ideal exit, this one came damn close anyway.

20

"EMALINE? WHERE DO you want us?"

I turned, looking over at all the activity before me. Finally, I located Robin, from Roberts Family Catering, standing by the back door, a dish wrapped in foil in her arms. "You can use the kitchen as a staging area," I told her. "What we don't have passed we'll put on the big table up at the front."

"Right," she said, gesturing to the girl behind her, who was pulling a cooler. They started across the floor, into the increasing chaos: guys from Everything Island, setting up small tables and chairs, Morris stacking beer and wine by the bar, Benji unloading flowers we'd bought at Park Mart, and Daisy arranging them in every vase I'd been able to get my hands on.

"Do we have cups?" Morris called out to me.

"Didn't I give them to you?"

He looked around. "Ummm . . ."

"Under the main table," Benji called out as he passed, dwarfed by a huge bundle of lilies. "They were in the way."

Morris bent down, locating them. "Thanks, dude."

"You're welcome. Be right back!"

And then, he was gone again, the only one truly running,

although we probably all should have been. I looked at my watch. It was two thirty, which meant I had only about two and a half hours to somehow pull all this together. The crazy thing was, after all I'd already managed to accomplish in the last few days, I was thinking I might actually do it.

It was hard to say what was the biggest surprise about working for Ivy. Not that she was a hard-ass, or a demanding, exacting perfectionist. These things I already knew. What still caught me off guard was the last thing I would have expected: it was fun.

Sure, she'd snapped at me a few times. And if you even tried to talk to her in the morning before she had any coffee, you got what you deserved. But underneath the brittle exterior, there was this crackling, tangible energy, so different from anyone I'd ever been around. I'd long watched my mother, grandmother, and even Margo as they worked, taking lessons on how to deal with problems. But Ivy was like a brand-new master class. I wasn't going to call it the Best Job Ever. I sure did like it, though.

"Watch the ceiling!" I heard her yell now, and turned to the other side of the Pavilion, where she was overseeing the guys we'd hired to hang the canvases. This was supposed to have been done the day before, but Theo and Clyde had been so indecisive about what to include we'd ended up cutting it way close. "I said *high*. Not as high as it could go, just go ahead and hit the ceiling."

There was a clunk as the painting being hoisted, one of the plant close-ups, bumped the air duct again. "Whoops," one of the guys said.

"Whoops," she repeated flatly. Then she looked at me. "Tell me again this is somehow not going to be a total disaster."

"Everything's under control," I replied. "Maybe you should let me take over. You still have to get ready so you can be here before anyone arrives, right?"

She looked up at the painting again, then the line of them already hung. "I'm still not sure how I'm going to schmooze this party and film at the same time."

"You're not," I said. "That's why we have Esther."

"Who is a college film student," she reminded me. "Not exactly an award-winning cinematographer."

"You said yourself it was mostly going to be crowd shots and candids," I pointed out. "You already got all the pieces and the interviews. This is just bonus."

She didn't look convinced. However, she was also not still clenching her jaw, which was progress. "Fine. I'm going to put on a black dress and say some Hail Marys."

"Perfect. I'll see you back here at four thirty sharp. And don't smoke any cigarettes. You'll just stink and hate yourself."

"Yes, Mom," she groaned, starting for the door.

As she left, I looked over to see Morris, who had watched this exchange, now looking at me. "What?" I asked.

He shook his head. "Nothing."

I felt something bump me, hard, from behind, then turned to find myself looking down at a small, flowering shrub. "Sorry," Benji said, his voice muffled by the leaves. "I can't really see around this."

I took it from him, placing it on a table behind me. "Safety first. Stick to the short stuff."

"Got it," he said, running back outside.

I smiled, watching him, as he approached the open door. Then I saw Theo, standing just inside, scanning the room as he took in all the bustle. I took a breath, then focused on my clipboard. Still, I could feel it when he spotted me.

To say things had been awkward between us for the last few days was an understatement. Ever since our argument and ensuing breakup in this same space, whenever we were forced to interact—which, because Clyde was crucial to both of our various tasks, was pretty often—the formality was palpable. It might have been the hottest month of summer, but with us in close quarters, the temperature dropped noticeably.

Ivy didn't seem aware of this, or if she was, she didn't care. All she was focused on was work. But Clyde, surprisingly, appeared alternately bemused and bothered by the friction. When he'd asked me if something had happened between Theo and me, I'd said only that we'd split up by mutual decision and could easily work together, and it was nothing to worry about. I assumed Theo was sticking to a similar story. Not that I was about to ask.

"Hey," Daisy called out to me now. I looked over to where she was standing on a stepladder, arranging hydrangeas in a vase. "Are we going for vertical or horizontal pop with these?"

"Pop?" I said.

She sighed. "Pop, as in zing, wow factor, eye-catching. Height or width?"

I just looked at her.

"Oh, never mind, I'll figure it out myself," she said, turning back to them.

"Thank you," I called out. I looked back at my list, crossing off both *Flower pick up* and *Bar stock*. Which left only about a hundred other things. My phone buzzed and I pulled it out, glancing at the screen. It was a text from my father.

Please tell Benji to be ready to go at 4.

OK, I wrote back. Will do.

This exchange was typical since Leah had returned to Connecticut for work a few days earlier. If he and I had to communicate, it was via text, and only about Benji. Which was just fine with me. I'd said everything else I needed to already.

"There's not enough space here. Do you not understand that we need room for people to gather so they can actually *see* the paintings?"

And this, ladies and gentlemen, was how Theo now spoke to me. I turned and looked at the wall he was studying. "The tables are too close?"

"There shouldn't even be tables," he said. "This is an art show, not a wedding reception."

"Where are people supposed to put their drinks and food?"

"They hold them. While they look at the *paintings*, which is the whole reason they are here in the first place." He shook his head, walking over to the wall. I followed him, watching as he seized one of the tables and started dragging it farther into the middle of the room. "What we need is space. Not to fill it."

"Ivy and I are handling the party," I told him, stopping the table with my hand. "You just focus on Clyde and the work."

"This *is* about the work," he shot back, nudging it again.

"Trust me. I've actually been to an art show or two. You want more room there."

For a moment, we just stared at each other. It's a table, I reminded myself. But, man, were these little battles exhausting.

"Emaline?" It was Luke, walking up behind him, pushing a wet-vac, COLBY REALTY printed on its side in marker. "Your mom told me you needed this?"

"Yes," I said, "thank God. Something's leaking back by the sink in the kitchen. Can you just stick it back there?"

"Got it," he said, glancing at Theo, who had taken advantage of this exchange and was moving the table around me. "Need anything else?"

"Everything else," I replied. "But I'm fine. Hey, you're coming tonight, right?"

He didn't hear me, as right then Morris upended a bag of ice into a metal cooler, the noise drowning out everything. Once Luke pushed the vacuum past us, Theo muttered, "I see we're back on good terms with the boyfriend. That was fast."

"He's helping out," I said. "Just like everyone else here."

"Must be nice," he replied. "Meanwhile I'm trying to successfully curate and launch a show totally on my own."

"Is that why," I said, pushing the table back, "you're rearranging the furniture?"

"You don't know what you're doing!" He threw up his hands. "Fine. Leave no room for anyone to gather and discuss. It's your funeral."

And with that, he stomped off. I adjusted the table, getting it back where I wanted it, then went back to my list. A moment later, I felt a tap on my shoulder. *Dear God*, I thought, bracing myself for another skirmish. But it was just Esther, the girl who was helping us film the party, standing there in a red sundress. She was a friend of Auden's and Maggie's I knew from high school, currently in her second year of film school in California.

"Hi," she said. "I'm early, sorry."

"You're perfect," I told her. "Come over here out of the chaos. Ivy left some stuff for me to go over with you."

We started over to the small bench I'd turned into my mobile office, passing Benji, who was now helping Morris rip open packs of napkins. Watching them, I had a flash of that other party, all the way back at the beginning of the summer, when I'd been forced to nag Morris to do a job he was actually getting paid for. Apparently I wasn't the only one who'd changed a bit since then.

"Hey," I said to Benji, "your dad says to be ready to go at four, okay?"

He looked at me. "Four? But the party starts at five."

I shrugged. "Just delivering the message."

"I want to be here, though," he persisted, looking at Morris, then back at me. "Can't I stay?"

"Sounds like he already has plans for you, bud," I told him.

This, clearly, was not good enough. "This sucks. I'll be the only one missing everything."

"Who's missing everything?" Luke asked, walking up. He nodded at Esther, who nodded back. Small towns.

"Me," Benji grumbled. "My dad's making me leave early."

"Bummer. I hear you," Luke told him. "I can't make it either."

I looked at him. "No?"

"Already had plans. Thanks for the invite, though," he said, ruffling Benji's hair. "Me and little man here will have to just get the recap later."

"I don't *want* the recap. I want to stay."

"Hey," Luke said. Benji looked at him, sullen. "Don't hassle your sister. She's got enough on her plate. Right?"

Benji bit his lip, scuffing his foot on the floor. "Okay."

"Okay." Luke caught my eye, smiled. "Good luck with everything."

"Thanks for your help," I replied.

"Anytime."

Across the room, there was another thump as a painting hit the ceiling. "Whoa," Esther said, as Benji walked away. "This place is nuts."

I looked at my watch again: almost four. "Yeah," I said to Esther, gesturing for her to follow me. "Come on. I'll catch you up."

Twenty minutes later, with Esther briefed and acquainting herself with Ivy's equipment, I rejoined Daisy, who was putting the finishing touches on the flowers. "So," she said, adjusting a rosebud that was sagging slightly. "What are you wearing for this gala?"

"Wearing?" I looked down. "Oh, right. I do need to change at some point."

"Emaline." She sighed. "*Please* tell me you have something cute and stylish already picked out."

"I'm a little busy," I said, gesturing around me. "I'm just going to run home and grab something. If I don't have to just wear this."

She gasped. "No. No way. Give me your keys, right now."

"Why?"

Instead of replying she held out her hand. Then she wiggled her fingers, insistent. I handed them over. "Back in fifteen," she called out over her shoulder. "Be ready to be fabulous."

"Nothing too crazy!" I hollered after her, but she ignored me. Of course.

Ivy, now dressed in a simple navy sleeveless shift, appeared next to me, already jumpy. "What's too crazy? What happened?"

"Nothing," I told her. "You look nice."

"I didn't smoke," she said. "If that's what you're asking."

"It was not," I replied. "But I'm glad. Esther's here. Let me introduce you."

"Who's Esther?"

"The film student," I reminded her. "She's been briefed and says she's worked with equipment like this before."

"Oh my God," she groaned, but she did follow me. "Tell me this is not going to be a total disaster."

"It's going to be great," I said. "Trust me."

At that moment, honestly, I was not entirely convinced. At four thirty, when there was still a painting not hung and the puddle in the kitchen was encroaching on the bar area, I was sure of it. By the time Daisy dragged me into the restroom to change at four fifty, I was saying some Hail Marys of my own.

"I know you're fashion-forward," I told her, as she hung up the garment bag she was carrying, "but I really don't want to look like a robot tonight."

"I would not dress you like a robot for an art opening," she replied, offended. "At least, not this kind of art. Hurry up, you've got, like, four minutes."

I squirmed out of my clothes, kicking off my flip-flops as she unzipped the bag. "I totally planned to go home and shower and do my hair, I swear. But the time got away from me, and then there was traffic—"

"Which is why," she said, "you need a dress that stops it. Luckily, I had one."

As I turned I was apprehensive, half convinced that I would turn to see the pink candy number for the Beach Bash. Instead, I was surprised to see her holding a short and sleeve-less ocean-blue dress, clearly vintage, with a full skirt. The color was bright but not loud; instead it looked cool, almost iridescent, like water itself. You sort of wanted to dive right into it.

"Daisy," I said, stepping closer and touching the bod-ice. "This is gorgeous. But do you think it might be too, you know . . . attention getting?"

"You're the one who always says you're tired of being a background player," she reminded me, turning it around and gesturing for me to step into it. I did, and she zipped up the back. "You want to be a star, you have to dress like one."

She turned me around again, stepping aside so I could see myself in the long mirror opposite the open stall. I wouldn't say I looked like a star, but I wasn't blending in with the scen-ery either. Plus, that color: I couldn't take my eyes off of it. She gathered my hair in her hands and twisted it up, securing it with a couple of bobby pins she pulled from her pocket. "So? What do you think?"

"It's perfect," I told her.

"I know," she replied, confidently. "Although I really wanted to do this metallic A-line thing I've been working on. But I resisted. When it comes to shoes, though, I will take no argument. You're wearing these."

She turned around to the garment bag, unzipped a side pocket, and pulled out a pair of silver strappy sandals. Now these were Daisy. I raised my eyebrows. "Really?"

"Emaline. Being a star also requires risk-taking shoes. It's Fashion 101. Put them on."

I did. To my luck or detriment, we'd always worn the same size in just about everything. Looking down, I had to admit they kind of worked. As far as I knew. "I have never worn silver anything before in my life."

"You can thank me later," she said, grabbing the bag and zipping it up. "You better run. It's five o'clock."

"It is?" I looked at my watch. "Crap. Let's go."

I literally did run down the hallway to the main room, hoping for only two things: that the paintings were all hung and, if not, that no one had yet arrived. It was my lucky day. I got both. And then, as a bonus, something else.

"Doing the lights," Morris called out. I looked over just in time to see him turn down the large, fluorescent ones overhead and plug in the cord connecting the smaller spots we'd been setting up all day. In an instant, the room went from bright and vast to small and intimate, each painting illuminated and defined. This was how I'd seen the Pavilion before. Such a difference, and for once, one I was more than happy to take full credit for.

"There are already people out front," Morris reported as Robin walked past me, tying on her apron. "Want me to open the door?"

I looked at Ivy, who was standing by the cameras, a nervous expression on her face. It was weird to see her so jumpy, but at the same time kind of nice. A reminder that not everyone is what they seem right at first glance. You needed those, now and then.

"Sure," I told him, giving Ivy a reassuring nod. "Let them in."

* * *

An hour later, the place was packed, we were already out of meatballs ("Everyone loves them," Robin said, sighing, before sending out more stuffed mushrooms), and, judging by the clumps of people in front of each painting, it appeared that Theo's concerns about traffic flow were not valid after all. For this reason, if nothing else, I was happy. Or as happy as I could be with two more hours to go.

"These fish things are good," Amber said to me, as we stood to the side of the bar, which I'd discerned had the best view of the entire room. Currently, I was watching Ivy as she took a lap around the room with Clyde, Esther following them with the camera. Theo, looking disgruntled, was sticking close to Clyde's elbow. The only time I'd seen him brighten, in fact, was when we'd been going over the night's schedule and

Clyde mentioned he wanted to "make a few remarks about up-coming events" at some point during the evening. Best Hiring Moment Ever, I could almost hear Theo thinking. Public and showy; pomp at its best.

"They're shrimp puffs," I told Amber now.

"Whatever. I've had, like, seven."

She popped another one in her mouth as my mom, hair still damp from her own rushed preparations, joined us. "Your dad is drinking a glass of white wine," she reported. "I feel like we should get documentation, as it will never happen again."

"Why isn't he having a beer?" I asked.

She shrugged, taking a sip off her own glass. "This didn't seem like a beer event. And they were walking past with them."

I scanned the room again. Sure enough, over by a painting featuring broad, horizontal stripes of varying shades of gray was my dad, in a dress shirt—i.e., one that buttoned up, and was tucked in—holding, but not drinking, a glass of wine.

"I'll be back," I told my mom and Amber, then cut behind the bar, reaching into the cooler for a longneck. "Doing okay?" I asked Morris, who was serving drinks, as Robin's bartender had never showed up.

"Yup," he replied, perennially calm, even with a huge crowd of people pressed in around him. "Did Clyde find you?"

"When?"

"A couple of minutes ago. He said he needed to ask you about something."

I looked across the room again, finding Clyde in front of the reedy painting Theo had been cataloging when we'd argued. He was gesturing at it, talking to Ivy, while Esther filmed. "I'll go ask him. Thanks."

"No prob," he replied, turning to his next customer. "Red wine? Okay, coming up."

I headed towards Clyde, uncapping the longneck in my hand on the way. En route, I stopped by my dad, who was now deep into a conversation with Roger from Finz about the slowness of the Colby building inspector. Without comment, I eased the white wine from his hand, replaced it with the beer, then patted his shoulder. He looked at it, then at me. "Oh, hey. Thanks."

"You're welcome," I said. Ditching the wine on a tray, I picked my way through the crowd, hearing snippets of conversation and laughter. The room was a bit warm, but not hot, and my sandals were already rubbing a blister. I was not complaining.

"—one of the first pieces I did when I returned here," Clyde was saying as I got within earshot. "I wasn't really thinking of this as a series since I was basically in the midst of a nervous breakdown. I was literally painting from my bed, because I couldn't get out of it. But in retrospect, it was key to this wider collection."

"So different from your previous work, to be sure," Ivy said, studying the painting as Esther moved around her. "Natural versus industrial, at the very least."

Clyde nodded. "I wasn't thinking that much, to be honest. Just recapturing something pure when I felt anything but."

"Which is why," Theo interjected, "it's so meaningful that

he picked this particular kind of plant to do in detail. It's not unintentional."

Clyde looked at him, then the painting. "What isn't?"

"That you chose *Verbus intriculatus*," Theo told him, taking a sip of his own drink. Red wine, naturally. To Ivy, he explained, "It's a plant native solely to this area. A sort of winter wheat, raised not for feed but for cover when the soil is overused and undernourished. It basically heals the ground."

We all looked at the painting again. I was trying to make out Clyde's expression, but honestly couldn't. There were quite a few people gathered around now, although whether because of the camera or the art history lesson was hard to say.

"So on a basic level," Theo continued, "it's a plant that coaxes something almost dead back to life. Which echoes what Clyde was saying earlier about his mind-set, the sense of exhaustion and sadness. And that it's captured in such close, painstaking detail . . . it conveys both a sense of defeat and perverse hope."

"Interesting," I heard someone murmur behind me.

"Defeat and hope," someone else agreed. "I wouldn't have ever gotten that."

I looked at Clyde again. This time, there was no question what he was feeling, and it wasn't defeat or hope. He looked pissed. I glanced at Ivy, who met my eyes for a second, then flicked her gaze to Esther, making sure she was filming.

"That's a lot to get from a plant," Clyde said to Theo. "Don't you think?"

"Not necessarily," Theo replied, confident as always. "You

do like to weave symbolism into your work. It's just a matter of cracking the code."

Clyde's eyes widened. *Uh-oh*, I thought. Then I felt the tap on my shoulder. I turned around to see Morris, his face flushed. Immediately, I glanced over at the bar, still crowded with people.

"Amber and your mom took over," he told me, before I could even ask. Man, things *had* changed. "Have you seen Benji?"

"Benji?" I asked. "He left at four, with my father."

"He was supposed to," he told me. "He never showed up at the car."

"He's gone?"

"I don't know," he replied. "He's just not with your father, who can't find him anywhere."

"Oh my God," I said, looking around. "He's got to be here someplace. You know he wanted to stay."

"Your mom and Amber looked already. Your dad's searching now. Me and Daisy are heading outside right now to check the boardwalk."

"Okay," I said, trying to think. "Where's my father?"

"Driving around, I think. But—"

We were interrupted, suddenly, by Clyde's voice. "Hey! Morris!"

Everyone was looking at us. Whoops. "Sorry for the disturbance," Morris said. "We just—"

"Can you answer a question for me?" Clyde asked him. "It'll only take a second."

Morris looked at me, and I shrugged. "Sure," he said.

Clyde stepped closer to the painting, pointing to one of the plants. "What is this?"

I saw Ivy look at Theo, who just took another sip of his wine.

"Beach grass," Morris replied.

"Where is it found, exactly?"

Morris looked at him like he was crazy. "Everywhere. You know that. You're always complaining there's so much of it outside your bedroom you can't even see the water."

I was pretty sure I heard Ivy snort.

Clyde smiled. "Exactly."

"Can I go now?" Morris asked. "I have something I have to do."

"Me too," I said. "Excuse us."

He turned, starting for the door, and I followed, taking in the crowd as I went. I was almost outside when I spotted Margo, eating a canapé by one of the gray paintings, and made a beeline for her.

"I need your help," I told her. "Benji's run off and my father can't find him."

"What?" She put her plate down on nearby table. "How long has he been missing?"

"An hour? Two? I have to go help look for him."

"Of course. I've got my car right outside, I can—"

"No," I told her. "I need you here."

"Here?"

I glanced around the room again, then at my watch.

"Things are running pretty smoothly right now, but we're low on food and Clyde still has to make a speech. He wants to do that in about ten minutes."

"Ten minutes," she repeated.

"Take this," I said, pushing my legal pad at her. "It's got the entire schedule on it. Check in with Ivy and tell her you're me until further notice. She will probably yell at you, but I know you can handle it."

"I . . ." She paused, then smiled. "Okay. Thank you, Emaline."

"Don't thank me yet," I said. "I have to go. Call me if you see Benji!"

She nodded, patting my arm as I went past her, towards the door. Right before I left, I turned to take one last gaze at what I'd done, so I would remember it. Then I went to look for my brother.

*   *   *

"I don't understand this," my father said, scanning the road again. "This town is *tiny*. Where could he possibly be?"

I didn't answer, instead I just looked hard along the side of the road, even though we'd already been through this neighborhood, which was just adjacent to the boardwalk, more than once. Morris and Daisy had covered from the Pavilion to Surfside and were now doubling back, after asking everyone at Abe's and Clementine's to keep an eye out as well.

"You called the arcade," I said, confirming. "And already looked at the mall?"

He nodded. "He's on foot, anyway. He can't have gotten far."

"It's been over two hours," I pointed out. "Should we go back to the hotel, in case he somehow got a ride back there?"

"Just called them, they haven't seen him. Anyway, that's the last place he wants to be, especially with us leaving tomorrow."

I turned to look at him. "You're leaving tomorrow?"

He nodded. "I was going to tell him at dinner tonight, but he overheard me talking to Leah on the way to see you this morning. I should have known he'd pull something like this."

I scanned the road again. "He probably just was upset, with the short notice and all."

"Your brother might be young, but he is a master negotiator," he informed me, turning onto another street. "He'll try to crack and improve any system to his advantage. Over time, I've learned I have to limit his window to do that, or he'll always find a way to better things in his favor."

Any other time, I would have been tempted to point out that Benji wasn't the only one who liked to be in control; he came by it honestly. But right then, all I could think was what an idiot I was.

"Dammit," I said, gesturing for my father to take the next left. "I know where he is."

"You do?"

I nodded. "Cut through here, it's right on the next block."

He pulled up in front of the office. I jumped out and ran up to the doors. They were locked, as we'd closed about a half hour earlier. I peered through the windows in the doors, looking for lights and movement, then pulled out my keys and let myself in.

"Benji!" I called out. "Hey! It's Emaline, come on out."

I searched the conference room, all the offices, the storage room, both bathrooms. Nothing. I couldn't believe I'd been so wrong. Eventually, since time was precious, I went back outside to rethink.

"No?" my father called from the car.

I shook my head. "I'm going to keep looking around here, though. Maybe do another loop up by the boardwalk and then come back?"

He nodded, then backed away and turned down the side street towards the Pavilion. I walked up to the main road, really starting to worry now. Yes, Colby was small and not like a big city in terms of danger. But it was still in the real world, regardless of what Theo might believe. Bad things happened. Just ask Rachel Gertmann.

I was just standing there on the grass, trying to think, when I heard a beep. When I looked up, Luke was turning in, a concerned look on his face.

"What's wrong?" he called out.

"Benji's missing," I told him. "We can't find him anywhere."

He parked, then climbed out of the truck. "Isn't Clyde's thing going on right now?"

"He was supposed to meet his dad at four, outside the Pavilion," I told him, scanning the road again. "But he never showed up."

"Emaline, it's okay. I'm sure he's fine."

"It's been over two hours," I said. "He's only ten."

"I know." He stepped closer and squeezed my arm. "Just take a breath. Let's think for a minute."

I exhaled, skipping the intake part. "We've looked all over. Surfside, the Pavilion, the sound, the boardwalk. I thought for sure he would have come here, because he loves this job so much, but I just turned the whole place upside down with no sight of him."

Luke thought for a minute. "Okay, so say we're Benji."

"Luke."

"Seriously. This works." He looked at me, nodding. "We're ten. We're pissed off. We go somewhere that's familiar and comforting, safe, but hard to find. Where would that be?"

"If I *knew*," I pointed out, "I would have him already."

"Just think for a second."

"Luke, for God's sake. I can't just—"

And then, just by chance, over his shoulder, I saw it. The bane of my existence, but possibly one of Benji's favorite places, ever.

"Hold on," I said.

I walked around Luke, breaking into a jog as I crossed the lot. The sandbar—my sandbox—was already set up for check-ins the next day. A pack of shrink-wrapped welcome packets sat just outside, two washed coolers stacked beside them, ready for cold drinks and ice. I climbed the two steps, then leaned over and peered down over the wall. Benji, sitting against the far wall with his knees pulled to his chest, looked up at me.

"I don't want everything to change," he said.

I bit my lip and glanced at Luke, giving him a nod. Then I opened the door, going inside, and sat down beside him. As always, the floor was dusted with a faint layer of sand. I could feel it on my feet as I slid off my shoes. "You really had us worried," I told him, my voice low. "Everyone is out looking."

He pulled his knees closer, not saying anything. Up close now, I could see he'd been crying, and it made him look so young I felt a lump form in my throat. "He's making me leave tomorrow. He didn't even tell me. I heard him saying it to my mom."

"I know," I said.

"I don't even start school for another three weeks," he went on, rubbing at his face. "What am I supposed to do all that time? Sit around and watch them get divorced?"

"Benji."

"I don't have anything there," he sputtered, tears filling his eyes. "Not like this."

Oh, man, I thought. I forced myself to take a breath. "I know how you feel."

"No, you don't," he said. "You get to stay here."

"For about two more weeks," I replied. "Then I have to move to a totally new place, with totally new people, and start a totally new life. I'm terrified."

"Luke will be there," he said, sulkily.

I stretched my legs out in front of me. "Yeah, but I'm not exactly his favorite person these days."

"But he's here, though. Isn't he?"

I looked down at him. "What's your point?"

He shrugged. "Just that he said he had plans, earlier. That he was missing the party, too."

"He just saw me looking for you and could tell I was worried," I said. "Look, I know you think you're all grown up and all, but you can't run off like that. Your dad is freaking."

"He's just mad because I'm not doing exactly what he wants," he grumbled, picking at the floorboard beside him. "He hates that."

I had to smile at this, although I quickly damped it down, as best I could. "I don't think anyone likes that much, actually."

"Are you still mad at him?"

"Who?"

"My dad."

It was not what I was expecting, so it took me a moment to answer. "No. Not really."

I was surprised, hearing myself say this, that it actually felt true. Was I sad about the way things stood, and did I wish, still, the spring and even this summer had gone differently? Yes. But the anger, somehow, had lifted, leaving behind a sense that I could deal with whatever came next for us, even if it was nothing at all. Which sounded bad, I knew. Having no expectations for some people in your life can be depressing, if not devastating. But with others, it's what is necessary. The hard part is not just figuring out which one applies, but accepting it.

"He's really bad at saying he's sorry or wrong, even when

he knows he is," Benji said now. I raised my eyebrows, and he explained, "That's what my mom always tells me when I get mad at him. Sometimes it makes it better."

"Yeah," I said. "I can see how it would."

We sat there for a minute, side by side, the sky still blue above us. I thought of the party still going on at the Pavilion, and wondered if Clyde had already made his big announcement, anointing Theo as he expected. By tomorrow, the show would be over, Ivy would start packing up, and Benji would be gone. All this thinking—consciously not thinking—about how things would end, and now, just like that, they were about to. It was the very nature of summer. So many long, lazy days when blissfully, nothing changes, and then everything does, all at once.

I heard a car approaching and I leaned over to look out a crack in the wall behind me. My father's Subaru was pulling in, parking beside the truck. Luke walked over, and my father rolled down the window. After a moment, they both looked over at the sandbox.

"Your dad's here," I told Benji. His shoulders sagged, his face reddening. "I know. But maybe just tell him what you told me."

"He'll still make me go," he grumbled.

"Probably," I agreed. "But at least he might understand why you don't want to. And sometimes, that's the best you can ask for. Okay?"

He nodded, and I pushed myself to my feet. My father was out of his car now, Luke standing nearby, both of them looking at me as I left the sandbar and walked over to them. As I got in earshot, my father said, "What? He wants to be forcibly removed now?"

"He's upset," I told him.

"*I'm* upset," he shot back. "We've got half the town looking for him. He needs to stop this nonsense and get in the car. I don't have time for this."

"Then *make* time," I said. Luke raised his eyebrows. I stepped closer to my father, lowering my voice. "He's your kid, he's scared, and he needs you to tell him everything is going to be all right."

"He's not a baby," he said. "He can handle the truth that is the world."

"He's *ten*, and he needs his dad." I could feel my throat get tight. "Please just make sure he gets that, if for no other reason than I'm standing here asking you. If you do, I swear to God, I will never trouble you for anything else."

"Hey," he said, sounding surprised. "I'm your dad, too."

"No, you're my father," I said. "I have a dad, and right now, Benji needs his. Not a lecture. Not fixing, because he's not broken. Just your attention and your patience and your time. Just *you*."

"Emaline," he said quietly.

I shook my head. "Go. *Please*."

I was crying now, why, I had no idea. The tears just came, carrying with them all the strain of these last few crazy days, this year, this summer. As my father looked at me, I knew, this time with certainty, that it was too late for us. But with Benji, he had so much time to do better. And it started right here, right now.

I didn't say any of this, of course. But as he finally turned and began to walk across the lot, it occurred to me that all I'd wanted from him was the unconditional love you get from family, that strong, innate connection so unlike anything else. For whatever reason—time, circumstance, distance—he wasn't able to give it to me himself. But he did give me Benji, and I would be forever grateful. With love like that, you can't get picky about how it finds you or the details. All that matters is that it's there. Better late than never.

21

I HAD TO admit, it *was* different.

"I'll swipe the card!" Benji yelled, running out ahead of me as we entered the station. He did, and I pushed through the turnstile, feeling a blast of hot, smelly city air as I did so. A moment later he joined me, and I peered down the dark tunnel, trying to get my bearings.

"Which one are we getting on, again?" I still hated not knowing where I was, or was going. Part of growing up in a berg, I supposed.

"The R. It's this way. Come on, I think that's one right there."

He grabbed my hand and we ran together along the platform, getting to the train just as the doors were closing. Inside, we found a single free seat, which he gallantly gave to me. He hung onto a pole instead.

"You're sure you have the invitation?" he asked me, for about the millionth time.

"I have the invitation," I told him. "But even if we didn't, I *bet* we could get in. We do know the artist's assistant."

"True," he said, taking a spin around the pole. It was mid-November, only three months or so since I'd last seen him, but

I'd swear he'd shot up a good foot. Add in his new haircut—a sort of a faux-hawk—and I'd almost not even recognized him when he and my father picked me up at the airport a few days earlier. Almost.

We'd planned this trip all the way back in August, when he and my father had left Colby. In the end, they'd stayed three more days, which allowed us to do all the big Colby things one last time: shrimp burgers, arcade, check-ins. On the last night, I'd kept my promise, emptying out our Summer Ending Tax jar, which held just enough for two tickets to the Surfside Ferris wheel. In the end, though, we didn't have to pay. High School Special.

As for my father, things had remained distant, especially as there was more distance between us. While I called and texted with Benji regularly—he loved that phone of his—I did not hear a thing from my father for two full months. Then, in the beginning of November, I opened up my e-mail to find a message. It had no subject, and no greeting, and just said this:

What are you reading for school that you love?
What do you hate?

For a full week, I left it in my inbox, where again and again I'd open it, scan these words, and then close it. I owed him nothing and hoped he knew to expect as much. But the one thing that had always worked for us was e-mail. So eventually, I wrote him a response, telling him that I liked Chaucer but found Milton impossible to understand. Within three hours, he'd written back. Since then, we'd kept up a steady discourse, solely about literature. It wasn't parenting, but I had that in spades with my mom's regular calls and texts. And he did know an awful lot about *Paradise Lost.*

"This is our stop," Benji called out now, as the train began to slow down. We followed a clump of other passengers out, then up the stairs, to my great relief. As a beach girl, being underground still felt weird to me. If I couldn't have water in sight, the sky was the next best thing.

"Okay," I said, pulling out the directions my father had printed out for us. "From the station, we go two blocks east, then three west. The gallery should be on the corner."

"This way," he said, turning right. "Follow me."

I did, the control freak in me requiring that I pull out my phone, where I'd programmed the address as well, to make sure we were going the right way. With all the noise and bustle of the city, I felt constantly uncertain. A year ago, it would have been my worst nightmare. But by now, after being the same old way for so long, I'd learned a little newness could be good for me.

My first semester at East U was a classic example. Even though it was only two hours from Colby, it *was* a different world. The campus was large, based on the edge of a city easily twice the size of Cape Frost, and I shared a dorm suite with three other girls. They were all nice and we got along fine, but I still found the training my mom and sisters had given me in my old room came in awfully handy when it came to our shared space. Despite my assumptions that it would be otherwise, no one else from my high school had ended up in my dorm or in any of my classes, which was both exciting and frightening all at once. No one had known me since kindergarten, so I could be anything or anyone. But no one had known me since kindergarten, so no one knew me, period.

Okay, maybe not no one. There *was* Luke, whose dorm was right down the block. He'd been a great comfort during those first, fierce days of homesickness, just as he had the night Benji ran off.

After my father and Benji went back to North Reddemane, Luke had driven me to the Pavilion, where I was able to catch the tail end of the party. He stayed, helping us clean up, and even went along when Ivy, a bit loopy on white wine and in a celebratory mood, insisted we all go dancing at Tallyho. There, she and Amber hit the floor together, with Morris and Daisy in tow, while I sat off to the side, nursing my blistered feet and a soda water.

"Thank you," I said to Luke, who was beside me, a watered-down beer in his hand.

"For what?" he asked.

"Helping with Benji, doing all this," I said, waving my hand.

He looked at me over the rim of his cup. "Don't thank me for Tallyho. Remember what happened earlier this summer."

"Oh, right." I put my hand over my mouth. "Sorry."

He made a face, sipping on his beer again. Out on the floor, Ivy was dancing with some sweaty guy in a tight red T-shirt, her head thrown back. Whoa.

"I was surprised to see you tonight, at the rental office," I said to Luke after a moment. "I thought you had plans."

"I did," he said.

"Oh. What happened?'

He looked at me. "Emaline. I was driving by and saw you in a total panic. Like I wasn't going to immediately stop and help you. Come on."

"Sorry," I said. He sat back. "No really, I am. I didn't mean to ruin your night."

"You didn't," he assured me. "But I probably ruined someone else's."

. I didn't know what to say to this. I sat there for a moment, watching everyone on the floor, then leaned over and kissed his cheek. Just as I was thinking how his skin tasted salty, familiar, he pulled away.

"Don't do that," he said. Not in a mean way, but firm. "Really. It's just going to complicate things."

"Okay," I said immediately. "I get it."

"Do you?" He turned to face me. "Because when it comes to you, Emaline, there can't be any halfway with me. And as far as I know you still have a boyfriend."

"We just broke up."

"*We* just broke up," he added. He looked down at his cup, then at me. "My point is, I don't want any more weirdness between us. Which means, honestly, not having anything between us. At least not now. All right?"

It was all right, strangely enough. In fact, it was just what I needed. Luke had been my love, but he'd also been my friend. That, despite everything, had not changed, even when I thought otherwise. We'd seen each other quite a bit over the remaining days of summer, and I was happy to just hang out, not worrying about what came next for us at East U. I truly believed that if we were meant to be, we would be. And there was no better way than jumping into a pool of thousands of strangers to find that out.

"This is it," I said to Benji now, as I spotted the gallery, a gray banner reading CLYDE CONAWAY: COLLECTED WORKS fluttering out front. Inside, it was bright and warm looking, people milling around. Seeing the paintings, the only thing familiar in this big foreign place, was like a comfort to me.

"Emaline!" Ivy called out as soon as we came in. She was in her classic black, skirt and top, her hair pulled back tight at her neck. Despite the city armor, I would always think of her that night at Tallyho, grinding with the guy in the T-shirt. Some things never leave you. "You made it!"

"Barely," I told her, as she hugged me, then Benji. "This place is so confusing."

"What? New York is the easiest city to navigate in the world. It's a grid, for God's sake."

"I just don't like not knowing where I am," I told her.

"Oh, God, no. Who does?" She took a sip of her drink, glancing around. "Let's look for Clyde. I know he is *dying* to see you guys."

We found him holding court in the back of the gallery, in front of one of the beach grass details. He had on a nice shirt and tie . . . and a Finz ball cap, well worn. When he saw me, he grinned. "There she is," he said. "My Colby girl."

"Like a fish out of water here," I said, hugging him.

"That makes two of us," he told me. "Have you seen my assistant yet?"

I bit my lip. "No. Not yet."

"Why do you look so nervous?" he asked.

"I don't know," I said, shrugging and glancing around. "It's still so, kind of weird. You know how I feel about him."

"I do," he assured me, waving at someone over my shoulder. "And it's fine."

The room was getting warmer as more people came in. Outside, the night was falling, cabs and cars passing with their lights on. It *was* pretty, I had to admit.

"New York during the holidays," Ivy said from beside me, looking out the window as well. "Nothing better."

"Except the beach in the fall," I replied. "Or anytime."

She made a face at me. "Just you wait. I'll make you a city lover yet."

"Don't be so sure."

"Oh, I am. When you get here in May, it'll be a whole new, wonderful world. Museums, theater, great food!" She sighed and took a sip of her wine. "Of course, you'll be working for me way too hard to actually enjoy any of that. But still, nice to know it's there."

"I'm not afraid to work," I told her.

"I know it. That's why you already have the job."

I smiled. All that hustling back in August had paid off, and not just with the hefty check Ivy had written me the day she left. She'd also extended the offer of employment the following summer, working for her here. It, too, was a new and scary prospect, which was just why I'd taken it. I would miss Colby, but it wasn't going anywhere. All the more reason why I should.

Benji, who'd gone off to find a drink, returned with two

bottled waters. "They aren't half-frozen. But good anyway."

"Perfect," I told him, uncapping mine. "To Clyde."

"To Clyde," he repeated, and we drank.

I still had one more person I needed to see, as my nervous stomach kept reminding me. I wasn't even sure why I felt like I had so much at stake, other than the fact that it was old habit. Even in a whole new world, some things never change.

"There he is!" Benji said, tugging at my sleeve.

I turned, looking where he was pointing. Sure enough, there across the gallery, in dark jeans and an untucked plaid shirt, was Morris. He was talking to two women in cocktail dresses, gesturing at the gray painting behind him, and for a moment I just watched him, marveling. When he finally looked over, seeing us, and grinned at me, I laughed out loud.

Because of Benji's disappearing act, I'd missed Clyde announcing the plans for this tour at the art show. Which was no big deal, as I'd already known about that. It was the other, less public choice he made that I knew, in the end, had probably qualified as Theo's Biggest Surprise Ever. Despite his glad-handing and mad ambition, or probably because of it, he was *not* the one chosen to come along for the ride. Instead, that was Morris, and it had been him even before he identified Theo's exotic plant as common beach grass. It had been what Clyde had wanted to talk to me about, before I found out Benji was missing, and in a way I was glad he'd never had the chance.

After all, my confidence in Morris's abilities was shaky to say the least. Which was why I'd stayed out of it as he began really working for Clyde, focusing instead on my own life, which is what I should have been doing all along. To my surprise, but not Clyde's, Morris turned out to be a quick study once inspired, the perfect mix of capable and familiar. Did he know everything about Clyde's oeuvre and the art world? No. But he didn't have to, either. All that was needed was for him to keep a schedule and do what he was asked, tasks I'd been struggling to get him to master for years. Somehow, though, Clyde was a good influence, not to mention role model, and Morris was doing well. At least if this event was any indication.

"Look at you," I said, as he came towards us. He high-fived Benji and gave me a hug. "You're wearing long pants!"

"It's winter," he told me. "Here, that means it's actually cold."

"Still, I'm impressed," I told him. "You look good."

"Yeah?"

I nodded. "And happy."

"Well, this one was a biggie," he said, glancing around. "You should meet the gallery owner. What a jerk. He's *totally* crackers."

I smiled. "You hear from Daisy lately?"

"Got a letter yesterday," he said, pulling a yellow envelope out of his shirt pocket. "Gonna answer it tonight."

"I still can't picture you writing letters," I admitted.

"I wouldn't for anyone else," he replied. "But I love that girl."

"Enough to get off the couch," I said, looking around.

"Yeah." He slid the letter back into his pocket. "Way off."

The day after the Beach Bash—where Daisy and I had

extended our Best-Dressed Couple streak, thanks to the candy dresses—Morris had indeed gone to break up with Daisy. He explained all his reasons, as well as why he felt it was what he had to do for her. And she informed him, flat out, that he was wrong. Typical Daisy: she wouldn't even do a breakup like everyone else. She *did* agree, however, that long-distance would be hard, and proposed that they try a different approach to staying together. Instead of talking and texting more, they'd go for the opposite tack, pledging for the entire fall to communicate only via time-honored, almost-obsolete handwritten correspondence. I knew from e-mailing with Clyde that Morris spent nights he wasn't working hunched over a legal pad, painstakingly detailing everything he was doing while away from her. It was an odd way to stay close, but then nothing about Daisy and Morris had ever made sense. It wasn't like I should have expected this to be the exception.

I felt my phone beep in my pocket and pulled it out, knowing already what I'd see. Sure enough, it was a text from my mom, the kind I'd gotten regularly since landing in New York.

Just tell me you are still alive please.

And well, I wrote back. At Clyde's show. Will call later.

This, I knew, would hold her over. For about fifteen minutes. She was better when I was at school, but not by much. It was still early days, though, and I knew she'd adjust eventually and realize the distance between us didn't really have to change anything. She still loved me to the moon. This was just the more.

"Let's get a picture," Clyde called out, gesturing for me, Morris, and Benji to come over to where he and Ivy were standing. Behind them was a broad canvas, one I hadn't seen before, made up of deep blues and greens, dotted with tiny specks of something I couldn't make out. I walked closer to the canvas, leaning in.

"Okay, everyone," the photographer, a tall girl with braids, called out. "Look here!"

Morris looped his arm over my shoulder, while Benji moved in beside me. Out on the street, traffic rushed past, night falling as everyone headed back to the place they called home. People were walking past the gallery, some looking in, some with their heads ducked down against the cold. Not for the first time since I'd been here, I thought of a boy in a sport jacket, raising a glass, who, despite everything else, had taught me something I needed to know about the difference between the superlatives and everything else. Any other girl might not have been so lucky.

The thing is, you can't always have the best of everything. Because for a life to be real, you need it all: good and bad, beach and concrete, the familiar and the unknown, big talkers and small towns. Otherwise, how could I have all these things and still be so close to my own Best After Ever? As close as this painting behind me, which as the flash popped, I reached a hand back towards, suddenly knowing what it was I'd seen on it earlier. It was just the lightest dusting, and another person might have mistaken it for something else. But I knew where I came from. No matter where I was, or what got me there, I would always feel at home when I touched sand.

JUST LISTEN

The best way out is always through.
                    —Robert Frost

JUST LISTEN

Chapter
ONE

I taped the commercial back in April, before anything had happened, and promptly forgot about it. A few weeks ago, it had started running, and suddenly, I was everywhere.

On the rows of screens hanging over the ellipticals at the gym. On the monitor they have at the post office that's supposed to distract you from how long you've been waiting in line. And now here, on the TV in my room, as I sat at the edge of my bed, fingers clenched into my palms, trying to make myself get up and leave.

"It's that time of year again. . . ."

I stared at myself on the screen as I was five months earlier, looking for any difference, some visible proof of what had happened to me. First, though, I was struck by the sheer oddness of seeing myself without benefit of a mirror or photograph. I had never gotten used to it, even after all this time.

"Football games," I watched myself say. I was wearing a baby-blue cheerleader uniform, hair pulled back tight into a ponytail, and clutching a huge megaphone, the kind nobody ever used anymore, emblazoned with a K.

"Study hall." Cut to me in a serious plaid skirt and brown

cropped sweater, which I remembered feeling itchy and so wrong to be wearing just as it was getting warm, finally.

"And, of course, social life." I leaned in, staring at the me on-screen, now outfitted in jeans and a glittery tee and seated on a bench, turning to speak this line while a group of other girls chattered silently behind me.

The director, fresh-faced and just out of film school, had explained to me the concept of this, his creation. "The girl who has everything," he'd said, moving his hands in a tight, circular motion, as if that was all it took to encompass something so vast, not to mention vague. Clearly, it meant having a mega-phone, some smarts, and a big group of friends. Now, I might have dwelled on the explicit irony of this last one, but the on-screen me was already moving on.

"It's all happening this year," I said. Now I was in a pink gown, a sash reading HOMECOMING QUEEN stretched across my midsection as a boy in a tux stepped up beside me, extend-ing his arm. I took it, giving him a wide smile. He was a sopho-more at the local university and mostly kept to himself at the shooting, although later, as I was leaving, he'd asked for my number. How had I forgotten that?

"The best times," the me on-screen was saying now. "The best memories. And you'll find the right clothes for them all at Kopf's Department Store."

The camera moved in, closer, closer, until all you could see was my face, the rest dropping away. This had been before that night, before everything that had happened with Sophie, before this long, lonely summer of secrets and silence. I was a mess, but this girl—she was fine. You could tell in the way she stared out at me and the world so confidently as she opened her mouth to speak again.

"Make your new year the best one yet," she said, and I felt my breath catch, anticipating the next line, the last line, the one that only this time was finally true. "It's time to go back to school."

The shot froze, the Kopf's logo appearing beneath me. In moments, it would switch to a frozen waffle commercial or the latest weather, this fifteen seconds folding seamlessly into another, but I didn't wait for that. Instead, I picked up the remote, turned myself off, and headed out the door.

I'd had over three months to get ready to see Sophie. But when it happened, I still wasn't ready.

I was in the parking lot before first bell, trying to muster up what it would take to get out and officially let the year begin. As people streamed past, talking and laughing, en route to the courtyard, I kept working on all the maybes: Maybe she was over it now. Maybe something else had happened over the summer to replace our little drama. Maybe it was never as bad as I thought it was. All of these were long shots, but still possibilities.

I sat there until the very last moment before finally drawing the keys out of the ignition. When I reached for the door handle, turning to my window, she was right there.

For a second, we just stared at each other, and I instantly noticed the changes in her: Her dark curly hair was shorter, her earrings new. She was skinnier, if that was possible, and had done away with the thick eyeliner she'd taken to wearing the previous spring, replacing it with a more natural look, all bronzes and pinks. I wondered, in her first glance, what was different in me.

Just as I thought this, Sophie opened her perfect mouth, narrowed her eyes at me, and delivered the verdict I'd spent my summer waiting for.

"Bitch."

The glass between us didn't muffle the sound or the reaction of the people passing by. I saw a girl from my English class the year before narrow her eyes, while another girl, a stranger, laughed out loud.

Sophie, though, remained expressionless as she turned her back, hiking her bag over one shoulder and starting down to the courtyard. My face was flushed, and I could feel people staring. I wasn't ready for this, but then I probably never would be, and this year, like so much else, wouldn't wait. I had no choice but to get out of my car, with everyone watching, and begin it in earnest, alone. So I did.

I had first met Sophie four years earlier, at the beginning of the summer after sixth grade. I was at the neighborhood pool, standing in the snack-bar line with two damp dollar bills to buy a Coke, when I felt someone step up behind me. I turned my head, and there was this girl, a total stranger, standing there in a skimpy orange bikini and matching thick platform flip-flops. She had olive skin and thick, curly dark hair pulled up into a high ponytail, and was wearing black sunglasses and a bored, impatient expression. In our neighborhood, where everyone knew everyone, it was like she'd fallen out of the sky. I didn't mean to stare. But apparently, I was.

"What?" she said to me. I could see myself reflected in the lenses of her glasses, small and out of perspective. "What are *you* looking at?"

I felt my face flush, as it did anytime anybody raised their voice at me. I was entirely too sensitive to tone, so much so that even TV court shows could get me upset—I always had to change the channel when the judge ripped into anyone. "Nothing," I said, and turned back around.

A moment later, the high-school guy working the snack bar waved me up with a tired look. While he poured my drink I could feel the girl behind me, her presence like a weight, as I smoothed my two bills out flat on the glass beneath my fingers, concentrating on getting every single crease. After I paid, I walked away, studiously keeping my eyes on the pocked cement of the walkway as I made my way back around the deep end to where my best friend, Clarke Reynolds, was waiting.

"Whitney said to tell you she's going home," she said, blowing her nose as I carefully put the Coke on the pavement beside my chair. "I told her we could walk."

"Okay," I said. My sister Whitney had just gotten her license, which meant that she had to drive me places. Getting home, however, remained my own responsibility, whether from the pool, which was walking distance, or the mall one town over, which wasn't. Whitney was a loner, even then. Any space around her was her *personal* space; just by existing, you were encroaching.

It was only after I sat down that I finally allowed myself to look again at the girl with the orange bikini. She had left the snack bar and was standing across the pool from us, her towel over one arm, a drink in her other hand, surveying the layout of benches and beach chairs.

"Here," Clarke said, handing over the deck of cards she was holding. "It's your deal."

Clarke had been my best friend since we were six years old. There were tons of kids in our neighborhood, but for some reason most of them were in their teens, like my sisters, or four and below, a result of the baby boom a couple of years previously. When Clarke's family moved from Washington, D.C., our moms met at a community-watch meeting. As soon as they realized we were the same age, they put us together, and we'd stayed that way ever since.

Clarke had been born in China, and the Reynoldses had adopted her when she was six months old. We were the same height, but that was about all we had in common. I was blonde-haired and blue-eyed, a typical Greene, while she had the darkest, shiniest hair I'd ever seen and eyes so brown they were almost black. While I was timid and too eager to please, Clarke was more serious, her tone, personality, and appearance all measured and thoughtful. I'd been modeling since before I could even remember, following my sisters before me; Clarke was a total tomboy, the best soccer player on our block, not to mention a whiz at cards, especially gin rummy, at which she'd been beating me all summer.

"Can I have a sip of your drink?" Clarke asked me. Then she sneezed. "It's hot out here."

I nodded, reaching down to get it for her. Clarke had bad allergies year-round, but in summer they hit fever pitch. She was usually either stuffed up, dripping, or blowing from April to October, and no amount of shots or pills seemed to work. I'd long ago grown used to her adenoidal voice, as well as the omnipresent pack of Kleenex in her pocket or hand.

There was an organized hierarchy to the seating at our pool: The lifeguards got the picnic tables near the snack bar, while the moms and little kids stuck by the shallow end and the baby (i.e., pee) pool. Clarke and I preferred the half-shaded area behind the kiddie slides, while the more popular high-school guys—like Chris Pennington, three years older than me and hands-down the most gorgeous guy in our neighborhood and, I thought then, possibly the world—hung out by the high dive. The prime spot was the stretch of chairs between the snack bar and lap lane, which was usually taken by the most popular high-school girls. This was where my oldest sister, Kirsten, was stretched out in a chaise, wearing a hot-pink bikini and fanning herself with a *Glamour* magazine.

Once I dealt out our cards, I was surprised to see the girl in orange walk over to where Kirsten was sitting, taking the chair next to her. Molly Clayton, Kirsten's best friend, who was on her other side, nudged her, then nodded at the girl. Kirsten looked up and over, then shrugged and lay back down, throwing her arm over her face.

"Annabel?" Clarke had already picked up her cards and was impatient to start beating me. "It's your draw."

"Oh," I said, turning back to face her. "Right."

The next afternoon, the girl was back, this time in a silver bathing suit. When I got there, she was already set up in the same chair my sister had been in the day before, her towel spread out, bottled water beside her, magazine in her lap. Clarke was at a tennis lesson, so I was alone when Kirsten and her friends arrived about an hour later. They came in loud as always, their shoes thwacking down the pavement. When they reached their usual spot and saw the girl sitting there, they slowed, then looked at one another. Molly Clayton looked annoyed, but Kirsten just moved about four chairs down and set up camp as always.

For the next few days, I watched as the new girl kept up her stubborn efforts to infiltrate my sister's group. What began as just taking a chair escalated, by day three, to following them to the snack bar. The next afternoon, she got in the water seconds after they did, staying just about a foot down the wall as they bobbed and talked, splashing one another. By the weekend, she was trailing behind them constantly, a living shadow.

It had to be annoying. I'd seen Molly shoot her a couple of nasty looks, and even Kirsten had asked her to back up, please, when she'd gotten a little too close in the deep end. But the girl didn't seem to care. If anything, she just stepped up her efforts more, as if it didn't matter what they were saying as long as they were talking to her, period.

"So," my mother said one night at dinner, "I heard a new family's moved in to the Daughtrys' house, over on Sycamore."

"The Daughtrys moved?" my father asked.

My mother nodded. "Back in June. To Toledo. Remember?"

My father thought for a second. "Right," he said finally, nodding. "Toledo."

"I also heard," my mom continued, passing the bowl of pasta she was holding to Whitney, who immediately passed it on to me, "that they have a daughter your age, Annabel. I think I saw her the other day when I was over at Margie's."

"Really," I said.

She nodded. "She has dark hair, a bit taller than you. Maybe you've seen her around the neighborhood."

I thought for a second. "I don't know—"

"That's who that is!" Kirsten said suddenly. She put down her fork with a clank. "The stalker from the pool. Oh my God, I *knew* she had to be way younger than us."

"Hold on." Now my father was paying attention. "There's a stalker at the pool?"

"I *hope* not," my mother said, in her worried voice.

"She's not a stalker, really," Kirsten said. "She's just this girl who's been hanging around us. It's so creepy. She, like, sits beside us, and follows us around, and doesn't talk, and she's always listening to what we're saying. I've told her to get lost, but she just ignores me. God! I can't believe she's only *twelve*. That makes it even sicker."

"So dramatic," Whitney muttered, spearing a piece of lettuce with her fork.

She was right, of course. Kirsten was our resident drama queen. Her emotions were always at full throttle, as was her mouth; she never stopped talking, even if she was well aware you weren't listening to her. In contrast, Whitney was the silent type, which meant the few words she uttered always carried that much more meaning.

"Kirsten," my mother said now, "be nice."

"Mom, I've tried that. But if you saw her, you'd understand. It's strange."

My mother took a sip of her wine. "Moving to a new place is difficult, you know. Maybe she doesn't know how to make friends—"

"She obviously doesn't," Kirsten told her.

"—which means that it might be your job to meet her halfway," my mother finished.

"She's *twelve*," Kirsten said, as if this was on par with being diseased, or on fire.

"So is your sister," my father pointed out.

Kirsten picked up her fork and pointed it at him. "Exactly," she said.

Beside me, Whitney snorted. But my mom, of course, was already turning her attention on me. "Well, Annabel," she said, "maybe you could make an effort, if you do see her. To say hello or something."

I didn't tell my mother I'd already met this new girl, mostly because she would have been horrified she'd been so rude to me. Not that this would have changed her expectations for my behavior. My mother was famously polite, and expected the same of us, regardless of the circumstances. Our whole lives were supposed to be the high road. "Okay," I said. "Maybe I will."

"Good girl," she said. And that, I hoped, was that.

The next afternoon, though, when Clarke and I got to the pool, Kirsten was already there, lying out with Molly on one side and the new girl on the other. I tried to ignore this as we got settled in our spot, but eventually I glanced over to see Kirsten watching me. When she got up a moment later, shooting me a look, then headed toward the snack bar, the new girl immediately following her, I knew what I had to do.

"I'll back in a second," I told Clarke, who was reading a Stephen King novel and blowing her nose.

"Okay," she said.

I got up, then started around by the high dive, crossing my arms over my chest as I passed Chris Pennington. He was lying on a beach chair, a towel over his eyes, while a couple of his buddies wrestled on the pool deck. Now, instead of sneaking glances at him—which, other than swimming and getting beaten at cards, was my main activity at the pool that summer—I'd get bitched out again, all because my mother was insistent we be raised as the best of Good Samaritans. Great.

I could have told Kirsten about my previous run-in with this girl, but I knew better. Unlike me, she did not shy away from confrontation—if anything, she sped toward it, before overtaking it completely. She was the family powder keg, and I had lost track of the number of times I'd stood off to the side, cringing and blushing, while she made her various displeasures clear to salespeople, other drivers, or various ex-boyfriends. I loved her, but the truth was, she made me nervous.

Whitney, in contrast, was a silent fumer. She'd never tell you when she was mad. You just knew, by the expression on her face, the steely narrowing of her eyes, the heavy, enunciated sighs that could be so belittling that words, any words, seemed preferable to them. When she and Kirsten fought—

which, with two years between them, was fairly often—it always seemed at first like a one-sided argument, since all you could hear was Kirsten endlessly listing accusations and slights. Pay more attention, though, and you'd notice Whitney's stony, heavy silences, as well as the rebuttals she offered, few as they were, that always cut to the point much more harshly than Kirsten's swirling, whirly commentaries.

One open, one closed. It was no wonder that the first image that came to mind when I thought of either of my sisters was a door. With Kirsten, it was the front one to our house, through which she was always coming in or out, usually in mid-sentence, a gaggle of friends trailing behind her. Whitney's was the one to her bedroom, which she preferred to keep shut between her and the rest of us, always.

As for me, I fell somewhere between my sisters and their strong personalities, the very personification of the vast gray area that separated them. I was not bold and outspoken, or silent and calculating. I had no idea how anyone would describe me, or what would come to mind at the sound of my name. I was just Annabel.

My mother, conflict-adverse herself, hated it when my sisters fought. "Why can't you just be *nice*?" she'd plead with them. They might have rolled their eyes, but a message sank in with me: that being nice was the ideal, the one place where people didn't get loud or so quiet they could scare you. If you could just be nice, then you wouldn't have to worry about arguments at all. But being nice wasn't as easy as it seemed, especially when the rest of the world could be so mean.

By the time I got to the snack bar, Kirsten had disappeared (of course), but the girl was still there, waiting for the guy behind the counter to ring up her candy bar. *Oh well*, I thought, as I walked up to her. *Here goes nothing.*

"Hi," I said. She just looked at me, her expression unreadable. "Um, I'm Annabel. You just moved here, right?"

She didn't say anything for what seemed like a really long while, during which time Kirsten walked out of the ladies' room behind her. She stopped when she saw us talking.

"I," I continued, now even more uncomfortable, "I, um, think we're in the same grade."

The girl reached up, pushing her sunglasses farther up her nose. "So?" she said, in that same sharp, snide voice as the first time she'd addressed me.

"I just thought," I said, "that since, you know, we're the same age, you might want to hang out. Or something."

Another pause. Then the girl said, as if clarifying, "You want me to hang out. With you."

She made it sound so ridiculous I immediately began backtracking. "I mean, you don't have to," I told her. "It was just—"

"No," she cut me off flatly. Then she tilted her head back and laughed. "No *way.*"

The thing is, if it had just been me there, that would have been it. I would have turned around, face flushed, and gone back to Clarke, game over. But it wasn't just me.

"Hold on," Kirsten said, her voice loud. "What did you just say?"

The girl turned around. When she saw my sister, her eyes

widened. "What?" she said, and I couldn't help but notice how different this, the first word she'd ever said to me, sounded as she said it now.

"I said," Kirsten repeated, her own voice sharp, "*what* did you just say to her?"

Uh-oh, I thought.

"Nothing," the girl replied. "I just—"

"That's my sister," Kirsten said, pointing at me, "and you were just a total bitch to her."

By this point, I was already both cringing and blushing. Kirsten, however, put her hand on her hip, which meant she was just getting started.

"I wasn't a bitch," the girl said, taking off her sunglasses. "I only—"

"You were, and you know it," Kirsten said, cutting her off. "So you can stop denying it. And stop following me around, too, okay? You're creeping me out. Come on, Annabel."

I was frozen to the spot, just looking at the girl's face. Without her sunglasses, her expression stricken, she suddenly *looked* twelve, just staring at us as Kirsten grabbed my wrist, tugging me back to where she and her friends were sitting.

"Unbelievable," she kept saying, and as I looked across the pool I could see Clarke watching me, confused, as Kirsten pulled me down onto her chair. Molly sat up, blinking, reaching up to catch the untied straps of her bikini.

"What happened?" she asked, and as Kirsten began to tell her, I glanced back toward the snack bar, but the girl was gone. Then I saw her, through the fence behind me, walking across the parking lot, barefoot, her head ducked down. She'd left all her stuff on the chair beside me—a towel, her shoes, a bag with a magazine and billfold, a pink hairbrush. I kept waiting for her to realize this and turn back for it. She didn't.

Her things stayed there all afternoon: After I'd gone back to sit with Clarke, and told her everything. After we played several hands of rummy, and swam until our fingers were pruny. After Kirsten and Molly left, and other people took their chairs. All the way up until the lifeguard finally blew the whistle, announcing closing time, and Clarke and I packed up and walked around the edge of the pool, sunburned and hungry and ready to go home.

I knew this girl was not my problem. She'd been mean to me, twice, and therefore was not deserving of my pity or help. But as we passed the chair, Clarke stopped. "We can't just leave it," she said, bending over to gather up the shoes and stuff them into the bag. "And it's on our way home."

I could have argued the point, but then I thought again of her walking across the parking lot, barefoot, alone. So I pulled the towel off the chair, folding it over my own. "Yeah," I said. "Okay."

Still, when we got to the Daughtrys' old house, I was relieved to see all the windows were dark and there was no car in the driveway, so we could just leave the girl's stuff and be done with it. But as Clarke bent down to stick the bag against the front door, it opened, and there she was.

She had on cutoff shorts and a red T-shirt, her hair pulled back in a ponytail. No sunglasses. No high-heeled sandals. When she saw us, her face flushed.

"Hi," Clarke said, after a just-long-enough-to-be-noticed

awkward silence. Then she sneezed before adding, "We brought your stuff."

The girl just looked at her for a second, as if she didn't understand what she was saying. Which, with Clarke's congestion, she probably didn't. I leaned over and picked up the bag, holding it out to her. "You left this," I said.

She looked at the bag, then up at me, her expression guarded. "Oh," she said, reaching for it. "Thanks."

Behind us, a bunch of kids coasted past on their bikes, their voices loud as they called out to one another. Then it was quiet again.

"Honey?" I heard a voice call out from the end of the dark hallway behind her. "Is someone there?"

"It's okay," she said over her shoulder. Then she stepped forward, shutting the door behind her, and came out onto the porch. She quickly moved past us, but not before I saw that her eyes were red and swollen—she'd been crying. And suddenly, like so many other times, I heard my mother's voice in my head: *Moving to a new place is tough. Maybe she doesn't know how to make friends.*

"Look," I said, "about what happened. My sister—"

"It's fine," she said, cutting me off. "I'm fine." But as she said it, her voice cracked, just slightly, and she turned her back to us, putting a hand to her mouth. I just stood there, totally unsure what to do, but as I looked at Clarke, I saw she was already digging into the pocket of her shorts to pull out her ever-present pack of Kleenex. She drew one out, then reached around the girl, offering it to her. A second later, the girl took it, silently, and pressed it to her face.

"I'm Clarke," Clarke said. "And this is Annabel."

In the years to come, it would be this moment that I always came back to. Me and Clarke, in the summer after our sixth-grade year, standing there behind that girl's turned back. So much might have been different for me, for all of us, if something else had happened right then. At the time, though, it was like so many other moments, fleeting and unimportant, as she turned around, now not crying—surprisingly composed, actually—to face us.

"Hi," she said. "I'm Sophie."

Chapter
TWO

"Sophie!"

Finally it was lunchtime, which meant that this, the first day of school, was now at least half over. All around me, the hallway was packed and noisy, but even with locker doors clanging and the droning of various announcements from the intercom, I could still hear Emily Shuster's voice, clear as day.

I looked down the hall to the main staircase and sure enough, she was coming toward me, her red head bobbing through the crowd. When she finally emerged about two feet from where I was standing, our eyes met, but only fleetingly. Then she was quickly moving on, down the hall to where Sophie was waiting for her.

Since Emily had been my friend first, I'd thought maybe, just maybe, she might still be. Apparently not. The lines had been drawn, and now I knew for sure I was standing outside of them.

I had other friends, of course. People I knew from my classes, and from the Lakeview Models, which I'd been doing for years now. It was becoming clear, though, that my self-imposed isolation during the summer had been more effective than I'd realized. Right after everything happened, I'd cut myself off entirely, figuring this was safer than risking people judging me. I blew off phone calls and avoided people when I saw them out at the mall or the movies. I didn't want to talk about what had happened, so it seemed safest not to talk at all. The result, however, was that now all morning, when I'd stopped to say hello to girls I knew, or walked up to groups of people chatting, I'd felt an instant coolness and distance, one that lingered until I made my excuses and walked away. Back in May, all I'd I wanted was to be alone. Now I'd gotten my wish.

My association with Sophie didn't help, of course. Hanging out with her made me a party to all her various social crimes and misdemeanors—and there were many—so there was a wide portion of the student body that was not exactly rushing to embrace me. To the girls Sophie had insulted and isolated while I stood by doing nothing, my own taste of this medicine was nothing short of deserved. If Sophie couldn't be ostracized, I was the next best thing.

Now I headed down to the main lobby, stopping in front of the long row of glass doors that looked out over the courtyard. Outside, the various cliques—jocks, art girls, pols, burnouts— were scattered across the grassy spaces and walkways. Everyone had a place, and once I'd known mine: the long wooden bench to the right of the main walkway, where Sophie and Emily were sitting. Now I was wondering if I should even go out at all.

"It's that time of year again," someone called out in a falsetto voice from behind me. There was a burst of laughter, and as I turned around, I saw a group of football players hanging out by the front office. A tall guy with dreadlocks was imitating the way I'd held out my arm to that guy in the commercial, while the rest of them snickered. I knew they were just goofing around, and maybe another time it wouldn't have bothered me. But now, I felt my face flush as I pushed the doors open in front of me and stepped outside.

There was a long wall to my right, so I headed toward it, looking for a spot, any spot, to sit down. There were only two people sitting on it, the distance between them just big enough to make it clear they weren't together. One was Clarke Reynolds. The other was Owen Armstrong. It wasn't like I had a lot of choices of seating or company, so I sat down between them.

The bricks were warm on my bare legs as I busied myself pulling out the lunch my mother had packed for me that morning: open-faced turkey sandwich, bottled water, and a nectarine. I uncapped the water, taking a big sip, before I finally allowed myself to take a look around. As soon as I glanced over at the bench, I saw Sophie was watching me. When our eyes met, she smiled a thin-lipped smile, shaking her head before looking away.

Pathetic, I heard her say in my head, then pushed this thought away. It wasn't like I wanted to sit with her, either. Then again, I never would have expected to find myself in my current company, either, with Clarke on one side and the Angriest Boy in School on the other.

At least Clarke I knew, or had once known. All the information I possessed about Owen Armstrong I'd gotten from a distance. Like that he was tall and muscular, with broad shoulders and thick biceps. And he always wore boots with thick rubber soles that made him seem even bigger, his steps heavier. His hair was dark and cut short, spiking up a bit at the top, and I'd never once seen him without his iPod and earphones, which he wore inside, outside, in class, out of class. And while I knew he had to have friends, I'd never seen him talk to anyone.

Then there was the fight. It had happened the previous January, in the parking lot before first bell. I'd just gotten out of my car when I saw Owen, backpack over his shoulder, earphones on as always, heading down to the main building. On the way, he passed Ronnie Waterman, who was leaning up against his car, talking with a bunch of his buddies. Every school has someone like Ronnie—a total jerk, famous for tripping people in the hallways, the kind of guy who yells "Nice ass!" when you walk past him. His older brother, Luke, had been his total opposite, captain of the football team and student-body president, totally nice and well liked, and because of this, people put up with his annoying little brother. But Luke had graduated the year before, and now Ronnie was on his own.

Owen was just walking along, minding his own business, and Ronnie shouted out something to him. When he didn't respond, Ronnie pushed off his car and crossed over to block Owen's path. Even from where I was standing, I could tell this was a bad idea; Ronnie wasn't small, but he was tiny compared to Owen Armstrong, who was a full head taller at least, not to mention much wider. Ronnie, however, didn't seem to notice this. He said something else to Owen, and Owen just looked at him for a second, then stepped around him. As he started walking again, Ronnie hit him in the chin.

Owen stumbled, but only slightly. Then he dropped his bag, pulling back his other arm and letting go in a solid arc, where it connected square in the center of Ronnie's face. I could hear it, that smack of fist against bone, from where I was standing.

Ronnie went down within seconds—his body first, knees buckling, then shoulders, followed by his head, which bounced slightly when it hit the ground. Owen, for his part, dropped his hand, stepped over him calm as you please, then picked up his bag and kept walking, the crowd that had gathered parting quickly, then scattering outright to let him through. Ronnie's friends were already gathering around him, someone was calling for the parking-lot guard, but all I could remember was Owen just walking away—same pace, same stride as before, as if he hadn't even stopped.

At the time, Owen was still relatively new; he had been at our school for a only month. As a result of this incident, he got suspended for another. When he came back, everyone was talking about him. I heard that he'd done time in juvenile hall, been kicked out of his previous school, and was in a gang. There were so many rumors that a few months later, when I heard he'd been arrested for fighting at a club over the weekend, I just assumed it wasn't true. But then he'd just disappeared, never coming back to school. Until now.

Up close, though, Owen didn't really look like a monster. He was just sitting there, in sunglasses and a red T-shirt, drumming his fingers on his knee and listening to his music. Even so, I figured it was best not to get caught staring at him, so after unwrapping my sandwich and taking a bite, I took a breath and turned my attention to my right side, and Clarke.

She was at the far end of the wall, a notebook open in her lap, eating an apple with one hand while scribbling something with the other. Her hair was pulled back at her neck in a simple elastic, and she was wearing a plain white T-shirt, army pants, and flip-flops, the glasses she'd started to wear the year earlier, small and tortoiseshell, perched on her nose. After a moment, she glanced up and over at me.

She had to have heard about what happened the previous May. Everyone had. As the seconds passed and she didn't turn away, I wondered if maybe she might have finally forgiven me. That perhaps, just as a new rift had started, I could mend an old one. It would be only fitting, now that we'd both been shunned by Sophie. It gave us something in common again.

And she was still looking at me. I put down my sandwich, then took in a breath. All I had to do, right now, was say something to her, something great, something that might—

But then, suddenly, she turned away. Pushed her notebook into her bag, zipping it shut, her body language stiff, her elbow extended in a sharp angle in my direction. Then she hopped down off the wall, slid her bag over her shoulders, and walked away.

I looked down at my sandwich, half-eaten, and felt a lump rise in my throat. Which was just so stupid, because Clarke had hated me forever. This, at least, was not new.

For the rest of lunch, I just sat there, making a point of not looking at anyone. When I checked my watch and saw I had only five minutes to go, I figured the worst part was over. I was wrong.

I was stuffing my water bottle into my bag when I heard a car pull into the turnaround at the end of the wall. I glanced over to see a red Jeep pulling up to the curb. The passenger door opened and a dark-haired guy climbed out, sticking a cigarette behind his ear as he ducked down, saying something to the person behind the wheel. As he shut the door and started to walk away, I got a look at the driver. It was Will Cash.

I felt my stomach physically drop, as if from a great height, straight down. Everything narrowed, the sounds around me falling away as my palms sprang into sweat, my heartbeat loud in my ears, *thump thump thump*.

I could not stop staring at him. He was just sitting there, one hand on the wheel, waiting for the car in front of him—a station wagon out of which some girl was unloading a cello or some other big instrument—to move along. After a second, he shook his head, irritated.

Shhh, Annabel. It's just me.

A million red Jeeps must have passed before my eyes in the last few months, and despite myself I'd checked each one for his face, this face. But only now, here, was it actually him. And while I had told myself that in broad daylight I could be strong and fearless, I felt as helpless as that night, as if even in the wide open, the bright light of day, I still wasn't safe.

The girl finally got her case out of the station wagon, then waved to the driver as she shut the door. As the car pulled forward, Will glanced over at the courtyard, and I watched his eyes move across the people there, barely seeming to register anyone in particular. Then he looked at me.

I just stared at him, my heart pounding in my chest. It lasted only a second, and I saw no recognition, nothing on his face but a blank stare, as if I were a stranger, just anyone. Then he was moving forward, the car a red blur, and it was over.

Suddenly, I was aware again of the noise and commotion around me: people bustling past to their next class, calling out to one another, tossing trash into the nearby can. Still, I kept my eyes on the Jeep, watching as it climbed the hill that led toward the main road, creeping away from me, bit by bit. And then, in the midst of all the noise and voices, movement and change, I turned my head, cupped a hand to cover my mouth, and threw up in the grass behind me.

When I turned back around a few moments later, the court-yard was mostly empty. The jocks had vacated the other wall, the grass beneath the trees was bare, Emily and Sophie had left their bench. It wasn't until I had wiped my mouth and glanced to my other side that I saw Owen Armstrong was still there, watching me. His eyes were dark and intense, and I was so startled that I quickly looked away. When I glanced back a minute later, he was gone.

Sophie hated me. Clarke hated me. Everybody hated me. Or, maybe not everybody.

"The Mooshka people *loved* your pictures," my mother was saying, her happy voice a complete contrast to how I felt as I sat in a long line of traffic, trying to get out of the parking lot after seventh period. "Lindy said they called her and were just raving."

"Really," I said, switching my phone to my other ear. "That's great."

I tried to sound enthusiastic, but the truth was I'd totally forgotten that a few days earlier my mother had told me that Lindy, my agent, was sending my pictures over to a local swimwear company called Mooshka Surfwear that was hiring for their new ad campaign. Suffice to say modeling was not my top concern these days.

"However," she continued, "Lindy says they'd like to see you in person."

"Oh," I said as the line crept another inch or so forward. "Okay. When?"

"Well," she replied, "actually . . . today."

"Today?" I said, as Amanda Cheeker, driving what looked like a brand-new BMW, totally cut me off, not even looking as she pulled out in front of me.

"Yes. Apparently one of their advertising heads is in town, but only until tonight."

"Mom." I inched forward incrementally, then craned my neck, trying to see who was causing the holdup. "I can't. It's been a really crappy day, and—"

"Honey, I know," she said, as if she actually did, which was totally not the case. Having raised three daughters, my mom was well versed in the politics of girls, which had made it easy for me to explain Sophie's sudden and utter disappearance from my life with the standard "She's just acting so weird," and

"I have no idea what happened." As far as she knew, Sophie and I had just drifted apart; I couldn't imagine what she would have thought if I told her the real story. Actually, I *could* imagine, which was why I hadn't and had no intention of doing so. "But Lindy says they're *really* interested in you."

I glanced in my side mirror, taking in my flushed face, flat hair, and the flecks of mascara around my eyes, the result of finally breaking down in tears in a bathroom stall after sixth period. I really did look as bad as I felt. "You don't understand," I said as I moved up barely one car length. "I didn't sleep well last night, I look really tired, I'm all sweaty—"

"Oh, Annabel," she said, and I felt a lump rising in my throat, reacting immediately to her soft, understanding tone, so welcome after this long terrible day. "I know, sweetie. But it's just one thing, and then you'll be done."

"Mom." The sun was in my eyes, and all I could smell was exhaust. "I'm just—"

"Listen," she said. "How about this. Come home, you can take a quick shower, I'll make you a sandwich and do your makeup. Then I'll drive you over, we'll get it done, and you won't have to think about it again. Okay?"

That was the thing with my mother. There was always a How About This, some deal she was able to manufacture and sell to you that, while being not very different from the original proposition, at least sounded better. Before, saying no had been my prerogative. Now, doing so would make me unreasonable.

"All right," I said as traffic finally started moving at a

decent pace. Up ahead, I could see the security guard waving people around a blue Toyota with a crushed back bumper. "When's the appointment?"

"Four o'clock."

I glanced at my watch. "Mom, it's three thirty right now, and I'm not even out of the parking lot. Where's the office?"

"It's at . . ." she said. I heard paper rustling. "Mayor's Village."

Which was a good twenty minutes away. I'd be lucky to get there on time if I headed straight there, and even then I'd need serious stoplight mercy. "Great," I said. "There's no way."

I knew I was being difficult, not to mention petulant. I also knew I'd go to the meeting and put on my best face, because being difficult and petulant was about as bad as I got when it came to my mother. After all, I was the nice one.

"Well," she said now, in her small voice. "I could call Lindy and tell her you just can't do it, if you like. I'm happy to do that."

"No," I said as I finally reached the top of the parking lot, putting on my blinker. "It's okay. I'll go."

I'd been modeling for as long as I could remember. Actually, it was even before that. I'd done my first shoot when I was nine months old, wearing onesies for a SmartMart Sunday circular, a job I'd gotten when my mother, her sitter having fallen through, had to bring me along to one of my sister Whitney's go-sees. The woman hiring asked her if I was available, my mother said yes, and that was that.

The whole modeling thing had started, though, with Kirsten. She was eight when a talent agent caught up with my mom and dad in the parking lot after her ballet recital, offering them a card and saying they should give him a call. My father had laughed, assuming it was a scam, but my mom was intrigued enough to take Kirsten in for an appointment. The agent had immediately set her up for an audition for a local car-dealership commercial, which she didn't get, followed by a print ad for Easter festivities at the Lakeview Mall, which she did. My modeling career began with onesies, but Kirsten could claim bunnies, or at least one very big one, leaning over to put a shiny egg in her basket as she, in a puffy white dress, smiled into the camera.

Once Kirsten started getting regular work, Whitney wanted to try it as well, and soon they were both making the rounds, often even going up for the same jobs, which only added to the natural friction between them. Their looks, though, were as distinct and different as their temperaments. Whitney was the beauty, with the perfect bone structure and haunting eyes, while Kirsten was somehow able to convey her bubbly personality with just one look. Whitney did better in print, but Kirsten popped on screen. And so on.

Because of this, by the time I started modeling, my family was well known on the local circuit, which consisted mostly of print ads for department and discount stores and regionally cast and shot commercials. While my dad chose to take a hands-off approach to us working—as he did to everything even vaguely girly, from Tampax to broken hearts—my mother thrived on it. She loved ferrying us to jobs, talking business with Lindy on the phone and gathering pictures to update our books. But when she was asked about it, she always pointed out first that it was our choice, not hers. "I would have been happy to have them making mud pies in the backyard," I'd heard her tell people a million times. "But this is what they wanted to do."

In truth, though, my mother loved the modeling, too, even if she didn't want to admit it. But I believed it was even more than that. In some way, I thought that it had saved her.

Not at first, of course. Initially, for her, our modeling was just a fun hobby, something for her to do when she wasn't having to work at my dad's office, which we joked was the most fertile place on the planet, as the secretaries were always getting pregnant, leaving it to my mom to answer the phones until he found a replacement. But then, the year I turned nine, my grandmother died, and something changed.

My own memories of my grandmother are distant, muted, based more on photographs I'd seen than on any real events. My mom was an only child and very close to her own mother, even though they lived on opposite coasts and saw each other only a few times a year. They talked on the phone almost every morning, usually while my mom had her midmorning cup of coffee. Like clockwork, if you came into the kitchen around ten thirty, you'd find her in the chair facing the window, stirring cream into a mug, the phone cocked between her ear and shoulder. To me, it always sounded like the most boring of conversations, solely about people I'd never met, or whatever my mom had cooked the night before, or even my own life, which sounded deadly dull, as well, relayed this way. For my mom, though, it was different. Crucial. How much so, we didn't realize until after my grandmother was gone.

It wasn't like my mom had ever been some pillar of strength. She was a quiet woman, soft-spoken, with a kind face—the sort of person you'd look for if you were out in public somewhere and something bad happened, an instant comfort. I'd always relied on my mom to be just that, exactly as she always had been, which was why the change in her in the weeks following my grandmother's funeral was so strange. She just got . . . quieter. Still. There was suddenly something haunted and tired about her face, so obvious that even I, at nine, could see it. At first, my dad just assured us that it was the normal grief process, that my mother was tired, and she'd be fine. But as time went on, she didn't get better. Instead she started sleeping later, and then later, until she sometimes didn't get out of bed at all. When she was up, I'd sometimes come into the kitchen midmorning to find her sitting in that same chair, empty mug in her hands, looking out the window.

"Mom," I'd say, and she wouldn't respond, so I'd say it again. Sometimes it took three times before she'd slowly begin to turn her head, but when she did I would suddenly feel scared, like I didn't want to see her face after all. Like in those few moments, she might have changed again, shifting deeper into someone I didn't recognize.

My sisters remembered this time better than I did, as they were older and therefore privy to more information. And in typical fashion, they each had their own way of dealing with it. It fell to Kirsten to take care of things around the house, like cleaning and making our lunches, when my mom wasn't up to it, which she did with her usual bravado, as if nothing was wrong at all. Whitney, on the other hand, I often found outside my mother's half-closed bedroom door, listening or peering in, but she'd always move on when I saw her, not meeting my eyes. As the youngest, I wasn't sure how to react, other than to just try not to make trouble or ask too many questions.

My mother's condition quickly grew to dictate our lives. It was the barometer by which we judged everything. In my mind, it all came down to the first glimpse I had of her each morning. If she was up and dressed at a decent hour and making breakfast, things would be okay. But if she wasn't and I found my dad in the kitchen instead, doing his best with cold cereal and toast, or even worse, if neither of them was in sight, I knew it was not going to be a good day. Maybe it was a rudimentary system, but it worked, more or less. And it wasn't like I had a lot else to go on.

"Your mother isn't feeling well," was all my dad would say when we asked after her as we sat around the dining-room table, my mother's place glaringly empty, or when she didn't emerge from her room all day, the only view of her a lump under the covers, barely visible in a sliver of light from the drawn shades. "We all just need to do the best we can to make things easy for her until she feels better. Okay?"

I remember nodding, and seeing my sisters doing the same. But *how* to do this was another thing entirely. I had no idea how to make things easier, or even if I'd done something to make them difficult in the first place. What I did get was that it was paramount that we protect my mom from anything that might upset her, even if I wasn't sure what those things were. So I learned another system: When in doubt, keep it out—out of earshot, out of the house—even if this meant, really, just keeping it in.

My mother's depression, or episode, or whatever it was—I never got a concrete term, which made it all the more hard to define—had been going on for about three months when my dad convinced her to go see a therapist. At first she went reluctantly, quitting after a couple of sessions, but then she started up again, and this time she stuck with it, continuing for the next year. Still, there wasn't some sudden change—one particular day that I came into the kitchen at ten thirty and there she was, bright and cheerful, like she'd been waiting for me to appear. Instead, it was a slow process, little increments, like moving a half a millimeter a day so that you only really notice progress from a distance. First she stopped sleeping all day, then she began to get up midmorning, then finally she started to cook breakfast every once in a while. Her silences, so noticeable at the dinner table and everywhere else, slowly became less extended, a little conversation here, a comment there.

In the end it was the modeling, though, that convinced me we were over the worst of it. Since my mom had been the one who got us to jobs and dealt with Lindy as far as scheduling and auditions, we'd all been working a lot less while she was sick. My dad had taken Whitney to a couple of jobs, and I'd had one shoot that was booked way in advance, but things had definitely slowed down—enough so that when Lindy called one day during dinner about a go-see, even she was assuming we'd take a pass.

"That's probably best," my dad said, glancing back at all of us at the table before taking the phone farther into the kitchen. "I just don't think the time's right."

Kirsten, who was chewing on a piece of bread, said, "Right for what?"

"A job," Whitney told her, her voice flat. "Why else would Lindy call during dinner?"

My dad was rummaging in the drawer by the phone now, finally digging out a pencil. "Well, okay," he said, grabbing a nearby notepad. "I'll just take down the info, but most likely . . . right. What was that address, again?"

My sisters were both watching him as he scribbled it down, probably wondering what the job was for, and for whom. But I was looking at my mom, who had her eyes on my dad as well, even as she drew her napkin out of her lap, dabbing the corners of her mouth. When he came back in, settling into his chair and picking up his fork, I waited for my sisters to ask for details. But instead, my mom spoke first.

"So what was that about?"

My dad looked at her. "Oh," he said, "just an audition tomorrow. Lindy thought we might be interested."

"We?" Kirsten said.

"You," my dad told her, scooping some beans onto his fork. "I told her it probably isn't a good time. It's in the morning, and I've got to be at the office. . . ."

He trailed off, not bothering to finish—not that he had to. My dad was an architect and busy enough with his own work, plus taking care of my mom and keeping up the house, without having to deal with running us all over town. Kirsten knew this, even though it was obvious she was disappointed. But then, in the quiet as we all went back to eating, I heard my mom take in a breath.

"I could take her," she said. We all looked at her. "I mean, if she wanted to go."

"Really?" Kirsten asked. "Because that would be—"

"Grace," my dad said, his voice concerned. Kirsten sat back in her chair, now quiet. "You don't have to."

"I know." My mom smiled, a wan smile, but a smile just the same. "It's just one day, though. One thing. I'd like to."

So the next day, my mom was up for breakfast—I remember that, clearly—and when Whitney and I left for school, she and Kirsten headed off to an audition for a local bowling alley commercial. Kirsten got the job. It was by no means her first ad, and not a very big one, as things went. But every time it ran afterwards, and I saw her bowl that perfect strike (edited in, as my sister was a terrible bowler, the queen of the gutter ball), I thought about that night at the table and how, finally, it seemed like things might be getting back to normal.

And they did, more or less. My mom started taking us around to auditions again, and while she wasn't always cheerful and perky, maybe she actually never had been in the first place. Maybe that, like so much else, I'd only imagined, or assumed. Still, as that year went on, I had trouble trusting that things were really getting better. As hopeful as I wanted to be, I always felt like I was holding my breath, sure that it wouldn't last. And even when it did, the fact that what had happened to my mom had come on so suddenly, with no beginning or true end, made it seem that much more likely to reappear in the same fashion. Back then, I always felt like it would take only one bad event, one disappointment, for her to leave us again. Maybe I felt that way still.

This was one reason why I hadn't yet told my mom I wanted to quit modeling. The truth was that all summer, when I went to go-sees, I felt strange, nervous in a way I never had before. I didn't like the scrutiny, having to walk in front of people, strangers staring at me. At one fitting for a swimsuit shoot in June, I'd kept cringing when the stylist tried to adjust my bathing suit, a lump rising in my throat even as I apologized and said I was fine.

Each time I got close to telling my mom about this, though, something would happen to stop me. I was the only one left modeling now. And while it is hard enough to take away something that makes a person happy, it's even more difficult when it seems like it's the *only* thing.

Which was why, when I got to Mayor's Village fifteen minutes later, I was not surprised to find my mother waiting for me. As I turned in, I was struck, as always, by how *small* she was. Then again, my perspective was a bit skewed, as I was five-eight, and even at that the shortest of my sisters: Kirsten had a half inch on me and Whitney was five-ten. My father loomed above all of us at six-two, leaving my mother to always look sort of odd when we were all together, like one of those which-one-of-these-is-not-like-the-other puzzles we used to do in elementary school.

As I pulled in beside her car, I saw Whitney was in the passenger seat, her arms crossed over her chest. She looked irritated, which was neither surprising nor new, so I didn't dwell on it as I grabbed my makeup bag from my purse and went around to meet my mother, who was standing by her bumper, the hatch open.

"You didn't have to come," I said.

"I know," she replied, not looking up as she handed me a Tupperware container with a plastic fork balanced on top of it. "Fruit salad. I didn't have time to make a sandwich. Sit down."

I sat, then opened the container, digging in the fork to take a bite. I realized I was starving, which made sense, considering I'd thrown up the small amount of lunch I'd managed to get down. God, what a crappy day.

My mother took my makeup bag from me and began to rummage through it, taking out an eye-shadow compact and my powder. "Whitney," she called out, "hand those clothes back here, would you?"

Whitney sighed loudly, then turned around, reaching for the shirts that were hanging from the hook on the door behind her. "Here," she said flatly, barely extending them over the backseat. My mother reached for them, her fingertips falling short, so I turned around to get them for her. As my hand closed over the hangers and I tried to pull them toward me, Whitney held on for a second longer, her grip surprisingly strong as our eyes met. Then she let go, suddenly, and turned back around.

I was trying to be patient with my sister. To remember, at times like this, that it wasn't *her* I was upset with, but her eating disorder. But at times like this, it looked a lot like Whitney, and vice versa, so it was hard to tell the difference.

"Have some water," my mother said now, handing me an open bottle as she took the shirts from me. "And look here."

I took a sip, staying still as she dusted powder across my

face. Then I closed my eyes, listening to cars go by on the highway behind us, as she applied shadow and liner before beginning to rifle through the shirts, the hangers clanking. I opened my eyes to see her holding a pink suede top out at me.

Shhh, Annabel. It's just me.

"No," I said. It came out harsher than I meant, my voice sharp. I took in a breath, forcing myself to sound more normal as I added, "Not that one."

She looked surprised, glancing at it, then back at me again. "Are you sure? It looks wonderful on you. I thought you loved this shirt."

I shook my head, then looked away quickly, focusing on a minivan that was passing by, one of those MY CHILD IS AN HONOR STUDENT stickers on the back window. "No," I told her again. She was still watching me, so I added, "It cuts me weird, or something."

"Oh," I heard her say. She offered me a blue scoop-neck instead. "Here," she said as I looked at it more closely, seeing a price tag hanging from it. "Hop in and change. It's three fifty."

I nodded, then got down off the bumper, walking around to the backseat door and pulling it open. I climbed in, bending down to pull off my tank top, and froze. "Mom," I said.

"Yes?"

"I don't have a bra."

I heard her heels on the pavement as she came around the car. "You don't?"

I shook my head, trying to stay low in the seat. "I had a tank top on; it's got one built in."

My mother thought for a second. "Whitney," she said. "Give—"

Whitney shook her head. "No way."

Now it was my mother's turn to sigh. "Honey, please," she said. "Just help us out, okay?"

And so, as we had for the last nine months or so, we had to wait, and worry, about Whitney. After what felt like a long silence, she finally pulled her arms up under her shirt, fumbled around, then drew a beige bra out of the collar, dropping it back behind her. I grabbed it off the floor, putting it on—we weren't exactly the same size, but it was better than nothing— then pulled the shirt over it. "Thanks," I said, but, of course, she ignored me.

"Three fifty-two," my mother said. "Let's go, honey."

I got out of the car, then walked back around to where she was waiting, holding my purse. She handed it to me, then looked at my face one last time, examining her handiwork. "Close your eyes," she said, reaching forward carefully to draw a clump of mascara off one of my eyelashes. When I opened them, she smiled at me. "You look beautiful."

"Yeah, right," I said, but then she gave me a look, so I added, "Thank you."

She tapped her watch. "Go ahead. We'll wait for you."

"You don't have to. I'll be fine."

The car's engine started suddenly as Whitney turned the key, and then she was rolling down the window, extending her arm outside. She was wearing long sleeves, as always, but you could see a bit of her wrist, pale and so thin, as she tapped her fingers on the side of the car. My mother looked at her, then back at me.

"Well, I'll at least wait for you to get inside," she said. "Okay?"

I nodded, then leaned forward to kiss her just above her cheek, so as not to smudge my lipstick. "Okay."

When I got to the building, I turned around. She lifted her hand, waving, and as I did the same I glanced beyond her at Whitney, whose face I could see framed in the side mirror. She was watching me, too, her face expressionless, and, like so often lately, I felt a twinge, something twisting in my stomach.

"Good luck," my mother called out, and I nodded, then looked back at Whitney. But she'd slid down in her seat and disappeared from view, leaving the mirror empty.

Chapter
THREE

Whitney had always been skinny. While Kirsten was volup-
tuous and curvy, and I was more wiry and athletic, my middle
sister had been born with the true model's body, tall and rail-
thin. Kirsten and I were always being told by photographers
that while we had pretty faces, we were too plump or too
short, respectively, to get serious print work. Early on, though,
it was clear Whitney had real potential.

So it only made sense that the summer after her senior year,
Whitney would move to New York to try her luck modeling
there. This was the same thing Kirsten had done two years earlier. After she'd begged my parents to let her move in with two
older girls she knew from our agency, they'd agreed on the condition that she also enroll in some college courses. Though at
first Kirsten had kept up the balance, once she'd gotten some
print work and a couple of commercials, school had fallen by
the wayside. Even with the work, though, she still earned the
bulk of her money with waitress and hostessing gigs.

Not that this bothered her all that much. Since high school,
when she discovered boys and beer—not necessarily in that
order—Kirsten's focus on modeling had dwindled consider-

ably. While Whitney always made sure to get plenty of sleep before a job and arrived on time without fail, Kirsten was much more likely to roll in late, with bedhead and a hangover. One time she'd showed up for a Kopf's prom dress shoot with a hickey so large they couldn't even totally cover it with make-up. When the ads ran, weeks later, she'd laughed as she point-ed it out to me—a brown circle, barely visible under the strap of her princesslike gown.

My mother had had higher hopes for Whitney. Two weeks after graduation, they packed her stuff and drove up to move her into the apartment where Kirsten was now living alone. To me, this cohabitation seemed like a bad idea from the start. My mom and dad, though, were firm: Whitney was only eighteen, and she needed some family looking out after her, and since my parents were already helping with Kirsten's rent, she couldn't really complain. (Although she did, of course.) Besides, my mom said, my sisters were older now, their vari-ous conflicts all in the past.

Once Whitney was moved in, my mom stayed on for a little while getting her settled, signing her up for a couple of courses and accompanying her to her first few appointments with agencies. Each night, she called after dinner to fill my dad and me in on what was going on, sounding happier than I'd ever heard her as she reported on celebrity sightings, meetings with agents, and the hectic, amazing pace of New York. Within a week, Whitney had her first go-see, landing her first job soon afterwards. By the time my mom left a month later, she was working much more than Kirsten ever had. Everything was going exactly as planned . . . until it wasn't.

My sisters had been living together for about four months when Kirsten started calling my mom and saying Whitney was acting strange. That she'd lost weight, hardly seemed to be eating at all, and was really snippy every time Kirsten tried to broach either topic. At first there didn't seem to be much cause for concern. Whitney had always been moody, and even my parents hadn't expected their living situation to go completely smoothly. Most likely, my mom reasoned, Kirsten was being overly dramatic, and if Whitney had lost a little weight, well, she *was* working in a very competitive market, which meant more pressure about her appearance. As she gained confidence, things would even out.

The next time we saw Whitney, though, the change in her was obvious. Before she'd looked lithe, elegant; now, she was gaunt, and her head seemed too big for her body, weighing down her neck. She and Kirsten flew down together for Thanksgiving, and when we picked them up from the airport, the contrast was startling. There was Kirsten, with her round cheeks and clear blue eyes, wearing a bright pink sweater, her skin warm against mine as she threw her arms around me, shrieking how much she'd missed us all. And beside her, Whitney, in sweatpants, a long-sleeved black turtleneck, no makeup, her skin pale. It was a shock, but at first no one said anything, instead just exchanging hellos and hugs and the basic how-was-the-trip banter. As we walked into baggage claim, though, my mother finally broke.

"Whitney, honey," my mother said. "You look *exhausted*. Is that cold you had still hanging on?"

"I'm fine," Whitney said.

"No, she isn't," Kirsten informed us flatly, pulling her suitcase off the carousel. "She doesn't eat. Ever. She's killing herself."

My parents exchanged a look. "Oh, no, she's just been sick," my mother said. She looked at Whitney, who was glaring at Kirsten. "Right, honey?"

"Wrong," Kirsten told her. To Whitney, she said, "Like we talked about on the plane: Either you tell them, or I will."

"Shut up," Whitney said, her voice clenched.

"Now, now," my father said. "Let's just get the bags."

This was typical. My father, the lone male in our estrogen-heavy household, had always dealt with any kind of emotional situation or conflict by doing something concrete and specific. Discussion of cramps and heavy flow at the breakfast table? He was up and out the door to change the oil on one of our cars. Coming home in tears for reasons you just didn't want to discuss? He'd go make you a grilled cheese, which he'd probably end up eating. Family crisis brewing in public place? Bags. Get the bags.

My mother was still studying Whitney, her face concerned. "Honey?" she said, her voice soft, as my dad yanked another suitcase off the belt. "Is this true? Is something wrong?"

"I'm fine," Whitney said again. "She's just jealous that I'm working so much."

"Oh, please!" Kirsten said. "I could give a *shit* about that, and you know it."

My mother's eyes widened, and again I thought of her amongst us, so small, fragile. "Watch your language," my dad said to Kirsten.

"Dad, you don't understand," she told him. "This is serious. Whitney has an eating disorder. If she doesn't get help, she'll—"

"Shut up!" Whitney shrieked, her voice suddenly shrill. "Just shut up!"

This eruption was so startling—we were only used to Kirsten freaking out, ever—that we all just stood there for a second, as if gauging whether it had really happened. But then I saw people in the crowd glancing over at us, making it clear. I saw my mother's face flush, embarrassed.

"Andrew," she said, moving closer to my father. "I don't—"

"Let's go to the car," my dad told us, picking up Whitney's suitcase. "Now."

We went. In silence, my mother and father walking ahead, his arm clamped over her shoulder, Whitney behind them, head bent down against the breeze, Kirsten and I bringing up the rear. As we walked, she slid her hand down to enclose mine, her palm warm in the cold. "They have to know," she said, but when I turned my head, she was looking away, and I wondered if she was actually talking to me at all. "It's the right thing to do. I have to do it."

When we got in the car, no one spoke. Not as we pulled out of the deck, not when we got on the highway. In the backseat, stuck between my sisters, I kept feeling Kirsten taking in a breath, like she might say something, but no words came. On my other side, Whitney was pressed up against the window, looking out, her hands in her lap. I kept staring at her wrists, which looked thin and knobby and pale against the black of her sweatpants. My parents, up front, both stared straight ahead, and occasionally I'd see my father's shoulder move, and I knew he was patting my mom's hand, consoling her.

As soon as we pulled into the garage, Whitney was pushing her door open. Within seconds, she covered the few feet to the door that led to the kitchen, disappearing inside and slamming it behind her. Beside me, Kirsten sighed.

"Okay," she said quietly as my dad cut the engine. "We need to talk."

They did, but I wasn't allowed to hear what they said. It was made clear to me ("Annabel, why don't you go do some homework?") that I was not to be part of this conversation. Instead, I stayed in my room, math book open in my lap, straining to make out some of what was happening downstairs. I could hear my father's low tones, my mom's higher ones, and the occasional indignant shift in tone from Kirsten. On the other side of my wall, Whitney, in her room, was silent.

Finally, my mom came upstairs, passing my room to knock on Whitney's door. When there was no reply, she said, "Whitney, honey. Let me in." Nothing. She stood there for what felt like a full minute or two before suddenly I heard the lock turn, and then the door open and shut again.

I went back downstairs, where I found Kirsten sitting at the kitchen table with my father, an untouched grilled cheese on a plate in front of her. "Look," she was saying as I opened the cabinet to pull out a glass, "she explains it all away really well. She'll have Mom brainwashed in three seconds."

"I'm sure that's not true," my dad told her. "Give your mother some credit."

Kirsten shook her head. "She's sick, Daddy. She hardly ever

eats, and when she does she's really weird about it. She'll eat one quarter of an apple for breakfast or, like, three saltines for lunch. And she works out all the time. The gym around the corner is open twenty-four hours, and sometimes I wake up and she's gone, and I know she's there."

"She might not be," my dad said.

"I followed her. A few times. She runs on the treadmill for hours. Look, I had a friend when I first moved to the city, her roommate was like this. She got down to eighty pounds or something; they had to put her in the hospital. It's serious."

My dad was quiet for a second. "Let's just get her side of things," he said finally. "And then we'll see where we are. And Annabel?"

I jumped. "Yes?"

"Maybe go finish that homework?"

"Okay," I said. I finished my water, then put my glass in the dishwasher and headed back upstairs. As I forced myself back to parallelograms, I could hear my mother talking to Whitney next door, her voice low and soothing. I was almost done with my work when her door opened.

"I know," my mom was saying. "How about this: Take a shower, and a nap, and I'll wake you up when it's time for dinner. Okay? Everything will look better then."

I heard a sniffle, which I assumed was Whitney agreeing to this, and then my mother was walking past my door again. This time, she looked in at me.

"Everything's all right," she said. "Don't worry."

Looking back, I don't doubt my mom believed this at the time. I learned later how Whitney had completely reassured her, saying she was just overworked and overtired, and while she had been working out more and eating less because she had found she was a little bigger than the girls she was going up against for jobs, it was by no means to extreme levels. If Kirsten thought she wasn't eating, she maintained, it was because they kept totally different hours, as Kirsten worked nights and Whitney worked days. Personally, she'd said, she felt that there was more to this than just concern. Since arriving in New York, Whitney had clearly been working more than Kirsten ever had, and perhaps that wasn't sitting well. Maybe she was just jealous.

"I am not jealous!" I heard Kirsten say, her voice angry, a few minutes after my mother went downstairs. "Don't you see, she's tricked you. Open your *eyes*!"

There was more, of course, but I couldn't hear it. And by the time I was called for dinner an hour later, whatever had happened was over, and we were back in default Greene family mode, pretending everything was just fine. And from the outside, I was sure it at least looked that way.

My father designed our house, and at the time it was the most modern one in the neighborhood. Everyone called it "The Glass House," although it really wasn't all glass, only the front. From the outside, you could see our entire downstairs: the living room, split by the huge stone fireplace, the kitchen beyond, and past that the pool in the backyard. You could also see the stairs and part of the second floor—the doorways to my room and to Whitney's, and the landing between them, split by the chimney. The rest was tucked away behind, out of sight. So while it seemed like you were seeing everything, you really weren't. Just bits and pieces that looked like a whole.

The dining room was right at the front of the house, though, so when we ate dinner, we were always in full view. From my seat at the table, I could always see when cars passing slowed down slightly, the drivers glancing in at us for this snapshot, a happy family seated around a hearty meal. But everyone knows looks can be deceiving.

That night, Whitney ate her dinner; it was the first time, but by no means the last, that I noticed this. Kirsten drank too many glasses of wine, and my mother kept saying how wonderful it was we were all together, finally. And repeat, for the next three days.

The morning they left, she sat them both down at the kitchen table and asked them each to make her a promise. She wanted Whitney to take better care of herself, get more sleep, and keep to a healthy diet. Kirsten she asked to keep an eye on Whitney and try to be sympathetic to the pressure she was under living in a new city and working so hard. "Okay?" she said, looking from one of them to the other, then back again.

"Okay," Whitney said. "I promise."

Kirsten, though, just shook her head. "It's not me," she said to my mother, pushing back her chair and standing up. "I warned you. That's all I'm going to say. I told you, and you are choosing not to listen to me. I just want us all to be clear on that."

"Kirsten," my mother said, but she was already gone, walking out to the garage, where my father was putting the suitcases into the car.

"Don't worry," Whitney said, getting up and kissing my mom on the cheek. "Everything's fine."

For a while, it seemed like it was. Whitney kept getting jobs, including a shoot for *New York* magazine, her biggest yet. Kirsten got a new hostessing gig at a very famous restaurant, and a cable TV commercial. If they weren't getting along, we didn't hear about it—instead of one weekly phone call where they passed the receiver between them, now they each called separately, Kirsten usually in the late morning, Whitney in the evenings. Then, about a week before they were due home for Christmas, we got a call during dinner.

"I'm sorry, what?" my mother said, the phone to her ear as she stood in the doorway that led from the kitchen to the dining room. My dad glanced over at her as she lifted her other hand, putting it over her free ear to hear better. "What did you say?"

"Gracie?" My dad pushed his chair back, getting to his feet. "What is it?"

My mom shook her head. "I don't know," she said, handing over the phone. "I can't . . ."

"Hello?" my dad said. "Who is this? . . . Oh . . . I see . . . Right . . . Well, that's a mistake, I'm sure. . . . Hold on, I'll find the right information."

As he put the phone down, my mother said, "I couldn't understand her, what was she saying?"

"There's a problem with Whitney's insurance card," he told her. "Apparently she was at the hospital today."

"The hospital?" My mother's voice crept up to that scary, shaky octave that always made my own heart instantly start beating faster. "Is she all right? What happened?"

"I don't know," my dad said. "She's already been discharged, there's just a problem with the billing. I have to find her new card. . . ."

As my dad went up to his office to look for it, my mom got back on the phone and tried to get information from the woman who'd called. Citing privacy reasons, though, she wouldn't tell much, only that Whitney had been brought in by ambulance that morning and left a few hours earlier. The minute my dad cleared up the billing issue, he called Kirsten and Whitney's apartment. Kirsten answered.

"I tried to tell you," was all she said. I could hear her voice from where I was sitting. "I tried."

"Put your sister on the phone," my father told her. "Now."

Whitney got on, and I could hear her talking quickly, her voice high and cheery, as my parents both leaned into the receiver, listening. Later, I'd get the story she told them: that it was no big deal, she'd just been really dehydrated—a result of an ongoing sinus infection—and fainted at a shoot. It sounded worse than it was, and the ambulance was just the result of someone panicking. She hadn't told us because she didn't want my mother to worry, and it really was nothing, nothing at all.

"Maybe I should come up there," my mother said. "Just to make sure."

No, Whitney said, there was no point, they'd be home for Christmas in two weeks, and that was all she needed, a real break, to get some sleep, and she'd be totally well again. "Are you sure?" my mother asked.

Yes. She was positive.

Before they hung up, my father asked to talk to Kirsten again. "Is your sister all right?" he asked her.

"No," Kirsten told him. "She's not."

But still, my mother didn't go. This was the biggest mystery, the one thing that, looking back, I could never quite figure out. For whatever reason, she chose to believe Whitney. It was a mistake.

When Whitney flew home for Christmas, she came alone, as Kirsten had to stay an additional few days for work. My dad went to the airport to pick her up, and my mom and I were in the kitchen, fixing dinner, when they returned. When I took my first glance at my sister, I couldn't believe my eyes.

She was so thin. Emaciated. It was obvious, even though she was wearing even baggier clothes than the last time I'd seen her, and more layers as well. Her eyes looked sunken in her face, and you could see all the tendons in her neck, moving like puppet strings whenever she turned her head. I just stared at her.

"Annabel," she said, annoyed. "Come give me a hug."

I put down the vegetable peeler I was holding, then moved tentatively across the room. As I wrapped my arms around her, I felt like I might break her, she felt so brittle. My father was standing behind her with her suitcase, and as I looked at his face I knew that he, too, was shocked by the change in her in only a month's time.

My mother did not acknowledge any of this, at least not out loud. Instead, as I let go of Whitney, she stepped forward, smiling, and pulled her close. "Oh, honey," she said. "You've had such a hard time."

As she leaned down over my mother's shoulder, Whitney

slowly closed her eyes. The lids seemed almost translucent, and I felt a shudder run through me.

"We're going to get you well," my mother said, "starting right now. Go freshen up, and we'll sit down for dinner."

"Oh, I'm not hungry," Whitney said. "I ate while I was waiting for my plane."

"You did?" My mother looked hurt. She'd been cooking all day. "Well, surely you can at least manage some vegetable soup. I made it specially for you, and it's just what you need to get your immune system up."

"Really, I just want to sleep," Whitney said. "I'm so tired."

My mom glanced at my dad, who was still looking at Whitney, his face serious. "Well, okay, then maybe you should lie down for a while. You can eat when you wake up. Okay?"

But Whitney didn't eat. Not that night, which she slept straight through, not stirring each time my mother came in with a tray. Not the next morning; she was up at the crack of dawn, claiming to have already eaten breakfast when my father, the earliest riser in our house, came downstairs to make his coffee. At lunch, she was asleep again. Finally, at dinner, my mother made her sit down with us.

It started the minute my dad began to serve. Whitney was sitting beside me, and as he started to carve the roast beef, putting pieces on plates, I was distinctly aware of how she was unable to sit still, twitching nervously, pulling at the cuff of her baggy sweatshirt. She crossed and uncrossed her legs, took a sip of her water, then tugged at her cuff again. I could feel the stress coming off of her, palpable, and as my father put a full plate in front of her heaped with meat, potatoes, green beans, and a big hunk of my mother's famous garlic bread, she lost it.

"I'm really not hungry," she said quickly, pushing it away. "I'm not."

"Whitney," my father said. "Eat your food."

"I don't *want* it," she said angrily, as across the table, my mother looked so hurt I could hardly stand it. "This is about Kirsten, isn't it? She told you to do this."

"No," my mother said, "this is about you, honey. You need to get well."

"I'm not sick," Whitney said. "I'm fine. I'm just tired, and I'm not going to eat if I'm not hungry. I won't. You can't make me."

We all just sat there, watching her as she tugged at her cuffs again, her eyes on the table. "Whitney," my father said, "you're too thin. You need—"

"Don't tell me what I need," she said, pushing back her chair and getting up. "You have no *idea* what I need. If you did, we wouldn't even be having this conversation."

"Honey, we want to help you," my mother said, her voice soft. "We want—"

"Then leave me alone!" She slammed the chair against the table, making all our plates jump, and then stomped out. A second later, I heard the front door open and shut, and then she was gone.

This is what happened next: After doing his best to calm my mother down, my dad got in the car and went out to look for Whitney. My mother took up a position in a chair in the foyer, in case he somehow didn't find her, and I quickly finished my dinner, then I covered all their plates with plastic wrap, put them in the fridge, and did the dishes. I was just finishing up when I saw my dad's car coasting back into the driveway.

When he and Whitney came back in, she wouldn't look at anyone. Instead, she kept her head low, eyes on the floor, as my father explained that she was going to eat some food and then go back to sleep, in the hopes that things would look better tomorrow. There wasn't a discussion of this deal, or how they had come about it. It was already decided.

My mother asked me to go upstairs then, so I didn't get to see Whitney eat her dinner, or hear if there were any more arguments about it. Later, though, when the house was so quiet I knew everyone else was asleep, I went downstairs. There was only one plate left of the three I'd wrapped up, and while it looked like it had been poked at since, it was nowhere near clean.

I got a snack, then went into the TV room, where I watched a rerun of a reality makeover show and some of the local news. When I finally headed back upstairs, it was that weird time of night when the moon was shining really brightly through the glass, lighting everything up. There was always something strange about seeing so much moonlight inside, and as I passed through it, I covered my eyes.

The hallway that led to my room and Whitney's was lit up as well, the only shaded part in the middle, from the chimney. As I stepped into that sudden dark, I smelled the steam.

Or felt it. All I knew was that suddenly, it was like the very air changed, becoming heavier and more moist, and for a second I just stood there, breathing it in. The bathroom was all the way at the other end of the hall, and there was no light beneath the door, but as I moved toward it, the steam got thicker and more pungent, and I could hear the sound of water splashing. It seemed so bizarre. I could understand leaving a faucet running, but the shower? Then again, Whitney had been acting weird ever since she got home, so anything was possible. I finally reached the half-open door, pushing it open.

Immediately it hit against something, then swung back at me. I eased it open again, the steam now thick in my face, already condensing on my skin. I couldn't see anything, and all I could hear was water, so I reached blindly to my right, my hand moving over the wall until I found the switch.

Whitney was lying on the floor, at my feet. It was her shoulder the door had hit when I first tried to open it. She was curled up, slightly, a towel knotted around her, her cheek pressed against the linoleum. The shower, as I'd suspected, was on full blast, and water was pooling in the bottom, too much for the drain to handle.

"Whitney?" I said, crouching down beside her. I couldn't imagine what she'd been doing here in the dark, alone, so late at night. "Are you—"

Then I saw the toilet. The lid was up, and inside was this yellowy mix, tinged with red that I knew, somehow, with one look, was blood.

"Whitney." I put my hand on her face. Her skin was hot, wet, and her eyelids fluttered. I reached down, shaking her shoulder. "Whitney, wake up."

She didn't. But she did move, just enough that the towel

came loose. And then, finally, I saw what my sister had done to herself.

She was all bones. That was the first thing I thought. Bones and knobs, every bump of her spine protruding and visible. Her hips poked out at angles, her knees were skinny and pale. It seemed impossible that she could be so thin and still be alive, and even more so that she'd been able to somehow hide this. As she shifted again, though, I saw it, the one thing that would stick with me forever: the sharpness of her shoulder blades as they rose out of her skin, looking like the wings of a dead baby bird I'd once found in our backyard, hairless and barely born, already broken.

"Daddy!" I screamed, my voice so loud in the tiny room. *"Daddy!"*

The rest of the night I remember only in bits and pieces. My father, fumbling to put on his glasses as he ran down the hallway in his pajamas. My mother behind him, standing in that one shaft of light at the other end of the hall, illuminated, her hands to her face as he pushed me aside, then crouched down beside Whitney, putting his ear to her chest. The ambulance, the swirling lights of which made the entire house seem like a kaleidoscope. And then the silence once it was gone, with Whitney and my mother inside, my father following in his car behind. I was told to stay where I was, and wait for word.

I didn't know what to do. So I went back to the bathroom and cleaned it up. I flushed the toilet, looking away as I did so, then mopped up the water that had spilled out on the floor, and took the towels I used down to the washing machine, putting them in. Then I went and sat in the living room, in all that moonlight, and waited.

It was my father who finally called two hours later. The sound of the phone ringing jerked me awake, and as I picked up the receiver, the sun was rising in the front of the house, the sky streaked with pinks and reds. "Your sister is going to be okay," he said. "When we get home, we'll explain what's happening."

After we hung up, I went back to my room and crawled into bed, sleeping two more hours until I heard the garage door open and knew they were home. When I came down to the kitchen, my mother was making a pot of coffee, her back to me. She had on the same clothes as the night before, her hair uncombed.

"Mom?" I said.

She turned around, and when I saw her face, my stomach dropped. It was just like all those years ago: her face so tired, eyes swollen from crying, her very features haunted. A sudden panic made me want to wrap myself around her, putting myself between her and the world and everything it could do to her, to me, to any of us.

And then it happened. My mother started crying. Her eyes welled up, and she looked down at her hands, which were trembling, and then she was sobbing, the sound seeming so loud in the quiet of the kitchen. I stepped forward, not knowing how to handle this. Luckily, I didn't have to.

"Grace." My father was standing in the doorway to the hall that led to his office. "Honey. It's all right."

My mother's shoulders were shaking as she drew in a breath. "Oh, God, Andrew. What did we—"

And then my father was moving across the room toward her, taking her in his arms, his big frame encompassing hers. She buried her face in his chest, the sobs muffled in his shirt, and I stepped back, over the threshold, out of sight, and sat down in the dining room. I could still hear her crying, and the sound was awful. But seeing it was worse.

Eventually, my dad got my mother calmed down and sent her upstairs to shower and try to get some rest. Then he came back down and sat across from me.

"Your sister is very sick," he said. "She's lost an extreme amount of weight and apparently hasn't been eating normally for months now. Her system just shut down last night."

"Is she going to be okay?" I asked.

He ran a hand over his face, taking a moment before answering. "The doctors feel," he said, "that she needs to go immediately to a treatment facility. Your mother and I . . ." He trailed off, looking past me, out at the pool. "We just want what's best for Whitney."

"So she's not coming back?"

"Not right away," he told me. "It's a process. We just have to see how it goes."

I looked down at my hands, which I had spread out in front of me on the table, the wood cool on my palms. "Last night," I said, "when I first saw her, I just . . ."

"I know." He pushed his chair out, standing up. "But she's going to get help now. Okay?"

I nodded. Clearly, my dad was not up for discussing the emotional impact of what had happened. He'd given me the facts, what prognosis there was, and that was all I'd get.

After a couple of days in the hospital, Whitney was transferred to a treatment center, which she hated so much she initially refused to speak to my parents when they visited. Still, it was helping her, as she began gaining weight, bit by bit, day by day. As for Kirsten, she arrived on Christmas Eve to find my parents exhausted and stressed out, me just trying to stay out of the way, and any hope of holiday cheer completely out of the question. Which did not prevent her from dropping a bomb of her own.

"I've made a decision," she announced as we sat at dinner that night. "I'm giving up modeling."

My mother, at the end of the table, put down her fork. "What?"

"I'm just not into it anymore," Kirsten said, taking a sip of her wine. "Truth be told, I haven't been for a while. And it's not like I've been working that much anyway. But I just decided to make it official."

I glanced at my mom. She was already so tired and sad, and this clearly was not helping. My dad was watching her, too. He said, "Don't do anything rash, Kirsten."

"I'm not. I've thought about it a lot." Of all of us, she was the only one still eating, scooping up a forkful of potatoes as she said this. "I mean, let's face it, I'm never going to be a hundred and five pounds. Or five-ten, for that matter."

"You've gotten plenty of work just as you are," my mom said.

"Some work," Kirsten corrected her. "It's by no means a living. I've been doing this since I was eight. I'm twenty-two now. I want to do something else."

"Such as?" my dad said.

Kirsten shrugged. "I don't know yet. I've got the hostess thing at the restaurant, and I have a friend who owns a salon who offered me a receptionist job. So the bills will be covered, for the most part. I'm thinking I might sign up for some classes or something."

My dad raised his eyebrows. "School," he said.

"Don't sound so surprised," Kirsten replied, although I had to admit, this was shocking to me, as well. Even before she'd stopped taking classes in New York, she'd never been much for academics. In high school the classes she hadn't missed because of modeling she skipped, usually preferring to spend her time with whatever scruffy, free-spirited boyfriend she had at the time. "Most girls my age have already graduated and have real careers. I feel like I've missed out on a lot, you know? I want to get my degree."

"You could take classes and still model," my mother said. "It doesn't have to be an either/or situation."

"Yes, it does," Kirsten replied. "For me, it does."

Under different circumstances, maybe my parents would have pushed to discuss this further. But they were tired, and while Kirsten might have been known best for her directness, her stubbornness ran a close second. It shouldn't have been all that surprising anyway, as she'd hardly been committed to modeling for years now. Coming so close to Whitney's collapse, however, it meant more. Especially to me, although I didn't realize it at the time.

Whitney stayed at the treatment center for thirty days, during which time she gained ten pounds. She wanted to return to

New York once she was released, but my parents insisted she move back home instead, as the doctors felt strongly a return to modeling would risk any progress she'd made, or would make. That was in January, and since then she'd been going to an outpatient program, seeing an additional therapist twice a week, and sulking around the house. Meanwhile, Kirsten had kept to her word, enrolling in some classes at a New York college while juggling her other two jobs. Surprisingly, given her high-school experience, she loved school, calling each weekend happy and bubbling over with details about her classes and what she was studying. Again, my sisters were at extremes and yet similar at the same time: Each was starting over, but only one by choice.

There were some weeks when it seemed like Whitney was really getting better, gaining weight, clearly on her way. And then there were others when she'd refuse to eat breakfast, or get caught doing forbidden crunches in her room late at night, and only the threat of having to go back into the hospital and be force-fed was enough to make her get back in line. Through it all, one thing remained constant: She would not talk to Kirsten.

Not when she called. Not even when she came home for a weekend in the spring. At first Kirsten was hurt, then angry, before finally retaliating with her own silence. The rest of us were stuck in the middle, filling the awkward pauses with chatter that always fell short. Since then, while my mom and dad had both traveled up to see her at various times, she'd made a point of not coming back home.

It was weird. As a kid, I'd always hated it when my sisters

fought, but them not talking at all was worse. Their complete and total lack of communication, now going on nine months, was scary in how permanent it felt.

The changes in my sisters over the last year were both evident and sensory. One you could spot on sight, while the other you heard about the moment you were in earshot, whether you wanted to or not. As for me, I found myself where I'd always been, stuck somewhere in the middle.

But I had changed, too, even if only I could tell. I was different. As different as my family was that night it all began from what we appeared to be—the five of us, a happy family, sharing a meal in our glass house—to anyone in a car passing by on the road outside, looking in.

Chapter
FOUR

For the first week of school, Sophie ignored me completely. Which was hard. But when she did begin to speak to me, I quickly realized I much preferred the silence.

"Whore."

It was always just one word. One word, said clearly and with enough spite to sting. Sometimes it came from behind me, floating over my shoulder when I wasn't expecting it. Other times, I could see her coming, and took it right in the face. The one thing that was always the same was that her timing was impeccable. The moment I started to feel a little better or have a half-decent moment in an okay day, she was right there to make sure it didn't last.

This time, she was walking by as I sat on the wall during lunch. Emily was with her—Emily was always with her, these days—and I didn't look at them, instead just focusing on the notebook in my lap and the history paper I was working on. I'd just written the word *occupation*, and I kept my pen to the page, making both *o*'s darker and darker, until Emily and Sophie passed.

There was a karmic aspect to this, although I didn't like to think about it. The truth was, it hadn't been that long ago that I'd been the one who walked alongside Sophie while she did her dirty work, when I was the person who, while not taking part in the slur, didn't stop it, either. Like with Clarke.

Thinking this, I looked up, glancing around the courtyard until I found her sitting at one of the picnic tables with a few of her friends. She was at the end of the bench, a textbook open in front of her, half listening to the conversation between the girls next to her as she flipped through the pages. Clearly, sitting alone on that first day for her had been optional. She hadn't come anywhere near the wall, or me, since.

But Owen Armstrong remained. Other people came and went from our wall, some in groups, some by themselves, but only he and I were there every single day. We always kept an understood distance between us—about six feet, give or take a few inches—that whoever arrived second was always sure to honor when they sat down. There were other constants, too. He never ate, that I saw; I always had a full lunch, courtesy of my mother. He seemed completely unaware, and uncaring, of what anyone else was doing, while I spent the hour convinced everyone was staring at and discussing me. I did homework; he listened to music. And we never, ever spoke.

Maybe it was because I was spending so much time alone. Or the fact that there were only so many minutes of my lunch hour I could spend doing homework. Whatever the reason, I'd become somewhat fascinated with Owen Armstrong. Every day, I made it a point to take a few sideways glances at him, cataloging something else about his appearance or habits. So far, I'd garnered quite a bit of information.

For instance, the earphones. He *never* seemed to take them off. Clearly, he loved music, and his iPod was always either in his pocket, his hand, or lying on the wall beside him. I'd also noticed that his reactions when he was listening varied. Usually he sat totally still except for his head bobbing, slowly and almost imperceptibly. Occasionally he drummed his fingers on his knee, and in very rare instances, he hummed along, barely loud enough for me to hear, and then only when no one was passing or talking nearby. Those were the times I wondered most what he was listening to, although I imagined it to be just like him, dark and angry and loud.

Then there was his appearance. His size, of course, you saw first: the height, the big wrists, the enormity of his mere presence. But there were little things, too, like his dark eyes, which were either green or brown, and the two identical rings—each flat, wide, and silver—he wore on the middle finger of each hand.

Now, as I glanced over at him, he was sitting with his legs stretched out in front of him, leaning back on his palms. A swath of sunlight was falling across his face, and his earphones were on, his head bobbing slightly, eyes closed. A girl carrying a piece of poster board walked past me, then slowed as she approached him, and I watched her as she carefully stepped over his feet, like Jack from "Jack in the Beanstalk" creeping past the sleeping giant. Owen didn't stir, and she scurried on.

I'd once felt this same way about Owen as well, of course. Everyone did. But there was something about our daily proximity that had made me relax, or at least not jump every time he looked my way. These days I was more worried about Sophie, who was a credible threat, or even Clarke, who had made it clear that yes, she still hated me.

It seemed odd that Owen Armstrong could seem somehow safer than the only two best friends I'd ever had. I was beginning to see, though, that the unknown wasn't always the greatest thing to fear. The people who know you best can be riskier, because the words they say and the things they think have the potential to be not only scary but true, as well.

I had no history with Owen. But Sophie and Clarke were different. There was a pattern here, some sense of connection, even if I didn't want to see it. It didn't seem fair or right, but I couldn't help but wonder if maybe all of this, and where I found myself, wasn't so accidental. Maybe it was just what I deserved.

After that night when Clarke and I returned her stuff to her at her house, Sophie started to hang out with us. It wasn't a specific invitation as much as she was just eased in. Suddenly there was a third beach chair, another hand dealt into the card game, one more Coke to carry when it was your turn to go get drinks. Clarke and I had been best friends for so long it was kind of nice to have a fresh take on things, and Sophie definitely provided that. In her bikinis and makeup, full of stories of the boys she'd dated in Dallas, she was totally different from us.

She was also loud and bold, completely unafraid to talk to guys. Or wear whatever she felt like wearing. Or say what was on her mind. She wasn't unlike Kirsten in this fashion, but while my sister's forthrightness always made me uneasy,

Sophie's was different. I liked it, almost envied it. I couldn't say what I wanted, but I could always count on her to speak up, and the events she set into motion—always a little risky, at least for me, but fun at the same time—were ones I never would have gotten to experience left to my own devices.

Still, there were moments when I felt uneasy around Sophie, although it was hard to put my finger on why, exactly. As much as we hung out and she became part of my day-to-day life, I couldn't forget how mean she'd been to me that first day at the snack bar. Sometimes I'd just look at her while she was telling a story, or painting her nails as she lay on the end of my bed, and wonder why she had done that. And in the next beat, if she'd do it again.

For all her bravado, though, I knew Sophie had her own problems. Her parents had just recently divorced, and while she'd mentioned repeatedly all the stuff her dad bought her when she lived in Texas—clothes, jewelry, anything she wanted—one day I'd overheard my mom and one of her friends discussing the divorce, which was apparently very ugly. Sophie's dad had left for a much younger woman, and there'd been a bitter battle over their house in Dallas. Mr. Rawlins supposedly wasn't in contact with Sophie or her mom at all. But Sophie never mentioned this, and I didn't ask about it. I figured if she wanted to talk about it, she would.

In the meantime, she hardly held back on anything else. For instance, she was always telling me and Clarke we were immature. Everything, apparently, was wrong: our clothes (so childish), our activities (boring), and our experiences (nonexistent). While she was interested in my modeling and seemed fascinated with my sisters—who both pretty much ignored her, as they did me—she was always giving Clarke a hard time.

"You look like a boy," she said one day when we all went to the mall. "You could look really cute, if you tried. Why don't you wear some makeup or something?"

"I'm not allowed," Clarke told her, blowing her nose.

"Please," Sophie said. "It's not like your parents have to know. Just put it on when you leave, take it off before you go home."

But Clarke wasn't like that, and I knew it. She got along well with her mom and dad, and wouldn't lie to them. Sophie, however, wouldn't let up. If it wasn't Clarke's lack of makeup, it was her clothes, or her constant sneezing, or the fact that she had to be home a full hour before either of us, meaning that whatever we did as a group always had to be cut short in order to make sure she got in on time. If I'd been paying more attention, maybe I would have seen what was happening. As it was, though, I just attributed it to us all getting used to one another, and figured everything would work out eventually—at least until that night in early July.

It was a Saturday, and we were all spending the night at Clarke's. Her parents were out at some symphony concert, so we had the house to ourselves to make a frozen pizza and watch movies. Typical Saturday. We'd preheated the oven, and Clarke was seeing what was on pay-per-view when Sophie arrived, dressed in a denim miniskirt, a white tank top that showed off her tan, and white sandals with thick heels.

"Wow," I said as she came in, her heels clacking against the floor. "You look nice."

"Thanks," she replied, as I followed her into the kitchen.

"You're pretty dressed up for pizza," Clarke told her, then sneezed.

Sophie smiled. "This isn't for pizza," she said.

Clarke and I looked at each other. I said, "Then what is it for?"

"Boys," she said.

"Boys?" Clarke repeated.

"Yeah." Sophie hopped up on the counter, crossing her legs. "I met a couple of guys today, walking home from the pool. They said they'd be hanging out there tonight and we should come meet them."

"The pool is closed at night," Clarke told her, sliding the pizza onto a cookie sheet.

"So?" Sophie said. "Everyone goes up there. It's not a big deal."

I knew instantly Clarke was not going to go for this. First, because her parents would kill her if they found out. Second, because she always followed the rules, even the ones everyone else ignored, like taking a shower before getting in the pool and always getting out of the water the second the lifeguard announced adult swim. "I don't know," I said as I thought this. "We probably shouldn't."

"Oh, come *on*, Annabel," Sophie said. "Don't be a wuss. Besides, one of these guys was asking about you specifically. He'd seen us together and asked if you would be there."

"Me?" I said.

She nodded. "Yeah. And he's *cute*. His name's Chris Pen-something. Penner? Penning—"

"Pennington," I said. I could feel Clarke looking at me; she was the only one who knew how I felt about him, the crush I'd had forever. "Chris Pennington?"

"That's it," Sophie said, nodding. "You know him?"

I glanced at Clarke, who was now making a point of focusing on putting the pizza in the oven, adjusting it on the rack. "We know who he is," I said. "Right, Clarke?"

"He's *so* hot," Sophie said. "They said they'd be there around eight, and they'd have some beers."

"Beers?" I said.

"God, calm down," she said, laughing. "You don't have to drink if you don't want to."

Clarke shut the oven with a bang. "I can't go out," she said.

"Oh, you can too," Sophie said. "Your parents won't even know."

"I don't *want* to," Clarke finished. "I'm staying here."

I just looked at her, knowing I should say the same thing, but for some reason, the words just didn't come. Probably because all I could think about was Chris Pennington, who I'd watched at the pool a million afternoons, asking about me. "Well," I said, forcing myself to speak, "maybe—"

"Then me and Annabel will go," Sophie said, hopping off the counter. "No big deal. Right, Annabel?"

Now Clarke did look at me. She turned her head, and I felt those dark eyes watching me carefully. Suddenly I felt that imbalance, that unevenness of three, with me left to choose which way to go. On the one side was Clarke, my best friend, and our entire routine, everything we'd always done and known. On the other was not only Sophie and Chris Pennington but this whole other world, unchartered and open, at least for a little while, this one night. I wanted to go.

"Clarke," I said, taking a step toward her. "Let's just go for a little while, like, a half hour. Then we'll come back and eat the pizza and do the movie and all that. Okay?"

Clarke wasn't an emotional person. She was instead a born stoic, extremely logical, her entire approach to life one of figuring out problems, stating solutions, and moving on. But in that moment, as I said this, I saw something rare on her face: surprise, followed by hurt. It was so unexpected, though, and gone so quickly, that it was hard to know if I'd really seen it at all.

"No," she said. "I'm not going." And with that, she walked across the room to the couch, sitting down and picking up the remote. A second later, she was scrolling through channels, images and color flickering across the screen.

"All right then," Sophie said with a shrug. Then she turned to me. "Come on," she said.

She started toward the front door, and for a second, I just stood there. Everything about the Reynoldses' kitchen and this night was so familiar: the smell of pizza in the oven, the two-liter Coke on the countertop, Clarke in her spot on the couch, my spot open and waiting for me beside her. But then I looked down the hallway to Sophie, who was now standing in the open door. Behind her, it was just barely dark, the streetlights flickering on, and before I could change my mind, I walked toward her and stepped outside.

Even years later, I remembered that night so well. Like how it felt, after climbing through the hole in the pool fence, to walk across the dark parking lot, right up to Chris Pennington, who smiled at me and said my name aloud. And the way the beer he'd brought tasted as I took my first sip, fizzy and light in my mouth. Then later, after he walked me around the back of the pool, how it felt to kiss him, his lips warm against mine, my back pressed up against the cool of the wall behind me. Or hearing Sophie laughing in the distance, her voice carrying over the still water from wherever she was with his best friend, a guy named Bill who moved away at the end of that summer. All of these things register, but there is one image, one moment, that rises above them all. That was later, when I glanced over the pool fence to see someone standing across the street, under a streetlight. A small girl with dark hair, in shorts and no makeup, who could hear our voices but not see us.

"Annabel," she called out. "Come on, it's late."

We all stopped talking. I could see Chris squint as he looked into the dark. "What was that?"

"Shhh," Bill said. "Someone's out there."

"It's not someone," Sophie said, rolling her eyes. "It's Ca-*larke*."

"Ca-w*hat*?" Bill said, laughing.

Sophie reached up, pinching her nose shut with two fingers. "Ca-*larke*," she repeated, her voice sounding so like Clarke's, stuffed up and adenoidal, that it was startling. I felt a pang in my chest as everyone laughed, and I looked back over at her again, knowing she could hear it. She was still there, across the street under the light, but I knew she would come no farther, and that it was my job to leave now and go to her.

"I better—" I said, stepping forward.

"Annabel." Sophie leveled her gaze at me. At the time this was new, but later I'd come to recognize her expression, a mix of annoyance and impatience. It was the look she'd give me a million times over the years, whenever I wasn't doing what she wanted. "What are you doing?"

Chris and Bill were both watching us. "It's just," I began, then stopped. "I should just go."

"No," Sophie said. "You shouldn't."

I should have just walked away, from Sophie, from all of it, and done the right thing. But I didn't. I told myself later it was because Chris Pennington had his hand on the small of my back and it was summer, and earlier, his lips on mine, hands in my hair, he had whispered to me that I was gorgeous. Really, though, it was this moment with Sophie, my fear of what would happen if I stood up to her, that stopped me. And shamed me for years to come.

So I stayed where I was, and Clarke went home, and later, when I tried to go back to her house, the lights were off, the door locked. I went up anyway, but unlike that night we'd gone to Sophie's, the door didn't open. Instead, Clarke left me waiting, as I had done to her, and eventually I went home.

I knew she was really mad at me. I assumed, though, that we'd work it out. It was just one night—I'd made a mistake; she'd come around. But the next day, when I walked up to her at the pool, she wouldn't even look at me and ignored my repeated hellos, turning away when I sat down on the chair beside her.

"Come on," I said. No response. "It was stupid of me to go. I'm sorry, okay?"

But it wasn't okay, clearly, as she still wouldn't look at me, giving me only her sharp profile. She was so mad, and I felt so helpless, I couldn't stand to sit there, so I got up and left.

"So what?" Sophie said when I went to her house and told her what had happened. "Why do you even care she's pissed?"

"She's my best friend," I told her. "And now she hates me."

"She's just a kid," she replied. I was sitting on her bed, watching her as she stood in front of her bureau mirror. She picked up her brush, giving her hair a few strokes. "And to be honest, she's kind of a nerd, Annabel. I mean, is that how you really want to spend your summer? Playing cards and listening to her sniffle? Please. You hooked up with Chris Pennington last night. You should be happy."

"I am," I said, although I wasn't sure this was true, even as I said it.

"Good." She put down her brush, then turned around, looking at me. "Now come on. Let's go to the mall or something."

And that was that. Years of friendship, all those card games and pizza nights and sleepovers, finished in less than twenty-four hours. Looking back, maybe if I had approached Clarke again, we could have worked things out. But I didn't. It was like the passing time and my guilt and shame opened up a chasm, wider and wider. Once, I might have been able to leap it, but eventually it was too distant to even look across, much less find a way to the other side.

Clarke and I would run into each other again, of course. We lived in the same neighborhood, rode the same bus, went to the same school. But we never spoke. Sophie became my best friend, although nothing ever happened with Chris Pennington, who, despite all the things he'd said in the dark that night, never talked to me again. As for Clarke, she found a new group of friends on the soccer team, which she joined in the fall, going on to be a starting forward. Eventually we were so different, and moving in such different crowds, that it was hard to believe we'd ever been close at all. In my photo albums, though, there was page after page of proof—the two of us at backyard cookouts, riding bikes, posing on her front steps, that ever-present pack of Kleenex between us.

Before Sophie, people knew who I was because of my sisters and my modeling, but it was only once we were friends that I was popular. And there was a difference. Sophie's particular brand of fearlessness was perfect for navigating the cliques and various dramatics of middle school and high school. The bossy girls and whispered comments that had always unnerved me didn't bother her at all, and I found it was much easier to cross the various social barriers once she'd already busted through them for me. Suddenly, everything I'd always watched and envied from a distance—the people, the parties, and especially the boys—was not only closer but altogether possible, and all because of Sophie. It made the other things I had to put up with, like her moodiness, and everything that had happened with Clarke, seem almost worth it. Almost.

At any rate, everything with me and Clarke and Sophie had happened ages ago. But this past summer, I'd found myself thinking about Clarke a lot, especially when I was alone at the pool. So much would have been different if I'd just stayed in that night, taken my spot beside her, and let Sophie go on without me. I'd made my choice, though, and I couldn't take it back.

Although sometimes, in the late afternoon, when I'd close my eyes and start to drift off, listening to kids splashing in the water and the lifeguard's whistle, it almost seemed like nothing had changed. At least until later, when I'd jerk awake to find myself in the shade, the air suddenly cooler, long past time to go home.

When I got home from school, the house was empty and the light on the answering machine was blinking. I pulled an apple out of the fridge, polishing it on my shirt as I walked across the room to play the messages. The first one was from Lindy, my agent.

"Hi, Grace, it's me, returning your call. Sorry it took so long, my assistant quit and I've had this useless temp manning the phones, it's been a total disaster. But anyway. No news yet, but I have a call in to the Mooshka office, so we'll hopefully hear something soon. I'll keep you posted, hope all is well, love to Annabel. Bye!"

Beep. I'd hadn't thought about the Mooshka go-see for days, but clearly it was on my mother's mind. I didn't want to think about it now either, so I moved on to the next message, which was from Kirsten. She was famous for leaving long, rambling missives, often having to call back for a part two when the machine cut off on her, so as soon as I heard her voice, I pulled out a chair.

"It's me," she began, "just calling to say hello, see what's going on. I am right this minute walking to class; it's a gorgeous day here. . . . Don't know if I told you guys, but I signed up for a communications class this semester, heavily recommended by a friend, and I am just loving it. It's taught with a psychology angle, and I'm just learning so much. . . . And the TA who runs my recitation is *brilliant.* I mean, a lot of times in lectures I just find myself zoning out, even if I feel the material is interesting, but Brian, he's just riveting. Seriously. He's even got me considering a minor in communications, just because I'm getting so much out of the class. . . . But there's also my film-making class, which really interests me, so I just don't know. Anyway, I'm almost to class now, hope all of you are well, miss you love you bye!"

Kirsten was so used to being cut off she always sped up at the end of her messages, so she blurted out this last part, barely beating the beep. I reached over, hitting the SAVE button, and the house was quiet again.

I stood, picking up my apple, and crossed through the dining room. When I got to the foyer I stopped, as I often did, to look at the big black-and-white photo that hung opposite the front door. It was a horizontal shot of my mom and the three of us girls, standing on the jetty near my uncle's summer house. Each of us was all in white: Kirsten in white jeans and a plain V-neck T-shirt, my mother wearing a sundress, Whitney in a bathing suit top and drawstring pants, me in a tank top and long skirt. We were all tan, the water spread out wide to the corners of the frame behind us.

It had been taken three years earlier during one of our extended family beach trips; the photographer was a friend of a friend of my father's. At the time it had seemed spontaneous, him casually suggesting we pose, but in fact my dad been planning it for weeks as a gift for my mother for Christmas. I remembered how we'd followed the photographer, a tall, lithe man whose name I forgot, out across the sand to the jetty. Kirsten had stepped up first, then extended her hand to help my mother, while Whitney and I brought up the rear. The rocks were hard to navigate, and I remembered Kirsten guiding my mom along the jagged edges until we got to a flat spot and gathered together.

In the picture, we are all intertwined: Kirsten's fingers are wrapped in my mother's, Whitney has her arm over her shoulder, and I'm in front, curved slightly toward my mom as well, my arm around her waist. My mother is smiling, as is Kirsten, while Whitney is just staring into the camera, her beauty, as usual, breathtaking. Even though I remembered smiling each time the flash popped, my expression in the final product is not one I recognize, my face caught somewhere between Kirsten's broad grin and Whitney's gorgeous hauntedness.

The picture was beautiful, however, the composition perfect. People always commented on it, as it was the first thing you saw when you walked in the door. In the last few months, though, it had started to look kind of eerie to me. Like I couldn't just see the fine white-on-black contrast, or the way our features repeated themselves, in different measure but always similar, across our faces. Instead, when I studied it, I saw other things. Like how Whitney and Kirsten stood so close to each other, no space between them. The way my own face looked different, more relaxed. And how small my mother seemed with all of us bent around her, pulling her closer, shielding her with our bodies, as if without us to hold her down, she might just fly away.

I picked up my apple, taking another bite just as my mother's car pulled into the garage. A second later I heard doors shutting and voices as she and Whitney came inside.

"Hello there," my mother said when she saw me, putting down the bag of groceries she was carrying on the counter with a thump. "How was school?"

"Fine," I said, stepping back as Whitney brushed past, not acknowledging me and taking the corner quickly, disappearing upstairs. It was Wednesday, which meant she'd just come from her shrink's, which always put her in a mood. I'd thought seeing a therapist was supposed to make you feel better, not worse, but apparently, it was more complicated than that. But then everything was more complicated for Whitney.

"There was a message from Lindy," I told my mom.

"What'd she say?"

"The Mooshka people haven't called yet."

My mom looked disappointed, but only for a moment. "Oh, well. I'm sure they will." She walked to the sink, turned on the faucet, and lathered up her hands with liquid soap, looking out the window at the pool. In the afternoon light she looked kind of tired—Wednesdays took a toll on her, too.

"And Kirsten called. She left a long message," I said.

She smiled. "You don't say."

"The upshot," I said, "is she likes her classes."

"Well, that's nice to hear," she said, drying her hands on a dishtowel. She folded it, putting it back by the sink, then came to sit down beside me. "So. Tell me something that happened to *you* today. Something good."

Good. I thought for a second about what was going on with

Sophie, my daily observations of Owen Armstrong, the fact that Clarke still hated me. None of these things fell under this heading, or anywhere near it. As the seconds ticked by, I could feel myself starting to panic, desperate for something to offer up to her to make up for the Mooshka people, for Whitney's mood, for everything. She was still waiting.

"There's this guy in my gym class," I said finally. "He's kind of cute, and he talked to me today."

"Really," she said, smiling. Score. "What's his name?"

"Peter Matchinsky," I told her. "He's a senior."

This was not a lie. Peter Matchinsky *was* in my gym class and he was kind of cute and a senior. And he had talked to me that day, although it was only to ask me what Coach Erlenbach had just said about our upcoming swim test. Normally, I didn't stretch the truth to my mom, but in the last few months I'd learned to forgive myself these little trespasses, because they made her happy. Unlike the real truth, which would be the last thing she wanted to hear.

"A cute senior," she said, sitting back in her chair. "Well. Tell me more."

And I would. Even though there wasn't much else. If I had to, I'd pad the edges of the story, filling it in, trying to make it substantial enough to nourish this need, her hunger for my life, at least, to somehow be normal. The worst part was that I had things I wanted to tell my mother, too many to count, but none of them would go down so easy. She'd been through too much, between my sisters—I could not add to the weight. So instead, I did my best to balance it out, bit by bit, word by word, story by story, even if none of them were true.

• • •

Most mornings before school, it was just me and my mom at breakfast, my dad only joining us if he got a late start to the office. Whitney never got out of bed before eleven if she could help it. So when I came down a couple of weeks later to find her showered, dressed, and sitting at the table with my car keys in front of her, I had a feeling something was up. I was right.

"Your sister's going to drive you to school today," my mother said. "Then she's going to take your car and do a little shopping, see a movie, and pick you up this afternoon. Okay?"

I looked at Whitney, who was watching me, her mouth a thin line. "Sure," I said.

My mother smiled, then looked from my sister to me, then back to my sister again. "Great," she said. "Everything works out."

She did her best to sound casual as she said this, but it was clear from her tone she was anything but. Since Whitney had come home from the hospital, my mother preferred to keep her both busy and within sight, which was why my sister was always dragged on errands and to my mother's appointments. Whitney was constantly arguing for more freedom, but my mom worried that given it, she'd binge or purge, or exercise, or do something else forbidden. Clearly, something had shifted, although what it was or why, I had no idea.

When we walked out to the car, I automatically headed for the driver's side, then stopped when I saw Whitney doing the same thing. For a second, we both just stood there. Then she said, "I'll drive."

"Okay," I told her. "That's fine."

The ride was awkward. I didn't realize until we were on the road how long it had actually been since I'd been alone with Whitney. I had no idea what to say to her. I could ask about shopping, but it might bring up body-image issues, so I tried to think of other topics. Seeing a movie? Traffic? I had no idea. So I just sat there, silent.

Whitney wasn't talking, either. I could tell it had been a while since she'd driven. She was being very cautious, pausing a beat longer at stop signs than necessary, letting people in front of us. At a red light, I looked across to see two business-men in an SUV staring at her. They were both in suits—one in his twenties, one my father's age—and instantly I felt defen-sive, protective of her, even though I knew she would have hated this if she knew it. Then, though, I realized they weren't looking at her because she was skinny, but because she was so striking. I'd forgotten that once, my sister had been the most beautiful girl I'd ever seen. The world, or at least some of it, still seemed to feel the same way.

We were about a mile from school when I finally decided to try and say something. "So," I said, "are you excited about today?"

She glanced at me, then looked back at the road. "Excited," she repeated. "Why would I be excited?"

"I don't know," I said as we turned into the school entrance. "Maybe because, you know, you have a whole day to yourself."

For a second, she didn't answer, focusing instead on pulling over to the curb. "It's a day," she said finally. "I used to have a whole life."

I wasn't sure what to say to that. "Okay, well, see you later!" seemed glib, if not totally inappropriate. So instead I just pushed open the door and reached into the back for my bag.

"I'll see you at three thirty," she said.

"Right," I said.

She put on her blinker, looking over her shoulder. I shut the door, and she eased into traffic and drove away.

I pretty much forgot about Whitney for the rest of the day, as I had a literature test that afternoon that I was totally nervous about. For good reason, as it turned out. Even though I had studied most of the night before *and* gone to the review session Mrs. Gingher offered at lunch, there had still been some questions that completely stumped me. There was nothing I could do but just sit there, staring at them and feeling like a total moron, until she announced time and I had to turn it in.

As I headed down the steps to the main building entrance to meet Whitney, I dug out my notes and started to go through them, trying to figure out what I'd missed. There was a big crowd making its way across the turnaround, and I was so engrossed that I didn't even see the parked red Jeep until I was walking right in front of it.

One minute I was scanning the notes I'd taken on Southern literature, trying to find a quote that had completely escaped me; the next, I was glancing up at Will Cash. This time, he'd seen me first. He was staring right at me.

I looked away, fast, quickening my pace as I walked in front of his bumper. I was almost to the curb when he called out to me. "Annabel," he said.

I knew I should just ignore him. But even as I thought this, my head was already turning, as if by instinct. He was sitting there, wearing a plaid shirt, unshaven, a pair of sunglasses perched on his forehead, as if they might slip down at any moment.

"Hey," he said. I was close enough to the car now to feel the A/C just barely wafting out the open window.

"Hi." Just one word, but it came out twisted, mangling itself as it squeezed up my throat.

He didn't seem to notice any of my nervousness as he slid an elbow out the window, then glanced over at the courtyard beyond me. "Haven't seen you around at the parties lately," he said. "You still hanging out?"

A breeze blew across me then, catching the edge of my notes, making them flutter, the sound like little wings. I tightened my fingers on the paper. "No," I managed. "Not really."

I felt a chill go up my neck, and I wondered if I was going to faint. I couldn't look at him, so I kept my eyes down, but in my side vision, I could see his hand, resting on the open window, and I found myself staring at it, the long tapered fingers drumming idly on the Jeep's door.

Shhh, Annabel. It's just me.

"Well," he said, "see you around, I guess."

I nodded, and then, finally, I was turning back around and walking away. I took in a breath, trying to remind myself that I was surrounded by people, safe here. But then I felt it, the ultimate proof otherwise: my stomach gurgling, rising up, the one response I could never control. *Oh my God,* I thought, quickly stuffing my papers into the top of my bag. I pulled it over my shoulder, not taking the time to zip it, then started walking toward the nearest building, praying that I could hold it together until I was to the bathroom. Or at least out of sight. But I didn't get that far.

"What was *that*?"

It was Sophie. She was right behind me. I stopped walking, but the bile kept rising. After so many times of her just saying one word, to hear these three was overwhelming. And then she was speaking again.

"What the hell do you think you're doing, Annabel?" she said.

Two younger girls scurried past me, their eyes wide. I tightened my hand around the strap of my bag, swallowing again.

"Didn't you get enough that night? You need more or something?"

Somehow, I started to move forward again. *Don't get sick, don't look back, don't do anything*, I kept telling myself, but my throat felt raw, my head light.

"Don't you ignore me," Sophie was saying now. "Turn around, bitch!"

All I wanted—all I'd ever wanted—was just to get away. To be somewhere small where I could crowd in and feel safe, all four walls pressed around me, no one staring or pointing or yelling. But here I was in the wide open, in full view. I might have just given in, letting her do whatever she wanted, like I had for weeks now, but then something happened. She reached out and grabbed my shoulder.

And something snapped in me. Snapped hard, like a bone, or a branch, a clean break. Before I even knew what I was doing, I'd whirled around and was facing her, reaching up with hands that I wasn't even sure were mine to push her away, my palms hitting her chest, hard, and knocking her backwards, stumbling. It was primal and immediate and surprised both of us, but most of all, me.

She lost her footing, her eyes wide, but then caught herself quickly and started toward me again. She had on a black skirt and a bright yellow tank top, her arms tan and wiry beneath it, her hair spilling loose over her shoulders. "Oh my God," she said, her voice low, and I somehow moved backwards, my feet thick underneath me. "You better—"

The crowd around us was closing in now, bodies jostling. Above the movement, I could hear the whirring of the security guard approaching on his golf cart. "Break it up," he called out. "Move on to the parking lot or bus area."

Sophie stepped closer to me. "You're a whore," she said, her voice low, and I heard a hiss from somewhere, that low *oooooh*, followed by the guard's voice, second warning.

"Stay away from my boyfriend," she said, her voice low. "Do you hear me?"

I just stood there. I could still feel the pressure of her chest against my hands, how it felt to push her, something solid giving way. "Sophie . . ." I said.

She shook her head, then stepped forward, brushing past me. Her shoulder hit mine, hard, and I stumbled, bumping someone behind me before righting myself. Everyone was staring, a blur of faces fluctuating, shifting, as she moved through them, and then their eyes all turned to me.

I pushed through the bodies beside me, one hand over my mouth. I could hear people talking, laughing, as the crowd gave way, bit by bit, and I finally reached the outer edge. The main building was right in front of me, a row of tall bushes in front of it that led around its back side. I ran toward them, their prickly leaves scraping my hands as I pushed through. I didn't make it far, and could only hope I was out of sight as I bent over, one hand clutching my stomach, and got sick in the grass, coughing and spitting, the sound rough in my ears.

When I was finished, my skin felt clammy, and there were tears in my eyes. It was horrible and embarrassing, and one of those moments when you just want more than anything to be alone. Especially when you suddenly realize you're not.

I didn't hear the footsteps. Or see the shadow. Instead, from where I was crouched on the ground, the green of the grass filling my vision, the first thing I made out were hands, a flat silver ring on the middle finger of each. One was clutching my notes. The other was reaching out for me.

Chapter
FIVE

Owen Armstrong looked like a giant, his hand enormous as it stretched toward me. Somehow I found myself extending my own back to him, and then he was folding his fingers over mine, pulling me to my feet. I stood steady for about a second before my head went light and woozy and I stumbled.

"Whoa," he said, reaching out to steady me. "Hold on. You better sit down."

He eased me back two steps, and I felt the building behind me, the bricks cool against my back. I slid down the wall slowly, until I was on the grass. From this new vantage point, he seemed even bigger.

Suddenly, he dropped his bag off his shoulder. It hit the ground with a clank, and then he was crouching down beside it, reaching in and digging around. I heard objects bumping against each other as they were moved and redistributed, and it occurred to me that maybe I should be concerned about this. Finally, his hand stopped digging, and he sat back, slightly. I braced myself as he worked his hand out of the bag, bit by bit, and came up with . . . a pack of Kleenex. A small one, bent and wrinkled, and he pressed them against his chest—which was enormous, oh my God—smoothing them out, before pulling one free and handing it to me. I took it the same way I'd taken his hand—in disbelief, and very carefully.

"You can have the whole pack," he said. "If you want."

"That's okay." My voice sounded hoarse. "One is fine." I pressed it to my mouth, taking a breath through it. He put the pack by my foot anyway. "Thank you," I said.

"No problem."

He sat down on the grass beside his bag. Because I'd gone to that review session at lunch, I hadn't seen him all day, but he looked pretty much the same as always: jeans, T-shirt fraying at the hem, thick-soled black wingtips, earphones. Up close—or closer—I could also see he had a few freckles, and that his eyes were green, not brown. I could hear voices rising up from the courtyard; they sounded like they were floating over our heads.

"So, um," he said, "are you okay?"

I nodded, the response instant. "Yeah," I said. "I just felt sick all of a sudden, I don't know . . ."

"I saw what happened," he said.

"Oh," I said. I felt my face flush. So much for trying to save face. "Yeah. That was . . . pretty bad."

He shrugged. "Could have been worse."

"You think?"

"Sure." His voice was not rumbly like I would have guessed, but instead low and even. Almost soft. "You could have punched her."

I nodded. "Yeah," I said. "I guess you're right."

"It's good you didn't, though. Wouldn't have been worth it."

"No?" I said, even though, truthfully, I hadn't even considered this.

"No. Not even if it felt good at the time," he said. "Trust me."

The weirdest thing of all was that I did. Trust him, that is. I looked down at the pack of tissues he'd given me, picking them up and taking out another one. Just as I did, I heard a buzzing from my bag. My phone.

I pulled it out, glancing at the caller ID. It was my mother, and I debated for a second whether I should pick up. I mean, it was weird enough to be sitting there with Owen without getting my mom involved. Then again, it wasn't like I had that much to lose at this point, considering he'd already seen me vomit—twice, actually—and freak out in front of half the student body. We were kind of past formalities. So I answered.

"Hello?"

"Hi, honey!" Her voice was loud, so much so that I wondered if Owen could hear it. I pressed the phone closer to my ear. "How was your day?"

By now, I'd detected the nervous shrillness that crept into her cadence when she was worried but pretending not to be. "It was fine," I said. "I'm fine. What's up?"

"Well," she said, "Whitney's still at the mall. She found some great sales, but then she missed the early movie. And she *really* wanted to see it, so she called to say she was staying later."

I switched the phone to my other ear as there was a burst of voices around the side of the building. Owen glanced over at them, but a second later they moved on. "So she's not coming to pick me up?"

"Well, no, as it turns out," she replied. Of course Whitney would push the limits the very first day she got her freedom. And of course my mother would say oh, yes, stay later, that's fine, but then completely freak out. "But I can come get you," she said now, "or maybe you could get a ride with one of your friends?"

One of my friends. Yeah, right. I shook my head, then ran a hand through my hair. "Mom," I said, trying to keep my voice even, "it's just that it's kind of late, and—"

"Oh, it's fine! I'll come get you right now!" she said. "I'll be there in fifteen minutes."

She didn't want to come, and we both knew it. Whitney might call, or show up. Or, even worse, not show up. Not for the first time, I wished both of us could just say what we meant. But that, like so much else, was impossible.

"It's fine," I told her. "I'll get a ride."

"Are you sure?" she asked, but already, I could hear her relaxing, thinking that this problem, at least, was resolved.

"Yes. I'll call if I can't."

"Do that," she said. And then, just as I might have been getting angry, "Thank you, Annabel."

When I hung up, I just sat there, holding my phone in my hand. Once again, everything was revolving around Whitney. It might have been just a day to her, but this one had really sucked for me. And now, I was walking home.

I glanced back up at Owen. In the time I'd been contemplating this newest problem, he'd pulled out his iPod and was messing with it. "So you need a ride," he said, not looking at me.

"Oh, no," I said quickly, shaking my head. "It's just my sister . . . she's being a pain."

"Story of my life," he said. He hit one last button, then slid it back in his pocket and stood up, brushing off his jeans. Then he reached down, grabbing his bag, and hoisted it over his shoulder. "Come on."

I'd endured a lot of scrutiny since the beginning of the school year. It was *nothing*, however, compared to the looks Owen and I got as we walked up to the parking lot. Every person we passed stared, most of them openly, with a few bursting into whispers—"Oh my God, did you see that?"—before we were even out of earshot. Owen, however, didn't seem to notice as he led me to an old-style blue Land Cruiser with about twenty CDs in the passenger seat. He got behind the wheel, then cleared them out and reached across to open the door for me.

I got in, then reached down for the seat belt. I was just about to pull it across me when he said, "Hold on. That's sort of busted," and gestured for me to hand it to him. When I did, he pulled it over me—his hand at what struck me as a very formal and polite distance from my stomach—then yanked up the buckle from the seat, holding it at an angle and sliding the belt in. Then, from the pocket on his own door, he pulled out a small hammer.

I must have looked alarmed—GIRL 17, FOUND DEAD IN SCHOOL PARKING LOT—because he glanced at me and said, "It's the only way it works." He tapped the buckle with the hammer three times in the center, before pulling at the belt to make sure it was locked in. When it was, he stuck the hammer back in the pocket and cranked the engine.

"Wow," I said, reaching down and giving it a little tug. It didn't budge. "How do you get it off?"

"Just push the button," he said. "That part's easy."

As we started through the parking lot, Owen rolled down his window, resting his arm there, and I took a look around the interior of the car. The dashboard was battered, the leather of the seats cracked in places. Plus, it smelled like smoke, faintly, although I could see the ashtray, which was partly open, was clean and filled with coins, not butts. There were some head-phones on the backseat, along with a pair of Doc Martens oxblood boots and several magazines.

Most of all, though, I saw CDs. *Tons* of CDs. Not just the ones he'd cleared out for me and dumped on the backseat floor, but stacks and stacks of others, some store-bought, many more clearly home-burned, piled haphazardly on the seats and the floor. I glanced back at the dashboard in front of me. While the car was dated, the stereo looked practically new, not to mention advanced, rows of lights blinking.

Just as I thought this, we reached the stop sign at the top of the parking lot and Owen put on his blinker, looking both ways. Then he reached out for the stereo, nudging up the vol-ume button with the side of his thumb before taking a right.

Even with all the lunches during which I'd studied him, and all the details I'd thereby managed to ascertain, there was still one unknown, and this was it: Owen's music. I had my hunches, though, so I braced myself for punk rock, thrash metal, some-thing fast and loud.

Instead, after a bit of staticky silence, I heard . . . chirping. Lots of chirping, like a chorus of crickets. This was followed, a moment later, by a voice chanting in a language I didn't understand. The chirping grew louder, then louder, and the voice did as well, so it was like they were calling to each other, back and forth. Beside me, Owen was just driving, nodding his head slightly.

After about a minute and a half, my curiosity got the better of me. "So," I said, "what is this?"

He glanced over at me. "Mayan spiritual chants," he said.

"What?" I said, speaking loudly to be heard over the chirping, which was really going now.

"Mayan spiritual chants," he repeated. "They're passed down, like oral traditions."

"Oh," I said. The chanting was so loud now it was verging on shrieking. "Where did you get this?"

He reached forward, turning the volume down a little bit. "The library at the university," he said. "I checked it out of their sound-and-culture collection."

"Ah," I said. So Owen Armstrong was spiritual. Who knew? Then again, who would have thought I would be sitting in his car, listening to chants with him? Not me. Not anybody. And yet, here we were.

"So you must *really* like music," I said, looking back at the stacks of CDs.

"Don't you?" he replied, switching lanes.

"Sure," I said. "I mean, everybody does, right?"

"No," he said flatly.

"No?"

He shook his head. "Some people *think* they like music, but they have no idea what it's really all about. They're kidding themselves. Then there are people who feel strongly about music, but just aren't listening to the right stuff. They're misguided. And then there are people like me."

I just sat there for a second, studying him. He still had his elbow out the window and was sitting back in his seat, his head just brushing the ceiling above him. Up close, I was realizing he was still kind of intimidating, but for different reasons. His size, yes, but other things, too—like those dark eyes and wiry forearms, plus his intense gaze, which he now turned on me for a moment before directing his attention back to the road. "People like you," I said. "What kind of people are those?"

He hit his blinker again and began to slow down. Up ahead, I could see my old middle school, a yellow school bus pulling out of the parking lot. "The kind who live for music and are constantly seeking it out, anywhere they can. Who can't imagine a life without it. They're enlightened."

"Ah," I said, like this actually made sense to me.

"I mean, when you really think about it," he continued, "music is the great uniter. An incredible force. Something that people who differ on everything and anything else can have in common."

I nodded, not sure what to say to this.

"Plus there's the fact," he went on, making it clear he didn't need me to reply anyway, "that music is a total constant. That's why we have such a strong visceral connection to it, you know? Because a song can take you back instantly to a moment, or a place, or even a person. No matter what else has changed in you or the world, that one song stays the same, just like that moment. Which is pretty amazing, when you actually think about it."

It *was* pretty amazing. As was this conversation, so wholly unlike anything I could or would have ever imagined. "Yeah," I said slowly. "It is."

We drove on for a second, in silence. Except for the chanting.

"What I mean to say," he said, "is yes. I like music."

"Got it," I said.

"And now," he said as we turned into the school's lot, "I'll apologize in advance."

"Apologize? For what?"

He slowed, finally stopping at the curb. "My sister."

There were several girls standing around the main entrance to Lakeview Middle, and I quickly scanned their faces, trying to guess which one was related to Owen. The girl with the instrument case and the braid, leaning against the building, an open book in her hands? The tall blonde with the big Nike duffel bag and the field-hockey stick, drinking a Diet Coke? Or the easiest bet, the dark-haired girl with the pixie cut, wearing all black, who was lying on a nearby bench, her arms crossed tightly over her chest, staring up at the sky with a pained expression?

Just then, though, I heard a clank right outside my window. When I turned my head, I saw a small, thin, dark-haired girl dressed head to toe in pink: ponytail tied with a pink ribbon, shiny pink lip gloss, hot-pink T-shirt, jeans, and pink platform flip-flops. When she saw me, she shrieked.

"Oh my God!" she gasped, her voice muffled by the window between us. "It's *you*!"

I opened my mouth to say something, but before I could, she disappeared from the window, a pink blur. A second later, the back door creaked open, and she scrambled inside. "Owen, oh my God!" she said, still at full, excitable volume. "You didn't tell me you were friends with Annabel Greene!"

Owen glanced at her through the rearview. "Mallory," he said, "take it down a notch."

I started to turn around to say hello, but she was already leaning forward, poking her head between my seat and Owen's, so close to me I could smell bubblegum breath. "This is unbelievable," she said. "I mean, it's you!"

"Hi," I said.

"Hi!" she shrieked, then jumped up and down a little bit in the seat. "Oh my God, I love your work. I really do."

"Work?" Owen said.

"Owen, come on." Mallory sighed. "She's a Lakeview Model, hello? And she's done tons of local ads. And that commercial, you know the one I love, with the girl in the cheerleading uniform?"

"No," Owen said.

"That's her! I can't believe this. I can't wait to tell Shelley and Courtney, oh my God!" Mallory grabbed her bag and unzipped it, pulling out a cell phone. "Oh! Maybe you can say hello to them, that would be so cool, and—"

Owen turned around in his seat. "Mallory."

"Just a sec," she said, pushing buttons. "I just want to—"

"Mallory." His voice was lower now, more stern.

"Hold on, Owen, okay?"

Owen reached out, taking the phone from her. She watched it leave her hands, eyes wide, then looked up at him. "Come on! I just wanted her to say hello to Courtney."

"No," he said, putting the phone on the console between us.

"Owen!"

"Put on your seat belt," Owen told her as he pulled away from the curb. "And take a breath."

After a short pause, Mallory proceeded to do both of these things, audibly. When I glanced back again, she was sitting there, in full pout mode, her arms crossed over her chest. When I looked at her, she brightened up immediately. "Is that a Lanoler sweater?"

"A what?"

She leaned forward, smoothing her fingers over the yellow cardigan I'd thrown on that morning. "This. It's gorgeous. Is it a Lanoler?"

"You know," I said, "I'm not—"

Her hand moved to my collar, pulling it down to check the tag. "It is! I knew it. Oh my God, I want a Lanoler sweater so *bad*, I have forever—"

"Mallory," Owen said, "don't be a label whore."

Mallory dropped her hand. "Owen!" she said. "R and R."

Owen gave her a look in the rearview. Then he sighed, loudly. "What I meant to say, Mallory," he said, sounding pained, "is that your focus on labels and material goods troubles me."

"Thank you," she replied. "And I understand and appreciate your concern. But, as you know, fashion is my life."

I looked at Owen. "R and R?"

"Rephrase and Redirect," Mallory told me. "It's part of his Anger Management. If he says something inflammatory, you can tell him it hurts your feelings, and he has to say it another way."

Owen was looking at her through the rearview, a flat expression on his face. "Thank you, Mallory," he said.

"You're welcome," she replied. Then she smiled at me, big, and bounced in the seat again.

For a second, we drove in silence, which gave me a moment to catch up, or try to, with all this newfound knowledge about Owen Armstrong's personal life. So far, only the fact that he'd been in Anger Management wasn't a surprise. Mallory, the music, and, of course, the fact that I was privy to either of these things were shockers in the biggest sense of the word. On the other hand, I wasn't sure what I'd been expecting. I mean, he had to have a family and a life. I'd just never really taken the time to picture it. It was like when you're a little kid and you run into your teacher or librarian at the grocery store or Wal-Mart and it's just so startling, because it never occurred to you they existed outside of school.

"So I really appreciate the ride," I said to Owen. "I don't know how I would have gotten home otherwise."

"It's no problem," he said. "I just have to make a couple of—"

This thought was interrupted, however, by the sound of Mallory sucking in a breath. "Oh my God," she said. "I'm going to get to see your *house*?"

"No," Owen said curtly.

"But we're taking her home! I'm here!"

"We're dropping you off first," he told her.

"Why?" she said.

"Because," Owen told her as we moved through an intersection, turning off the main road, "I have to go by the station, so Mom said to bring you by the store."

Mallory sighed, sounding pained. "But Owen—"

"No buts," he said. "It's already decided."

Another thump as Mallory slumped, dramatically and dejectedly, against the seat behind her. "It's so not fair," she said a second later.

"Life isn't fair," Owen told her. "Get used to it."

"R and R!" she said.

"No," Owen said. Then he reached forward, nudging up the volume on the radio, and the chirping started up again.

We drove along with just the Mayan chants for a few minutes, long enough for me to actually start to get used to them. Then, suddenly, I felt breath in my ear. "When you did that commercial," Mallory asked, "did you get to keep the clothes from that?"

"Mallory!" Owen said.

"What?"

"Can you just relax and listen to the music?"

"This isn't music! This is crickets and screaming." To me she said, "Owen is a total music Nazi. He won't let anyone listen to anything other than the weird stuff he plays on his radio show."

"You have a radio show?" I asked Owen.

"It's just a local thing," he told me.

"It's his *life*," Mallory said dramatically. "He spends all week getting ready for it, worrying about it, even though it's on when normal people aren't even up yet."

"I'm not playing music for normal people," Owen said. "I'm playing music for people who are—"

"Enlightened, we know," Mallory said, rolling her eyes. "Me, personally? I listen to 104Z. They play all the top-forty stuff, lots of good songs you can dance to. I like Bitsy Bonds. She's my favorite singer. I went to her concert last summer, with all my friends? It was *so* fun. Do you know her song 'Pyramid'?"

"Um," I said. "I don't know."

Mallory sat up straighter, tossing back her hair. "'Stack it up, higher and higher, the sun's above, it's full of fire, kiss me here so I'll know you did, baby I'm falling, pyramid!'"

Owen winced. "Bitsy Bonds isn't a *singer*, Mallory. She's a product. She's fake. She has no soul; she doesn't stand for anything."

"So?"

"So," he said, "she's more famous for her belly button than her music."

"Well," Mallory said, "she does have a *great* belly button."

Owen just shook his head, clearly bothered, as he turned off the main road into a small parking lot. There was a row of stores to the left, and he turned into a space in front of one that had a mannequin in the front window wearing a poncho and some flowing earth-toned pants. The sign on the door said DREAMWEAVERS. "Okay," he said. "We're here."

Mallory made a face. "Great," she said sarcastically. "Another afternoon at the store."

"Your parents own this place?" I asked.

"Yes," Mallory grumbled as Owen picked up her phone from the center console, giving it back to her. "It's *so* unfair. Here I am, obsessed with clothes, and my mom has a clothing store. But it's all stuff I wouldn't ever wear in a million years. Not even if I was *dead*."

"If you were dead," Owen told her, "you'd have bigger problems than what you were wearing."

Mallory looked at me then, her expression grave. "Annabel, seriously. It's all, you know, natural fabrics and fibers, Tibetan batiks, vegan shoes."

"Vegan shoes?" I said.

"They're awful," she whispered. "Awful. They're not even *pointy*."

"Mallory," Owen said. "Please get out of the car."

"I'm going, I'm going." Still, she took her time gathering up her bag, undoing her seat belt, and unlocking the door. "It was really nice to meet you," she said to me.

"You, too," I said.

She slid out, shutting the door behind her, and started into the store. As she pushed the door open, she looked back, then waved at me excitedly, her hand blurring. I waved back, and then Owen was pulling away, back to the main road. Without Mallory, the car seemed smaller, not to mention quieter.

"Again," he said, as we slowed for a red light, "I'm sorry."

"Don't be," I told him. "She's cute."

"You don't live with her. Or have to listen to her music."

"104Z," I said. "All the hits, with less of the lip."

"You listen to that station?"

"I have before," I said. "Especially when I was in middle school."

He shook his head. "It would be different if she had no access to good music. If she was deprived of culture. But I've made her tons of CDs. She just won't listen to them. Instead, she chooses to fill her head with that pop crap, listening to a station where they pretty much just play the occasional songs between commercials."

"So on your show," I said, "it's different."

"Well, yeah." He glanced over at me, shifting gears as we headed back onto the main road. "I mean, it's community radio, so there aren't commercials. But I think you should be responsible about what you're putting out there for people to hear. If it can be pollution or art, why wouldn't you choose art?"

I just looked at him. Clearly, I had really misjudged Owen Armstrong. I wasn't sure who I'd thought he was, but it wasn't this person sitting beside me.

"So where do you live?" he asked me, switching lanes as we approached a stoplight.

"The Arbors," I said. "It's a few miles past the mall; you can just—"

"I know it," he said. "The station is just a couple of blocks from there. I have to stop in there for a second, if that's okay."

"Sure," I said. "That's fine."

The community radio station was in a squat, square building that had once been a bank. There was a metal tower beside it, as well as a somewhat droopy banner hanging across the front entrance. WRUS it said in big black letters. COMMUNITY RADIO: RADIO FOR US. There was a big window in front, on the other side of which I could see a man sitting in a broadcast booth wearing headphones and speaking into a microphone. There was a lit-up sign in the corner of the window that said O AIR: apparently, the N was burned out.

Owen pulled into a space right up front, then cut the engine before turning around in his seat to pick through some CDs on the floor. After gathering up a few, he pushed open the door. "Back in a sec," he said.

I nodded. "Okay."

Once he disappeared inside, I started checking out some of the handwritten names on the CD cases, none of which I recognized: THE HANDYWACKS (ASSORTED), JEREMIAH REEVES (EARLY STUFF), TRUTH SQUAD (OPUS). Suddenly, I heard a beep, then turned my head to see a Honda Civic pulling into the spot next to me. Which wouldn't have been noteworthy, really, except the driver had on a bright red helmet.

It wasn't the kind football players wear, exactly, but something a little bigger, with more padding. The guy wearing it looked to be about my age and was dressed in a black sweatshirt and jeans. He waved at me, and I waved back, tentatively, and then he was rolling down his window.

"Hi," he said. "Is Owen inside?"

"Yeah," I said slowly. His eyes were big, blue, and longlashed in the small cutout of the faceplate, and his hair was past his shoulders, pulled back in a ponytail that was poking out from under the helmet. "He said he'd be back in a second."

He nodded. "Cool," he said, sitting back in his seat. I was trying not to stare at him, even though it was kind of hard. "I'm Rolly, by the way," he said.

"Oh. Hi. I'm Annabel."

"Nice to meet you." He reached down to his cup holder, picking up a paper cup with a straw poking out of it and taking a sip. He was just putting it back when Owen came out of the building.

"Hey," Rolly called out to him. "I was just driving by and saw your car. I thought you had to work today."

"At six," Owen told him.

"Oh. Well, that's cool," Rolly said, sitting back in his seat with a shrug. "Maybe I'll come by or something."

"Do that," Owen said. "And Rolly?"

"Yeah?"

"You know you still have your helmet on, right?"

Rolly's eyes widened, and he lifted up his hands to his head, carefully. Then his face flushed, almost as red as the helmet. "Oh," he said, pushing it off. Underneath, his hair was matted down, and there were creases across his forehead. "Yeah. Thanks."

"No problem. I'll see you in a bit."

"Okay." Rolly put the helmet on the seat beside him, smoothing a hand over his head as Owen climbed back behind the wheel. As we backed away, I waved at him again, and he nodded, smiling, his face still slightly pink.

Once back on the main road, we drove for a moment before Owen said, "It's for his job. Just so you know."

"The helmet," I said, clarifying.

"Yeah. He works at this self-defense place. He's an attacker."

"An attacker?"

"The one people practice on," he told me. "You know, once they learn the techniques. That's why he has to wear padding."

"Oh," I said. "So . . . you guys work together?"

"No. I deliver pizzas. This is it, right?" he asked as we came up on the entrance to my neighborhood. I nodded and he put his blinker on, then turned in. "He does the radio show with me."

"Does he go to Jackson?"

"Nope. The Fountain School."

The Fountain School was an "alternative learning space," also known as the Hippie School. It had a very small student body and an emphasis on personal expression, and offered electives like batik and Ultimate Frisbee. Kirsten had dated several somewhat crunchy guys from there, back in the day.

"Left or right?" Owen asked as we came up to a stop sign.

"Straight. For a while," I told him.

As we headed farther into my neighborhood, not talking, I got the same feeling I'd had that morning with Whitney, like I should at least attempt to make conversation. "So," I said finally, "how'd you end up with a radio show?"

"It's something I've always been sort of interested in," Owen said. "And right after I moved here, I heard about this course they have at the station where they teach the basics. After you take it, you can write up a show proposal. If they approve it, they give you an audition and, if they like what you do, a time slot. Me and Rolly got ours last winter. But then I got arrested. So that put us back a bit."

He said this so nonchalantly, as if he was talking about a vacation to the Grand Canyon, or attending a wedding. "You got arrested?" I asked.

"Yeah." He slowed for another stop sign. "I got in a fight at a club. With some guy in the parking lot."

"Oh," I said. "Right."

"You heard about it?"

"Maybe something," I said.

"So why'd you ask?"

I felt my face get hot. Ask a bold question, you'd better be prepared to answer one. "I don't know," I said. "Do you believe everything you hear?"

"No," he said. Then he looked at me for a moment, before turning back to the road. "I don't."

Right, I thought. Okay. So I wasn't the only one who had heard some rumors. It was only fair, though. Here I'd had all these assumptions about Owen based on what had been said about him, but it hadn't occurred to me that there were stories about me out there as well. Or at least one.

We drove on in silence through two more stop signs. Then, finally, I took a breath and said, "It's not true, if that's what you were wondering."

He was downshifting, the engine grinding as we slowed to take a corner. "What isn't?" he said.

"What you heard about me."

"I haven't heard anything about you."

"Yeah, right," I said.

"I haven't," Owen said. "I'd tell you if I had."

"Really."

"Yeah," he said. I must have looked doubtful at this, because he added, "I don't lie."

"You don't lie," I repeated.

"That's what I said."

"Ever."

"Nope."

Sure you don't, I thought. "Well," I said. "That's a good policy. If you can stick to it."

"I don't have a choice," he replied. "Holding stuff in doesn't really work for me. Learned that the hard way."

I had a flash of Ronnie Waterman going down in the parking lot, his head bouncing off the gravel. "So you're always honest," I said.

"Aren't you?"

"No," I told him. This came so easily, so quickly, it should have surprised me. But for some reason, it didn't. "I'm not."

"Well," he said as we approached another stop sign, "that's good to know, I guess."

"I'm not saying I'm a liar," I told him. He raised his eyebrows. "That's not how I *meant* it, anyway."

"How'd you mean it, then?"

I was digging myself a hole here, and I knew it. But still, I tried to explain myself. "It's just . . . I don't always say what I feel."

"Why not?"

"Because the truth sometimes hurts," I said.

"Yeah," he said. "So do lies, though."

"I don't . . ." I said, then trailed off, not sure exactly how to put this. "I just don't like to hurt people. Or upset them. So sometimes, you know, I won't say exactly what I think, to spare them that." The ironic thing was that saying this out loud was actually the most honest I'd been in ages. If not ever.

"But that's still a lie," he said. "Even if you mean well."

"You know," I replied, "I find it really hard to believe you're always honest."

"Believe it. It's true."

I turned to face him. "So if I were to ask you if I looked fat in this outfit," I said, "and you thought I did, you'd say so."

"Yes," he said.

"You would not."

"I would. I might not say it that way, exactly, but if I thought you didn't look good—"

"No way," I said flatly.

"—and you'd *asked*," he continued, "I'd tell you. I wouldn't just offer it up, though. I'm not a hateful person. But if you asked for my opinion, I'd give it."

I shook my head, still not believing him.

"Look," he said, "like I said, for me, not saying how I feel when I feel it is a bad move. So I don't do it. Look at it this way: I might be saying you're fat, but at least I'm not punching you in the face."

"Are those are the only options?" I asked.

"Not always," he replied. "Just sometimes. And it's good to know your options, right?"

I could feel myself about to smile, which was just so strange that I turned my head as we came up to another stop sign. There was a car parked on the street ahead, halfway down, facing us. A second later, I realized it was mine.

"Still straight?" Owen asked.

"Um, no," I told him, leaning closer to the glass. Sure enough, it was Whitney behind the wheel. She had a hand to her face, her fingers spread to cover her eyes.

"Then . . . what? Right? Left?" Owen asked. He dropped his hand from the wheel. "What's wrong?"

I looked at Whitney again, wondering what she was doing so close to home, parked. "That's my sister," I said, nodding at the car.

Owen leaned forward, looking at her. "Is . . . is she okay?"

"No," I said. Maybe not lying was contagious; this reply came out automatically, before I could pick other words to explain. "She's not."

"Oh," he said. He was quiet for a second. "Well, do you want to—"

I shook my head. "No," I told him. "Take a right."

He did, and I slid down slightly in my seat. As we passed Whitney, it was clear she was crying, her thin shoulders shaking, her hand still pressed to her face. I felt something catch in my own throat and then we were moving on, leaving her behind.

I could feel Owen watching me as we reached the next

stop sign. "She's sick," I said. "She has been for a while now."

"I'm sorry," he said.

This was what you were supposed to say. What anyone would say. The weird thing was, after everything he'd just told me, I knew Owen meant it. Honest, indeed.

"Which is yours?" he asked me now, as we turned onto my street.

"The glass one," I told him.

"The glass—" he began, but then stopped, as it came into view. "Oh. Right."

It was the time of day when the sun hit the glass just so, the golf course reflected almost perfectly in the second story. Downstairs, I could see my mother standing at the kitchen counter. She'd started walking to the door when we pulled up, then stopped when she realized it was just me and not Whitney. I thought about my sister, sitting two streets over, and my mom, worrying here at home, and felt that familiar pull in my stomach, a mix of sadness and obligation.

"Man," Owen said, looking up at it. "That's really something."

"People in glass houses," I said. I looked back in at my mother, who was still at the counter, watching us. I wondered if she was curious about Owen or too distracted to even notice I was in a car she didn't recognize, much less with a boy. Maybe she thought it was Peter Matchinsky, that nice senior from my gym class.

"Well," I said, reaching down for my bag. "Thanks for the ride. For everything."

"No problem," he said.

I heard a car coming up behind us, and a second later, Whitney was pulling into the driveway. It wasn't until she parked and got out that she looked up and saw me and Owen. I lifted my hand, waving at her, but she ignored me.

I knew already what would happen when I went inside. Whitney would be stomping around, ignoring my mother's cheerful, leading questions. Eventually she'd get fed up and go upstairs, slamming her door, and then my mom would be upset, but pretend not to be. Even so, I'd worry over her until my dad got home, at which time we'd all sit down for dinner and pretend everything was fine.

Thinking this, I looked back at Owen. "So when is it?" I asked. "Your radio show."

"Sundays," he replied. "At seven."

"I'll listen," I told him.

"In the morning," he added.

"Seven in the *morning*?" I asked. "Really?"

"Yeah," he replied, picking at the steering wheel. "It's not the ideal time slot, but you take what you can get. Insomniacs are listening, at least."

"*Enlightened* insomniacs," I said.

He looked at me for a second, as if I'd somehow surprised him, saying this. "Yeah," he said, and smiled. "Exactly."

Imagine that, I thought. *Owen Armstrong smiling*. In a bizarre day, this was the most surprising thing yet. "Well," I said, "I guess I should go."

"Okay. I'll see you around."

I nodded, then reached down, undoing the seat belt. Sure enough, one click and I was free. Harder to get in than out, like so little else.

As I shut the door behind me, Owen put the car into gear, beeping the horn once as he drove off. Sure enough, as I turned to look up at my house, Whitney was climbing the stairs, taking the steps two at a time. My mother was still at the kitchen island, staring out the back window.

I don't lie, Owen had said, with the same flat certainty someone else might tell you they didn't eat meat or know how to drive. I wasn't sure I could even fathom it, but I still envied Owen his easy bluntness, the ability to open himself out into the world instead of folding deeper within. Especially now, as I headed inside, where my mother was waiting for me.

Chapter
SIX

"Okay, girls, quiet down. Attention here, please! We're getting ready to start, so listen for your name. . . ."

I'd been doing Lakeview Models since I was fifteen. Every summer, tryouts were held to pick sixteen girls for mall promotions like posing with cub scouts at a Pinewood Derby event or handing out balloons at the Harvest Festival Petting Zoo. The models also appeared in print ads, did fashion shows, and were part of the annual Lakeview Mall calendar, which was distributed along with the new phone book every year. That was what we were shooting today. We were supposed to have been done the day before, but the photographer was slow, so we'd all been called back now, on a Sunday afternoon, to finish.

I yawned, then sat back against the potted plant behind me, taking a look around the room. The newer girls were all together in a corner, talking too loudly, while a couple of people I knew from previous years were gossiping about some party. The only two seniors sat apart from everyone else, one with her head back, eyes closed, the other flipping through an SAT prep book. Finally, across the room from me, also sitting alone, was Emily Shuster.

I'd met Emily at the last calendar shoot. She was a year younger than me and had just moved to town. She didn't know anyone, and while everyone was waiting around, she'd come and sat down next to me. We started talking, and just like that, we were friends.

Emily was, in a word, sweet. She had short red hair and a heart-shaped face, and when I'd invited her out with me and Sophie that night after the shoot, she'd been thrilled. When I pulled up to her house, she was already outside waiting, her cheeks pink from the cool air, as if she'd been there awhile.

Sophie was less enthusiastic. Plainly put, she had issues when it came to other girls, especially pretty ones, even though she herself was gorgeous. Whenever I had Lakeview Model stuff, or landed a big job, she always got a little moody. There was stuff about her that bothered me, too. Like how she sometimes snapped at me and acted like I was stupid, and often wasn't nice to other people unless she had a reason to be—and sometimes, not even then. The truth was, my friendship with Sophie was complicated, and at times I wondered why she was my best friend, when more often than not I was either tiptoeing around her or having to ignore one barbed comment or another. But then I'd remember how much things had changed for me since we'd started hanging out—from that night with Chris Pennington on, so much had happened that I never would have experienced otherwise. And really, when you came down to it, I didn't have anyone else. Sophie made sure of that, too.

The night I met Emily, we were going to a party at the A-

Frame, a house just outside of town that was rented by a few guys who'd gone to Perkins Day, the local private school, a couple of years earlier. They had a band called Day After, and after graduation they'd stuck around, playing club dates and trying to get a record deal. In the meantime, they had parties almost every weekend that attracted a mix of high-school students and various locals.

From the moment the three of us walked into the party that night, I could feel people looking at Emily. She *was* a beautiful girl, but being with us—especially Sophie, who was well known not only at our school but at Perkins Day, as well—made her suddenly that much more noteworthy. We weren't even halfway to the keg when Greg Nichols, an obnoxious junior, made a beeline for us.

"Hey, guys," he said, "what's up?"

"Go away, Greg," Sophie told him over her shoulder. "We're not interested."

"Speak for yourself," he said, completely undeterred. "Who's your friend?"

Sophie sighed, shaking her head.

I said, "Um, this is Emily."

"Hi," Emily said, flushing.

"Hel-lo," Greg replied. "Let me get you a beer."

"Okay," she said. As he walked off, glancing back at her, she turned to me, her eyes wide. "Oh my God," she said. "He's really cute!"

"No," Sophie told her. "He's not. And he's only talking to you because he's already hit on everyone else here."

Emily's face fell. "Oh," she said.

"Sophie," I said. "Honestly."

"What?" she said as she picked some lint off her sweater, scanning the crowd. "It's true."

It probably was. But that didn't mean she had to *say* it. This was typical Sophie, though. She believed everyone had a place, and it was her job to make sure you knew yours. She'd done it with Clarke. She did it with me. And now, it was Emily's turn. But while I'd just stood by all those years earlier, this time I felt I had to do something, if only because I was the reason Emily was even there in the first place. "Come on," I said to her. "Let's go get a beer. Sophie, you want one?"

"No," she said curtly, and turned away from me.

By the time I got a drink and went to look for her, she'd disappeared. *So she's pissed*, I thought. *That's nothing new, I'll smooth it over in a second.* But then Greg Nichols had reappeared, and I didn't want to leave Emily alone with him. It took us twenty minutes to extricate ourselves, at which point I left Emily with some girls she knew and finally went looking for Sophie. I found her on the back porch, smoking, alone.

"Hi," I said, but she ignored me. I took a sip of my beer, looking out over the swimming pool below the deck. It was empty and covered in leaves, a lawn chair parked at the bottom.

"Where's your friend?" she asked me.

"Sophie," I said. "Come on."

"What? It's just a question."

"She's inside," I said. "And she's your friend, too."

"No," she said, snorting. "She's not."

"Why don't you like her?"

"She's a freshman, Annabel. And she's—" She stopped,

taking another drag of her cigarette. "Look, if you want to hang out with her, go ahead. I don't."

"Why not?"

"I just don't." She turned, looking at me. "What? We don't have to be joined at the hip, you know. You don't have to do everything I do."

"I know that," I said.

"Do you?" She exhaled, a stream of smoke billowing out between us. "Because, really, you've never done *anything* without me. From the day we met, I'm the one who's gotten all the guys, found out about all the parties. Before you met me, you were just sitting around passing tissues to Ca-larke Rebbolds."

I took another sip from my cup. I hated when Sophie was like this—nasty, all sharp edges. I hated it even more when I thought it was my fault, which clearly this was. "Look," I told her, "I just invited Emily along because she doesn't know any-one."

"She knows you," she said. "And now Greg Nichols."

"Funny."

"I'm not being funny," she told me. "I'm just telling it like it is. I don't like her. If you want to hang out with her, go ahead. I'm not interested." Then she dropped her cigarette on the deck, grinding it out with her boot, turned around, and went inside.

I felt uneasy watching her go, nervous. Like maybe she was right, that without her I really would be nothing. A part of me knew this wasn't true, but there was this small sliver of doubt, nagging like a splinter. With Sophie, it was always all or nothing. You were either with her—or, more specifically, following her—or against her. There was no in between. So while being her friend was often hard, being on her bad side would be much, much worse.

I glanced at my watch, realizing Emily had to be home soon, and went to look for her, working my way through the party until I found her talking to a girl from the models. I hung out with them for a while, letting Sophie cool down. By the time we had to leave, I figured her little mood had passed.

When I went to look for her, though, she'd disappeared again. She wasn't outside. Or in the kitchen. Finally I turned down a hallway and spotted her at the other end, opening a door. She saw me, then turned away, slipping inside. I took a deep breath, then headed toward it, knocking twice.

"Sophie," I said. "It's time to go."

No answer. I sighed, crossing my arms over my chest, and stepped closer to the door. "Okay," I said, "I know you're mad at me, but let's just go, and we can talk about it later. All right?"

Still nothing. I looked at my watch again—if we didn't leave soon, Emily would be late for curfew. "Sophie," I said, reaching down for the knob. It wasn't locked, so I turned it, slowly, pushing it open and starting to step inside. "Just—"

I stopped speaking. And walking. Instead, I just stood there, in the half-open door, staring at Sophie, who was leaning against the wall opposite, a boy pressed against her. He had one hand under her shirt, the other moving down her thigh, and his head was ducked down, his lips on her neck. As I jerked back over the threshold, startled, he turned and looked at me. It was Will Cash.

"We're busy," he said, his voice low. His eyes were red, his lips inches from her shoulder.

"I—" I said "—I'm sorry . . ."

"Go home, Annabel," Sophie told me, moving her hand up into his hair, her fingers moving through where it curled, just barely, over his collar. "Just go home."

I stepped back, shutting the door, and just stood there in the hallway. Will Cash was one of the Perkins Day guys. He played guitar in the band and was a senior that year. While he was cute—very cute, the kind of guy you couldn't help but notice—he also had a reputation for being sort of a jerk, as well as a serial dater, at least in the short term. He was always with one girl or another, but never for long. Sophie, for her part, preferred jocks and clean-cut types and hated anyone even slightly alternative. Clearly, though, she was making an exception. At least for the time being.

That night, I tried to call her several times, but she never answered. The next day, around noon, when she finally called me, she didn't even mention Emily or what had happened between us. All she wanted to talk about was Will Cash.

"He's amazing," she told me. She'd given me the barest of details before announcing she was coming over, as if this subject was too big for a simple phone discussion. Now, she was sitting on my bed, flipping through an old *Vogue*. "He knows everybody, he's this amazing guitar player, and he's so freaking smart. Not to mention sexy. I could have kissed him all night long."

"You looked happy," I said.

"I was. I *am*," she said, turning a page and leaning in to

examine a shoe ad. "He is just what I need right now."

"So," I said, keeping Will's hit-and-run reputation in mind, "you're gonna see him again?"

"Of course," she said, like this was a stupid question. "Tonight. The band's playing at Bendo."

"Bendo?"

She sighed, reaching up to pull her hair back behind her neck with one hand. "It's a club, over on Finley?" she said. "Come on, Annabel, you have to have heard of *Bendo*."

"Oh," I said, although I hadn't. "Yeah."

"They go on at ten," she said, flipping another page. "You can come, if you want."

She wasn't looking at me as she asked this, and her voice was flat, no intonation. "No," I said. "I can't. I have to be up early tomorrow."

"Suit yourself," she said.

So that night, I sat at home, and Sophie went to Bendo to see the band, after which, I heard later, she went back to the A-Frame and slept with Will. Despite all her bragging and talk, he was her first, and from then on, he was all she cared about.

For me, though, it was difficult to see the appeal. While Sophie claimed that Will was sweet and funny and hot and smart (as well as a million other adjectives) none of these things really came to mind whenever I found myself face-to-face with him. Will *was* good-looking and incredibly popular. But he was also hard to read, the kind of guy who is just attractive enough that a warm personality is almost required to make him approachable. Will didn't have that. Instead, he came off as standoffish, as well as eerily intense, and whenever I found myself having to make conversation with him—in the car, when Sophie ran in to pay for gas, or at parties, when we both were looking for her—I felt nervous, entirely too aware of how he stared at me or let long silences fall between us.

Even worse, it was like he knew he unsettled me, almost as if he *liked* it. Usually I attempted to make up for my uneasiness by talking too much or too loudly, or both. And when I did, Will would just keep his eyes level, no expression on his face, as I floundered on endlessly before finally sputtering to a stop. I was sure he thought I was stupid. I *sounded* stupid, like a little girl trying too hard to impress. At any rate, I did my best to avoid him, although it wasn't always possible.

Other girls, though, didn't seem to have this problem, and because of it, dating Will turned out to be a full-time job, even for a girl as hardworking as Sophie. From the very start, there were rumors, and it seemed like everywhere they went Will knew someone, usually female. Add in the fact that they went to different schools, which made the stories we heard second- or thirdhand of his wandering eye and—if the constant rumors were to be believed—hands that much harder to confirm. Plus there was the being-in-a-band factor. Plainly put, Sophie had her work cut out for her, and their relationship quickly became defined by a recognizable cycle: Will interacts in any way with some girl, rumors abound, Sophie goes after said girl, then after Will, they argue, break up, get back together. And on and on.

"I just don't understand why you put up with this," I said to her late one night as we drove too fast through a strange neighborhood, yet again looking for the house of some girl she'd heard had been flirting with Will at a party.

"Of course you don't," she snapped, running a stop sign as we took a sharp right. "You've never been in love, Annabel."

I said nothing to this, because it was true. I'd dated a few guys but had never had anyone serious. Although, if this was love, I thought, as we screeched around another curve, Sophie leaning across me to scan house numbers, her face flushed, I had to wonder if that was really such a bad thing.

"Will could have any girl he wanted," she said, slowing down a bit as we approached a row of houses on the left. "But he chose me. He's *with* me. And I will be damned if I let some bitch decide she's going to change that."

"They were just talking, though," I said. "Right? I mean, that doesn't mean anything, necessarily."

"Just talking, alone, at a party, in a room with no one else, is *not* just talking," she snapped. "If you know a guy has a girlfriend—especially if that girlfriend is me—there's absolutely no reason you should be doing anything with him that could be taken the wrong way. It's a choice, Annabel. And if you make the wrong one, you have only yourself to blame when there are consequences."

I sat back in my seat, keeping quiet as she pulled up in front of a small white house. The front porch light was on, and there was a red Jetta in the driveway, a Perkins Day field hockey sticker on the back bumper. If I'd been bolder—or just very stupid—I might have pointed out that it couldn't just be that all the girls in town had it in for Sophie's relationship, that Will had to have *some* culpability in all the rumors. But then I looked at her face, and something in her expression reminded me of that day at the pool all those years ago, when she'd shown up and immediately zeroed in on Kirsten being her friend. It didn't matter that my sister ignored her or was outright rude to her. When Sophie decided she wanted something, she wanted it. And for all the drama, being with Will had made her more envied than ever. She didn't have to follow the most popular girl around anymore. She *was* the most popular girl. Because of this, I wondered if the way she saw Will wasn't, really, all that different from how I saw her; while staying could be difficult, doing without entirely would be much, much harder.

So I'd sat there in the car as she got out, dodging the thrown brightness of the porch light as she walked up the driveway to the Jetta. I wanted to look away as she took the key clutched in her hand and dragged it across its pretty red flank, spelling out what this girl now was to her. But I didn't. I watched, the way I always did, only turning away as she came back toward me, when I was already a partner to the crime.

The irony was that even though I'd seen Will and Sophie go through their drama enough times to know it by heart, I was still completely surprised when I suddenly found myself a part of it. One bad move on one night, and the next thing I knew it was *me* she was after—me who was the slut, the whore—and me cut out, not only of her life, but the one I'd come to know as my own, as well.

• • •

"Annabel," Mrs. McMurty, the director of the Models, said now as she passed behind me, "you're up next, okay?"

I nodded, then stood up, brushing myself off. Across the room, I could see one of the new girls, a tall brunette, posing awkwardly with a large blue serving platter from the kitchen store. The calendar shoot was always kind of weird. Each girl got a month, and you had pose with products from a particular store in the mall. The year before, I'd been unlucky enough to draw Rochelle Tire and got stuck with whitewalls and radials.

"Hold it out, like you're offering something," the photographer said, and the girl reached forward, extending her neck. "Too much," he said, and she flushed, then pulled back.

I started up toward where the photographer was, working my way around a few girls who were leaning against the wall. I was almost there when Hillary Prescott stepped in front of me, blocking my path.

"Hey, Annabel."

Hillary and I had started in the Models together. While initially we'd been kind of friends, I'd quickly learned to keep my distance, as she was a huge gossip. She was also an instigator, more than happy to not only report the dish but stir it up as well.

"Hi, Hillary," I said. She was unwrapping a stick of gum, which she now popped in her mouth, then offered the pack to me. I shook my head. "What's going on?"

"Not much." She reached up, twisting a strand of hair around her finger, looking at me. "How was your summer?"

If it had been anyone else, I would have offered up my standard answer—"Fine"—without even thinking. But since it was Hillary, I was on my guard. "Good," I said, keeping my voice curt. "How was yours?"

"Totally boring," she replied, sighing. She chewed her gum for a moment: I could see it, pink and shiny, on her tongue. "So what's up with you and Emily?"

"Nothing," I said. "Why?"

She shrugged. "It's just, you guys always used to hang out. Now you're not even talking to each other. Just seems kind of weird."

I glanced over at Emily, who was examining her fingernails. "I don't know," I said. "Things change, I guess."

I could feel her looking at me, and I knew, despite her questions, that she knew exactly what had happened, or most of it. Still, I'd be damned if I filled in the rest of the details. "I better go," I told her. "I'm up next."

"Right," she said, narrowing her eyes at me as I stepped around her. "See you later."

I took my place against the wall, then settled to wait again, yawning. It was two in the afternoon, but I was exhausted. And it was all Owen Armstrong's fault.

That morning I'd happened to wake up briefly and glance at the clock right at 6:57 A.M. Just as I was about to roll back over, I remembered Owen's show. He'd been on my mind a lot that weekend, if only because I was suddenly aware of every little white lie I told, from the "Fine" I replied when my dad asked me how school was on Friday to how I'd nodded when my mom asked me the night before if I was excited about getting back to the Models. Cumulatively, it seemed like a lot of dishonesty, enough so that I found myself wanting to keep my word whenever possible. I'd told Owen I would listen to his show. So I did.

When I first turned it on at seven sharp, I could hear only static. I leaned closer to the radio, pressing my ear to it, just as there was an explosion of noise: a sudden burst of guitar, a clanging of cymbals, followed by someone screaming. I jerked, startled, whacking the radio with my elbow and knocking it off the bed. It hit the floor with a bang but kept playing, now at full blast.

Whitney started banging on the other side of the wall as I grabbed it, turning it down as quickly as I could. When I finally pulled it back to my ear—carefully this time—the song was still going, the words the singer was saying (or screeching, really) indecipherable. I had never heard music like this, if it was even music at all.

Finally, with a burst of cymbals, it was over. The next song, though, was no better. Instead of thrashing guitars, it was some sort of electronic piece, consisting of various beeps and blips with a man talking over them, reciting what sounded, to me anyway, like a shopping list. Plus, it went on for five and a half minutes, which I knew because I was watching the clock the entire time, praying for it to finish. When it finally did, Owen came on.

"That was Misanthrope with 'Descartes Dream,'" he said. "Before that, we had Lipo with 'Jennifer.' You're listening to Anger Management, here on WRUS, your community radio station. Here's Nuptial."

Which was another long techno piece, followed by something that sounded like old men reciting poems about whaling ships, their voices gruff and uneven, after which came a solid two minutes of very drippy-sounding harp music. It was such a mishmash, I couldn't even begin to adjust to it. Instead, for a full hour, I sat there, listening to song after song, waiting for one I could actually either a) understand or b) enjoy. It didn't happen. Clearly, I was not going to be enlightened. Just exhausted.

"Annabel," Mrs. McMurty called out, jerking me back to the present. "We're ready for you."

I nodded, then stepped over to stand in front of the backdrop, which was now decorated with several plants: a spider plant, some ferns, and a big palm tree in a pot with wheels. Clearly, this year I'd drawn Laurel's Florals. At least it was better than tires.

The photographer was one I hadn't met before, and he didn't say hello as I stepped in front of him, too busy messing with his camera as a prop guy pushed the rolling pot closer to me. A frond brushed my cheek.

The photographer glanced up at me. "We need more plants," he said to Mrs. McMurty, who was standing off to the side. "Or else I'm just going to have to shoot really close."

"Do we *have* more plants?" Mrs. McMurty asked the prop guy.

He glanced into the adjoining room. "A couple of cacti," he said. "And one ficus. But it's looking kind of sick."

There was a pop as the light meter went off. I reached up,

trying to push the frond out of my face. "Good," the photographer said, coming closer and moving it back. "I like that. Kind of a reveal thing. Do it again."

I did, holding back a sneeze as a branch tickled my face. Behind the photographer, I could see the other girls watching me—the new models, the seniors, Emily. But while I'd had so much trouble lately with being stared at, in this setting it was familiar, what was supposed to happen. If only for a few minutes, I could stop thinking of everything inside to focus only on the surface: one glimpse, one glance, one look. This one.

"Good," the photographer said. A cactus was moving closer in my side vision, but I kept my eyes on him as he moved around me, the flash popping as he directed me to come out, emerge, again and again.

That night, after my mom had gone to bed, and Whitney was locked away in her room, I went downstairs for a glass of water. My dad was sitting in the den just beyond the kitchen, the TV on in front of him, his feet up on the ottoman. When I flicked on the light, he turned around.

"You," he said, "are just in time for a great documentary on Christopher Columbus."

"Really," I said, pulling a glass out of the cabinet.

"It's fascinating," he said. "You want to watch with me? You might just learn something."

My dad loved the History Channel. "It's the story of the world!" he always said, when the rest of us complained about having to watch yet another show about the Third Reich, the fall of the Berlin Wall, or the Great Pyramids. Usually he capitulated, allowing himself to be outvoted, and was subsequently subjected to the Style Network, HGTV, or an endless series of reality shows. When he was alone later at night, though, the TV was all his. Still, he always seemed eager for company, as though history was even better when you had someone to share it with.

Usually, that someone was me. While my mom went to bed early, Whitney claimed boredom, and Kirsten always talked too much no matter what you were watching, my dad and I were a good match in the evenings, sitting together as history unfolded before us. Even if it was a show I knew he'd seen before, he still acted interested, nodding and saying, "Hmm," and "You don't say," as if the narrator could not only hear him, but required this feedback to continue.

In the last few months, though, I'd stopped watching with him. I wasn't sure why, but each time he asked, I suddenly felt tired, too tired to keep up with world events, even if they had already happened. There was something so heavy about the burden of history, of the past. I wasn't sure I had it in me to keep looking back.

"No thanks," I said now. "It's been a long day. I'm pretty tired."

"All right," he said, sitting back and picking up the remote. "Next time."

"Yeah. Definitely."

I picked up my water and walked over to his chair, and he leaned sideways, offering his cheek for me to kiss good night. After I did, he smiled, then hit the volume button, the sound of the narrator rising as I walked out of the room.

"In the fifteenth century, explorers yearned for . . . "

Halfway to the stairs I stopped, taking a sip of my water, then turned back and looked at him. The remote was now on his stomach, the light of the TV flickering across his face. I tried to picture myself retracing my steps, moving back to take my place on the couch, but I just couldn't. So I left him there alone to watch history repeat, the same events retold again and again, on his own.

Chapter
SEVEN

The entire weekend, I'd wondered what to expect when I next saw Owen at school. If anything would be different after what had happened on Friday, or we'd go back to our shared silence and distance, as if nothing had happened. A few minutes after he sat down, he made the choice for us.

"So. Did you listen?"

I put my sandwich down, turning to face him. He was in his normal spot, wearing jeans and a black crewneck. His iPod was out as well, earphones hanging around his neck.

"To your show?" I said.

"Yeah."

I nodded. "I did, actually."

"And?"

Despite the fact that I'd spent most of the weekend realizing how often I fibbed or outright lied to keep the peace, my first instinct at this moment was to do just that. Honesty in principle was one thing. In someone's face, another.

"Well," I began. "It was . . . interesting."

"Interesting," he repeated.

"Yeah," I said. "I'd, um, never heard those songs before."

He just looked at me, studying my face for what felt like a very long time. Then he startled me by standing up and taking three strides, quickly closing the distance between us before sitting down beside me. "Okay," he said. "Did you really listen?"

"Yeah," I said, trying not to stammer. "I did."

"I don't know if you remember," he said, "but you *did* tell me that you lie."

"I didn't say that." He raised an eyebrow. "I said I often hold back the truth. I'm not doing that this time, though. I listened to the whole show."

He still didn't believe me, it was obvious. And not exactly surprising.

I took a breath. "'Jennifer' by Lipo. 'Descartes Dream' by Misanthrope. Some song with a lot of beeping—"

"You *did* listen." He sat back, nodding his head. "Okay, then. Now tell me what you really thought."

"I told you. It was interesting."

"Interesting," he said, "is not a word."

"Since when?"

"It's a placeholder. Something you use when you don't want to say something else." He leaned a little closer to me. "Look, if you're worried about my feelings, don't be. You can say whatever you want. I won't be offended."

"I did. I liked it."

"Tell the truth. Say something. Anything. Just spit it out."

"I—" I began, then stopped myself. Maybe it was the fact that he was so clearly on to me. Or my sudden awareness of how rarely I was honest. Either way, I broke. "I . . . I didn't like it," I said.

He slapped his leg. "I *knew* it! You know, for someone who lies a lot, you're not very good at it."

This was a good thing. Or not? I wasn't sure. "I'm not a liar," I said.

"Right. You're *nice*," he said.

"What's wrong with nice?"

"Nothing. Except it usually involves not telling the truth," he replied. "Now. Tell me what you really thought."

What I really thought was that I felt very unsettled, as if somehow, Owen Armstrong had figured me out, and I hadn't even realized it. "I liked the show format," I said, "but the songs were kind of . . ."

"Kind of what?" He waggled his fingers at me. "Give me some adjectives. Other than interesting."

"Noisy," I said. "Bizarre."

"Okay." He nodded. "What else?"

I looked at his face carefully, gauging it for signs that he was offended, or bothered. There were none, so I continued. "Well, the first song was . . . painful to listen to. And the second, the Misanthrope one . . ."

"'Descartes Dream.'"

"It put me to sleep. Literally."

"That happens," he said. "Go on."

He said this so easily, like he wasn't bothered in the least. So I did. "The harp music sounded like something you'd hear at a funeral."

"Ah," he said. "Okay. Good."

"And I hated the techno."

"All of it?"

"Yes."

He nodded. "Well. Okay, then. That's good feedback. Thank you."

And that was that. He pulled out his iPod and started pushing buttons. No tantrums, no hurt feelings, no offense. "So . . . you're okay with that?" I asked.

"That you didn't like the show?" he replied, not looking up. "Yeah."

He shrugged. "Sure. I mean, it would have been cool if you had. But most people don't, so it's not exactly surprising."

"And that doesn't bother you," I said.

"Not really. I mean, at first, it was kind of disappointing. But people recover from disappointment. Otherwise we'd all be hanging from nooses. Right?"

"What?"

"Hey, what about the sea shanty?" he asked. I just looked at him. "The men chanting about sailing the open sea. What was your take on that one?"

"Weird," I said. "Very weird."

"Weird," he repeated slowly. "Huh. Okay."

Just then I heard voices, and footsteps, and turned my head just in time to see Sophie crossing the courtyard with Emily. I'd been so distracted by what had happened with Owen on Friday that initially, I'd forgotten about the confrontation that preceded it. That morning, though, on the way to school, the dread set in as I began wondering what would happen. But so far, I'd only crossed paths with Sophie once, at which point she'd glared at me, mumbling a "slut" as she went by. Same old, same old.

Now, though, she glanced over at me, her eyes widening slightly before she nudged Emily with her elbow. Then they were both staring at me, and I felt my face flush as I looked down at my backpack at my feet.

Owen, for his part, did not notice this as he put his player down, running a hand through his hair. "So you didn't like any of the techno?" he asked. "Like, not even one aspect?"

I shook my head. "No," I said. "Sorry."

"Don't be sorry, it's your opinion. There's no right and wrong in music, you know? Just everything in between."

Just then, the bell rang, surprising me. I was so used to lunch being interminable, but this one had flown by. I reached down, balling up what was left of my sandwich as Owen hopped off the wall, slipping his player in his pocket and grabbing his earphones.

"Well," I said, "I guess I'll see you around."

"Yeah." He started to put on his earphones as I grabbed my bag, sliding off the wall. "See you later."

As he walked away, I took another look at the bench. Sure enough, Sophie and Emily were still staring. I watched as Sophie said something, and Emily smiled, shaking her head. I could only imagine what they would say about us, what stories they would come up with. None of them could be weirder than the truth: that Owen Armstrong and I just might be friends.

Thinking this, I glanced over, finding him in the crowd. He'd put on his earphones and was headed up to the arts building, his bag over his shoulder. They'd been watching him, too, but he hadn't even noticed. If he did, I was pretty sure he wouldn't care anyway. And for that, more than the honesty, the directness, and everything else, I envied him most of all.

I didn't get the Mooshka job. This was neither upsetting nor surprising, at least to me, although my mother did seem disappointed. Personally, I was just relieved the whole thing was over, and ready to move on. But the next day, as I took out my lunch, a note fell out with it.

> *Annabel,*
>
> *I just wanted to tell you that I'm so proud of you for all you've accomplished, and not to be discouraged about the Mooshka campaign. It was very competitive, Lindy said, and they did think highly of you. She and I have arranged to talk today about some other things she's lining up, which sound very exciting. I'll fill you in tonight. Have a great day.*

"Bad news?"

I jumped, startled, then glanced up to see Owen was standing in front of me. "What?"

"You looked stressed," he said, nodding at the note in my hand. "Something wrong?"

"No," I said, folding the note and putting it down beside me. "Everything's fine."

He walked over to the wall, sitting down not right next to me, as he had the day before, but not as far away as he once had, either. I watched him as he slid his iPod out of his pocket, then leaned his palms back on the grass beside us, surveying the courtyard.

I was aware, during all of this, that with my last response, I hadn't exactly been honest with him. Of course, he never would have known this. Or cared, probably. Still, for some reason, I felt the need to Rephrase and Redirect. As it were.

"It's just this thing with my mom," I said.

He turned his head, and I wondered if maybe he thought I was crazy, or had no idea what I was talking about. "Thing," he repeated. "Just so you know; that's a *serious* placeholder."

Of course it is, I thought. Still, I clarified. "It has to do with my modeling."

"Modeling?" He looked confused. "Oh, right. Like Mallory was talking about. You were in a commercial or something?"

"I've been doing it since I was a kid. Both my sisters did it, too. But lately, I've been wanting to quit."

And there it was. The one thing I'd only said in my head, now finally out there, and to Owen Armstrong, of all people. This was so big a step for me that I probably could have stopped right there. But for whatever reason, I continued.

"And anyway," I said, "it's complicated, because my mom's really into it, and if I quit, then she'll be upset."

"But you don't want to do it anymore," he said. "Right?"

"Yeah."

"So you should tell her that."

"You say that like it's easy," I said.

"Isn't it?"

"No."

There was a burst of laughter from the doors to our left as a group of freshmen came out, talking too loudly. Owen looked over at them, then back at me. "Why not?" he asked.

"Because I don't do confrontations."

He glanced over at Sophie, who was sitting on her bench with Emily, then slowly slid his eyes back to me.

"Well," I added, "I don't do confrontations *well*."

"What happened between you two, anyway?"

"Me and Sophie?" I asked, although I knew what he meant. He nodded. "It was just . . . we had a falling-out over the summer."

He didn't say anything; I knew he was waiting for more details. "She thinks I slept with her boyfriend," I added.

"Did you?"

Of course he would ask, point-blank. But still, I felt my face flush. "No," I said. "I didn't."

"Maybe you should tell her that," he said.

"It's not that simple."

"Huh," he said. "Call me crazy, but I'm sensing a theme here."

I looked down at my hands, thinking again that I had to be awfully simple for him to deduce so much about me in less than a week. "So if you were me," I said, "you would—"

"—just be honest," he finished. "On both counts."

"You say that like it's easy, too," I told him.

"It's not. But you can do it. It just takes practice."

"Practice?"

"In Anger Management," he said, "we had to do all this role-playing stuff. You know, to get used to handling things in a less volatile way."

"You role-played," I said, trying to picture this.

"I had to. It was court-ordered." He sighed. "But I have to say, it was kind of helpful. You know, so that when and if something similar did happen, you had some kind of road map for dealing with it."

"Oh," I said. "Well, I guess that makes sense."

"All right, then." He slid a little closer to me. "So say I'm your mom."

"What?" I said.

"I'm your mom," he repeated. "Now tell me you want to quit modeling."

I could feel myself blushing. "I can't do that," I said.

"Why not?" he asked. "Is it so hard to believe? You think I'm not a good role-player?"

"No," I said. "It's just—"

"Because I am. *Everyone* wanted me to be their mother in group."

I just looked at him. "I just . . . It's weird."

"No, it's hard. But not impossible. Just try it."

A week earlier, I hadn't even known what color his eyes were. Now, we were family. At least temporarily. I took in a breath.

"Okay," I said. "So—"

"Mom," he said.

"What?"

"The more accurate the exercise, the more effective it is," he explained. "Go all out, or don't go at all."

"Okay," I said again. "Mom."

"Yes?"

This is so weird, I thought. Out loud, I said, "The thing is, I know that the modeling thing is really important to—"

He held up a hand in the STOP position. "R and R. Rephrase and Redirect that."

"Why?"

"*Thing*. Like I said, major placeholder, super vague. In confrontations, you have to be as specific as possible, to avoid misunderstandings." He leaned a little closer to me. "Look, I know it's weird," he said. "But it works. I promise."

This was little comfort, though, as I proceeded to cross over from simply uncomfortable to borderline humiliated. "I know my modeling is very important to you," I said, "and that you really enjoy it."

Owen nodded, gesturing for me to go on.

"But to be honest . . . " I reached up, tucking a piece of hair behind my ear. "It's just that lately, I've been thinking about it a lot, and I feel like . . ."

The thing was, I knew this was just a game. Practice, not real. But even so, I felt something seizing up in me, like an engine sputtering to a stop. I had too much at stake here— failing would not only reveal my weakness about confrontation, but embarrass me in front of him, as well.

He was still waiting.

"I can't do it," I said, and looked away.

"You so had it, though!" he said, slapping the wall with the palm of his hand. "You were right there."

"I'm sorry," I said, picking up my sandwich again. My voice sounded tight as I said, "I just . . . I can't."

He looked at me for a moment. Then he shrugged. "All right," he said. "No big deal."

We sat there, both of us silent for a second. I had no idea what had just happened, but it did feel like a big deal, suddenly. Then I heard Owen take in a breath.

"Look," he said, "I'm just going to say this: It's got to suck, you know? Keeping something like that in. Walking around every day having so much you want to say, but not doing it. It's gotta make you really mad. Right?"

I knew he was talking about modeling. But hearing this, I thought of something else, the thing I could never admit, the biggest secret of all. The one I could never tell, because if the tiniest bit of light was shed upon it, I'd never be able to shut it away again.

"I should go," I said, stuffing my sandwich back into the bag. "I . . . I have to talk to my English teacher about this project I'm supposed to be doing."

"Oh," he said. I could feel him watching me, and made a conscious effort not to look back. "Sure."

I stood up, grabbing my bag. "I'll, um, see you later."

"Right." He picked up his iPod. "See you around."

I nodded, and then, somehow, I was walking away, leaving him behind. I waited until I was at the main doors to look back.

He was just sitting there, head ducked down, listening to his music like nothing had happened at all. I had a flash of my first impression of him—that he was dangerous, a threat. I knew now he wasn't, at least not in the ways I'd thought then. But there *was* something frightening about Owen Armstrong:

he was honest and expected the same from everyone else. And that scared me to death.

When I first walked away from Owen, I felt relieved. But it didn't last.

The real truth, I realized as the day wore on, was that even though I hardly knew Owen, I'd actually been *more* honest with him than anyone else in a long time. He knew about what had happened between me and Sophie, about Whitney's illness, and that I hated modeling. This seemed like an awful lot to reveal to someone who, in the end, I couldn't even risk being friends with. But I didn't know it for sure until I saw Clarke.

It was after seventh period, in the hallway, and she was opening her locker. Her hair was in two spriggy pigtails, and she had on jeans, a black shirt, and shiny Mary Janes. As I watched, a girl I didn't know passed behind her, saying her name, and Clarke turned, smiling, and said hello back to her. It was all totally normal, just another moment in another day, but something in it struck me, and I found myself going back, back, all the way to that night down by the pool. Another time I'd been afraid of conflict, afraid to be honest, afraid even to speak. I'd lost a friend then, too. The best friend, really, I'd ever had.

It was too late to try and alter what had happened between me and Clarke, but there might still be time to change something else. Maybe even me. So I went to look for Owen.

In a school of over two thousand students, it was easy to lose yourself, not to mention someone else. But Owen definitely stood out in a crowd, so when I couldn't find him or the

Land Cruiser, I figured I'd missed him. When I got into my car and pulled out onto the main road, though, I spotted him. He was on foot, walking down the center of the median, his backpack over one shoulder, earphones on.

It wasn't until I was right up to him that it occurred to me this might be a mistake. But you get only so many do-overs in this life, so many chances to, if not change your past, alter your future. So I slowed down and lowered my window.

"Hey," I called out, but he didn't hear me. "Owen!" Still no response. I moved my hand to the center of my steering wheel and pushed down, hard, on the horn. Finally, he turned his head.

"Hey," he said as someone behind me beeped angrily before whizzing past. "What's up?"

"What happened to your car?" I asked him.

He stopped walking, then reached up, pulling the earphone out of his left ear. "Transportation issues," he said.

This is it, I told myself. *Say something. Anything. Just spit it out.*

"Story of my life," I told him, then reached over, pushing open my passenger door. "Get in."

Chapter
EIGHT

The first thing that Owen did when he got in my car was bump his head on what I hadn't realized—until that particular moment anyway—was a pretty low ceiling. "Oof," he said, reaching up to rub his forehead just as one of his knees whacked the dashboard. "Man. This is a small car."

"Is it?" I said. "I've never really noticed, and I'm five-eight."

"Is that tall?"

"I used to think so," I said, glancing at him.

"Well, I'm six-four," he replied, trying to push his seat, which was already back as far as it would go, even farther away from the dashboard. Then he moved his arm, trying to balance it on the window, but it was too big, so he changed position, crossing it over his chest, before finally letting it drop to hang beside him. "So I guess it's all relative."

"You okay?" I asked.

"Fine," he said, altogether unbothered, as if this sort of thing happened all the time. "Thanks for the ride, by the way."

"No problem," I said. "Just tell me where you're going."

"Home." He moved his arm again, still trying to fit into the seat. "Just keep straight. You don't have to turn for a while."

We rode without talking for a few minutes. I knew this was the time to say what was on my mind, to explain myself. I took in a breath, bracing myself.

"How do you *stand* it?" he said.

I blinked. "I'm sorry?"

"I mean," he said, "it's just so silent. Empty."

"What is?"

"This," he said, gesturing around the car. "Driving in silence. With no music."

"Well," I said slowly, "to be honest, I didn't realize we were, actually."

He sat back, his head bumping the headrest. "See for me, it's immediate. Silence is so freaking loud."

This seemed either deep or deeply oxymoronic. I wasn't sure which. "Well," I said, "my CDs are in the console in the center if you—"

But he was already pulling it open and taking out a stack of CDs. As he began to work his way through them, I glanced over, suddenly nervous.

"Those aren't really my favorites," I said. "They're just the ones I have in here right now."

"Huh," he said, not looking up. I turned back to the road, hearing the cases clacking as he flipped through them. "Drake Peyton, Drake Peyton . . . so you're into that frat-boy hippie rock stuff?"

"I guess," I said. This was bad, I thought. "I saw him live summer before last."

"Huh," he said again. "More Drake Peyton . . . and Alamance. That's alt-country, right?"

"Yeah."

"Interesting," he said. "Because I wouldn't have pegged you for . . . Tiny? This is his most current album, right?"

"I got it over the summer," I said, slowing for a red light.

"Then it is." He shook his head. "You know, I have to admit, I'm surprised. I never would have pegged you for a Tiny fan. Or any rap, for that matter."

"Why not?"

He shrugged. "I don't know. Bad assumption, I guess. Who made you this one?"

I glanced at the disc he was holding, immediately recognizing the slanting print. "My sister Kirsten."

"She's into classic rock," he said.

"Since high school," I said. "She had a Jimmy Page poster on her wall for years."

"Ah." He scanned the track list. "She has good taste, though. I mean, there's Led Zeppelin here, but at least it's not 'Stairway to Heaven.' In fact," he said, sounding impressed, "'Thank You' is my favorite Led Zeppelin song."

"Really?"

"Really. It's got that kind of cheesy, power-ballad feel. Kind of ironic, yet truthful. Can I put it on?"

"Sure," I said. "Thanks for asking."

"You gotta ask," he said, reaching forward and sliding the CD into my stereo. "Only a real asshole takes liberties with someone else's car stereo. That's serious."

The player clicked a couple of times, and then I heard music, faintly. Owen reached forward for the volume button, then glanced at me. When I nodded, he turned it up. Hearing the opening chords, I had a pang of missing Kirsten, who, during her rebellion-filled senior year, had developed a passion for seventies-era guitar rock, which, at its height, had her listening to Pink Floyd's *Dark Side of the Moon* on repeat for what seemed like weeks at a time.

Thinking this, I looked back over at Owen, who was drumming his fingers on his knee. Kirsten, of course, would never hesitate to say what was on *her* mind. So with her song playing in my ears, I decided to follow suit. Or try to. "So about today," I said. He looked over at me. "I'm sorry about what happened."

"What happened?"

I fixed my eyes on the road ahead, feeling my face flush. "When we were doing the role-playing, and I freaked out and walked away."

I was expecting an "It's okay" or maybe a "Don't worry about it." Instead, he said, "That was freaking out?"

"Well," I said. "I guess. Yeah."

"Huh," he said. "Okay."

"I didn't mean to get so upset," I explained. "Like I said, I just don't do confrontations very well. Which I guess was obvious. So . . . I'm sorry."

"It's all right." He tried to sit back again, his elbow knocking the door. "In fact . . ."

I waited for him to finish this thought. When he didn't, I said, "What?"

"It's just, to me, that wasn't really freaking out," he said.

"No?"

He shook his head. "To me, freaking out is raising your voice. Screaming. Veins bulging. Hitting people in parking lots. That kind of thing."

"I don't do that," I said.

"I'm not saying you should." He reached up, running a hand through his hair; as he did so, the ring on his middle finger caught the light, glinting for a second. "It's just a semantic issue, I guess. Take this next right."

I did, turning onto a tree-lined street. All the houses were big, with wide front porches. We passed a group of kids in a cul-de-sac playing roller hockey, then some moms on a corner, grouped around a pack of strollers.

"This is it, up here," he told me. "The gray one."

I slowed down, then pulled over to the curb. The house was beautiful, with a wide front porch with a swing, and bright pink flowers in pots lining the steps. A yellow cat was lying on the front walk, stretched out in the sunshine. "Wow," I said. "Great house."

"Well, it's not glass," he said. "But it's okay."

We sat there for a second, our situation now reversed from last time, me waiting for him to go inside. "You know," I said finally, "I just wanted to say you were right about what you said earlier. It is kind of hard to hold a lot in. But for me . . . it's sometimes even harder to let it out."

I wasn't sure why I felt compelled to bring this up again. Maybe to finally explain myself. To him, or to me.

"Yeah," he said. "But you gotta get stuff out. Otherwise it just festers, and eventually, you just blow."

"See, that's the part I can't deal with," I said. "I can't take it when people are angry."

"Anger's not bad," he said. "It's human. And anyway, just because someone's upset doesn't mean they'll stay that way."

I looked down at my steering wheel, picking at the edge. "I don't know," I said. "In my experience, when people I'm close with have gotten upset with me, that's it. It *is* forever. Everything changes."

Owen didn't say anything for a second. I could hear a dog barking from some house down the street. "Well," he said, "maybe you weren't as close with them as you thought."

"Meaning what?"

"Meaning that if someone is really close with you, your getting upset or them getting upset is okay, and they don't change because of it. It's just part of the relationship. It *happens*. You deal with it."

"You deal with it," I said. "I wouldn't even know how to do that."

"Well, that makes sense," he said. "Considering you never let it happen in the first place."

The CD was still going, now playing a song by Rush as a minivan drove past us, kicking up some leaves. I had no idea how many minutes had passed while we'd been sitting there. It seemed like a long time.

"You sure have a lot of answers," I said.

"I don't," he replied, reaching down to twist one of his rings around his finger. "I'm just doing the best I can, under the circumstances."

"How's that going?" I asked.

He glanced up at me. "Well, you know," he said. "It's day to day."

I smiled. "I like your rings," I said, nodding at his hands. "Are they the exact same?"

"Sort of. And not really." He reached down, sliding the one off his left hand and handing it to me. "They're kind of a before-and-after thing. Rolly made them for me. His dad's a jeweler."

The ring was heavy in my palm, the silver thick. "He made this?"

"Not the ring," he said. "The engraving. On the inside."

"Oh." I tilted the ring slightly, peering along the interior curve. There, in all capital letters, in formal, very elegant type, it said GO FUCK YOURSELF. "Nice," I said.

"Classy, huh?" he said. He made a face. "That was me pre-arrest. I was a little . . ."

"Angry?"

"You could say. He made this one when I finished the Anger Management course." He slid the ring off his other middle finger, then held it up to my face. In the same type, same size, it said OR NOT.

I laughed. "Well," I said, handing it back to him. "It's always good to know your options."

"Exactly." Then he smiled at me, and I felt another flush come over my face, but not the embarrassed or anxious kind—a different sort entirely. One I never would have thought I'd feel around Owen Armstrong. Ever. The moment was broken, however, by a voice.

"Annabel!"

I looked to my right—it was Mallory. Sometime during this exchange, she'd appeared at Owen's window, where she was now smiling widely and waving. "Hi!"

"Hi," I said.

She gestured for Owen to put his window down, which he did, slowly, and clearly somewhat reluctantly. As soon as there was a space big enough, she stuck her head in. "Oh my God, I love your shirt! Is that from Tosca?"

I glanced down. "Maybe," I said. "My mom got it for me."

"You're so lucky! I love Tosca. It's, like, my favorite store in the whole world. Are you coming in?"

"Coming in?" I asked.

"To the house. Are you staying for dinner? Oh, you *totally* have to stay for dinner!"

"Mallory," Owen said, rubbing a hand over his face. "Please stop shrieking."

She ignored him, sticking her head in even farther. "You could see my room," she said, her eyes wide, excited. "And my closet, and I could show you—"

"Mallory," Owen said again. "Back away from the car."

"Do you like my outfit?" she asked me. She stepped back so I could see it: plain white tee, short jacket over it, rolled-up jeans, and shiny boots with thick soles. After doing a little spin, she stuck her head back in the window. "It's inspired by Nicholls Lake; she's my favorite singer right now? She's, like, punk."

Owen sat back, his head bonking against the headrest. "Nicholls Lake," he said in a low voice, "is *not* punk."

"Yes, she is," Mallory told him. "And see? Today, so am I!"

"Mallory, we've talked about this. Remember? Did we not discuss the true definition of punk?" Owen said. "Have you even *listened* to that Black Flag CD I gave you?"

"That was so loud," she said. "And plus you can't even sing along. Nicholls Lake is better."

Owen took in another shuddering breath. "Mallory," he said. "If you could just—"

Just then, a tall dark-haired woman—Owen's mom, I assumed—appeared in the doorway of the house, calling her. Mallory shot her an annoyed look. "I have to go in," she announced, then leaned in even farther, so her face was inches from Owen's. "But you'll come over another time, right?"

"Sure," I told her.

"Bye, Annabel."

"Good-bye," I said.

She smiled, then stood up, and waved at me. I waved back, and Owen and I watched her climb the front stairs and head down the walk, turning to look back at us every few steps or so.

"Wow," I said. "So she's punk, huh?"

Owen didn't answer me. Instead, all I could hear was him inhaling, loudly, several times in a row.

"Is this you freaking out?" I asked.

He exhaled. "No. This is me annoyed. I don't know what it is about her. There's just something about sisters. They can make you freaking crazy."

"Story of my life," I said.

Another silence. In every one that fell, I told myself this

time, he was going to get out and leave, and this would be over. And each time, I wanted it to happen even less.

He said, "You say that a lot, you know."

"What?"

"'Story of my life.'"

"You said it first."

"Did I?"

I nodded. "That day, behind the school."

"Oh." He was quiet for a moment. "You know, when you think about it, that's kind of a weird thing. I mean, it's meant to be sympathetic, right? But it's kind of not. Like you're telling the other person there's nothing unique about what they're saying."

I considered this as a couple of kids on Rollerblades whizzed past, hockey sticks over their shoulders. "Yeah," I said, finally, "but you could also look at it the other way. Like you're saying no matter how bad things are for you, I can still relate."

"Ah," he said. "So you're saying you relate to me."

"No. Not at all."

"Nice." He laughed, turning his head to look out the window. I caught the quickest flash of his profile, and remembered all those days I'd spent studying him from a distance.

"Okay," I said. "Maybe a little."

He turned back, facing me, and I felt it again. Another pause, just long enough for me to wonder what, exactly, was happening. Then he pushed the door open. "So," he said, "um, thanks again for the ride."

"No problem. I owed you."

"No," he said, "you didn't." He untangled himself from the seat. "I'll see you tomorrow, or something."

"Yeah. See you then."

He got out, shutting the door behind him, then grabbed his bag and started up the steps. I watched him until he went inside.

As I pulled away from the curb, the whole afternoon seemed so strange, surreal. There was so much filling my head, too much to even begin to understand, but as I drove, I suddenly realized something else was bothering me: The CD had stopped and there was no music. Before, I probably wouldn't have even noticed, but now that I had, the silence, if not deafening, was distracting. I wasn't sure what this meant. But I reached forward and turned on the radio anyway.

Chapter
NINE

Beauty and the Beast. The Odd Couple. Shrek and Fiona. I had to hand it to the rumor mill: Over the next couple of weeks, they came up with lots of names for me and Owen and whatever it was we were doing every day on the wall at lunch. For me, it was harder to define. We weren't together by any means, but we weren't strangers. Like so much else, we fell somewhere in the middle.

Whatever the case, some things now were just understood. First, that we'd sit together. Second, that I'd always give him a hard time about not eating anything—he'd confessed to me he spent his lunch money on music, always—before sharing whatever I'd brought. And third, that we would argue. Or not argue, exactly. *Discuss.*

Initially, it was only about music, Owen's favorite subject and the one about which he felt the most strongly. When I agreed with him, I was brilliant and enlightened. When I didn't, I had the Worst Taste in Music in the World. Usually the most spirited exchanges came at the beginning of the week, as we discussed his radio show, which I now listened to faithfully every Sunday morning. It was hard to believe that once I'd been so nervous to tell him what I thought. Now, it came naturally.

"You've got to be kidding!" he said one Monday, shaking his head. "You didn't like that Baby Bejesuses song?"

"Was it the one that was all touch-tones?"

"It wasn't all touch-tones," he said indignantly. "There was other stuff, too."

"Like what?"

He just looked at me for a second, half of my turkey sandwich poised in his hand. "Like," he said, then took a bite, which meant he was stalling. After taking his time chewing and swallowing, he said, "The Baby Bejesuses are innovators of the genre."

"Then they should be able to put together a song using more than a phone keypad."

"That," he said, pointing at me with the sandwich, "is I-Lang. Watch it."

I-Lang meant Inflammatory Language. And like R and R and placeholders, it had become part of my daily vocabulary. Hang out with Owen long enough, and you got an Anger Management tutorial, free of charge.

"Look," I said, "you know I don't like techno music. So maybe, you know, you should stop asking me my opinion of techno songs."

"That is such a generalization!" he replied. "How can you just rule out an entire genre? You're jumping to conclusions."

"No, I'm not," I said.

"What do you call it, then?"

"Being honest."

He just looked at me for a second. Then, with a sigh, he took another bite of the sandwich. "Fine," he said, chewing. "Let's move on. What about that thrash metal song by the Lipswitches?"

"Too noisy."

"It's supposed to be noisy! It's thrash metal!"

"I wouldn't mind the noise, if there were other redeeming qualities," I told him. "It's just someone wailing at the top of their lungs."

He popped the last bit of crust into his mouth. "So no techno and no thrash metal," he said. "What's left?"

"Everything else?" I said.

"Everything else," he repeated slowly, still not convinced. "Okay, fine. How about the last song I played, the one with glockenspiel."

"The glockenspiel?"

"Yeah. By Aimee Decker. There was a stand-up bass, and some yodeling at the beginning, and then . . ."

"Yodeling?" I said. "Is that what that was?"

"What, now you don't like *yodeling*, either?"

And on and on. Sometimes, it got heated, but never to the point where I couldn't handle it. The truth was, I looked forward to my lunches with Owen, more than I ever would have admitted.

Between our discourses on early punk, big band and swing, and the questionable redeeming qualities of techno music, I was learning more and more about him. I now knew that although he'd always had a passion for music, it wasn't until his parents divorced a year and a half earlier that he'd become, to use his word, obsessed. Apparently the split had been pretty ugly, with accusations going back and forth. Music, he told me, was an escape. Everything else was ending and changing, but music was this vast resource, bottomless.

"Basically," he said one day, "when they wouldn't talk to each other, I got stuck in the middle, doing all the go-between work. And of course, it was always the *other* one who was terrible and inconsiderate. If I agreed, I was screwed, because someone got offended. But if I disagreed, that was taking sides, too. There was no way to win."

"That must have been hard," I said.

"It sucked. That's when I started really getting into the music thing, all the obscure stuff. If nobody had heard it, nobody could tell me what I was supposed to think about it. There was no right and wrong there." He sat back, waving away a bee that was circling around us. "Plus, around that same time, there was this college radio station out in Phoenix that I started listening to—KXPC. There was this one guy who had a late-night shift on the weekends . . . he played some seriously obscure shit. Like tribal music, or seriously underground punk, or five full minutes of a faucet dripping. Stuff like that."

"A faucet dripping," I said. He nodded. "That's music?"

"Obviously not to everyone," he replied, shooting me a look. I smiled. "But that was kind of the point. It was, like, this whole uncharted territory. I started writing down the stuff he was playing, and looking for it at record stores and online. It gave me something to focus on other than all the stuff going down at home. Plus, it came in handy when I needed to drown out the screaming downstairs."

"Really? Screaming?"

He shrugged. "It wasn't that bad. But there were definitely some freak-outs on both sides. Though, to be honest, the silence was worse."

"Worse than screaming?" I said.

"Much," he said, nodding. "I mean, at least with an argument, you know what's happening. Or have some idea. Silence is . . . it could be anything. It's just—"

"So freaking loud," I finished for him.

He pointed at me. "Exactly."

So Owen hated silence. Also on his list of dislikes: peanut butter (too dry), liars (self-explanatory), and people who didn't tip (delivering pizza didn't pay that well, apparently). And those were only the ones I knew about so far. Maybe it was because of his stint in Anger Management, but Owen was very open about the things that pissed him off.

"Aren't you?" he asked one day, when I pointed this out to him.

"No," I said. "I mean, I guess I am about some things."

"What makes you mad?"

Instinctively, I looked over at Sophie, who was on her bench, talking on her cell phone. Out loud I said, "Techno music."

"Ha-ha," he said. "Seriously."

"I don't know." I picked the crust of my sandwich. "My sisters, I guess. Sometimes."

"What else?"

"I can't think of anything," I said.

"Please! You're seriously saying the only thing that bugs

you is siblings and a genre of music? Come on. Are you not human?"

"Maybe," I said, "I'm just not as angry as you are."

"Nobody's as angry as I am," he replied, hardly bothered. "That's a fact. But even *you* have to have something that really pisses you off."

"I probably do. I just . . . can't think of one right this second." He rolled his eyes. "And besides, what do you mean no one's as angry as you are? What about Anger Management?"

"What about it?"

"Well," I said, "wasn't the point that you not be angry anymore?"

"The purpose of Anger Management isn't to make you not angry."

"No?"

He shook his head. "No. Anger is inevitable. Anger Management is just what it sounds like: It's supposed to help you deal with it. Express it in a more productive way than, say, hitting people in parking lots."

If at first I'd doubted it, I didn't now: Owen was always this honest. Ask a question, you got an answer. For a while, though, I'd tested him, soliciting his opinion on various things, like my clothes ("Not your best shade," he told me about a new peach-colored shirt), his initial impression of me ("Too perfect and completely unapproachable"), and the state of his love life ("Nonexistent, currently").

"Is there anything you won't tell someone?" I finally asked him one day, just after he'd told me that, while my new haircut looked fine, he preferred it longer. "Like, at all?"

"You just asked me what I thought," he pointed out, help-ing himself to a pretzel from the bag between us. "Why ask me, if you don't want me to be honest?"

"I'm not talking about my hair. I'm talking in general." He gave me a doubtful look, popping the pretzel into his mouth. "Seriously. Do you ever think to yourself, maybe I shouldn't say this? Maybe it's not the right thing to do?"

He considered this for a second. "No," he said finally. "I told you. I don't like liars."

"It's not lying, though. It's just not telling."

"You're saying there's a difference?"

"There is," I said. "One is actively deceiving. The other is just not saying something out loud."

"Yes, but," he replied, pulling out another pretzel, "you're still participating in a deception. Except it's just to yourself. Right?"

I just looked at him, turning this thought over in my mind. "I don't know," I said slowly.

"In fact," he continued, "that's worse than lying, when you really think about it. I mean, at the very least you should tell yourself the truth. If you can't trust yourself, who can you trust? You know?"

I would never have been able to tell him so, but Owen inspired me. The little white lies I told on a daily basis, the things I kept in, each time I was not totally honest—I was aware of every one now. I was also cognizant of how good it felt to actually be able to say what I thought to someone. Even if it was just about music. Or not.

One day at lunch, Owen put his backpack on the wall

between us, unzipped it, and pulled out a stack of CDs. "Here," he said, pushing them toward me. "For you."

"Me?" I said. "What is this?"

"An overview," he explained. "I planned to do more, but my burner was acting up. So I could only do a few."

To Owen, "a few" CDs meant ten, by my count. Looking at the top few, I saw that each had a title—TRUE HIP HOP, CHANTS AND SHANTIES (VARIOUS), TOLERABLE JAZZ, ACTU-AL SINGERS ACTUALLY SINGING—with the tracks listed beneath in a neat block print. It occurred to me that they were probably the result of a pointed discussion about stoner rock we'd had the day before, when Owen decided that maybe my knowledge of music was so "stunted and wanting" (his words) due to a lack of exposure. So here was his remedy: a personal primer, divided into chapters.

"If you really like any of these," he continued, "then I can give you more. When, you know, you're ready to go in depth."

I picked up the stack, flipping through the rest of the titles. There was one for country music, the British Invasion, folk songs. When I reached the one at the very bottom, though, I saw that the cover was blank, except for two words: JUST LISTEN.

Instantly, I was suspicious. "Is this techno?" I asked him.

"I can't believe you'd just assume that," he said, offended. "God."

"Owen," I said.

"It's not techno."

I just looked at him.

"The point is," he said as I shook my head, "that all the others are set lists, set concepts. An education, if you will. You should listen to them first. And then, when you've done that, and you think you're ready, really ready, put that one on. It's a bit more . . . out there."

"All right," I said. "I'm *officially* wary now."

"You might totally hate it," he admitted. "Or not. It might be the answer to all life's questions. That's the beauty of it. You know?"

I looked down at it again, studying the cover. "'Just Listen,'" I said.

"Yeah. Don't think, or judge. Just listen."

"And then what?"

"And then," he said, "you can make up your mind. Fair enough, right?"

This did seem fair to me, in fact. Whether it was a song, a person, or a story, there was a lot you couldn't know from just an excerpt, a glance, or part of a chorus. "Yeah," I said, sliding it back to the bottom the stack. "Okay."

"Grace," my father said, glancing at his watch again. "It's time to go."

"Andrew, I know. I'm almost ready." My mother bustled across the kitchen, picking up her purse and putting it over her shoulder. "Now, Annabel, I'm leaving money for pizza tonight, and tomorrow you girls can make whatever you want. I just went shopping, so there's plenty of food. Okay?"

I nodded, as my dad shifted in the doorway.

"Now," my mom said, "what did I do with my keys?"

"You don't need your keys," my father told her. "I'm driving."

"And I'm going to be in Charleston all day tomorrow and

half of Monday while you're in meetings," she replied, putting her purse down again and starting to dig through it. "I might need to get out of the hotel for a while."

My father, who by my count had already been standing in the open door to the garage for a full twenty minutes, leaned against the doorjamb, exhaling loudly. It was Saturday morning, and my parents were supposed to have left for South Carolina for the long weekend, and some big architecture conference, ages ago. "Then you can use mine," he told her, but she ignored him and began taking stuff out of her purse, laying her wallet, a pack of Kleenex, and her cell phone on the counter. "Grace. Come on." She didn't budge.

When my dad had first proposed this trip, he'd pitched it as a great getaway to one of their very favorite cities. When he was in meetings, she could shop and see the sights, and in the evenings, they'd eat at the best restaurants and enjoy some quality time together. It had sounded great to me, but my mother had hesitated, not sure she wanted to leave me and Whitney alone. Especially since Whitney had been in a worse mood than usual since the week before, when she'd started a new therapy group. Against her wishes. With, in her words, a "freak."

"Whitney, please," my mother had said one night at dinner, when the subject first came up. "Dr. Hammond thinks this group could really help you."

"Dr. Hammond is an idiot," Whitney replied. My father shot her a look, but if she saw this, she ignored it. "I know people who have worked with this woman, Mom. She's a nutcase."

"I find that hard to believe," my dad said.

"Believe it. She's not even a real psychiatrist. A lot of the doctors in my program think she's way out there. Her methods are really unorthodox."

"Unorthodox how?" he asked.

"Dr. Hammond," my mom said, and this time, Whitney rolled her eyes at his name, "says that this woman, Moira Bell, has had great success with many of his patients *because* she takes a different approach."

"I'm still not getting what's so different about this woman," my dad said.

"She does a lot of hands-on exercises," my mother told him. "It's not just sitting and talking."

"You want an example?" Whitney put down her fork. "Janet, this girl I know from the hospital? When she was in Moira Bell's group, she had to learn how to make fire."

My mother looked confused. "Make fire?"

"Yeah. Moira gave her two sticks, and her assignment was to rub them together until she made fire. Until she could make fire consistently, every time she did it."

"And what, exactly," my dad said, "was the purpose of this exercise?"

Whitney shrugged, picking up her fork again. "Janet said it was supposed to have something to do with being self-sufficient. She also said Moira Bell was crazy."

"That does sound different," my mother said. She looked worried, like she was picturing Whitney burning the entire house down.

"I'm just saying," Whitney said, "that it's going to be a waste of time."

"Give it a try," my dad told her. "Then make up your mind."

Her mind, though, had clearly already been made up, at least judging by how the rest of the night went—all her typical slamming, sighing, and sulking tacked up a notch. The next day, after attending the group as scheduled, she'd come back in one of the worst moods yet. Now, she'd been back twice, and while she hadn't yet burned down the house, my mother was still nervous. I kind of was as well, since I was the one stuck behind with her.

My dad, though, felt it was time to trust Whitney with more responsibility. She'd never be independent if my mother kept hovering, he said, and they'd only be gone for two days. He'd even called Dr. Hammond, who signed off on the arrangement. Still, my mother wasn't convinced, which was why she was stalling now, going through her purse contents yet again as my father glanced at his watch.

"I just don't understand," she said, opening the purse wider. "I had them last night, and I can't imagine where they've gotten to. . . ."

Just then, I heard the front door shut. A moment later, Whitney came around the corner, wearing yoga pants, a T-shirt, and sneakers, her hair pulled back in a ponytail. In one hand, she was carrying a bag from Home & Garden. In the other, my mother's keys.

"Ah," my father said, walking over to my mom. "Mystery solved." He picked up the purse, pushing everything on the counter back into it. "Let's go. Before we lose anything else."

They went, finally, and I watched from the kitchen table as

they backed up the driveway. The last glimpse I got of my mom, she was turning her head to look back at the house as they drove away.

Once they were gone, I pushed out my chair, standing up, then looked over Whitney, who was messing with whatever she'd bought at Home & Garden, her brow furrowed as she studied the bag's contents. "Well," I said. "I guess it's just the two of us."

"What?" she said, not looking up at me.

All around me, the house felt empty. Quiet. It was going to be a long weekend. "Nothing," I told her. "Never mind."

Luckily, I had other things to do besides be ignored by my sister. Well, one thing.

The Lakeview Mall Fall Fashion Show was the next weekend, and that afternoon, I had to go to a meeting about the rehearsal schedule. When I got to Kopf's, it was in the midst of a typically hectic Saturday, complete with an in-store appearance by a pop singer named Jenny Reef, who was doing a promotion with, of all things, Mooshka Surfwear. The juniors department was packed with girls, a long line snaking all the way back to lingerie while a bouncy pop song played on a constant loop from a nearby boom box.

"Annabel!"

I turned around, and there was Mallory Armstrong. She was smiling big and coming toward me at a fast clip, her progress impeded somewhat by the poster, CD, and camera she was carrying. Following behind her at a more leisurely pace was her mom, whom I recognized from the day I'd dropped Owen at his house. "Hi!" Mallory said. "I can't believe it—are you a Jenny Reef fan, too?"

"Um," I said as another throng of girls rushed past us to get in line, "not really. I had to come in for a meeting. . . ."

"For the Models?"

"Yeah," I said, "actually. We have this fashion show next weekend."

"The Fall Fashion Show. I know! I'm so excited, I'm totally coming," she said. "Can you believe Jenny Reef is, like, here? She signed my poster!"

She unrolled it so I could see. Sure enough, there was Jenny Reef, looking very surferesque and Californian, posing on a beach. There was a guitar stuck in the sand on one side of her, a surfboard on the other. Written beneath it, in black sharpie, it said: TO MALLERY. HANG TEN WITH ME AND MOOSHKA SURFWEAR. LOVE, JENNY.

"Wow," I said as her mom walked up to us. "That's cool."

"And I got a free CD and a picture!" Mallory said, bouncing slightly on the balls of her feet. "I wanted to get a Mooshka T-shirt, too, but . . ."

"But you already have a thousand T-shirts," her mom finished for her. Looking at her, I could see where Owen got his height: She was taller than me, with dark hair pulled back at the neck, and was wearing jeans and a knitted pullover. I took a quick glance at her shoes, noting that they were not pointy, and wondered if they were vegan. "Hi," she said to me. "I'm Teresa Armstrong. And you are?"

"Mom!" Mallory shook her head. "This is Annabel Greene, I can't believe you don't recognize her."

"I'm sorry," Mrs. Armstrong said. "Should I?"

"No," I said.

"*Yes*," Mallory said, turning to her mom. "Annabel's from the Kopf's commercial, the one I'm, like, obsessed with?"

"Ah," her mom said, smiling politely. "Right."

"And she's friends with Owen. *Good* friends."

"Really," Mrs. Armstrong said, sounding surprised. She smiled at me. "Well. That's nice."

"Annabel's in the fashion show I was telling you about next weekend," Mallory explained. To me she said, "Mom isn't very into fashion. But I'm trying to educate her."

"And I," Mrs. Armstrong said with a sigh, "am trying to get Mallory more interested in issues, and less in pop stars and clothes."

"Hard to do," I said.

"Almost impossible." She pushed her purse farther up onto her shoulder. "But I'm doing my best."

"Hello Kopf's shoppers!" a voice suddenly boomed from a speaker overhead. "Thank you for coming out today for our exclusive in-store appearance by Jenny Reef, sponsored by Mooshka Surfwear! Please join us in a few minutes, at one o'clock, when Jenny will perform her newest single, 'Becalmed,' in the Kopf's Café, located adjacent to the men's department. We'll see you there!"

"Did you hear that? She's performing!" Mallory grabbed her mom's hand. "We *have* to stay."

"We can't," Mrs. Armstrong told her. "We have to be at the women's center at one thirty for group."

"Mom," Mallory groaned. "Please not today. Please?"

"We have a mother-daughter discussion group," Mrs. Armstrong explained to me. "Once a week, we get together, six moms and six girls, and discuss issues that are pertinent to our personal growth. The group is led by this wonderful women's studies professor from the university, Boo Connell? It's really—"

"So totally boring," Mallory finished for her. "Last week I fell asleep."

"Which was very unfortunate, because the topic was menstruation," Mrs. Armstrong said. "It's a manifestation of many changes and beginnings for women. . . . The discussion was really fascinating."

Mallory gasped. "Mom! You are not talking about getting your period with Annabel Greene!"

"Menstruation is nothing to be embarrassed about, sweetie," her mom said as Mallory flushed a deeper shade of pink. "I'm sure even models get their periods."

Mallory put a hand to her face. "Oh," she said, "my God." Then she closed her eyes, as if she wanted to disappear, or maybe was pretending she already had.

"I should go," I said, the voice coming over the loudspeaker again. "It was, um, nice to meet you."

"You, too," Mrs. Armstrong said.

I smiled at Mallory, who was still standing there looking mortified. "See you later," I said.

She nodded. "Okay. Bye, Annabel."

I started back toward the conference room. I'd only taken a couple of steps, though, when I heard Mallory hiss, "Mom, I can't believe you did that to me."

"Did what?"

"*Humiliated* me like that," Mallory said. "You owe me an apology."

"Honey," Mrs. Armstrong said, sighing, "I'm really not clear on what the problem is. Maybe if you . . ."

I didn't get to hear the rest, as I was passing through the cosmetics department, where a mob of women were getting makeovers, and their voices drowned everything out. When I reached the conference room, though, I turned back to see Mallory and her mom were still where I'd left them. Mrs. Armstrong had squatted down in front of her daughter and was listening, nodding occasionally, as Mallory spoke.

Inside the conference room, I could hear Mrs. McMurty telling everyone to quiet down, that it was time to get started. Still, I stayed where I was a moment longer, watching as Mrs. Armstrong finally stood and she and Mallory started toward the exit. Mallory didn't look particularly happy, but when, after a few steps, her mom reached down for her fingers, she didn't pull away. Instead, she wrapped her hand around her mom's, quickening her pace, and they walked out the doors together.

When I got home later that afternoon, Whitney was out on the front steps. There was a row of four small flowerpots lined up in front of her, a bag of potting soil beside them, and she was sitting there, a small shovel in one hand, with an annoyed expression on her face.

"Hi," I said as I headed up the walk toward her. "What are you doing?"

She didn't answer me at first, instead just ripping open the potting-soil bag and plunging the shovel in. But then, as I stepped around her, toward the door, she said, "I have to plant herbs."

I stopped walking. "Herbs?"

"Yeah." She scooped some thick soil out of the bag, dropping it into one of the tiny pots with a thunk, some spilling over the sides. "For my stupid therapy group."

"Why herbs?"

"Who knows?" She filled another pot, just as messily, then reached up, wiping her face. "This is what Mom and Dad are paying Moira Bell one fifty an hour for, to tell me to grow some freaking rosemary." She picked up a stack of seed packets from beside her foot, flipping through them. "And basil. And oregano. And thyme. Money well spent, right?"

"It does seem kind of weird," I said.

"Because it *is*," she replied, scooping out more dirt for the third pot. "It's also stupid and a waste of time and not going to work. It's almost winter. You can't grow stuff in winter."

"Did you tell her that?"

"I tried to. But she doesn't care. She doesn't care about anything except making sure she makes you look like an ass." She dumped dirt into the last pot, making it wobble, but it didn't fall over. "'You can grow them inside,' she said, all chirpy. 'Just find a sunny window.' Yeah, right. I'll kill these things in days. And even if I don't, what the hell am I supposed to do with a bunch of herbs?"

I watched as she picked up the basil packet, ripping it open, and dumped out some seeds into her hand. "Well," I said, "you can use them to cook, or something."

She'd been about to plant the seeds, but now she looked up at me, her expression flat, unreadable. "Cook," she repeated. "Right."

I felt my face flush. Again, I'd managed to say something wrong, even when I hadn't really thought I'd said anything at all. Thankfully, the phone began to ring inside, and I headed to get it, grateful for a reason to shut a door between us.

By the time I reached the kitchen, the machine had already picked up. There was a beep, and then Kirsten came on.

"Hello?" she said, her voice loud, as always. "Anybody there? It's me, pick up if you are. . . . God, where is everyone? And I had good news, too. . . ."

I picked up the receiver. "What good news?"

"Annabel! Hi!" Her voice jumped a couple of octaves, a marked contrast to Whitney's flat monotone. I sat down, getting comfortable—if Kirsten's messages were long, actually being on the phone with her could kill an entire afternoon. "I'm so glad you're home, how are you?"

"Okay," I said, sliding my chair a bit to the right. Looking across the dining room, I could see Whitney shaking seeds into a flowerpots, her brow wrinkled as she concentrated. "How are you?"

"Fabulous." Of course she was. "You know that filmmaking class I was telling you about? The one I'm taking this semester?"

"Yeah," I said.

"Well," she continued, "we had to do a five-minute short for our midterm grade, right? They only pick two to be shown for this, like, showcase night that everyone goes to. And mine got picked!"

"That's great," I said. "Congratulations."

"Thank you." She laughed. "I have to tell you, I know it's just this school thing but I am so psyched. This class, and the communications one I'm taking . . . I mean, they've just really changed the way I look at things. Like Brian says, I'm learning to tell, but also to show. And I—"

"Wait," I said. "Who's Brian?"

"The TA in my communications course. He helps the professor run the class, and handles the smaller discussion group I'm in on Fridays. He's amazing, just so smart. God! Anyway, I'm really proud of this piece I did, but now I have to get up and introduce it next weekend in front of everyone. I am so nervous I can't even tell you."

"Nervous?" Of all the adjectives I would have used to describe my sister, this would never have been one of them. "You?"

"Well, yeah," she said. "Annabel, I have to get up and talk about my film in front of total strangers."

"You used to get up and walk in front of strangers," I pointed out. "In bathing suits, even."

"Oh, that's different," she said.

"How?"

"Because that's just . . ." She trailed off, sighing. "This is personal. Real. You know?"

"Yeah," I said, although I wasn't sure I did, really. "I guess."

"Anyway, it's a week from today. So you'll have to think good thoughts for me. Okay?"

"Sure," I said. "So . . . what's it about?"

"My short?"

"Yeah."

"Oh. Well, it's kind of hard to explain. . . ." she said before, of course, commencing to do just that. "Basically, though, it's about me. And Whitney."

I looked outside again at Whitney, who was ripping open another seed packet, wondering how she'd react to this. "Really," I said.

"I mean, it's a fictional thing, of course," she said. "But it's based on that time when we were kids, out on our bikes, and she broke her arm. Remember? I had to ride her home on my handlebars?"

I thought for a second. "Yeah," I said. "Wasn't that . . . "

"Your birthday," she said. "Your ninth birthday. Dad missed the party to take her to the hospital. She got back with her cast just in time for cake."

"Right." It was coming back to me. "I do remember that, actually."

"Well, it's basically about that. But different. It's hard to explain. I can e-mail it to you, if you want. I mean, I'm still tinkering with it, but you could get the general idea."

"I'd love to see it," I said.

"You'll have to tell me if it's terrible, though."

"I'm sure it isn't."

"I guess I'll find out on Saturday." She sighed. "Anyway,

look, I better go. I just wanted to tell you guys about it. Everything okay there?"

I looked out at Whitney again. She'd put another layer of soil into the pots and had now picked up a hose to water them, her eyes narrowed as the drops sputtered out. "Yeah," I said. "Everything's fine."

As I hung up the phone, I heard the front door open. A moment later, when I crossed through the foyer, Whitney was lining her flowerpots up in the dining-room window. I stood in the archway, watching her arrange them on the sill in a neat row, brushing off their rims with her fingers. When she was done, she stood up, planting her hands on her hips. "Oh, well," she said. "Here goes nothing."

"Or not," I said.

She glanced over at me, and I wondered if she was going to snap at me or make a typically sarcastic remark. "We'll see," she said, then dropped her hands and started toward the kitchen.

As she turned on the faucet and began washing her hands, I walked over to the window to look at the flowerpots. The dirt in them was black and fragrant, spotted with fertilizer, and I could see beads of water here and there, glinting in the sunlight. Maybe it was a stupid exercise, and you couldn't grow things in winter. But there was something I liked about the idea of those seeds, buried so deep, having at least a chance to emerge. Even if you couldn't see it beneath the surface, molecules were bonding, energy pushing up slowly, as something worked so hard, all alone, to grow.

Chapter
TEN

By that afternoon, my mother had already left two messages: one letting us know they'd arrived at their hotel, and the other reminding me where she'd left the pizza money, a subtle hint to make sure that we (i.e., Whitney) ate dinner. *Message received*, I thought as I walked down to the kitchen. The money was on the counter with a list of several places that delivered. My mother was nothing if not prepared.

"Whitney?" I called up the stairs. No answer. Which didn't mean she wasn't there, just that she probably didn't feel like responding. "I'm ordering the pizza. Is cheese okay?"

Another silence. *Fine*, I thought. *Cheese it is.* I picked a number at random and dialed.

After ordering, I headed up to my room and settled in to listen to the discs Owen had made me, beginning with one entitled PROTEST SONGS (ACOUSTIC AND WORLD). I made it through three tracks about unions before nodding off, only to wake up with a start when I heard the doorbell ring.

I sat up just as Whitney passed my room and padded down the stairs to answer it. After brushing my teeth, I followed her.

When I got to the foyer, she was standing at the door, which was open, blocking my view of both her and whoever was on the other side. Still, I could hear their voices.

". . . not so much their newer stuff, but the earlier albums," she was saying. "I have a couple of imports I got from a friend that are awesome."

"Really," another, deeper voice—a guy—replied. "UK imports, or somewhere else?"

"UK, I think. I'd have to check."

Maybe it was because I'd just woken up, but there was something familiar about some part of this scene, although I couldn't put my finger on exactly what it was.

"What do I owe you again?" Whitney asked.

"Eleven eighty-seven," the guy replied.

"Here's a twenty. Just give me five back."

"Thanks." I took another step. Now, I was sure I knew that voice. "The thing about Ebb Tide," it continued, "is that they're really an acquired taste."

"Totally," Whitney said.

"I mean, most people don't even . . ."

I stepped around the door, and sure enough, it was Owen. Standing there on the mat in front of my door, earphones dangling around his neck, counting out dollar bills into my sister's hand She was nodding as he spoke and looking at him with a much warmer expression than she'd given me in, oh, a year. When he saw me, he smiled.

"See," he said to Whitney, "case in point. Annabel is *not* an Ebb Tide fan. She hates techno, in fact."

Whitney looked at me, then back at Owen again, clearly confused. "She does?"

"Yup. Despite my best efforts to convince her otherwise," he said. "She's very stubborn, once she's made up her mind. Totally honest, totally opinionated. But I guess you already know that."

Whitney just looked at me as he said this, and I knew what she was thinking: that this was not me at all, not by a long shot. It didn't sound exactly right to me either, but for some reason, her incredulousness bothered me.

"Anyway," he said now, bending down to the plastic carrier at his feet and unzipping it to pull out a pizza box. "Here you go. Enjoy it."

Whitney nodded, still looking at me, and took it from him. "Thanks," she said. "Have a good night."

"You, too," Owen replied as Whitney turned, walking into the dining room toward the kitchen.

I stepped into the center of the open doorway, watching Owen as he shoved the wad of money in his hand into his pocket, then picked up the carrier. He had on jeans and a red T-shirt that said SLICE O'CHEESE! Of all the numbers for pizza places my mom left me, I'd called this one. Who knew? But I had to admit, I was happy to see him.

"Your sister," he said to me now, "is an Ebb Tide fan. She has *imports*."

"And that's good?"

"*Very* good," he replied. "It's almost enlightened. Imports take effort."

"Do you talk about music with every single person you meet?"

"No," he said. I just looked at him. Behind me, I heard Whitney cut on the TV.

"Well, not always. In this case, I had on my earphones, and she asked me what I was listening to."

"And it just so happened to be a band she knows and loves."

"That's the universality of music," he said cheerfully, switching the carrier to his other arm. "It's a bonding thing. It brings people together. Friend and foe. Old and young. Me and your sister. And—"

"Me and your sister," I finished for him. "And your mom."

"My mom?" he asked.

"I met her today, at the mall. At the Jenny Reef thing."

His face fell. "You went to see *Jenny Reef*?"

"I *love* Jenny Reef," I said, and he winced. "She's much better than Ebb Tide."

"That," he said, his voice serious, "is not *even* funny."

"What's wrong with Jenny Reef?" I said.

"Everything is wrong with Jenny Reef!" he shot back. *Here we go*, I thought. "Did you even *see* the poster she signed for Mallory? With the product plug in her autograph? I mean, it's so abhorrent that anyone could consider themselves an artist and then sell out so completely to the corporate machine, in the name of—"

"Okay, okay, calm down," I said, figuring I should fess up before he popped a vein. "I didn't go to see Jenny Reef. I had a meeting for the Models at Kopf's."

He sighed, shaking his head. "Thank God. You had me worried there for a second."

"What happened to there being no right and wrong in music?" I asked him. "Or does that not apply to teenage pop stars?"

"It applies," he said flatly. "You're entitled to an opinion about Jenny Reef. It would just dismay me if you were really a fan."

"But have you really given her a chance? Remember," I said, holding up my hand, "don't think or judge. Just listen."

He made a face at me. "I *have* listened to Jenny Reef. Not necessarily by choice, but I have. And my opinion is that she's a publicity whore who has allowed her music, if that's even what you want to call it, to be hijacked and compromised in the name of materialism and big business."

"Well," I said. "As long you don't feel too strongly about it."

Suddenly I heard a low buzz, and he reached around to his back pocket, pulling out a cell phone, glancing at the screen. "Pie up, gotta go," he said, stuffing the carrier under his arm. "You know, as much as you might want me to, I can't just stand here and argue with you about music all night."

"No?" I said.

"No." He stepped back from the door. "However, if you want to continue this discussion some other time, I'd be more than happy to do so."

"Like Tuesday?"

"Sounds good." He started down the steps. "I'll see you then, okay?"

I nodded. "Bye, Owen."

"And don't forget the show tomorrow!" he called out over his shoulder as he headed for his truck. "We're doing all techno. A full hour of dripping faucets."

"Are you joking?"

"Maybe. You'll have to listen to find out, though."

I smiled, then stood there, watching him as he climbed inside the Land Cruiser. He turned the stereo on first, then put the car in gear. Of course.

When I got to the living room, Whitney was settled on the couch, drinking a bottled water. The pizza was on the counter. She didn't say anything, her eyes on the TV—which was showing something about a sitcom actress who'd had a cocaine problem—as I helped myself to a plate and a slice and sat down at the table in the kitchen.

"Are you . . ." I began, then stopped myself. "Aren't you hungry?"

She kept her eyes on the TV as she said, "I'll eat in a minute."

Fine, I thought. My mother wouldn't be happy, but then again she wasn't here. And I was starving. As I began to take a bite, though, Whitney muted the TV and said, "So how do you know that guy?"

"He goes to my school," I said, then swallowed. She was watching me, so I added, "We're friends."

"Friends," she repeated.

I thought of Mrs. Armstrong's surprised smile as she reacted to this same word, hours earlier. "Yeah," I said. "We sometimes hang out at lunch."

She nodded. "Is he friends with Sophie, too?"

"No," I said. I didn't know why, but instantly, my guard was up, and I wondered why she was asking this. Or, actually, why we were even talking at all, when she'd been the one who'd been so resistant to my attempts at conversation all day long. But then I remembered her face when Owen had described me as honest, how clear it was this surprised her, so I added, "I'm not really friends with Sophie these days."

"You're not?"

"No."

"What happened?"

Why do you care? I wanted to ask. Instead, I said, "We had a fight last spring. It got kind of ugly. . . . We don't really talk."

"Oh," she said.

I looked back down at my plate, wondering why I had suddenly decided to share this with Whitney, of all people. It seemed like a mistake, and I sat there, waiting for her to say something snarky or mean, but she didn't. Instead, she just turned back to the TV, and a moment later, I heard the volume come on.

On the screen, the actress was now telling her story, dabbing her eyes with a Kleenex as she did so. I looked from her to Whitney, who was sitting in my father's chair. Who knew she was an Ebb Tide fan, that she had imports, that she was possibly, in Owen's view anyway, enlightened? On the other hand, though, it wasn't like she knew that much about me, either. Maybe we could have remedied this over a long weekend, but we weren't. Instead, we just sat there, together but really apart, watching a show about a stranger and all her secrets, while keeping our own to ourselves, as always.

The next morning, Owen kicked off his show with a techno song that went on, no joke, for a full eight and a half minutes. All of which I spent telling myself that I was fully entitled to go back to sleep, and yet somehow not able to do so.

"That was Prickle with 'Velveteen,'" he said, when it was finally over. "Off of their second disc, *The Burning*, which is probably one of the best techno records ever released. Hard to believe some people don't even like that kind of music, isn't it? You're listening to Anger Management. Got a request? Call us at 555–WRUS. Here's Snakeplant."

I rolled my eyes, but didn't roll over. Instead, I listened to the entire show, as was my habit now, while Owen played some rockabilly, some Gregorian chants, and a song in Spanish he described as "like Astrid Gilberto, and yet not." Whatever that meant. Finally, in the last few moments before eight o'clock, I heard the beginning of notes of a song that sounded familiar. Although why I wasn't sure until he came on again.

"This has been Anger Management, here on your community radio station, WRUS, 89.9. We'll wrap up today with a long-distance dedication to a regular listener, to whom we say: Look, don't be ashamed of the music you love. Even if, in our humble opinion, it's not really music at all. We know why you really went to the mall yesterday. See you next week!"

Only then did it hit me: It was the Jenny Reef song, the one they'd been playing nonstop at the mall the day before. As it began, I sat up, grabbing for my phone.

"WRUS, Community Radio."

"I did not go to the mall to see Jenny Reef," I said. "I told you that yesterday."

"Are you not enjoying the song?"

"Actually," I said, "I am. It's better than just about everything else you played."

"Funny."

"I'm not joking."

"I'm sure you aren't," he said. "Which, frankly, is just plain sad."

"Almost as sad as you playing Jenny Reef on your show. What is this, all the hits with none of the lip?"

"It was meant to be ironic!"

I smiled, reaching up to tuck a piece of hair behind my ear. "Just keep telling yourself that."

He sighed loudly, the noise filling the receiver. "Enough about Jenny Reef. Answer me this. How do you feel about bacon?"

"Bacon?" I repeated. "Which song was that?"

"It's not a song. It's a food. You know, bacon? Pork product? Sizzles in a frying pan?"

I actually pulled the phone away from my ear, looked at it, then put it back.

"What do you say? You up for it?" he was saying.

"Up for what?" I asked.

"Breakfast."

"Now?" I said, glancing at the clock.

"What, you have plans already?"

"Well, no, but—"

"Cool. Pick you up in twenty minutes."

And then he just hung up. I put the phone back on its base, then turned, looking at myself in the mirror over my bureau. *Twenty minutes*, I thought. *Okay.*

In nineteen and a half, I'd managed to shower, throw on some clothes, and get out to my front stoop, where I was waiting when Owen pulled into the driveway. Whitney was still asleep, allowing me to forgo an explanation, which was handy since I didn't exactly have one. As I walked over to the car, Rolly, who was in the front passenger seat, pushed open his door and got out, leaving it open for me.

"You remember Rolly, right?" Owen said.

"Yeah," I said, as he nodded at me. "But you don't have to move. I can sit in back."

"It's no problem," he told me, climbing into the backseat. "Besides, I have to make sure I have all my gear for later."

"Gear?" I said as I got in, shutting the door behind me. Owen gestured for me to put on my seat belt, which I did, letting him work the hammer to get it buckled.

"For work. I've got to do a class today," Rolly explained. As I turned around, I saw he was holding the same red helmet he'd been wearing the first time I saw him. Also on the seat were several pads of all sizes: a large one that looked like something an umpire would wear, several that were tube-shaped, and some thick gloves. "It's an intermediate level. Gotta make sure I'm well covered."

"Right," I said as Owen shifted into reverse, backing out of my driveway. "So, how do you end up with a job like that?"

"Same way as most," he replied, putting the pad down. "I

answered an ad. Initially, I was just helping out answering phones and enrolling people for classes. But then one guy got a groin injury and quit, so I got promoted to attacker."

"Or demoted," Owen said. "Depending on how you look at it."

"Oh, no," Rolly told him, shaking his head. He had a really sweet face, I was noticing. Where Owen was big and broad, more the attacker style, Rolly was smaller and wiry, with bright blue eyes. "Attacking is *much* better than clerical work."

"It is?" I asked.

"Sure. I mean, for one, it's exciting," he said. "And another, you really get to meet people on such a personal level. There's a real bonding in someone beating the crap out of you."

I glanced over at Owen, who was switching gears with one hand and adjusting the stereo with the other. "You can look at me all you want," he said, keeping his eyes on the road. "I am not commenting on that."

"Fighting brings people together," Rolly said. "In fact, a lot of the women who take my classes come up and hug me afterwards. People connect with me. It's happened tons of times."

"But only once," Owen added, "that really mattered."

Rolly sighed. "True," he said. "Very true."

"Meaning what?" I asked.

"Rolly's in love with a girl who punched him in the face," Owen explained.

"Not the face," Rolly corrected him. "The neck."

"Apparently," Owen told me, "she has a mad right hook."

"It was impressive," Rolly agreed. "It was at this expo I worked, at the mall? We had a table, you know, and people could enter a drawing for a free class, and take a hit at me, for fun."

Owen put on his turn signal, shaking his head.

"Anyway," Rolly continued, "she comes up with some friends, and Delores—that's my boss—starts her spiel about the classes and invites them to hit me. Her friends won't do it, but she steps right up. Looks me in the eye. And wham! Right in the collarbone."

"You had your pads on, though, right?" I said.

"Of course!" he said. "I'm a professional. But still, even through the pads, you can tell when someone packs a wallop. And this girl did. Plus, she was gorgeous. Lethal combination. But before I can even say anything, she just smiles at me, says thanks, and walks away. Gone. Just like that. I never even got her name."

We were merging onto the highway now, picking up speed. "Wow," I said. "That is quite a story."

"Yeah," he said, nodding, his expression solemn. He put his hands on top of the helmet in his lap, folding them carefully. "I know."

Owen rolled down his window, letting some air in. Then he took in a deep breath. "Oh, yeah," he said. "We're almost there."

I turned around; all I could see was highway. "Where?"

"Two words," Owen said. "Double bacon."

Five minutes later, we were pulling into the parking lot of the World of Waffles, a twenty-four-hour breakfast place right off the interstate. *So they like breakfast*, I thought. Then the breeze shifted, and suddenly I smelled it: bacon. The scent was pungent, heavy, and inescapable.

"Oh my God," I said as we headed inside. Owen and Rolly were taking deep, full breaths on either side of me. "That is—"

"Great, I know," Owen said. "It didn't used to be like this. I mean, they had bacon, but not at this level. But then this new place opened up on the other side of the highway—"

"The Morning Café," Rolly said, wrinkling his nose. "So subpar. Famously soggy pancakes."

"—and they had to get competitive. So now, every day is Double Bacon Day." He stepped up, pulling the door open for me. "Great, right?"

I nodded, then stepped inside. The first thing I noticed was that the smell was stronger, if that was even possible. The second was that the room, which was small and crammed with tables and booths, was freezing.

"Oh," Owen said once he glanced over and saw I had my arms wrapped around myself. "Forgot to warn you about the cold thing. Here." He shrugged off the jacket he was wearing, handing it to me. I started to protest, but he said, "They keep it cold so people don't stay too long. Believe me, if you're chilly now, you'll be frozen in ten minutes. Take it."

I did, then slipped it on. Of course it was huge on me, the cuffs completely covering my hands. I pulled it tighter around me as we followed a tall, slim waitress whose name tag said DEANN to a booth by the window. Behind us, a woman was quietly nursing a baby, her head ducked down. On our other side, there was a couple about our age eating waffles, both in running clothes: The girl had blonde hair and an elastic around her wrist, while the guy was taller and darker, the bottom part of a tattoo just visible under his shirtsleeve.

"I recommend the chocolate-chip pancakes," Rolly told me after Deann had brought coffee and left us to examine the menu. "With lots of butter and syrup. And bacon."

"Ugh," Owen said. "I keep it basic: eggs, bacon, biscuit. Done."

Pork seemed to be required, so when Deann returned I ordered a waffle and, yes, bacon. Although I wasn't sure I needed it; I felt like I'd already eaten an entire side just by breathing.

"So you guys do this every week," I said, taking a sip of my water.

"Yeah." Owen nodded. "Since the first show. It's a tradition. And Rolly always pays."

"That's not tradition," Rolly said. "It's because I lost a bet."

"How long do you have to pay?"

"Forever," Rolly told me. "I had my chance, and I blew it. And now I pay. Literally."

"It's not really forever," Owen said now, tapping his spoon against his water glass. "Just until you talk to her."

"And when is that going to happen?" Rolly asked.

"The next time you see her."

"Yeah," he said glumly. "The next time."

I looked at Owen. "The girl with the hook," he explained. "In July, we saw her out at a club. First time we ever saw her anywhere. And Rolly'd been talking about her nonstop since she clocked him—"

Rolly flushed. "Not *nonstop*."

"—and here's his chance," Owen finished. "But he can't act."

"The thing is," Rolly said, "I'm a big believer in the perfect moment. They don't come around that often."

This deep thought was punctuated—or interrupted, depending on how you looked at it—by Deann arriving with our food. I had never seen so much bacon in my life; it was crammed around the edge of the waffle, literally falling off my plate.

"So there I am," Rolly said, beginning to butter his pancakes, "trying to figure out an in, and her sweater falls off the back of her chair. It's like it's meant to be, you know? But I freeze up. I can't do it."

Beside me, Owen had already popped a piece of bacon in his mouth and was chewing it while peppering his eggs.

"The thing is," Rolly said, "it's a big deal when you finally get the chance to do the one thing you want to do—need to do—more than anything. It can kind of scare the crap out of you."

He pushed the syrup over to me, and I picked it up, putting some on my waffle. "I bet," I said.

"Which is why," Owen said, "I said that if he picked up the sweater and talked to her, I'd pay for breakfast forever. And if he *didn't* do it, he had to foot the bill."

Rolly took another bite of his pancakes. "I actually got up and started over there. But then she turned around, and I—"

"Choked," Owen said.

"Panicked. She saw me, and I got all flustered, and I kept walking. Now I have to pay for breakfast for eternity. Or, until I actually make good on the bet, which is unlikely because I haven't seen her since."

"Wow," I said. "That's quite a story."

He nodded somberly, just as he had earlier in the car. "Yeah," he said. "I know."

By the time we left an hour later, all the bacon was gone and I was so full I thought I would bust. Back in the car I reached for my seat belt, pulling it across me, then stopped just short of the buckle as Owen slid it in for me, then grabbed the hammer again. His hands were right at my waist as he tapped its center, his head ducked down by my shoulder. I looked at his dark hair, the sprinkle of freckles by his ear, those long lashes, but then he was already done, pulling away.

All the way into town, I watched Rolly in the side mirror as he put on his padding for work: first the big chest piece, then the tubes on his arms and legs, gradually growing more substantial and less recognizable in front of my eyes. He put on the helmet just as we pulled up to the strip mall where EmPOWerment! was located.

"Thanks for the ride," he said, opening the door and easing himself down to the ground. The padding on his legs was so thick he had to take short, halting steps, his arms held out to his sides. "I'll call you later."

"Sounds good," Owen told him.

As we drove home, the scenery blurring past, I thought back to that first day, and how strange it had been to find myself with him. Now it was almost normal. Outside, the neighborhood was quiet, a few sprinklers going, a man in his robe padding out down the driveway to pick up his paper, and I found myself remembering what Rolly had said earlier about the perfect moment. This seemed like one, suddenly, the right time to say something to Owen. To thank him, maybe, or just to let him know how much his friendship had meant to me in the last couple of weeks. But just as I was getting up the nerve to say something, he beat me to it.

"So. Have you listened to any of the CDs I burned for you?"

"Yeah," I said as we turned onto my street. "I actually started the protest song one yesterday."

"And?"

"Fell asleep," I told him. He winced. "But I was really tired. I'll try it again and let you know."

"No rush," he said, pulling up in front of my house. "These things take time."

"No kidding. You gave me a lot to listen to."

"Ten CDs," he replied, "is not a lot. It's barely a smattering."

"Owen. It's, like, a hundred and forty songs. Minimum."

"If you want a real education," he continued, ignoring this, "you can't just sit and wait for the music to come to you. You have to go to the music."

"Are you suggesting some sort of pilgrimage?"

I was joking. Judging by the serious look on his face, however, he was not. "You could call it that," he said.

"Uh-oh," I said, sitting back in my seat. "What would *you* call it?"

"Going to a club to see a band," he replied. "A good band. Live. Next weekend."

The first thing that popped into my mind was a question: *Are you asking me out?* The second, following rapidly behind, was that if I actually asked it, he'd answer in full truth, and I was not sure I wanted that. If he said yes, it would be . . . what? Great. And terrifying. If he said no, I'd feel like an idiot.

"A good band," I repeated instead. "Good according to who?"

"To me, of course."

"Oh."

He raised an eyebrow. "And to *others*, too," he said. "It's Rolly's cousin's band."

"Are they—"

"No. Not techno," he answered flatly. "They're more kind of a loose rock, original songs, somewhat jokey but solidly alternative."

"Wow," I said. "That's quite a description."

"The description means nothing. It's the music that counts," he said. "And the music, you will like. Trust me."

"We'll see," I said, and he smiled. "So when is this loose-rock-original-songs-somewhat-jokey-but-solidly-alternative band playing?"

"Saturday night," he replied. "It's an all-ages show, at Bendo. There's an opener, so they'll go on around nine."

"Okay."

"Okay, as in you'll go?"

"Yeah."

"Cool."

I smiled as, behind him in my house, I saw Whitney appear at the top of the stairs. She had on her pajamas and was yawning, one hand to her mouth, as she started down to the foyer, her shadow stretching across the wall beside her. Once at the bottom of the stairs, she crossed into the dining room, then bent down over her flowerpots in the front window. After a moment, she reached out, pressing down the soil in one of them, then turned another so the opposite side faced the light. Then she sat back on her heels, her hands in her lap, and studied them.

I glanced at Owen, who was watching her as well, and wondered what this looked like to him. From the outside, it had to seem so different from what it really was. Move on to the next house and you'd see something else, another glimpse, another story. This one wasn't even mine to tell, but for whatever reason, I found myself wanting to do it anyway.

"They're herbs," I said to Owen. "She just planted them yesterday. They're, um, part of her therapy."

He nodded. "You said she was sick. What's wrong? If you don't mind my asking."

"She has an eating disorder," I told him.

"Oh."

"She's a lot better than she was," I added. And this was true. In fact, I'd watched her eat two pieces of pizza the night before. Much later than I ate, and only after blotting off any semblance of grease, and then cutting them into many small pieces. But she did eat them, so that had to count for something. "I mean, when we first found out, it was really bad. She was in the hospital for a while last year."

We both watched as Whitney stood up, brushing a piece of hair out of her face. I wondered if she suddenly looked different to Owen, as if knowing this information had changed her to him. I studied his expression, but there was no way to tell.

"That must have been hard," he said, as she turned, starting around the dining-room table. "Watching her go through that."

As Whitney stepped through the archway to the kitchen, she disappeared. A second later, I spotted her again, crossing in front of the island. That was the thing I always forgot about being outside our house, how it seemed like you could see everything, but certain things were blocked out, hidden. "Yeah," I said. "It was. It was awful. It really scared me."

This time, I didn't think about the fact that I was telling the truth. I didn't have that moment when I felt myself take the leap, daring to be honest. Instead, it just happened. Owen turned and looked at me, and I swallowed, hard. Then, as I so often found myself doing when I had his attention, I continued.

"The thing about Whitney," I said, "is that she was always really private. So you never knew if anything was wrong with her. My sister Kirsten, she's the total opposite, the kind of person who always volunteers *too* much information. So, like, when Kirsten was unhappy, you knew it even if you didn't want to. Whereas with Whitney, you had to draw it out of her. Or figure it out some other way."

Owen looked back at the house, but Whitney had disappeared again. "What about you?" he said.

"What about me?"

"How can they tell when something's wrong with you?"

They can't, I thought, but I didn't say this. Couldn't say this. "I don't know," I said. "I guess you'd have to ask them."

A big SUV blew past us then, kicking up a bunch of leaves that had been raked to the curb. As they fluttered across the windshield, I glanced back over at my house to see Whitney climbing the stairs again, a bottled water in her hand. This time, she glanced outside. When she saw us, she slowed her steps, briefly, before continuing on to the landing.

"I should go in," I said, reaching down to undo my seat belt. "Thanks again for breakfast."

"No problem," Owen said. "Don't forget about the pilgrimage, okay? Saturday. Nine o'clock."

"Got it." I opened my door, sliding out, then shut it behind me. As I walked around the front bumper, he cranked the engine, then waved at me. It wasn't until I got halfway down the driveway that I realized I was still wearing his jacket. I whirled around, only to see him taking the corner, a blue blur, disappearing. Too late.

I unlocked the front door, stepping inside, then slid the jacket off, folding it over my arm. There was something clunky in the outside pocket, and I reached in, my fingers groping until they brushed a solid object. Even before I pulled it out, I knew what it was: Owen's iPod. It was nicked and scratched beyond all belief, a faint crack across the screen, his earphones wrapped around it. And despite the cold of the World of Waffles, it was warm in my hand.

"Annabel?"

I jumped, then looked up; Whitney was at the top of the stairs, staring down at me. "Hi," I said.

"You're up early."

"Yeah," I said. "I, um, went out for breakfast."

She narrowed her eyes at me. "When did you leave?"

"A while back," I said, starting up the stairs. As I got to the landing, she stepped aside, just barely, so I had to squeeze past her. I heard her sniff once. Then twice. *Bacon*, I thought.

"I better go start on my homework," I said, heading toward my room.

"Okay," she said slowly. But she stayed where she was, still watching, as I shut my door behind me.

Because I had never once seen Owen without his iPod, I assumed he would notice its absence pretty quickly. So when the phone rang later that afternoon, I picked it up expecting to hear him already in deep music withdrawal. But it wasn't Owen; it was my mother.

"Annabel! Hi!"

When my mother was nervous, her cheerfulness quotient skyrocketed. The line was almost crackling from her forced perkiness. "Hi," I said. "How's your trip going?"

"Just fine," she said. "Right now your father's playing golf, and I just got my nails done. We've been so busy, but I figured I should check in. How are things going?"

This was actually her third call in thirty-six hours. But I played along anyway.

"Good," I said. "Not much is happening."

"How's Whitney?"

"Fine."

"Is she there now?"

"I don't know," I said. I sat up, then got off the bed, walking to my door and opening it. "I can check—"

"Did she go out?" she asked.

"I'm not sure," I said. *God*, I thought. "Hold on." I stepped out into the hallway, then put the phone to my chest, listening for a second. I didn't hear the TV, or any noise from downstairs, so instead I walked a few paces to Whitney's door, which was closed, but not entirely. I knocked, lightly.

"Yeah?"

When I pushed it open, she was sitting on her bed, cross-legged, writing in a notebook in her lap. "Mom's on the phone," I said.

She sighed, then reached out her hand, palm up, and I stepped over, giving her the receiver. "Hello? . . . Hi. . . . Yes, I'm here. . . . I'm fine. . . . Everything's fine. You don't have to keep calling, you know."

Then my mother said something, and Whitney sat back against her headboard. As she listened, offering up a series of mmm-mhms and uh-huhs, I glanced out her window. Even though our rooms were adjacent, her view of the golf course, where a man in checked pants was now taking a practice swing, looked totally different to me, like it might have been another place altogether.

"Yeah, okay," she was saying now, reaching up to smooth a hand over her hair. Looking at her, I thought again how beautiful she was—even in jeans and a T-shirt, no makeup, she was breathtaking. So much so that it was hard to believe she could ever have looked at herself and seen anything else. "I'll tell her. . . . Okay. . . . Bye."

She dropped the phone from her ear, hitting the OFF button. "Mom says she'll see you tomorrow," she said. "They'll be back by dinnertime."

"Oh," I said as she handed the receiver back to me. "Right."

"And we can either eat spaghetti for dinner tonight or go

out." She sat back, pulling her legs up to her chest, then looked at me. "What do you want to do?"

I hesitated, wondering if this was a trick question. "I don't care," I said. "Spaghetti is fine."

"All right. I'll fix it in a little while."

"Okay. I can help, if you want."

"Whatever," she said. "We'll figure it out later." She leaned forward, picking up a pen from beside her foot and uncapping it. I could see now that the top page of the notebook in her lap was filled with her print, and I wondered what she was writing. After a moment, she looked up at me. "What?"

"Nothing," I said, realizing I was still standing there, staring at her. "I'll, um, see you in a bit."

I went back to my room and sat down on my bed, picking up Owen's iPod. It seemed strange, and maybe kind of wrong, to have it here in my room, not to mention in my hands. Still, I found myself unwrapping the earphones, then hitting the power button. After a second, the screen blinked to life. When the menu appeared, I clicked on SONGS.

There were 9,987 to choose from. *Good God*, I thought, as I scrolled down through the list for a minute, titles blurring past. I remembered what he'd said about drowning things out. It was what he'd done during the divorce, but also every day, I realized, when he walked around with his earphones on. Ten thousand songs could fill a lot of silence.

I clicked back to the menu, then scrolled to PLAYLISTS. Another long list popped up: A.M. SHOW 8/12, A.M. SHOW 8/19, CHANTS (IMPORTED). And then: ANNABEL.

I lifted my finger off the button. It was probably just one of the CDs he'd made for me, I thought. But still, I found myself hesitating, the same way I had earlier in the truck. Wanting to know, but not. This time, though, I broke.

When I clicked on the button, the screen changed, pulling up a list of songs. The first one was "Jennifer" by a band called Lipo. Which sounded slightly familiar. As was "Descartes Dream," by Misanthrope, the second song, which I went ahead and clicked on. It only took a moment to recognize it as one of the songs from the first show of Owen's I'd listened to. Not liked, but listened to. And discussed with him afterwards.

They were all there. Every song we'd ever talked or argued about, listed in careful order. The Mayan chants, from the first day he'd given me the ride. "Thank You," by Led Zeppelin, from when I'd picked him up. Entirely too much techno, every thrash metal song. Even Jenny Reef. As I listened to a bit of each, I thought of all the times I'd seen Owen with his earphones on and wondered what he was listening to, much less thinking about. Who would have ever guessed that it might have been me?

I glanced over at the clock—it was 4:55. Owen had to be missing this by now. No big deal. I'd just drive over to his house and drop it off. Easy.

Halfway down the stairs, though, I heard a crash, followed by a muttered "shit." When I poked my head into the kitchen, Whitney was shoving a saucepan back into the cupboard.

"Everything okay?" I asked.

"Fine." She stood up, brushing her hair out of her face. On the island in front of her, there was a jar of pasta sauce, a box of spaghetti, a cutting board with a red pepper and a cucumber on it, and a bag of lettuce. "Are you going out or something?"

"Um," I said. "I was . . . just for a little while. Unless you want me to—"

"No, I'm fine." She picked up a box of spaghetti, her eyes narrowing as she read the back of it.

"Oh. Okay," I said. "Well, I'll be back by—"

"It's just . . ." She put the box down. "I'm not sure which pot I'm supposed to use for pasta."

I put Owen's coat down on the table, then crossed the room to the cabinet next to the stove. "This one," I told her, pulling out the large stock pan and the strainer pot that fit inside of it. "It's easier to drain that way."

"Oh," she said. "Right. Sure."

I carried it to the sink, filling it up with water, and put it on the stove. I could feel her watching me as I turned on the burner. "It'll take a while," I told her. "If you cover it, it cuts down the time some."

She nodded. "Okay."

I walked back over to the chair where I'd left Owen's coat, then stood there, watching, as she took a smaller pot out of the cabinet and put it on the stove. Then she picked up the pasta sauce, popping off the top and dumping it in. All of this she did very slowly and deliberately, as if she were splitting atoms. Which wasn't really all that surprising, as Whitney hardly ever cooked for herself. My mother monitored all her meals, fixed her snacks and sandwiches, even the cereal she ate for breakfast. I realized that if this was weird for me to watch, it had to be really strange for her to do. Especially alone.

"Do you want me to help?" I asked her as she pulled a spoon out of the drawer by the stove and stuck it into the pasta sauce, stirring it tentatively. "I don't mind."

For a minute, she didn't say anything, and I wondered if I'd offended her. But then, not turning around, she said, "Sure. I mean, if you want to."

So that night, for the first time I could remember, I fixed dinner with my sister. We didn't talk much, other than her asking me the occasional question (what temperature to put the oven on for garlic bread, or how much spaghetti to make) and me answering (350, all of it). I set the table while she tackled the salad in her typically slow and methodical way, cutting up the vegetables so carefully and grouping them by color on the cutting board. Once everything was done, Whitney and I sat down together in the dining room, just the two of us. As I slid into my seat, I glanced over at her flowerpots in the windowsill.

"They look good there," I said as she sat down.

"I guess," she replied, picking up her napkin. Her plate was mostly salad, with only a tiny bit of pasta, but I didn't say anything, if only because I knew my mom would have. "Now they just have to actually grow."

I twirled some spaghetti around my fork, then took a bite. "This is good," I told her. "Perfect."

"It's pasta," she said with a shrug. "It's easy."

"Not always," I told her. "If you don't cook it enough, it's crunchy in the middle. And if you cook it too much, it's mushy. It's a fine line."

"Really," she said.

I nodded. For a moment, we were both quiet, just eating. I looked over at the pots again, the golf course beyond, so green it was almost unreal.

"Thank you," Whitney said.

I wasn't sure if this was for the cooking compliment, or the salad, or just sticking around. I didn't care, either. I was just happy to take it, for whatever it was.

"You're welcome," I said, and she nodded, as outside, a car drove past, then slowed, the driver glancing in at us before moving on.

Chapter
ELEVEN

"It's Annabel!"

I had not even taken my finger off Owen's doorbell, but somehow Mallory was already on the other side. Then the knob rattled and the door swung open.

At first, I almost didn't recognize her, as she was wearing an incredible amount of makeup: base, eyeliner and shadow, way too much rouge, and fake eyelashes, one of which was unpasted and sticking to her eyebrow. She also had on a tight, strapless black dress and very high-heeled sandals, on which she was teetering as she gripped the doorknob.

Grouped around her, all staring at me, were four other girls, also dressed and made up: a short, dark-haired girl with glasses, wearing a black dress and wedge heels; two identical redheads with green eyes and freckles, each in jeans and high-cut crop-tops; and a chubby blonde in what looked like a prom dress. In the small space of the doorframe, the smell of hairspray was overpowering.

"Annabel!" Mallory shrieked, jumping up and down. Her hair, done up high above her head in some sort of faux-Mohawk, did not move. "Hi!"

"Hi," I said. "What are you—"

Before I could finish, she reached out, grabbing my hand and yanking me over the threshold. "You guys," she said as the other girls stepped back, still staring, "oh my God, this is Annabel Greene, can you even believe it?"

The blonde in the prom dress, studying me with her very pink lips pursed, said, "You were in that commercial."

"Duh!" Mallory told her. She reached up, finally adjusting her eyelash. "She's the Kopf's girl. And a Lakeview Model."

"What are you doing here?" one of the redheads asked.

"Well," I said, "I was in the neighborhood, and—"

"She's friends with my brother. *And* with me." Mallory squeezed my hand again, her palm hot against mine. To me she said, "You're just in time for our photo shoot. You can help us with our poses!"

"Actually, I can't stay," I said. "I just stopped in for a second."

This was what I'd told Whitney, too, after dinner. That I had something to bring by a friend's, and I'd be back within the hour. She'd just nodded, although she was looking at me sort of strangely, like she was wondering if I might come home smelling of bacon.

"Do you like my outfit?" Mallory asked now, striking a pose, one hand behind her neck, eyes turned up to the ceiling. She held it for a moment, then resumed her normal standing position. "We're doing all these different looks. I'm Evening Elegant."

"We're Daytime Casual," one of the redheads told me, planting a hand on her hip. Her sister, who had more freckles, nodded, her face solemn.

I looked at the dark-haired girl with the glasses. "Classy Workplace," she mumbled, tugging at her black dress.

"And I," the blonde announced, twirling so her dress swished, "am Fantasy Engagement."

"You are not," Mallory said. "You're Nighttime Formal."

"Fantasy Engagement," the blonde insisted, taking another spin. To me she added, "This dress cost—"

"Four hundred dollars, we know, we know," Mallory said, annoyed. "She thinks she's a big deal just because her sister was a debutante."

"When are we taking pictures?" one of the redheads asked. "I'm tired of being Daytime Casual; I want to wear a dress."

"In a second!" Mallory snapped, irritated. "First Annabel has to see my room. Then she can advise us on our looks."

She started to pull me toward the stairs, the other girls clomping along behind us. "Is Owen here?" I asked.

"Somewhere," she said as we started up the steps. The dark-haired girl was beside me now, studying me with a serious expression, while the other three whispered behind me. "You should see the pictures we took last time at Michelle's, they were so good! I had this one where I was European Flair? It was fabulous."

"European Flair?" I asked.

She nodded. "I wore a beret and a plaid skirt, and posed with a loaf of French bread. It was awesome."

"I want to be European Flair," the girl in black said. "This dress is boring. And how come you always get to be Evening Elegant?"

"Just wait a second!" Mallory hissed as we came up on a

closed door. She stepped in front of it, clasping her hands to her chest. "Okay," she said. Her eyelash had come loose again. "Prepare yourself for the ultimate model experience."

This did not sound very promising. I glanced behind me; the other girls were all staring at me, still. I turned back to Mallory. "All right," I said slowly.

She reached down, twisting the knob, then pushed the door open. "Here it is," she said. "Can you believe it?"

I couldn't. The wall in front of me, like the ones on either side, was covered from top to bottom with pictures from magazines. Model after model, ad after ad, celebrity after celebrity. There were blondes, brunettes, redheads. High fashion, prom fashion, casual fashion, showbiz fashion. One beautiful, high-cheekboned face after another, striking a pose this way, that way, every possible way. There were so many pictures, cut out and edges overlapping, that you couldn't even see the wall behind them.

"Well?" Mallory said. "What do you think?"

Truth be told, it was all completely overwhelming, even before she pulled me forward, pointing at one specific face. It was only after I moved closer that I realized it was mine.

"See," she said, "this is from the Lakeview Models calendar last year, when you were April, and posed with the tires? Remember?"

I nodded, and then she was pulling me a few feet to the right, pointing again. Meanwhile, the other girls had scattered, the redheads flopping onto the nearby bed, where they were flipping through a stack of magazines, while the blonde and the dark-haired girl jockeyed for position on the chair that faced a nearby vanity.

"And this," Mallory said, her finger inches from the wall, "is the Boca Tan ad that was in the program for a basketball game I went to last year at the university. See, your hair is blonder there, right?"

"Right," I said. I looked slightly orange, as well. So strange. I'd forgotten all about that. "It sure is."

Another tug, and the photos blurred as we moved again, this time in the opposite direction, coming to a stop on the far left. "But this one," she said, "is my all-time favorite. That's why I have it right next to my bed."

I leaned in closer. It was a collage of shots from the Kopf's back-to-school commercial: me in the cheerleader uniform, on the bench with the girls behind me, at a desk, on the arm of the cute boy in the tux. "Where did you get photos?" I asked her.

"It's a screen capture," she said proudly. "I burned the commercial to a DVD, then uploaded it and saved the images on my computer. Cool, huh?"

I leaned in, looking even more closely, remembering, as I did each time I saw the commercial, that day in April when I'd shot it. I was so different then; everything was different then.

Mallory dropped my hand, leaning in beside me. "I just love that commercial," she said now. "At first, it was because of the cheerleading outfit, because I was really into that this summer? But then it was all about the clothes, and the story. . . . I mean, it's great."

"The story," I said.

"Yeah." She turned to look at me. "You know, that you're this girl, and you're going back to high school after a great summer."

"Oh," I said. "Right."

"At first, it's, like, all the stuff that happens right at the beginning of school. Like cheering at the big game. And studying for tests, and hanging out with all your friends on the quad."

Hanging out with all my friends on the quad, I thought. *Right.*

"And then," she said, "it ends with the first dance, where you get the hot guy, which means the *rest* of the year will be even better." She sighed. "It's like you have this great life, and get to do all this cool stuff. All the stuff high school should be. You're like—"

I looked at her again. Her face was inches from the pictures, still staring. "The girl who has everything," I said, remembering the director's words.

She turned to face me, nodding. *"Exactly,"* she said.

I wanted to tell her, right then, that this wasn't true. That I was far from the girl who had everything; that I wasn't even that girl in the pictures, if I ever had been. No one's life was really like that, one glorious moment after another, especially mine. A real set of snapshots from my back-to-school experience would be something else entirely: Sophie's pretty mouth forming an ugly word, Will Cash smiling at me, me alone behind the building retching in the grass. This was the real truth about me going to back to school. The story of my life.

I heard heavy footsteps in the hallway, then a heavy sigh. "Mallory, I told you, if you want me to take pictures, let's go ahead and do it. I've got a show to work on and I don't—"

I stood up; Owen was standing in the open doorway. When he saw me, his eyes widened. "—have all night," he finished. "Hey. What are you doing here?"

"She came for my party," Mallory told him.

Owen narrowed his eyes. "You came for this?"

"You're helping with the photo shoot?" I replied.

"No," he said. "I just—"

"We needed a photographer," Mallory explained to me, "for the group shots. And now we have a stylist, too! This is perfect." She clapped her hands. "Okay, everyone, downstairs and into position. We'll do our group pictures first, then move on to individual. Who has our shoot list?"

The dark-haired girl got up off the chair by the mirror, reaching into her pocket to pull out folded piece of paper. "Here," she said.

"Okay," Owen said as Mallory took it from her, "tell me why you're really here."

"Fashion is my life," I told him. "You know that."

Mallory cleared her throat. "Daytime Casual first," she said, pointing to the redheads, "followed by Workplace Classy, Evening Elegant, and Nighttime Formal."

"Fantasy Engagement," the blonde corrected her.

"Downstairs!" Mallory said. "Let's go!"

The redheads got off the bed, heading for the door, the dark-haired girl in the black following along. The blonde, in comparison, took her time, shooting me a look as she passed.

"Hi, Owen," she said as she walked by him, the hem of her dress dragging on the carpet.

Owen nodded at her, a flat expression on his face. "Hello, Elinor," he said. At the sound of her name, her face flushed pink and she picked up speed, darting out the door and down the hallway, where she was greeted with a burst of giggling.

Mallory followed her friends, then stopped in the doorway, turning back to look at us. "Owen," she said, "I'll need you downstairs in five, ready to shoot. Annabel, you can style and supervise."

"Watch the tone, Mallory," Owen told her. "Or you'll be taking self-portraits."

"Five minutes!" she said. Then she clomped down the hallway, her voice rising up as she continued to order her friends around.

"Wow," I said to Owen as their voices faded. "This is quite a production."

"Tell me about it," he said, sitting down on the edge of the bed. "And mark my words: it will end in tears. It always does. These girls have no concept of thinking toward the middle."

"Thinking toward what?"

"The middle," he repeated as I sat down next to him. "It's an Anger Management term. It means not only thinking in extremes. You know, either I get what I want or I don't. Either I'm right or I'm wrong."

"Either I'm Fantasy Engagement or I'm Nighttime Formal," I added.

"Right. It's dangerous to think like that, because nothing is totally cut-and-dry," he said. "Unless, apparently, you're thirteen."

"Miss Fantasy Engagement does seem like a bit of a diva."

"Elinor?" He let out a breath. "She's a piece of work."

"She seems to like you quite a bit."

"Stop it," he said, shooting me a dark look. "That's I-Lang. Big-time."

"You know that whole model-photographer-hookup thing," I said, bumping him with my knee. "It's practically required."

"Why are you here, again?"

"I just came by to drop this off." I held up his jacket. "I forgot to give it back to you this morning."

"Oh," he said. "Thanks. But you could have waited until Tuesday, if you wanted."

"I would have," I told him, reaching into the pocket and pulling out the iPod, "except for this."

His eyes widened. "Oh, man," he said, taking it from me. "That I would have missed."

"I figured you probably were already."

"Not yet," he said. "But I was about to start planning next week's show, so pretty soon, I would have. Thanks."

"You're welcome."

There was a burst of noise from downstairs, what sounded like someone either cheering or wailing. "See?" Owen said, pointing at the open door. "Tears. Guaranteed. No middle."

"Maybe we should just hide out here," I said. "Might be safer."

"I don't know," he said, glancing around at the walls. "Looking at all these pictures gives me the creeps."

"At least you're not in them," I told him.

"You? There are ones of you here?"

I pointed at the pictures from the commercial, and he got up, walking over to look closer. "It's nothing special," I said. "Really."

He studied the pictures long enough that I began to regret pointing them out. "It's strange," he said finally.

"Gee," I said. "Thanks a lot."

"No, I mean, you don't look like you, or something." He paused, leaning in a little closer. "Yeah. I mean, you look familiar, but not like the same person at all."

I sat there for a second, a little weirded out, because actually this was how I felt, too, when I looked at the older ads I'd done, especially the Kopf's commercial. That girl *was* different from who I was now, more whole and unbroken and okay than the one I saw in the mirror these days. I'd just thought I was the only one who noticed.

"No offense," Owen said.

I shook my head. "It's fine."

"I mean, it's a nice picture." He peered at it again. "I just think you look better now."

At first, I thought maybe I'd heard him wrong. "Now?" I said.

"Yeah." He glanced up at me. "What did you think I meant?"

"I don't . . ." I began, then stopped. "Never mind."

"You think I'd tell you that you looked better here?"

"Well," I said, "you *are* honest."

"I'm not a jerk, though," he replied. "You look good. You just don't look like you. You look . . . different."

"Different bad," I said.

"Different different."

"Super vague," I pointed out. "Placeholder. *Double* place-holder."

"You're right," he said. "What I mean is, looking at this, I think, *Huh, that's not Annabel. That doesn't look like her at all.*"

"What do I look like?"

"Like this," he said, nodding at me. "My point is, I don't know you as someone who gets their picture taken in a cheer-leading outfit. Or even as a model, period. That's not you to me."

I wanted to ask him to explain further, to say what I was to him, exactly. But then I realized maybe he just had. I already knew he thought of me as honest, direct, even funny—all things I had never thought about myself. Who knew what else I could be, what kind of potential there was in the differences between that girl and the one he saw now. So many possibilities.

"Owen!" Mallory yelled up the stairs. "We're ready for you now!"

Owen rolled his eyes. Then he walked over, holding out his hand to help me to my feet. "Okay," he said. "Come on."

Looking up at him, I realized that this, too, was part of my real back-to-school days: Along with Sophie and Will and every-thing horrible, there was Owen, reaching out a hand to me. And now, as I reached up, closing my fingers over his, I was grate-ful more than ever for something, finally, to hold on to.

Owen was right about the tears. Within an hour, we had a melt-down.

"It's not fair!" said the dark-haired girl, whose name I now knew was Angela, her voice wavering.

"You look good," Mallory told her, adjusting her boa. "What's the problem?"

I knew. In fact, it was pretty obvious. While Mallory and the others were alternating between Evening Elegant and Nighttime Formal (or, depending on how you looked at it, Fantasy Engagement), Angela had been continually assigned Workplace Classy, which was clearly the least favorite of the chosen looks. Now, she looked down at her plain black skirt, black blouse, and flats. "I want to do Evening Elegant," she protested. "When is it my turn?"

"Owen!" Elinor, the blonde, called out, tugging a tube top down over her stomach. "Are you ready for me?"

"No," Owen muttered as she moved in toward him, tossing her hair and putting a hand on her hip. "Not even close."

The shoot was quite a production. Not only had the girls pushed back the furniture in the living room and draped a white sheet over the mantel for a backdrop, there was also a dressing and makeup area (the powder room) and background music (mostly Jenny Reef, Bitsy Bonds, and Z104; Owen's offer to put together a mix was roundly rejected).

"It will be your turn," Mallory, who was now in a gold bathing-suit top and sarong, the boa over her shoulders, told Angela. "But Workplace Classy is very important. Someone has to do it."

"Then why don't you?"

Mallory sighed, blowing her bangs out of her face. "Because my look is better suited to evening," she explained as the redheads, who'd moved on to swimwear, practiced for the beach action shots by tossing a soccer ball back and forth.

"With your glasses, you look better doing serious corporate looks."

I glanced at Angela, whose upper lip was now trembling slightly. "You know," I said, "maybe she could take off her glasses."

"I'm ready!" Elinor said to Owen. "Go ahead! Get the shot!"

Owen, who was standing in front of the couch, winced as he lifted the camera to his eye. In my experience, models did not ever boss the photographer, but that was clearly not the case here. Instead, Owen just kept his finger on the shutter pretty much nonstop, taking shot after shot as the girls arranged themselves every which way. Now, as Elinor blew a kiss to the camera, and to him, he looked appalled.

As a stylist, I'd been told it was my job to stay in the powder room/dressing area and supervise wardrobe, which consisted of the piles of clothing and shoes that were scattered on the countertops, floor, and nearby stairs. After my few early suggestions—less cleavage and makeup, for starters—had been completely ignored, I'd been mostly watching Owen and trying not to laugh.

"You know," he said now, as Elinor dropped to the floor and began to writhe toward him, her elbows clunking across the hardwood, "I'm thinking we're about done here."

"But we haven't even gotten the group shots!" Mallory said.

"Then you better get those together," he told her. "Your stylist and photographer get paid by the hour, and you can't afford us for much longer."

"Okay, fine," Mallory grumbled, tossing her boa over one shoulder. "Everyone together in front of the backdrop, now!"

The redheads grabbed their ball and headed over, while Elinor got to her feet, pulling up her tube top again. I looked at Angela, who was standing in the archway to the living room, arms crossed over her chest, her upper lip seriously shaking now. Three could be a crowd, I thought. But so could five.

"Hey," I said, and she turned around, looking at me. "Come on. Let's get you into something else."

I could hear Mallory telling everyone how to stand as Angela followed me back to the powder room, where I surveyed the options. "This is cute," I said, picking up a red skirt. "What do you think?"

Angela sniffled, then reached up, adjusting her glasses. "It's all right," she said.

"And maybe we can pair it with . . ." I glanced around, then grabbed a black top with spaghetti straps. "This. And some really high heels."

She nodded, taking the skirt from me. "Okay," she said, starting down the hallway to the side bedroom there. "I'll go change."

"You do that," I told her. "I'll find the shoes."

"Angela!" Mallory yelled. "We need you in here!"

"Just a sec," I called out, bending down and rummaging through the pile of shoes by my feet. I'd picked out one strappy sandal and was looking for its mate when I felt someone watching me. When I glanced up, Owen was standing there, holding the camera.

"One sec," I said. "We're changing our look."

"I heard." He stepped into the powder room, leaning against the door and watching me as I finally found the shoe, wedged under a puffy parka. "That was nice of you. Helping her out."

"Well," I said, "modeling can be an ugly business."

"Yeah?"

I nodded as I stood up, glancing down the hallway for Angela, then leaned against the opposite side of the doorframe, facing him, the shoes dangling from my hand. After a moment, he lifted up the camera to his eye. "Don't," I said, putting my hand over my face.

"Why not?"

"I hate having my picture taken."

"You're a *model*."

"That's why," I told him. "It's gotten old."

"Come on," he said. "Just one."

I dropped my hand but didn't smile as his finger moved to the shutter. Instead, I just looked at him, through the lens, as the flash popped. "Nice," he said.

"Yeah?"

He nodded, turning the camera over to look at the display on the back. I stepped closer, looking down at it as well. Sure enough, there I was, the doorframe behind me. My hair was unbrushed, a few strands loose around my face, I had on no makeup, and it wasn't my best angle. It also wasn't a bad picture. I moved in closer, studying my face, the faint light behind it.

"See?" Owen said. I could feel his shoulder against mine, his face only inches away, as we both peered down at the image. "*That's* what you look like."

I turned my head to say something to this—what, I had no

idea—and his cheek was so close, right there. I looked up at him, and then, before I knew what was happening, he was turning his head slightly, bending down to me. I closed my eyes, and then his lips were right there, soft on mine, and I stepped closer, pressing myself against—

"I'm ready for my shoes."

We both jumped, startled; Owen bonked his head on the doorframe. "Shit," he said.

Heart pounding, I looked down at Angela, who was staring up at us, her expression serious. "Shoes," I said, handing them over. "Right."

Owen was rubbing his head, his eyes closed. "Man," he said. "That smarts."

"Are you okay?" I asked. He nodded, and I reached out, touching his temple, then kept my fingers there for a moment, his skin warm, smooth to the touch, before taking my hand away.

"Owen!" Mallory yelled from the living room. "We're ready! Let's go!"

Owen pushed off the doorframe and started into the living room while Angela, now strapped into her shoes, slowly made her way along behind him. I stayed where I was for a moment, then glanced at myself in the powder-room mirror, amazed at what had just happened. I studied my reflection for a second, then stepped away from it, out of my own sight.

When I got to the living room, all drama had been forgotten, and the group shot was in full swing, all five girls posing wildly as Owen moved dutifully around them. I leaned in the archway, watching as each girl vamped in her own way: a hip shimmy, an arched neck, fluttering lashes.

The song playing in the background was the kind Owen hated: all poppy, bouncy beats, a girl's perfectly engineered voice sliding effortlessly over the instruments. Mallory reached over to the CD player on the floor beside her, cranking the volume, and the girls all shrieked, beginning to dance, their hands waving over their heads. Owen stepped aside as they bounced and twirled, then turned the camera on me, holding it there as the girls blurred past between us. I wasn't sure exactly what he was seeing, but now I had an idea. So this time, I smiled.

When I pulled into my driveway later that night, all the lights in the house were off except in Whitney's room. I could see her in the chair by her window, sitting with her feet tucked up under her. She had that same notebook open in her lap and was writing, her hand moving slowly across the page. For a moment I just sat there, watching her, the one thing I could make out in the dark.

I'd left Owen's just in time. Elinor, Angela, and the twins had tired of both the photo shoot and Mallory's bossiness and were on the verge of some sort of fashion mutiny, the house was a wreck, and Owen's mom—apparently a bit of a neat freak—was due home at any moment. I'd offered to stay and help clean up, or play peacemaker, but he declined.

"I can handle it," he said, as we stood on the front steps. "If I were you, I'd get out while I could. It's only going to go downhill from here."

"So optimistic," I said.

"No," he replied as, inside, I heard an indignant shriek, followed by a door slamming. He turned his head, glancing toward the door, then back at me. "Just realistic."

I smiled, then moved down one step, pulling my keys out of my pocket. "So I'll see you at school, I guess."

"Yup," he said. "See you then."

Neither of us moved and I wondered if he would kiss me again. "Okay," I said, feeling my stomach flip-flop. "I'm, um, going."

"Right." He stepped a little closer to the edge of the step where he was standing, and I moved forward on mine, meeting him halfway. As he leaned down to me and I closed my eyes, I could hear something, a *thunk-thunk-thunk* noise, growing both louder and closer. The doorknob rattled, and we both jumped back as Mallory, wearing thick wedge heels, a black catsuit, and the green boa, burst out onto the porch.

"Wait!" she said, clomping across to me, her hand outstretched. "Here. These are for you."

She handed me a stack of pictures, so fresh from the printer I could smell ink. The one on the top was of her in her gold bathing-suit top, the shot taken close with the feathers from the boa framing her face, drifting upwards toward the edges. I flipped through the next few, which featured a couple of group poses, Elinor writhing on the floor and, finally, Angela in the outfit I'd picked out for her. "Wow," I said. "These are great."

"They're for your wall," she said. "So you can look at me sometimes."

"Thank you," I told her.

"You're welcome." She turned to Owen. "Mom just called from the car. She'll be home in ten minutes."

"Right." Owen sighed. To me he said, "I'll see you later."

I nodded, and then they were walking inside, where I could hear the other girls arguing, Mallory waving at me one last time before shutting the door. A moment later, he said something, and the girls quieted down, quick. By the time I started down the steps, I couldn't hear a thing.

Now, I got out of my car and started up the walk, Mallory's pictures in my hand. The entire ride home all I'd been able to think about was Owen's face, coming closer to mine, how it felt when he'd kissed me, barely long enough to count and yet still unforgettable. I felt my face flush as I pushed open the door, then started up the stairs.

"Annabel?" Whitney called out when I got to the top. "Is that you?"

"Yeah," I said. "I'm back."

As I reached for my door, hers opened and she stepped out into view. "Mom called again," she said. "I told her you'd gone to a friend's house. She asked who, but I said I didn't know."

For a moment we just looked at each other, and I wondered if I was supposed to explain myself further. "Thanks," I said finally as I pushed my door open and turned on the light. I put the pictures on the bureau, then shrugged off my coat, tossing it over my desk chair. When I turned back around, she was standing in my doorway.

"I told her maybe you'd call her when you got in," she said. "But you probably don't have to."

"Okay," I said.

She shifted slightly, leaning against the doorjamb. As she did so, she saw the pictures. "What are these?" she asked.

"Oh, nothing," I said. "They're just . . . they're silly."

She picked them up, cradling them in her open hand as she worked through them, her expression moving from impassive to curious to, at one shot of Elinor sprawled on the floor, somewhat horrified.

"My friend's little sister was having a modeling slumber party," I said, walking over to stand beside her as she kept moving through the stack. There were the redheads, side by side, doing a mirror-image pose, and Angela in her black dress, the dreaded Workplace Classy. There were a few more of Mallory as well, doing a full range of looks: pensive, dreamy, and, perhaps due to something Owen had just said, annoyed. "They get all dressed up and take shots of themselves."

Whitney paused to study a shot of Elinor in her white dress, looking pensive. "Wow," she said. "That's quite a look."

"It's called Fantasy Engagement."

"Huh," she said, flipping to the next picture, which was Elinor again, this time sprawled on the floor, mouth half open. "What's that called?"

"I don't think that has a name," I said.

She withheld further comment, flipping to the next shot, which was of Mallory in a red top, facing the camera. Her lips were pursed, her eyelashes enormous. "She's kind of cute," she said, tilting the picture slightly. "Good eyes."

"Oh, God," I said, shaking my head. "She'd *die* if she heard you say that."

"Really."

I nodded. "She's model-obsessed. You should see her room. It's all pictures from magazines, everywhere you look."

"She must have been thrilled you were there, then," she said. "A real-live model."

"I guess," I said, watching as she kept flipping, past a series of group shots: all the girls' faces pressed together, then each of them looking a different direction, as if waiting for five separate buses. "It was kind of weird for me, actually."

Whitney was quiet for a second. Then she said, "Yeah. I know what you mean."

Like so much else that had happened that weekend, I found myself in this unexpected moment with my sister almost holding my breath. Finally I said, "I mean, we never did that, you know? When we were kids."

"We didn't have to," she said as Angela's picture came up, her dark eyes so serious, skin pale in the camera's flash. "We had the real thing."

"Yeah," I said. "But this might have been more fun. Less pressure, anyway."

I felt her cut her eyes at me as I said this, and too late I realized she thought I was talking about her. I waited for her to snap or say something nasty, but she didn't, instead just handing me back the pictures. "Well," she said. "I guess we'll never know."

As she stepped out into the hallway I looked down at the pictures; Mallory's boa shot was back on top. "Sleep well," I said.

"Yeah." She glanced over at me, the light behind her, and I was struck by the simple perfection of her cheekbones and lips, so striking and accidental all at once. "Good night, Annabel."

Later, when I got into bed, I picked up the pictures again, then sat back in bed, flipping through them. After going through the stack twice, I got out of bed and went to my desk, digging around in the top drawer until I found some pushpins. Then I tacked the pictures up, in rows of three, on the wall above my radio. *So you can look at me sometimes*, Mallory had said, and as I turned off my light I did just that. The moon, coming in, was slanted across them, making them bright, and I kept my eyes on them as long as I could. At some point, though, I could feel myself falling asleep, and I had to turn away, back to the dark.

Chapter
TWELVE

My mother returned from her first vacation in over a year rested, manicured, and rejuvenated. Which would have been great, if her newfound energy hadn't been directed at the one thing I least wanted to think about, but now could not avoid: the Lakeview Models Fall Fashion Show.

"So you've got to be at Kopf's today for a fitting, tomorrow for a rehearsal," she said to me as I poked at my breakfast before school. "And the final run-through is on Friday. Your hair appointment is on Thursday, and I booked your nail stuff for Saturday morning, early. Okay?"

After an entire weekend to myself, not to mention the last few months with very few work commitments, this did not sound okay. It sounded painful. But I didn't say anything. As much as I was dreading the week and the show, at least I had something to look forward to afterwards, which was going to Bendo with Owen.

"You know, something occurred to me this weekend," my mom continued. "The Kopf's people are probably just about to start casting for the spring campaign. So this show is a great opportunity for them to see you in person, don't you think?"

Hearing this, I felt a twinge of dread, knowing I should tell her I wanted to quit modeling. But then I had a flash of me and Owen on the wall, role-playing this very scenario, and how even when it was just a game I hadn't been able to get the words out. Across from me, my mother was sipping her coffee, and I knew that this, right now, was the perfect moment. She'd dropped a sweater, and I could just pick it up. But like Rolly, I froze up. And stayed silent. I'd do it later, I told myself. After the show. I would.

At the same time that I was walking down a runway at the mall, modeling winter clothes, my sister Kirsten would also be in front of a crowd, albeit for a different reason. The day before, she'd finally e-mailed her short piece to me as promised. Because I was used to Kirsten explaining—if not overexplaining—everything that was any part of her life whatsoever, the message she'd sent with it took me by surprise.

Hi, Annabel, here it is. Let me know what you think. Love, K.

At first, I'd actually scrolled down through the body of the e-mail, looking for the rest of the message—if my sister was long-winded on the phone, her e-mails were equally verbose. But there was nothing else.

I hit the DOWNLOAD NOW button, then watched as blue squares filled up the screen. When it was done, I clicked on PLAY.

The first shot was of grass. Green, beautiful grass, just like the kind on the golf course across the street, i.e., totally chemically induced, filling the screen from one side to the other. Then the camera pulled back, back, to show it was the yard in front of a white house with pretty blue trim, and two figures on bikes blurred past.

The camera cut, and we were suddenly facing two girls as they rode toward us. One, a blonde, looked to be about thirteen; the other, a brunette, was thinner and more slight, lagging a little bit behind.

Suddenly the girl in front looked back at the other, then began pedaling faster, pulling away from her. As she did so, the camera cut back and forth between her pedaling, wind blowing back her hair, and pretty images of the neighborhood: a dog asleep on the sidewalk, a man picking up his paper, the blue, blue sky, a sprinkler sending water in an arc over a flower bed. As she kept on, picking up speed, the images came faster and faster, repeating, until the camera cut to a shot of the road ahead, coming to a *T*. She skidded to a stop, then turned around. Behind her, in the distance, you could just see a bike lying in the middle of the road, one wheel spinning, the smaller girl sitting beside it, holding her arm.

The next shot was of the blonde skidding to a stop beside her. "What happened?" she asked.

The younger girl shook her head. "I don't know," she said.

The blonde pushed herself over, closer. "Here," she said. "Get on."

In the next shot, the smaller girl was balanced on the handlebars, holding her arm, as the blonde pedaled up the street. Again the camera cut between them and images of the neighborhood, although both were different now: the dog lunging and barking as they passed, the man stumbling as he reached for his paper, the sky gray, the sprinkler hissing as water splatted a nearby car, then ran in streaks down the side. It was the same, and yet so different, and when the house rose up in the distance, it looked different, too. The blonde pedaled up the driveway, the camera pulling back as she did so, then stopped as the younger girl slid off the handlebars, holding her arm tight against her. They dropped the bike onto the grass and started toward the house. They climbed the steps. The door opened for them, but you couldn't see who was on the other side. As they disappeared inside, the camera panned down until the grass filled the screen again, side to side, scarily green and bright and fake. And then it was over.

I just sat there for a moment, staring at the screen. Then I hit PLAY and watched it again. And a third time. I still wasn't sure what to make of it, even as I reached for the phone and dialed Kirsten's number. But when she answered, and I told her I liked it but didn't get it, she wasn't upset. Instead, she said that was the whole point.

"What, that I be confused?" I asked.

"No," she said, "that the meaning not be spelled out. It's supposed to be left up to your interpretation."

"Yes, but *you* know what it means," I said. "Right?"

"Sure."

"And that is?"

She sighed. "I know what it means to *me*," she said. "For you, it's going to be different. Look, film is personal. There's no right or wrong message. It's all what you take from it."

I looked at the screen again, which I'd paused on the last shot of that green grass. "Oh," I said. "Okay."

It was just so bizarre. Here was my sister, queen of the

overshare, holding out on me. Holding *back*. I was used to having to guess with some people, but never Kirsten, and I wasn't sure I liked it. She, however, sounded happier than I'd heard her in months.

"I'm just so glad you liked it. And had such a strong reaction!" She laughed. "Now all I need is for everyone there on Saturday to feel the same way, and everything will be great."

Great for you, I thought, when we hung up a few minutes later. As for me, I was still confused. And, I had to admit, intrigued. Enough to watch the film two more times, studying it frame by frame.

Now, as my father came into the kitchen, running late, and my mom jumped up to bustle around him, I brought my plate to the sink, running some water over it. Through the window in front of me, I could see Whitney sitting on a chaise by the pool, a cup of coffee beside her. Normally she was sleeping at this hour, but lately she'd started getting up early. It was just one recent change among many.

At first the shifts were small, but still noticeable. She'd recently become somewhat social—a couple of days earlier she'd gone out for coffee with people from Moira Bell's group—and had also begun working a few mornings a week at my dad's office answering phones, filling in for yet another pregnant secretary. When she was home, she'd started to spend at least some of her time outside her room. It happened in stages: First her door went from always being shut to slightly ajar, to finally being open occasionally. Then I noticed she was hanging out in the living room instead of shut away upstairs. And just the previous day I'd come home from school to find her sitting at the dining-room table, books stacked all around her, writing on a legal pad.

I'd been ignored for so long that it was still my tendency to hesitate before addressing Whitney. This time, though, she spoke first.

"Hey," she said, not looking up. "Mom's out running errands. She said not to forget about rehearsal at four thirty."

"Right," I said. Her arm was crooked across the pad, her pen making a scratching noise as it moved across the paper. In the window, her herb pots were in full sunlight, although they hadn't shown any sign of sprouting yet. "What are you doing?"

"I have to write a history."

"A history?" I repeated. "Of what?"

"Well, actually, it's two histories." She put down her pen, stretching her fingers. "One of my life. And one of my eating disorder."

It was weird to hear her say this, and after a moment, I realized why. Even though it had pretty much dominated our family dynamic for almost a year, I'd never heard Whitney acknowledge her problem out loud. Like so much else, it was known but not discussed, present but not officially accounted for. From the way she said it, though, so matter-of-factly, it sounded like she, at least, was used to it.

"So they're two separate things?" I asked.

"Apparently. At least according to Moira." She sighed, although this time, when her therapist's name came up, she sounded more tired than annoyed. "The idea is that there is some separation, even if it doesn't always seem like it. That we had a life before we had a disorder."

I moved closer to the table, glancing at the books stacked beside her. *Starving for Attention: Eating Disorders and Adolescents* was the title of one; there was a slimmer volume called *Hunger Pains* beneath it. "So you have to read all those books?"

"I don't *have* to." She picked up her pen again. "They're just to fill in the factual stuff, if I need it. But the personal history is all my memories. We're supposed to do it one year at a time." She nodded at the pad in front of her. On the top line, I could see she'd written ELEVEN (11). There was nothing else on the page.

"Must be kind of weird," I said. "Thinking back, year by year."

"It's hard. Harder than I thought it would be." She opened a book by her elbow, flipping through the pages, then shut it. "I don't remember that much, for some reason."

I glanced over at her pots again, the sun spilling across them. On the other side of the window and across the street, the golf course was green and bright.

"You broke your arm," I said.

"What?"

"When you were eleven," I said. "You broke your arm. You fell off your bike. Remember?"

For a moment she just sat there. "That's right," she said finally, nodding. "God. Wasn't that, like, right after your birthday?"

"*On* my birthday," I told her. "You got back in your cast just in time for cake."

"I can't believe I forgot that," she said. She shook her head again, looking down at the paper before picking up her pen and clicking it open. Then she began to write, her script filling the top line. I started to mention Kirsten's movie, and how it had reminded me of this, but then I stopped myself. She'd already filled three lines and was still going; I didn't want to interrupt. So I backed out of the room and left her to it. When I passed by again an hour later, she was still going, and this time she didn't look up. She just kept writing.

Now as I turned away from the sink, I looked over at my mother, wondering if I asked her about what had happened on that day, my ninth birthday, just a month or two before her own mother died, what she would remember. The green, green grass, like Kirsten. That it happened just before my party, like me. Or, like Whitney, nothing at all, at least at first. So many versions of just one memory, and yet none of them were right or wrong. Instead, they were all pieces. Only when fitted together, edge to edge, could they even begin to tell the whole story.

"Get in."

I looked at Owen, raising one eyebrow. A minute earlier, I'd been walking across the Kopf's parking lot to my car, leaving yet another fashion-show rehearsal, when someone screeched into the space beside me. I'd looked over, startled, expecting to see a white kidnapper van. Instead, it was Owen in the Land Cruiser, already reaching over to push the passenger door open.

"Is this an abduction?" I asked.

He shook his head, gesturing impatiently with one hand for

me to get in the car, while adjusting the stereo with the other. "Seriously," he said, as I slowly climbed into the seat. "You have *got* to hear this."

"Owen," I said, watching him continue to push buttons on the console, "how did you know I was here?"

"I didn't," he replied. "I was just up at that light, heading home, when I looked over and saw you. Check this out."

He reached for the volume knob, turning it up. A second later, a whooshing sound filled my ears, followed by what sounded like a violin, but at rapid speed, and electrified. The result was a noise that would have been unsettling at a normal volume. Cranked as it was, though, I felt the hairs on my neck stand on end.

"Great, right?" Owen said, grinning widely. He was bobbing his head as the chords bounced over us. In my mind, I pictured one of those cardiac monitor machines, each sound causing my own heart to spike, the needle jumping off the screen.

I could feel myself wincing even as I said—or yelled— "What is this?"

"They're called Melisma," he yelled back as there was a boom of bass, loud enough to shake my seat. Over at the next car, a woman loading her squirming toddler into a car seat glanced over at us. "It's a music project. These awesome string players, synthesized and blended with various world beats, influenced by—"

Then he said something else, which was drowned out by a sudden burst of rapid drumbeats. I watched his lips move until it subsided, picking back up as he said, "—really a collaborative thing, this whole new music initiative. Incredible, right?"

Before I could answer, there was a bang of cymbals, followed by a fizzing noise. Call it reflex, or self-preservation, or just common sense, but I just couldn't help myself: I pressed my palms over my ears.

Owen's eyes widened, and I realized what I'd done. As I dropped my hands, though, the song suddenly ended, so the sound of them hitting the seat on either side of me was incredibly loud. Especially compared to the awkward silence that followed.

"You did not," Owen said finally, his voice low, "just cover your ears. Did you?"

"It was an accident," I said. "I just—"

"That's *serious*." He reached forward, shaking his head, and turned down the CD. "I mean, it's one thing to listen and respectfully disagree. But to shut it out entirely, and not even give it a chance—"

"I gave it a chance!" I said.

"You call that a chance?" he asked. "That was five seconds."

"It was long enough to form an opinion," I said.

"Which was?"

"I covered my ears," I told him. "What do *you* think?"

He started to say something, then stopped, shaking his head. Beside us, the woman in the minivan was now backing out. I watched her slide past his window. "Melisma," Owen said after a moment, "is innovative and textured."

"If by textured you mean unlistenable," I said quietly, "then I agree."

"I-Lang!" he said, pointing at me. I shrugged. "I can't believe you're saying that! This is the perfect marriage of instrument and technology! It's unlike anything anyone's ever done before! It sounds incredible!"

"Maybe in the car wash," I muttered.

He'd drawn in another breath, to continue this rant, but now he let it out, one big whoosh, then turned his head to look at me. "What did you just say?"

Like covering my ears, this had happened without my really realizing it. There had been a time when I was painfully aware of everything I said or did around Owen. The fact that this was no longer the case was either good or very bad. Judging by the look on his face—a mix of horrified and offended—I had a feeling it was probably the latter. At least right at this moment.

"I said . . ." I cleared my throat. "I said, maybe it sounds incredible in the car wash."

I could feel him staring at me, so I busied myself picking at the edge of my seat. Then he said, "Which means what?"

"You know what it means," I said.

"I truly do not. Enlighten me."

Of course he'd make me explain it. "Well," I said slowly, "you know, everything sounds better when you're driving through the car wash. It's just, like, a fact. Right?"

He didn't say anything, just stared at me.

"My point is," I said, clarifying, "it's not my thing. I'm sorry. I shouldn't have covered my ears; that was rude. But I just—"

"Which car wash?"

"What?"

"Which is this magical listening station, whereupon all musical worth is decided?"

I just looked at him. "Owen."

"Seriously, I want to know."

"It's not any one car wash," I said. "It's the car-wash phenomenon. You really don't know about it?"

"I don't," he repeated. Then he reached down, shifting into reverse. "But I will. Starting now."

Five minutes later, we were pulling up to 123SUDS, the automated drive-through car wash that had been down the street from my neighborhood for as long as I could remember. I'd grown up going there fairly often, mostly because my mom loved it. My dad would always tell her that the only way to get a car truly clean was to do it by hand—as he often did, on warm sunny days, in the driveway—and that 123SUDS was a waste of time and money. But my mom didn't care. "It's not about the wash, anyway," she'd tell him. "It's the *experience*."

Going there was never really planned. Instead, we'd just be passing by and she'd suddenly turn in, sending my sisters and me scrambling to collect change from the floorboards and center console to feed into the machine. We always chose the basic wash, skipping the hot wax, sometimes adding on the optional Armor All on the tires. Then we'd roll up all the windows, sit back in our seats, and go in.

There was just something about it. Driving into that dark bay, the water suddenly whooshing down like the biggest and most sudden thunderstorm ever. It would beat across the hood and trunk, pouring down the other side of your window, washing all the pollen and dust away, and if you closed your eyes you could almost imagine you were floating along with it. It was eerie and incredible, and when you spoke you always whispered, even if you didn't know why. More than anything, though, I remembered the music.

My mother loved classical stuff—it was all she played in her car, which drove my sisters and me nuts. We'd beg for regular radio, anything from this century, but she was stubborn. "When you drive, you can listen to whatever you like," she'd say, then crank up Brahms or Beethoven to drown out our irritated sighs.

But in the car wash, my mother's music sounded different. Beautiful. It was only then that I could close my eyes and enjoy it, understanding what it was that she heard every time.

When I finally got my own license, I could play whatever I wanted, which was great. But still, the first time I went through 123SUDS alone, I flipped around my radio dial to find something classical, for old times' sake. Just as I was rolling in, though, the station faded and my tuner jumped to the next one, which was playing a loud, twangy country song, also not something I would have chosen on my own. But it was strange. Sitting there, the brushes moving overhead, water spilling down my window, even the song that was playing—something about driving an old Ford under a full moon—sounded perfect. As if it didn't matter what was on, but instead how hard I was listening, there in the dark.

I told Owen all this on the ride over, explaining how since then, I'd been convinced that anything sounded good at the car wash. He looked dubious, however, as he pushed quarters into the cashier station, and I had to wonder if my theory was about to debunked.

"So what now?" he asked as the machine spit out his

receipt and the red light beside the bay dropped to green. "We just drive in?"

"You've never done this?" I asked him.

"I'm not much for car upkeep simply for aesthetics' sake," he said. "Plus, I think there's a hole in my roof."

I motioned for him to drive forward and he did, over the slight bump and up to the yellow line, faded over time, that said STOP HERE. Then he cut the engine. "Okay," he said. "I'm ready to be impressed."

I shot him a look. "You know," I said, "this is your first time, so for full effect, you really need to recline."

"Recline."

"It adds to the experience," I told him. "Trust me."

We both eased back our seats, settling in. His arm was resting against mine, and I thought of being at his house the other night, and how I'd come so close to kissing him, twice. As the machine began to whir behind us, I reached forward and turned on the CD again. "All right," I said as the jets came on overhead. "Here we go."

The water was pattering at first, then began to move down the glass in front of us in a wave. Owen shifted in his seat as a drop fell from over his head, landing on his shirt. "Oh, great," he said. "There *is* a hole in the roof."

He grew quiet, though, as the next cut on the CD began with a soft murmuring, followed by some plucking of strings. There was also a bit of buzzing, but with the water moving over us, the inside of the car seeming smaller, then smaller still, it seemed to dissipate, fading out behind us. I could hear the hum of the brushes as they moved in closer to the car, intermixed with the sad, sloping chords of a violin. Already I could feel it happening, that slowing of time, everything stopping for this one moment, here, now.

I turned my head to look over at Owen. He was lying there, watching as the brushes drew big, soapy circles across the windshield in front of us, his gaze intent. Listening. I closed my eyes, focusing on doing the same. But all I could think was that it felt like my whole life had changed—again—in just the few weeks I'd known Owen; and not for the first time, I wanted to tell him so. Find the right words, string them together in the ideal way, knowing that here they would have the best chance of sounding perfect.

I turned toward him again, thinking this, and opened my eyes. He was looking right at me.

"You were right," he told me, his voice low. "This is great. Seriously."

"Yeah," I said. "It is."

Then he shifted, moving closer to me, and I felt his arm press against mine, his skin warm. And then, finally, Owen kissed me—really kissed me—and I couldn't hear anything: not the water, the music, or even my own heart, which had to be pounding. Instead, it was just silence, the very best kind, stretching out forever, or only a moment, and then it was over.

Suddenly, the car wash was quiet, the music finished. Above me, I could see one big drop, dangling precariously over our heads. I kept my eyes on it until dropped, landing with a plunk on my arm just as a horn beeped behind us.

"Whoops," Owen said, and we both sat up. He cranked the engine as I glanced back at a guy in a Mustang who was waiting, windows already up, by the entrance. "Hold on."

When we pulled out of the bay, the sun was bright, catching the pools of water as they broke up, sliding off the hood. With the kiss, and the dark, I felt like I was still underwater, the brightness startling.

"Man," Owen said, blinking as he pulled over by the curb, "that was really something."

"Told you. Everything sounds better in the car wash."

"Everything, huh?"

He was looking at me as he said this, and I had a flash of his face just moments earlier, staring up at the windshield, listening so carefully. Maybe sometime, I would be able to say everything I'd thought at that moment. And even more.

"I wonder," he said now, running a hand through his hair, "if it works for techno."

"Nope," I said flatly.

"You're sure."

"Oh, yeah." I nodded. "Positive."

He raised an eyebrow at me. "Yeah, well," he said, pulling away from the curb and starting around the building again. "We'll see."

"Did you hear?"

It was six o'clock on the Saturday of the fashion show, and I was sitting in the makeshift dressing room at Kopf's, waiting. For the last few hours, while getting my hair and makeup done and my outfit fitted and tweaked, I'd managed to ignore the chatter around me. Instead, I focused on getting through this show so I could move on to the one I really cared about, at

Bendo, with Owen. It had been working just fine. Until now.

I looked to my left, where Hillary Prescott had just sat down beside a girl named Marnie. Like me, they were already done with hair and makeup, which left them with nothing to do but drink bottled water, examine their reflections, and gossip.

"Hear about what?" Marnie asked. She was a thin girl with a long face and high cheekbones. When I'd first seen her I thought she looked like Whitney, somewhat, although she was more pretty than beautiful.

Hillary glanced over one shoulder, then another, the classic double-check. "What went down last night at Becca Durham's party," she said.

"No," Marnie said, dabbing a finger over the gloss on her lips. "What happened?"

Hillary leaned in a little closer. "Well," she said, "from what I heard, there was total drama. Louise told me that about halfway through the party—"

She stopped talking, suddenly, staring at the mirror facing us just as Emily Shuster walked in. She had her arms crossed over her chest, her head ducked down slightly, and her mom was with her. I only got one quick glance, but that was all it took to see Emily looked terrible: Her face was puffy, her eyes red, rimmed with dark circles.

Hillary, Marnie, and I all watched as she and her mom passed, continuing toward Mrs. McMurty, who was on the other side of the room. Then Hillary said, "I can't *believe* she showed up here."

"Why?" Marnie asked. "What happened?"

Not my problem, I thought, turning my attention back to

the history notebook I'd brought with me to get some studying in during the downtime. As I did so, though, I felt a piece of hair stick to my cheek. I looked up at the mirror to brush it away just as Hillary leaned in a little closer.

"She hooked up with Will Cash last night," she said, her voice low, but not that low. "In his car. And Sophie caught them."

"No way," Marnie said, her eyes wide. "Are you *serious*?"

Because I was looking at my reflection, I was able to actually see myself react as I heard this. I watched myself blink, my mouth fall open just slightly before I shut it, quick, and looked away.

"Louise was inside," Hillary was saying now, "so she only heard about it. But apparently Will had driven Emily there, and someone saw them. When Sophie heard, she *freaked*."

Marnie glanced over at Emily, who was now standing with her back to us while her mom spoke to Mrs. McMurty. "Oh my God," she said. "What did Will do?"

"I don't know. But Louise said that Sophie had kind of suspected something lately. Like Emily had been flirting with him, always acting silly when he was around."

Silly, I thought. *Or just nervous.* I had a flash of Will's intense, flat stare, how slowly the time seemed to pass whenever we were alone in the car waiting for Sophie. Behind me, people were passing by, other models talking, the same noise and commotion. But all I could hear were these two voices, and my own heartbeat.

"God," Marnie said. "Poor Sophie."

"No kidding. They were supposed to be best friends." Hillary sighed. "I guess you can't trust anybody."

I turned my head. Sure enough, they were both looking at me. I stared back at them, and Marnie blushed, shifting her gaze elsewhere. But Hillary kept her eyes on me for a long moment before pushing back her chair and standing up, then shaking out her hair and walking away. After picking at her water bottle for an uncomfortable few moments, Marnie got up and followed her.

For a moment, I just sat there, trying to process what I'd heard. I looked at Emily, who was now sitting in a chair across the room. Her mom, standing beside her, was saying something, her face serious, and Mrs. McMurty, next to her, was nodding. Mrs. Shuster's hand was on Emily's shoulder, and every once in a while I saw her squeeze it, the fabric bunching, then unbunching.

I closed my eyes, swallowing over the lump that had risen in my throat. *She hooked up with Will Cash last night. Sophie freaked. They were supposed to be best friends. I guess you can't trust anybody.*

No, I thought, *you can't.* I had a flash of the last few months, my quiet summer, starting school alone, that awful day in the courtyard when I'd pushed Sophie away. Maybe I couldn't have changed any of that. But now, too late, I was realizing I might have been able to change something. Or one thing.

I tried to study, tried to think about Owen and what came next. But every time I managed to distract myself for even a moment, I'd find myself looking up and across the room, where Emily was sitting in front of a mirror. She'd been so late they were having to make her up quickly, a hairstylist and makeup person working in tandem, stepping around each other. In the room between us, people kept passing by, their voices high, movements busy, as the time to the show counted down, but Emily kept her gaze straight ahead, looking at herself and no one else.

When they called us out of the dressing room, she didn't walk out with the rest of us. Instead, she showed up after we were all in our places to take her spot second in line, three people ahead of me. There was a digital clock on a nearby mall directory—it was 6:55. Several states and miles away, Kirsten was getting ready to show her piece, and I had a flash of that green, green grass, suddenly not so perfect anymore.

Usually, this was the time I was the most nervous, these last few minutes before I had to walk. Ahead of me, Julia Reinhart was tugging on the hem of her shirt, and behind me I could hear one of the freshman models complaining that her shoes were too tight. Emily wasn't saying a word, her eyes on the slit in the curtain.

The music started—it was loud and poppy, total Z104 material—and Mrs. McMurty came around the corner, looking frazzled, her clipboard in hand. "One minute!" she said, and the girl at the front of the line, one of the seniors, tossed her hair, squaring her shoulders.

I stretched out my fingertips, taking a deep breath. Now, in the mall itself, everything felt brighter and more open. All I had to do was get through this, get out, and go find Owen, moving forward into what I wanted, not what I'd been.

The music stopped for a moment, then began again. We were starting. Mrs. McMurty made her way up the stairs to stand by the curtain, then pulled it aside and motioned for the first girl to step through. As she did, I caught a glimpse of the crowd—so many people in the chairs on either side, and more standing behind them.

When it was Emily's turn, she headed out with her head high, her spine ramrod straight, and as I watched her I wished I was like everyone else out there, who would see only a beautiful girl in beautiful clothes, nothing more or less. Another girl went out, then Julia, after which point Emily returned, walking off the other side of the stage to the dressing room. Then it was my turn.

When the curtain opened, all I could see at first was the runway stretched out in front of me, a blur of faces on either side. The music was pounding in my ears as I began to walk, trying to keep my eyes straight ahead, but still, I caught the occasional glimpse of the crowd. I saw my parents on the left, my mother beaming at me, my dad's arm around her. Mallory Armstrong was sitting with the red-haired twins from her party a few rows back on the other side. In the split second our eyes met, she waved excitedly, hopping up and down in her seat. I kept going, down the runway. When I got to the very end, I saw Whitney.

She was leaning against a planter in front of the vitamin store, a good fifty feet from the back of the fashion-show crowd. I hadn't even known she was coming. But what surprised me more than this was the look on her face, which was so sad that it almost knocked the wind out of me. When our eyes met, she stepped forward, sliding her hands in her pockets, and for a moment I just stared at her, feeling a tug in my chest. And then I had to turn back.

I could feel a lump rising in my throat as I willed myself forward, toward the curtain. I'd been through enough. I didn't want to think about anything that was happening or had happened, to Emily, or to me. I just wanted to be on the wall with Owen, talking music, and be the girl he saw, who was different, and in a good way. All the good ways.

I was at the midpoint of the runway by now, halfway there. Four more changes, four more trips, a grand finale, and this would be over. It wasn't my job to save anyone, anyway. Especially since I hadn't even been able to save myself.

"Annabel!" I heard a voice call out, and I glanced to my left to see Mallory, smiling widely as she lifted her camera to her face, her finger moving to the shutter. The redheads were waving, everyone was watching, but as the flash popped, all I could think of was that night in her room with Owen, looking at all those faces on the wall and not even recognizing my own.

I turned back to face forward, and then Emily stepped out from behind the curtain. As I saw her, I heard Kirsten's voice in my head, explaining why she was scared to show her film: *This is personal*, she'd said. *Real*. This moment was, too, even if you couldn't tell at first glance. It was fake on the outside, but so true within. You only had to look, really look, to tell.

The weird thing was that all fall, at school, rehearsals, anytime we passed, Emily wouldn't meet my eyes. It was like she didn't want to see me at all. But this time as we approached each other, I could feel her staring at me, willing me to turn my head, pulling my gaze in her direction. I fought it as hard as I could. But just as she passed me, I gave in.

She knew. I could tell with one glance, one look, one simple instant. It was her eyes. Despite the thick makeup, they were still dark-rimmed, haunted, and sad. Most of all, though, they were familiar. The fact that we were in front of hundreds of strangers changed nothing at all. I'd spent a summer with those same eyes—scared, lost, confused—staring back at me. I would have known them anywhere.

Chapter
THIRTEEN

"Sophie!"

It was the annual end-of-year party, the previous June, and I was late. Emily's voice, saying this, was the first thing I heard when I stepped in the door.

At the time I couldn't see her—the foyer was packed, the stairs crowded with people as well—but then, a moment later, she rounded the corner, a beer in each hand. When she saw me, she smiled. "There you are," she said. "What took you so long?"

I had a flash of my mother's face an hour earlier, how her eyes had widened when Whitney pushed back her chair, then slammed it against the table, making all our plates jump. This time, the issue had been chicken, specifically the half a breast my father had deposited on Whitney's plate. After cutting it up into quarters, then eighths, then impossibly small sixteenths, she'd pushed it all to the side before commencing to eat her salad, chewing each bite of lettuce for what seemed like ages. My parents and I acted like we weren't watching this, like we weren't even aware, keeping a conversation about the weather somehow aloft among the three of us. Still, a few minutes later, when Whitney dropped her napkin on her plate, I watched it drift down, draping the chicken like a magician's scarf as she willed it to disappear. No luck. My father told her to finish her food, and then she exploded.

By this point, we should have been used to her dinnertime histrionics—she'd been out of the hospital for several months, during which time they'd become routine— but there were still times when the volume and suddenness of her outbursts took us all by surprise. Especially my mom, who always seemed to take every raised syllable, every slam or crash, even the numerous sarcastic sighs like personal attacks. This was why I'd lingered after dinner, standing in the kitchen as my mother washed dishes. I could see her face reflected in the window over the sink, and I kept watching it closely, the way I always did when she got upset, worried I might see something besides her features that I recognized.

"I got held up at home," I told Emily now. "What'd I miss?"

"Not much," she said. "Have you seen Sophie?"

I looked around, past the clump of people beside us and into the living room, where I spotted her on a short couch by the window, a bored expression on her face.

"This way," I told Emily, taking one of the beers from her as I worked through the crowd over to the couch. "Hey," I called out to Sophie, over the din of a nearby TV. "What's going on?"

"Nothing," she replied, her voice flat. She nodded at the beer. "Is that for me?"

"Maybe," I said. She made a face at me, and I handed it over, then sat down as she took a sip, her lipstick staining the rim.

"God, I love your shirt, Annabel," Emily said. "Is it new?"

"Yeah. Pretty new." I reached up, running my hand over the pink suede top my mom and I had found at Tosca earlier the day before. It had been expensive, but we figured the whole summer's worth of wear I'd get out of it justified the price. "I just got it this week."

Sophie exhaled loudly, shaking her head. "This," she announced, "is officially the worst last-day-of-classes party ever."

"It's only eight thirty," I told her, looking around the room. There was a couple making out on a nearby armchair, and I could see a group of people sitting around the dining-room table playing cards. Music was coming from somewhere, probably out back, the bass thumping beneath our feet. "Things could improve."

She took another swig of her beer. "Doubtful. If this is any indication, this summer's going to be the worst yet."

"You think?" Emily said, sounding surprised. "There were some cute college guys outside."

"And you'd want to date a college guy who hangs out at a high-school party?" Sophie said.

"Well," Emily replied, "I don't know."

"Like I told you," Sophie said. "Lame."

There was a burst of noise to our left, and I turned to see a group of people pushing their way into the foyer. I saw a girl I recognized from my P.E. class, a couple of guys I didn't know, and, bringing up the rear, Will Cash.

"See? Things are looking up already," I said to Sophie. Instead of looking pleased, though, she narrowed her eyes.

They'd had some spat earlier in the week, but I'd thought it was resolved as much as anything ever was between them. Apparently not. Will only nodded at Sophie before following the people he'd come with down the hallway to the kitchen.

Once he was out of sight, she sat back, crossing her legs. "This sucks," she announced, and this time, I knew better than to disagree.

I stood up, holding my hand out to her. "Come on," I said. "Let's go circulate."

"No," she said flatly. Emily, who had started to get up, sat down again.

"Sophie."

She shook her head. "You two go. Have a fabulous time."

"So you just want to stay here and sulk?"

"I'm not sulking," she said, her voice cold. "I'm just sitting."

"Fine," I said. "I'm going to get another beer. You need anything?"

"No," she said, her eyes on the dining room, where Will was talking to the guy at the head of the table who was dealing out cards.

"You want to come with me?" I asked Emily. She nodded, putting her beer on the coffee table, and followed me down the hallway.

"Is she okay?" she asked me as soon as we were out of Sophie's earshot.

"She's fine," I told her.

"She seems upset," she said. "Before you got here, she was barely even speaking to me."

"She'll warm up," I told her. "You know how she is."

We walked through the kitchen and out onto the porch to the keg, which was surrounded by a few older guys. "Hey," one of them, who was tall and thin and smoking a cigarette, said to me. "Let me get you a beer."

"I'm okay," I said, giving him a mild smile as I picked up a cup and filled it myself.

"You two go to Jackson?" another asked Emily, who was standing off to the side, her arms crossed over her chest. She nodded, her eyes on me. "Man, these freshmen get hotter every year."

"We're not freshmen," I said as I turned away from the keg. A curly-headed guy was standing right in front of me now, blocking my path. I said, "Excuse me."

He looked at me for a second before moving aside. "Hard to get, huh?" he said as I stepped past him. "I like that."

I walked back into the kitchen, and Emily followed, shutting the door behind us.

"Those weren't the ones I was talking about earlier," she said quietly.

"I know," I said. "Those guys are at every party."

We started back to Sophie, but a bunch of people had just come in, and the hallway was packed with bodies and noise. I tried to push my way through, only to get stuck about halfway to the living room, with people crammed on all sides of me. I turned my head, looking for Emily, but she'd been waylaid by a loud girl named Helena we knew from the Models who, from the looks of it, was yelling in her ear.

"*Excuse* me," some girl I didn't recognize snapped as she

pushed past me, her elbow cracking against mine. I felt a splash, then looked down to see beer—hers or mine, it was hard to say—running down my leg. Suddenly the hallway seemed even smaller, not to mention hotter. So when a space opened up to my left, I took it, turning into a small alcove under the stairs where I could finally breathe.

I leaned back, pressing myself against the wall, and took a sip of my beer as people continued to push past. I was getting ready to go back into the throng when Will Cash walked by. He glanced over at me, then stopped.

"Hey," he said. Two guys passed him going the other way. One of them reached up, ruffling his hair, and Will made a face. "What are you doing?"

"Nothing," I said. "Just—"

He turned, then ducked under to where I was. There was barely enough room for both of us in the alcove—it was the kind of place for a small table, or maybe a piece of art—but I still tried to move to my left, putting some space between us.

"Hiding out, huh?" he asked. He wasn't smiling as he said this, even though I was pretty sure he meant it as a joke. That was the thing with Will. You just could never tell. Or I couldn't, anyway.

"It just . . . got a little crazy out there," I said. "Have you, um, caught up with Sophie yet?"

He was still looking at me, that flat gaze, and I felt myself flush again. "Not yet," he said. "How long you guys been here?"

"Oh, I didn't come with them," I replied as Hillary Prescott walked past. When she saw us, she slowed her pace, staring at us for a moment before moving on, disappearing around the corner. "I just got here . . . I got held up at home."

Will didn't say anything, just kept staring at me.

"You know how it is," I said, taking another gulp of my beer as a bunch of girls passed by, laughing loudly. "Family drama and all that."

I had no idea why I was telling him this, just as I had no idea why I did anything I did around Will Cash. Something about him unsettled me to a point where I felt so tentative that for some reason I compensated by being entirely too open.

"Really," he said now, his voice flat.

I felt my face flush again. "I should go catch up with Sophie," I said. "I'll, um, see you around, I guess."

He nodded. "Yeah," he said. "See you."

I didn't even wait for a break in the crowd, instead just pushing forward, bumping some football player who was passing and following him back toward the kitchen, where I found Emily leaning against the island, her cell phone pressed to her ear.

"Where'd you go?" she asked, flipping it closed and slipping it back into her pocket.

"Nowhere," I said. "Come on."

When we got back to the living room, Sophie was still on the couch, but now she wasn't alone. Will had joined her, and from the looks of it, they were having some sort of argument. Sophie was saying something, her face pinched, while Will seemed to be only half listening, glancing around the room as she talked.

"Better not bug them right now," I said to Emily. "We'll

come back. Anyway, I have got to pee. Any idea where the bathroom is?"

"I thought I saw one over there," she said, nodding toward a nearby hallway. "Come on."

There was a bathroom there, but also a line, so we decided to try our luck on the second floor. We were navigating a long hallway when I heard someone yell out my name.

I stopped, then doubled back to an open door we'd just passed to see Michael Kitchens and Nick Lester, two seniors I'd spent all semester suffering through art history with, playing pool.

"See?" Nick said. "I told you I saw Annabel!"

"What do you know," Michael, who was bent over the table about to take a shot, said. "And here I thought you were just hallucinating."

Nick turned around, then put a hand to his heart when he saw me. "No, it's Annabel," he said. "Annabel, Annabel, Annabel Greene."

"You promised when the year was over, you'd let that go," I told him. He'd done some senior project on Poe and had bugged me with this line endlessly. "Remember?"

"No," he said, grinning at me.

Michael took the shot, the balls splitting apart with a clank. "Nick's drunk," he informed us. "Consider yourself warned."

"I'm not drunk," Nick said. "I'm just cheerful."

"Is there a bathroom in here?" I asked. "We've been looking for one everywhere."

"Right over there," Michael told me, nodding across the room.

"Come on," I said to Emily, and she followed me inside. "This is Nick and Michael," I said, handing her my beer. "And this is Emily. I'll be back in a sec, okay?"

She nodded, looking a bit nervous. "Do you play?" Michael asked her, gesturing at the table.

"Kind of," she said.

He walked over to the wall, pulling off a stick for her. "Yeah, right," he said. "You say that, and then you'll beat me in ten seconds."

"She does have that pool-shark look to her," Nick said. Emily laughed, shaking her head. "It's always the quiet ones."

"Just go easy on me," Michael said to her. "That's all I ask."

By the time I came out of the bathroom two minutes later, Emily was holding her own. She was also in full-on flirt mode with Michael, who seemed more than happy to reciprocate. Which left me with Nick, who sat down beside me on the near-by couch and announced he had something to say.

"You know," he said as he took a sip of his beer, "since school is over now and all, I just think you should know that I'm aware of how you feel about me."

"How I feel about you," I repeated.

"Dude," Michael called out from the right corner pocket. "Stop before you say something you regret."

"Shhh," Nick told him, waving his arm. He turned back to me. "Annabel," he said, his voice serious, "it's okay that you have a crush on me."

"Oh, God," Michael groaned. "I'm so embarrassed for you right now."

"I mean, it makes sense," Nick said, slurring slightly as I

tried not to smile. "I'm a senior. An older man. It makes sense you'd look up to me. But . . ." Here he paused, taking another swig of his beer. "It's not going to work out."

"Oh," I said. "Well. It's better to know now, I guess."

Nick patted my hand, nodding. "I'm really flattered, but it doesn't matter how much you love me. I just don't feel that way about you."

"Like hell," Michael said, and Emily laughed.

"I understand," I told Nick.

"You do?"

"Totally."

He was still patting my hand, although, at this point, I was not sure he was aware of it. "Good. Because I'd really like, if you can get past your feelings, for us to remain friends."

"Me, too," I said.

Nick sat back, tipping his bottle to his mouth. Then he brought it back down, turning it up. One drop fell out. "Empty," he announced. "I need another."

"You really don't," Michael said, then winced as Emily shot the cue ball, knocking two of his stripes into a pocket.

"How about a water?" I asked Nick. "I was just about to get one for myself."

"A water," he repeated slowly, as if this was a foreign concept. "Okay. Lead the way."

"We'll be back," I said to Emily as I got to my feet, Nick then doing the same with considerably more trouble. "You need anything?"

She shook her head, bending down for another shot. "I'm good," she said.

"Too good," Michael said as two more of his balls disappeared. "'Kind of' play, my ass."

Nick and I only made it about halfway down the hallway before he announced he'd changed his mind. "Too tired," he said, plopping down next to a bedroom door. "Need to rest."

"Are you okay?" I asked him.

"Dandy," he replied. "You just go get that, that . . ."

"Water," I said.

"Water . . . and I'll meet you right here. 'Kay?" He sat back, his head bonking the wall. "Right here."

I nodded, then continued on to the stairs. On the way, I stopped to look down at the living room below, which was now considerably more crowded. Sophie was gone from the couch, as was Will, which I figured was either a good sign or a really bad one.

Downstairs, I located two bottled waters, then stopped to talk to a few people. When I got back to the hallway, Nick wasn't there. I figured he'd headed back to the game room. I was just about to do the same when I heard a voice.

"Annabel."

It was soft and faint. I turned. There was a bedroom to my right, the door slightly ajar. Handy if you were stumbling or, even worse, puking. *Poor Nick*, I thought. I stuck one water in my back pocket, opened the other one, then pushed the door open and stepped inside.

"Hey," I said. "Did you get lost?"

As I stepped over the threshold into the dark, I had my first prickling sense that something wasn't right. It was just how the room felt, like the entire space around me was unsettled. I stepped back, reaching for the knob, but I couldn't find it, my fingers only touching wall. "Nick?" I said.

Then, suddenly, I felt something bump up against my left side. Not furniture, or an object, but something alive. Someone. *It's Nick*, I told myself. *He's drunk*. But at the same time I started moving my hand behind me, faster now, searching for the light switch or doorknob. Finally, I felt the knob. Just as I was twisting it, though, I felt fingers closing over my wrist.

"Hey," I said, and even though I was trying to act casual, my voice sounded scared. "What's—?"

"Shhh, Annabel," a voice said, and then the fingers were moving up my arm, over my skin, and I felt another hand on my right shoulder. "It's just me."

It wasn't Nick. This voice was deeper, and not slurring at all, each syllable enunciated perfectly. As I realized this, I panicked, my hand gripping tighter around the water bottle in my hand.The top popped off, and suddenly I felt cold seeping into my shirt, onto my skin. "Don't," I said.

"Shhh," the voice said again, and then the hands were off me. A second later, they covered my eyes.

I jerked forward, trying to pull away. The water bottle, now half empty, fell from my hands, hitting the carpet with a dull thud, and his hands grabbed me by my shoulders, hard. I kept wriggling, trying to get loose and turn around, toward the door, but my hands were flailing in empty air. It was like the walls had slid back, out of reach; there was nothing to hold on to.

I could hear myself gasping, my breath beginning to sputter as he locked an elbow around my neck, pulling me up against him. My legs came up off the ground and I started kicking them, making contact with the door once—*bang!*—before he dragged me backwards a couple of steps. Then his other hand was moving around to my stomach, pushing aside my shirt, and thrusting down my jeans.

"Stop it," I said, but then his arm—warm, and smelling of sweat—was covering my mouth, blocking the sound. His fingers were sharp as he pushed aside my underwear, going deeper and deeper, his breath now hard little bursts in my ear. I was still trying to get away, squirming, even as his fingers probed farther, and then he was inside me.

I bit down on the skin of his arm, hard. He yelped, then yanked his arm off my mouth, pushing me forward. As I felt my feet under me, I reached for the wall, trying to get my bearings, my fingers only barely raking some solid surface before he grabbed the waistband of my jeans and turned me around to face him. Instinctively I put my hands out in front of me, shielding myself, but he pushed them aside, roughly, and then I was down.

In a second—it seemed impossible he could move so fast—he was on top of me, his fingers fumbling open the snap of my jeans. I could feel carpet beneath me, scratchy on my back, as I tried to push him away, the smell of wet suede filling my nostrils as he put one hand on my chest, his palm flat against my skin to hold me down, and began pulling down my jeans with the other. I was digging into the floor with my elbows, putting all I had into rising up, but I couldn't move.

I heard him unzip, and then he was back on top of me. I tried to push against his shoulders, throwing every bit of my weight against him, but he was so heavy, pressing into me, push-ing one of my legs up—this was really happening—and then, just as I felt him on my leg and twisted myself one last, desper-ate time, I saw something: a tiny sliver of light, falling across us.

It was like a thread through the dark, and in it, I saw a bit of his back, freckled; the fine blond hair on the arm that was thrown across me; the tiniest bit of dark pink suede; and then, just before he pushed off me, his eyes, blue, the pupils widen-ing, then narrowing, then widening again, as the light stretched wider. And then he was scrambling to his feet.

I sat up, my heart pounding, and pulled up my pants. Somehow, I was able to focus on zipping them, as if this, now, was the most important thing in the world. I had just gotten it when the light overhead clicked on, and there, standing in front of me, was Sophie.

She saw me first. Then she turned her head and looked at Will Cash, who was now sitting on the bed behind me. "Will?" she asked. Her voice was high, tight. "What's going on?"

Will, I thought. I had a flash of his arm covering my mouth, his hands over my eyes, then another of him earlier, standing so close to me in the alcove. *It's Will.*

"I don't know." He shrugged, then ran a hand through his hair. "She just . . ."

Sophie stared at him for a long moment. From the hallway behind her, I could hear laughter, and I had a flash of Emily and Michael still playing their game. Still waiting for me.

Sophie turned to me. "Annabel?" she said, then stepped forward, into the room, her hand still on the doorjamb. "What are you doing?"

I felt like I'd been shattered, everything that had just happened a fragment, no part of a real whole. I got to my feet, smoothing down my top over my stomach. "Nothing," I said, the word coming out in a gasp. I tried to swallow. "I was—"

Sophie cut her eyes back at Will, and even though she hadn't interrupted me, I stopped talking. He stared right back at her. Not a flinch. Not one. "Somebody," she said, "had better start explaining this. Right now."

But nobody said anything. Later, this would strike me as so surprising, that at that moment I was actually waiting for someone else to define this, as if I hadn't been there, had no words for it at all.

"Will?" Sophie said. "Say something."

"Look," he said, "I was waiting for you, and then she came up here . . ." He trailed off, shaking his head, but kept his eyes on her. "I don't know."

Sophie turned her attention back to me, and for a moment we just looked at each other. She had to see something was wrong, I thought. I shouldn't have to tell her. I wasn't some other girl, like the ones we'd driven around looking for all those nights. We were best friends. I honestly believed that. Then.

Her mouth pursed. I watched the lips come together. "You *slut*," she said.

It seemed so stupid, later. But I actually, honestly thought I'd heard her wrong. "What?" I said.

"You're a goddamn whore." Her voice was rising now, still shaky but gaining strength. "I can't believe you."

"Sophie," I said. "Wait. I didn't—"

"You didn't what?" she said. Behind her, I could see shadows, stretching forward across the opposite wall of the hallway. People were coming, I thought. People were hearing this. People would know. "You think you can just fuck my boyfriend at a party and I won't find out?"

I felt my mouth open, but no words came. I just stood there, staring at her, and then Emily appeared behind her in the doorway, her eyes wide. "Annabel?" she asked. "What's going on?"

"Your friend's a slut is what's going on," Sophie told her.

"No," I said. "It's not like that."

"I know what I saw!" she screamed. Emily, behind her, stepped backwards. Sophie leveled a finger at me. "You have always wanted what I have!" she said. "You've always been jealous of me!"

I felt myself flinch. Her voice was so loud it was like it was shaking my bones. I was so confused, and scared, and even though through everything else, I had not cried—how had I not cried?—now I felt a lump begin and then swell in my throat.

Sophie pushed through the door, taking two big strides until she was right in front of me, and the room seemed to shrink—Will, Emily, everyone else disappearing from my peripheral vision—until it was just her narrowed eyes, her finger still jabbing, so much anger and fury.

"You're so done," she said. Her voice was shaking. "It's over for you."

"Sophie." I shook my head. "Please. Just—"

"Get out of my face!" she said. "Get out!"

And then, as quickly as it had fallen away, my view came back and I saw everything. The crowd of faces that had somehow gathered in the hallway. Will Cash, in my side vision, still sitting on the bed. The sea-foam green of the carpet beneath my feet, the yellow glare of the light overhead. It was hard to believe that only moments earlier, all of these things had been cloaked in such a thick darkness, so hidden I wouldn't have been able to recognize a single one. But now, like me, they were exposed.

Sophie was still standing in front of me. It was quiet all around us. I knew I could have broken the silence, could have spoken up. It was only my word against his, and now hers. But I didn't.

Instead, I walked out of that room and everyone watched me. I could feel their eyes as I stepped around Sophie, then pushed out into the hallway and started for the stairs. Once in the foyer, I went to the door, pushing it open, then stepped out into the night, crossing the damp grass to my car. I did all of this very carefully and with purpose, as if having control over these actions would somehow balance out what had just happened.

The one thing I didn't do, though, all the way home, was look at myself. Not in the side mirror. Not in the rearview. At every stoplight, every time I downshifted, I picked a point up ahead—the bumper of the car in front of me, a distant building, even the broken yellow line of the road—to focus on. I did not want to see myself like this.

When I got home, my dad was waiting, like always, sitting up by himself. I could see the light from the TV, pale and flickering, the minute I stepped inside.

"Annabel?" he called out as the volume on the set began to

decrease, bit by bit, before falling silent entirely. "Is that you?"

I stood there for a second in the foyer, knowing that if I didn't show my face he'd suspect something. I reached up, brushing back my hair with my fingers, then took a breath and stepped into the living room. "Yeah," I said. "It's me."

He turned in his chair to look at me. "Good night?" he asked.

"It was okay," I said.

"There's a great show on," he said, nodding at the TV. "It's all about the New Deal. You interested?"

Any other night, I would have joined him. It was our tradition, even if I only sat down for a few minutes. But this time, I just couldn't.

"No, thanks," I said. "I'm kind of tired. I think I'll just go to bed."

"All right," he said, turning back to the TV. "Good night, Annabel."

"Good night."

He picked up the remote and I turned away, walking back into the foyer, where the moonlight was slanting in the window over the door and falling on the picture of me and my mother and sisters on the opposite wall. In that bright light, you could see every detail: the distant caps of the waves, the slight tinge of gray to the sky. I stood there for a moment, studying each of us, taking in Kirsten's smile, Whitney's haunted gaze, the way my mother cocked her head slightly to the side. When I got to my own face, I found myself staring at it, so bright, with dark all around it, like it was someone I didn't recognize. Like a word on a page that you've printed and read a million times, that suddenly looks strange or wrong, foreign, and you feel scared for a second, like you've lost something, even if you're not sure what it is.

The next day, I tried to call Sophie, but she wouldn't answer. I knew I should go over to her house, explain myself in person, but each time I began to I had a flash of being in that room, that hand over my mouth, the bang of my foot kicking the door, and I just couldn't do it. In fact, whenever I thought about what had happened, my stomach twisted and I felt bile rising in my throat. Like some part of me was trying to push it up and out, purging it from my body entirely in a way I could not seem to do on my own.

The alternative wasn't good either, of course. I'd already been labeled a slut, and who knew how the story had grown in the hours since. But what had really happened was worse than anything Sophie could make up and pass on.

Even so, deep down, I knew I hadn't done anything wrong. That this wasn't my fault, and in a perfect world, I could tell people what happened and somehow not be ashamed. In real life, though, this was harder. I was used to being looked at—it was part of who I was, who I'd been as long as I could remember. But once people knew about this, I was sure they'd see me in a different way. That with every glance, they'd no longer see me, but what had happened to me, so raw and shameful and private, turned outward and suddenly scrutinized. I wouldn't be the girl who had everything, but the girl who'd been attacked, assaulted, so helpless. It seemed safer to hold it in, where the only one who could judge was me.

Still, I had times when I wondered if this was the right decision. But as the days passed, and then weeks, it seemed like even if I could have told my story, now it was too late. Like the longer the distance from it, the less people would be willing to believe it.

So I did nothing. But a couple of weeks later, I was with my mother at the drugstore, picking up a few things, when she said, "Isn't that Sophie?"

It was. She was at the other end of the aisle, looking at magazines. I watched her turn a page, wrinkling her nose at something she saw there. "Yeah," I replied. "I think so."

"Then go say hello. I'll get this," she said, taking the list from me. "Just catch up with me up front, okay?" And then she was gone, shifting her basket farther up her arm and leaving us alone.

I should have just followed her. But for whatever reason, I found myself walking toward Sophie, coming up behind her just as she stuffed the magazine—which had a cover entirely devoted to the latest high-profile celebrity breakup—back onto the rack. "Hi," I said.

She jumped, startled, then turned around. When she saw me, she narrowed her eyes. "What do you want?"

I hadn't planned what I was going to say, but even if I had, this would have made it harder. "Look," I said, glancing over to the next aisle, where my mother was examining an aspirin display, "I just wanted to—"

"Don't talk to me," she said. Her voice was loud, much louder than mine. "I have nothing to say to you."

"Sophie," I said. I was almost whispering now. "It wasn't what you think."

"Oh, so you're psychic now, and not just a slut?"

I felt my face flush at this word, and instinctively looked over again at my mom, wondering if she'd heard it. She'd glanced up, and now smiled at us and moved on farther down to the next aisle.

"What, is there a problem, Annabel?" Sophie said. "Let me guess. Just the regular family drama?"

I just looked at her, confused. Then I remembered: This was what I'd said to Will in the alcove that night, for what reason I still didn't know. Of course he'd tell her, use this, the stupidest of confessions, against me. I could just imagine how he'd spun it, me confiding in him, then following him upstairs. *I don't know*, he'd said that night as I waited for him to explain himself. *She just* . . .

"If you know a guy has a girlfriend—especially if that girlfriend is me—there's absolutely no reason you should be doing anything with him that could be taken the wrong way," Sophie had said to me, all those months ago. "It's a choice, Annabel. And if you make the wrong one, you have only yourself to blame when there are consequences."

In her mind, it was that simple. I knew this wasn't true, but I felt a flicker of doubt and fear as the pieces came together, building against me, my worst fears realized. What if even if I had told, or did tell, nobody believed me? Or even worse, blamed me for it?

My stomach twisted, that familiar taste filling my mouth.

Sophie glanced over at my mom, watching her for a second, and I had a flash of her that night at dinner, wincing as Whitney slammed her chair into the table. I'd been so worried about her that night, so many nights, and I couldn't imagine what she'd make of this if it ever got back to her.

"Sophie," I said again. "Just—"

"Get away from me," she said. "I never want to see you again."

Then she pushed past me, shaking her head, and walked away. Somehow, I managed to turn around and make my way back down the aisle, the shelves blurring as I passed them. I saw a woman with a kid on her hip, an old man pushing a walker, some stock clerk examining a price gun, and then, finally, my mom, standing by a sunscreen display, looking for me.

"There you are," she said as I approached. "How's Sophie?"

I forced myself to take in a breath. "She's good," I said. "Fine."

It was the first lie I told my mother about Sophie, but by no means the last. Then, I'd still thought everything I felt about that night—the shame, the fear—would fade in time, healing like a onetime gash to a single, barely noticeable scar. But that hadn't happened. Instead, the things that I remembered, these little details, seemed to grow stronger, to the point where I could feel their weight in my chest. Nothing, however, stuck with me more than the memory of stepping into that dark room and what I found there, and how the light then took that nightmare and made it real.

That was the thing: Once, the difference between light and

dark had been basic. One was good, one bad. Suddenly, though, things weren't so clear. The dark was still a mystery, something hidden, something to be scared of, but I'd come to fear the light, too. It was where everything was revealed, or seemed to be. Eyes closed, I saw only the blackness, reminding me of this one thing, the most deep of my secrets; eyes open, there was only the world that didn't know it, bright, inescapable, and somehow, still there.

Chapter
FOURTEEN

"Hey," Owen said, smiling as he turned around to face me. "You made it."

And I had. I was there, at Bendo, standing in front of the stage. How, though, I wasn't exactly sure. In fact, everything since Emily and I had finally come face-to-face was a bit of a blur.

Somehow, I'd managed to finish the fashion show, modeling three other outfits and clapping as Mrs. McMurty pretended to be both totally embarrassed and completely surprised to be coaxed onstage for flowers, just like every other year. Afterwards, I'd gone backstage, where my parents were waiting.

When my mother saw me, she pulled me in for a hug, her hands smoothing over my back. "You were fantastic," she said. "Absolutely gorgeous."

"Although that dress is a little low-cut," my dad added, eyeing the white sheath I'd worn for the formal segment, the last one of the show. "Wouldn't you say?"

"No," my mom said, swatting him as she pulled away from me. "It's perfect. You were perfect."

I forced a smile, but my mind was still reeling. There were

so many people behind the stage, so much noise and commotion, but all I could think about was Emily. *She knew*, I thought as my mom said something about finding Mrs. McMurty. *She knew*.

I reached up, tucking a piece of hair behind my ear. I felt nervous, jumpy, the noise of the crowd and the heat of all those bodies not helping, and now my mother was talking again.

". . . just wonderful, but we should get home. Whitney's fixing dinner, and I told her we'd be there ten minutes ago."

"Whitney?" I said as my dad nodded at a man in a suit as he passed, saying his name. "She's not here?"

My mom squeezed my shoulder. "Oh, sweetie, I'm sure she would have liked to come, but it's still hard for her, I think. . . . She wanted to stay home. But we loved it. We really did."

With everything that had happened with Emily, I felt crazy, but I knew one thing: That had been my sister, watching me from a distance as I reached the end of the runway. I would have bet my life on it.

I felt a hand on my arm, and turned to see Mrs. McMurty standing there, a tall, gray-haired man in a suit beside her. "Annabel," she said, smiling, "I want you to meet Mr. Driscoll. He's the head of marketing for Kopf's, and he wanted to say hello."

"Hi," I said. "It's nice to meet you."

"And you as well," he replied, reaching out his hand. His palm was dry and cool. "We're all big fans. We loved you in the back-to-school commercial."

"Thank you," I said.

"Great show." He smiled, nodding at my mom and dad, and

then he and Mrs. McMurty were moving on, through the crowd. My mother watched them go, her face flushed.

"Oh, Annabel," she said. She squeezed my arm again, not saying anything else, but I got the message. Loud and clear.

Just then, over my mom's head, I saw Mrs. Shuster, a coat folded over her arm, standing by the back edge of the stage. She looked at her watch, then glanced around, worried. A second later, her face relaxed, and I saw Emily walking toward her. Her hair was still up, her makeup on, but she'd changed back into regular clothes and wasn't talking to anyone as she made her way through the crowd.

"Um, I should go change," I said to my parents. "These shoes are killing me."

My mom nodded, then leaned in, giving me another kiss. "Of course," she said as Mr. Driscoll walked past again, this time without Mrs. McMurty. My mom watched him go, then said, "I'll put aside a plate for you, all right?"

"Actually," I said, "um, some of us were going to go out for pizza. You know, to celebrate the show being over, and all."

"Oh," my mom said. "Well, I know you must be exhausted, so don't stay out too long. Okay?"

I nodded as, behind her, I watched Mrs. Shuster reach out to Emily, handing her the coat and standing there, her face somber, as Emily shrugged it on. Then she slid her hand down her daughter's arm, rubbing it slightly, and they started toward the mall exit. I turned my attention back to my mother, quickly. "I won't be too late," I said.

"Eleven at the latest," my father said as he leaned down to give me a hug. "Right?"

"Right," I replied.

The entire time I was changing out of my outfit, then walking to my car and driving across town, I told myself I had to
push what had happened with Emily out of my mind. I'd been
looking forward to going to Bendo, and I was determined to
enjoy it. Or try to.

Starting right now.

"So," I said as Owen turned back to the stage, "what'd I miss?"

"Not much," he replied as someone bumped me from
behind. As I pitched forward he reached out, grabbing my arm.
"Whoa," he said. "Watch the footing, this place is kind of a mad-
house." There was a burst of feedback from the stage in front
of us, and a group of people to our left let loose with a loud
chorus of boos. Owen leaned his head down closer to my ear.
"How was the fashion show?"

I didn't want to lie to him. At the same time, though, I knew
I couldn't tell him what had really happened—not here, not
tonight. Maybe not ever. "It's over," I replied, which was, technically, true.

"That good, huh?" he said as a tall girl in a sequined top,
holding a drink, pushed past us, splattering as she went.

I smiled. "Pretty much."

"Well, never fear. When the band comes on, your night will
improve."

"You think?"

"I know," he said just as he got bumped, hard this time, by
a guy in a black coat who was passing by, a cell phone pressed
to his ear. Owen glanced at him, and the guy shrugged, hardly

bothered, and kept walking. "Okay. Time for a space break. Come on."

He turned and started back through the crowd, and I did my best to follow him as he led me to an open booth against the wall.

"Have a seat," he said, gesturing for me to slide in. "The view isn't as good, but at least no one's elbowing you in the spleen."

I could hear what sounded like someone tuning up, followed by a burst of feedback. "The opener," Owen said, nodding toward the stage. "They were supposed to go on a half hour ago, but—"

This thought was interrupted by Rolly, who suddenly slid in beside him, landing with a thump on the bench. "Oh," he said, breathless, "my God."

"Finally," Owen said, turning to look at him. "Where the hell have you been, man? I was beginning to think you'd been abducted or something."

"No," Rolly replied. "You are not going to *believe* what just happened."

"He went to get drinks about a half hour ago," Owen explained to me. "I mean, I know the crowd is big, but that's ridiculous. And where's my water?"

Rolly shook his head. "Dude. She's here."

"What?"

Rolly took in a breath, then held up his hands, palms facing out. *"She's here,"* he said again. Then he paused, letting this sink in before adding, "She's here, and she smiled at me."

"For thirty minutes?" Owen asked.

"No. Only for a moment."

"This is the girl that punched you?" I asked, clarifying.

"Yes."

"I can't believe you didn't get my water," Owen said.

"Would you just forget about that for a second?" Rolly pulled a hand through his hair. "I don't think you're getting the significance of this situation."

"So you talked to her," Owen said.

"No. Here's what happened." Rolly took a deep breath. "I was on my way to the bar and then, suddenly, there she was. Boom! Popped up right in front of me, like an apparition or something. But just as I'm about to speak to her, someone steps between us. And the next thing I know, she's gone, walking away, surrounded by people. Since then I've been hanging back, waiting for the perfect in to present itself. I mean, it has to be just right."

"Why don't you offer to go get her a water?" Owen suggested. "You can pick up one for me while you're at it."

Rolly just looked at him. "What is up with you and this water thing?"

"I'm thirsty," Owen told him. "And I was going to go, but you offered. *Insisted*, I might add."

"I will get you a water!" Rolly said. "But first, if you don't mind, I'd like to meet my destiny in the most ideal way possible."

There was another burst of feedback from the stage. Owen sighed. "Look," he said, "maybe you should just forget about the ideal moment."

Rolly just looked at him. "I'm not following," he said.

"It's taken a long time for you to see her again, right?"

Owen said. "And who knows how much longer until the perfect moment. Maybe you should just do it. That way—"

Rolly's eyes widened, suddenly. "Oh, shit," he said. "There she is."

Owen leaned out of the booth slightly. "Where?"

"Don't look!" Rolly said, yanking him back in. "God!"

Owen looked down at his sleeve, which Rolly was clutching. Rolly moved his hand.

"Okay," he said quietly. "She's standing by the door. In the red."

I watched as Owen leaned out of the booth again, took a quick glance behind me, then sat back straight again. "Yep, that's her," he reported. "Now what?"

"My point exactly," Rolly said. "I need an in."

By this point, I had to admit that the suspense was killing me. "I'm just going to do a quick over-the-shoulder survey of the room," I said to Rolly. "Okay?"

He nodded, and Owen shot him a look. "She's a girl," Rolly explained. "They can look without looking."

When I first turned around, all I could see was a heavyset guy in a Metallica shirt. But then he moved slightly, and I saw that there was a girl behind him. She had shiny black hair and was wearing little retro glasses, a red sweater and jeans, a beaded bag pulled across her. But I didn't need to see any of these things, really; I knew her with one glance.

"Wait," I said, turning back to Rolly. "The girl . . . it's Clarke?"

For a moment, Rolly just looked at me. Then he leaned across the table so quickly that I drew back, startled, bumping my head on the booth behind me. "Is that her name?" he asked. His face was now inches from mine. "Clarke?"

I nodded, carefully. "Um . . . yeah."

After staring at me for another second he moved back, slowly, until he was sitting upright. "She has a *name*. And it is Clarke. Clarke . . ." He trailed off, looking at me again.

"Reynolds," I said.

"Clarke Reynolds," he repeated. "Wow." He looked like he was in a trance. Then, suddenly, his eyes widened, and he snapped his fingers. "That's it! That's my in. You."

"Me?"

He nodded vigorously. "You know her."

"No," I said quickly. "I don't."

"You knew her name," he pointed out.

"We were friends once. It was—"

"You're *friends* with her?" he asked. "This is perfect!"

"It's really not," I said, shaking my head.

"You go up and talk to her, and then I'll walk by and you can introduce me. It's organic. It's ideal!"

"Rolly, seriously," I said. "I'm not the person to get you close to Clarke."

"Annabel." He leaned across the table again, sliding his hands out to mine. "Annabel, Annabel, Annabel Greene."

Shhh, Annabel. It's just me. I felt a chill run up my neck.

"Please," Rolly said. "Just hear me out."

I looked at Owen, who just shook his head. When I moved my right hand forward, Rolly instantly grabbed it.

"This girl," he said solemnly, his palm hot, "is my destiny."

"Okay," Owen said, "now you're officially freaking her out."

"Rolly," I said. "This thing is—"

"Please, Annabel," he said. He put his other hand on mine, so my fingers were completely enclosed. "Please just introduce me. That's all I'm asking. One shot. One chance. *Please.*"

I knew I should tell him the real reason he did not want me to be his in, or any part of whatever happened, or didn't, between him and Clarke. Not just because he deserved to know it, but also because up until now I had been truthful with Owen—and all things having to do with Owen—and holding this back would mean that for the second time that night, I wasn't being the honest girl he thought I was. If I ever had been.

At the same time, looking at Rolly's hopeful face, I could feel myself wavering. On a night when what I'd done, or not done, was suddenly looming large, this seemed like a tiny way to somehow, in some distant way, make up for it. I couldn't fix the past, or change what had happened to Emily, but with this, maybe, I could help someone else's future.

"All right," I said. "But I'm just warning you: It might not work."

Rolly beamed, then hurriedly motioned for Owen to get out of the booth before sliding out himself. "I'll just go over by the bar," he said, "and wait until you've made contact. Then I'll casually happen by, and you can introduce us. Okay?"

I nodded. Already I was regretting agreeing to this, which Rolly most likely sensed, as he bolted out of there, fast, so I couldn't change my mind.

"You sure you want to do this?" Owen asked me as I got to my feet.

"No." I glanced over at Clarke, who was now sitting with a group of people at a table. "I'll be back in a second."

As I turned away, I felt his hand on my arm. "Hey," he said. "Are you okay?"

"What?" I asked. "Why?"

"I don't know." He dropped his hand, then looked at me. "You just seem . . . I don't know. Not yourself, or something. Everything all right?"

And here I'd thought I was hiding it. But like the difference between the picture on Mallory's wall and my face in the picture he took, this contrast—between who I'd been and who I felt myself becoming, again, with each step I took or was forced to take backwards—was obvious. To both of us. Which was why this time, I didn't hesitate and try to be honest, instead just going with what came naturally.

"I'm fine," I told him, but I could feel him watching me as I walked away.

Clarke was talking to a girl with blonde hair wearing heavy dark eyeliner, and didn't see me until I was right up on her. She glanced up, half smiling, reacting to something her friend had just said. When she saw me, she immediately affected her normal thin-lipped, stoic expression. It wasn't like I could turn back now, though. So I just dove in.

"Hi," I said.

At first, she didn't say anything, her silence stretching out long enough that I thought she might turn away, ignoring me completely. But just as the pause was getting excruciating, she said, "Hello."

Someone from down the table said something to the

blonde girl, and she turned away, leaving us alone. Clarke was still looking at me, a flat expression on her face. I had a flash of her at the pool, all those years ago, a hand of cards spread out between her thumb and forefinger.

"Look," I blurted out, "I know you hate me, okay? But the thing is—"

"Is that what you think?"

I stopped in mid-breath. "What?"

"You think I hate you?" she asked. Her voice, I noticed suddenly, was clear. Crystal. Not a sniffle to be heard. "Is that what you think the problem is here?"

"I don't know," I said. "I mean, I just thought—"

"You don't know," she repeated. Her voice was sharp. "Really."

Just then, I felt it: a hand clapping onto my shoulder with such force it almost sent me spilling forward onto the table. "Annabel! Hello!"

It was Rolly. When I turned, he was standing there with a wow-how-about-this expression, as if we were long-lost friends who hadn't seen each other in eons. At the same time, I could feel a dampness from his hand, already seeping through to my shoulder.

"Hi," I said, trying to sound casual.

"Hi!" he replied, doing no better than I had. "I'm going to go to the bar in a second to get some waters. You want one?"

Clarke was looking at us, her eyes narrowed. *Better get to it*, I thought.

"Sure," I said. "Thanks. Oh, um, Rolly, this is Clarke. Clarke, this is Rolly."

Rolly shot out his hand. "Hi," he said as Clarke, more slowly, offered up her own. "Really nice to meet you."

"You, too," Clarke said flatly. She turned back to me. "You were saying?"

"So you're here for Truth Squad, right?" Rolly said, looking from me to Clarke, then immediately back to Clarke again. "They're really good, have you heard them before?"

"Um," Clarke said, "no. I haven't."

"Oh, they're *great*," Rolly gushed. I took a step to the side, and he immediately moved into the space I'd been standing in, closer to her. "I've seen them tons."

"You know, I better see if Owen wants a drink," I said. Clarke shot me a look; now, she was definitely pissed. "I'll, um, be back in a minute. Or two."

And then I got out of there, quick. When I got back to Owen, he'd been joined by a guy with short dark hair and an intense look on his face.

"—a total shambles," the dark-haired guy was saying as I slid in. "It was better when we did the booking ourselves. At least then, we had some say in the dates, and the venues. Now we're just their pawns, in their sick little corporate game."

"That sucks," Owen said.

"It does." The guy shook his head. "At least the single's getting some airplay nationally. I mean, that's what they *say*. Who knows if it's true or not."

I glanced over at Clarke's table. Rolly was still standing up, talking animatedly, while Clarke seemed markedly less so as she listened to him.

"Annabel," Owen said, "this is Ted. Ted, Annabel."

"Hi," Ted replied, barely glancing at me.

"Hi."

From the stage, there was a thumping noise as someone tested the microphone. "Hey," a voice said. "This thing on?" Someone from the crowd booed in response.

Ted sighed, "See," he said, "this is what I'm talking about. These jokers were only supposed to do a mini set, and they haven't even started yet."

"Who are they?" Owen asked him.

"I don't even know," Ted said, clearly disgusted. "The original openers came down with some kind of intestinal flu, so they booked these guys to fill in."

"Should have just had you go on early," Owen said. "It *is* an all-ages show. Plus everyone's here to see you guys."

"My point exactly," Ted replied. "Plus, if we had longer sets, we could try out some of the new stuff I've been writing. It's, like, a total change for us."

"Really."

Ted nodded, suddenly looking much more animated. "I mean, it's not so far from our regular stuff. Just a little slower, with some more technical touches. Reverb, and all that."

"Technical?" Owen said. "Or techno?"

"It's hard to say," Ted replied. "It's kind of its own thing. Maybe we'll be able to get a couple in the second set. Tell me what you think, okay? It's, like, supposed to be out there but still accessible."

Owen glanced at me. "You know, if that's what you're after, you should ask Annabel what she thinks," he said. "She hates techno."

They were both looking at me now. "Well," I said. "Actually—"

"So if she likes it," Owen said, "it's not too far out there. If she hates it, though, it won't float with the masses."

"And she'd say if she hated it," Ted said.

"Yup." Owen nodded. "She's dead honest. Doesn't hold back."

As he said this, I felt some part of me just sink. Because I so wanted this to be true, enough that, once, I'd actually believed it was. But now, I just sat there, feeling them both looking at me, and felt like the biggest liar of all.

There was a burst of guitar music from the stage, followed by a few drumbeats. Finally, the opening band was starting. Ted made a face, then pushed himself out of the booth. "I can't tolerate listening to this crap; I'm going back. You want to come with?"

"Sure," Owen said. I heard someone yowl, and more feedback. To me he said, "Come on."

I followed him and Ted along the back of the crowd, passing Clarke's table on the way. Rolly was still there, talking excitedly, waving his hands as he did so. Clarke was listening to him, however, so that had to count for something.

Ted led us to a door by the bar, then down a hallway so dark I could barely make out the restrooms as we passed them. When he pushed open a door with a hand-lettered sign that said PRIVATE, the sudden bright light spilling out made me squint.

The first thing I saw inside was a guy with curly black hair crouching on the floor, reaching under a nearby couch. When he saw us, he got to his feet, breaking into a wide smile. "Owen! What's up, man?"

"Not much," Owen said as they shook hands. "What about you?"

"Same old, same old." The guy held up a cell phone and battery. "Just busted my phone. Again."

"This is Annabel," Owen said.

"Dexter," he said, offering his hand. To Ted he said, "What's the word?"

"The opener just went on," Ted replied as he walked over to a small fridge, pulling out a beer. "Are you guys pretty much ready?"

There were two guys at a nearby table, playing cards. One of them, a redhead, said, "Do we look ready?"

"No."

"Well, looks can be deceiving. Because we are."

The other guy at the table laughed, throwing down a card as Ted shot him a look, then plopped on the couch, propping his feet on the table in front of him.

"So," Dexter said, sitting down on the opposite end of the couch. He put the phone on his knee, then picked up the battery, examining it. "What's new on the local music scene?"

"Nothing worth talking about," Owen told him.

"No kidding," Ted said. "You should see the frat-rock cover band that's playing now. Total Spinnerbait wannabes."

"Spinnerbait?" I said.

"They're a band," Owen told me.

"Hate Spinnerbait!" the redhead said, throwing down a card with a smack.

"Now, now," Dexter said, placing the battery carefully back on his phone. When he removed his hand, though, it fell off again, hitting the floor with a clack. He bent down, picking it up. "That's the thing that's great about this town," he said, putting it on again. "There are so many bands to choose from."

"Doesn't mean any of them can play," Ted said.

"True. But variety is always a good thing," Dexter said as the battery fell off again. He turned the phone over, trying to fit it on that way: no go. "In some places," he said, "you really only have a few choices and that"—the battery fell off again— "sucks."

"Dexter." I turned around to see a blonde girl sitting in a chair in the corner of the room. She was holding a yellow highlighter, and a textbook was open in her lap. I hadn't even seen her. "Do you need help?" she asked him.

"Nope. I'm good. Thanks, though."

She got up, sticking the pen in the book and the book under her arm, then walked over to him. "Give it to me."

"No, I've got it," Dexter said, turning the phone over again. "I think it's busted for good this time, actually. Maybe something broke out of it."

She held out her hand. "Let me try."

He handed it over. Then, as we all watched, she looked at it for a second, stuck the battery in, and pushed down. There was a click, and then a trilling sound as the phone came on. She handed it back to him, then sat down on the couch.

"Oh," he said, turning the phone over and staring at it. "Thanks, honey."

"No problem." She opened her book—*Statistics for*

Business Applications, the spine said—then smiled at us. "I'm Remy," she said.

"Oh! Sorry!" Dexter said. He reached down, smoothing a hand over her hair. "This is Owen and Annabel. This is Remy."

"Hi," I said, and she nodded, pulling out the highlighter again.

"Remy's slumming, touring with us over her fall break," Dexter explained. "She goes to Stanford. She's *very* smart."

"Then why's she with you?" the redhead called out from the table.

"I have no idea," Dexter replied as Remy rolled her eyes, "but I think it's my mad make-out skills." He leaned over, planting a series of loud, sloppy kisses on her cheek. She winced, trying to push him away, but then he fell into her lap, his long legs splaying out across the couch.

"Stop," she said, laughing. "God."

From outside, we could suddenly hear more feedback, followed by booing. "Hopefully, they're cutting that set short," Ted said. "Would anyone else like to perhaps, I don't know, get ready for our show?"

"No," the redhead said.

"Absolutely not," the other guy added.

Ted glowered at them. Then he put down his beer on the table with a clank, walked to the door, and pulled it open. Once he was out in the hallway, he slammed it behind him. Hard.

The redhead threw down his cards. "Gin!" he said, lifting his hands over his head in a victory salute. "Finally!"

"Aw, man," the other guy said. "I was close, too."

"Off," Remy said, and Dexter disentangled himself from

her lap, getting to his feet. In the process, he dropped his phone again. This time, though, the battery stayed put.

"Ted's right," he said, although Ted was now gone. "We should get organized. Owen, you guys sticking around after?"

Owen glanced at me. "Sure," he said.

"Cool. We'll catch up with you then, all right?"

"Sounds good."

Then, everyone was suddenly in motion: Dexter sliding his phone into his pocket, the redhead pushing out his chair while the other guy gathered up the cards. Owen led me back into the hallway, where we passed Ted, who was leaning against the wall, still looking annoyed. Owen told him to have a good show as we passed, and he mumbled something in return, but I couldn't make it out.

On the way back to our booth, I glanced over at Clarke's table. She was still there, looking at the stage, but Rolly was gone. *Oh well*, I thought. *I tried.*

"All right," Owen said as we sat down. From the stage, I could hear the openers winding up their set. "Now comes the real music. You'll like this."

I nodded, leaning back against the wall and tucking a piece of hair behind my ear. When I glanced over at Owen, he was staring at me. "What?" I said.

"Okay," he said. "Something *is* up with you. What's going on?"

I froze. Here it was, the direct question. Maybe I could answer. Just say something, spit it out, finally. Maybe—

"I mean," he said, "when have you ever just assumed you'll

like what I like? This could be Ebb Tide Two about to come on here. You have a fever or something?"

He was smiling as he said this, and I tried to smile back. Deep down, though, I could suddenly feel the weight of all my withholding, so many lies and omissions.

"I'm fine," I said as someone played a few guitar chords. "Stop distracting me. I need to concentrate on the music."

The crowd was huge now, much bigger than for the previous band, and pretty soon all I could see was backs and shoulders. Owen got to his feet. "You should stand up," he said.

"I'm okay," I said.

"Part of seeing a band live is actually *seeing* them," he said. And then he held out his hand.

Ever since I'd left the mall I'd been trying to forget about what had happened between me and Emily on the runway. But looking up at Owen, it all came back. Not just the day that led up to this, but all the ones since he'd done this the first time, offering not only his hand but a friendship that had saved me. I'd been so alone and scared and, yes, angry, and somehow Owen had seen it, even when everyone else had chosen to look away and act like it wasn't happening. Just like I'd done, and was doing, to Emily tonight.

He was still holding out his hand. Waiting.

"I'm, um, going to go to the bathroom," I said, pushing off the wall and out of the booth. "I'll be back in a second."

"Wait," he said, dropping his hand. He glanced at the stage. "The band's coming on. . . ."

"I know. I'll be right back."

Then I started walking before he could say anything else. Mostly because I couldn't bear to lie again. But also there was that sourness in my mouth, something rising up. I had to get out of there.

The crowd was impossibly thick now, body after body in my way as I tried to get to the door. Meanwhile, Truth Squad started with a song that, judging by the amount of people who immediately began to sing along, a lot of the crowd knew; the lyrics had something to do with potatoes.

I kept pushing on, moving sideways through a crowd of people all facing forward, just one profile after another after another, some turning slightly, annoyed as I pushed past, others ignoring me entirely. Finally, the crowd began to thin. I was almost to the door when someone grabbed my arm.

"Annabel!" It was Rolly. He was smiling, his grin wide, and carrying an armful of bottled waters. "I'm in!"

I just looked at him as the crowd suddenly burst into cheers and applause. "What?"

"In," he said, holding up a water. "I went to get her a drink, even. It's working! Finally, it's really happening! Can you believe it?"

He was so happy, his face flushed. "That's great," I managed. "Actually, I was just—"

"Here," he said, cutting me off. He stuck one of the waters it in his shirt pocket, another under his arm, and then handed me the remaining two. "For you and Owen. Tell him I said he was right. About everything. Okay?"

I nodded, then he flashed me a thumbs-up and was gone. As I watched him disappear into the crowd, I wished I'd thought to give him a message for Owen, as well. I looked across the crowd, knowing he was somewhere on the other side, waiting for me. But now the distance seemed so vast and impossible, too much in between. So with my mouth sour and palms wet, I headed for the door.

Once outside, the cold air hit me like a smack, gravel crunching beneath my feet as I left the building behind me. It was all too familiar, this bubbling up inside me, my throat burning, never enough time to get away. I barely made it to my car before I was dropping to my knees, the waters spilling to the ground as I smoothed my hair back with my hand. This time, though, as I felt my stomach clench, my body retch, nothing came up. All I could hear was the raspy sound of my own breathing, my heart thumping in my ears, and in the distance, barely audible but still somehow playing, music.

Chapter
FIFTEEN

"Okay," my mother said, loosening a cart from the row in front of the automatic doors. She set her purse in the front, then pulled out her list, unfolding it. "Here we go."

It was the second week of December, and we were at Mayor's Market, where I'd been recruited to help with the grocery shopping for Kirsten's homecoming dinner. It was not something I was all that excited about, unlike my mother, who was in full-on holiday mode. But still, as she pushed the cart toward the doors, smiling at me, and they slid open, I tried my best to smile back. It was all about trying, these days.

The last month and a half had been a total blur. The only thing I was fully aware of was how completely things were back to how they had been when the school year began. It was like the time I'd spent with Owen hadn't happened at all. Yet again, I was alone at school, modeling even though I didn't want to, and somehow completely unable to do anything about either.

The Sunday after that night at Bendo, I woke up right at seven, just in time for Owen's show. It was only once I opened my eyes that I remembered this morning was different and turned away from the clock, trying to will myself back to sleep. But I could feel some part of myself stubbornly waking up, bit by bit, and then everything was flooding back.

He had to be furious with me. After all, I'd just bolted, no explanation, nothing. The worst part was I knew it was wrong, even as it was happening, and yet I still couldn't stop myself. The only way to fix it would be to explain openly and honestly why I'd left, and I just could not do that. Even for him.

As it turned out, though, whether we discussed that night or not wasn't entirely up to me. The next day, our first day back at school, Owen made the decision for us.

I was in my car, having just parked, when he suddenly appeared at my driver's-side window. He announced himself by knocking: three hard raps, *boom boom boom*. I jumped, then turned. Once he saw he had my attention, he dropped his hand and started around my front bumper to the passenger door. As he opened it I sucked in a breath, the way they say you should do if your car is ever immersed in water, one last gasp to hold you over. And then he was in.

"What *happened* to you?"

As I'd expected, there was no hello. No stony silence for me to fill. Just the one thing that had been on his mind for, oh, thirty-six hours or so. Even worse, he was looking at me so intently—angrily—that I couldn't keep my eyes on him for more than a moment. His mouth was a thin line, his face flushed, his unsettled presence filling the small space around us.

"I'm sorry," I said, and as the words came out I heard my voice break. "I just . . ."

This is the problem with dealing with someone who is

actually a good listener. They don't jump in on your sentences, saving you from actually finishing them. Or talk over you, allowing what you do manage to get out to be lost or altered in transit. Instead, they wait. So you have to keep going.

"I don't know what to say," I finally managed. "I just . . . don't."

He was quiet for what felt like a long time. *This is excruciating*, I thought. Then he said, "If you didn't want to be there on Saturday, you could have just told me."

I bit my lip, looking down at my hands as a couple of guys passed by my window, yelling something about football practice. "I wanted to be there," I said.

"Then what happened?" he said. "Why did you just bolt? I didn't know what was going on. I waited for you."

There was something in these last few words that made my heart just break. *I waited for you.* Of course he had. And of course he would tell me this, because unlike me, Owen didn't keep secrets. With him, what you saw was really what you got.

"I'm sorry," I said again, but even to me it sounded so lame and weak, meaningless. "I just . . . There was a lot going on."

"Like what?"

I shook my head. This was what I could not do, get into this place where I was backed up to a wall, no choice but to tell the truth. "It's just a lot of stuff," I said.

"Stuff," he repeated, and I thought in my head, *Placeholder.* But he didn't say this out loud.

Instead he exhaled, turning his head toward the window. Only then did I allow myself to really look at him, taking in all the familiar things: the strong line of his jaw; the rings on his fingers; his earphones, looped loosely around his neck. Distantly, through one of them, I could hear music, and I wondered out of habit what he was listening to.

"I just don't get it," he said. "I mean, there has to be a reason, and you just don't want to give it. And that's just . . ." He stopped, shaking his head. "It's not like you."

For a moment, everything was very quiet. No one was passing, no cars driving up the row behind us. So silent as I said, "It is, though."

Owen looked at me, shifting his bag to the other leg. "What?"

"It is like me," I said. My voice was low, even to my ears. "This is just like me."

"Annabel." He still sounded annoyed, like this could never be true. So wrong. "Come on."

I looked down at my hands again. "I wanted to be different," I said to him. "But this is how I really am."

I'd tried to tell him that first day. I'd said I didn't always tell the truth, that I didn't handle conflict well, that anger scared me, that I was used to people just disappearing when they were mad. Our mistake was that we'd both thought I was capable of changing. That I *had* changed. In the end, though, that was the biggest lie of all.

The first bell sounded then, long and loud. Owen shifted in his seat, then put his hand on the door handle.

"Whatever it is," he said, "you could have told me. You know that, right?"

I knew as Owen sat there, one hand on the door, he was waiting for me to be the bold girl he'd wanted to believe I was, to just tell him. He waited longer than I thought he would have before pushing the door open and getting out.

And then he was gone. Walking across the parking lot, his bag over one shoulder, already lifting his earphones to his ears. Almost a year ago I'd watched him this same way, just after he punched Ronnie Waterman out. Then, I'd been awed, and slightly scared, and I felt the same way now as I realized what my silence and fear had cost me, yet again.

I waited until second bell, when the courtyard was nearly empty, before I finally got out of my car and headed to class. I didn't want to see Owen; I didn't want to see anyone. All morning, I walked through the halls in a fog, deliberately blocking out the voices around me. At lunch, I went to the library and sat in a carrel by the American History section, books spread out in front of me, not reading one word.

As the period was winding down, I packed up my stuff and went to the bathroom. It was empty except for two girls I didn't know, standing by the sinks, who started talking as I went into a stall.

"All I'm saying," one said as a faucet was turned on and water began to splash, "is that I don't think she's lying."

"Oh, come on." The other girl's voice was high, and more nasal. "He could date any girl he wanted. It's not like he's desperate. So why would he do something like that?"

"Do you really think she'd go to the cops if he hadn't?"

"Maybe she just wants attention."

"No way." The faucet cut off, and I heard paper towels being yanked from the dispenser. "She and Sophie were best friends. And now everyone knows? Why go through all that for a lie?"

I froze. They were talking about Emily.

"What did he get booked for?" the first girl asked.

"Sexual assault. Or second-degree rape, I don't know which."

"I can't believe he actually got *arrested*," the other girl said.

"At the A-Frame!" her friend replied. "Meghan said when the cops pulled up, people were running in all directions. Everyone thought it was a beer bust."

"Not hardly." I heard a backpack pocket unzip. "Have you seen Sophie?"

"Nope. I don't think she came today," the other girl said. "Shit. Would you?"

They were leaving now, their heels clicking across the floor, so I didn't get to hear the response to this. Instead, I stood in the stall, one hand on the wall beside me, where someone had written I HATE THIS PLACE in blue ballpoint pen. I dropped my hand, then put down the toilet seat and sat, trying to piece together what I'd just heard.

Emily had gone to the cops. Emily had pressed charges. Emily had *told*.

This realization was so big I just sat there, hands locked in my lap, stunned. Will had been arrested. People knew about this. Ever since Saturday night, I'd assumed Emily, like me, had stayed silent and scared, sucked this story in and held it there. But she hadn't.

As the afternoon wore on and I actually started listening to the people around me, I got the rest of the story. I heard that Emily was supposed to get a ride from the A-Frame to the party with Sophie, but she'd gotten held up, so Will offered to drive her instead. That he'd parked on the street and then, depending on who you believed, either jumped on her or was surprised when she made a move on him. That a woman walking her dog past saw something happening and threatened to call the cops if they didn't move on. That this was how Emily had gotten out of the car and, after getting a ride home, told her mom everything. That she'd spent Saturday morning at the police station, filing charges. That when the cops came for Will on Saturday night, he cried when the cops cuffed him. That Will's dad bailed him out within hours, then hired him the best lawyer in town. That Sophie was telling everyone that Emily had always been hot for Will, and when he wasn't interested, she cried rape. And that while Sophie was not at school today, Emily was.

I didn't see her until just after final bell. I was pulling a notebook out of my locker when I felt a sudden, strange hush fall over the normal end-of-the-day commotion. It didn't get entirely quiet, just quieter. When I turned my head, I saw her coming down the hallway toward me. She wasn't cowering or alone. She had two girls with her, one on either side, both of them people she'd been friends with before Sophie. I'd just assumed that I had no one after what had happened, that everyone would just accept Sophie's side of the story. It hadn't even occurred to me that somebody would believe mine.

For the next few days, what happened between Emily and Will remained the hot topic, although I was doing my best not to pay attention to it. At times, though, this was impossible, like the day I was in my English class, doing some last-minute cramming before a midterm, and Jessica Norfolk and Tabitha

Johnson, who sat behind me, started talking about Will.

"What I heard," said Jessica, who was junior class treasurer and not, I thought, the gossip type, "is that he's done it before."

"Really?" Tabitha replied. She'd sat behind me all year and always clicked her pen, which drove me nuts. She was doing it now.

"Yeah. There were rumors when he was at Perkins Day, apparently. You know, girls who said similar stuff had happened to them."

"But nobody ever had him *arrested*."

"Well, no," Jessica said. "But it means that it could be, you know, a pattern."

Tabitha, still clicking her pen, sighed through her teeth. "God," she said. "Poor Sophie."

"I know. Can you imagine dating someone and then this?"

A lot of these conversations I'd overheard came back to Sophie, which wasn't surprising. She and Will were one of those couples people knew about, if only for their frequently public dramatics. So it was odd she wasn't at school that first day. If Emily surprised me, though, Sophie did, too. Not only by not showing up, but by how she acted when she finally did.

She didn't station herself in the courtyard to make it clear she was unaffected by what had happened. Or confront Emily in public, as she had me. In fact, the first time I saw her she was alone, walking down the hallway with her cell phone pressed to her ear. At lunch, when I glanced out the library window, she wasn't on her bench—which was populated instead by some sophomore girls I didn't even know—but sitting on the curb by the turnaround, waiting for a ride. As for

Emily, she was sitting at a picnic table, drinking a bottled water and eating some potato chips, surrounded by people.

So Sophie was alone. I was alone. And Owen was alone, or so I was assuming. Occasionally before or after school, I'd catch a glimpse of him, towering over everyone else as he cut across a pathway or disappeared around a corner. Sometimes when I saw him, all I wanted to do was tell him everything. The thought would crash over me like a wave, sudden and unexpected. In the next moment, though, I'd already be telling myself that he probably didn't even want to hear it, now. Watching him walking across the courtyard with no expression, earphones on, it was like he was receding, back, back, to the person he'd been to me before all this. Just a mystery, a boy I didn't know at all, one more face in the crowd.

If school was stressful, home was not much better. At least not for me. For everyone else in my family, however, things were just great. My mother, next to me, was at this moment pushing her cart through the bounty that was the Mayor's Market produce department, so happy the entire family was finally getting together. While Kirsten had talked about coming for Thanksgiving, she'd opted instead to stay in the city, ostensibly to work some extra shifts and catch up on schoolwork. Later, though, she'd mentioned eating a turkey dinner with Brian, her TA; however, in very non-Kirsten fashion, she hadn't offered more details. Now she was finally coming home early for Christmas, and my mom was going all out.

"We're doing two kinds of potatoes," Mom said to me, gesturing for me to pull a couple of plastic bags from the dispenser. "I'm doing my creamed casserole, and Whitney's doing some kind of roasted potatoes with olive oil."

"Really," I said, handing the bags over to her.

"It's some recipe Moira gave her," she said. "Isn't that *great*?"

It was. My own problems aside, I could not help but be impressed with Whitney's recent progress. A year ago everything had started; now, while she was still by no means cured, the changes in her were yet again evident, but they were all good ones.

First, she'd started cooking. Not a lot, and not constantly; it had started slowly, after the dinner she'd made for me. Apparently Moira Bell was big into natural foods and organic cooking, and when Whitney told her about making spaghetti, she'd lent her a couple of cookbooks. My mother's meals tended toward the creamy and hearty: lots of casseroles with cream of mushroom bases, heavy sauces, meats, and starches. Whitney's interest, not surprisingly, leaned in a different direction. She'd started by contributing salads to our dinners now and then, going to the farmer's market and loading up with vegetables, which she'd spend ages slicing and dicing. Her dressings were vinaigrettes, swirled with herbs; reach for the Thousand Island or ranch and she'd shoot you a look suggesting that you don't. Then, the weekend of the fashion show, she made grilled salmon with a lime sauce for my parents, followed by steamed green beans with fresh lemon to replace the gooey casserole with french-fried onion topping we normally had for Thanksgiving. My mother was a great cook, the kind who worked on instinct, with no real measurements, only pinches and dashes. When Whitney cooked, she was all about exactitude, and her natural bossiness—about the dressing, or how yes, we could live without butter on every side dish—was just part of the process. But even at its most annoying, it was still an improvement, and we were all eating better. Whether we liked it or not.

She was also writing. She'd finished her official history by the end of the October, but since then she'd kept at it, often sitting at the dining-room table scribbling on a notepad, or curling up by the fire chewing her pencil. So far she hadn't let me read anything she'd written, although it wasn't like I'd asked, either. Still, the couple of times I'd found her notebook on the stairs, or the kitchen table, I'd been tempted to open it, just to see what was within all those carefully written lines. But I didn't. After all, I could understand about keeping things to yourself.

The most amazing thing, though, was the herbs. After sitting in the window doing absolutely nothing for a couple of months, the rosemary had suddenly sprouted just before Halloween. It was just one tiny, green shoot, but in the next week the others followed suit. Whitney checked on them every single day, testing the dampness of the soil with her fingers, turning them slightly for the optimum amount of light. Where I'd once thought of my middle sister as a closed door, these days when I pictured her I saw another image: her hands, curved around a chopping knife, or a pen, the handle of a watering can, moving across the plants, helping them grow.

Kirsten, meanwhile, had not only survived the showing of her piece to her professors and classmates but emerged victorious, winning the first-place prize in the competition. I'd expected her to call and regale us with one of her typical monologues, full of stream-of-consciousness details, but instead she'd left a message—telling us about the win and that she was very pleased with it—that clocked in at under two minutes, which had to be a record for her. It was so strange we were all convinced something must be wrong, but when I called her back, she said it was just the opposite.

"Things are great," she told me. "Just great."

"Are you sure?" I asked. "Your message was awfully short."

"Was it?"

"I thought the machine had cut you off, at first," I said.

She sighed. "Well, that's not altogether surprising, I guess. I've really been doing a lot of work on how I convey myself these days."

"You are?" I asked.

"Well, sure." She sighed again, a happy sigh. "It's amazing what I've learned this semester. I mean, between the filmmaking and Brian's class, I'm learning a lot about the true meaning of communication. It's really opened my eyes."

I waited for her to go on, to explain. Especially about Brian. But she didn't. Instead, she told me she loved me and had to run, and that she'd see me soon. And then we hung up. In under four minutes.

Kirsten may have been mastering the art of true communication, but I was failing miserably. Not just with Owen, but with my mother as well, as I'd somehow, in the midst of everything else that was happening, agreed to do another Kopf's commercial.

It happened the same week I'd heard about Emily's pressing charges. When I got home from school that Friday, my mother was waiting for me at the door.

"Guess what!" she said, before I even stepped over the threshold. "I just got a call from Lindy. The Kopf's people contacted her yesterday morning. They want you for their new spring commercial."

"What?" I said.

"Apparently they were very pleased with how the fall campaign went. Although, I have to say, I think your meeting that man from marketing last weekend didn't hurt. They're shooting in January but they want to see you in December for a fitting. Isn't it great?"

Great, I thought. The truth was, a couple of months ago this would have been a much bigger deal. A couple of weeks ago, maybe I might have even been able to stop it. But now, I just stood there, and barely managed to nod.

"I told Lindy I'd call her as soon as I told you," she said, going into the kitchen and picking up the phone. As she dialed, she added, "From what Lindy said, the ad skewed really well with younger girls, and that's what really won the Kopf's people over. You're a role model, Annabel! Isn't that something?"

I thought of Mallory's room, the screen captures lined up on the wall. And then her face staring into the camera, the feathers from the boa floating up to the edges.

"I'm no role model," I said.

"Sure you are," she replied, so easily. She turned and looked at me, smiling again as she shifted the phone to her other ear. "You have so much to be proud of, honey. You really do. I mean—

Lindy? . . . Hi! It's Grace, I've been trying to get through . . . is
your receptionist out? . . . Still? . . . That's horrible. . . . Yes, I've
just talked to Annabel, and she's thrilled. . . ."

Thrilled, I thought. *Not quite.* And not a role model, either.
Not that it mattered. As long as someone else thought I was
those things, that was all that counted.

October had folded into November and then December
somehow without my even noticing, the days getting shorter
and colder, Christmas music suddenly on the radio. I went to
school, I studied, I came home. Even when people did try to
talk to me at school, I barely replied, so used to my isolation
that now I preferred it. At first, on weekend nights, my mom
and dad seemed curious as to why I didn't go out or have plans.
But after a few times of telling them I was just so tired from the
Models and school and trying to catch up on my schoolwork,
they stopped asking.

Still, I was aware of what was happening around me. I
knew from the rumor mill that Will's trial was coming up, and
there was still talk that some girls from Perkins Day would
come forward with stories similar to Emily's. As for Emily herself, she seemed to be doing well. She certainly wasn't hiding
out. In fact, I saw her everywhere—in the halls, the courtyard,
hanging out in the parking lot—always with a bunch of girls
around her. A week or so earlier, in the hallway between classes, I'd caught a glimpse of her standing by her locker, laughing
at something. Her cheeks had been flushed, her hand covering
her mouth. It was just one moment, one thing, but for some
reason it stuck with me, all that day and into the next. I could
not get it out of my mind.

Sophie was not faring so well. Usually when I saw her, she was alone, and she now left for lunch almost every day, a black car sliding to a stop to pick her up. It wasn't Will, and I wondered if they were still together. Because I hadn't heard otherwise, I assumed they were.

It seemed like a million years ago now that school had begun, and I'd been so scared of her. Now when I saw Sophie, I just felt tired and sad for both of us. Only when I saw Owen did I feel a twinge of something like loneliness. But even though we weren't talking, I was still listening, in my own way.

Not to the radio show, although I still found myself waking like clockwork at seven A.M. on Sundays, a bad habit that proved impossible, for whatever reason, to break. Even harder to shake was the music itself. Not just his music, either, but all music.

I wasn't sure when it had started, exactly, but suddenly I was very aware of silence. Everywhere I went, I needed some kind of noise. When I was in the car, I instantly turned on my stereo; in my room, I hit the light switch first, my CD player ON button second. Even in class, or sitting at the table with my parents, I'd always have to have some song in my head, repeating itself again and again. I remembered Owen telling me how music had saved him in Phoenix, that it drowned everything out, and it was the same for me now. As long as I had something to listen to, I could blur the things I didn't want to think about, if not block them out completely.

It took a lot of music to do this, though, and after a few weeks, I'd burned through my entire collection multiple times. Which was why, on a recent Saturday night, I'd broken down and pulled out the stack Owen had burned me. *Desperate times*, I thought as I opened up the PROTEST SONGS one again and stuck it in.

I still didn't love it. Some of the songs were strange, and others I didn't understand. But while I'd expected it to be weird to listen to Owen's music, I found a surprising comfort instead. There was something nice about picturing him picking the songs for me, organizing them so carefully, hoping I'd be enlightened. If nothing else, they proved we had been friends, once.

For the past few weeks I'd been working my way through the discs, song by song, listening to every single track until I knew them all by heart. Each time I finished with one, I felt sad, knowing there were only that many more left before this, too, was over. Because of this, I was planning to save the one that said JUST LISTEN. Like Owen had been to me once, it was a total mystery, and sometimes one I thought maybe was best unsolved. Still, I pulled it out every once in a while, just turning it in my hands before sliding it back to the bottom of the stack and leaving it there.

When my mom and I finally headed out into the Mayor's Market parking lot, I was surprised to see it was snowing. The flakes were the big, fat kind, too pretty to stick or last, but we both stopped still for a moment, looking up at them as they fell. By the time we got in the car and pulled out of the lot, they were already slowing, some catching the wind, blowing in circles. My mom turned on the wipers as we sat at a stoplight, watching the flakes hit the windshield.

"It's beautiful, isn't it?" she said. "There's something about snow that just makes everything seem so fresh and new. Don't you think?"

I nodded. The light was a long one, and even though it was barely five P.M., it was already getting dark. My mom glanced over at me, smiling, then reached forward to the radio. As she twisted the volume, filling the car with classical music, I turned my head to the side. The window was cool against my cheek, those pretty flakes still falling, as I closed my eyes.

Chapter
SIXTEEN

The library carrel where I was spending my lunches was deep in the far right corner, out of sight and away from most foot traffic. I wasn't used to having company. Which was why when Emily came looking for me thirty minutes into the last lunch before Christmas break, I saw her first.

Initially, she was just a flash of red in the corner of my eye, blurring past once, then twice. I glanced up from my English notes, which I had spread out in front of me, doing some last-minute cramming, then looked around me: nothing. Same quiet shelves, same rows of books. A moment later, though, I heard footsteps. When I turned around, she was standing at the end of the stack just behind me.

"Oh," she said. Her voice was quiet but audible. "There you are."

Like I'd been lost. Misplaced, only now turning up, like a sock you find long after you've assumed it was eaten by the dryer. I didn't say anything, too distracted by a rising panic. I'd picked my spot because it was secluded, faced the wall, and was tucked away from everything, the same reasons it was the last place you wanted to find yourself trapped.

Emily started toward me, and without even realizing it I leaned back, bumping the carrel behind me. She stopped, crossing her arms over her chest.

"Look," she said. "I know things have been weird between us this year. But I . . . I need to talk to you."

Somewhere nearby, I could hear voices, one male, one female, chatting as they moved through the stacks. Emily heard it, too, turning her head at the sound, until it faded. Then she grabbed a nearby chair, dragging it closer to me, and sat down. Her voice was barely a hush as she said, "I know you've heard what happened. What Will did to me."

She was so close I could smell her perfume, something fruity and floral.

"Afterwards," she continued, keeping her green eyes level on me, "I started thinking about you. And that night at the party, back when school ended last year."

I could hear myself breathing, which meant she probably could, too. Behind her, the trees beyond the window shifted, and a shaft of sunlight spilled across the shelves of books, dust dancing within it.

"You don't have to talk to me about it," she said. "I mean, I know you hate me and all."

I thought of Clarke, looking up at me from that chair at Bendo. *Is that what you think?* she'd replied, when I'd said this same thing to her.

"But the thing is," Emily said, "if something did happen . . . something like what happened to me, it could help. Make it stop, I mean. Make him stop."

I still hadn't said a word. I couldn't. Instead, I just sat

there, immobile, as she reached into the pocket of her jeans, pulling out a small white card.

"This is the name of the woman who's been working on my case," she said, holding the card out to me. When I didn't reach for it immediately, she put it on the table, beside my elbow, faceup. The name was in black, a seal of some sort on the top left-hand corner. "The trial starts on Monday, but they're still wanting to talk to people. You could just call her and tell her . . . whatever you wanted. She's really nice."

The one thing that scared me more than anything, the reason I hadn't been honest with Owen about what was really bothering me that night at Bendo—she made it sound easy. If I couldn't tell him, the one person I actually thought could take it, how on earth could I be expected to confide in a stranger? There was no way. Even if I wanted to. Which I didn't.

"Just think about it," she told me. Then she took in a breath, like she might add something, but didn't, instead just pushing herself to her feet. "I'll see you around, okay?"

She pushed the chair back into place, then started down the nearest row of shelves. After taking a couple of steps, though, she turned back to face me. "And Annabel?" she said. "I'm sorry."

These two words just hung there for a moment in the air between us, and then she was walking away, disappearing around the empty carrel on the far end of the row. *I'm sorry*. It was the same thing that I wanted to say to her, that I'd wanted to say ever since that Saturday night at the fashion show. What did she have to apologize for?

But even as my mind grappled with this, trying to work the

logic, I could feel it, a visceral reaction to what had just happened, her coming closer than anyone to the truth. My truth. And just like that, I could feel something rising up inside me. I looked around, wondering where on earth I could get sick quietly and discreetly. But then something else happened: I started to cry.

Cry. Really cry, the way I hadn't in years, the kind of full-out sobbing that hits you like a wave, pulling you under. Suddenly the tears were just coming, sobs climbing up my throat, my shoulders shaking. I turned around clumsily, trying to hide myself, banging my elbow on the edge of the carrel, and the business card Emily had left fell to the floor, fluttering end over end before landing at my feet. I put my head in my hands, pressing my palms over my eyes to shut out everything, even as the tears continued. I cried and cried, there in the library, tucked away in the corner, until I felt raw inside.

I was so scared about being discovered, but nobody came. Nobody heard. In my own ears, though, my sobs sounded primal and scary, like something I would have turned off if I'd been able to. Instead all I could do was just ride it out, until it—and I—was done.

When that happened, I dropped my hands and looked around me. Nothing had changed. The books were still there, the dust dancing in the light, the card at my feet. I reached down for it, closing my fingers over one edge and lifting it up. I did not read it, or even glance at it. But I did slide it into the pocket of my bag, stuffing it down and away just as the bell rang and the period ended.

• • •

For the rest of the day, you could just feel the pre–holiday-break restlessness in the air, everyone counting down until vacation officially began.

After finishing my exam late, I headed to my locker, then to the bathroom, which was empty except for a girl who was leaning in close to the mirror, putting on liquid blue eyeliner. Soon after I went into the stall, I heard her leave, and I thought I was alone. When I came out, though, Clarke Reynolds, in jeans and a TRUTH SQUAD T-shirt, was leaning against the sink.

"Hi," she said.

My first instinct was to look behind me, which was crazy, as well as kind of stupid, as I could see in the mirror there was no one there.

"Hey," I said.

I stepped around her, to the next sink down, and turned on the water. I could feel her watching me as I rinsed my hands and pumped the soap dispenser, which was empty as always. "So," she said, as again I realized there was no stuffiness to her voice whatsoever, "are you okay?"

I turned off the water. "What?"

She reached up, adjusting her glasses. "It's not really just me asking," she said. "I mean, it is, obviously. But Owen's wondering, too."

Hearing her say Owen's name was so strange that it took me a moment to wrap my mind around it. "Owen," I repeated.

She nodded. "He's just . . ." She trailed off. "Concerned, I guess, is the word."

"About me," I said, clarifying.

"Yeah."

Something wasn't right here. "And he asked you to talk to me?"

"Oh, no." She shook her head. "He's just mentioned it to me a few times, so I got to wondering, and . . . then I saw you today. After lunch. You were leaving the library, and you just looked really upset."

Maybe it was because she'd brought up Owen. Or because at this point, I really didn't have that much to lose as far as she and I were concerned. Whatever the reason, I just decided to be honest. "I'm surprised," I said. "I didn't think you'd care if I was upset."

She bit her lip for just a second, something I suddenly remembered her doing a million times when we were younger. It meant I'd caught her off guard. "Is that what you really think?" she said. "That *I* don't like *you*?"

"You don't," I said. "You haven't, since that summer with Sophie."

"Annabel, come on. You were the one who blew me off, remember?"

"Yeah, but—"

"Yeah, but nothing. *You* don't like *me*, Annabel." Her voice was even, level. "That's the way it's been since that summer."

I just stared at her. "But you won't even look at me in the halls," I said. "You never have. And that first day, on the wall—"

"You hurt my feelings," she said. "God, Annabel. We were best friends and you totally dumped me. How did you expect me to feel?"

"I tried to talk to you!" I said. "That day at the pool."

"And that," she shot back, pointing at me, "was the *only* time. Yeah, I was mad. It had just happened! But then you never came around, you never called. You were just gone."

It was like Emily saying "I'm sorry" to me, a total reversal of how I saw things, which seemed crazy and impossible to process.

"So why now?" I said. "Why talk to me now?"

She sighed. "Well," she said slowly, "I have to be honest. Rolly's a big part of it."

Rolly, I thought. Then I remembered that night, him clutching those waters. *Tell Owen he was right about everything,* he'd said, so excited. "You and Rolly?" I said.

She bit her lip again, and I could have sworn she blushed, but only for a second. "We're talking," she said, reaching down to tug at the hem of her TRUTH SQUAD T-shirt, which, now that I noticed, looked awfully worn for someone who had only just seen the band for the first time a month and half earlier. "Anyway, that night at the club, when he got you to introduce him to me, you said that I hated you. It got me thinking about everything that had happened with us all those years ago. And with Owen talking about you . . . you've been on my mind. So when I saw you today, and you were—"

"Wait," I said. "Owen talks about me?"

"He hasn't said all that much," she told me. "Just that you guys were friends, and then something happened, and now you're not. Forgive me for saying so, but it sounded, I don't know, a little bit familiar to me. If you know what I mean."

I felt myself flush, imagining Clarke and Owen discussing

me and my avoidant behavior. How embarrassing.

"It's not like we discuss you," she added, as if I'd said this aloud. Which was another thing that I now remembered about Clarke: She could always kind of read my mind.

Clarke was worried about me. Emily was apologizing to me. This was a weird day.

"So are you?" Clarke asked now, as a group of girls came in, cigarettes already out, their faces falling when they saw us there. They grumbled, huddled, then walked back out, presumably to wait until we'd left. "Okay, I mean?"

I just stood there, wondering how to answer this. I realized that for the last few weeks I hadn't been missing just Owen, but also that part of me that had been able to be so honest with him. Maybe I couldn't do that here. But I didn't have to lie, either. So I went for the place I was working toward always: the middle.

"I don't know," I said.

Clarke looked at me for a moment. "Well," she said, "do you want to talk about it?"

I'd had so many chances. Her, Owen, Emily. For so long, I'd thought all I needed was someone to listen, but that wasn't really true at all. It was me that was the problem. I did this. And now, I did it again. "No," I said. "But thanks anyway."

She nodded, then pushed off the sink, and I followed her out of the bathroom. In the hallway, as we prepared to go our separate ways, she reached down to her bag, pulling out a pen and scrap of paper. "Here," she said as she scribbled on it, then handed it to me. "My cell number. Just in case you change your mind."

Her name was written beneath it, in the hand I still recognized—clean, block-print, the same little swoop on the final *E*. "Thanks," I said.

"No problem. Merry Christmas, Annabel."

"You, too."

As we walked away from each other, I knew I probably wouldn't call her. Still, I unzipped my bag, stuffing the paper in with the card Emily had given me. Even if I never used either, for whatever reason, it was nice to know they were there.

Another holiday, another trip to the airport. Just like I had about a year earlier, I sat in the backseat, behind my parents, as we headed down the highway, a plane rising from one corner of the windshield to the other as we took the exit. Whitney had stayed home, ostensibly to get dinner ready. So it was just the three of us waiting behind the barricade for Kirsten to emerge from the gate.

"There she is!" my mother said, waving as my sister appeared wearing a bright red coat, her hair pulled back in a ponytail. Kirsten smiled, waving back as she walked toward us, the wheels of her suitcase whizzing across the floor.

"Hello!" she said, immediately reaching up to hug my dad, then moving on to my mom, who was already teary-eyed, the way she always was at arrivals and departures. When it was my turn she hugged me tight, and I closed my eyes, breathing in her scent: soap, cold air, and the peppermint of her shampoo, all so familiar. "I am so happy to see you guys!"

"How was the trip?" my mom asked as my dad took the

handle of her suitcase and we started across the terminal. "Any trouble?"

"None," Kirsten said, linking her arm in my mine. "It was all good."

I waited for her to continue, but she didn't. Instead, she just smiled at me, then slid her hand down around mine, squeezing it as we stepped out into the cold.

On the ride home, my parents peppered Kirsten with questions about school, which she answered, and Brian, which she evaded cheerfully, blushing occasionally. The new Kirsten I'd noticed on the phone was clearly in evidence. Her responses, while not curt, were much briefer than any of us were used to, so much so that weird silences kept falling after she spoke, while the rest of us waited for her to start up again. But she didn't, just sighing instead, or looking out the window, or squeezing my hand, which she was still holding, which she held all the way home.

"I have to say," my mother said as my dad turned into our neighborhood, "there's something different about you, honey."

"Really?" Kirsten asked.

"I can't put my finger on exactly what it is . . ." my mother said, looking pensive. "But I think . . ."

"She's letting the world get a word in edgewise?" my dad finished for her, glancing at Kirsten in the rearview. He was smiling. And right.

"Oh, Daddy," Kirsten said. "I didn't used to talk *that* much, did I?"

"Of course not!" my mother told her. "We always loved to hear what you had to say."

Kirsten sighed. "I've just learned a lot about being more concise. As well as making an effort to hear what's being said to me. I mean, do you realize how few people actually *listen* these days?"

I did. In fact, I'd spent the time between school and leaving for the airport finishing up the last tracks of Owen's OLD SCHOOL PUNK/SKA CD, the final labeled one in the stack he'd given to me. After this, I only had JUST LISTEN left to go, which made me sad. I'd gotten used to spending some time each day or night hearing a few tracks here or there. The act was like ritual, a weird kind of steady comfort, even when the music wasn't.

While I listened, I usually just lay on my bed with eyes closed, trying to lose myself in what I was hearing. Today, though, as the CD began with the pumping beats of a reggae-style song, I'd pulled my backpack onto my bed, taken out the card Emily had given me and Clarke's number, then laid them in front of me on the bedspread. As the music played, I studied each one, as if it was important to commit them to memory: the slightly raised type of the D.A. assistant's name, ANDREA THOMLINSON, the lines across the middle sections of the two sevens in Clarke's number. I told myself I didn't have to do anything with either of them. They were just options. Like Owen's two rings, two messages. And it was always good to know your options.

When we got home, it was already dark, but the house was lit up, and I could see Whitney in the kitchen, stirring something on the stove. As we coasted down the driveway, Kirsten squeezed my hand again, and I wondered if she was nervous. But she didn't say anything.

Inside, the house was warm, and I realized I was starving. Kirsten took in a deep breath, closing her eyes. "God," she said as my dad led the way in, "something smells amazing."

"That's Whitney's stir-fry," my mother told her.

"Whitney cooks?" she asked.

I looked ahead to see Whitney standing in front of the island. She had a dishtowel in her hands. "Whitney cooks," she said. "It should be ready in about five minutes."

"You are in for a treat!" my mom said to Kirsten, her voice a little bit too loud. "Whitney is a natural in the kitchen."

"Wow," Kirsten said. Another silence fell. Then she said to Whitney, "You look great, by the way."

"Thanks," Whitney replied. "So do you."

So far, so good. Beside me, my mother smiled.

"I'll put your bag upstairs," my dad told Kirsten, who nodded.

"And I'll get the salad together," my mom said, "and then we can all sit down and catch up. In the meantime, you girls can go upstairs and freshen up. How's that sound?"

"Good," Kirsten said, looking at Whitney again. My father turned, heading for the stairs with the suitcase. "Sounds great."

Upstairs, I sat in my room, listening to the noises around me. Kirsten's room had been pretty much untouched since she'd left, so it was weird to hear activity—drawers being opened and closed, the bumping of furniture being moved around—from that side of the wall. On the other, there were the Whitney noises I was used to: the creak of her bed, the low hum of a radio. When my mom called up to us that everything was ready, we all came out into the hallway together.

Kirsten had changed her shirt and let her hair down. She

glanced back at me, then at Whitney, who was behind me, pulling a sweater over her head. "Ready?" she asked, as if we were going farther than just the table. I nodded, and she started down the stairs.

When we came into the dining room, the food was already out: the stir-fry heaped on a big platter, a bowl of brown rice, my mother's salad, with the dressing, of course, to Whitney's specifications. Everything smelled great, and my father was standing at the head of the table as we all took our places around him.

Once we sat, my mom poured Kirsten a glass of wine, and my dad, a true meat-and-potatoes person, asked Whitney to please explain, if she could, exactly what we were eating.

"Tempeh and vegetable stir-fry," she said, "in peanut hoisin sauce."

"Tempeh? What's that?"

"It's good, Daddy," Kirsten told him. "That's all you need to know."

"You don't have to eat it if you don't want to," Whitney said. "Although it is pretty much the best thing I've ever made."

"Just give him some," my mom said. "He'll like it."

My dad looked dubious, though, as Whitney picked up a spoon, putting some onto his plate. As she added the sides, I looked around the table at my family, so different now from a year ago. We would probably never be the way we had been again, but at least we were all together.

As I thought this, I caught a glimpse of lights. Sure enough, in the window behind the row of herbs, a car was passing. As it slowed, the driver looking in at us, I thought again how you

326 ◄ Sarah Dessen

could never really know what you were seeing with just a glance, in motion, passing by. Good or bad, right or wrong. There was always so much more.

The rule in our house was that if you didn't cook, you cleaned up, so after dinner Kirsten, my dad, and I ended up in the kitchen together on dish duty.

"That," Kirsten said, handing me a soapy pan to rinse, "was delicious. The sauce was to die for."

"Wasn't it?" my mother, who was sitting at the kitchen table drinking a cup of coffee—but still yawning—replied. "And your father had *thirds*. I hope Whitney noticed. That's the best compliment you can give a cook."

"I never cook," Kirsten said. "Unless ordering in counts."

"It does," my dad told her. He was supposed to be helping, although so far all he'd done was take out the garbage and take a long time to replace the bag. "Calling for delivery is my favorite recipe."

My mom made a face at him as Whitney, who had disappeared upstairs after dinner, walked in wearing her jacket, her keys in hand. "I'm going out for a little while," she said. "I won't be late."

Kirsten, her hands in the water, turned and looked at her. "Where are you going?"

"Just to this coffee shop to meet some people," Whitney told her.

"Oh," Kirsten said, nodding. Then she turned back to the sink.

"Do you . . ." Whitney paused. "Did you want to come?"

"I don't want to intrude," Kirsten told her. "That's okay."

"It's all right," I heard Whitney say. "I mean, if you don't mind hanging out there for a little while."

Again, I felt it: this tentative, careful peace between my sisters—not exactly flimsy, but not set in stone, either. My parents exchanged a look. "Annabel, you want to come?" Kirsten said. "I'll buy you a mocha."

I could feel Kirsten's eyes on me as she asked this, and I thought of her squeezing my hand earlier, and how she was maybe more nervous than she seemed. "Sure," I said. "Okay."

"Wonderful!" my mother said. "You all go and have fun. Your dad and I can finish cleaning up."

"Are you sure?" I asked. "We're only about halfway through—"

"It's fine." She stood up, then came over, gesturing me and Kirsten out of the way as she rolled up her sleeves. I looked over at Whitney, standing in the archway. How I'd gotten in the middle of this I wasn't sure. But here I was. "Just go."

"Hello, and welcome to open-mike night, here at Jump Java. I'm Esther, and I'll be your emcee tonight. If you've been here before, you know the rules: Sign up at the back, keep it down when someone's reading, and most importantly, tip your barista. Thank you!"

When we arrived, I'd figured this was just something that happened to be going on. But as Whitney's friends from her group waved us over, it was clear it was no coincidence.

"So are you ready?" a girl named Jane, who was tall and very thin, wearing a red sweater with a pack of cigarettes poking out of the front pocket, said to Whitney after we got our coffees and had introductions. "And, more importantly, are you nervous?"

"Whitney doesn't get nervous," Heather, the other girl, said. She looked to be about my age and had short black hair, cut spiky, and a variety of piercings in her nose and lip. "You know that."

Kirsten and I exchanged a look. "What would you be nervous about?" she asked Whitney, who was sitting beside me, rummaging through the purse in her lap.

"Reading," Jane told her, taking a sip from the mug in front of her. "She's signed up for tonight."

"She had to sign up," Heather added. "It was a Moira Must."

"Moira Must?" I said.

"It's something from our group," Whitney explained, pulling some folded papers from her purse and putting them on the table in front of her. "You know, like an assignment. Moira's one of my doctors."

"Oh," Kirsten said. "Right."

"So you're reading something you wrote," I said. "Like part of your history?"

Whitney nodded. "Kind of."

"All right, we're ready to get started," Esther said. "And first up, we have Jacob. Welcome, Jacob!"

Everyone applauded as a tall, skinny guy wearing a black knit cap wound his way through the tables to the microphone. He opened a small spiral notebook, then cleared his throat. "This is called 'Untitled,'" he said as the espresso machine hissed from behind us. "It's, um, about my ex-girlfriend."

The poem he began to read started with images about daylight and dreaming. Then it began to build quickly, his voice rising until it was just a staccato list of words that he spit out, one right after another. "Metal, Cold, Betrayal, Endless!" he was saying, as the occasional bit of spit arced over the mike. I glanced at Whitney, who was biting her lip, then at Kirsten, who looked completely entranced.

"What is this?" I whispered.

"Shhh," she said.

Jacob's poem went on for what seemed like a long time before ending, finally, with a series of long, breathless gasps. When he was done, we all sat there for a second before deciding it was okay to clap.

"Wow," I said to Heather. "That was really something."

"Oh, that's nothing," she said. "You should have been here last week. He did ten minutes on castration."

"It was disgusting," Jane added. "Compelling, but disgusting."

"Next up," Esther said, "we have a first-time reader. Everyone, please, give it up for Whitney."

Jane and Heather immediately burst into loud applause, and Kirsten and I followed suit. As Whitney walked up to the mike, I watched the crowd reacting to her, their heads turning, then double-taking, at her beauty.

"I'm going to read a short piece," she said, her voice kind of faint. She stepped closer to the microphone. "A short piece," she repeated, "about my sisters."

I felt myself blink, surprised, and looked at Kirsten. I

wanted to say something, but I kept quiet, not wanting to be shushed again.

Whitney swallowed, then looked down at her papers, the edge of which I could see fluttering, just barely. She looked scared, and it suddenly seemed too quiet. But then she began.

"I am the middle sister," she read. "The one in between. Not oldest, not youngest, not boldest, not nicest. I am the shade of gray, the glass half empty or full, depending on your view. In my life, there has been little that I have done first or better than the one preceding or following me. Of all of us, though, I am the only one who has been broken."

I heard the chime over the door sound, and turned in my seat to see an older woman with long curly hair come in and stand at the back. When she saw Whitney at the microphone she smiled, then began to unwind her scarf from around her neck.

"It happened on the day of my youngest sister's ninth birthday party," Whitney continued. "I'd been sulking around the house all day, feeling alternately ignored and entirely too hassled, which was pretty much my default setting, even at eleven."

Kirsten's eyes widened as, at the table next to us, a man laughed loudly, and I heard other chuckles as well. Whitney flushed, smiling. "My older sister, the social one, was going to ride her bike down to the neighborhood pool to meet some friends and asked me to come along. I didn't want to. I didn't want to be with anyone. If my older sister was friendly, and my younger sweet, I was the darkness. Nobody understood my pain. Not even me."

There was another laugh, this time from someone across the room, and she smiled. So Whitney could be funny. Who knew?

"My older sister got on her bike and headed for the pool, and I started to follow. I *always* followed, and once we were riding, I started to get angry about it. I was tired of being second."

I looked at Kirsten again; she was watching Whitney so intently, as if no one else was even there. "So I turned back. And suddenly, the road was empty ahead of me, this whole new view, all mine. I started to pedal as fast as I could."

I could hear Heather's spoon clinking as she added another packet of sugar to her coffee, as I sat silent, unmoving.

"It was great. Freedom, even the imagined kind, always is. But as I got farther away, and didn't recognize what was ahead of me, I started to realize the distance I was covering. I was still going full speed, away from home, when my front wheel suddenly sank, and I was flying."

Beside me, Kirsten shifted in her seat, and I moved my chair closer to her.

"It's a funny feeling, being suddenly airborne," Whitney said. "Just as you realize it, it's over, and you're sinking. When I hit the pavement, I heard the bone in my arm break. In the moments afterwards, I could hear the wheel of my bike, ticking as it spun. All I could think was what I always thought, even then: that this was just not fair. To get a taste of freedom, only to instantly be punished for it."

I looked back at the woman by the door. She was watching Whitney with full concentration.

"Everything hurt. I closed my eyes, pressing my cheek to the street, and waited. What for, I didn't know. To be rescued. Or found. But no one came. All I'd ever thought I wanted was to be left alone. Until I was."

I swallowed, hearing this, then looked down at my coffee mug, sliding my fingers around it.

"I don't know how long I lay there before my sister came back for me. I remember staring up at the sky, the clouds moving past, and then hearing her calling my name. When she skidded to a stop beside me, she was the last person I wanted to see. And yet, like so many times before and since, the only one I had."

Whitney paused, taking a breath.

"She lifted me up and settled me onto her handlebars. I knew I should be grateful to her. But as we pedaled toward home, I was angry. With myself, for falling, and with her for being there to see it. As we came up the driveway, my younger sister, the birthday girl, burst out of the house. When she saw me, my arm dangling useless, she ran back inside yelling for my mother. That was her role, always, as the youngest. She was the one who told."

I remembered that. My first thought had been that something had to be really wrong, because they were together, so close to each other. And that never happened.

"My father took me to the emergency room, where the bone was reset. When we got home, the party was almost over, presents unwrapped, the cake just being served. In the pictures taken that day, I am holding my arm over my cast, as if I don't trust it to keep me together. My older sister is on one side, the hero; my younger, the birthday girl, on the other."

I knew that picture. In it, I am wearing my bathing suit, a piece of cake in my hand; Kirsten is grinning, one hand on her hip, which is jutting out.

"For years, when I looked at the snapshot, all I could see was my broken arm. It was only later that I began to make out other things. Like how my sisters are both smiling and leaning in toward me, while I am, as always, between them."

She took a breath, looking down at her papers.

"It was not the last time I would run away from my sisters. Not the last time I thought being alone was preferable. I am still the center sister. But I see it differently now. There has to be a middle. Without it, nothing can ever truly be whole. Because it is not just the space between, but also what holds everything together. Thank you."

I just sat there, a lump rising in my throat, as applause began all around me, first here and there, and then everywhere, filling the room. Whitney flushed, pressing a hand to her chest, then smiled as she stepped out from behind the microphone. Beside me, Kirsten had tears in her eyes.

As Whitney made her way toward our table, people nodding at her as she passed, I was so proud of her, because I could only imagine how hard it must have been to read this piece aloud. Not just for strangers, but us, as well. But she'd done it. Sitting there, watching my sister, I wondered which was harder, in the end. The act of telling, or who you told it to. Or maybe if, when you finally got it out, the story was really all that mattered.

Chapter
SEVENTEEN

The clock beside my bed, glowing red, said 12:15. Which meant that, by my count, I'd been trying to fall asleep for three hours and eight minutes.

Ever since Whitney's reading the previous night, all the things I'd been trying to push away—my falling-out with Owen, Emily giving me the detective's card, Clarke talking to me again—were suddenly haunting me. The house felt full and busy, my parents were more relaxed than they'd been in months, and my sisters were not only talking to each other but actually getting along. This sudden harmony was so unexpected, it just made me seem that much more out of sorts.

The night before, on the way home from the coffee shop, Kirsten had told Whitney about her film, and how it was similar to the piece she'd read. Whitney wanted to see it, so tonight before dinner, Kirsten had set up her laptop on the coffee table and we all assembled to watch.

My parents sat on the couch with Whitney perched on the arm beside them. Kirsten took a seat at an angle, motioning for me to sit closer, but I'd just shook my head, hanging back. "I've already seen it," I told her. "You sit there."

"I've seen it a million times," she replied, but took the spot anyway.

"This is so exciting!" my mother said, looking around at all of us, and I didn't know if she meant that we were all there together, or the film itself.

Kirsten took in a breath, then reached forward to push a button. "Okay," she said. "Here it is."

As the first shot of that green, green grass, came up, I tried to keep my eyes on it. But slowly, I found myself looking instead at my family. My father's face was serious, studying the screen; my mom, beside him, had her hands curled in her lap. Whitney, on my dad's other side, had pulled a leg to her chest, and I watched the light flicker across her face as the piece continued.

"Why, Whitney," my mother said as the girls pedaled down the street, "this is kind of like that essay you let us read a while back, isn't it?"

"It is," Kirsten said softly. "Weird, right? We just figured it out last night."

Whitney didn't say anything, her eyes on the screen as, in the distance, the camera showed the smaller girl, now off her bike, the wheel spinning. Then there were the scarier images of the neighborhood: the lunging dog, the old man getting his paper. When it finally ended with that last flash of green, we were all quiet for a moment.

"Kirsten, my goodness," my mother finally said. "That was incredible."

"Hardly incredible," Kirsten replied, tucking a piece of hair behind her ear. But she did look pleased. "It's just a beginning."

"Who knew you had such an eye?" my father said, reaching across to squeeze her leg. "All that TV-watching finally paid off."

Kirsten smiled at him, but her real attention was on Whitney, who hadn't said anything yet. "So," she asked, "what did you think?"

"I liked it," Whitney told her. "Although I never thought you'd left me behind."

"And I never would have guessed you turned back," Kirsten replied. "It's so funny."

Whitney nodded, not saying anything. Then my mother sighed and said, "Well, I never realized that day was such a big deal for either of you!"

"What, you don't remember Whitney breaking her arm?" Kirsten asked.

"Your mother has a selective memory," my dad told her. "I, however, have distinct recollection of the collective trauma."

"Of course I *remember* it," my mom said. "I just . . . had no idea it had resonated with you both so much." She turned, glancing around behind her until her eyes found me. "What about you, Annabel? What do you remember about that day?"

"Turning nine," my father said. "Right?"

I nodded, because they were all watching me. In truth, though, I wasn't sure what I recalled most about that day, as so much of it had been retold now, through other eyes. It had been my birthday, I'd had a cake, I'd run to tell my mom Whitney was hurt. But the rest, I wasn't sure of.

All through dinner I watched my family: Kirsten telling stories about the intense people in her filmmaking class,

Whitney explaining the details of the sushi rolls she'd been working on all afternoon, my mother's cheeks, pink and flushed, as she laughed. Even my father was relaxed, clearly happy to have everyone together, under such better circumstances. It was a good thing, and yet I felt strangely disconnected. As if I were now a car on the street outside, slowing down to stare, with nothing in common at all but proximity, and barely that.

Now, I pushed back the covers, getting up, then went to my door, easing it open. The hallway was silent and dark, but as I suspected, there was a light visible from the stairs. My dad was still up.

As soon as he saw me crossing the living room, he muted the TV. "Hey there," he said. "Can't sleep?"

I shook my head. On the screen, I could see the grainy black-and-white images of an old news report, two men shaking hands over a table. Behind them, a crowd was clapping.

"Well," he said, "you are just in time to help me decide. It's either this fascinating show on the beginning of World War One, or something on A&E about the Dust Bowl. What do you think?"

I looked at the TV, which he'd flipped to the other channel. It showed a bleak landscape, a car moving slowly across it. "I don't know," I said. "They sound equally compelling."

"Hey," he said. "Don't knock history. This stuff is important."

I smiled, moving to the couch and sitting down. "I know," I said. "It's just hard to get excited about it. I mean, for me."

"How can you not get excited about this?" he asked. "It's

real. This isn't some silly story somebody made up. These are things that actually happened."

"A long time ago," I added.

"Exactly!" he said, nodding. "That's my point. That's why we *can't* forget it. No matter how much time has passed, these things still affect us and the world we live in. If you don't pay attention to the past, you'll never understand the future. It's all linked together. You see what I'm saying?"

At first, I didn't. But then, I looked back at the screen, those images moving across it, and realized he was right. The past did affect the present and the future, in the ways you could see and a million ones you couldn't. Time wasn't a thing you could divide easily; there was no defined middle or beginning or end. I could pretend to leave the past behind, but it would not leave me.

Sitting there, I could suddenly feel myself getting more anxious, even as I tried to focus on the images on the screen. My mind was racing, too fast to even think, and after a few minutes I went back to bed.

This is crazy, I thought as I found myself again staring at the ceiling, my sisters quiet in their rooms on either side. I closed my eyes, the events of the last few days blurring across my vision in bits and pieces. My heart was pounding. Something was happening I didn't, or couldn't, understand. I sat up, kicking off the covers; I needed something to calm me down, or just even take away these thoughts, if only for a little while. Reaching over to my bedside drawer, I grabbed my headphones and plugged them into my CD player, then went to my desk. In the bottom drawer, after digging through all the CDs Owen had made me, I finally found it: the yellow disc that said JUST LISTEN.

You might totally hate it, Owen had told me. *Or not. It might be just what you need. That's the beauty of it. You know?*

When I hit the PLAY button, all I could hear was static, and I settled in, closing my eyes, and waited for the first song to begin. It didn't. Not in the next few minutes, not ever. Then I realized: the CD was blank.

Maybe it was supposed to be a joke. Or something profound. But as I lay there, it only seemed like silence filling my ears. And the thing was, it was so freaking loud.

It was the weirdest thing, so different from music. The sound was nothing, empty, but at the same time, it pushed everything else out, quieting me enough that I began to be able to make out something distant, hard to hear. But it *was* there, albeit softly, coming to me from some dark place I'd never seen but still knew well.

Shhh, Annabel. It's just me.

But these words were only the middle of the story. There was a beginning here, too. And I knew suddenly that if I stayed where I was, in all that quiet, and didn't run from it, I would hear it. I'd have to go back, all the way to that night at the party when I'd first heard Emily call out Sophie's name, but that was okay. It was the only way, finally, to get to the end.

All I'd ever wanted was to forget. But even when I thought I had, pieces had kept emerging, like bits of wood floating up to the surface that only hint at the shipwreck below. A pink shirt, a rhyme with my name, the feeling of hands on my neck. Because that is what happens when you try to run from the past. It doesn't just catch up: it overtakes, blotting out the future, the landscape, the very sky, until there is no path left except that which leads through it, the only one that can ever get you home.

I understood now. This voice, the one that had been trying to get my attention all this time, calling out to me, begging me to hear it—it wasn't Will's. It was mine.

Chapter
EIGHTEEN

"This is WRUS, your community radio station. It's seven fifty-eight, and this is Anger Management. Here's one final song."

There was a twang, followed by a burst of feedback. Something experimental, different, and not altogether listenable. Just another Sunday on Owen's show.

It was not, however, just another Sunday for me. Somewhere between sliding on my headphones the night before and now, something had changed. After lying there for a long time, letting myself retrace the steps of that night at the party, I'd drifted off into that silence, the voice inside my head finally talked out. When I'd woken up at seven, my headphones were still on, and I could hear my heart in my ears. I sat up, sliding them off, and the quiet around me did not, for once, seem empty and vast. Instead, for the first time in a while, it felt like it already was full.

When I'd first turned on the radio, the show had just started with a blast of old-school metal, someone wailing over some heavy-duty guitars. After following up with what sounded like a Russian pop song, Owen finally came on.

"That was Leningrad," he said, "and this is Anger

Management. I'm Owen. It's seven oh-six, thanks for hanging out with us. Got a request? A suggestion? Issues? Call us at 555–WRUS. Here's Dominic Waverly."

The song that followed was a techno one, beginning with several bouncy beats, seemingly out of sync, which eventually blended together. All those other Sundays I'd listened so intently, wanting to like or at least understand what I was hearing. When I hadn't, I'd never hesitated to tell Owen. If only I'd been able to just tell him everything else, as well. But you can't always get the perfect moment. Sometimes, you just have to do the best you can, under the circumstances.

Which was why I was now in my car, pulling out of my neighborhood, heading toward WRUS. It was 8:02 when I turned into the lot. The Herbal Prescription, the syndicated show that followed his, was just starting. I parked between Owen's and Rolly's cars, then reached over to the passenger seat for the CD there and went inside.

The station was quiet, a voice murmuring about ginkgo biloba as I made my way across the lobby. To my right, at the end of a hallway, I could see the booth, enclosed in glass. As I approached, the first thing I saw was Rolly at the controls in the little room adjacent to it; he had on a bright green T-shirt and a baseball hat turned backwards, his headphones over it. Clarke was beside him, drinking from a to-go coffee cup, the Sunday paper crossword puzzle in front of her. They were talking, and neither of them noticed my arrival. When I turned to the main booth, though, Owen was looking right at me.

He was sitting at the microphone, a stack of CDs spread out in front of him. Judging by the look on his face, he was not happy to see me. It was worse than the day in the parking lot. Which made it that much more important that I push the door open and go inside. So I did.

"Hi," I said.

He just looked at me for a second. "Hey," he said finally, his voice flat.

There was a buzz, and then Rolly's voice came from over my head. "Annabel!" he said, his sunny tone a distinct contrast to Owen's barely tolerant one. "Hey! What's going on?"

I looked over him, lifting a hand to wave. He waved back, as did Clarke. He was leaning in to say something else to me when he glanced at Owen—who was glaring at him—and slowly drew back, deciding against it. There was a click, and the microphone went off again.

"What are you doing here?" Owen asked me.

Of course he would come right out with it. "I need to talk to you," I said.

Out of the corner of my eye, I was aware of some sudden movement in the other room. I looked over to see Clarke hurriedly stuffing her newspaper into a bag, while Rolly took off his headphones, standing up. *Who's conflict-adverse now*, I thought as they exited the room at a breakneck pace, Rolly slapping the light off as he went.

"We're, um, going to go ahead to the bacon," he said to Owen as they passed behind me. "See you there?"

Owen nodded, and Rolly smiled at me again before turning away. Clarke lingered for a moment, her hand on the open door. "You okay?" she asked.

"Yeah," I said. "I'm fine."

She pulled her bag over her shoulder, giving Owen a look I couldn't make out. Then she was running to catch up with Rolly, linking her hand with his, and they disappeared around the corner into the lobby.

When I looked back at Owen, he was packing up as well, coiling the cord around his headphones. "I don't have much time," he said, not looking at me. "So if you've got something to say, go ahead and say it."

"Okay," I said. "It's—" My heart was beating fast, and I felt sick. Normally this was where I stopped, chickened out, and turned back. "It's about this," I said, holding up the CD in my hand. My voice sounded shaky, so I cleared my throat. "It was supposed to blow my mind? Remember?"

He glanced at it again, his expression wary. "Vaguely," he said.

"I listened to it last night," I said. "But I wanted to be, um, sure that I got it. Your intention, I mean."

"My intention," he repeated.

"Well, you know," I said, "there's a lot left up to interpretation." My voice sounded more solid now, finally. The power of music, indeed. "So I just wanted to make sure I really, you know, got it."

We just stared at each other, and it was all I could do not to look away. But I managed. And then, after a moment, he stuck out his hand for the CD.

He looked at the case, then turned it over. "There's no track listing on here," he said.

"Don't you remember what you put on it?"

"It was a long time ago." He shot me a look. "And I made you a lot of CDs."

"Ten," I told him. "I listened to them all."

"Really."

I nodded. "Yeah. You told me you wanted me to before I put that one on."

"Ah," he said. "So now you care about what I want."

Outside, I could see Rolly and Clarke in his car, backing out of their parking space. He was saying something, and she was laughing, shaking her head.

"I always cared about that," I said to Owen.

"Really? It's been kind of hard to tell, by the way you've been avoiding me for the last two months." He reached out to the console in front of him, hitting a button. The drawer slid open, and he put the disc in.

"I figured that *was* what you wanted," I said.

"Why?" he said. He reached down, nudging up a knob beneath the player.

I swallowed, hard. "You were the one who got out of the car in the parking lot that day and walked away," I told him. "You'd had it with me."

"You ditched me at a club and wouldn't even tell me why," he shot back, his voice rising. He turned the knob a bit more. "I was pissed, Annabel."

"Exactly," I said, and now I could hear static over our heads. "You were pissed. I'd let you down. I was not what you wanted me to be—"

"—and so you just bolted," he finished, hitting the knob

again. The static grew louder. "Disappeared. One argument, and you're out of there."

"What did you want me to do?" I said.

"Tell me what was going on, for one," he said. "God, tell me *something*. It's like I said, I could have handled it."

"Like you were handling my not saying anything? You were furious with me."

"So what? I was entitled," he said. He glanced at the console again. "People get mad, Annabel. It's not the end of the world."

"So I was supposed to just explain myself, and let you be mad at me, and then maybe you might have gotten over it—"

"I would have gotten over it."

"—or not," I said, glaring at him. "Maybe it would have changed everything."

"That happened anyway!" he said. "I mean, look at us now. At least if you'd told me what was going on, we could have dealt with it. As it was, you just left everything hanging, no resolution, nothing. Is that what you wanted? That I be gone for good, rather than just mad for a little while?"

I just stood there as he said this, the words sinking in. "I didn't," I said. "I didn't realize that was an option."

"Of course it was," he said, looking up at the speaker overhead; the static was even louder now. "Whatever it was, it couldn't have been that bad. All you had to do was be honest. Tell me what really happened."

"It's not that easy."

"Is this? Ignoring and avoiding each other, acting like we

were never friends? Maybe for you. It's sucked for me. I don't like playing games."

As he said this, I felt something in my stomach. It wasn't the clenching sickness I was used to, though. More of a slow simmer. "I don't like that, either," I said. "But—"

"If it's so big that it's worth all this," he said, waving his hand to include the studio, the static, and us in the midst of it all, "all this crap and weirdness that's happened since then, it's too big to keep inside. You know that."

"No," I said, "*you* know that, Owen. Because you don't have problems with anger—yours or anyone else's. You just use all your little phrases, and everything you've learned, and you're always honest and you never regret a thing you say or how you act—"

"Yes, I do."

"—and I'm not like that," I finished. "I'm just not."

"Then what *are* you like, Annabel?" he shot back. "A liar, like you told me that first day? Come on. That was the biggest lie of all."

I just looked at him. My hands were shaking.

"If you were a liar, you would have just lied to me," he said, glancing at the monitor again as the static grew louder. "You would have just acted like everything was fine. But you didn't."

"No," I said, shaking my head.

"And don't tell me this is easy for me, because it's not. These last couple of months have sucked, not knowing what's going on with you. What is it, Annabel? What's so bad you can't even tell me?"

I could feel my heart beating, my blood pulsing. Owen turned back to the console, raising the volume of the CD even higher, and as the sound filled my ears it hit me, all at once, what this feeling was. I was angry.

Really angry. At him, for attacking me. At myself, for waiting until now to fight back. At every other chance I hadn't taken. All these months, I'd been having this same reaction, but I'd blamed it on nerves, or fear. It wasn't.

"You don't understand," I said to him now.

"Then tell me, and maybe I will," he shot back, pushing the empty chair in front of him toward me. "And what," he said, his voice loud, "is going *on* with this CD? Where's the music? Why can't we hear anything?"

"What?" I said.

He pushed a few buttons, swearing under his breath. "There's nothing on this," he said. "It's blank."

"Isn't that the point?"

"What?" he said. "What point?"

Oh my God, I thought. I reached forward for the chair he'd pushed toward me, then eased myself down into it. Here I'd thought this gesture was so deep, so profound, and it was just . . . a mistake. A malfunction. I was wrong, all wrong.

Or not.

It was all so loud, suddenly. His voice, my heart, the static, filling the room. I closed my eyes, willing myself back to the night before, when I'd been able to hear the things I'd kept silent for so long.

Shhh, Annabel, I heard a voice say, but it sounded different this time. Familiar. *It's just me.*

Owen began to turn down the volume, and the static above us receded bit by bit. There comes a time in every life when the world gets quiet and the only thing left is your own heart. So you'd better learn to know the sound of it. Otherwise you'll never understand what it's saying.

"Annabel?" Owen said. His voice was lower now. Closer. He sounded worried. "What is it?"

He had already given me so much, but now I leaned toward him, asking him for one last thing. Something I knew he did better than anyone. "Don't think or judge," I said. "Just listen."

"Annabel? We're just about to start the movie. . . ." My mother's voice was soft; she thought I'd been sleeping. "You about ready?"

"Almost," I said.

"Okay," she said. "We'll be downstairs."

The day before, I hadn't just told Owen about what happened to me at the party. I told him everything. The stuff with Sophie at school, Whitney's recovery, Kirsten's movie. Agreeing to do another commercial, talking with my dad about history, and listening to his blank CD the night before. He just sat there, listening to every single word. And when I was finally done, he said the two words that usually don't mean anything, but this time, said it all.

"I'm sorry, Annabel," he told me. "I'm so sorry that happened to you."

Maybe this was what I'd wanted, all along. Not an apology—and certainly not one from Owen—but an acknowledgment. What mattered most, though, was that I'd gotten through it, finally—beginning, middle, and end. Which did not, of course, mean it was over.

"So what are you going to do?" he asked me later, when we were standing by the Land Cruiser, having had to leave the booth to make room for the next show, which was hosted by two cheery local realtors. "Are you going to call that woman? About the trial?"

"I don't know," I said.

I knew that in any other circumstance he'd be telling me exactly how he felt about this, but this time he held back. For about a minute.

"The thing is," he said, "there aren't a whole lot of opportunities in life to really make a difference. This is one of them."

"Easy for you to say," I said. "You always do the right thing."

"No, I don't," he replied, shaking his head. "I just do the best I can—"

"—under the circumstances, I know," I finished for him. "But I'm scared. I don't know if I can do it."

"Of course you can," he said.

"How can you be so sure?"

"Because you just did," he said. "Coming here, and telling me that? That's huge. Most people couldn't do it. But you did."

"I had to," I said. "I wanted to explain."

"And you can do it again," he replied. "Just call that woman and tell her what you told me."

I reached up, running a hand through my hair. "There's more to it than that," I said. "What if she wants me to come

testify or something? I'd have to tell my parents, my mom. . . .
I don't know if she can take it."

"She can."

"You don't even know her," I said.

"I don't have to," he replied. "Look, this is important. You know that. So do what you have to do, and then go from there. Your mom just might surprise you."

I felt a lump rise in my throat. I wanted to believe this was true, and maybe it was.

Owen dropped his bag to the ground, then crouched down beside it, rummaging around. I had a flash of him that day behind the school, doing this same thing, and how I'd had no idea in the world what he would come up with, what on earth Owen Armstrong had to offer me. After a moment, he pulled out a picture.

"Here," he said, handing it to me. "For inspiration."

It was the one he'd taken of me the night of Mallory's photo shoot. I was standing in the powder-room doorway, no make-up, my face relaxed, the yellow glow of the light behind me. *See*, he'd said then, *that's what you look like*, and as I stared down at it, it seemed like proof, finally, that I was not the girl from Mallory's wall or the Kopf's commercial or even the party that night in May. That something in me had changed that fall, because of Owen, even if I only now could really see it.

"Mallory told me to give it to you," he said. "But . . ."

"But?" I said.

". . . I didn't," he finished.

I knew maybe I shouldn't ask. But I did anyway. "Why not?"

"I liked it," he said with a shrug. "I wanted to hang on to it."

It was the picture I was holding that afternoon when I finally got up the nerve to call Andrea Thomlinson, the woman whose card Emily had given me. I left a message on her voice mail, and she called back within ten minutes. Emily was right: She was nice. We talked for forty-five minutes. And when she asked if I'd come to the courthouse the next day, in case they needed me, even though I knew what it meant to do so, I agreed. As soon as we hung up, I called Owen.

"Good for you," he said when I told him what I'd done. His voice was warm, pleased, and I pressed the receiver closer, letting it fill my ear. "You did the right thing."

"Yeah," I said. "I know. But now I have to get up in front of people. . . ."

"You can do it," he said, and when I sighed, not at all sure of this, he said, "You can. Look, if you're nervous about tomorrow—"

"If?" I said.

"—then I'll go with you. If you want."

"You'd do that," I said.

"Sure," he replied. So easily, no question. "Just tell me where and when."

We arranged to meet at the fountain in front of the courthouse, just before nine. I knew that even without him, I still wouldn't be alone. But it was nice to have options.

Now, I took one last look at the picture, then slid it into my bedside-table drawer.

On my way to the living room, where my family was gathered, I stopped to look at the photo in the foyer. As always, my eyes were drawn to my own face first, then those of my sisters, and finally my mother, looking so small between us. But I saw it differently now.

When that picture was taken, we were all gathered around my mother, sheltering her. But that was just one day, one shot. In the time since, we had arranged and rearranged ourselves so many times. We'd all gathered around Whitney, even when she didn't want us to, and Kirsten and I had gotten closer when she pushed us both away. We were still in flux, as had been clear at the table that night as I watched my mother and sisters come together again. Then, I'd been convinced I was on the outside, but really, I'd always been within arm's reach. All I had to do was ask, and I, too, would be easily brought back, surrounded and immersed, finding myself safe, somewhere in between.

I walked across the living room to where my family was gathered around the TV. No one saw me at first, and I just stood there for a second, looking at them all together. Finally, my mom turned her head, and I took in a breath, knowing that whatever I saw in her face, I could do this. I had to.

"Annabel," she said. Then she smiled before moving over to make a place for me beside her. "Come join us."

For a moment I hesitated, but then I looked at Whitney. She was watching me, her expression serious, and I thought of that night a year ago, when I'd pushed open a door and flipped a switch, exposing her to the light. What had happened to her had scared me to death, but she'd survived it. So I kept my eyes on her as I crossed the space between and took my seat.

My mother smiled at me again, and I felt a wave of sadness and fear come over me, knowing what I was about to do. *You about ready?* she'd asked me earlier, and then, I hadn't been. Maybe I never would be. But there was no way around it now. So as I got ready to tell my story again, I did what Owen had done for me so many times: I reached out a hand, to my mother and my family. And this time, I pulled them through with me.

Chapter
NINETEEN

When I first got into the courtroom, I could only see Will Cash in glimpses. The back of his head here, the arm of his suit there, a profile, fleeting. At first this was frustrating and made me even more nervous, but as the time grew closer to when I'd be called, I began to think this was a good thing. Pieces and parts were always easier to process. The full picture, the entire story, was another thing entirely. But you just never knew. Sometimes, people could surprise you.

Telling my family had been harder, in the end, than telling Owen. But I did it. Even through the hard parts, even when I heard my mother catch her breath, could feel my father's eyes narrowing, felt Kirsten shaking beside me, I kept on. And when I felt myself really wavering, I looked at Whitney, who never flinched. She was strongest of us all, and I kept my eyes on her, all the way to the end.

My mother had surprised me most. She had not fallen apart, or crumpled, although I knew hearing what had happened to me was not easy for her. Instead, while Kirsten cried, and Whitney helped my dad find Andrea Thomlinson's card in my room so he could call her for more details, my mother sat beside me, her arm around my shoulder, just smoothing her hand over my head, again and again.

That morning, on the way to the courthouse, I'd sat in the backseat between my sisters, watching my parents. Every once in a while my mother's shoulder would move, and I knew she was reaching over to pat my father's hand, as he had done to her on another drive, on another day when secrets had begun to come out, not so long ago.

All my life, I realized, I'd only seen my parents one way, as if it was the only way they could be. One weak, one strong. One scared, one bold. I was beginning to understand, though, that there were no such things as absolutes, not in life or in people. Like Owen said, it was day by day, if not moment by moment. All you could do was take on as much weight as you can bear. And if you're lucky, there's someone close enough by to shoulder the rest.

When we walked up to the courthouse it was just before eight forty-five, and I scanned the crowd in the square around the fountain, looking for Owen. He wasn't there. Not then, and not after my mother and I met with Andrea Thomlinson in a nearby office to go over my story again. Not even when the courtroom opened and we filed inside, taking our seats just down the row from Emily and her mom. I kept looking for him, thinking he would slide in at the last minute, just in time, but he didn't. It was so not like him, and it worried me.

An hour and a half later, the prosecutor called my name. I stood up, my palm slick on the bench in front of me as I slid my hand along its back, walking past my sisters to the end of the row. Then I stepped out into the aisle and was on my own.

As I crossed the floor I finally had a clear view of everything—the crowd, the judge, the prosecutors and defense attorneys—and I made a point of focusing only on the bailiff, who was waiting for me by the witness stand. I took my seat, feeling my heart pounding as I answered his questions and the judge turned, nodding at me. It was only after the prosecutor stood and started toward me that I finally let myself look at Will Cash.

It wasn't his fancy suit I noticed first. Or his new haircut, short and schoolboyish, which was probably intended to make him look young and innocent. The look on his face—narrowed eyes, pursed lips—didn't really register, either. The only thing I could see, actually, was the black circle around his left eye, the redness of the cheek beneath. Someone had tried to cover it up with makeup, but it was still there. Clear as day.

"State your name for the record," the prosecutor asked me.

"Annabel Greene," I said. My voice was shaking.

"Are you acquainted with William Cash, Annabel?"

"Yes."

"Could you point him out to me, please?"

After being silent for so long, I felt like I had talked so much in the last twenty-four hours. But with any luck, this would be the last time for a while. Which was maybe why it wasn't so hard to quiet myself, to take in that first breath, to begin.

"There," I said, raising my finger and pointing at him. "He's right there."

• • •

When it was finally over, we walked through the dark of the courthouse lobby into a noontime sun so bright it took my eyes a moment to adjust. When they did, Owen was the first thing I saw.

He was sitting on the edge of the fountain, wearing jeans and a white T-shirt, a blue jacket over it, his earphones hanging around his neck. It was lunchtime, and the square was packed with people crossing back and forth: businessmen with briefcases, students from the university, a bunch of preschoolers walking in a line, all holding hands. When Owen saw me, he stood up.

"I think," my mother was saying, running a hand down my arm, "that we should all go get something to eat. What do you think, Annabel? Are you hungry?"

I looked at Owen, who was watching me, his hands now in his pockets. "Yeah," I told her. "Just give me one second."

As I started down the steps, I could hear my father asking where I was going, and my mother responding she had no idea. I was sure they were all watching me, but I didn't look back as I crossed the square, walking up to Owen, who had the strangest look on his face, one I'd never seen before. He was shifting in place, clearly uncomfortable.

"Hey," he said quickly, as soon as I was in earshot.

"Hi."

He took in a breath, about to speak, then stopped, running a hand over his face. "Look," he said. "I know you're pissed off at me."

The weird thing was that I wasn't. While initially, I'd been surprised, then worried when he hadn't shown up, the entire experience had been so overwhelming—although cathartic— that I'd kind of forgotten about it once I got up on the stand. I opened my mouth to tell him this, but he was already talking again.

"The basic fact is that I should have been here. I have no excuse. There is no excuse." He looked down at the ground, scuffing his foot across the pavement. "I mean, there is a reason. But it's not an excuse."

"Owen," I said. "It's—"

"Something happened." He sighed, shaking his head. His face was flushed, and he was still fidgeting. "Something stupid. I made a mistake, and—"

Then, and only then, did I put it altogether. His absence. This shuffling embarrassment. And Will Cash's black eye. *Oh my God*, I thought.

"Owen," I said, my voice low. "No way."

"It was an error in judgment," he said quickly. "And something I regret."

"Something," I repeated.

"Yes."

A businessman talking loudly on a cell phone passed us, talking about mergers. "Placeholder," I told him.

He winced. "I thought you might say that."

"Come on," I said. "You *knew* I would say that."

"Fine, fine." He pulled a hand through his hair. "I was having an in-depth discussion with my mother. One that I could not easily extract myself from."

"A discussion," I repeated. "About what?"

Again, he flinched. This was killing him. And yet I could not help myself. After being on the other side of the truth for so long, I realized I kind of liked asking the questions.

"Well," he said, then coughed. "Basically, I'm supposed to be under punishment right now. For the foreseeable future, in fact. So I had to negotiate a furlough. It took longer than I expected."

"You're grounded," I said, clarifying.

"Yes."

"For what?"

He winced, then shook his head, looking over at the fountain. Who knew the truth could be so hard for Owen Armstrong, the most honest boy in the world. But if I asked, he would tell. That I knew for sure.

"Owen," I said as he squirmed, noticeably, his shoulder wriggling, "what did you do?"

He just looked at me for a minute. Then he sighed. "I punched Will Cash in the face."

"What were you *thinking*?"

"Well, clearly I wasn't." He flushed a deeper red. "I didn't intend to do it."

"You punched him by accident."

"No." He shot me a look. "Okay, you really want to know?"

"Am I not asking?"

"Look," Owen said, "the truth is, after you left yesterday, I was really pissed off. I mean, I'm human, right?"

"You are," I agreed.

"I really only wanted to get a good look at him. That was all. And I knew he sometimes plays with that shitty Perkins

Day band that was in a showcase last night at Bendo, so I figured he might be there. And he was. Which, really, when you think about it, is despicable. What kind of a person goes to a club—to see a shitty band, no less—the night before he's due in court? It's—"

"Owen," I said.

"I'm serious! Do you know how much they *suck*? Seriously, even for a cover band they're pathetic. I mean, if you're going to just come out and admit you can't write your own songs, at least be able to play other people's well. . . ."

I just looked at him.

"Right," he said. He ran a hand through his hair again. "So anyway, he was there, I got a look at him, end of story."

"Clearly," I said sternly, "that is *not* the end of the story."

Owen continued, reluctantly. "I watched their set. Which, as I said, sucked. I went out for some air, and he was outside smoking a cigarette. And he starts talking to me. Like we know each other. Like he's not the freaking scum of the earth, a total fucking asshole."

"Owen," I said softly.

"I could feel myself getting more and more pissed off." He winced. "I knew I should breathe, and walk away, and everything else, but I didn't. And then, when he finished his cigarette, he clapped me on the shoulder and turned to go back inside. And I just—"

I took a step closer to him.

"—snapped," he finished. "I lost it."

"It's okay," I said.

"I knew even when I was doing it I'd regret it," he said.

"That it wasn't worth it. But by then it was already happening. I'm really pissed off at myself, if you want to know the truth."

"I know."

"It was just one punch," he grumbled, then added quickly, "which doesn't make it okay. And I'm so freaking lucky the bouncer just broke us up and told us both to get out of there, and didn't call the cops. If he had . . ." He trailed off. "It's just so stupid."

"But you told your mom anyway," I said.

"When I got home, she could tell I was pissed. So she asked me what happened, and I had to tell her—"

"Because you're honest," I said, taking another step.

"Well, yeah," he said, looking down at me. "She was livid, to say the least. Laid down this hardcore punishment, totally deserved, but then today, when I tried to leave to come here, things got kind of sticky."

"It's okay," I said again.

"It's not, though." Behind him, the fountain was splashing, sunlight glinting off the water. "Because I'm not like that. Anymore. I just . . . freaked out."

I reached up, brushing his hair out of his face. "Huh," I said. "Really."

"What?"

"I don't know." I shrugged. "It's just to me, that's not freaking out."

"It's not," he said. Then he just looked at me for a second. "Oh," he said finally. "Right."

"I mean, to me," I said, moving closer, "freaking out is different. More of a running away, not telling anyone what's wrong, slowly simmering until you burst kind of thing."

"Ah," he said. "Well, I guess it's just a matter of semantics."

"I guess so."

People were still moving all around us, on their way here and there, filling up their lunch hour however they could before the rest of the day began. I knew that somewhere behind me, my family was waiting, but still I reached my hand down to brush his.

"You know," Owen said, as his fingers found mine, "it sure seems like you have all the answers."

"Nah," I told him. "I'm just doing the best I can, under the circumstances."

"How's that going?" he asked.

There was no short answer to this; like so much else, it was a long story. But what really makes any story real is knowing someone will hear it. And understand.

"Well, you know," I said to Owen now. "It's day by day."

He smiled at me, and I smiled back, then stepped closer, turning my face up to meet his. As he leaned down to kiss me, I closed my eyes and saw not the flat black of the dark but something else. Something brighter, closer to light, shining small but ever steady. More than enough to go on as a part of me pushed up and out, finally, to meet it there.

Chapter

TWENTY

I slipped on my headphones, then looked over at Rolly. When he flashed me a thumbs-up, I leaned into the microphone.

"It's seven fifty, and you're listening to your community radio station, WRUS. If you're looking for Anger Management, it will return in"—I glanced at my notepad, where, above my neatly written playlist, there was a big number two, followed by an exclamation point—"two weeks. In the meantime, I'm Annabel, and this is Story of My Life. Here's The Clash."

I kept my headphones on, watching Rolly until the first notes of "Rebel Waltz" were audible. Then I finally let out the breath I felt like I'd been holding forever, just as the speaker over my head popped and Clarke came on.

"Nice," she said. "You barely sounded nervous."

"That's still nervous," I told her.

"You're doing great," Rolly said. "And I don't know why you get so worried anyway. It's not like you're walking in front of people in a bathing suit." Clarke turned, shooting him a look. "What?" he said. "It's true!"

"This is harder," I said, sliding off my headphones. "Much harder."

"Why?" he asked.

I shrugged. "I don't know," I said. "It's more real. Personal."

And it was. In fact, I'd been terrified when Owen had first asked me to fill in when his mom decided that taking away the radio show was the only sufficient punishment for what he'd done to Will Cash. But once he'd convinced me that Rolly (and Clarke) would be there to help with the technical stuff and make sure I stayed on time every week, I'd agreed to try it at least once. That had been four weeks ago, and while I was still nervous, I was also having fun. So much that Rolly was already bugging me to take the community radio prep course and apply for my own time slot, but I wasn't quite ready for that yet. But never say never.

Of course, Owen was still involved with the show. When I'd first started subbing for him, he'd insisted that I stick to his playlist, even when it meant forcing music I hated on the masses. After the first week, though (and once he realized that he really couldn't stop me), he'd relented, and I'd started putting my own songs in here and there. There was something really great about being able to put something out into the world—a song, an introduction, even my voice—and let people make of it what they wanted. I didn't have to worry about how I looked, or if the image of me people had fit who I really was. The music spoke for itself and for me, and after so long being watched and studied, I was finding I liked that. A lot.

Rolly knocked on the glass between us, then signaled to me to get the next song ready to go. It was a Jenny Reef single, for Mallory—my first true fan—who made a point of setting her alarm each week so she could call in a request. I cued it up, then waited until The Clash began to fade out before hitting the button to begin its bouncy beats (a segue that I knew would annoy Owen, who for various reasons insisted on listening to the broadcast of the show in the car, alone). Once it had fully started, I shifted in my chair, glancing over at the row of pictures I had lined up next to my monitor. When I'd first started, I'd been so nervous I figured I could use all the inspiration I could get. So I'd brought in the shot of Mallory with the feather boa circling her face, to remind me at least one person was listening. The one of me Owen had taken, so I'd keep in mind that it didn't matter if she was the only one. And then one more.

It was shot of me and my mother and sisters, taken at New Year's. Unlike the one in the foyer, it was hardly professional, with no dramatic vista behind us. Instead, we were all standing at the kitchen island. We'd just been talking, about what I couldn't even remember, and then Kirsten's boyfriend Brian—with the class over, they were now free and clear to make their relationship public—was telling us to look here, and the shutter snapped. It was not a great picture in the technical sense. You can see the flash in the window behind us, my mother has her mouth open, and Whitney is laughing. But I loved it, because it was what we looked like. And best of all, this time no one was in the middle.

Every time I looked at it, I was reminded how much I liked this new life, without a secret hanging over me. It was a fresh start, and now I didn't have to be the girl who had everything, or nothing, but another girl altogether. Maybe even the one who told.

"Two minutes until next break," Rolly said now, and I nodded, sliding my headphones back on. As he leaned back from the microphone, Clarke reached over, ruffling his hair. He smiled at her, making a face as she went back to the Sunday crossword, which she made a point of trying to complete every week during the hour the show was on. Clarke was competitive, even with herself. It was one of many things I'd forgotten about her, but was now remembering—like how she always sang along with the radio, refused to watch scary movies, and could make me giggle uncontrollably over the stupidest things—as we cautiously worked our way back into a friendship. It wasn't like it had been, but then neither of us would have wanted that anyway. As it was, we were just happy to be hanging out. Everything else, we took day by day.

This was how I was dealing with everyone and everything lately, taking the good when it came, and the bad the same way, knowing each would pass in its own time. My sisters were still speaking, as well as occasionally still arguing. Kirsten was in her second filmmaking class, working away on a piece about, strangely enough, modeling, which she promised would "rock our world" (whatever that meant). In January, Whitney had enrolled in classes at the local university, where, along with a few requirements, she was taking two writing classes, one on memoir, the other fiction. In the spring, with her doctor's blessing, she was moving into her own apartment, a place she'd made sure had enough light for some plants. In the meantime, her herbs were still in the windowsill, where I made a point to pass them whenever I could, reaching down to smooth their pungent leaves between my fingers, releasing their scent to linger to the open air behind me.

As for my mother, she had accepted all these changes with a few tears—of course—as well as a strength that continually surprised me. I'd told her, finally, that I was done with modeling, for good, and while it was hard for her to let go of that part of my life, and her own, she'd compensated by taking a part-time job with Lindy, who was still desperately in need of a receptionist. It was a good fit. Now she sent other girls out to calls and dealt with clients, keeping one foot in the world where she, out of all of us, always felt the most comfortable.

Still, I knew it would probably be hard for her when the new Kopf's commercial began running in a few weeks. From what I heard, they'd stuck to the same idea as the one I'd done, focusing on the Ideal Girl as she moved through spring sports and prom. It probably would have bothered me, for all the reasons the other one had, if not for the girl they'd picked to replace me: Emily. After all, if anyone could be a role model, it was her.

As far as Emily and I went, we weren't exactly friends. But we both knew what we'd been through would link us forever, whether we liked it or not. Whenever we passed each other in the hallway now, we made a point of saying hello, even if that was all we said. This was more than I could say for Sophie, who studiously ignored both of us. After Will's conviction and sentencing for second-degree rape—six years, although he'd probably be out earlier—she'd laid low for a while, clearly uncomfortable with being the subject of so much discussion. There were times when I saw her alone in the halls, or at lunch, and thought that ideally, I'd be able to go up to her, heal this rift, do for her what she'd never done for me.

Or not.

Thinking this, I looked down at my thumb, slipping off the thick silver ring there to read these same words. It was too big for any of my fingers, and I'd had to wrap some tape on it so it would fit, but it was just fine for now while I was still figuring out what I wanted on the one Rolly had promised me. Until then, Owen had said I could hold on to his, if only to remind me that it's always good to know your options.

"Thirty seconds," Rolly said in my headphones.

I nodded, moving my chair closer to the microphone. As the seconds counted down, I looked out the window to my left and saw a blue Land Cruiser turning into the lot. Right on time.

"And . . ." Rolly said, "you're on."

"That was Jenny Reef, with 'Whatever,'" I began, "and this has been Story of My Life, here on WRUS. I'm Annabel. The Herbal Prescription is next. Thanks for listening. Here's one last song."

The opening notes of Led Zeppelin's "Thank You" came on, and I pushed back my chair. Then I closed my eyes to listen, as I did every time I heard this song, my own little ritual. Just as the chorus began, I heard the door open and, a moment later, felt a hand on my shoulder.

"Please tell me," Owen said, flopping down dramatically in the chair beside me, "that I did not just hear Jenny Reef on my show."

"It was a request," I said. "And besides, you said I could play what I wanted as long as we called the show something else."

"Within *reason*," he said. "I mean, you just have to keep in mind that my listeners are going to be confused. They're still tuning in, and they expect quality. If possible, enlightenment. Not commercial, mass-produced crap sung by a teenager completely controlled by corporate marketing."

"Owen."

"I mean, there's room for some irony, but it's a delicate balance. Too much either way and you lose all credibility. Which means that—"

"Are you even listening to what I'm playing now?" I asked.

He stopped in mid-rant, then looked up at the speaker overhead, listening for a second. "Oh," he said. "Well, this is what I mean. This is my—"

"Favorite Led Zeppelin song," I finished for him. "I know."

In the booth, Clarke rolled her eyes.

"Okay, fine," Owen said, moving his chair closer to mine. "So you played some Jenny Reef. I thought the rest of the show was pretty good. Although I'm not sure about the juxtaposition you did in the second pairing—"

"Owen."

"—following up that Alamance track with the Etta James. It was a bit much. And—"

"Owen."

"What?"

I leaned closer to him, pressing my lips to his ear. "Shhh," I said.

He started to say something else—of course—but stopped as I slid my hand over to his, locking his fingers in mine. It wasn't over. Eventually, he'd make his point, or at least argue it into submission. But for now, the chords were building overhead, the chorus starting up again. So I moved closer to Owen, leaning my head on his shoulder to listen, as we settled into the sunlight coming through the window beside us. It was bright and warm, catching the ring on my thumb as Owen reached for it, spinning it slowly, slowly, as the song played on.

ACKNOWLEDGMENTS

It takes a village to see a book from beginning to end, and I am lucky to have good neighbors. Thanks to Leigh Feldman, the most honest person I know, and the fabulous Regina Hayes, who always takes my best and makes it so much better. Joy Peskin gave her perspective and experience when I needed it most. I am also indebted to Marianne Gingher and Bland Simpson at UNC–Chapel Hill, who gave me the second best job I've ever had and, more importantly, continue to understand why writing is the first. I'm grateful to Ann Parrent at WCOM 103.5 Community Radio, and Jeff Welty, dashing vegan criminal defense attorney, for facts and information, and to my parents for yet again talking me down off the ledge. But in the end, this book, like all the others, is really for Jay, who gave me Bob Dylan, Tom Waits, Social Distortion, and a million other songs still playing. Thanks for listening.

TURN THE PAGE TO READ AN
EXCERPT FROM SARAH DESSEN'S

ONCE AND FOR ALL

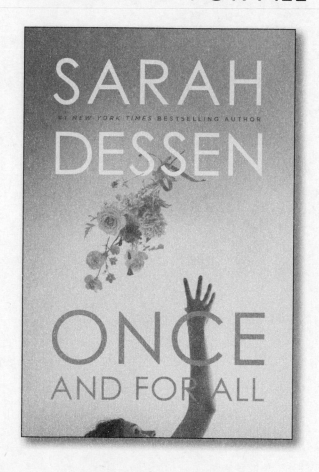

THE SAND WAS chilly on my feet as I stepped onto it that August night. With the music still audible from the patio, I hooked the straps of my shoes onto my thumb, then slid my phone into the pocket of my dress. Ahead, the beach was flat and dark, dotted with the lights from hotels and, farther along, houses. Thinking I'd only go a little way before I turned around, I started walking.

If he hadn't been wearing that white shirt, bright almost to the point of glowing, I might not have even seen him. But he was. The boy who had asked me to dance, standing by the water's edge. I couldn't miss him. No, more than that. I can never picture him in anything else.

The real surprise, though, was that he saw *me*. When you come across someone on the beach at night, contemplating the ocean, you don't exactly interrupt. It's one of those unwritten rules. So I'd just walked behind him, keeping my head down, when I heard him say, "All done for the night?"

It's funny, the details you remember from the things you cannot forget. The sand cool on my feet. The weight of my shoes, shifting as they swung in my hand. And again, that shirt bright in contrast to my own black dress, so dark I wondered later how he'd seen me at all.

We stood there a second, facing each other. His shirttails, now untucked, were ruffling in the wind. I'd never had this feeling before, that something big was about to happen, and there was nothing I had to do but wait for it. A beat. Then another. Finally, Ethan stepped back from me, away from the thrown brightness of the hotel and into the dimness of the beach beyond. The wind blew my hair, the straps of my shoes twisting around each other as he smiled at me, then gestured for me to join him there.

I didn't hesitate. So much of life is not being sure of anything. How I wished, later, I'd been able to savor them, those few steps and moments when for once, I just knew.

Behind us, I heard a swell of music, something easy and slow; it had to be deafening by the bonfire. Where we were, though, it was caught in the wind and carried, just distant enough to seem ghostlike. Or maybe that was the wrong word. Perhaps I wouldn't have used it at that moment, but only now.

Ethan walked out a little farther into the sand and water, the wind catching that white shirt, again sending the back billowing behind him. It was like he was glowing, more alive than anything I'd ever seen, when he turned back to me, holding out his hand. "Okay, I'll only ask once more, I promise. Want to dance?"

Could I hear the music, still? In my memory, the answer is yes. But in retrospect everything is perfect, as are all the other details of this night. At that moment, though, everything was brand-new, including the way I felt as I stepped forward, locking my fingers into his as he pulled me in closer. Me and Ethan, dancing in the dark at the end of the world. It was like I'd waited all my life to have something like this, and I knew even then, at the start, that it would be hard, so hard to lose. The big stuff always is.